# FORGET
# ME NOT,
## STRANGER

CW00867017

## By the same author

*A Thing beyond Forever*
*That Kiss in the Rain*
*How About a Sin Tonight?*
*Ex*

## Stranger Trilogy
*Marry Me, Stranger*
*All Yours, Stranger*

# NOVONEEL CHAKRABORTY

# FORGET ME NOT, STRANGER

RANDOM HOUSE INDIA

Published by Random House India in 2016
1

Random House Publishers India Pvt. Ltd
7th Floor, Infinity Tower C, DLF Cyber City
Gurgaon – 122002
Haryana

Random House Group Limited
20 Vauxhall Bridge Road
London SW1V 2SA
United Kingdom

978 81 8400 730 5

Typeset in Requiem Text by Manipal Digital Systems, Manipal

Printed at Thomson Press India Ltd, New Delhi

A PENGUIN RANDOM HOUSE COMPANY

*For . . .*

*The two souls I can't name.*
*One happens to be the most prized experience of my life.*
*The other, the most significant event.*

*Three things can't be long hidden:*
*the sun, the moon and the truth*

The Buddha

# Prologue

She was lost in the dark, dense forest. It was worse since she wasn't alone. Someone was following her, and had been for quite some time.

Her eyes were used to the darkness by now. She kept running, unsure of the direction. She had not seen the face of the person she was running from but she had an eerie feeling she would be cornered the moment she stopped. And so she ran, even though her legs were about to give way. She paused for a moment to catch her breath, and turned to look. Some dead leaves crackled in the distance and fear woke up in her guts once again.

Rivanah Bannerjee started running again. She checked her phone for the umpteenth time but there was still no network. She quickly checked the messages she had sent Danny. None of them had been delivered yet. She couldn't even shout for help because, for one, there was nobody in the forest and, two, it would only alert her follower and help track her down all the more easily. Just as she was about to collapse from exhaustion, Rivanah noticed a light in the distance. From where she was standing, Rivanah couldn't say what the source of the light was. But a light in the middle of the forest gave her hope. She took a deep breath and ran towards it with gusto. As she approached the light, she saw that it was inside what looked like an abandoned house. A huge banyan tree had spread its branches all over the wooden house—like a curse hanging above it.

When she reached the house, she peeped in through the window. Her breathing slowly regained a normal pace. There were four lanterns, one at each corner of the room, giving it a hauntingly erotic ambience. The room was barely furnished otherwise.

Right in the middle of the room was a naked man on his knees with his back to her. Around the man's neck were wrapped two shapely female legs. The man's mouth was right between the girl's legs. The girl suddenly popped her head up—her eyes were rolled back in ecstasy. As Rivanah got a good look of the girl's face, her heart stopped. She was staring at her own image! The Rivanah who was clutching the man's hair with both hands suddenly looked directly at the Rivanah peeping in through the window.

'Hello, Hiya!' the Rivanah inside the house said to the one outside. The man paused for a moment but didn't turn. He slowly held her throat with both hands and said aloud, 'Death is the ultimate orgasm, Mini.' He tightened his grip on her throat. Rivanah started to lose her senses. She could feel the pressure of the man's hands choking her windpipe. She tried to break free but couldn't. There was nobody who could help her except for her own 'image' standing by the window, helpless. The Rivanah at the window felt her feet turn to ice. She desperately wanted to escape. She felt her breath becoming shorter as if the man was pressing her throat instead of the girl's inside. An acute survival instinct finally gave her the energy to move. Rivanah went around the house looking for the main door. When she found it, she couldn't push it open. She banged hard, kicked it a few times but it wouldn't budge. The Rivanah inside the house was choking. The kicks on the door were relentless now and grew more intense. Finally the door crashed open and Rivanah ran towards the man who was holding the naked Rivanah by her throat. Before she could reach him, the man turned around to face her.

She opened her eyes wide. All she could see was a whitewashed ceiling with a static white fan. She saw Danny lying by her side, his face turned away from her. For a moment Rivanah thought she was still in her nightmare. She forcibly turned Danny's face towards her. She relaxed.

'What happened?' Danny asked in a sleepy voice.

'Nothing,' Rivanah said, feeling guilty for having disturbed his sleep. It was a nightmare, after all—a super-weird one all right, but a nightmare nevertheless.

'Go back to sleep,' she said. Danny obediently closed his eyes.

A quick look at her phone told her it was 10.45 in the night. Rivanah was about to get up to fetch some water when she heard a bell ring a couple of times. She ambled to the window and noticed an ice-cream wallah within the building premises. A family of four was buying ice creams from him. The sight made her miss her college days when Ekansh, her ex-boyfriend, would come over to her place at midnight and together they would have ice creams from a particular joint run by Ekansh's friend. Though the thought of Ekansh made her feel sour, a sudden urge to have ice cream possessed her. One look at Danny and his open mouth and soft snores told her he wouldn't come along. She picked up her wallet and quietly slipped out of the flat.

She bought herself a bar of khatta-meetha-aam-flavoured ice cream. After finishing one, she bought another to take back to her flat. By then the family of four had gone. Taking the money from Rivanah, the ice-cream wallah too turned to make an exit from the building premises.

As Rivanah walked towards her building entrance, there was a loud splash. Somebody had thrown a bucketful of water on her from above. Drenched from head to toe, she angrily looked up to reprimand the culprit but saw no one.

'Asshole!' she screamed out. There was a strange smell emanating from her clothes. She sniffed—and stopped dead in her tracks. What she had mistaken for water was, in fact, kerosene! Rivanah looked up again. Something like an arrow was travelling fast towards her. A flaming arrow.

'Oh my God!' she gasped, knowing well it wasn't a dream any more. The smell of the kerosene was real. The fire was real. She was real. Her fear was real. Rivanah had only a few seconds to move before the fiery missile touched her and burnt her to the ground. But her feet seemed to have frozen with fear. Just like in the nightmare. As the fireball neared her, her mind had already started a countdown—5—4—3—2 . . .

# 1

'Hey, you should call Aunty back. She has already called thrice,' Ishita said once Rivanah came out of the shower.

'I don't know why Mumma keeps worrying even though I'm in Kolkata, my hometown,' Rivanah said, picking up her phone. Rivanah was feeling sick ever since she had come back to Ishita's PG from Hiya's house in Agarpara. She could feel fear flutter in her guts. *Will the stranger really kill her? Was he a stalker cum serial killer?*

Ishita had been coaxing Rivanah to eat something but she didn't feel like it. Rivanah tried to sleep but feared that when she opened her eyes, she would see the stranger standing right in front of her, waiting to kill her. *Just like he must have compelled Hiya Chowdhury to kill herself*, she thought. Ishita had asked her to take a long, warm shower in order to relax. It sounded like a good idea. And now that she was done with the shower, Rivanah was indeed better.

'Hello, Mumma, what happened?' She finally called her mother back.

'Mini, come home. Now!' Her mother sounded petrified.

Rivanah's heart skipped a beat. Something terrible must have happened.

'What's wrong, Mumma?' Rivanah sounded equally terrified.

There was no response for a moment and then her mother said calmly, 'Nothing. I'm just feeling lonely. Come home now, Mini!'

This was strange. Suddenly her mother sounded as if everything was all right. 'You scared me, Mumma. Anyway, I'm coming home. And I'm bringing Ishita along.'

'No, not now,' Mrs Bannerjee shot back instantly.

'Why?'

'We have to go out for lunch to your baba's colleague's place.'

'Today?'

'Yes, today. In fact, in a few hours. So come home immediately.'

'Okay, Mumma. I'm coming.' *Why did her mother sound so . . . unlike herself?*

'What happened?' Ishita asked, entering the room with two cups of green tea. She gave one to Rivanah.

'No, thanks. I need to go now. Have a luncheon to attend,' Rivanah said, combing her hair in front of a full-length mirror in the room.

'With Ekansh?'

Rivanah shot her a glance and sighed, 'Baba's colleague.'

'Okay, I get it,' Ishita said, sipping her green tea. Rivanah shrugged.

'Your mother wants to introduce you to another of your arranged-marriage guys.'

Rivanah rolled her eyes realizing Ishita was right. How could she have missed that?

'Wish me luck,' Rivanah said, and left.

A few hours later, Rivanah's father met her and her mother outside the Esplanade metro station, and they drove in his Alto to Kalikapur. Rivanah didn't say much during the journey. It was obvious in the way her mother had asked her to 'dress properly' while she herself wore her latest buy—a Baluchari sari. They could try but Rivanah had no intention of getting married just yet. She was sure her parents hadn't told her the real reason for the luncheon fearing she wouldn't go with them.

The Bannerjee family were received warmly by Manick Dutta on their arrival.

'So nice to see you, Mr Bannerjee,' he said, hugging Rivanah's father. Rivanah thought it was odd that he referred to her father by his surname. Generally all his colleagues addressed him by his first name.

'It's been a while since I met your family,' Mr Dutta added.

*Been a while? When did he meet Mumma and me?* Rivanah wondered. *He must be confusing us with someone else*, she

3

thought. Soon all of them settled on a spacious L-shaped couch. It was a posh and neatly kept flat.

'My wife and son will be here soon. They have gone to the AC market. As you already know, Rishabh is here only for a week, and his mother prefers shopping with him.'

*So his name is Rishabh—the man my parents want me to spend the rest of my life with.* She noticed a couple of family photos in frames on either side of the huge LED television. Mr Dutta's son looked much older than she was. *If that is really his son in the photograph,* she thought and casually glanced at Mr Dutta. He was smiling at her.

'How are you doing, Mini?'

*Calling me by my nickname when we are meeting for the first time? This is a first,* thought Rivanah.

'I'm good, uncle. How are you?' Rivanah said, maintaining a warm smile.

'I'm good too. How long will you be in Kolkata?'

'A few more days.'

'That's nice.'

A servant came in with a tray carrying three glasses of water. The Bannerjees took a glass each and sipped on the water idly, waiting for Mr Dutta's wife and son to return. In the meantime, Mr Dutta shot a volley of questions at Rivanah. It was evident from the nature of the questions that he wanted to judge her as a person.

'When do you go to office?'

'What do you do on weekends?'

'How many friends do you have?'

'Do you have more male friends than females?'

Questions that were none of his business and yet she had to answer them because that was why she had been brought there: to answer whatever the boy's family asked. As time passed, Rivanah became increasingly bored and, as a result, started yawning more and more, to a point when it became embarrassing.

'Do you want to sleep for a bit, Mini?' Mr Dutta asked.

Rivanah glanced at her parents once and then at Mr Dutta.

'No, uncle, it is just that I haven't slept well for the last few days, with all the travelling.'

'Totally understandable. Youngsters these days have a mad schedule indeed,' Mr Dutta sympathized.

'Why don't you take a short nap? You'll look fresh by the time Mr Dutta's family gets back,' Mr Bannerjee chipped in.

*Look fresh in front of Mr Dutta's son, that's the whole point*, Rivanah thought.

'We will wake you up the moment Rishabh and his mother arrive.'

Rivanah gestured to her mother to come along for a second. 'Bhola, show madam the bedroom,' Mr Dutta said aloud.

The servant immediately appeared from the kitchen and escorted both Rivanah and Mrs Bannerjee to the master bedroom.

'Isn't it odd to sleep like this at someone else's place?' Rivanah said, keeping her voice in check.

'And what was it that you were doing sitting there? Yawning away like anything.' Her mother sounded cross.

'I'm sorry but I couldn't help it. I'm feeling very sleepy.'

'Then just sleep. I will wake you up when his son and wife come,' she said and walked out of the room. Rivanah sighed with yet another wide-mouthed yawn. She sat down on the bed. A moment later she lay down closing her eyes, telling herself she will not sleep. But she dozed off as soon as her head hit the pillow. When Rivanah woke up, she wondered why the interior of the room was so familiar. And then it hit her—she was lying in her own bedroom.

# 2

'Mumma!' Rivanah screamed as she sat upright with a jolt. Her mother came running, looking worried.

'What happened, Mini?' she asked.

'How did I come to my room? And did Mr Dutta's son and wife ever come?'

'What are you talking about, Mini?' her mother asked, looking aghast. 'You came back from your friend's place, had lunch and slept like a log.'

'Like a log? How many hours has it been?' Rivanah got off her bed and picked up her mobile phone from her study table.

'It is 9.30 p.m.!' she said aloud.

'I thought you were tired so I didn't wake you up,' her mother said and then, turning back, added, 'Come along now. Dinner is almost ready.'

'Mumma, tell me you are kidding.' Rivanah stopped her mother.

'Kidding about what, Mini?'

'You, Baba and I had gone to Mr Dutta's place for lunch today, right? I was feeling sleepy, so I went to his bedroom to sleep. What happened after that?'

Her mother's worried look was back.

'What are you talking about, Mini? Are you all right?' Rivanah looked hassled as she left her mother in the room and rushed to her father downstairs. He was sitting at the dining table waiting for dinner to be served. He was holding a copy of Tagore's *Gitanjali*. He dog-eared the page he was reading and looked up to see his daughter standing right in front of him.

'Tell your mother I'm very hungry,' he said.

'Baba, didn't we go to Mr Dutta's house today for lunch?'

Mr Bannerjee looked at her for a moment. Then, removing his specs, he said, 'We were supposed to but he had some work, so we didn't go. Why, what happened?'

Rivanah's jaws dropped.

'I don't know what she is talking about,' Mrs Bannerjee joined them.

'What is she saying?' Mr Bannerjee looked at his wife.

'That we went to Mr Dutta's place and she felt sleepy and . . .'

'Did you have a nightmare, Mini?' Mr Bannerjee asked Rivanah, cutting his wife short.

Rivanah, for a trice, seemed lost. Then she nodded. *Was it all a dream? Her coming home, going to Esplanade metro station with her mother and then being picked up by her father, going to Mr Dutta's house, him saying his wife and son are out.* Rivanah immediately called Ishita.

*The number you have called is not reachable right now.*

She checked her call log and found a call from her mother during the day.

'See, you called me in the morning,' she said, showing the phone to her mother.

'Of course, I did. I called and asked you to come over because we had to go to Mr Dutta's house. But the meeting was cancelled by the time you came home. Then you slept until you woke up a few minutes back,' her mother said, with a surety even Rivanah couldn't question.

A frustrated Rivanah sat with a thud in the chair right opposite her father.

'You should eat properly,' her mother said and moved towards the kitchen to serve them dinner. Rivanah didn't notice Mr and Mrs Bannerjee exchanging a furtive glance.

'This is what is wrong with your generation,' Mr Bannerjee started, 'You think money is everything and compromise on your health in the process. All this forgetfulness happens when you eat junk all day. These American food joints are spoiling our kids and their future, I tell you.'

Rivanah pushed her chair back and got up to leave.

'Mini?' Mr Bannerjee sounded worried.

Rivanah went straight to her room and opened her wardrobe to look for the salwar suit she had worn to Mr Dutta's place. She remembered it distinctly. *It couldn't possibly be a dream*, she thought, furiously ruffling through her wardrobe but she didn't find what she was looking for. Disappointed, she turned around to see her mother standing by the door.

'Can you tell me what's wrong with you?' Mrs Bannerjee asked.

'Mumma, where's that salwar suit that we bought the last time I was here?'

'Which one?'

'The peacock-green one with the red border.' Rivanah could have easily referred to it as the one she wore to Mr Dutta's place but she didn't.

'Oh that! It's in my wardrobe.'

Rivanah glared at her mother. 'What is my dress doing in your wardrobe, Mumma?'

'I had given it to be washed and kept it all ironed after you left. Forgot to put it back.'

Rivanah wasn't convinced.

'Show me,' Rivanah said and walked out of her room. Her mother followed.

Her mother opened the wardrobe in the master bedroom and there in one of the shelves lay her neatly ironed dress. 'Now do you believe me?' Mrs Bannerjee said, sounding hurt. Rivanah nodded and after thinking for a moment muttered under her breath, 'I'm sorry, Mumma. Let's have dinner. Baba is waiting.' *Maybe I am turning paranoid*, Rivanah thought.

All through dinner, her parents kept talking but Rivanah wasn't listening. She tried Ishita's number a couple of times but each time the automated voice told her the phone was not reachable. After dinner Rivanah checked her phone again. There were two missed calls from Danny and one message from Ekansh. Rivanah read the message first.

*Hi, what's up?*

The time of the message was 4.46 p.m. She checked the time of Danny's calls: 3.30 p.m. and 7.58 p.m. Rivanah immediately called Danny. He picked up on the fourth ring.

'Hey baby, where are you?'

'Hi! I'm sorry, Danny. I just dozed off in the afternoon.' Rivanah decided against recounting to him the confusing events of the day.

'You didn't send me your convocation pictures. How was the event?'

Images of her, along with Ishita, following her colleague Argho to her deceased college-mate Hiya's house flashed before her eyes.

'Hello?' Danny was waiting for her response.

'Oh, sorry. The event was great. I have few pictures on Ishita's phone. I shall ask her to share them with me. I will WhatsApp you.'

'Ishita?' Danny sounded clueless.

'The girl because of whom we met,' Rivanah said and remembered how Ishita had told her about this hot guy who had swept her off her feet at first sight. How they had had a bet to woo this guy. And that hot guy was now her boyfriend. Certain memories take your soul out for a sunbath. Her meeting Danny for the first time wrapped in only a towel was one such memory.

'Oh! Now I remember. Your old roomie?'

'Right. She is working here in Kolkata now.'

'That's good. And when are you coming back? I miss you.'

A smile featured on Rivanah's face. Nothing can beat the feeling of being desired by someone. 'I miss you too. Just a couple of days more and I'll be there.'

'Now that will give me a good night's sleep.' He kissed her over the phone. She kissed him back. After the Nitya incident, when Rivanah had wrongly doubted his loyalty, Danny had suddenly become this close-to-perfect boyfriend. Which girl would not desire someone who is hot, caring and gives ample space to you to the extent that even if he had an inkling that you were in touch with your ex, he still doesn't ask you awkward questions. But the other important question was: was she a close-to-perfect girlfriend to him? Rivanah was yet to confess to Danny about what had happened in the flat between Ekansh and her—that they had made love as if nothing had ever gone wrong between them. And it was scary because this feeling was like a seed which could proliferate into a gigantic tree with innumerable forbidden branches sprouting fresh leaves of illicit desires.

'Hello? You there?'

'Yes, yes. I'm here.' Rivanah came out of her momentary trance.

'I said I love you.'

'I love you too, Danny,' she said and cut the line. She sat on her bed lost in thoughts when her phone buzzed with a WhatsApp message.

*How are you? No response?*

It was Ekansh again. He was online. So was she now. Rivanah replied.

*I'm good. How are you? And Tista?*

She sent it and fixed her eyes below Ekansh's name on WhatsApp where it was written: *online*. Then it changed to *typing . . .* and then *online* again. A response came:

*Can we please meet?*

*Sure. Tomorrow around noon?*

*Now?*

*Now? It's past 10! Mumma and Baba won't allow it.*

*Like old times?*

He shouldn't have used those words: old times. Not now, not ever. She knew what he meant though. It wasn't the first time Ekansh wanted to meet her at a time when moving out of her house was next to impossible. Back when they were in college and in a relationship, she would sneak out of the house after her parents had slept. Rivanah typed out a four-letter word and pressed Send. Her message read: *Okay*.

13

# 3

Rivanah waited until her parents were done watching their favourite Bengali soap and retired to bed. When her mother came to leave a bottle of water in the room, Rivanah feigned drowsiness and wished her goodnight. Once her mother left, switching the lights off, Rivanah waited for some more time before sneaking out. This was such a familiar routine. The fact that she was still good at it told her how invested she had been in what Ekansh and she had called a 'relationship'. And love. Does love end when a relationship ends? Or does a relationship end because love has ended? And what were Ekansh and Rivanah into now? She didn't dare name it. But was this too because of what they had been earlier? Isn't the aftermath of love also . . . *love*?

Her mind still full of such thoughts, Rivanah took the keys out from under the old shoe rack beside the terrace door, unlocked the door and closed it gently behind her. Theirs was a two-storeyed house, so the terrace wasn't at a huge height. All she had to do was jump from the cemented parapet; Ekansh would catch her. She felt an awkwardness clinch her muscles. It is one thing to write 'like old times' in a message but it wasn't old times. They weren't a couple any more.

'Jump,' Ekansh said softly. Rivanah nodded and jumped as he caught her in his arms. He held her the way he used to and yet it felt different. She quickly severed herself from any kind of bodily touch from him. They quietly walked to Master da's tea stall where boys from the locality were playing carom while gossiping and drinking lemon tea. As they neared the stall, Rivanah stopped. What if the boys told on her? She would become the talk of the town by the next morning. How had she dared to do such things before? And why was she fighting it now? Was it because she really felt Ekansh and she shouldn't be seen together or because she didn't want those 'old times' to replay?

'Let's not go there,' she said. Ekansh gave her a look of understanding and took a lane leading to a small park. She followed. Sitting on a lonely bench in the park, the distance between them was palpable. Rivanah could almost see their past selves on a bench on the other part of the park. But unlike their present, their past selves' hands were clasped together.

'Why are we here, Ekansh?' Rivanah asked abruptly.

'Tista's surgery is tomorrow.' There was a forlorn look on Ekansh's face. As if he already knew what was going to happen inside the operation theatre the next day.

'But you told me earlier there's a 30 per cent chance of survival. I'm sure she will make it,' she said.

'What if Tista dies, Rivanah? Will you marry me?' Ekansh blurted. Rivanah couldn't help but give him a shocked look.

'I'm sorry. I don't mean it the way it sounds.'

'Then what did you mean, Ekansh?'

'I haven't slept since we both came back to Kolkata.'

Rivanah could tell he was telling the truth by the look in his eyes—tired, withdrawn and somewhat lifeless. She had noticed it when she met him that night in her flat in Mumbai but she didn't say anything lest he interpreted as concern. Though Rivanah had deliberately chosen to meet Ekansh at this hour, she didn't want him to read too much into it.

'All I keep thinking about is what will happen if Tista doesn't survive the surgery,' Ekansh said.

'Have you been really thinking that, Ekansh?'

'Yes.'

'No.'

'What do you mean no?'

'You have been thinking of what will happen to *you* if Tista doesn't survive the surgery. And hence your question to me. You are simply being selfish.'

Ekansh sat back on the bench and looked at the night sky.

'This was always my problem, wasn't it? I was always selfish in love. When I was in love with you, and now when I'm in love with Tista.'

In the silence, Rivanah could hear a frog croaking somewhere close by, and at a distance she could again see their old selves laughing, her head on his shoulder. He used to love it when her hair fell on his face. Then Rivanah saw their old selves turn quiet suddenly. She remembered that, back then, every time they became quiet, they would end up speaking at the same time. 'Ekansh.' This time, it was only she who spoke. He didn't look at her.

'Tista will be all right. And then we will stop meeting like this,' she said.

Ekansh turned his head towards her quizzically.

'What?' she shrugged.

'Can't we . . . ?'

'No, we can't be friends any more,' Rivanah responded to his incomplete question.

'Tell me honestly, Rivanah—don't you want to be my friend?' By now Ekansh had turned around and was facing her.

She took her time to answer. 'No, I don't.'

'Then what are you doing here?' He didn't know why he held her hand while saying it. She didn't know why she didn't push it away. She slowly looked down and then drew her hand out of his grasp.

'I'm guilty of the same thing I'm accusing you of. I too am selfish,' she said, choking up.

'Aren't we all, in one way or the other?'

*Maybe he is right*, Rivanah wondered, but kept mum. She stood up and asked, 'What time is the surgery tomorrow?'

17

'They will take her in the OT around ten in the morning.'

'I'll try to see her before that,' Rivanah said, and walked away. She saw Ekansh's shadow stand up and follow her but she didn't turn back. While moving out of the park she noticed the old Rivanah and Ekansh breaking from a tight embrace and kissing passionately. She could feel a lump in her throat.

Ekansh helped Rivanah climb on to the cemented parapet and then left. Rivanah locked the terrace door, kept the keys under the shoe rack and went downstairs to her room. She opened the door noiselessly. Once inside her bedroom, she let out a long sigh. Ekansh's query echoed in her mind: *What if Tista doesn't survive the surgery tomorrow?* Her relationship with Danny won't be accepted by her parents anyway. Rivanah shook her head vigorously. *What the hell am I thinking?* She was about to lie down on her bed when the lights in her room came on. Before she could speak, she heard a man say, 'Where were you, Mini?'

Rivanah looked up and got the shock of her life.

# 4

'You scared me!' Rivanah exclaimed. For a moment, she had thought it was the stranger in her room. Her heart was still racing with fear. Her parents were standing by her wardrobe staring at her.

'Where did you go, Mini?' Mr Bannerjee repeated.

'I went outside.'

'How did you go? We checked the main door. It was locked from the inside.' Mrs Bannerjee sounded exasperated.

'Oh, Mumma, I meant I was in the terrace. Why would I go outside at this hour?'

'I checked the terrace,' Mr Bannerjee said. 'You were not there.'

'Of course I was there. Did you check the portion behind the water tank?' Rivanah was trying her best to sound confident. Mr and Mrs Bannerjee exchanged a thoughtful glance. 'The network wasn't holding up here, so I went there to talk to Ishita,' Rivanah lied. 'But why are you two so worked up about it?'

Mrs Bannerjee came to Rivanah, caressed her head and said, 'Nothing. We just panicked not seeing you in your room. That's all. Now sleep, Mini. You anyway keep working all the time in Mumbai.'

Rivanah, to make things look normal, kissed her mother and climbed back into bed.

'Goodnight, Baba. Goodnight, Mumma.'

'Goodnight.' Her father left the room. Her mother pulled a thin blanket over her, and, switching off the lights, followed her husband out. Rivanah finally relaxed. She had forgotten her phone in the room itself. When she checked it, she found there was only one new message. It was from Ekansh.

*Thank you for being there.*

The message had come a few minutes after she had come back into her house. Had she met him for his sake? Or was it because her own damaged self was seeking a repair through proximity to Ekansh? Would Ekansh really want to get back with her if Tista didn't survive the surgery? She immediately hated herself for having such a filthy thought. And then a filthier question occurred in her mind: Whom would she ultimately choose if given the option—Ekansh or Danny? On an impulse, Rivanah typed a response to Ekansh:

*See you at the hospital tomorrow.*

To Danny, she messaged: *I love you. Goodnight.*

After sending both messages, she switched off her phone to avoid any further communication with the world and shut her eyes tight. She dozed off after murmuring a short prayer for Tista's well-being.

Next morning, Rivanah reached the hospital around ten. Tista's entire family was there. So was Ekansh. He came towards Rivanah the moment he saw her.

'What happened?' she said, seeing everyone crowding outside the room.

'The nurse is dressing her up for the OT,' Ekansh said.

'Dressing?'

'They need to wear a different uniform for the OT.'

'Oh, okay,' Rivanah said, and went ahead to greet Tista's parents and a few relatives who had seen her the other time she had come to the hospital.

'Any idea how long the surgery will take?' she asked Ekansh.

'Two hours minimum—if there are no complications,' he said and brushed his hand against her. *Was it an accident?* Rivanah didn't know. She felt as if Ekansh wanted her to hold him. They exchanged a furtive glance and her presumptions were confirmed. Rivanah intentionally stood slightly away from him. The fact that he too took couple of steps back told her his guard was up as well. Rivanah saw two people walking towards them. They were Ekansh's parents and she knew them well. Especially his father who used to joke that Rivanah spared them the pain of finding a daughter-in-law for their good-for-nothing son. Rivanah touched their feet. They blessed her like old times, but it was very awkward. Before his parents could speak, Ekansh came forward and told them that Tista was Rivanah's friend as well. They gave them an unsure smile and went ahead to greet Tista's parents. Rivanah was itching to ask Ekansh what reason he had given his parents for their break-up. Had he told them the truth? Or had he fabricated a web of lies to keep his image intact?

A nurse emerged from Tista's room and asked, 'Who is Rivanah here?'

Everyone turned to look at Rivanah as if a judge had pronounced an unexpected death sentence.

'Tista wants to have a word with you before the operation,' the nurse said. Rivanah glanced at Ekansh who gestured her to go ahead. As she took a couple of steps towards the room, the nurse spoke up, 'Make it short. I have to take her into the OT in a minute.' The nurse waited outside while Rivanah, all eyes still on her, went inside Tista's room.

Once inside, Rivanah shut the door behind her. She saw Tista lying on the bed in a green hospital dress. The way she looked at Rivanah scared her. She looked like a doppelganger of the Tista she had met for the first time in her Mumbai flat.

'Hi, Tista,' Rivanah said with a forced smile and went to stand by the bed.

The response came after few seconds. 'Hi, Rivanah di.'

'All will be good. Don't worry.'

'Rivanah di, do you still love Ekansh?'

22

There was a momentary shock in Rivanah's eyes but she couldn't tell if she hid it well.

'Who told you . . . ?' Rivanah immediately realized her response shouldn't have started with those words.

'For how long?' Tista asked, looking blankly at Rivanah.

'We were together for four or five years before we broke up.'

'Did you guys break up because of me?'

'No! No, Tista. You came into the picture much later.'

For a few seconds, neither spoke, neither moved. Then Rivanah noticed a teardrop roll down Tista's cheek.

'When Ekansh came to our flat for the first time, did you guys . . . ?' Tista's voice trailed off. And the trailing voice brought back the memory of the evening Rivanah had locked deep in her conscious, labelling it as 'so what?' But now with Tista inquiring about it the label had changed into 'why'. Did Tista know what happened between her and Ekansh that evening? How could she unless Ekansh had told her about it? Or the . . . ?

'I will have to take her to the OT now,' the nurse interrupted. She was followed by two ward boys who entered the room with a stretcher. They picked Tista up and lay her on the stretcher. All the while, Tista's eyes were fixed on Rivanah. Even though Rivanah was seeking an accusation in Tista's eyes, she couldn't find any. And it made the guilt inside her churn her guts. She felt like throwing up.

As Tista was taken away, Rivanah too rushed out. She didn't stop for Ekansh. While he was busy with Tista, Rivanah took the elevator and went downstairs. She sat down on one of the seats in the waiting area and immediately broke down. A few people sitting beside her gave sympathetic glances, assuming some acquaintance of hers must be in a serious condition—not knowing it was her conscience on the ventilator.

Earlier she had to deal only with the fact that she couldn't tell Danny what had happened between Ekansh and her that evening, but now her guilt discovered a stepsister named shame. Rivanah buried her face in her lap as she sobbed and shuddered. Someone in the seat behind her was staring at her. If Rivanah had turned around and looked, the person would have caught her attention. But she didn't even lift her head. A few seconds later the person stood up and left. Rivanah was still sobbing when she heard someone say:

'The heart leads but the mind misleads, Mini.'

Rivanah's sobs paused instantly. In a flash, she turned around only to see a small recorder on the seat right behind her. She rubbed her eyes and stood up. She went to the row of seats behind her and picked up the recorder. She fast-forwarded it, rewound it but all there was in the recorder was a single sentence in a male voice.

*The heart leads but the mind misleads, Mini.*

She kept the recorder in her bag, knowing only too well who must have placed it on the seat. She was sure her chance to catch the person was long gone. Her phone flashed 'Ekansh calling' but she didn't answer the call. Feeling slightly dizzy, she went out, wary of the people around her, and took a cab home. She slept till evening. Once her parents left for a function, she went to take a shower. Sitting naked on the bathroom floor under the shower, she only had one thing on her lips—a prayer for Tista. Ekansh had called her again, but she didn't dare pick up the phone. The surgery must have ended but she didn't have the courage to find out how it went. If Tista had died, Rivanah would die of guilt. If Tista lived, she would perish in shame. She was about to burst into tears again when her eyes snapped open. The water from her shower was still cascading down her body. But Rivanah could smell something. She stood up in a flash and turned off the shower. *Something is surely burning*, she thought, quickly wrapping herself in the towel. She unlocked the bathroom door and was about to step out into her room when the sight in front of her shocked her. There was a bonfire in the middle of her room, with flames licking the ceiling. She could feel the heat and knew the fire would soon engulf her as well, and yet she couldn't move. Fear had clouded her instinct for survival.

*The stranger is here to kill me. I'll die in no time. Just like Hiya Chowdhury*, she thought. As the fire in the room grew,

Rivanah's eyes fell on one of the many windows in her room. It had a word written on it in red:

*Your*

She looked at the next window.

*End*

Then the next one:

*Is*

The fourth window:

*Coming*

And then the last:

*Soon.*

Rivanah collapsed on the floor.

# 5

M r and Mrs Bannerjee had rushed home after a panic call from their neighbour. By the time they reached, there was already a small crowd gathered around the front door, along with a stationary fire engine with its siren on. The firemen informed Mr Bannerjee that everything was under control; they had arrived before the fire could do some real damage. When Mr and Mrs Bannerjee went inside, they found their daughter huddled up in a corner of her room.

'Someone was here, Mumma,' Rivanah said, bursting into tears.

While Mrs Bannerjee hugged and tried to console her, Mr Bannerjee called up the police who arrived within half an hour. By then Rivanah had come out of shock and was able to speak clearly.

'Do you have any idea how the fire started?' Police Inspector Rajat Das asked Rivanah. He was the younger brother of one of Mr Bannerjee's colleagues.

'I don't know. I was in the bathroom. I smelt something and came out to see my room engulfed in fire,' she recounted, with fear still lurking in her heart.

'Do you have enemies? Or did you fight with someone recently? Anything untoward?' Inspector Rajat urged on.

Rivanah was lost in thoughts.

'I'm asking because we have found some words on the window panes.'

'What words?' Mr Bannerjee was confused.

'It said: Your end is coming soon.'

Mr and Mrs Bannerjee exchanged a worried glance.

'Mini,' Mr Bannerjee said, 'are you hiding anything from us?'

Rivanah couldn't tell them about the Stranger. Who knew what he would do if she involved the police this time. Forget the Stranger, she had a few skeletons of her own to hide from her parents. She looked at her father and shook her head.

'Hmm.' Rajat stood from the chair.

'Don't worry,' he said, facing Mrs Bannerjee, 'We shall be quick with the investigation. I'll let you know if something comes up.' He turned to Mr Bannerjee and said, 'Do accompany us to lodge an FIR.'

'Certainly.' Mr Bannerjee followed Rajat to the door.

Rivanah was wondering whether she should tell the police about Argho. It was evident what his or the Stranger's intention was: to kill her. What if she didn't live long enough to tell them the name?

As Inspector Rajat took his leave, Rivanah blurted out, 'Argho has been following me.'

'Argho? Who is he?' Rajat came up to her once again. Her parents were behind him.

'He works with me in Mumbai.'

'You never told us about this guy Argho before!' Mr Bannerjee said.

'And why has he been following you?' Mrs Bannerjee was quick to ask.

'I don't know,' Rivanah said, feeling her mind go blank.

'There has to be some reason for taking his name?' Rajat asked.

Rivanah was in two minds. If she told the police that she thought Argho was the Stranger, then she would have to tell them the entire story. What if the Stranger killed her if she confessed? Rivanah swallowed a lump and said, 'I'm not sure. I saw him glancing at me in the office.'

'Just glancing at you? Hmm. Anyway, do you know where he lives in Mumbai?' Rajat asked.

Rivanah nodded.

'What's his full name?'

'Argho Chowdhury.'

'Did he follow you here to Kolkata?'

'Yes.'

'How are you sure?'

'He was there in the recently held convocation in my college a few days back.'

'Did he study with you in college?'

'No.'

29

'Then what was he doing in the convocation?'

Rivanah took her time before saying, 'I don't know.'

'Hmm. Any idea where he lives in Kolkata?'

Rivanah shot him an incredulous look and shook her head. For a second, she thought of giving the inspector the phone numbers of the Stranger she had stored, but knew it would be useless since he never used them under his name.

'Hmm, you said he works with you. So it won't be difficult to hunt him down and check if your suspicion is right.'

Inspector Rajat finally took his leave followed by Mr Bannerjee. Her mother stayed back with her.

'I don't know what we have done to anyone to deserve all this.'

'I'm not hurt, Mumma,' she said trying to emotionally shelter her mother. I'm not hurt *yet*, she said to herself.

'Can I please have some water? I'm very thirsty.'

'Yes. You should have some salt water, actually. You are perspiring a lot,' Mrs Bannerjee said and sauntered away. Mr Bannerjee came back and said, 'You should have told us about Argho before.'

'Baba, even I didn't know it would come to this. In fact, I don't have solid reason to suspect him. It's just that when the inspector asked if I have anyone in my mind, only his face came to me.'

'But why would he do such a fatal thing? Does he have a grudge against you?'

'I don't know, Baba. I'm sure if the police nab him he will confess whatever it is. If he is the guilty one, that is.'

'Did he do anything during or after the convocation?'

'Nothing.'

'Hmm.' Mr Bannerjee went away.

Rivanah picked up her phone and went to her Contacts. She had to talk to someone. She scrolled down till she stopped at a name: *Danny*. And right below it was *Ekansh*. Calling Danny would have been the right thing to do. But right things always had consequences. What if Danny sensed her unsettled tone and asked questions? Telling him one thing would invariably lead to telling him a lot of things, which she knew would complicate their relationship. Ekansh too could ask questions but with him she now had the luxury to dodge them. Rivanah tapped on Ekansh's name. She anyway had to inquire about Tista's surgery. She had already ignored it for too long. The phone was answered on the second ring but Ekansh didn't speak.

'Ekansh, you there?'

'Hmm.' He sounded grim.

'What happened? How was the surgery?' Rivanah said, feeling a tinge of guilt that she couldn't be there with him when the surgery happened.

'Tista hasn't gained consciousness as yet. She is under observation for twenty-four hours. I . . .'

Rivanah could sense he was crying.

'Where are you right now?'

31

'Home,' he said in a choked voice.

She knew he needed her. *Did Tista tell him that she knows?* The emotional desperation to be there for Ekansh made her uncomfortable. But a truth from within struck the bell of her conscience—Ekansh was more a part of her now, when they were separated, than when they were together. Whether she accepted this truth or not was a different story.

'Ekansh, I'm coming to your place,' she said in one breath and cut the line.

Though she tried to coax her father, he wouldn't let her leave the house on her own—not after what had happened. Rivanah had to lie that an urgent office work had come up, else she wouldn't have insisted. They reluctantly agreed. Mr Bannerjee dropped her at Ekansh's place. She didn't tell him it was his place to avoid unnecessary questions. Her father offered to wait outside but she promised to call him once she was done. After Mr Bannerjee drove away, she walked for half a kilometre and reached Ekansh's actual house. The lights were off. She pushed the gate open and noticed a faded board on it: Beware of dog. Ekansh used to have a bulldog named Engineer. It was a joke between Ekansh and her that engineers studied to become MNC dogs. Every time she entered through the gate, Engineer would come and wag his tail until she put him on her lap and let him lick her face. The dog had died the year they graduated but the board had remained intact. Ekansh probably never got a pet after that. She rang the doorbell, and Ekansh's mother answered the door. If she was surprised to see Rivanah, she didn't show it.

'Hello, aunty,' Rivanah blurted awkwardly.

'How are you, Rivanah?' Ekansh's mother usually called her Mini. *The way we address people tells us so much about our relationship with them*, she thought.

'I'm okay, aunty. Is Ekansh—?'

'He is in his room,' his mother answered before she could finish.

Rivanah walked in as she closed the door behind her. Sensing she wasn't very inclined to talk, Rivanah took the stairs to Ekansh's room. As she stood outside the door, she took a deep breath to negate the flashes from the past which were becoming clearer and clearer every second. This was the room in which they had secretly kissed so many times.

Rivanah knocked on the door.

'Mom, I told you to leave me alone.' Ekansh's pitch had an irksome tinge to it.

'It's me, Ekansh.'

Ekansh let her in and shut the door. Before she could say anything, he hugged her tightly, almost crushing her ribs. The way his hands gripped her back always aroused her before—and it was no different now.

'Ekansh . . .' she murmured. He half broke the hug and then tore away from her, probably sensing she was uncomfortable.

33

'Any news of Tista?' Rivanah asked quickly, not wanting to give time for memories to return. After all, Tista was the reason they were together in his room. Whatever they had between them was not supposed to be set on fire again. *Deep relationships probably never die*, she thought, *and always have the potential to be rekindled.*

'Not yet,' he said. 'Tell me she will be all right.'

Rivanah had never seen Ekansh behave like a kid. It just told her how much he loved Tista. During their relationship, she had never believed Ekansh could love anyone more than he loved her. But now, getting a glimpse of his love for Tista, she had mixed feelings. She wasn't sad about it. But she wasn't happy either.

'She will be all right.' Rivanah understood that Tista hadn't told Ekansh anything yet, or else that would have surely been his first question to her.

A few silent moments and a stare later, Ekansh added, 'Thanks for coming here. I needed you.'

Words like these from your ex can steal your peace, especially when the real you knows you aren't over him completely.

'I'm going to Mumbai the day after.'

Ekansh sat down beside the window without a word. He was staring at the floor. Rivanah could tell he was thinking hard.

'I know it is still early, but do you have any idea when Tista will be discharged?'

'Rivanah . . .' Ekansh raised his head and looked straight at her. It wasn't a normal look. It looked like something of uber importance had dawned on him and she was interrupting that realization. She had a hunch that whatever he was about to say could alter a lot of choices in her life. It made her heart beat faster.

'Just say it . . .' Rivanah said.

Ekansh shook his head and said, 'Nothing.'

*There was most definitely something but why won't he say it?* Rivanah wondered.

'You can be honest with me, Ekansh,' she said, feeling her throat go dry as she spoke.

'That's the problem. If we are always absolutely honest, we won't be able to live in peace.'

'Why do you say that?' Rivanah frowned slightly.

'It's because peace is an illusion created by either ignorance or acceptance.'

*What are you trying to ignore, Ekansh? Or accept, for that matter?* She desperately wanted to ask him but didn't, since she understood his point. She was oscillating between honesty and peace herself as far as her confession to Danny was concerned. Thinking about Danny, she wondered if she should tell Ekansh about her conversation with Tista. One look at Ekansh, however, and she knew he wouldn't be able to handle it.

'I'm not sure when I'll be in Mumbai,' he said.

'I get it. Let me know when you visit Tista next. I need to see her once.' *And apologize to her with all my heart,* she said to herself, knowing full well a verbal apology would not be good enough to cleanse the dirt of guilt within her.

Rivanah's father came to pick her up from exactly where he had dropped her. Later in the night, when Rivanah joined her parents at the dining table, Mr Bannerjee gave her a bunch of papers.

'What's this, Baba?'

'One of Rajat's constables was here when you were out. It has the names of the passengers who travelled to Mumbai from Kolkata yesterday. The name you'd mentioned . . .'

'Argho Chowdhury,' Rivanah chipped in.

'Right. Argho's name is on the list, and the police have confirmed from the CCTV footage that he did go through the security check at the airport yesterday.'

*He couldn't have set fire inside my bedroom*, she thought.

'If he has flown back to Mumbai, then what am I to check in these papers?'

'These papers have the names of passengers who flew from Kolkata to Mumbai after the incident. The police want to know if you recognize any name.'

Rivanah kept flipping through the pages, going through each name with utmost focus. She paused on one name: Prateek Basotia.

# 6

Rivanah gave the papers back to her father saying, 'I don't know anyone from the list.' She had to first check if Prateek, her school senior and ex-colleague, was indeed the Stranger or not. But if he was, why would he call her to his place like he had done months back and then humiliate himself by recording his own self in a compromising manner only to help her out?

'What happened, Mini?' Mr Bannerjee asked.

'Nothing. I think I'll retire now. Goodnight, Baba, goodnight, Mumma,' said Rivanah, pushing her chair back. She got up and walked straight to her room.

Once inside, she opened Facebook and unblocked Prateek from her blocked list. She immediately went to his profile. His cover photo was of a woman's mehendi-adorned hands with a wrist full of red bangles. Her hand was holding a man's hand. The profile picture was of Prateek with a girl. A look at his About Me section confirmed her guess. His relationship status was 'Married to: Rati Agarwal Basotia'. Rivanah clicked on the hyperlink and Prateek's wife's profile opened. She appeared to be a typical Marwari girl with a domestic vibe. A casual glance at her timeline told Rivanah that she had checked-in at the Yellow Chilli restaurant in Bangur Avenue with Prateek Basotia at . . . Rivanah saw the time. It was about the same time the attack had taken place. Had Prateek paid someone to do it? He had all the reasons to be upset with her. Rivanah scrolled down Prateek's timeline. He had got married three months back. On a hunch she ran to her parents' room.

'Baba?' Rivanah said. The lights in the room were off. Both her parents woke up, startled.

'What happened, Mini?'

'Relax. I just wanted to check the passengers list once again,' she said, switching the lights on.

'It is right below that book,' Mr Bannerjee said pointing towards a table. Rivanah picked it up.

'Keep it with you tonight,' Mr Bannerjee said sleepily. Rivanah nodded and took the papers with her. She switched the lights off before leaving the room.

Back in her room, Rivanah opened the page which had Prateek's name on it. And right below was: Rati Agarwal Basotia. The two had clearly travelled together from Kolkata to Mumbai. Why would a guy who got married few months back take such a big risk of attacking a girl because of a grudge? What will he get out of it? It wasn't Argho if the police were to be believed, and now it was almost clear that Prateek's name was a coincidence. Then it could only mean the Stranger was still at large . . . unless . . . there were not one but several people involved. The thought itself made her heart skip a beat. What if there were not one but multiple Strangers? As Rivanah lay in bed, she kept wondering if she was missing out on any detail from the first day she had landed in Mumbai. An hour later, she fell asleep with a myriad of directionless thoughts.

Rivanah woke up late the next morning. She saw a few missed calls from both Ekansh and Danny. She called Danny while brushing her teeth and rushed through breakfast, still on the call, mostly listening to the latest news from his shoot. By the time she reached the hospital, it was around 10.30 a.m. The scene didn't look good. Tista's parents—especially her mother—were hysterical. Other relatives were trying to calm her down but in vain. She took a couple of steps towards them but nobody noticed her. She could see Ekansh's parents standing with Tista's relatives. With her heart beating harder, she went to the nurse who was writing something on a paper.

'What happened, sister?'

'The patient collapsed.'

'Collapsed?' Rivanah's throat had gone dry by then.

'Tista died early morning.'

Rivanah thought her heart had stopped for a moment. *Tista can't die. Tista shouldn't die. Tista hasn't died.* Tears started rolling down her cheeks. The nurse made a soft announcement that the body would be in the room for another half hour maximum.

Rivanah slowly turned towards the cabin door. It was a couple of metres away from her but she had to summon all her energy to be able to come up to it.

Standing by the door, she could see Ekansh sobbing beside Tista's bed. No medical equipment was attached to her body any more. Her eyes were shut. Rivanah wouldn't have guessed if she didn't already know. She still hoped Tista would miraculously open her eyes— and she would get a chance to apologize to her. At that instant, Rivanah knew nothing would give her more joy than seeing Tista and Ekansh together and happy. Tista's calm visage told her coming back to life was still possible while Ekansh's ashen face confirmed the improbability of it. Ekansh lifted his head when she entered the room. She had once believed Ekansh loved her truly and had changed her perception of him over the years, believing he could not be loyal to anyone. But he had surprised her with his behaviour towards Tista. A person can be good as well as bad, black and also white. Our experience of the person is only a way to perceive him or her. And perceptions come with inherent limitations, Rivanah now knew.

She placed a hand on Tista's forehead, caressing it. Ekansh grasped Rivanah's other hand. He tightened his grip; it hurt but she didn't move. Ekansh looked up at her and said, 'She knew.'

Those weren't just words but a pyre on which Ekansh's life would station itself. The fire of guilt shall

40

slowly lick his conscience all his life like it would lick hers. Till those words were spoken by him they had shared a past, but from now on, Ekansh and Rivanah would share the same fire of guilt in them. She wanted to talk to him but stopped herself when Ekansh's mother stepped into the room. Rivanah quickly managed to free her hand from his grasp. Ekansh's mother asked him to come out with her; he followed her out. Rivanah too left Tista's room but didn't see Ekansh or his parents.

Back from the hospital, Rivanah was too dazed to think clearly. She picked up her phone several times to call Ekansh but didn't know what they would talk about. At night, he messaged her saying he wanted to meet. Rivanah had just finished packing for her flight the next morning. She agreed and asked him to pick her up from her place. She convinced her parents that she was going to her friend's place like the other day for some office work and the friend would pick her up and drop her back as well.

'What is your friend's name and phone number?'

Rivanah gave them Ekansh's number but told them the name was Pooja, someone they knew.

Ekansh picked her up and they drove to the Kankurgachi footbridge. Neither uttered a word during the ride. Danny had called but Rivanah told him she was out with family and would call him back the moment she reached home. The two climbed the bridge and sat on the steps. The footbridge was a lonely place during the day. Even more so at night.

'Why did you tell her?' Ekansh asked.

'What?' Rivanah wasn't expecting this question.

'Why did you tell Tista what happened between us that evening?' Ekansh asked sternly.

*I didn't,* Rivanah thought. *Someone else did. But I can't tell you who that someone is.*

'Was this your revenge?'

'Revenge?'

'Because I ditched you.'

'You really think I'm capable of doing something so cheap, Ekansh? Like, really?'

'I don't know. How else did she come to know?'

'If you don't know, how would I know?' Rivanah raised her pitch a bit. It was frustration shielded as anger—frustration of not being able to tell Ekansh about the Stranger. She stood up, paced the bridge, came back calm and said, 'Maybe she just understood it. A girl's sense is very strong in these matters.'

'She understood it the day she died? You think I'm going to believe that?'

'What are you trying to say, Ekansh? Please be clear.'

'I said what I wanted to say. I know what I did to you wasn't good, but by telling Tista what happened between us that evening, you have scarred me for life.'

'I haven't scarred you for life, your own karma has.'

'What bullshit!' Ekansh stood up to face Rivanah.

'Bullshit? If I had told her about this, why would I not confess to you? I was always there whenever you needed me. Back then, when we were in a relationship, and now, when we aren't. But at both times you have shocked me with your behaviour.' The irritation was evident in her face. They could have done this over phone too if all Ekansh had in mind was blaming her unnecessarily.

'I know you were and are there for me, but that doesn't mean I'm going to believe you on this. There is no way a third person could have known what happened between us that evening in the flat. I know I didn't tell Tista anything. That leaves only one person who could have.'

Rivanah shot an angry glance at him.

'Do me a favour now. Please don't get in touch again,' Rivanah said and started stepping down the bridge's staircase. Ekansh caught up with her calling her name, 'Rivanah . . . listen, Rivanah.'

'There is nothing to listen. Be it love or friendship, if you can't trust the other person, there is no reason why you should be together,' she said.

'All right. Go. If you think that by putting the blame on a girl's sixth sense you would be able to absolve yourself, then you are mistaken. Just imagine me telling your boyfriend about what happened between us. Only then you will understand my pain.'

With that Ekansh had blown the lid off Rivanah's anger.

'It's a free world, Ekansh Tripathi,' she said, turning back. 'Do as you please.' She finally climbed down the footbridge stairs.

'Thank you for the suggestion,' Ekansh shouted behind her.

Rivanah didn't care to turn. She hailed a cab standing nearby and was on her way home. Her phone rang flashing Ishita's name. Rivanah wiped the tears from her eyes and took the call. 'Where were you, girl?' she asked.

'Sorry, I was at a remote place with my office team. Didn't have network coverage there. I just received a missed call alert. Did you find a lead to Hiya Chowdhury?'

'Now who on earth is Hiya Chowdhury? What are you talking about, Ishita?' Rivanah said. There was total silence from Ishita's side.

## 7

'Though I would have liked to go with you, Mini, I couldn't manage to get leave,' Mr Bannerjee said, kissing his daughter's forehead. Rivanah's parents were seeing her off at the airport.

'Don't worry, Baba. I can take care of myself. I'll be all right,' Rivanah said. Though her father's anxiety was to be expected, especially after the attack, this time he seemed more uncomfortable than last time she flew to Mumbai. She hugged him hoping it would help. So much had happened after the Stranger's attack that it didn't seem as threatening to her now as it had then.

'Take care, shona.' Mrs Bannerjee kissed her daughter's cheeks. And whispered in her ears, 'I have packed a box of nalen gurer sandesh for Danny. Baba doesn't know.' Rivanah couldn't help but kiss her mother back.

'I'll miss you both,' she said.

Right then one of the security personnel came up to Mr Bannerjee and asked him to move his car from the gate since he wasn't allowed to park there.

'You guys leave now. I'll call you right after my security check,' Rivanah said.

She waved her parents goodbye and waited till they drove out of sight. Then she walked briskly with her luggage to the departure gate nearby; Ishita was waiting for her there.

'Just tell me you were joking on the phone last night?' said Ishita the moment Rivanah reached her. Ishita couldn't make head or tail of what Rivanah was talking about when she had said she didn't know who Hiya Chowdhury was, so she had decided to meet her in person this morning.

'No, I wasn't. Who is Hiya Chowdhury? And why would I joke about someone whose name I'm hearing for the first time?' Rivanah was as genuine as she was on phone the previous night. Ishita showed her phone to Rivanah. There was a WhatsApp message Ishita had sent to Rivanah a couple of days before. It read:

*I'm off for few days. Let me know if you come to know anything about Hiya.*

*Why isn't this message there in my phone when Ishita's WhatsApp shows a blue tick?* Rivanah was clueless.

'I haven't read this message of yours,' Rivanah said aloud.

'Well, someone did.'

*Was it the Stranger?* Rivanah wondered. Ishita took a few minutes to relay all that Rivanah had told her regarding the Stranger and Hiya after she reached Kolkata. She also recounted how they had followed Argho to Hiya's house, met her parents and realized Rivanah's life could be in danger since they both believed the Stranger might have killed Hiya.

*I remember the Stranger*, Rivanah wondered, *I also remember Argho but why don't I remember Hiya Chowdhury and the visit to her house then? Ishita can't be lying about this girl named Hiya. Why would she?*

'Now don't tell me you have forgotten it all?' Ishita looked a little unnerved.

Rivanah nodded. 'I really don't remember any of this.'

'Oh my God. Does the Stranger practise some black magic shit?'

Rivanah swallowed a lump remembering the fire in her room. *Your end is coming soon.* Was the Stranger really going to kill her? But why? What harm had she done to him? On the contrary, she had always done whatever he had asked of her—except, she hadn't confessed to Danny yet. The Stranger had already avenged that by telling Tista about it. What more did he want?

'I think you should go now,' Ishita said, looking at the board. It was time for security check.

'Yeah, I suppose I should.'

'But I'm really worried for you, dear. Just take care and let me know if I can help. If something out of the ordinary happens, do inform Uncle and Aunty,' Ishita instructed, hugging her friend. Once she broke the hug, Rivanah pulled her luggage and went inside. She went

Novoneel Chakraborty

straight to the security check and realized she hadn't collected her boarding pass. She could sense a tension brewing within her and it made her head reel. She sat down for a moment holding her head. Nothing was making sense. If Ishita was to be believed, she already knew a lot about Hiya, so then why could she not remember anything? Just then her phone rang. It was her father.

'We just reached home. Are you done with your security check, Mini?'

'Yes, Baba. All done,' she somehow managed to speak.

'Good. Call me once you board,' he said and hung up.

Rivanah knew she couldn't sit there for long. She went to collect her boarding pass. Right after the security check, she saw Danny's missed call on her phone. Only she knew how much she craved to be in his strong arms that moment, safe and sound. She immediately called him back.

'Hey baby.' He answered on the first ring.

'I love you, Danny.'

'Whoa, I'm having a morning wood and your voice isn't helping much.'

Rivanah managed a smile. 'Just hold it. I'll be there in three hours.'

'I'm not a fucking Viagra that I will hold-on for that long without you here. So give me enough reason to prolong my hard on,' Danny said naughtily.

48

He didn't know she wasn't quite in the mood.

'Actually Danny . . .'

'Airports have washrooms, right?'

*He is really in the mood now*, Rivanah thought, and decided it would be better to tell him about what was troubling her when they met.

'Hold on, cowboy,' she said and cut the line. Rivanah located the ladies' washroom, went straight inside the toilet and shut the door. She quickly raised her top to expose her royal-blue bra and clicked a pouting selfie showcasing her soft cleavage. She sent the picture to Danny.

*That's such a lifesaver. Thanks, baby. Have a safe flight back. Your cowboy is waiting. In fact, both your cowboys are waiting.* He WhatsApped back with a wink emoticon.

She replied with three kiss emoticons. And then sat on the toilet sink trying to think clearly. *Why the hell can't I remember Hiya Chowdhury? Who deleted Ishita's message from my phone?* Nothing made sense; she gave up. Rivanah slept through the entire flight.

By the time she reached her flat in Lokhandwala, Andheri West, she had prepared herself to meet Danny with as much eagerness as he had voiced on phone few hours back. She noticed the door was already slightly ajar. With a frown she pushed the door open and was taken aback. The entire room was stuffed with heart-shaped balloons. There were so many that she couldn't even step inside. She caught hold of a balloon and read what was written right across the centre: *Will you marry me?*

She checked two more balloons, and they all had the same thing written on them. A smile touched her face. This was completely unexpected.

She called out to Danny. 'Baby, you there? How do I come in?'

'If your answer is yes,' Danny said from somewhere inside the flat, 'take the lighter kept under the doormat and burst the balloons to come in.'

She picked up the lighter, and burst the first balloon. Then she burst another one, and another one. She managed to squeeze into the flat and close the main door behind her.

'Keep coming,' Danny said.

With a smile, Rivanah punctured another one with the lighter. Slowly it turned into a game she was starting to enjoy. The more balloons she burst, the deeper she went into her own flat. Finally she saw Danny right in the middle of the room, where he had positioned himself amidst the balloons.

'How did you do that?' she said, checking him out. He was in his boxer shorts. Only his boxer shorts.

'Do you think I'm in the mood to talk?' Danny said and lifted her. He took her to the bedroom where he had sprinkled rose petals all over the bed.

'I must say I'm impressed,' she said as Danny placed her on the bed.

'Now time to impress me,' he said and tugged down his boxers. He was kneeling on the bed while Rivanah was lying on her back looking at him. Her eyes slowly went down to his raging hard-on. She moistened her dry lips with the tip of her tongue. After the weeks-long dry spell, a sexual monsoon loomed large as Rivanah pushed him on the bed with her feet. She then sat on top of him, putting both her legs on either side. In a flash, she removed her tee. As she bent down to kiss him, he unhooked her bra. It came off as she sat straight again. She was getting aroused slowly. She started rubbing her pelvis on his hard-on, turning it even harder. He unbuttoned her jeans, unzipped it and, with her help, tugged it down along with her panties. He was surprised how wet she was. As he held his penis, she lifted her back only to sit on it gently, allowing it to quite deftly go inside her. With her hands on his chest, Rivanah shut her eyes tight and started slowly moving her pelvis. As the initial pain of insertion slowly turned into pleasure, her mind kept switching between pleasure and reality. Though she didn't like how things had ended with Ekansh, she now felt it was for the best. With Ekansh in her life, she had to constantly juggle between whether to tell Danny the truth or not, but now when she was sure of not seeing Ekansh's face ever again, she could well bury the sexual slip in her subconscious labelling it as 'a nothing'.

Danny flipped her without warning, and from her being on top, it changed into the missionary position.

Danny took her legs on his shoulders, rubbing his face on her calf, while Rivanah still had her eyes shut, clutching the bed sheet tight with both hands. His intense and strong thrusts felt like he was making her disappear. With every passing moment, she felt as light as a feather. All her defences seemed conquered, all her filters seemed compromised. If Danny had probed at that moment she would have confessed what had happened between Ekansh and her in the flat. Feeling his breath on her face, she opened her eyes. Danny had leaned forward and was now close to her. His lips pursed hers, and in no time, he took her tongue in his mouth. She understood that confession was the easy part. What was difficult was the explanation. Why were she and Ekansh intimate in the flat even though they had broken up long before that? Until that moment, she had sworn to herself she hated Ekansh up to the hilt. How could she dress the complex thoughts that propelled her to first indulge in the act with all her heart and then keep it a secret from Danny with words? *How does one explain the plausibility of such a thing?* Rivanah wondered, as she felt Danny squeezing her boobs with both his hands and sucking on her nipples alternately. He had increased his pace by now and she had wrapped her legs tightly around him to escalate her pleasure. Soon the thrusts became even harder, the moans louder, and they both climaxed as Danny came inside her. Both were panting as he looked at her and said, 'Sorry, I came inside you.'

'It's okay. I'm on my safe period. Hopefully!' she winked at him. He kissed her. Danny flipped her once again, bringing her on top of him. She placed her ears on his chest and could hear his heart beat fast. He held her tight in his arms. They slept in that position for a good five hours. When she woke up with a start, it was close to lunchtime. The fact that she should have been at work made her sit up. But right then, a strong pull made her collapse on the bed again.

'No office today,' Danny said in a groggy tone.

'Why?'

'Because I said so. One more day of leave won't change anything.'

Rivanah looked at him and caressed his already ruffled hair. To her, he seemed like the most desirable man on the planet. She picked up her phone and texted her teammate to manage without her for one more day. Next, she called her parents and told them she had reached Mumbai safely and would have called sooner had she not slept. The moment she put the phone down, Danny pulled her towards him and pinned her hands to take control of her.

'Relax. I'm not going anywhere,' she said, with a warm smile.

'Yes, you are,' Danny said.

'Huh?'

'To fairyland.'

Before she knew it, Danny was kissing his way to her navel. She somehow managed to push him away saying, 'Let's eat something first.' She climbed down and took out a pair of shorts and a spaghetti top from her wardrobe. She could sense Danny's eyes on her all the time. It made her blush. As Rivanah went to the kitchen to fix a meal, Danny came from behind and scooped her up, lifting her off the kitchen floor.

'Danny!'

Before she could say anything, he took her to the bathroom and placed her under the shower. As the water came cascading down, she knew how much he had missed her. And with every kiss, she realized how much she too had missed him.

'I want to eat her first,' he said. She knew what he meant as he went down on his knees, putting the tip of his tongue on her belly button. Rivanah gripped his hair tightly. He had always been passionate in his lovemaking. The pleasure hormones released by Danny's touch made her feel lucky, accepted, wanted and thoroughly desired. Danny stood up. As they smooched under the cold shower, she realized whatever had happened was for good. Now she won't have to fight guilt. Ekansh was finally history and so was whatever had transpired between them.

After a prolonged fondling under the shower, they finally had lunch. Having catered to the two most basic requirements of human beings—sex and food, they collapsed on the bed. Rivanah and Danny slept in a tight embrace, as if never wanting to let go. Listening to Danny's soft snores, she too closed her eyes.

Rivanah woke up startled and anxious. She had had a nightmare . . . *someone was following her . . . she was running in a forest . . . all alone . . . discovering a wooden house . . . and then seeing herself in a sexual act with a man whose face was hidden . . . and as he tried to press her throat and kill her . . .* Rivanah relaxed when she realized she was lying beside Danny. It had been some time since she had had a nightmare. In the silence of the room, she could hear her heart beating fast. Danny shifted slightly asking her if there was any problem. She said no and asked him to go back to sleep, got down from the bed to fetch some water when she heard a bell ring a couple of times. She went to the window and saw an ice-cream wallah who had brought his small van inside their building—Krishna Towers—for eager children. An intense desire for ice cream propelled her to leave Danny alone in the flat and rush out to get one.

As she was coming back after buying an ice cream for herself, just when she was about to step into her wing, someone threw a bucket full of water on her—or so she thought. Looking up towards the terrace, she hurled an abuse at whoever it was. But she stopped dead when a staunch smell of kerosene infiltrated her nostrils. She had been drenched in kerosene! And when she looked up again, she saw a flaming arrow approaching her. She knew she had to move away or else . . .

# 8

The arrow fell right beside Rivanah's feet. The ground where the kerosene had spilt caught fire immediately. Survival instinct pushed Rivanah to dash towards the building entrance. The fire trailed her rapidly. It was about to touch her when one of the two security guards seated at the entrance came and poured an entire bottle of water on it, extinguishing the trail. The guard looked up at Rivanah who was screaming her lungs out. He tried to calm her down but her screams only escalated. A few residents of the colony peeped out of their windows. Rivanah stopped her screams and said, 'He will kill me.'

'Take her to her flat,' one of the inhabitants shouted at the guard from the first-floor flat.

'Is there someone living with her?' asked another.

'Call the police maybe,' said a third.

A woman who lived on the ground floor took Rivanah to the elevator with the help of one of the guards and then to her flat, while the other guard went to the terrace and the other flats to try and find out who could be behind all this.

Danny was shocked to see Rivanah shuddering when he opened the main door all confused. She hugged him tightly. The guard felt awkward and, without clarifying, left the couple and went up to the terrace to join his colleague. Danny closed the door behind.

'What happened, baby? When did you go out? And why are you smelling of . . .' Danny sniffed and added, 'kerosene?'

'He tried to kill me.'

'*He*?' Danny's heart skipped a beat. 'Who is this *he*?'

'Argho Chowdhury.'

'Who is this guy?' Danny said, cupping her face and compelling her to make an eye contact.

'He works in my office.' *And I am sure he is the Stranger.* But she couldn't tell Danny that.

'Why the hell would he try to kill you? Are you hiding anything from me, Rivanah?' Danny's eyes showed evidence of genuine care. And what she had for him was a lie.

'No.'

A guilt-laden no. That's all she could manage before averting her eyes.

'Then is he a lunatic to try to kill you?'

Rivanah looked up at him and said softly, 'I'm scared, Danny.'

He hugged her tighter.

'You don't have to be as long as I'm with you,' he whispered in her ears. 'First, take a shower and get rid of this smell.'

57

Danny guided her to the shower and closed the bathroom door. Rivanah took off her clothes and stood under the shower. The image of the fireball flashed in front of her eyes. What if she had not seen it coming? She would have had burnt to death by now. She slowly applied the shower gel to get rid of the kerosene smell, all the while trying to get a grip on herself. *Why the hell does Argho want to kill me? Revenge? For what? Have I forgotten something the way I forgot about Hiya Chowdhury a few days back? Am I suffering from amnesia or Alzheimer's?*

Rivanah came out of the shower after almost an hour. She was feeling and smelling fresh. Danny was working on his laptop.

'How are you feeling now?' he asked.

'Better.' She came to him and kissed him on the cheeks.

'For you,' he said as he pushed a mug with steaming black coffee towards her.

'Thanks.'

'The guards told me they didn't notice anyone or anything odd in the terrace.'

*I was sure they didn't*, Rivanah thought.

'Now tell me what you haven't told me yet,' Danny said.

Rivanah's heart skipped a beat.

'Who is Argho?' he said.

Rivanah swallowed a lump and then spoke, 'I think he is the Stranger.'

There was a deep frown on Danny's face.

'You mean . . .'

Rivanah nodded as if she had read his mind.

'Why didn't you tell me before?' He sounded cross.

'I never thought it would come to this.'

'That's not the point. The point is that you didn't tell me about it.'

'I'm . . . sorry . . . Danny.' Only she knew she was apologizing for more than one thing.

In the silence that followed, they stood hugging each other with Danny caressing her back.

'I was just talking to a friend. He said he has good connections with the police.'

'Hmm,' Rivanah said, feeling Danny break the hug. As they settled on the bed, Rivanah picked up her phone. *Should I message the Stranger and ask him what the fuck he wants from me?* She scrolled down her Contacts. It had been some time since she had had any sort of communication with him. But was there any point in messaging him? He had made his intention clear: he wants her dead—for reasons best known to him. If Ishita was to be believed, they had together guessed that the Stranger may have killed Hiya as well and projected the entire incident as a suicide and was now pinning it all on Rivanah. *But . . . why?* She heard Danny's phone buzz.

'My friend messaged saying he will take us to his uncle who is the assistant commissioner of Mumbai,' Danny said.

'Thanks, Danny,' Rivanah said. It was time something was done about the Stranger.

# 9

Rivanah was the first to wake up the next morning. Giving a peck to a sleeping Danny, she went to fetch the milk packets and the day's newspaper from her doorstep. As she crossed the living room to reach the kitchen, she noticed a sketch board. She frowned; she hadn't noticed it lying there before. She tossed the newspaper on the sofa and sauntered to the kitchen to put the milk packets in the fridge and then came right back to stand in front of the board. There was a sketch of a pair of eyes, a nose, lips and ears but the contour of the face was missing. *Danny never told me he sketches*, she wondered and checked the sketches under the first one. Each of them had her name signed at the bottom-right corner. She was about to turn around when she felt a pair of hands around her waist.

'What are you doing, baby?' It was Danny.

'Did I sketch these?'

'Of course, you did,' Danny said and licked the back of her ears subtly. It tickled her senses but her mind was elsewhere. If she had sketched them, why didn't she remember it? Just like she didn't remember Hiya Chowdhury? Why did Ishita have to relay everything she had experienced herself only days back? Rivanah was deeply immersed in her thoughts.

'What happened?' Danny said, sensing a certain stiffness in her.

'Nothing.'

'Not in the mood?'

She gave him a weak smile.

'I understand. Anyway, get ready,' he said, giving her a peck on the cheek. 'We need to go to the police first. Then I have to meet the producer of my film.'

'How is the film going, Danny?' Rivanah said and felt a tad guilty for not having asked sooner. She had been so preoccupied with what was happening in her own life that she had forgotten that Danny's life too, somewhere, touched her. The last time she had inquired about him was when she had talked to him on phone from Kolkata.

'So far so good. Two more shoot schedules left. One in Mumbai and the other one in Delhi.'

'Great. By the way, I have to go to office today. I can't take any more leaves.'

'That's why I said, get ready quickly.'

Danny and Rivanah picked up his friend from Bandra, and together they went to the friend's uncle's place in Mumbai Central. All through the drive, Rivanah kept quiet but her mind was constantly probing the reason for her forgetfulness. First Hiya, and now the sketches. This, she understood, had to be the second dot—forgetting Hiya was the first. But she had never forgotten the Stranger. Were these two dots exclusive of the Stranger? Or, would she get the third dot only when she joins the first two properly? Every question was a dead end and it made her all the more frustrated. Moreover, now she only knew as much about Hiya Chowdhury as Ishita had relayed to her. What about the stuff she may have known earlier? How the hell had she become so forgetful?

Danny's friend took them to his uncle, Assistant Commissioner Dharmesh Waghdhare, whose house had a constant influx of constables. At fifty-five, Mr Waghdhare had a rather amicable personality for a police officer. He met the trio over breakfast. It was Danny who narrated what had happened the previous night.

'So nobody has seen the person who threw kerosene on her?'

'No. I asked the security guards and other people this morning, but nobody saw any one,' Danny said.

'Aren't there any CCTV cameras in your building?'

'No, sir.'

'Do you suspect anyone?'

Rivanah glanced at Danny and then said, 'There is a senior in my office.'

'Argho Chowdhury,' Danny added.

'And why would he do such a thing? Spurned lover, you think?' Dharmesh asked, finishing his poha and taking a sip from his mango shake.

'I never got any love-struck vibes from him, which is why I'm all the more confused—why would he do something like this?' Rivanah wondered aloud, fully aware that she wasn't making much sense. She wanted to disclose the Kolkata incident to Waghdhare and that a complaint had already been registered with the Kolkata Police, but, because of Danny's presence, she didn't. She had still not told him about it and disclosing it now would only put a strain on his trust. According to the Kolkata Police, Argho had an alibi. He flew out of Kolkata a day before the incident. But he could have bribed someone else to come to her house and create the deadly mess.

'Hmm, you don't seem to know of any possible reason, but you still think Argho could be trying to kill you? That's a big allegation,' he said. Waghdhare had years of experience which had sharpened his instinct for crime. He felt Rivanah was hiding something. Or that some important part of the puzzle was missing.

'The thing is, I can get this Argho guy picked up for interrogation, but I would rather catch him red-handed. If he is guilty, that is.' He looked at all of them one by one as he spoke. 'So I'll ask one of my men to follow him for a week or so. Let's see what comes up.'

'What if he attacks again?' Rivanah blurted.

'My man will be there. Any suspicious activity, and Argho Chowdhury will be taken into custody.'

Rivanah moistened her dry lips anxiously and glanced at Danny. 'So we will leave now, uncle,' his friend said, as he stood up.

'Sure,' Dharmesh said and turned to Rivanah to say, 'My man will contact you in some time. Give him all the details of Argho Chowdhury, and when you are in office, make sure you don't make it obvious that he's a suspect. Also, remain alert always.'

'Sure, sir,' Rivanah said, and left with Danny who dropped her to her office. Once Rivanah was in, she was extra conscious of Argho's presence. Though their cubicles were far apart, if she pushed her chair back a little, Argho's cubicle would be visible to her.

Argho came in half an hour late. The promised phone call from the policeman came within minutes of Argho's arrival in the office. Rivanah told him whatever she could about Argho. The policeman, Sadhu Ram, asked her to calm down and to make sure her suspicion wasn't obvious. The rest he would manage since he had already collected Argho's photograph, address and phone number. Though Rivanah had piles of work, she kept her eyes on Argho. If he went to the washroom, she excused herself and paced up and down right in front of the men's washroom. She was sure Argho would message her from inside the washroom from one of the Stranger's numbers. But nothing happened. Instead, there was a momentary, awkward eye contact with Argho when he came out of the washroom.

'Hey, congrats,' he said.

'Huh?' Rivanah was stumped.

'I saw you at the convocation ceremony in Kolkata.'

'Oh!' She could feel a cold sweat forming right behind her ears. 'Thanks,' she managed to say. *What else did he see? Ishita and me following him to his cousin Hiya's place?* she wondered as Argho moved on.

Once she was back at her cubicle, they exchanged a few casual glances, but nothing out of the ordinary. Rivanah was slightly embarrassed by the thought that if Argo was really the Stranger, then he had seen her in all kinds of nudity; both physical and emotional. How do you face a person in that case? Later in the day, she somehow controlled the itch to keep an eye on him, reminding herself that all will be clear in a week's time. *One week*, Rivanah leaned back on her chair and wondered, *and finally the whole mystery will end.* Talking of mysteries, it struck her that she should continue sketching if she knew the craft. The sketches at her place told her she wasn't exactly a novice. But one more issue still remained: why did she forget about the sketches, like she had forgotten about Hiya?

'Come on, let's go,' Rivanah heard one of her team members say. She opened her eyes and sat up straight on her chair and saw most of the employees rushing off somewhere. She quickly caught up with one of them.

'What happened? Fire drill?' Rivanah tried to guess.

'No, yaar,' Rekha, her teammate, said. 'You weren't here last week. It was announced that Samir Bajaj would deliver a lecture on successful business start-ups. He is here.'

'Samir Bajaj?'

'The entrepreneur of the year: Samir Bajaj. Of Bajaj Corps.'

'Oh,' Rivanah said, making a face as she followed Rekha to the boardroom. The whole thing sounded dead boring to her.

The boardroom was packed with employees, making Rivanah feel claustrophobic. The two chairs in the centre were reserved for Samir Bajaj and the CEO of her company, Anil Khanna. There were a few mineral-water bottles kept in the front, a bouquet and couple of small trays with Ferrero Rochers on it. They were her weakness. She went near the chairs and as others were busy chit-chatting and tapping on their mobile phones Rivanah picked up a handful of chocolates and stealthily went and stood in a corner.

The lecture was exactly as Rivanah had predicted: BORING. Sometime in the middle of it, she managed to step out of the boardroom, popped one of the chocolates into her mouth and went back to her cubicle. There was nobody in the entire floor except for few office boys. She had last seen Argho in the boardroom with his colleagues. Rivanah thought of checking her Facebook but what she saw on her desktop monitor made her go numb. A Word doc was open and had bold, red-coloured words in font size 36:

*It's farewell, Mini.*

Before she knew, Rivanah was already sweating in the air-conditioned floor of her office. Out of fear, she walked briskly to the boardroom again. She didn't dare to turn and check if anyone was watching or following her. The moment she entered the boardroom, she heard people applauding. The session was finally over. She noticed Argho on the opposite side. He did look at her but Rivanah couldn't guess if it was an intentional gaze or a casual one. Mr Bajaj and Mr Khanna walked out of the boardroom together. Everyone else started to file out too. Once the crowd became thin, she went towards the exit only to be stopped by someone.

'You left these,' the man said. He had few Ferrero Rochers in his hand. It was the same greenish-eyed man who had saved her in the elevator and once more in the backstairs. He had an amused expression on his face; he had obviously seen Rivanah stealing the other Ferrero Rochers from the plate.

'I'm sorry. Actually, I can't resist these,' she said apologetically.

'It's okay. Stealing chocolates isn't a crime.' He flashed a smile and Rivanah's mind buzzed with a new-crush alert. She took the chocolates from him.

'Thanks,' she said.

The man turned and started walking away, when she stopped him saying, 'Excuse me! I'm Rivanah Bannerjee.' She extended her hand for a handshake.

'Call me Nivan,' he said and shook her hand with a firmnesss that evoked certain forbidden thoughts in Rivanah's mind. Before she could follow him further to know which department he worked in, she remembered she had something more important waiting. Rivanah called Sadhu Ram, clicked a picture of the Word document on her screen, and sent it to him on WhatsApp as directed. He asked her to be extra alert.

Rivanah was expecting a call from Sadhu Ram but it didn't come. She left office early and took a cab home. She noticed a bike was always moving parallel to her cab. The rider whose head was hidden inside a mercury-coated helmet kept looking sideways. Rivanah's heart was in her mouth. There was no prize for guessing who this rider could be. What if he attacked her? She rolled up the window of the cab and asked the driver to go faster, but it didn't matter how fast he drove, the rider was always parallel to her. Did he come to know about the police guy following him? Rivanah was getting nervous with every passing second. She kept Sadhu Ram's number open on her phone.

Finally, at one of the traffic signals, the rider halted right next to Rivanah's cab and climbed down the bike. Her heart almost stopped. She checked if the cab's door was locked; it was. The rider came right up to the window and removed his helmet. It was Ekansh. For a moment, she didn't know how to react. Next, out of rage, she rolled down the cab's window. But before Rivanah could ask him why the hell he was stalking her like a fool, he said, 'I have found a way to apologize to Tista.'

Somehow he didn't look like his former self.

# 10

'What the hell are you talking about, Ekansh?' Rivanah said. Before she could get around to asking him why he was following her, the traffic light turned green. Vehicles behind them were honking, with drivers hurling abuses at them for holding up the traffic on a busy street. Ekansh wasn't ready to go back to his bike. Rivanah didn't know what to do, nor did the cab driver. He kept inching the cab ahead while Ekansh kept jogging alongside.

'Ekansh!' Rivanah rebuked, 'Get your damn bike and meet me at the other side of the signal.' To the driver she said, 'Bhaiya, signal ke aage side kar dijiye.'

The cab driver mentally abused Ekansh for cutting his drive short. Once he crossed the signal and parked the car, Rivanah paid the fare and got down. Ekansh by then had parked his bike right behind the cab. She went straight to him.

'What's your problem, Ekansh?'

'Rivanah, I'm sorry,' he said, removing his helmet once again.

'Why are you doing this to me? We are done. Like *done*! Let's not re-establish contact ever again.'

'Can we please sit and talk?'

'No! We can't!' Rivanah was furious. She looked around only to realize her pitch was loud enough to attract attention. Heads were turning in their direction. It made her uncomfortable.

'Okay, let's go,' she said.

She wanted to be done with this once and for all. Rivanah rode pillion as they headed to the nearest CCD outlet.

'Tell me, what is it?' Rivanah snapped, once Ekansh had placed his order.

'Firstly, I'm sorry,' Ekansh said.

'Your sorry irritates me, Ekansh. You always say sorry but you are never really sorry. So please cut the crap and tell me why you were following me. You were saying something about Tista?'

'I couldn't sleep after Tista passed away. I felt restless all the time thinking that Tista knew what happened and I couldn't even say sorry to her.'

'Again sorry? Listen, you either come straight to the point or I'm out of here.'

Ekansh understood that Rivanah was losing patience. 'I won't be able to live in peace if I don't apologize to her.'

Rivanah stared at Ekansh like he had lost it completely. 'Didn't Tista die in front of both of us?'

Ekansh nodded.

Novoneel Chakraborty

'Then what is this "I want to apologize to her" bullshit?'

'Planchette.'

'What?' Her disbelief pushed her to reconfirm with him.

'I will call upon her soul and apologize.'

She knew what a planchette was. Once or twice during college, some friends had talked about it eagerly, but nobody had ever tried it. Rivanah didn't even know if it was real. *Can souls be really recalled?* Rivanah knew she couldn't be a part of this nonsense.

'Ekansh, I can't help you in this, and please don't follow me or try to contact me again. I'm sorry for whatever happened with Tista, I really am, but I too have a life. Let me live it peacefully,' she said and started to walk away.

'Don't you want to apologize to Tista too?' he asked. His high pitch made the other customers look at them with curiosity. She gave him a you-are-incorrigible look and stormed out.

Rivanah knew she was being rude but she didn't care. To cut all ties, one had to be rude at times. She had already tried it the other way and it hadn't worked.

Once Rivanah reached home, she called Danny. He didn't answer but a minute later messaged that he was in a meeting and would call back right after it ended. Loneliness brought the memory of Tista. Her face started flashing in front of Rivanah along with Ekansh's last words to her: *Don't you want to apologize too?* Ekansh's guilt was spreading its roots deep in her as well. She had chosen to ignore it, Ekansh hadn't. But now, after meeting him, she was forced to pay attention to it. And who was responsible for this guilt? Who had told Tista about the unplanned 'escapade' between Ekansh and her?

Rivanah called up Sadhu Ram. 'Sadhu Ramji, any news yet?'

'Just been two hours. As of now, nothing. Argho Chowdhury lives in Andheri East. I'm right outside his building.'

'All right.'

'Don't worry, I shall let you know if I get anything.'

'Okay, thank you.'

Rivanah thought of messaging the Stranger; it didn't matter to her then if it was Argho. He owed her an explanation as to why he had told Tista and made everyone's life miserable. Including the one who was dead.

*Why did you tell Tista the truth?* Rivanah tapped her phone hard to write the message and sent it to all the numbers she had saved of the Stranger.

*Why didn't you tell Danny the truth?* came the Stranger's reply. Rivanah frowned, reading the message, and dialled the number from which she had received it, pressing her phone against her ears.

'Hello, Mini,' the Stranger said in a male voice.

'Get this right: I will not tell Danny the truth, okay?'

'Then I will,' the Stranger replied in a poised manner.

73

'You will not!' Rivanah brought the phone in front of her mouth and almost screamed at it.

'I sure will.' The tone remained unaffected.

A few seconds of silence later, Rivanah added, 'Please. I beg you. I'm done with Ekansh. Telling Danny the truth may not go well. I just don't want to take a chance.'

'If you don't take a chance, you will never know how true your love is.'

'I already know how true our love is, so please spare me.'

'You have no idea, Mini, how much these assumptions of yours excite me to prove you otherwise.'

Rivanah swallowed a lump.

'You are simply impossible,' she said and hung up.

The next second the Stranger messaged back: *Guilty as charged.* A pissed-off Rivanah put her phone away and opened her laptop to distract herself. There was no way she was going to tell Danny about what had happened between Ekansh and her. Definitely not now, when everything was back on track between Danny and her. She was about to log in to her Facebook when another message popped up on her phone.

*Please!*

It was a WhatsApp from Ekansh. Rivanah didn't care to reply. She put her phone on silent mode and continued logging on to Facebook. She checked her phone again. There was a missed call from Ekansh. *This guy has turned nuts! Does he really think I will help him with . . .*

*what was the word . . . planchette?* She wondered and, after a thoughtful moment, typed the word on Google. For the next one hour, Rivanah read whatever Google had to offer on planchette. And most of them were real life incidents—or so the articles claimed. There was one particular article which piqued her interest the most. It said that a planchette was done by a group of relatives to connect with the spirit of a person who was murdered. And they claimed that through planchette they identified who the murderer was. It sounded like a television script but it intrigued her. Could it be true? If yes, then all her problems would end in one go. Was it worth a try? What will she lose even if it's a bluff? Rivanah picked up her phone and stared at Ekansh's name for some time before finally dialling his number. He answered on the second ring itself.

'Hi. I knew you would call.'

She ignored the comment and came straight to the point.

'I shall help you communicate with Tista, but I have a condition.'

'What condition?'

'You too will have to help me communicate with someone.'

'Who?'

'Hiya Chowdhury.'

75

# 11

The plan seemed perfect. Rivanah would go to Ekansh's place right after office. And together they would call upon the spirit of Tista first and then Hiya through planchette, and help each other get rid of their personal burdens. Ekansh wanted to apologize while Rivanah wanted to ask Hiya who her killer was. Ekansh enquired why she wanted to know who killed Hiya when the entire college knew she committed suicide; Rivanah simply put forward her second condition: no questions. But she didn't let Ekansh go without asking him a few questions of her own.

'Was Hiya my friend?' she asked.

'She was your batchmate. The topper.'

'What else do you know about Hiya and me?'

'What do you mean?'

'Just answer me, Ekansh.'

'Nothing more. But why are you asking me? Whatever I know, you too should know, right? In fact, you would know more since she was your batchmate, not mine.'

Rivanah didn't answer. Now, standing by the window of her bedroom, she wondered how she could answer something she didn't remember about herself.

Danny called for her attention.

'Can we go for dinner tomorrow night? Maybe I'll get free early,' he said, sipping on green tea while phone-browsing.

'Sure, we can.' She didn't want to refuse now and raise an alarm. But she knew that she would have to call Danny after work and, on the pretext of an important meeting, go straight to Ekansh's place to finish the chapter of the Stranger's identity once and for all. Then she would come back to be with Danny. Forever. *Forever: the root of all flowery assumptions in a love story*, she thought and knew no one could sever oneself from this concept since it is forever that makes the fight for love worth it. Somewhere, the fact that she was ready to remain committed to Danny forever helped her justify her lie to him. And what was the truth anyway? That Ekansh and she had fucked that night in the flat? It was one of those random slips which . . . Rivanah checked her thoughts . . . well, it wasn't a random slip. Such vulnerability towards someone happens when that someone defines almost the whole of your past. And more often than not, it is a permanent vulnerability. After all, time isn't a strong-enough detergent to wash off certain spots of memories.

*The planchette though*, Rivanah thought, *was her best bet to clean up her life once and for all.* First, she wouldn't meet

Ekansh ever again after this, and second, she would know who the Stranger is since she was sure he was the one who had killed Hiya. She would then move on with Danny to happier and less-confusing times.

The next day Rivanah went to her office on time. Seeing Argho reminded her that she had received no intimation from Sadhu Ram. She wanted to call him but stopped herself, deciding it was better to give Sadhu Ram his own time. Not like he would hold on to information. Tonight something would anyway come up. Only nine hours remained before they dabbled in planchette.

In the afternoon, she received a message from Ekansh asking if their plan was still on. She wanted to clarify that it was his plan, and that she was only helping him, but sent a dry 'yes' instead. She didn't want to give him any signal to lurch on to and initiate something which may progress into anything even remotely close to a relationship.

After work, Rivanah called Danny and told him she had a meeting and wouldn't be able to join him for dinner. But she promised she would prepare his favourite dish the moment she was home. Danny said he would wait. Rivanah took a cab and rushed to Ekansh's place. He was putting up at an out-of-town friend's place in Santa Cruz.

Ekansh opened the door before Rivanah could press the doorbell.

'I saw you coming into the building,' Ekansh said. She gave him a tight smile noticing his dark circles were more pronounced than ever but chose not to comment. He looked desperate. She didn't know what weighed on him more—Tista's death or his guilt. *Did our break up ever weigh on him?* Rivanah thought and stepped into the rather tiny flat.

'You want to drink some water?' he said.

'Let's go through this quickly, please.'

Ekansh looked at her and nodded.

'I have arranged everything. Come on in,' he said.

After a slight hesitation she followed him inside. It was a small, dimly lit bedroom with no furniture. A rolled-up mattress lay in one corner. In the middle of the room, she noticed, was the Ouija board used for planchette, as Google had told her a day back. It was an ancient portal to connect to the dead. Till that moment, she had been eager, but now, as she saw the Ouija board, she felt scared. Would Tista's and Hiya's spirit actually come to them? Her throat went bone dry.

'I need some water,' she told Ekansh. He was busy placing a candle at each corner of the Ouija board.

'Sure.' He stood up and went out of the bedroom. Rivanah came forward and knelt down to notice a coin at the centre of the board. There was a sound and Rivanah's heart was in her mouth. She turned to see Ekansh bringing her a glass of water.

'I'm sorry.' He realized he had petrified Rivanah.

'It's okay.' It was not. She nervously took the glass of water from him and gulped it down in one go.

'So how do we go about it?'

Ekansh kept the glass away and sat down beside the Ouija board. He took a deep breath and said, 'We both sit opposite each other.'

Rivanah sat down right opposite Ekansh. He brought one of the corner candles and put it at the centre of the board and said, 'We need to put our index fingers on the coin.' He put his finger on it. Rivanah followed. He stretched his hand saying, 'We must hold our hands.'

Rivanah wasn't sure.

'It's important, Rivanah.'

Reluctantly she stretched her hand. Ekansh clasped it.

'We need to close our eyes and call upon whom we want to first.'

'Tista.' Rivanah wanted to say Hiya's name first but the hair on her nape had stood up at the thought of it.

'We need to call Tista to our mind with utmost attention and focus.'

'How will we know she is here?'

'This candle will extinguish on its own,' he said, glancing at the candle in the centre.

*On its own . . .* the thought made Rivanah's tension rise up, shortening her breaths.

'And with these letters and numbers, we can interact with her,' Ekansh said, gesturing at the Ouija board. Rivanah swallowed a lump. *How can Ekansh be so cool about all this?* she thought. He looked like he dealt with spirits on a regular basis. Perhaps he was more concerned about his apology than anything else. *Typically selfish Ekansh*, Rivanah concluded.

'Let's close our eyes and start chanting her name,' he said and closed his eyes. Rivanah too closed her eyes and together in their minds they started chanting Tista's name. Rivanah started having flashes of all the good times she had spent with Tista, especially that scene with her questioning eyes, as she looked at her before going in for the surgery. She could never forget those eyes. They had an accusation in them, as if her trust had been breached. And rightly so. Had she not let the sexual slip happen with Ekansh that evening in the flat then . . . Rivanah felt Ekansh's grasp tighten. On an impulse, she opened her eyes and found him staring at the candle. Its flame had died. Rivanah could hear her own heart beating. Her body was mildly shivering. Was it real? Was Tista's spirit in the room? Suddenly she felt a haunting energy in the room. It freaked her out.

'Tista, are you there?' Ekansh spoke up. He sounded brittle. Rivanah didn't move. She only kept moving her eye balls from right to left, scared to see an apparition. She suddenly felt Ekansh pushing her finger which was on the coin. And before she could even fight it, the coin was already moved to the right, to the space in the Ouija board marked 'yes'. One glance at Ekansh and she knew he wasn't pushing the coin at will. Or was he? There was something eerie in the air and Rivanah felt she couldn't breathe any more. Her hands and legs felt heavy and muscles stiff.

'I'm sorry, Tista,' he said. Rivanah could sense his lips shiver and voice shudder as he spoke, 'I know I broke your trust. But I'm apologizing now.'

Nothing happened.

'Will you please—?'

One of the windows in the room opened suddenly. Rivanah was about to stand up but Ekansh held on to her tightly. She was profusely sweating by now. *I'm not doing this again*, Rivanah promised herself, as she heard Ekansh speak again. She had never felt her heart beating so hard.

'Will you please forgive me, Tista? I love you and I mean it.' Ekansh was staring at the coin hoping it would move to his left. A moment later, their fingers on the coin felt a push to the 'yes' part of the board. Was it really a spirit or was it Ekansh's own guilt manipulating him to push the coin, Rivanah couldn't tell.

'Thank you so much, Tista, for liberating me from this guilt. I miss you.'

Rivanah was glaring at Ekansh. He understood why.

'Goodbye, Tista,' he said and the next moment he let Rivanah's hand go.

'Are we done?' she whispered.

'Yes. Should we call upon Hiya?'

'No!' Rivanah stood up.

'What happened?'

'I changed my mind. And I'm leaving.'

Ekansh could tell she was scared. Rivanah walked to the drawing room with Ekansh behind her. *It was a foolish idea to even participate in this*, she thought. One more minute, and she would have fainted there.

'What's the matter, Rivanah?'

'Nothing. And, by the way, we are now officially done. Please don't try to contact me.'

'I thought we—'

'Just don't do that, Ekansh. We are done. Period,' she said and was about to storm out when her phone rang. It was Danny. She gestured Ekansh to keep quiet, with a finger on her lips, and took the call.

'Hey, baby.' For Danny, she was having a long day at office. She tried her best to sound tired.

'Hey, where are you?'

'Office. I told you I have a long meeting.'

'Hmm.' He didn't sound convinced.

'What happened?'

'Someone just messaged me saying you are with Ekansh at his place. I was pretty confident you weren't, but I was passing by your office, so thought I'd stop over.'

How could she underestimate this 'someone', Rivanah cursed herself and said, 'Where are you now?'

'I'm right outside your office. Can you come out for a minute?'

Rivanah pressed the mute button quickly and looking at Ekansh said, 'You need to help me out. Fast!'

# 12

'Give me five minutes. I'll be downstairs,' Rivanah told Danny on phone and disconnected. She wasn't sure if it was Argho who had messaged Danny, but she decided she would take care of it later. First, she had to reach Danny.

'But we can't reach your office in five minutes,' Ekansh said, picking up his friend's bike keys from the key holder near the main door.

'We'll have to,' Rivanah said and rushed out of the flat. Ekansh followed.

They zoomed to her office on Ekansh's friend's bike. The traffic was intense and they had to stop at almost every signal. Rivanah's tension grew by the minute as she constantly kept checking the time on her watch. *What if Danny calls back? With such a cacophony of horns all around, he'll immediately know I'm not inside the office.* Four minutes after they had left, they had only crossed half the distance. She told Ekansh to speed up. He looked at her via the rear-view mirror and changed the gear. He didn't stop at any signal even though most were red. When they were just one traffic signal away from her office, Ekansh was cornered by three traffic policemen.

'Damn! Not now,' Rivanah lamented. As Ekansh stopped his bike and took off his helmet, he turned around and said, 'You take an auto and leave. I'll sort this out.'

Rivanah didn't waste another second. While she was climbing down the bike, Danny called again. She let the phone ring for a bit while she hailed an autorickshaw and then cut the call. She immediately WhatsApped him:

*Two minutes, baby. Meeting is getting over.*

*Okay.*

She prayed hard that she would make it on time. *No more Ekansh. No more visiting the past. No more lies to Danny.* Rivanah didn't like one bit of what she was doing. And to negate the dislike, she kept telling herself, *I will make up for it. I really will.*

As the autorickshaw took a turn from the Linking Road signal, she noticed a Xylo near the main gate of her office building. Danny was sitting on the driver's seat perusing his phone. Even if she wanted to, she couldn't afford to get down from the autorickshaw there. She asked the driver to go around the office building and eventually got down near the back gate. She paid the fare and WhatsApped Danny:

*Where are you? I'm at the back gate.*

*Oh, I'm at the front. Wait, I'm coming,* Danny replied. Waiting for him, Rivanah wondered what a fool she had been to have involved herself with Ekansh for the planchette. *Like always!* Every time she convinced herself she had improved, she ended up doing some stupid act or the other. And her instinct told her it would continue till she was done with Hiya. Or maybe till Hiya was done with her. She would have herself died of fear in Ekansh's flat had she been there for a minute longer. She wanted to know who had killed Hiya Chowdhury and who the Stranger was, but not this way. This way, she would only die and join Hiya wherever she was. Rivanah saw a Xylo taking a turn on the back lane. She waved and walked towards it.

'I had a talk with Sadhu Ram,' Danny said the moment Rivanah got into the car and wore her seat belt. She looked at him expectantly.

'He said Argho is presently at his flat in Andheri. I also passed him the number from which I received the message. Sadhu Ram got it checked. It came from the tower closest to Argho's place.'

'Goddamn it! Can't we just get him?'

'I asked him the same thing. But we need more definite clues to round Argho up since the number wasn't registered in his name.'

'Oh!' She took Danny's phone and checked the message:

*Rivanah is alone with Ekansh at his friend's flat in Santa Cruz.*

She swallowed a lump because every word of it was true. She checked the number next. A chill ran through her spine. It was Ekansh's Mumbai number which, she was sure, the Stranger had duplicated and used to message Danny.

'Do you recognize the number?' Danny asked.

Rivanah shook her head hesitatingly.

'I ran it via Truecaller. It did throw up a name—Ekansh,' he said.

Rivanah frowned as if it was news to her.

'Anyway, where do you want to go for dinner?' Danny asked, shifting the gear.

'Home.'

'Huh?'

'Remember, I'm supposed to prepare dinner for us tonight,' she said smiling.

'Oh yes. Sounds super.'

Rivanah leaned back on her seat, switched on the FM to a channel which was playing a soft romantic number and tried to relax, hoping Danny would not probe further, when she heard him speak.

'Don't take it otherwise, Rivanah, but is there something that I should know but you aren't telling me?'

Rivanah glanced at him not knowing how or where to hide her emotions. *Yes, there are things I haven't told you yet. But, trust me, they aren't important. Not any more. Those things involve me—and only me. I know what involves one involves the other too in a relationship, but, trust me, I won't let it affect what we share with each other.* She locked her jaws tight in order to gulp her emotions before they made their presence obvious.

'Has that scoundrel been disturbing you a lot?' he asked.

Rivanah spoke after a pause, 'Not really.'

'What do you mean?'

87

'I think he knows I have been to the police so I haven't heard anything from him again. Nothing after the kerosene episode.'

'Hmm.'

Danny surprised Rivanah by clasping her hand gently. He looked at her as he drove on a rather empty lane.

'I don't want a veil between you and me, Rivanah. If we love each other, we shouldn't have filters. You get my point?'

*Do I get his point? Or do I already know what he means but can't believe in it enough to implement it?* But Rivanah found herself nodding in agreement. The only filter that love is capable of building in us is secrecy. When we are in love, we don't want our own selves to be an enemy of our relationship. And the more we stick to this want, the more vehemently the filter of secrecy is built. Though it is to protect something we long to have—the relationship—it is also potent enough to destroy it.

Once they reached their flat, Rivanah went to the kitchen to prepare lemon rice and pepper chicken, which they had with red wine. Every time Danny appreciated the preparation, Rivanah's guilt got a massage. Done with dinner, she went closer to him and, making herself comfortable in his lap, wine glass in hand, asked, 'Danny, you know I love you, right?'

'Yeah? I never knew that! Mind explaining?' he said, with an amused smile.

Rivanah looked into his eyes and held his chin in her hand, tilting his face a bit, and then planted a hard kiss on his lips. The moment their tongues met, she pushed herself inside his mouth and within seconds squeezed the blood out of his lips.

'You want more proof, mister?' This time a wicked amusement reflected in her face.

'I don't mind,' Danny said, maintaining eye contact. Rivanah slowly emptied the entire glass of red wine over his forehead and then started tracing it as the wine cascaded down his face. She licked his forehead, his cheeks, his ears, his chin and finally she came back to his lips from where she sucked the blood out from the tiny wound she had made seconds back. They were about to smooch again when Rivanah's phone rang. She pursed Danny's lips as she picked up her phone. He broke the kiss and asked, 'Who is it?'

Rivanah cut the call and said, 'Nobody.' She proceeded to kiss him when the phone rang again and Ekansh's name appeared on the screen. Danny caught Rivanah glancing at the phone in a spiteful way.

'Why don't you just take it?'

Rivanah understood even Danny was affected by it as much as she was. She picked up on the last ring.

'I'm sorry to disturb you, Rivanah . . .'

*When will he stop using that goddamn sorry word!* Rivanah wondered.

'I came out with you in a hurry,' Ekansh said over phone. 'I forgot my driver's licence. And now they have locked me up at the Goregaon police station.'

'What?' Rivanah couldn't hide her shock.

'Could you please come and bail me out?' Ekansh said. 'I called all my friends here in Mumbai. Nobody is available right now. The ones in Navi Mumbai will take forever to reach.'

'Uh-huh.' Rivanah kept shooting furtive glances at Danny trying to maintain a calm demeanour.

'Okay,' she said.

'Thanks a lot.'

'Okay. See you in some time. Bye.' She hung up and gave an exasperated look at Danny.

'Office call and you have to go,' he said.

Rivanah nodded.

'Then why are you looking so guilty about it? Work first. Should I drop you? It's already eleven.'

'I will take an auto or a cab. Don't worry. I'll be back soon. And . . .' she took his face in her hands and, kissing his nose, said, 'I will make up for this real soon.'

'You better! And be safe. Call if need be,' Danny said. *Only a woman knows how much a man's concern can turn her on*, she thought.

'I will,' she said, kissing the tip of his nose with a smile.

Soon Rivanah was in a cab heading towards the Goregaon police station. The traffic had eased out in the last hour. As her cab took a left turn from Mega Mall, a biker joined them from behind. The biker had his head covered with a helmet just like Ekansh had a day before.

*What the fuck!* Rivanah thought. *When will this guy understand we are done with each other?* She asked the driver to stop the cab. The driver slowed down first and then halted the cab on the left. Rivanah got down immediately and turned to see the biker had stopped right behind the cab.

'What's wrong with you, Ekansh?' In the calmness of the night, it sounded like a shout even though it wasn't quite.

The biker rode the bike to reach her.

'What? Will you explain this?' she said, first shrugging and then putting both her hands on her hips.

'You are going to have it from me if you tell me you lied about the lock-up thing.' The biker didn't move except for stretching his right hand towards her. His fist was closed. She noticed the biker was wearing gloves. A familiar smell reached her—It's Different, Hugo Boss. Rivanah's heartbeats slowed down. His fist opened and . . . *Is he going to slash my throat?* Rivanah thought and felt her knees lose strength by the second. The hand caressed her cheeks. She saw something drop to the ground. She looked down. It was a white piece of cloth. Before she could lift her head, she heard the biker speed away. There was no way to note down the number on the plate. It was only seconds after the biker left that Rivanah regained her composure and picked up the white cloth. In black embroidery it read:

*People use love to justify their dishonesty. You ONLY have two more days to confess, Mini.*

# 13

'Madam, chalna hai ki nahi?' the cab driver asked, realizing Rivanah was standing like a fool even after the rider had long gone.

Rivanah nodded and got into the cab again. *Was it Argho? Is he really going to tell Danny the truth if I don't confess in two days?* Rivanah kept wondering as the cab drove to the Goregaon police station. Standing outside the station entrance, for a moment Rivanah didn't know why she was there. Her phone buzzed with Danny's call. She picked it up on an impulse.

'Did you reach office?' Danny asked.

'No,' Rivanah blurted.

'What? It's been half an hour. Didn't you get a cab or what?'

It was then that she remembered the lie she had cooked up and made up an excuse for her slip up, 'I meant I'm about to enter the office building.'

'Oh, okay. Call me once you leave. I'm not sleeping until you are back.'

'Sure.'

Rivanah cut the call, paid the cab driver and then got out of the cab. She went straight inside the police station.

There were two vest-clad constables sitting and laughing outside a lock-up. The old man inside the lock-up, a convict by the looks of it, too was laughing with the constables. There was no sign of Ekansh. Rivanah went to the inspector sitting with his legs on the table and flipping through a foreign issue of *Maxim*. Rivanah coughed to get the inspector's attention. He looked up at her, startled. He kept the magazine aside and withdrew his legs from the table, shooting an inquiring look at Rivanah.

'I'm here to meet Ekansh Tripathi,' Rivanah said. The inspector's reply was blocked out by the beep of a WhatsApp message on her phone. It was from Ekansh:

*Thank you.*

'Please excuse me,' Rivanah told the inspector and called up Ekansh.

'Hey, nice to get your call,' Ekansh said picking up the phone.

'Where the hell are you?'

'I'm on my way home. Why?'

'Who bailed you out?' Rivanah asked. By then she had already started walking away from the inspector and towards the entrance. The inspector kept staring at Rivanah cluelessly.

'You sent a lawyer and bailed me out ten minutes ago.'

'What?'

'Why are you sounding so surprised?'

'Did you tell anyone about the incident except me?'

'No. Why would I?'

Only one person could have known where Ekansh was.

'Is something up?' Ekansh asked.

The inspector saw Rivanah step out of the police station. He was too lazy to ask her why she was there in the first place. He picked up the magazine again.

'No, nothing,' Rivanah said and continued, 'Ekansh, I want you to listen carefully to what I'm about to say next.'

'I'm listening.'

'I want you to delete my number after I disconnect this call. Whatever we shared—good, bad, ugly—it is all in the past and we should put it behind us and move on. Do you get what I'm trying to tell you?'

'Hmm. You don't want us to be in touch any more.'

'Precisely.'

'But I need you, Rivanah.'

Rivanah rolled her eyes and continued, 'Please don't say things like that. When you had me, you never needed me. Now when you can't have me, you shouldn't need me.'

'But—'

'Ekansh, this is for our own good. I expect you to understand this and ask no further questions. Stay good.'

'So this is it? We become strangers?'

The last word sent a shiver down Rivanah's spine. What if the Stranger was watching her?

'Yes, this is it. We don't become strangers. We simply stop believing the fact that we are not an option for each other any more.'

There was silence at the other end.

'Goodbye, Ekansh. Take care,' Rivanah said, expecting a reply but he said nothing. She disconnected the line. A few seconds later, she deleted Ekansh's number as well as his chat messages from her phone. She looked around for a cab but couldn't find any. She opened her phone and tapped on the Ola app. There was a cab available within 5 minutes. While booking the cab, she heard something and looked up. At a distance, there was a bike with its headlights on. The rider was intentionally accelerating the bike to draw attention. In the darkness, she couldn't tell who it was and yet she knew it could only be one person. Her phone rang with an unknown number. She swallowed a lump and put the phone against her ears.

'Hello, Mini,' said a man's voice.

'What do you want?' Rivanah's voice was shivering.

'I want you to know your own worth, Mini.'

'That's what you have been telling me for a long time now. I want a different answer. And a correct one.'

There was silence. Rivanah was looking straight at the biker and knew the person would have his eyes on her.

'So, you won't answer?' she asked.

'So, you won't confess?' the Stranger shot back.

Rivanah became quiet for few seconds and then said, 'I will confess, but I want something in return. You can't always push me to do anything you want.' Though Rivanah was putting forth a condition, she couldn't sound confident about it.

'What is it?'

'I want to see you. As in, I want to see your face.'

There was silence at the other end.

'The moment you reveal your identity to me, I shall confess to Danny,' Rivanah said, knowing it was akin to Hobson's choice for the Stranger, so even though he was being given the freedom to make a free choice, only one option was actually being offered. There was no way the person on the bike was going to reveal his identity to her. Finally she had trapped the Stranger in some sort of dilemma. Her face broke into a sly smile.

'I shall meet you, Mini.'

The smile disappeared from Rivanah's face.

'You mean you are going to reveal your identity?'

'I shall reveal my identity to you.'

Rivanah swallowed hard and said, 'Now?'

'Soon. You will know when I do.'

'But no tricks. No masks. No nothing.'

'Promise. No tricks. No masks. No nothing,' the Stranger said.

'I'll wait,' Rivanah said and noticed her Ola cab had come up. The biker switched the headlight off and allowed the darkness to absorb him.

Rivanah got into the cab and was on her way to her flat.

'Bhaiya, AC on kar dijiye please,' she told the driver wiping the sweat off her brow.

'Madam, AC on hai,' the driver said.

And yet she was sweating profusely. She took out the wet, fragranced tissue from her purse and rubbed her face and nape with it. She kept looking behind to see if the Stranger was following her, but could spot no one. Something struck her. She took her phone and dialled Sadhu Ram's number. He picked up the phone and sounded groggy.

'Yes, madam.'

'What is Argho doing now?'

'He came back to his flat two hours back. I'm sitting right outside his apartment gate.'

'Oh okay, thank you,' Rivanah said and cut the line. *Argho can't be the Stranger then,* she thought. What she and Sadhu Ram didn't know was that Argho's bike was missing from the apartment's garage that moment.

97

# 14

There was an unusual buzz in Rivanah's office. Everyone, especially her own team members, looked happy and energetic. Rivanah soon found out that one of their important clients was happy with the software that her team had developed and had hence thrown a party for all of them after office hours. The news, however, didn't excite Rivanah much. She would have skipped the party if she had a choice. The moment she sat on the chair in her cubicle, her eyes fell on a pamphlet placed at her desk. It read: *Self-defence classes for women*. She looked around and saw the same pamphlet on every female employee's desk. Rivanah saved the phone number given on the pamphlet and folded it neatly before keeping it in her purse. The place was near her residence. She made a mental note of giving it a shot in a day or two. With the Stranger making his fatal intent clear more than a couple of times, self-defence may come in handy, she thought.

All through the morning, Rivanah kept checking her phone from time to time, constantly debating with herself whether the Stranger would actually reveal his identity to her. And if so, where would they meet? But no message came from the Stranger. It wasn't only about his revelation this time. There was a consequence to the revelation as well. If the Stranger actually revealed his identity, she would have to confess the truth to Danny. The fear of the consequence kept convincing her that the Stranger, as always, wouldn't reveal himself after all. It was one of those ploys of his to put her on the back foot. Rivanah was too mentally preoccupied to pry on Argho during office hours until she received a phone call from Sadhu Ram.

'Why did you call me last night?' Sadhu Ram asked.

'What?' The question had come out too abruptly for Rivanah to make any sense of it.

'What made you call me?'

'I wanted to check if Argho was at home.'

'Why suddenly?'

'Someone had followed me on a bike.'

'Why didn't you tell me this last night?' asked Sadhu Ram.

'I would have but you told me Argho was at his flat, so I thought . . . why, what happened?'

'I'm keeping a track of the kilometres his bike has been driven so that I know if he has driven without me knowing. Last night when I checked, it read 1203 kilometres, and this morning when he drove to office it read 1250 kilometres. And he drove straight from his house to the office which is only twenty kilometres.'

Rivanah was quiet. She knew what Sadhu Ram was hinting at.

'It means he had taken the bike somewhere last night without my knowledge,' Sadhu Ram said.

The obvious interpretation was: Argho *was* the Stranger. For the first time in the morning, she pushed her chair back and stood up to have a look at Argho. He was in his cubicle working with his back to her.

'Hello? Are you there, madam?' Sadhu Ram spoke over the phone.

'Yes, yes, I'm here.' Rivanah sat down on her chair and continued, 'What do we do now?'

'Did you notice anything last night that would prove it was Argho following you on bike?'

Rivanah thought for a moment. She hadn't seen the biker's face or even noticed the model of the bike. In fact, she didn't know Argho had a bike.

'I don't remember much except that the biker's helmet was black.'

'Hmm. That's not much of a help. Please update me immediately if anything happens. Even if you are remotely suspicious of anything, just let me know.'

'I sure will.'

The phone call ended. Rivanah once again glanced at Argho, who was still working, and thought: *If this guy is the Stranger, then he needs to be given the best actor award.*

Before moving out with her team around 8 p.m. to the Little Door eatery in Andheri West, where the client party was supposed to take place, Rivanah called Danny up who told her he too would be late. Rivanah, on one hand, was in no mood to party, but on the other hand, didn't want to go back to an empty home so early. Reluctantly she asked Danny to pick her up on his way home post the party. A part of the pub was cordoned off for the office team. When Rivanah reached there with her teammates it was rather quiet, but within an hour the place started warming up with people, alcohol and music. After Rivanah had her third Budweiser, she excused herself to go to the loo.

Just as she was about to pull up her panties after relieving herself, her phone beeped with a message.

*I'm at the party. See you soon.*

It was from one of the numbers belonging to the Stranger. Rivanah couldn't get up from the seat. *Is he really out there in the party? Is he someone I know?* Just then she heard a knock on the door.

'Are you done?' a female voice asked.

Rivanah quickly pulled up her panties, flushed and moved out. She washed her hands, wiped it dry and then, taking a deep breath, stepped outside. The music seemed even louder now. Her eyes were zeroing-in on each and every person in the restaurant. Some were drinking by the bar, some were sitting on couches in the corners and some dancing on the floor. The disco lights made it impossible for her to recognize anyone besides her colleagues whose faces she was familiar with. Finally she located Argho. He was by the bar outside in the open where people were allowed to smoke. Rivanah immediately called Sadhu Ram.

'Hello, I just received a message on my phone saying the Stranger is here.' She was careful nobody overheard her.

'Don't worry, I'm already keeping an eye on anyone who so much as approaches you. Just act as if all's well.'

'Thanks,' Rivanah said sounding relieved. She turned around to locate Sadhu Ram but couldn't see him. She turned to see Argho standing right behind her. She would have spilt his drink had he not pulled his hand back on time.

'Oops, sorry,' she said.

'Not a problem. Enjoying the party?'

'Yes.'

'Good. See you around,' said Argho and went inside. *Too casual,* Rivanah thought feeling an urge to keep an eye on him but knew Sadhu Ram was on it anyway. She went up to her teammates and picked up her beer pint which she had left mid-way before excusing herself to the restroom.

'Shots time, everyone!' one of her teammates screamed coming in with a tray full of tequila-shot pegs, lime and salt. Everyone picked up their pegs except for Rivanah.

'Don't tell me you aren't going to have it?' asked Rekha, the teammate she was closest to.

'Not tonight.'

'Not tonight? Then when? Come on!'

'Please . . .'

'If you aren't drinking, I won't either.'

'Don't be a spoilsport, Rivanah,' said another teammate.

'What's happening?' It was their US client, Mark Gems. Everyone stood up seeing him.

'Rivanah says she won't drink,' Rekha complained.

'What?' Mark sounded almost offended.

'No I mean, I—' Rivanah mumbled.

'What if there's a prize? 500 dollars to the one who gulps down the maximum shots!' Mark announced. There was a collective joyous hoot.

Rivanah was in a fix. She couldn't say no to her client while she knew she wouldn't be able to resist the temptation of the tequila shots if she tasted one. *I won't go for more than two*, she promised herself.

'All right,' she said resigning to the situation.

'That's the spirit girl!' Mark said as her teammates lined up in front of the table they had kept the shots on.

'On the count of three . . .' Mark said and continued, '1—2—3!'

There were seven of them, including Rivanah, and each one of them picked up their peg, did a bottoms-up and sucked on the lime dipped in salt. Mark gestured to one of the waiters who readied another set of shots for them. After each round, the pepping continued and the pressure got to Rivanah. After a total of seven rounds, only three people were left. One of them was Rivanah. The taste of tequila diluted her resolve. By the ninth round, only Rivanah and another guy, Sudhir, were left. On the tenth, Rivanah backed out. Sudhir was declared the winner of 500 dollars by Mark.

'Now just make sure Sudhir doesn't take the 500 dollars home. Your drinks are on him,' Mark said, winking at the group. Everyone laughed out.

'Let's burn the floor now. Come on!' Mark said and made the entire group hit the dance floor. Rivanah's head was already reeling. She thought she was in control but in reality she was high from the numerous tequila shots she had consumed. Rivanah wanted to simply sit by a chair outside but she was pulled to the dance floor by Mark.

The in-house DJ changed the song from a slow one to a fast Punjabi number. Rivanah started grooving to the beats of the music with her teammates. The tequila shots had invaded her conscience. The fact that the Stranger could be watching her flew out of her mind. After a long time she was this drunk. Every problem seemed trivial. Every guilt seemed avoidable. She felt as free as a bird. It was almost as if the alcohol had turned her into a child once again and everything in life was only a wish away. Just then her eyes fell on the guy who had saved her twice: once in the elevator, then at the backstairs. He had also noticed her stealing chocolates from the boardroom. Rivanah was having trouble recollecting his name. But she was very clear about one thing: she had a huge crush on him. He was busy chit-chatting with a male colleague by the in-house bar with a drink in his hand. Rivanah stopped dancing.

'What are you looking at?' Rekha screamed in her ears to negate the sound of the music.

'Who is that guy?' Rivanah asked her. Rekha followed her gaze and replied, 'That's Nivan. VP, sales.' Rivanah held her gaze for some time, the way a naughty thought makes you do, and then moved out of the dance floor. Tipsily, she headed straight towards Nivan.

'Excuse me,' she said. Nivan, along with the male colleague, turned to look at her.

'I wanted to thank you,' Rivanah said in a tipsy voice.

Nivan exchanged a clueless look with the male he was talking to.

'What for?' Nivan asked.

'You saved me some time back.'

'OH. KAY,' Nivan said, by now convinced she was extremely drunk.

'I'll get a refill,' the male sitting beside Nivan said and excused himself.

'So I really wanted to pay back tonight,' muttered Rivanah as she tried to stand upright.

'Really?' an amused Nivan asked.

'Yes. By dancing with you. May I?' Saying so, she pulled Nivan to the dance floor. Once there looking at him in the eye, she whispered, 'Thank you.'

Some of the office people had stopped dancing. It was quite a sight after all—Rivanah pulling the VP, sales, to the floor for a dance. But more than being concerned, it was entertainment for them. As if by a divine plan the music turned into a raunchy English number. Rivanah turned around, gyrating her pelvis rather sexually against Nivan. Before Nivan could think of what to do, Rivanah placed his hands on her waist. Though she was inebriated yet his touch made her labia twitch. Her hips were almost rubbing on to his pelvis as she wildly grooved to the English number. Nivan leaned forward and whispered in her ears, 'I'm overwhelmed with your payback. And I think I don't deserve more than this,' he said with a half-smile.

'No more?' Rivanah asked.

'No more,' Nivan said. Looking over at her teammate, Rekha, he said, 'Take care of her.'

'Sure, sir,' Rekha replied, going red in the face.

Nivan excused himself to rejoin the male colleague he had left at the bar.

Rekha took Rivanah outside in the open while she kept blabbering 'I want to pay back Nivan'. Rekha made her sit by a chair and went to get her a glass of water. Rivanah was finding it difficult to focus. If she was drunk before hitting the dance floor, she now felt sloshed. She placed her head on the table in front of her and shut her eyes. She felt like she was levitating in the air. She could hear the DJ had changed the song inside. She was about to stand up to dance on her own when she heard a voice.

'Hello, Mini.'

# 15

Rivanah kept staring at the blurry image of the person in front of her. She tried hard to make out the face, but everything seemed hazy. The voice was of a male, she was sure of that. Even the face seemed familiar but . . .

'I've been waiting to meet you, Mister Stranger . . .' she slurred.

'I'm here, Mini. Right in front of you. Revealing myself as promised,' the Stranger said.

'But . . . but . . .' She stretched her hand to touch him. She wanted to convince herself it was all real. Her fingertips traced his forehead to his nose to his lips to his chin.

'Who are you?' she asked.

'Who are you, Mini?' he asked back.

'I'm Rivanah Bannerjee.'

'That's only a name, Mini. And names don't define people.'

Rivanah kept looking at the blurry image of the Stranger, wishing she had not drunk so much, wishing she could hug the Stranger and explain that making out with Ekansh was a slip on her part, that she isn't a bad girl, after all, even if she isn't ready to confess anything to Danny yet.

'Do you love me?' she asked. She had no idea why she had asked him that question.

'Love? Does any one of us even know what love is? We all try to understand it. And the point where we think we have understood it is also the point where we let go of the chance to understand it completely.'

'I love Danny,' she said.

'I'm sure you do.'

'I don't want to confess.'

'You'll have to.'

'Why?'

'I told you something in the very beginning, Mini. Do you remember it?'

'What?'

'Know. Your. Worth.'

'Will I ever know my worth?'

'I wouldn't have wasted my time otherwise.'

Rivanah wanted to reach out for his hand but she frowned, hearing someone shout out her name.

'Rivanah!' It was Smita, another colleague of hers. Rivanah turned around.

'You burnt the dance floor, yaar,' Smita said. Rivanah turned back to look at the Stranger.

'Done partying?' She felt someone tap her shoulder. She turned around and saw it was Danny. There was no sight of the Stranger.

'Huh?' Rivanah wasn't ready for Danny. *What is he doing here?*

'Hi, I'm Danny. Rivanah's boyfriend.'

'I'm Smita. Her colleague.'

'Good to meet you, Smita. Is the party over? May I take Rivanah home?'

'Yeah sure. We are wrapping up right now.'

'But I want to stay and talk to him,' a sloshed Rivanah blabbered. Danny and Smita exchanged a clueless glance.

'Talk to whom?' Danny asked.

'Nobody,' Rivanah said. Danny understood how much under the influence of alcohol she was. He helped her into the car and drove straight home.

Next morning, she woke up remembering nothing. The memory of the Stranger coming and talking to her by the bar in the open seemed so distant that she wasn't sure if it was a memory or a wishful thought. When she checked her phone, it had seven missed calls from Sadhu Ram. She looked around for Danny. Before she could locate him, his phone buzzed. It was Sadhu Ram.

'Hello, where are you guys? I have been calling all day.'

'We were sleeping. What happened?'

'I regained consciousness only an hour back. Are you safe?' Sadhu Ram sounded genuinely concerned.

'Yeah, I'm all right. But what do you mean you regained consciousness?'

'I was knocked out last night.'

'Knocked out?'

'I had gone to the washroom while the party was on, after which I don't remember anything. The Little Door guys took me home.'

*Shit!*

'When I woke up, I was sure something must have happened to you.'

Rivanah was lost in a trance.

'Hello? You there?'

'Yes, I'm here. Where was Argho at the time?'

'He had already moved out of the party. I have already checked. He stayed with a friend in Bandra after he left the party. He has a strong alibi.'

'Does that mean he isn't the—?'

'That's what it seems like as of now. I think it is someone who is very close to you . . .'

Just then Danny came out of the bathroom in his boxers.

'Nothing like a cold shower,' he said and noticed Rivanah holding his phone to her ear.

'Whose call is it?' he asked.

*Someone close to you,* she thought, and vaguely remembered how Danny had suddenly appeared in front of her at the party.

'Sadhu Ram,' she blurted.

Danny took the phone from her and talked to Sadhu Ram. He recounted the same story to him. Danny hurled his phone on the bed after disconnecting the call and looked at her.

'Did anything happen last night at the Little Door?'

*I was talking to the Stranger and then I saw you in his place*, Rivanah wondered and said aloud, 'No. I don't remember anything strange.'

'Can you tell me what time I reached the party?' Danny asked in an interrogative tone.

Rivanah said she wouldn't know.

'I thought so. Even if something had happened, you wouldn't be able to tell.'

Rivanah kept staring at Danny as he wore his tee.

'When did you come last night?' she asked. Danny paused for a trice and said, 'I don't remember the exact time. Should be around 12.30. Why?'

'Just like that.'

'I haven't seen you so sloshed before.'

Rivanah hung her face in utter disappointment. She knew she shouldn't have drunk so much. *Damn the client, damn those tequila shots and damn her teammates. And, above all, damn her own self.* She remembered nothing concrete. Not even whether the Stranger had approached her or not. If he had not, then all was fine. But if he had, then she knew what was coming next. She had to respect her part of the deal. She hadn't received any message from the Stranger yet. Rivanah got ready and left for work, hoping against hope that there was more time.

'You were amazing last night,' Smita said. Rivanah immediately threw a what-are-you-talking-about glance at her. Smita took out her phone and showed her a video of Rivanah gyrating her hips against Nivan. She might

111

have enjoyed it the previous night but in the morning it looked plain vulgar to her.

'No, I didn't do that!' she said, feeling flabbergasted to say the least. She took the phone in her hand and watched the entire clip. By the time the video ended, her expression had changed to one of utter embarrassment. *What would Nivan think of me? A cheap despo!* Rivanah immediately deleted the clip.

'Arrey, why did you delete it?' said Smita, snatching the phone back.

'Isn't it obvious?' Rivanah shot back. 'Did I do anything else?'

'Well, after you went and pulled Nivan to the dance floor and danced like crazy with him, I don't think there was much left to do. And it's good you didn't. Your boyfriend was there shortly after.'

'You met Danny?'

'Yes. You are lucky to have such a caring boyfriend.'

'Thanks.' *I indeed am,* Rivanah thought. But first things first.

'Did you say his name was Nivan?' When he had told her his name for the first time, she hadn't registered it, but she was too tongue-tied to ask him again.

'Uh?'

'The guy I danced with last night.'

'Yes. Nivan; VP, sales.'

*Oh god!* This gets worse. I had a sexy dance with my VP with no memory of it.

'I need to apologize to him.'

'Well, even I think you should, though he didn't look too offended. Still, you never know.'

Rivanah knew where the Sales head's cabin was. She just didn't know who occupied the cabin until today. She excused herself and went straight to the cabin. With every step forward, she felt her heart beating faster. The man inside the cabin wasn't just her senior at work. He was someone on whom she had had a secret schoolgirlish crush.

'Hi sir, I'm sorry for last night. I wasn't in my senses and . . .' Rivanah kept mumbling the apology to herself softly while preparing herself to knock on the door. The moment she knocked, she heard a voice very close to her ears.

'You dance really well.'

Rivanah turned around and saw Nivan standing very closely behind her. Nivan took a step back and she wondered why. She wasn't complaining about the closeness. The thought made her feel guilty but the pleasure in the guilt made her go red in the face.

'Thank you,' she mumbled.

'You're welcome. Please excuse me,' Nivan said. Rivanah moved so he could enter his cabin but the moment he tried to step inside, she stopped him by his arm. He looked back at her. She let go of his hand immediately.

'I'm sorry for this. And for last night,' she said.

'Last night?'

*Does he really not remember or is he intentionally pushing it?*
'I'm sorry to have pulled you to the dance floor and . . .'

'That's fine. You were drunk. I got that.'

Rivanah smiled at him saying, 'Thanks.'

Nivan went inside his cabin while Rivanah traipsed towards her cubicle like a little girl who had spoken to her crush for the first time. She hoped her apology was enough to take care of the embarrassment she had caused herself and probably him too. She casually checked her phone which displayed a couple of WhatsApp messages from Danny and a message from one of the Stranger's number. She checked the time. It had come a minute back. She stopped dead in her tracks.

*I kept my promise, Mini. I was right there in front of you last night. We had a little chit-chat too. Now it's your turn.*

Rivanah missed a heartbeat. He must be lying. He couldn't have possibly revealed himself to her when she wasn't in her senses. Or was it all planned? Or was it all a . . .

*You are bluffing.* She messaged back.

*LOL* was the response.

Rivanah stared at the message for some time and then typed back:

*What was the colour of my dress last night?* She waited impatiently for a response.

He replied: *Pink.*

But she was wearing a purple dress . . . Rivanah paused. Her undergarments were pink. Rivanah swallowed hard.

*How do you know that?* she messaged.

*Why do you always forget that I have my ways, Mini?*

Did the Stranger really come in front of her?

'Shit!' she blurted out.

'Any problem?' It was Argho. Rivanah was quick to realize she was blocking his way. She shook her head and moved aside to let him pass. And she kept looking at him. When will she know for sure if Argho was the Stranger or not?

Rivanah went back to her cubicle and was about to call Danny and ask him not to believe in any message or call unless it was actually from her. Chances were the Stranger may manipulate Danny the way he did by messaging about her presence in Ekansh's flat the other night. Just then, her desk phone rang. It was from the security guard, informing her that there was a parcel in her name.

'I'm coming,' Rivanah said, put the receiver down and went to the security post.

A large parcel was waiting for her. She took it after signing in the register and then tore it open. It was a white, one-piece dress in floral print. A sudden smile appeared on her face, the kind that happens when you aren't prepared for something but really like it when it happens. Her phone vibrated with a message:

*I'm sure you'll look beautiful in this dress.*

Rivanah couldn't believe the Stranger had gifted her that dress. She had known the Stranger for a good while but he still didn't stop surprising her. Admiring the dress, she started walking towards her cubicle when she messaged back: *Thank you. But why this gift?*

*You should look beautiful when you confess an ugly truth to Danny.*

Rivanah paused reading the Stranger's message. Another message popped up precisely then:

*Don't disappoint me, Mini.*

There was nothing she could think of except: *Why this dress in particular? Why the dramatics?*

*The dress is bugged, Mini. I want to hear you confess.* The message popped in her phone as if the Stranger had read her mind.

*Coming in front of me when I was sloshed wasn't part of the deal. You have cheated me.* She messaged back sitting on her chair in her cubicle feeling a restlessness brewing in her.

*The deal was that I would come in front of you. Then you would confess. I didn't ask you to drink. My part of the deal is done, Mini. It is time for you to comply.*

Rivanah read and re-read the message. No, she can't simply comply, she kept telling herself. A message popped up after some time.

*9 p.m. tonight, Bungalow 9, Bandra. I've booked a table for Danny and you.*

After Rivanah read the message for the third time, she smiled. It wasn't the end of road for her after all, she thought. She had a plan to catch the Stranger.

She called Danny and told him that she had booked a table for them at Bungalow 9. Danny promised her he would be there directly from work. Next, Rivanah called Sadhu Ram and noted down his email, immediately after which she created a new email address for herself. She couldn't trust anything or any medium any more. She wrote Sadhu Ram an email where she mentioned all the details—from her dress being bugged to the venue and time Danny and she were supposed to meet. She also wanted to clear her doubts regarding a bugged dress. How far should a person be if he wanted to hear a conversation?

Sadhu Ram confirmed that chances were the person would either be inside or just around the restaurant. Rivanah asked him to stay away from the scene in case the Stranger already knew who he was. After sending the last mail to him she sat back in her chair waiting for the clock to strike 9. She stared at the floral dress she had placed on her table.

'That's a lovely one!' Rekha said, seeing the dress. 'Where did you order it from?'

'It's a gift,' Rivanah said with a tight smile. A few seconds later she picked up the dress and tried to feel it. She felt the microphone placed inside the cloth around the shoulder. The Stranger had taken the trouble to not only buy the dress but stitch the microphone inside. Rivanah sighed. Tonight she would finally know who the Stranger was.

## 16

Rivanah reached Bungalow 9 before Danny. She had changed into the floral dress in her office itself. She was escorted by one of the restaurant managers to the table reserved. She looked around to see if she could locate any familiar face but found none. Rivanah settled down and ordered a beer to calm her nerves. She kept checking her phone with every sip. Around 9.15 p.m., Danny was escorted inside by the same manager. As he came to the table, Rivanah stood up. They hugged, pecked each other on the cheek and took their seats.

'You look lovely,' Danny complimented.

'Thank you.'

'Why don't I remember you buying this dress?'

'That's because I bought it today itself. I wanted to literally look like your better half.'

'You look way better, my better half,' Danny said and leaned forward to kiss her cheek again.

A waiter came and placed the beverage menu on the table along with the food menu. Danny took the former while Rivanah picked up the latter.

'I want some red wine,' Danny said and looked at Rivanah inquiringly.

'I'm done drinking for the night,' she said sipping the last bit of beer from her pint. She couldn't afford to get drunk tonight.

'You suddenly sound so health conscious,' Danny said and added, 'Remember how you used to go to the gym once?'

'Yes,' Rivanah said. The time when the two had connected for the first time seemed long time ago.

'I never went there to get a good figure,' she said with a naughty amusement on her face.

'Is it? Then what for?' Danny responded with the same naughtiness in her tone.

'I wanted to set my life right,' she said and blew him a kiss.

Rivanah helped Danny choose his red wine while she zeroed-in on a sushi platter.

Danny picked up his glass of red wine and gestured at her. Rivanah knew how Danny would do a 'cheers' with her. She smiled naughtily and asked, 'Here too?'

'Why not?' Danny whispered back.

'Okay,' Rivanah said. She took a small sip from his glass. He followed suit and they kissed letting the liquid merge.

'Cheers!' Danny said, breaking the kiss and gulping down the wine she had in her mouth.

'Cheers!' Rivanah repeated, conscious of the fact that the Stranger was privy to every word of their conversation.

'So, why this sudden dinner plan? Any more surprises coming up?' Danny said gazing into her eyes. Rivanah's guilt broke the gaze. She took another sip from his glass even though she had said she wouldn't drink.

'I'm a little worried about something.' She paused seeing Danny's expectant face. And then continued, 'There's a friend of mine . . .' she said, with her throat drying up every second, 'who loves her boyfriend a lot. Like, genuinely. But she had a slip.'

'Slip?'

'She cheated on him. Just once. Not wilfully, though. It just happened. She didn't intend to cheat on him, and in her heart she still loves her boyfriend. Only her boyfriend.' Rivanah stopped suddenly, realizing she was justifying this 'friend' of hers a little too much.

'Hmm, and whom did she cheat on him with?'

'Her roommate's boyfriend,' she said, looking at Danny who was lost in thought while sipping his wine.

'Actually, the roommate's boyfriend was an old friend of hers,' Rivanah corrected herself. Danny still didn't respond.

'I mean the roommate's boyfriend was this girl's ex,' Rivanah finally blurted out. Danny shot a sharp glance at her as if he had already judged this imaginary friend of hers.

'If it was her ex, then I'm sure it wasn't just a slip. Like, if I meet my ex and it ends up in a . . . wait a minute. Did you mean she simply kissed him when you said she slipped, or did she fuck her ex?'

'They . . .' She took yet another sip from Danny's glass and said, 'They fucked.'

'Whoa, then it obviously isn't a slip. By the way, are you sure you don't want to have wine?'

Rivanah shook her head and said, 'Why do you think that?'

'Because you are drinking all of mine,' Danny said in a lighter vein.

'Not that. Why do you think it was not a slip? How are you so sure?'

'You slip with strangers but you don't slip with people you already know. Especially your ex.'

Rivanah frowned. It didn't make sense to her. She probably didn't want it to make sense. All she wanted to hear from him was: it was just a slip, why bother? And since it didn't come the way she desired from Danny, Rivanah felt all the more frustrated.

'Anyway, what's up with this friend of yours?' Danny asked.

'She is in a fix whether to tell her present boyfriend about it or not.'

'Hmm. Okay.'

By then, the waiter laid out the sushi platter. But instead of the platter, Rivanah's eyes were on Danny.

He was about to say something when she cut him short saying, 'What do you reckon? What should the girl do? Tell her boyfriend everything?'

'I don't know. If it is not important, then she probably shouldn't,' he said, gobbling up a sushi.

'It's yum—' but before he could finish his sentence, she shut his lips with a kiss. He had finally said what she wanted to hear. There was no reason whatsoever for her to confess anything. Danny's opinion was, of course, more important and valuable to her than the Stranger's demand which now seemed all the more futile. The slip wasn't important for her so there was no reason why she should tell Danny about it. Period. She knew this from day one. It was the Stranger who had pushed her to believe otherwise. She took a bite of the sushi wondering if the Stranger had heard Danny's point of view. But he wouldn't know she wasn't going to comply with him. Doesn't matter what he said, he hadn't kept his part of the deal. Coming in front of her when she was in an inebriated state was a sheer breach. And now he would get in return exactly that—a breach. Danny took out his phone, stretched his hand and the two of them squeezed together beaming ear to ear for a selfie. Rivanah grabbed the phone from him to see how the selfie had come out. They looked happy together. No confession was bigger than the happiness that seemed to emanate from the selfie for her.

'What are you looking at?' Danny asked, taking the phone from her. Rivanah simply smiled and said, 'I love you.'

'I love you too.'

The waiter was back. 'Would you like to order your main course, sir?' he asked Danny.

'Certainly.'

'You order. I'll be back from the restroom,' Rivanah said.

'But what do you want to have?'

'I chose starters. You choose the main course for us,' she said with a heart-warming smile and headed towards the restroom.

In the restroom, Rivanah received a call from Sadhu Ram's number.

'Where are you?' Rivanah said the moment she picked up the call.

'Hello, Mini.'

Rivanah almost bit her own tongue.

'The first thing you will do after you step out of the restroom is confess,' the Stranger said.

'No, I won't. Didn't you hear? It is not important for Danny.'

'It is important for you, Mini.'

'No, it is not. Who are you to decide what's important for me and what's not?' Rivanah was surprised at the way she was talking to the Stranger. *But this is what is needed,* she told herself. This person was responsible for the life-threatening incidents in her life only weeks back, but she couldn't take it all lying down. A couple of seconds later she heard the line cut. She looked at her phone expecting another call but all that came was Danny's WhatsApp stating he was getting bored. Rivanah quickly stepped out. She was about to join Danny at the table when five men barged into the restaurant. She identified one of them. It was Sadhu Ram. She looked at the others. *Probably his men*, she thought, until she looked at the one who was right in front of Sadhu Ram. She knew this man too. It was Argho Chowdhury.

'We caught him red-handed with an ear piece,' Sadhu Ram said with a victorious smile.

## 17

Rivanah, Danny, Sadhu Ram along with his men and Argho were at the Bandra police station. The way the entire thing had played out reminded Rivanah of Abhiraj and how he was caught at Starbucks some time back. The difference being previously it wasn't the Stranger who was caught.

'So, it's all very simple: confess everything, or else we will do things our way,' Sadhu Ram said, oddly relaxed.

'Confess what?' Argho shouted. 'I don't know why I've been brought here! Rivanah, what nonsense is going on?'

'Talk to me, not to the girl,' said Sadhu Ram, holding Argho's chin up. He was handcuffed and made to sit on a chair in the middle of a cell, while Rivanah, Danny and the inspector in charge of the police station were standing in a circle around him.

'What were you doing at Bungalow 9?'

'I had a date.'

'With whom? Where's the girl?' Sadhu Ram took Argho's phone from his subordinate. They had confiscated it from him at the restaurant.

Argho looked at Sadhu Ram and said uncomfortably, 'I don't know her.'

Sadhu Ram smirked as if he was expecting it. 'That, I believe. You won't know her because there was no date. I have been following you for a week now, but haven't seen you with any girl.'

'You have been following me? For what?'

'Forget that and answer me first. Who is this girl you just mentioned?'

'We connected on Tinder,' Argho said. He was speaking softly now.

'Tinder? I know Tardeo but where is Tinder?' Sadhu Ram said, looking at his subordinates for clues.

'It is a dating app,' Rivanah spoke up. 'It is an app that you can download for free in your phone. You have to sign in through your Facebook account, after which you can find a match with prospective people.'

'I have to check your phone. What's the password?' Sadhu Ram gave the phone to Argho after unlocking the handcuffs. He made a pattern on the screen to unlock it. Sadhu Ram took the phone away and went to Rivanah. She tapped on it few times and opened Tinder. There were five matches.

'Which one?' Sadhu Ram asked Argho.

'Kanika Negi.'

'Does the name ring a bell?' Sadhu Ram asked Rivanah. Negative.

Sadhu Ram scrolled down and, along with Rivanah, read through the messages on the Tinder chat screen. There had been around fifty messages exchanged between Argho and Kanika. It was evident they didn't know each other and had casually decided to meet up at Bungalow 9 that night. That couldn't have been a coincidence; Rivanah was sure of it. The moment they reached the first message—a 'Hi' from Argho—a new message popped up right at that instant. Both Sadhu Ram and Rivanah read it and looked at each other with fright. The message read:

*Argho is innocent. Mini is not.*

The next instant, Kanika unmatched Argho from Tinder. And her profile wasn't live any more.

'Who is Mini?' Sadhu Ram asked.

'I am,' Rivanah said, her throat going dry.

'You are Mini?'

'It's her nickname,' Danny butted in.

It was clear now that Argho wasn't the Stranger. Or at least he wasn't alone in this.

'Why did the message say you are the culprit?' Sadhu Ram looked at Rivanah.

'I . . .' She glanced at Danny and said, 'I have no idea.'

'Hmm.' Sadhu Ram turned towards Argho and said, 'What about the difference in the kilometre reading on your bike?'

'What difference? I only use my bike sometimes, not every day.'

'I know you don't use it every day but—'

Sadhu Ram told him about how he had found there was a difference in the kilometre reading on his bike that particular day. As the two argued over the matter, Rivanah understood once and for all: Argho wasn't the Stranger. He was a pawn in an elaborate game. Just like she was. She couldn't help but feel astounded at how elaborate the game really was!

'What about the ear piece?' Sadhu Ram asked. Rivanah could tell even Sadhu Ram sounded frustrated now.

'That's my ear piece. Kanika asked me to put it on as a mark of identification.'

Argho took the phone from Rivanah and showed them the message where Kanika had written: *Put on an ear piece. I'll recognize you with it.* The same Kanika whose profile had been deactivated now.

'Madarchod!' Sadhu Ram shouted, stamping his foot on the ground. He simply couldn't take it that twice the Stranger had made a complete fool out of him. He apologized to Rivanah for the curse. Half an hour later, Sadhu Ram and the inspector on duty let Rivanah and Danny go. Argho was also allowed to leave as it was evident he was being set up.

'But you may have to come up to the station if summoned,' the inspector on duty said.

'Sure. I'm not guilty of anything, so why wouldn't I cooperate?' Argho said taking his phone from Sadhu Ram.

Outside, Rivanah and Danny were waiting for Argho. As he appeared, Rivanah apologized to him.

'As you already know there has been some confusion. I'm really sorry for this,' she said.

'I didn't know you had a police guy behind me! What is this all about?'

Rivanah felt pushed to tell him about his cousin Hiya's connection but held herself back at the last moment. By now it had become a long story. *Too long indeed*, she thought and said, 'Honestly Argho, even I'm yet to figure it out.'

'I completely fail to understand how I can be roped into something this serious about which I have no clue!'

Rivanah shot an embarrassing look at Danny so he could bail her out of the situation. He understood.

'We are sorry, Argho. It's just that even we have been misled. I hope you understand. Rivanah's intention wasn't to malign you in any way. It was all a misunderstanding. There's a stalker who is creating trouble. Probably the same person who connected with you via Tinder—Kanika Negi.'

Argho stood there looking around as if he still needed to be convinced.

'If the person wanted to frame me, then why would he or she message saying I'm innocent?' Argho argued.

Rivanah wanted to speak but didn't. It wasn't about Argho, she knew. It was about her. Only she knew the subtext of the last message from 'Kanika Negi'. Argho was just a tool to mislead her, corner her and make her do things which the Stranger wanted.

'I hope it gets sorted out for you fast,' Argho said looking at Rivanah. 'Whatever it is.'

'I hope so too.'

Argho took a cab and left. Danny climbed into his car. Rivanah excused herself and, taking a couple of steps away from the car, called her father.

'Baba, did Inspector Rajat Das get in touch with you?'

'No, what happened?'

'Nothing. I think we should take the complaint against Argho back.'

'How can you be so sure?'

'I am, Baba. Please take the complaint back.'

'Hmm. But if not Argho then who attacked you?'

'I don't know. Let them find the person if they can. But it wasn't Argho.'

'Okay, I will talk to Rajat.'

Rivanah talked to her mother for a minute and then joined Danny in the car. After a short distance, Danny stopped the car at a street corner.

'What happened?' Rivanah asked. She had just put on some music to distract herself. Danny switched it off. Their eyes met.

'Why didn't you tell me?' Danny asked. There was a sudden harshness in his tone. She knew why.

'I was about to Danny.'

'About to? When? I thought you'd planned the dinner for me. For *us*. I thought you had dressed up for me. But—surprise, surprise—it wasn't!' He now sounded cross. *And rightly so*, Rivanah thought.

'The dress, the look, it was all for you, Danny.'

'Shut up. Even the dress was bugged. You knew it. I didn't. Why?'

'It was just . . . just . . .' Rivanah couldn't think of anything to say. And with that, she knew she had given Danny enough reason to raise a finger at her. And at her love towards him.

'That's because you don't trust me.'

'It is nothing like that. Sadhu Ram asked me not to involve anybody.'

'Anybody? Okay, so after being in a relationship for more than a year now, I'm *anybody* to you. Great!' Danny started the engine and put the car on gear.

'I'm sorry, Danny.'

'Don't I-am-sorry me.'

Rivanah saw that Danny felt the same disgust she had felt every time Ekansh said sorry to her.

'I genuinely—'

'Rivanah, I will tell you this once.' Danny cut her short, glancing intently at her and continued, 'I don't like the fact that you hide things from me. If there's anything, just let me know. Share it with me. Anything at all, okay?'

Rivanah had to clear her throat mildly before nodding. When they reached their apartment, Danny climbed out of the car saying, 'Please lock the car before coming. You always seem to forget.' He was gone before she could say anything.

In the silence of the garage, Rivanah could feel the sting of Danny's words. Everything in her life was an irony. The one she loved first—Ekansh—had ditched her, the one who loved her next—Danny—was being kept in the dark by her. She reclined the car seat and shut her eyes, desperately wishing everything to be okay when she suddenly opened her eyes again. *Hello, Mini.* The entire car echoed with the two words. In a flash, she turned back and saw a small phone placed on the back seat. It had been connected to the car's Bluetooth. The Stranger had heard her entire conversation with Danny before he got out of the car. She quickly took the phone in her hand.

'You just awarded yourself a storm, Mini. Be ready now.'

Rivanah shut her lips so tight with fear that they turned white. Swallowing a lump, she said, 'No please, we can negotiate this, right?'

'I'm not in the mood to negotiate any more, Mini.' The line went dead. Rivanah saw a bike vroom past right in front of her car and out of the garage. She could neither see the number plate, nor the model, though she knew who it was. The one she knew nothing about.

# 18

That night, Rivanah tried her best to win Danny over, but he wouldn't warm up to her touches or her deliberate conversation-initiating queries. She knew she should have shared everything with him but it had all happened so quickly that she had decided to tell him later. She had been confident that he would be all ears. She wasn't expecting this cold shoulder. The way he reacted told her how less we know our partners. Living with them day in and day out, we create our own biased versions of them and start projecting our interpretations of the person on to their personality—which more often than not is far from reality. Like she would never know if Danny and Nitya had ever been close or not. Like Danny still didn't know Rivanah had things hidden from him. Rivanah wanted to discuss this with someone, but she was sure it couldn't be the Stranger. *He may have shown her glimpses of his good soul, but overall he was a sadist*, Rivanah concluded. But then . . . who else could she talk to?

While going to the office the next day, Rivanah tapped ten digits on her phone and then pressed on the call button. She had deleted Ekansh's number but she remembered it by heart.

'Hi Rivanah. I knew you would call,' Ekansh said, picking up the call almost immediately. *Does he really mean what he said? He knew? Does Ekansh know me more than Danny does?* Rivanah brushed aside these thoughts and said, 'Ekansh, I want to ask you something. But promise me that you will answer to the point.'

'I promise,' he said after a pause.

'If Tista was alive, would you have told her about what happened between us that evening?'

'Look, Rivanah, we have . . .'

'Just answer the question, Ekansh,' Rivanah said and added softly, 'Please . . .'

She could hear him breathing.

'No, I wouldn't have told her.'

Rivanah sighed. She needed this reassurance to validate what she was doing with Danny. She told herself that anyone in love would have done the same thing. Sometimes, lies are the only way to keep a relationship running like a well-oiled machine.

'Thanks,' she said and hung up before Ekansh could say anything else. She thought he would call her back but he didn't. *He probably knew*, Rivanah wondered, *that she would herself call him when needed—the way she did minutes ago*.

In office, there were a few awkward glances exchanged between Rivanah and Argho, but neither said anything. He was Hiya's cousin, but till now he had showed no inclination whatsoever in trying to know if anything had happened between Hiya and Rivanah. He would have told Sadhu Ram during the interrogation in case he knew something. Or was he too smart for the police? Rivanah tried to forget the last thought.

For most of the day, Rivanah kept sending emotional messages to Danny but there was no response from him. In the end, she thought she would resolve it the way most couple fights get resolved: with time, by doing nothing about it at the moment. But she was in for a surprise. An hour before her work was about to get over, she got a gift pack from the security. There was no name on it. She tore open the gift wrap to reveal a small box. She unlocked it and found two pearl earrings along with a note saying: *Game for a fresh start?*—D.

She immediately called Danny up. He answered on the third ring.

'Danny, you dog, I'm going to kill you,' she said and heard him laugh. 'Stop laughing. This isn't funny. I have been messaging you all day like a moron.'

'Serves you right,' Danny said, with a hint of amusement in his voice.

'Really? Meet me tonight and I'll show you what suits you!'

'Is that a promise?'

'Like hell it is.'

'I shall be waiting.'

'You better.'

'Love you loads.'

'Love you back. When are you reaching home today?'

'Latest by eight. And you?'

'Should be there by nine.'

'Great.'

Rivanah then Googled 'best sexual surprises for boyfriend' on her desktop. A series of links appeared but just as she was about to open one, a beep on her phone stopped her. It was a WhatsApp message. The message was in the form of an image. The image was a Google map pinning her office as 'Address A'. A blue line from this point led to a point somewhere in Kalyan which was in the outskirts of Mumbai. The end pin was labelled, to her utter shock, 'Hiya Chowdhury'. She maximized the image on her phone. The message was obvious: Hiya, or some link to her, was in Kalyan. And Kalyan was a good two hours away from where Rivanah was at the moment. She quickly calculated: she had four hours before she had to reach her flat, just in time for Danny. Or should she go there with Danny? But what if that irks the Stranger and she misses out on the vital information on Hiya? Once again it was a catch-22 situation for Rivanah. There was no other friend whom she could request to follow her secretly, just in case there was danger. Ekansh's name crossed her mind but she wasn't sure. Only a few seconds later, she dialled Danny's number on an impulse.

'Hey baby, I'll be home by nine. Some work has come up. I'll call you the moment I'm done.'

'In office itself?'

'No.' She swallowed a lump. 'But somewhere nearby.' *If she said Kalyan, there can't be any excuse for her to be there at this hour*, she thought. Yet another lie. *But this would be the last*, she promised herself.

'Just call me once around nine,' she said, sounding pensive.

'Why?'

'I'll wrap it up quickly then,' she said, keeping the real reason from him. Just in case something happened, someone should have the right doubt at the right time.

'All right. I'll call you at nine,' Danny said.

'Thanks. Muah. Love you.'

Rivanah took a cab to Andheri railway station, took the metro till Ghatkopar and then a local train from the central line to reach Kalyan. Exhaustion made her doze off in the train itself. She was woken up by a fellow passenger when Kalyan—the last station on the line—arrived. Little did she know that someone was following her.

Once she came out of the rather busy Kalyan railway station, she took a cab without knowing where to go. She glanced at the image of the map once and told the cab driver she would guide him to the destination. Half a minute later, the person following her also hailed a cab and asked the driver to follow hers.

After about twenty five minutes, Rivanah reached the spot marked on the map. From inside the cab she tried to look out. There was nothing around. She opened the car's door and stepped out. She had no idea where she was. She tried to extract her location via Google but realized her mobile Internet wasn't working.

'Madam, rukna hai ya jaun?' the cab driver popped his head out of the window and asked. She knew there wasn't any chance of getting public transport in such a place and—her eyes fell on an ATM a few metres away. Strangely, the light inside the ATM was flickering.

'Madam?' the driver egged on.

Rivanah quickly took out her purse. To her surprise, she was short of the fare. In fact, all she had was a ten rupee note. She frowned, not remembering how much she was carrying. She told the driver she would need to take money out of the ATM, realizing this could well be part of the plan. *Was the clue to Hiya inside the ATM? Was the flickering of light a ploy to attract my attention? Did someone empty my wallet when I dozed off in the train so that I have no option but to use the ATM?*

'Bhaiya, main ek minute mein aati hun. Paise nikalne hai,' she told the cab driver, who made a face. Rivanah proceeded towards the ATM. Another cab had stopped at some distance behind her. The person following her stepped out of the cab and noticed her going towards the ATM. The person waited for her to enter the ATM.

Rivanah went close to the ATM entrance and tried to look through the glass door. There was nobody inside, and the lights were still flickering. She gently pushed the door open, still looking around, and slowly stepped inside. Why would the Stranger call her to such a place with Hiya marked on the map? *There has to be something to it*, she wondered, and glanced at the ATM screen. It was out of order. She sensed something was wrong. Just like the Planchette idea, this too seemed like a mistake.

*You awarded yourself a storm* . . . the Stranger's words came rushing to her. *Shit, shit, shit. Why the hell did I come here!* Rivanah thought, feeling anxious, and immediately turned around to leave. She paused, hearing her name being called out. It was a male voice. She froze. Was it the Stranger? But the voice was very familiar.

'Rivanah!' the voice called out again. She suddenly felt energy gushing to her feet as she turned around in a flash to see Ekansh.

'What are you doing here?' Rivanah looked to his right where there was a tiny room for the security guard. He was probably inside the room when she came in.

'I was waiting for you,' he said.

'For me? Why?' Looking at him, she felt scared like never before. Somehow he didn't seem like himself.

'You said you know how to connect to Tista,' he blabbered, as if he was under some spell.

'I did? What nonsense are you talking? How did I communicate with you?' She almost knew the answer.

'Through messages,' he said confused, and showed her his phone. Rivanah read the messages:

*Hi Ekansh, I know of a way of communicating with Tista. Don't call me or message me back. If you are interested then just meet me at 7.30 at this address . . .*

She didn't read the rest. It was yet again a case of SIM card duplication. The ease with which the Stranger duplicated SIM cards told Rivanah how dangerous technology was and how fatal its impact could be if in wrong hands. It was clear the Stranger was up to some game once again by calling Ekansh and her at the same spot, but why? She wanted to rush back home, to Danny. *Nothing was going to be revealed to me about Hiya. It is all a joke, a sick joke which the Stranger has been playing on me since my arrival in Mumbai.* Rivanah turned towards the door without saying anything to Ekansh. He held her hand. She turned to glance at him and said, 'Leave me, Ekansh, and go home. It wasn't me messaging you.'

'What do you mean?' His grip turned tighter. She had neither the time nor the intention to clarify anything.

'Someone was just messing with you. Chuck it and go.' It was the best excuse she could come up with. She again turned around to leave but he pulled her towards him. They came dangerously close, with Ekansh still gripping her hand while placing the other hand around her waist to hold her tight.

'What do you think of yourself, Rivanah?' Ekansh asked. His grip was hurting her as he continued, 'You can call me anytime, cut the phone line without saying anything, tell Tista about us, call me to a secluded ATM in the name of Tista, and then say it was all a joke? I won't allow you to treat me as if I'm some piece of shit.' The strength with which he held her not only hurt Rivanah but surprised her as well.

'Ekansh, it wasn't me. It's someone who is playing with me. Now leave me.'

'Who is it?'

'I don't know.'

'Just like you didn't know who told Tista the truth, right?'

'Shut up and leave me,' she said, trying to release herself from his grip.

Just outside the ATM, the person who had been following Rivanah to Kalyan station and then to the ATM pushed open the door. It was Danny.

Danny first looked at Rivanah, then at Ekansh, and then the way he was holding her. Ekansh let go of Rivanah. She was too dumbstruck to speak.

'I was outside your office when you called me. I kept telling myself that you love me too much to lie to me. Especially after we had both decided you won't hide anything from me.' Danny sighed and added, 'I tried to make you as comfortable as I could but still this sluttish behaviour—why? You could have just told me you are done with me,' Danny said, looking acutely hurt. It was evident he had misinterpreted the entire scene. But the word 'sluttish' stabbed Rivanah deeply. This name-calling was the last thing Rivanah expected from Danny.

'I think I should leave,' Ekansh mumbled awkwardly. He looked at Rivanah. Whatever anger his eyes were carrying against her a moment back suddenly changed into sympathy. Neither Rivanah nor Danny cared to look at him. As Ekansh stepped outside and shut the door, Rivanah asked in an injured tone, 'Why would you call me a slut, Danny? That too in front of Ekansh?'

'I didn't call you a slut. I just said your behaviour is that of a slut. Ask yourself why I said that. If you were not a slut, you wouldn't have lied to me to be here with your ex. God knows how many more times you guys have been together.'

'Who said I lied to you? I myself didn't know Ekansh was supposed to be here.'

'Yeah sure, like I'm going to believe you,' Danny said, without caring to look at her as he talked.

'You have to, because it's the truth. I came here because I was sent this,' Rivanah tapped her phone to show him the Google map image the stranger had sent her. He looked at it and then said, 'Okay. Look into my eyes and answer two questions.'

'Ask me anything.' Rivanah knew she was going to cry any moment now.

'Were you with Ekansh as the message claimed the night I came to your office?'

It took her some time but she nodded. Danny swallowed hard.

'But that's because . . .' she started.

'Don't explain,' he said and continued to look straight into her eyes, 'Is there anything that you think I should know as far as you and Ekansh are concerned?'

Rivanah looked down.

'Look at me, goddamnit!' he shouted.

Rivanah slowly lifted her head up and then nodded.

'What is it?'

She was crying now as she spoke, 'I just can't tell you.' But she didn't have to, for Danny knew: that she and Ekansh were still in a relationship.

'Is it what I think it is?'

'I simply can't tell you about it,' Rivanah said, feeling shame and humiliation squeeze all the pain out of her core.

'So let me rephrase. It wasn't sluttish behaviour. You are a slut. That's what it is,' Danny said in a concluding tone.

'Please don't say that, Danny. I love you.'

'Shut the fuck up.'

'You just can't come here, interpret everything wrongly and call me names, Danny. You have to listen to me. Your inference isn't the whole story.'

'I. Don't. Care. Any more,' he said, locking his jaws.

Rivanah felt a sudden anger honking hard within her. But she didn't know what she was angry about: the fact that she didn't tell Danny about the matter or the fact that his reaction was exactly how she thought any man would react. *Any man!* If this was any man's reaction, then what did Danny mean when he said he loved her? Any man would have labelled her a slut misinterpreting the scene or the truth which she nested within her—but not the one who loved her, for that man would have actually understood it was indeed a slip and respected the fact that she too had the right to explain. *In an ideal world, that is.* If she was a slut, then she would have continued fucking Ekansh, fucking every other man she came across without feeling guilty about it. But her love for Danny was exactly why she couldn't confess to him in the first place. But by saying she was a slut, did Danny think he had washed his hands off the relationship, off her?

'So you are saying there's nothing for me to react to, right?' Danny said.

'Right.' Rivanah said it more out of anger than anything else. She knew he had the right to react but she had a problem with the way he was reacting—like someone who never knew her.

'If you really think there's nothing for me to react, then why don't you tell me the truth yourself?' Danny asked.

*I don't mind your reaction, Danny. I just don't get how you have already decided what my intention was and given it a name,* she thought, but couldn't say it aloud. *Anybody would reach conclusions about you in no time, but when your closest one too does it, then what's left to say? Conclusions are made very swiftly, but to*

144

*break them one needs time*, she thought. And Danny didn't seem to be in the mood to give her time.

There was silence as Danny waited for her to speak. She knew whatever she said now would be twisted by him, turned into an arrow and darted right back at her.

'You continue to be quiet and still don't want me to react the way I'm doing. Awesome!' Danny said.

As he was about to leave, Rivanah blurted out, 'Ekansh and I slept with each other some time back.'

Danny stood frozen for a few seconds and then turned around to look at her. 'Were we together then?'

Rivanah nodded like a programmed machine and hung her head in shame. She looked up when she heard a loud bang. Danny had smashed his hand on the ATM door creating a crack in the glass. She immediately took his hand in hers to check the extent of the injury.

'Stay. Away,' he said pushing her back. His touch had never felt so condescending.

'Remember how you walked out on me because of Nitya?' Danny asked, facing away from her. He then turned around and, looking straight at her, said, 'I think it is time to walk out again. Just that, this time, it will be me walking out on you.'

'Why aren't you listening to me?' Her frustration was evident in her tone. 'It is not what it sounds like.'

'You just said you fucked your ex when we were in a relationship. To me, it sounds pretty simple.'

'It just happened, Danny. It. Just. Happened. I have avoided Ekansh since then.'

'I saw a minute back how much you guys have avoided each other. Meeting in a secluded ATM after you told me you had some office work? I don't know what you call it, but for me this is sluttish behaviour.'

'Please don't say that. Had I been a slut, I would have continued to sleep with Ekansh. But I never did that.'

'And you think that, after what I saw here and whatever you confessed, I'm going to believe you? Do you understand, Rivanah, I can't turn a blind eye to your acts any more?'

*Who is this Danny?* Rivanah wondered. *How can the person I love so dearly behave like a stranger? One sight of me with Ekansh, and Danny has already judged me? Can one be so blinded by love?*

'I love you, Danny. Only you. Why aren't you getting it?' Rivanah blurted out.

Danny smirked and said, 'That's what I thought too. And would have continued to think all my life, had I not been led to this place.'

'The one who led you to this place led me here as well,' she said.

'That changes nothing.'

Rivanah mentally cursed the Stranger for having stirred this and said aloud, 'Let's just go home, sit down and talk it out. I can explain everything. Then I'm sure you will understand.'

'I'm sorry, but I can't be associated with a lying whore,' Danny said and turned to leave. He knew the last part was little too much but he didn't care. If this was too much, then what was that she confessed? A raging frown appeared on Rivanah's face. On an impulse, she followed him.

'You really want to know what a whore is, Danny?' Rivanah shouted. This was the first time she had raised her voice this high in front of someone she loved.

'I'll show you and then you can walk out on me,' Rivanah said, her entire body shaking. She saw Ekansh in the distance, perhaps waiting for a cab. She crossed Danny and called out to Ekansh. Ekansh was taken aback seeing Rivanah come up to him.

Before Ekansh could speak, Rivanah grabbed him by his collar, pressed her lips against his and with one hand clicked a picture of them kissing. She broke the kiss the next second and sent the picture to Danny on WhatsApp. Looking towards Danny, who was still beside the ATM, she shouted, 'Check your phone, Danny, to know what a real whore is like.' Rivanah smashed her phone on the ground. It broke into pieces but it wasn't the only thing that broke.

'Rivanah!' Ekansh called out. She turned and said, 'Don't you follow me.' And walked out of his sight.

She found a cab at a distance and told the driver to take her to Dahisar.

It was the same area where she had taught Mini's Magic 10. The destination didn't matter to her. All she wanted was to cry alone. It was already dark when she reached the place three hours later. Looking around, the only lonely spot she could see was the skywalk. She climbed the stairs and took the empty bench under a light, feeling progressively suicidal. *What was left?* she asked herself. *A big nothing. How do you build anything from that big nothing and still call it life?* Rivanah cried.

It was over with Ekansh long ago, and now it was over with Danny too. Next time it won't be 'falling' in love for her. From here on, it would be suffering in love. But did she have the energy to suffer in love again? She wiped her tears and tried to breathe, but her nose was slightly blocked. Sitting under one of the lamp posts, she thought she heard footsteps coming towards her. She peered into the darkness but didn't see anybody. She sighed and was about to bury her face in her hands again when she heard a voice say, 'Hello, Mini.'

Rivanah slowly looked up—in anticipation. And fear. And disgust.

# 19

For a split second, Rivanah thought she had simply imagined the voice, before she noticed the tips of someone's shoes at the edge of the light. The light overhead did not fall on his face, and most of him was shrouded in darkness, but it didn't take her long to guess who this someone could be.

'Is that you?' Rivanah said aloud. Her voice was brittle.

The response came after few seconds.

'Yes, Mini.'

Her eyes were transfixed on the shining black tips of the shoes. Rivanah stood up, expecting the Stranger to take a step back. But he didn't. Rivanah took a step towards him. He was still. Slowly, she began inching towards the Stranger. With every step, her heart beat faster. And every beat felt heavy with anxiety. When she stood close to him, she could smell his deodorant—It's Different from Hugo Boss. *It is indeed him!* But his face and body remained shrouded in darkness. Rivanah took the final few steps and stood only inches away from the tips of the shoes. Breathing had become difficult. The fact that the Stranger hadn't moved told her he wanted her to unmask him. She was about to reach out when two hands shot out and, before Rivanah could understand what was happening, she was turned around forcefully and blindfolded. Rivanah felt him tightening the blindfold. Slowly, the Stranger pulled her into the darkness, away from the sight of any pedestrian.

'I . . .' Rivanah started, but she felt a finger on her lips and a whisper right next to her left ear, 'Ssshhh.' She felt a little aroused even in her state of emotional distress.

'Pain is a seed, Mini. And it often grows into a tree we call strength. A seed of strength has been sown in you today, Mini. You have no idea how emotionally stable a tree this will become,' the Stranger whispered. His breath tickled her ear as she allowed this idea to take root in her. She could feel his cotton shirt as she grabbed it tight with both hands. Not able to hold herself back any more, she buried her face in the Stranger's chest and cried her heart out. She knew it would be useless to try to get rid of the blindfold.

'I never wanted to tell Danny the truth because the incident didn't compromise my love for him. Please say you know this. Please . . .'

'I know, Mini,' the Stranger whispered back.

'Then why did you do this to me? Why did you lead Ekansh, me and Danny to the ATM today? This is an irreparable damage. I don't think Danny will ever understand why I couldn't confess. It was only out of love.'

'I know Danny will never understand it.'

Rivanah frowned. She tried to touch the Stranger's face but he wouldn't let her.

'You have to tell me why you did this to me!' she said.

'First, you tell me, Mini, what's love if it doesn't let you give your loved one some time to explain? If it stands like a wall between you and your beloved? There are already a lot of walls in a relationship, Mini. What's rare is a freeway for trust.'

Rivanah listened hard as the Stranger continued, 'This confession of yours wasn't a test for you, Mini, it was a test of Danny's love. He is hurt not because you didn't confess to him but because you supposedly cheated on him. He doesn't want to give you a chance to explain. It's difficult to be with someone who prefers his own assumptions to his partner's reality.'

Rivanah wasn't sure what she felt at that moment.

'Ekansh ditched me, Danny didn't understand me. And I loved both with all my heart. What else can I do apart from loving someone honestly? I have tried the best I could, and it didn't work. What else remains for me to give anyone? I somehow managed to come to terms with Ekansh's betrayal but this . . . how will I be able to forget this scar, this hurt that Danny has given me by not understanding me?'

'To forget a hurt, Mini, we subconsciously seek a bigger and deeper hurt. Happiness is a vacation. Hurt is our home.'

'I was so confident nothing will go wrong between Danny and me.' She choked. For the first time, she felt the Stranger's hand caressing her back. Somehow she couldn't blame the Stranger any more for stirring the storm he did in the ATM, because otherwise she would have continued to live a lie.

'You will have to learn to let go, Mini. Life's not about what you have. It's about how much and how easily you let go of what you have.'

There were footsteps. The Stranger placed one hand on Rivanah's mouth, the other behind her back, and drew her closer to his chest. She could hear his heartbeat. It sounded normal. Hers definitely was not. The embrace calmed her. And he was . . . she lifted her head and felt his breath on her face. As she tasted her own tears, her lips parted. She didn't know whether the Stranger was looking at her—she wished he was. But when she felt a thumb caressing her lips, she was sure he was looking at her. She didn't know which was scarier: the comfort she was feeling in the arms of a stranger or a stranger making her this comfortable. But she knew whichever of the two it was, it was the most compelling fear she had ever felt.

Two young boys walked past them, chatting cheerfully, not noticing them in the dark. Once their voices became faint, the Stranger slowly released Rivanah from his grip. They stood a few inches apart.

'Why do you keep breaking me and then making me at the same time?'

The Stranger didn't respond immediately. Rivanah thought he was gone. She stretched her hand and relaxed when she felt him.

'That's what true love is, isn't it?' the Stranger asked. 'Helping the other person grow by constantly breaking and making them at the same time? Not the way you want them to be but the way they ought to be.'

'Do you mean you love—' Rivanah felt a finger on her lips before she could finish.

'That's not important, Mini. What is important is why you forgot about Hiya all of a sudden after you visited Mr Dutta in Kolkata? Ask yourself that. And get an answer soon. Time is running out.'

'But you won't kill me, right?'

There was no response. She couldn't touch him any more with her hands. Rivanah quickly opened her blindfold. She looked around and found herself all alone on the skywalk. Why did she forget about Hiya after visiting Mr Dutta? Did she really visit Mr Dutta? Wasn't it supposed to be a dream? Her parents had confirmed it for her. The Stranger must be kidding.

# 20

Rivanah had little choice but to return to the flat she shared with Danny. She used the spare key to unlock it. She was sure she would find him inside and had no clue how to handle the situation. But instead of Danny, she found a Post-it note on the refrigerator. It read:

*I know it sounds rude but you haven't left me with any other option. Please leave by tomorrow. Thanks.*

It wasn't just rude. It was formal. Way too formal. And that was more hurtful. Two people claiming to be in love until few hours back now behaving like strangers. Rivanah threw the note in the dustbin and went to the bedroom. By then she had realized Danny wasn't home. He wouldn't be till the next day—till she left. In only a few hours she had become an emotional disease he couldn't bear to see. She switched on the night lamp in the bedroom and looked at the nicely made bed. They had made love on the bed time and again, whispering promises to each other and confessing their love. What were those promises and confessions? Just a momentary illusion squeezed out by the hunger of the body? Rivanah sat on the bed and caressed the bed sheet. The place which once had the fragrance of their togetherness would have the stain of her tears tomorrow. But would the stains be prominent enough to be noticed by Danny? Rivanah doubted it as a teardrop fell on the bed sheet. She lay down on the bed, clutching the bed sheet tight, and quietly cried her way to sleep.

Rivanah woke up in the morning, took a little more than an hour to pack all her stuff except for the ones gifted to her by Danny and pasted a blank note on the refrigerator. She didn't have anything to say and hoped Danny would understand. She had finally understood men. They would demand chance after chance when they were at fault but wouldn't give a woman any chance—it didn't matter if she was at fault or not. Their straying is always accidental but a woman's straying is part of her personality. Most importantly, a man's mistake is a woman's sin.

There was a surprise waiting for her in front of the main door. Her mobile phone. The one she had smashed to the ground the previous evening. She picked it up trying to guess who could have kept it there. There was no damage to it. Did the Stranger buy her a new phone, same model? Switching it on she realized it was her phone; all repaired.

Initially Rivanah thought she'd go to Meghna's place, dump her stuff and head to office but decided against it midway. She couldn't trouble her every time she was in a spot. Especially since Rivanah had never bothered to keep in touch with her. The kind of spite she had felt seeing Riju with Meghna last time eventually steered her mind off. With no clue where to go at such short notice, Rivanah went to the office with her luggage. When her colleagues enquired about the reason for such a sudden shift, she made up excuses.

Rivanah thought she could find temporary accommodation with the colleagues she was close to, but they all gave some excuse or other. She talked with two or three brokers for a rented place, but nothing was available immediately. In the end she thought of putting up at a hotel near her office until she found a flat. She booked a room. Rivanah was surprised—she wasn't as disarrayed as she thought she would be. She even faked a perfectly normal tone while talking to her mother. The Rivanah who had come to Mumbai wouldn't have been able to be so composed and practical after a break-up. It was the Rivanah who had stayed in Mumbai and fought whatever had come her way.

In the evening, as she dragged her luggage into the office elevator on her way out and pressed the ground floor button, a foot stopped the door from closing. She looked up to see Nivan.

'Hey,' he said and entered the elevator.

'Hey.' Rivanah was glad to see him. Nivan glanced at her luggage and said, 'Did you just rob our office?'

Rivanah smiled and replied, 'House issues. Need to find a place ASAP.'

'Oh. Didn't the landlord give you any notice?'

Rivanah's smile went dry as she said, 'Not really.'

'That's quite indecent on his part.'

Rivanah nodded in agreement. The elevator door opened on the ground floor. 'See you,' Nivan said and stepped out of the elevator before she could reply. She dragged her luggage out and went out of her office building to fetch an autorickshaw. Had it not been for her luggage, she could have walked the distance. To her dismay, no auto was ready to take her to the hotel such a short distance away. A pitch-black BMW came to halt right in front of her. Rivanah didn't notice who was inside it until the window rolled down. It was Nivan. And her stupid smile was back.

'Where are you going to put up tonight?' Nivan asked trying to lean sideways away from the steering wheel in order to make eye contact.

'Hotel Hometel. It's very close—'

'I know where Hometel is,' he cut her short. 'But I think I've a permanent solution for you.'

'You do? I'm listening.'

'I own an empty flat right opposite the one I live in. You can stay there if it is okay with you.'

'Thanks, but I think it would be a problem for you.'

'Not really. I'm anyway thinking of letting the flat out. Might as well start with you.'

*So it's not charity*, Rivanah thought, and said, 'In that case, I don't mind.'

Nivan got out of the car and helped her put the luggage in the boot. Rivanah cast furtive glances at Nivan all through their ride, but not once did she see him return any. She would have loved it if he had asked her something. That would have given her the licence to ask him some as well without sounding like a probing psycho.

Nivan lived in a posh locality near the Lokhandwala market in Andheri West. Five minutes from Krishna Towers where she lived with Danny. *Used to live with Danny*, she corrected herself. Once inside the society premises, she knew she wouldn't be able to afford the rent there. The Residency Enclave was visibly an upscale area. She thought it'd be rude if she refused outright since Nivan was concerned enough to have driven her to the place.

He lived on the sixteenth floor. Flat number 1603. He pressed the doorbell and they exchanged a formal smile.

The door was opened by an old female servant. She took Nivan's laptop bag as a Labrador rushed towards him, wagging its tail.

'Meet Xeno,' Nivan told Rivanah.

'Say hello to . . .' Nivan told Xeno, caressing him, and then turned to Rivanah saying, 'It's Rivanah, right?'

'Yes.'

'Say hi to Rivanah,' Nivan spoke into Xeno's ears.

'Niv!' A lady called out from one of the rooms inside.

'Please be comfortable, and give me a minute,' Nivan told Rivanah and went in as Xeno sniffed her. She patted its head lovingly and walked to the huge white sofa and sat down. Xeno too sat down right beside her feet on the Kashmiri carpet. The servant who had opened the door came with a glass of water. While sipping the water, a tiny part of her was praying that the woman who called Nivan inside was his mother. Or aunt. Or whoever except . . . her eyes fell on a lot of photographs, mostly of Nivan and another girl. But before she could take a closer look at the pictures, Nivan came out into the drawing room.

'Let's go,' he said and went towards the main door. Rivanah kept her glass on the tray on the centre table. As she followed Nivan, Xeno followed her.

It was flat no. 1604, right opposite his, as Nivan had said. Rivanah realized there was no nameplate on the front door as she saw him switch on the lights. He asked Rivanah to follow him inside. She did along with Xeno.

It was a well-furnished flat. There was a little dust in the air, which told Rivanah it must have been closed for some time, but it was a cosy place nonetheless. Nivan went to a corner and pressed a button. Slowly the curtains which Rivanah had been mistaking for wallpaper drew themselves to one side bringing alive a breathtaking view of the Versova beach. Rivanah's jaw fell open as she went close to the glass wall. She could see the evening horizon in the distance as the sun almost set in its lap. It was almost a dream flat for her but soon reality set in. She couldn't afford such a place.

'Give me eighteen thousand a month for this, and it's all yours. No brokerage. No advance,' she heard Nivan say. Rivanah immediately turned around to look at him.

'Okay. How many tenants will you allow?' she asked.

'It's all yours. No sharing business.'

A smile of disbelief escaped her. 'You must be kidding?' Rivanah said.

'No, I'm not,' Nivan said kneeling down to caress Xeno.

'This flat's rent, considering the locality, should be around eighty thousand a month. And you are asking me to pay eighteen with no other roommates? That has to be a joke.'

'What you mentioned is the market rate. But the rent is decided by someone else.'

'Someone else? Who?'

'The landlady.'

'Oh, I thought you owned the place.'

'I own the place but someone else rules it,' Nivan said with a faint smirk.

'May I know who that landlady is?'

'You'll get to know soon. I hope you liked the place though.'

'I love it. And I can't thank you enough, sir.'

'Call me Nivan. And we'll make an agreement by noon tomorrow.'

Rivanah smiled and said, 'Thanks, Nivan.'

'Don't mention it. You can have a look at the entire flat first.'

'Sure,' Rivanah said and went in. It was a fully furnished two-bedroom flat. *Only a blind person can say no to this one*, Rivanah thought, and paused at the bedroom entrance seeing something.

'All good?' Nivan startled Rivanah.

'A sketch stand?' Rivanah said, looking at the sketch stand in the bedroom.

'It belongs to the one who stayed in this flat before you. Been some time. I didn't want to throw it away, actually. After all, it's art and I appreciate it.'

Rivanah walked up to the sketch stand. There were sheets on it. The first sketch was of a woman's face.

'I can get this removed if it's too much of a bother,' Nivan offered.

'Let it be,' Rivanah said as she touched the sheet. She neither knew nor remembered that it was her own sketch of Hiya Chowdhury's face. 'It's lovely,' Rivanah added.

## 21

Rivanah ordered from Subway that night. She was so tired because of the constant shuttling that she had no strength to cook. Only when the sub and diet Coke arrived did it strike her that she had not eaten a morsel in the last twenty-four hours. Post dinner, she called up her mother. Since her Kolkata trip, the frequency of her mother's calls had increased as well. After the attack, she understood their concern. The police hadn't been able to find a lead. Though she talked to her mother for almost half an hour, she didn't say a word about what had happened between Danny and her. She could well imagine her father's reaction once he knew: *I told you so!* And never again would she be able to convince him about her choice in the future—*if* she has a choice in the future. Lying down in bed, Rivanah's eyes fell on the sketch stand next to her with the face of a girl. Rivanah had brought her own sketch stand when she had left Danny's place, but had instructed the guard to discard it since she wouldn't need it. She had no idea what it was doing at Danny's house in the first place—she definitely couldn't remember sketching anything. But Danny had said she was the one who had sketched those faces. And now, lying on the bed gaping at the sketch, she felt there was something familiar about it. But what was it? The Stranger's last question to her before he disappeared popped up in her mind: *Why did you forget about Hiya after meeting Mr Dutta?* Why would her parents deny something which had happened for real? Or was the Stranger up to some mind games again? Rivanah immediately picked up her phone and called her mother. It was 10.30 p.m. She didn't care that they might be asleep.

'Mumma?'

'Mini? Is everything all right?' her mother asked, sounding anxious.

'Yes, all is fine. Tell me, Mumma, did I ever sketch before?' Rivanah asked.

There was silence.

'Mumma?'

'Mini?' Her father came on the line.

'Baba? Where's Mumma? What happened?'

'That's what I want to know. What happened? Why are you asking about sketching at this odd hour?' Her father sounded as anxious as her mother.

'Everything is fine. I just wanted to know if I sketched before or not.'

'Yes, you used to sketch. But you left that hobby long back.'

*Long back?* 'Hmm. Okay. Goodnight, Baba.'

'Are you sure everything is okay, Mini?'

'Yes. Goodnight, Baba.'

'Goodnight, Mini,' her father said, still sounding concerned.

Rivanah kept staring at the sketch and then shut her eyes to sleep.

The next morning, before going to office, Nivan's agent had come to take her signature on the rental agreement. Rivanah didn't see Nivan leaving for office around the time she did, though she secretly wished he had. His presence—she had realized in the car with him the other day—made her disconnect with the mess her life was. The sight of him was a sweet escape. But one thing she had promised herself: even if she felt attracted to him, she wouldn't fall for him. In fact, she wouldn't fall for any man again. After two failed relationships, Rivanah didn't want to take a chance. Not so soon. Not ever, if possible.

In the office, Rivanah was surprised to know that she and Nivan had become a couple overnight for most of her teammates.

'Don't lie! Rohit saw you guys together. Didn't he give you a lift yesterday?' asked one.

'Yeah, but—'

'How is he in bed?' asked another inquisitive co-worker.

'Shut up! I needed a place to stay so—'

'OMG! You are staying with Nivan?' said another colleague almost having a heart attack.

164

'No! Someplace close to his.' Rivanah intentionally lied to avoid any further questions.

'Did you find out anything about him?' Rivanah understood she wasn't the only one crushing on Nivan. He was quite a hit with the office females. Twice while fetching hot cappuccino for herself, Rivanah came across Nivan, but his body language was so formal that she wondered if he was the same person who had given her a lift and lent out his flat at half the market rate.

During the day, whenever her phone buzzed with a message, Rivanah thought it would be Danny, but it never was. When she checked her WhatsApp during lunch, she saw Danny's display picture wasn't visible to her. He must have deleted her number. *So easily?* It scared her. Are relationships that brittle? Or are humans that unpredictable? Rivanah remembered how her cousin Meghna and Aadil broke up after almost a decade of being together. The worst part of such an experience is that it no longer lets you be in control of your own life, blinding you in the process.

She deleted Danny's number. A supposed intimate connection between two human beings was finally over with one tap of a finger on a mechanical device.

In the evening, Rivanah went straight to her flat, feeling mentally exhausted. The moment she unlocked the door, a pleasant smell hit her. She followed it to the dining table where she saw a bowl covered with a plate.

It was payesh. And this one smelt exactly the way her mother used to make it. Rivanah scooped out some with her index finger, and licked it, relishing the taste. *But who kept it here?*

Rivanah picked up the bowl and went to Nivan's door and rang the doorbell. The servant opened the door.

'Hi, I wanted to know if you kept this inside the flat,' Rivanah said.

The female servant nodded and gestured her to come inside.

'No, I'm fine. Just wanted to know if it was you. Did you prepare it?'

The servant suddenly grabbed her hand and tried to pull her inside the flat. It didn't take much time to understand that she was dumb. She gestured Rivanah to sit down, closed the main door, and scampered inside. Xeno came running towards Rivanah, wagging its tail. The servant came into the drawing room pushing a wheelchair on which sat a pristine-looking girl. She was smiling at Rivanah. *Is she the one who called Nivan the other day from the bedroom?* Rivanah wondered.

'Hi,' the girl said as the servant brought her close to Rivanah.

'Hi. I'm Rivanah Bannerjee. I stay—'

'I know. I'm Advika,' the girl interrupted. Her words came out slurry.

*And what's your relation with Nivan?* Rivanah thought, but said, 'Nice to meet you,' extending her right hand.

166

Instead of the right, Advika lifted her left hand saying, 'I'm sorry, Rivanah, my right side doesn't function.'

'Oh!' Rivanah looked at her, pulling back her hand slightly, but Advika's left hand grasped it. It was unusually warm. They shook hands.

'Actually, I found this in my house.' She showed her the bowl and continued, 'I have no idea how it got there.'

Advika smiled, eyeing the servant, and said, 'I'd asked her to send some for you.'

'But—' Rivanah started but was cut short again.

'I love cooking. But now I can't do so myself; I only get to supervise. Is it any good?' Advika said.

'It is awesome. Just the way my mother prepares it.'

'Thank you.'

'You stay alone here?' Rivanah asked.

'Not alone. Nivan stays with me.'

'Oh, yes. That was so silly of me to ask,' Rivanah said awkwardly.

'Nivan told me about you though.'

'He did?' she asked in surprise.

'The way you made him dance at the office party. I would've loved to witness it in person.'

Rivanah desperately wanted to disappear into thin air.

'Trust me, I've known Nivan for a long time. And I'm yet to see him dance. You must be some girl to have made it possible.'

*Yeah, some girl I'm! Someone with no limits to her stupidity,* Rivanah thought.

'Thank you,' Advika said.

'Huh?' Rivanah wasn't prepared for it.

'Thank you for making Nivan happy. Of late, he's been quite stressed. He seldom shares his problems with me. But since that dancing incident, he has been happy. I can feel it. And I'm sure you are the reason for it.'

*I am? I can't be the reason for my own happiness, how can I make someone else happy?* Rivanah thought and said, 'Well, I'm sure there's a better and more legitimate reason for him to be happy.'

Advika was about to respond when Rivanah's phone rang. It was her mother.

'Excuse me,' Rivanah apologized and picked up the call.

'Mumma, what happened?'

'It's Baba here,' said Mr Bannerjee in a grave tone. Rivanah stood up and went a little away from Advika so she could speak to him privately.

'Baba, why do you sound so serious?'

'I just came back from office, so I'm a little tired. Anyway, Mini, some office work has come up in Mumbai. Mumma and I are coming over there tomorrow. What's your address? I misplaced the paper on which you wrote it down when you were here.'

*Sudden work in Mumbai?* Something wasn't right.

# 22

Rivanah took her leave from Advika soon after the phone call. She couldn't sleep properly that night. There were too many questions haunting her. Was her parents' sudden visit actually because of office work? Or were they coming to check on her? Also, what would she tell them about Danny? She'd never told them she was living with him in the first place. And now she won't have to, but should she come out clean about her relationship with him, even if it was a thing of the past now?

Upon their arrival, Mr and Mrs Bannerjee's first impression of their daughter's new place was good. But they were not in favour of the fact that she was living alone.

'What if you fall sick? There should be one roommate at least,' Mrs Bannerjee said.

'Your mother is right, Mini,' Mr Bannerjee chipped in, making himself comfortable on the sofa. He was happy there weren't any of those horrible bean bags in sight that he so greatly despised. 'I have spread the word.

Someone will join me soon,' Rivanah lied while serving her parents water.

'Which branch will you have to go to, Baba?' Rivanah asked, trying to figure out if there really was any office work.

'Wait, I have to show you something,' Mr Bannerjee said and brought out a newspaper from his bag. *Why was he evading my question?* Rivanah wondered, as he opened the newspaper's entertainment supplement. He pointed at a particular picture and gave the supplement to Rivanah.

'See.'

She took it from him with a frown. It didn't take long for her to identify Danny in the photograph. He was with three girls and two boys. The photograph was part of a feature whose headline read 'Newbies in Bollywood'. She took half a minute to go through the article. It was the first unofficial announcement of the movie Danny was doing. *Finally he has made it*, she thought. Just when she was out of his life.

'Don't tell me, Baba, you guys came to Mumbai for this?' Rivanah said.

'Of course not. But it's good to know that Danny's movie will be coming out soon,' Mr Bannerjee said.

Rivanah glanced at her mother who beamed at her as if she was happy that her daughter would now be allowed to marry the guy of her choice.

'It doesn't matter,' Rivanah said. While reading the article, she had decided it was useless to keep them in the dark.

'What do you mean?' Mrs Bannerjee's smile disappeared at once.

'We broke up.'

Mr Bannerjee threw an incredulous look at his wife and said the expected; 'I told you!'

Rivanah sat back on the sofa trying to shut her mind because she knew most of what was going to be said. And when it was over, Rivanah said, 'This is what you guys wanted anyway. Why dissect it more?'

Both Mr and Mrs Bannerjee understood their daughter had a point. Mr Bannerjee quietly went inside to change while Mrs Bannerjee came close to her daughter and asked, 'One last question, Mini.'

'What?'

'Why did you two break up?'

Rivanah rolled her eyes and said, 'That's because we stopped loving each other.' She carried their luggage to the guest bedroom while her mother mumbled under her breath, 'Stopped loving each other? How ridiculous!'

When Rivanah came out of the bedroom, she saw her parents gaping at the sketch stand.

'What happened?'

'Who sketched this?' Mr Bannerjee asked. He sounded as grave as he did on the phone when he had informed her about his Mumbai trip.

'Someone who used to stay here before me.'

'What?' Mr Bannerjee said in shock.

'That's what the landlord told me. But why do you look so unconvinced? Have you seen the sketch somewhere?'

Before Mr Bannerjee could speak, his wife spoke up, 'How will we see the sketch before? You sketched it in Kolkata also, so your baba must have thought—'

'What? I sketched this in Kolkata? When?' Rivanah said, looking at her parents. She noticed her father shooting an angry glance at her mother as if she had crossed a line, and then he said, 'Not exactly this, but you used to sketch facial portraits during your schooldays.'

There was an awkward silence in the room for some time.

'Is this our room?' Mr Bannerjee asked.

'No. This is mine. Yours is the other one. I have kept the luggage inside.'

'Good. And you shouldn't keep other people's stuff with you. It's not good manners,' Mr Bannerjee said, pointing to the sketch one last time, and then went away.

'Your baba is right.' Mrs Bannerjee came to her daughter and grasped her hand. 'One can't trust anyone or anything.'

'What are you talking about, Mumma? It's just a sketch stand for God's sake. Anyway, I'm going to take a bath now and then I have to rush to office. Everything is in the kitchen, Mumma. By the way, when do you have to go to office, Baba?' Rivanah wanted an answer.

'What's the hurry?' Mr Bannerjee said, unlocking his suitcase and averting his eyes.

'Baba, look at me,' Rivanah said. 'There's no office work, right?'

Mr Bannerjee looked down at the suitcase making the answer evident.

'Can't we come to just see you, Mini?' Mrs Bannerjee joined them in the bedroom.

'Of course, Mumma, you can. Any time. But what's the reason to lie?'

'We thought you may ask us to delay the visit if we were coming only to see you,' Mrs Bannerjee said.

'Okay, whatever. You guys take rest now,' she said and went to take a bath.

Rivanah reached her office and immediately messaged the Stranger: *Is the question you wanted me to ask myself and my parents' Mumbai visit connected?*

The Stranger's response made Rivanah's heart skip a beat: *Very much.*

Rivanah couldn't believe the fact that her own parents were probably part of something sinister. Did they know who the Stranger was? Her fingers trembled as she typed a message back: *How are the two connected?*

*I shall only provide you with the dots. You'll have to draw the line yourself, Mini.*

*Damn!* She was frustrated about the whole thing. And scared too, knowing her parents were hiding something on which perhaps two of the biggest questions in her life depended: one, what connected her to Hiya Chowdhury, and two, who the hell was this Stranger? A direct confrontation with her parents on this, she now knew, wouldn't fetch the kind of results she wanted. Rivanah kept pondering over this all day. In between, she checked Danny's Facebook profile. As expected, the Add as a Friend button showed up. She had been ousted from there too. *If that's what you want, Danny,* she thought and logged out.

Rivanah received a call from Sadhu Ram inquiring if anything untoward had happened after they had caught Argho at Bungalow 9. Rivanah informed him she would like to take the complaint back, realizing the Stranger puzzle wasn't going to end with the help of police. In fact, it would only become more complicated. She would have to solve it on her own. *If at all it is solvable,* she thought.

In the evening, when Rivanah reached her place, she ran into Nivan taking a stroll with Xeno in the society premises.

'You came early?' Rivanah said, kneeling down to pat Xeno on the head.

'I was in Bangalore for a meeting. Came a few hours back. How is it going?'

'All good.'

'I'm sure. I heard your parents are here,' she heard Nivan say.

'Oh yes, they are.'

'Nice. See you around,' he said and pulled Xeno away. He had taken a couple of steps when Rivanah rushed to him.

'Do you, by any chance, remember who your last tenant was?' Rivanah asked.

'Well, it was a guy.'

'Okay.' Rivanah's hair on her nape rose. *Was it the Stranger?*

'What did he look like?' Rivanah asked, anxious.

'Don't mind me asking, but what's up? Is there any problem?'

Rivanah immediately realized her mistake. 'I'm sorry I'm being rude,' she said and tried to act all normal. 'My father saw the sketch stand and wanted me to return it to the person who left it there since he doesn't like to use other people's things.'

'To be honest, it has been some time the guy lived here. And I was in the US at that time. I don't really remember him clearly. But I think if he left the sketch stand here, it must mean it wasn't important to him or else he would have come back.'

*Makes sense*, Rivanah thought.

'If you want I can get it removed.'

'It's okay. It's a sketch stand, after all. Not a time bomb.' Rivanah managed a smile. Nivan too smiled back. He finally walked away with Xeno while Rivanah entered the building. By the time she reached the sixteenth floor, she had an idea—as the Stranger had said— to join the dots.

Rivanah remained quiet all through dinner. She told her parents she had had a long day in office and would

175

retire early. She waited for her parents to sleep, after which she tiptoed into their room. She looked around and soon found her father's phone on the bedside table. It was an old phone without any password protection. She quickly unlocked it and went to Contacts and scrolled down. Rivanah sighed in relief, seeing what she was hoping for: Manick Dutta's phone number. She typed a message to him: *It was nice to meet you the other day. Hope you are doing fine.*

Rivanah sent it, praying that Mr Dutta was awake. It was only 10.45 p.m., after all. Not everyone slept early like her parents. Putting the phone on mute, she waited impatiently for a response. Her father turned around in his sleep. Rivanah froze. She had an excuse ready: if any of the two woke up, she would tell them she had come to look for a hairclip. But neither woke up.

Two minutes later, a message came in from Mr Dutta: *The pleasure is mine. It was indeed nice to meet you and family the other day. I hope Rivanah is all right.*

*She is fine. Thank you.* Rivanah messaged back, now certain that the visit to Mr Dutta's house wasn't a dream as she was made to believe by her parents. *But why? What happened at Mr Manick Dutta's place which had to be kept a secret from me by my own parents?* Rivanah deleted all the messages and put the phone back on the side table.

# 23

'I s there anything that you are hiding from us, Mini?' Mr Bannerjee asked.

It was next morning. The three were at the dining table having breakfast. Mr Bannerjee was reading the *Economic Times* while Mrs Bannerjee was leafing through the entertainment section. She glanced at her husband and then at her daughter, anticipating a response from the latter.

The word 'hiding' made Rivanah look up for the first time since she had joined her parents for breakfast. She couldn't sleep after reading Mr Dutta's message. What was it her parents were hiding from her? Why would her own parents hide anything from her in the first place? And now her father was asking her what *she* was hiding?

'Nothing, why?' she said.

'You seem lost. Didn't you sleep well?'

'Office pressure,' she said and noticed her parents exchanging looks. *This exchange of looks*, Rivanah surmised, *has happened too many times since they came here.*

'Don't let your health get affected, shona,' Mrs Bannerjee said. They resumed eating in silence.

'I'll get ready for office.' Rivanah went to her room after breakfast, while Mrs Bannerjee cleared the table and took the leftovers back to the kitchen. Just then, Mr Bannerjee heard two screams—one came from the bedroom and the other from the kitchen. Mr Bannerjee didn't know where to go. He scampered to the kitchen and realized his wife was standing with her hands on her hips while the washbasin tap was flowing with full gusto.

'Why don't you close the tap? You are wasting water.'

'It won't close.'

Mr Bannerjee came to inspect the tap and splashed water all over him in the process. He understood the knot in the tap had become loose.

'Why did you open it so hard?' he asked, irritated. 'We have to bring a plumber for this.'

Rivanah dashed into the kitchen, asking, 'Where did you put the sketch, Mumma? Why isn't it there on the sketch stand?'

'I just kept it—'

'And what's this?' Rivanah asked, gaping at the water gushing out of the tap. Her father had tied a piece of cloth over the tap, controlling the force of the water somewhat.

'Call a plumber, Mini,' Mr Bannerjee said.

'I have no idea where from. Wait, let me ask Nivan.'

'Who is Nivan?' Mrs Bannerjee was instantly curious.

'My landlord,' Rivanah said and left the kitchen.

Nivan answered the doorbell. He was in a tee and shorts, coffee mug in hand.

'Hey,' he said.

'Hi,' she replied, while trying hard not to register the boyish charm he exuded. She failed miserably.

'Do you know a plumber around here? The kitchen tap has gone bonkers.'

'Oh.' Nivan kept the coffee mug on the wooden shoe rack and came out of the flat.

'Let me check.'

'A plumber would do actually,' Rivanah said, feeling embarrassed about her senior trying a role shift.

'It's okay.'

Rivanah reluctantly led him inside the flat and into the kitchen where her parents were still fidgeting with the tap. Rivanah made a quick introduction as Nivan went towards the kitchen window, opened it completely and stretched his hand out.

'Its main knob is outside,' he said and the water stopped immediately. Nivan drew his hand in and said, 'I shall send the plumber in some time.'

'Thank you so much, Mr Nivan . . .' Mr Bannerjee was fetching for a surname and Rivanah knew exactly why.

'Mallick. Nivan Mallick.'

'It is nice to meet you, Mr Mallick.'

'Same here, sir,' Nivan said.

'Thanks for taking such good care of my daughter. She told me everything,' he said with a smile. Though it was a lie—*she told me everything*— Rivanah knew where the discussion was heading and wanted to stop her father right there but couldn't.

'Your daughter deserves every bit of it.'

'Why don't you join us for dinner tonight if it's not much of a problem?'

*There!* She knew it.

'Baba, he is a busy man.' Rivanah had to barge in now.

'Why, don't busy people have dinner?' he said and laughed, aptly joined by his wife.

'I would love to. I love Bong food.' Nivan said.

'Khoob bhalo! Then at 9 tonight?'

'Sure.'

Rivanah escorted Nivan to the main door and shut it after him. She was about to rush to the kitchen but she noticed her parents were already in the drawing room.

'Very nice boy,' Mr Bannerjee said.

'Shotti!' Mrs Bannerjee confirmed her husband's sentiments.

'He is my senior in office, Baba.'

'Senior? What's his designation?'

'VP, sales.'

'VP? This is even better. At such a young age. He must be what, 28–29? Max 30. A real achiever indeed. He must have good genes.'

Rivanah knew arguing would be a waste of time. She changed the topic. 'Where's the sketch, Mumma?'

'I have kept it inside the wardrobe.

'Why? Was it biting you?'

'Why keep someone else's sketch in the open?'

'Uff, tumi je ki koro na!' Rivanah walked off.

In the office, Rivanah thought the best way to avoid the impending dinner disaster would be to somehow request Nivan not to come for dinner. She didn't have his phone number yet. And going to his cabin for such a lame thing would be too much. She went through her mails to check if any of them had Nivan's official mail ID. She found it in one of the group emails. She immediately wrote to him: *May I have your mobile number?*

A minute later, Nivan replied with his phone number. Rivanah saved it on her phone and checked if he was available on WhatsApp. He was. She typed carefully: *Sorry to disturb you like this, but I hope my parents didn't offend you in any way.*

His reply came soon enough: *Offended? Not at all. Looking forward to some delicious Bong food tonight.*

And Rivanah knew an acute embarrassment was only hours away.

Mrs Bannerjee surprised Rivanah with the number of food items she had prepared for dinner.

'Mumma, he is coming alone, not with the whole colony. Why have you prepared so much food?'

'I know, but what will he think of us if we don't give him options?'

The acute embarrassment was confirmed as far as Rivanah was concerned. Not because she had any problem with so many food items, but because she knew what the intention behind impressing Nivan was.

The doorbell rang shortly after nine. Mr Bannerjee welcomed Nivan. The dinner didn't go as badly as Rivanah had imagined. Nivan loved everything that was served to him. Mr Bannerjee found the perfect pal in Nivan to discuss his latest obsession: politics. Seeing Nivan talk with her father, she remembered how Danny too had once come for dinner only to be cold-shouldered by her father. *How lifesaving it would be if one already knew whether a relationship would go the distance or not, before commencing it. We can always change the road we take but we can't undo the steps we took.*

It was around 10.30 when Nivan finally left. Rivanah let out a sigh of relief as she joined her parents on the couch in the drawing room.

'Mini,' Mr Bannerjee said and continued once Rivanah looked up at him, 'I think Nivan is a good guy.'

'Hmm.' Rivanah said.

'I think we should meet his parents too.'

'Huh?'

'He is young, highly qualified, seems very decent, knowledgeable, well settled, and he is not married.'

Rivanah was in an instant dilemma: whether to feel happy about all this or to rue over the fact that her father actually made such enquiries.

'Baba, don't tell me you asked him if he was married.'

'I did when you went to the kitchen to fetch more water for him.'

'But why?'

'What why? It is pretty evident what your choice of guys is like. I think you should focus on your job and let us select your life partner. And don't worry, we won't give you any reason to cry about this.'

'I know that, Baba, but I don't even know Nivan.'

'You always told us you knew Ekansh and Danny. What was the result? Marriage is about taking as much time as possible to know the person. You youngsters end up knowing everyone so quickly that you get bored and itch to move on to someone else.'

'This is not what happened with Ekansh or Danny.'

'You told us what happened between Ekansh and you, but what happened with Danny?' Mrs Bannerjee was curious.

Rivanah threw a helpless look at her mother and then said, 'Nothing. I'm feeling tired. Goodnight.' As she hit the bed, her father's words echoed in her mind: *and he is not married.* Why did that sound so appealing? In the Stranger's words: was she yet again seeking a bigger and deeper hurt in Nivan in order to get over the one given by Danny? It had been some time since the Stranger had contacted her. And with the house-hunting and shifting and her parents' arrival, she didn't get the time to contact him more than once. She knew now was the time.

*You there?* she messaged on one of the stored numbers.

*You bet*, was the immediate response.

A smile lit up her face. *How are you?*

*I'm good, Mini. Thank you for asking. How are you?*

*I'm . . . I don't know. Tell me, you wanted to kill me some time back, and now you don't contact me at all. Why are you so unpredictable?*

*I'm unpredictable because you know nothing about me, but in your mind you have heaps of presumptions about me.*

*Why don't you clear those presumptions then?*

*I will when I'm in the mood, Mini.*

*You never will, I know.*

*That too is a presumption.*

*Haha. Okay, what if I say I know you are aware of the fact that I live right next to Nivan's flat. Would you call it a presumption?*

*No. I will call it duty. My duty is to know whatever you are up to.*

*I knew that. What if I tell you I've been thinking about Nivan? Do you think I'm doing so because I'm somewhere seeking a bigger and deeper hurt?*

*Perhaps.*

*What should I do then?*

*Be wary of Nivan. He is hiding something.*

For the first time during the chat, Rivanah's expression changed into a deep frown. *What is it?*

*It is something that may bring you and me closer. Goodnight, Mini.*

Rivanah messaged back couple of times but there was no response. *What could Nivan possibly be hiding that may bring the Stranger closer to me?* Rivanah wondered and replayed the entire evening in her mind from the time he came in. She stopped at a particular moment when he had asked her if the sketch stand had to be removed. Rivanah had said no, after which he had asked if she had found anything else that belonged to the previous tenant. She had said no then, but the truth was that she had not checked the flat thoroughly.

Rivanah got up with a start, closed her room's door lest her parents noticed, and switched on the light. She checked the wardrobe, behind it, under the bed, below the mattress. While lifting the mattress, she noticed the bed had boxes for storage. Three out of the four boxes were empty. In the fourth box, she found a stack of books. They were some old Harold Robbins and Irving Wallace books. She was about to put them back in the box when she noticed something white peeping out of one of the books. She opened the particular novel and her jaw dropped immediately. It was a white piece of cloth with a message embroidered in black thread. She quickly opened the other books and all of them had a similar white cloth on which some message was embroidered in black. The sight made her stomach churn.

# 24

The radium hands of the clock in Rivanah's bedroom showed it was 3.15 a.m. As she tossed and turned in bed, Rivanah felt she couldn't move her hands properly. She got up and tried to move one hand but realized it was tied to the other.

'Fuck!' she gasped.

A sound made her look towards the window. She saw a man's silhouette, clear against the moonlight by the room's window. He had a shiny object in his hand.

'Hello, Mini,' the man said.

She knew who it was. She had asked him on the skywalk if he wanted to kill her. The sight of the shiny, pointy object told her he did. She tried to jump out of the bed and fell on the floor. Her feet were free but her hands were tied. She was about to scream when she heard the Stranger say, 'If you call your parents, I'll kill you in two seconds, but if you keep quiet and cooperate I shall tell you who I am.'

Rivanah, still on the floor, was already breathing hard. Her lower lip quivered. And her silence told the

Stranger what her decision was. With each step he took towards her, her heartbeat quickened. He bent down and picked her up in his arms, as if she were a feather. His strength aroused her and eclipsed her fear even. The mask covering his face revealed only his eyes, lips and the tip of his nose. She knew she had seen those eyes before.

He took her to the drawing room, never breaking eye contact.

The Stranger placed her close to the glass wall. Before her feet could find the floor, he pursed her lips with his. In a second, his tongue barged into her mouth. The hunger with which he was exploring her mouth broke the slumber created by fear in her, and every inch of her body awoke to an overtly sexual dawn. She wanted to see who this Stranger was but her hands were still tied together. He broke off the kiss and, looking straight into her eyes, tore open her nightdress. The buttons flew open, and he doffed the shirt as she raised her hands above her head. Rivanah rarely wore a bra at night, and her breasts were now out in the open. Her instinct was to cover them with her hands but they were pinned above her head with such power that she didn't even try. The Stranger squeezed her breasts with his free hand and whispered in her ears, 'I'm going to untie you now. I hope you know what you have to do.' With a deadly twinkle in his eyes, he slowly pulled a string and her hands came free. She put her arms around him immediately and pulled him closer to cover her breasts with his chest. Holding him around his neck

187

with one hand, her other hand slithered downwards till it reached his groin. As she massaged his erect penis over his jeans, she pulled his face closer to hers and this time explored his mouth herself with a renewed hunger. The Stranger grasped her hand over his groin. He made her unzip his jeans, and then tug it down, along with his underwear, till his knees. She could feel the tip of his erect penis poking her lower abdomen over her shorts as the two smooched harder. The Stranger scratched her thighs and reached for the elastic of her shorts. Slowly, he rolled both her shorts and panties down together. Grabbing her bare butt with his strong hands, he lifted her till both her legs were resting on his arm. Next, he brought her down so that she could hold his penis and guide it inside her. She obliged and let out a loud moan as he entered her. She heard some noise in her parent's bedroom. *What if my mother comes out in the drawing room right now? What will I tell her?* The forbidden nature of her act made Rivanah even more excited. As the Stranger kept moving his pelvis against hers with vigour, Rivanah kept glancing at her parents' door, hoping nobody came out, while her heart wanted the Stranger to keep going. The way he was looking at her told her he knew what was on her mind . . .

*After this, you'll have to remove the mask. You'll have to tell me who you are. I promise I won't tell anyone anything. Not even my parents or the police. I have paid enough price to deserve your identity now, Stranger. Even if you want to kill me after this, do it. I wouldn't*

*mind, but here's one last wish: I want to die in your arms, Stranger.*
*I want to die in your arms, looking deep into your eyes as you lead me*
*to a crushing climax where life and death merge to become eternity . . .*

'Mini?' Mrs Bannerjee called out from her room. By
the time she came into Rivanah's bedroom inquiring
who she was talking to at such an odd hour, Rivanah
was sound asleep—or faking it, to be more precise.
Mrs Bannerjee came to her, caressed her forehead and
then returned to her room. Once Rivanah was sure her
mother had gone, she opened her eyes. Her heart was
racing. She couldn't believe she had spoken the words
out loud, with her parents in the very next room. She
removed her hand from between her legs, tugged her
panties up and sat up. Her fantasy had ended abruptly.
She felt a little empty, but she didn't want to do it again.

Rivanah went into the washroom and shut the door.
Switching on the lights, Rivanah stared at her reflection
in the mirror. She saw someone who had no clue what
was happening in her life. After she had found the pieces
of white cloth inside the books, Rivanah had been shell-
shocked for some time. They had the same messages that
she had received from the Stranger in the beginning. Was
it the Stranger who had stayed in this flat before her?
Her parents were surely hiding something. The Stranger
wouldn't tell her anything directly, so where did that
leave her? Whom could she talk to? She felt a stifling
restlessness which wouldn't let her sleep or even be at
peace. She wanted a distraction. The Stranger had come

into her life once in a while, and it ended in a raunchy fantasy. But the questions still remained: whom could she talk to about the pieces of cloth? And why would the Stranger say Nivan was hiding something?

The next morning, her mother complained that Rivanah hadn't taken a day off work to spend time with her parents, like she had done the last time they had come to Mumbai.

'But, Mumma, I don't have many leaves. And I've just joined this company,' she said but promised herself to take her parents out for dinner at least.

At work, she kept thinking of how she could find out more about the pieces of cloth in the bed box. She was surprised when Nivan messaged her asking her to come to his cabin whenever she was free. Rivanah went to him immediately.

'Good morning, Rivanah,' he said.

'Hello, Nivan.'

'Sorry to have disturbed you during work hours.'

'Not a problem,' she said and wondered if she should tell him about the pieces of cloth.

'You look like you have something to share?' Nivan said.

'Actually, I stumbled upon some white pieces of cloth in my bed box.'

'White cloth?' Nivan looked interested.

'Pieces of cloth with messages embroidered on them.'

'That's weird.'

Nivan clearly had no idea how those could have ended up in the bed box. Rivanah decided to drop the matter and take it up on her own later.

'Anyway, you called me. Anything important?' she said.

'Yes. I looked for the agreement which I had with the previous resident of the flat.'

*You are a saviour, Nivan*, Rivanah thought. 'Thank you so much.'

Nivan picked up a document and gave it to Rivanah, saying, 'Never mind. This is the agreement. The tenant's name is Ekansh Tripathi.'

Rivanah looked down at the name on the document. For a moment, her mind went blank. She slowly lifted her face, still unable to think properly.

'Your expression tells me you know the person.'

'Umm . . .' She felt her throat had dried up by then. 'Not really,' she lied.

'Okay. He has a phone number if you can read it in the agreement. If you want you call him up and talk about the sketch stand.'

There was no response from Rivanah.

'Hello? Everything okay?' Nivan said, leaning forward.

'Yeah,' Rivanah nodded, looking stumped. 'Yeah, right. I'll call him.'

'Great.'

She took her leave. Back in her cubicle, Rivanah had only one question on her mind: *when* would Ekansh

Tripathi leave her life? She had deleted his number but it was still etched in her mind. She matched it with the one in the agreement—they were the same. She dialled, but before it could connect, Rivanah cut the call. She still wasn't sure if she should give Ekansh another excuse to enter her life. Especially since what happened the last time they met had altered her life drastically. She put these thoughts away and dialled again. The call was answered on the third ring.

'Hi, Rivanah. What's up?' he said in a formal tone.

That voice . . . that 'Hi Rivanah' . . . that 'what's up' . . . they were like the evil chant of a witch to crack open her box of memories, which had nothing but pain and suffering in the form of beautiful snapshots of the past.

'Did you ever live in the Residency Enclave, B wing, flat no. 1604?'

'What?'

'Please answer me.'

There was a pause.

'I think so.'

'Did you or did you not?'

'I did. For some time when I . . .' He stopped midway.

*You were cheating on me.* Rivanah completed his sentence in her mind.

'But Tista once told me you lived in Navi Mumbai.'

'That was after this. Why are you asking?'

192

Rivanah quickly checked the date on the agreement. The stay in the Residency Enclave was indeed dated well before she had moved in with Tista.

'Hello? You there, Rivanah?' Ekansh said.

'Please don't ever take my name,' she said and asked, 'Did you keep a sketch stand in the flat?'

'A sketch stand? I never used to sketch, you did. Why are you asking me all this? And what about Danny? Is everything okay? Look, I'm really sorry for my behaviour that day.'

The mention of Danny's name pushed her to remember how she had kissed Ekansh and sent the picture of it to Danny. Disgust clouded her.

'Yeah. All is fine. Bye.' She cut the line. Ekansh called back. Rivanah ignored the call, and later blocked the number. *Whom should I trust? Ekansh? The guy who has already given me the biggest reason in the past not to trust him?* A dreaded thought occurred to her at that moment: what if Ekansh was the Stranger? A mild headache hit her and she started massaging her forehead.

'Hey, what happened? You okay?' Smita enquired.

'Nothing,' Rivanah muttered. She somehow managed to get back to work.

In the evening, Rivanah left office later than usual. She called her parents and asked them to come over to Red Box in Andheri itself. She met them downstairs, and together they went up to the restaurant. Though she maintained a smile all through the dinner, there was too much on her mind for her to enjoy. They were done in two hours and took an autorickshaw home. As they were about to walk into the elevator, they bumped into Nivan. Greetings were exchanged. But Rivanah sensed something wasn't right about him. When she reached the sixteenth floor, she received a message from Nivan: *Come downstairs, please.*

With a slight frown, Rivanah told her parents she would join them in few minutes and took the elevator down. The moment she stepped out of the elevator, she noticed Nivan's BMW right outside the building. He was behind the wheel. She walked up to him, but before she could enquire, he said, 'Get inside.'

Rivanah got in and asked, 'What happened?'

Nivan pointed to something on the dashboard as he shifted the gear. Rivanah noticed there were two Post-it notes stuck on it.

The first one read: *I lied to you.*

The one right beside it read: *I'd kept the pieces of cloth in the books inside the bed box.*

They had driven out of the Residency Enclave by then.

# 25

Reading the two Post-it notes, Rivanah got goosebumps all over her body. She sat stiff as Nivan drove the car rather unsteadily. Perhaps he too was unnerved by something. For the first few minutes, Rivanah kept quiet, hoping Nivan would clarify what he meant when he said he kept the pieces of cloth inside the bed. Was he the Stranger? It sounded absurd.

'Could you please—' she began, but Nivan grabbed her hand. She stopped. He moved his hand from the gear and quickly stuck another Post-it on the dashboard. Rivanah looked down to realize he had a bunch of those notes beside the gear. The note said: *Sshhh.*

Nivan stuck another one.

*I have checked myself and the car. Are you sure you aren't bugged? Just nod if you aren't. Or else, check.*

Rivanah remembered how her dress had been once bugged by the Stranger. She tapped the edges of her shirt, the sleeves, the shoulder, the buttons, the trouser and finally her footwear. Nothing seemed suspicious. She nodded to Nivan. He put another note on the dashboard:

*Don't talk till I stop the car.*

Nivan drove to the western express highway and then, paying the toll, entered the 7-km-long Worli Sea Link. At night, the city skyline on both sides of the Sea Link made Mumbai look like a teenager's first love: too good to be real.

The car slowly came to a halt in the middle of the Sea Link. They both stepped out. Nivan went in front of the car and opened the bonnet. Rivanah joined him.

'Are you being pursued by someone?' Nivan asked, without looking at her. She nodded hesitantly.

'Same here,' he muttered.

'What do you mean?' Rivanah said, as a breeze ruffled her hair. She tucked her hair behind her ears. Nivan looked around and then, staring at the car's engine in front of him, said, 'Two years ago, it started with a rather harmless note saying: *Be ready, Nivan.*'

The scene inside the Meru cab when she arrived in Mumbai for the first time flashed in her mind: *Be ready, Mini.*

'Then one message after another started coming in. Pieces of white cloth in which the messages were embroidered in black thread.'

Nothing made sense to Rivanah.

'I went to the police as well but it didn't help. The person isn't just a stalker. He made me do weird things like . . .'

'Like?' Rivanah's throat was dry.

'Like . . .' Nivan glanced at Rivanah and said, 'Make sure you were employed in our company.'

*While I was left with no other option but to seek your company out,* Rivanah thought and said aloud, 'Do you mean you always knew who I was?'

'You were just a name to me, and one of the tasks I was given by this . . .'

'Stranger.' Rivanah completed his sentence for him.

Nivan nodded.

'And you had to do it?' she asked.

Nivan nodded again. Just like she *had to* do what the Stranger wanted.

'So I had kept the cloth pieces inside the bed box. Those were given to me. Did you get them as well?'

'Yes. I did,' Rivanah said, matching Nivan's soft tone. 'But didn't you try to find out who the Stranger is or why he is pursuing you?'

'I tried my best but couldn't. I don't even try to trace him any more. But I am sure my moves are under observation,' he said in a resigned tone.

*Hence the Post-it notes,* Rivanah thought and said, 'Are you still in touch with the Stranger?'

'I was never in touch with him. It was he who never left me.'

They fell silent.

'I sensed it the day you came to my cabin and told me about the pieces of cloth. And tonight, I only wanted to make sure if it was what I thought it was. That you too are a victim of this mysterious frenemy, who coincidentally we both refer to as the Stranger,' Nivan said as he closed the bonnet.

'Let's go back. Please don't mention this conversation to the Stranger, in case you are in touch with him.'

Rivanah nodded. As they got back inside the car, Rivanah was tempted to ask Nivan if he had a personal secret because of which the Stranger was in his life—just like Hiya was her secret which the Stranger wanted her to pursue. And whether his and her secrets have a link. Rivanah took one of the Post-it notes. Nivan's eyes followed Rivanah as she opened the glovebox. She found a pen and immediately scribbled on the slip. She showed it to Nivan.

*Is the Stranger making you seek some secret?*

She sensed a tinge of discomfort on Nivan's face as he stepped on the accelerator and murmured, 'I can't tell you.'

*Which means there is one*, Rivanah concluded. She checked her phone which she had left inside the car. There were five missed calls from her father's number. She didn't call back.

When Rivanah returned to her flat, her parents kept hounding her, enquiring where she had disappeared. They stopped bothering her when she told them she was with Nivan. It seemed to make them happy. But Rivanah wasn't happy. After what Nivan had told her, she only had one priority now: to find out about Hiya Chowdhury. That's the link to the Stranger. And why would he involve Nivan in the scheme of things? So many times she was on the verge of inquiring about Hiya—and the sketch—to her parents, but she didn't. If her parents were to tell her something, they would have done so by now. She would have to find out in a different way.

Retiring to her room, Rivanah put the sketch back on the sketch stand and kept staring at it. Was the sketch the sole clue in the entire puzzle? On a hunch, she stood up, removed the sketch and stared at the blank page on the stand. She took a deep breath and walked to her dressing table. She brought her eye pencil and stood in front of the sketch stand once again. Letting her instinct take over, she started sketching. When she was done, Rivanah's sketch quite resembled the one that had been on the stand earlier. It scared her, but she knew she was right. The sketch was a clue. She took a good picture of the sketch and uploaded it on Facebook with a question: *Whom does she resemble?*

She kept refreshing the page but there came no likes or comments. Frustrated, she slumped on her bed again. It was around 4.30 a.m. when her eyes opened suddenly. She checked her phone. There was one comment on the picture. She immediately tapped on the notification. Someone by the name of Binay Das had liked the picture and left a comment: *Isn't that our college-mate Hiya?* And Rivanah knew she was closer to unveiling the mystery than she had ever been. She left a message for Binay asking him to call her on her number the moment he saw the message.

She couldn't get much sleep that night. It was 8 a.m. when her phone rang.

'Hi, this is Binay here. How are you doing, Rivanah? It has been so long. Where are you?'

She remembered Binay from college as someone who would take fifty words to say what could be said in five.

'Binay, don't get me wrong, but I need to know something urgently. We will talk properly later.'

'Sure. What happened?'

'You commented on the picture I put up.'

'That's Hiya Chowdhury, right?'

'What do you know about her?'

'About Hiya? The usual, that she was our batch topper and the one who committed suicide.'

'That's it?'

'And you two were fierce competitors.'

*Just the kind of information I am looking for.* 'Anything else?' she said.

'Ummm. Can't think of anything else right now. Why do you need to know about Hiya, all of a sudden?'

'Just like that.'

'Okay. Where are you, by the way?'

'Mumbai.'

'Great, I'm in Pune. I can come down this weekend if you—'

'I'm really busy this weekend, Binay. I'll call when I'm free. You take care. Bye.' She quickly cut the line and blocked the number. She had no room in her life for guys who mistook her friendliness for availability.

Rivanah now had two clues: she had sketched Hiya's face again and again, and the two had been fierce competitors in college. The fact that her father told her she used to sketch in school could well be a lie. But why would this sketch and stand be in this flat? And a sketch stand was in the Krishna Towers flat as well. Something told her she was there and yet not there.

'Didn't you sleep properly?' her mother asked walking into her room.

'Yes, I did. Let me go for a bath, Mumma. Need to go to office early today.'

Mrs Bannerjee sensed something was not all right.

'You better be back early today,' Mrs Bannerjee said, as her daughter entered the bathroom. 'Your baba and I are leaving tonight, remember?'

The latching of the bathroom door was the only response.

At work, Rivanah wrote down the supposed dots on a piece of paper. Telling Nivan about it verbally could be risky. Writing it down was the best option—like they had done in the car the other night.

*Parents are hiding something . . . Hiya Chowdhury's sketch in my flat . . . she's my college-mate who hanged herself . . . I was able to sketch her face even though I supposedly stopped sketching long back . . . Hiya was my competition in college, but I don't remember anything about her . . . in fact, recently I forgot all about her, though I had gone to unearth the missing link in Kolkata . . . father's colleague—Mr Dutta—seems a shady character . . . Argho Chowdhury is Hiya's cousin, but I doubt he is involved in this. These are the dots which, I'm sure, lead somewhere. What do I do? Please suggest.*

Rivanah reread it and, once convinced she had written whatever she had in mind, went to Nivan's cabin. A look at her and Nivan knew it wasn't an official visit. She quietly passed the note to him. He read the note and seemed pensive for some time. Finally he wrote back on the paper:

*Your past is in Kolkata. Don't you think going there will take us closer to the mystery?*

Rivanah read the note and then looked up at Nivan.

'You can ask Nivan to stay with us. Why else have we built so many rooms in our house? Only for guests to come and stay,' said Mr Bannerjee the moment Rivanah told them she and Nivan would be returning with them to Kolkata on account of some office work.

'Thanks for this, Nivan. I really needed someone to—' Rivanah had told Nivan when he said he would accompany her to Kolkata. He had cut her short and said, 'There's nothing to thank me for. You forget that we both are victims. And my itch to know who this Stranger is just as strong as yours. He made me manipulate your selection in the company. I really want to know how you and I are related. If at all, that is.'

Rivanah could identify with Nivan's sentiments. The fact that they were sailing in the same boat gave her hope. Of late, she had been missing Danny. Or was she missing someone's safety net around her? Was it again the Cinderella Syndrome popping up like the psychiatrist had once told her? It was worse that she couldn't talk to the Stranger. It wasn't the time to engage in any philosophical prattle with him. It was time to end whatever shit he had been involving her in.

The Bannerjee family met Nivan after the security check in the airport. Mr Bannerjee was extra talkative to him. Rivanah had requested her family not to ask Nivan to stay at their place because it looked thoroughly unprofessional. Mrs Bannerjee, on the other hand, whispered to her daughter, 'Mini, is something going on between you two?'

'No, Mumma,' Rivanah said and excused herself to go and fetch a Coke. Anything to avoid her parents. This was something she had expected to happen. Nivan and the Bannerjee family split up and went to their assigned seats after boarding. Rivanah's parents fell asleep soon after take-off, while Rivanah watched darkness fall outside the window. In a matter of just two years, she was done with two guys—Ekansh and Danny—and now, suddenly, the rest of her life looked like those white balls of cloud—empty. She felt an urge to cry but checked herself. She went to the lavatory and looked at herself in the small mirror and wondered if she hadn't really changed. Life had only dug out another Rivanah from within her. *Not Life*, she corrected herself, *there was another name for it—the Stranger.* Since she had come to Mumbai, her life had been all about him. She hoped this visit to Kolkata would end the mystery. Rivanah was walking back to her seat when she heard her name. She turned around and saw Nivan sitting in the last row. The entire row was empty. Rivanah gladly joined him.

'Did the Stranger get in touch?' he asked.

'Not after last time.'

'I thought so. It only means we are following what he wants us to follow.'

'I agree.'

'I was wondering if you know anyone in Kolkata who would be able to give us any information about Hiya Chowdhury.'

Rivanah thought for a minute and said, 'Ishita, a friend of mine. She was the one who told me I'd forgotten about Hiya suddenly.'

'Hmm, okay. This forgetting part confused me, actually. How can a person forget something all of a sudden, unless it is some sort of amnesia?'

'I know. But the weirdest thing is, although I'd forgotten everything about Hiya, I remembered the Stranger.'

Nivan's eyes remained on Rivanah for some time as if he was trying to figure out what the reason could be.

'Anyway, we should meet your friend first,' he said.

'Sure.'

Rivanah soon joined her parents and found them still asleep. She didn't wake them up lest they probed her more about Nivan.

The flight landed on time. Nivan headed to ITC Sonar Bangla, while Rivanah and her parents took a cab home. She couldn't wait to call Ishita. Once home, Rivanah went straight to the terrace and called her.

'Hey babe, what's up?'

Rivanah could hear loud music. 'Go to a quieter place.'

'Give me a second.'

As Rivanah held on, Ishita spoke a few seconds later.

'Better?'

'Much better. I'm in Kolkata.'

'Cool. Let's catch up tomorrow then?'

'Yes. Can we catch up in the morning itself?'

'I have to go to work, my dear.'

'It's urgent.'

Ishita thought for a second and said, 'Can you come down to sector 5?'

'I can come anywhere.'

'Great. There's a CCD near my office. Let's meet there. 10?'

'Absolutely.'

'All fine?'

'Almost fine. Let's talk tomorrow.'

Rivanah then dialled Nivan's number but had to end the call abruptly since she heard someone say two words.

'Hello, Mini.'

Rivanah looked towards the water tank which was not very well lit. She was sure the voice had come from there. Fear written all over her face, Rivanah tried to locate the obvious source of the voice.

'How come you are here?' she blurted.

'I go wherever you go, Mini,' the Stranger said. He was merely a voice coming out from somewhere near the water tank. In a flash, Rivanah leapt towards the switchboard and pressed the switch for the light above the water tank. Nothing happened—except, a lightbulb rolled towards her.

'Try, try, try till you succeed,' the voice said. Rivanah picked up the bulb cursing herself for thinking she was smarter than the Stranger.

'What do you want?' she said.

'I'm happy for you. Finally you are getting where I always wanted you to.'

'Do you mean I'm close to finding the link between me and Hiya?'

'I only say things. What I mean depends on how smartly you interpret my words, Mini.'

'And when am I going to—' Rivanah stopped as her phone flashed 'Nivan calling'. She silenced the call and continued, 'When will I see who you really are?'

'Trust me, knowing my identity isn't going to help you in any way.'

'Would it hurt you if I get to know you?'

'Maybe.'

'But this is unfair,' Rivanah said. She waited for a response but there was none. *Is he gone?* Rivanah took a few unsure steps towards the water tank and then walked more confidently. But there was no sign of him. She was about to turn to leave when the Stranger leapt out of the darkness and held her tightly from behind so she had her back to him, pressing her mouth with one hand while grabbing both her wrists with another. She tried to free herself but he was too strong for her. Using his thumb and index finger of the hand which was pressing her mouth he clipped her nose. Her entire body was trying to break free but in vain. He appeared to be enjoying the fact that she was growing more and more breathless by the second. Her resistance became even stronger, and she knew that if she didn't breathe in the next five to ten seconds, she would die. A mental countdown had begun. And just when it reached 1, the Stranger released her. She inhaled as much oxygen as she could while the Stranger whispered in her ears, 'Remember this experience, Mini. I'll tell you later why.'

As he released her, Rivanah sat down on her knees trying to catch her breath. She wanted to look for the Stranger but felt stifled. She was sure the Stranger had disappeared by then. Her phone once again flashed 'Nivan calling'. She picked up.

'Hey, did you get through to your friend?'

'Yes.' She was still gasping for air.

'What happened?' Nivan sounded concerned.

'He was here.'

'What? Are you all right?'

'Now I am. Don't worry.'

'What did he say?'

'He knows what we are looking for.'

'We? He said that?'

'No. He meant me, but I'm sure he knows.' Rivanah finally stood up.

'I'm sure too.'

'Ishita will meet us tomorrow morning. I'll message you the address.'

'Okay. I'll wait. You take care. See you.'

Rivanah heard her mother calling her downstairs. 'Mini, what are you doing on the terrace?'

'Mumma, a bulb on the terrace has fused. We need to replace it,' Rivanah said and went downstairs, the Stranger's last words still echoing in her mind: *I will tell you later why.*

Next morning, Rivanah and Nivan took a cab to the CCD where Ishita was already waiting for her.

'It's lovely to see you, babes.' Ishita hugged Rivanah immediately and then went slightly stiff seeing Nivan.

'Tell me he is your cousin and is here to bride-hunt,' Ishita whispered in Rivanah's ears. The latter broke the hug with an amused face and said, 'Ishita, meet Nivan, my senior at work.' The two shook hands. As Nivan sat down, he realized the girls were still standing. He excused himself and stood back up.

'Please excuse us,' Rivanah said as Ishita pulled her towards the washroom. The moment they entered, Ishita asked, 'Is he your—'

'No! Though I didn't tell you I'm single now.'

'You are fucking Nivan?'

'Shut up, no!'

'What happened with Danny?'

'Same thing that happened with Ekansh. Life! We broke up because of my alleged infidelity.'

'What the fuck! Seriously?'

Rivanah nodded.

'And what exactly is Nivan doing here with you?'

Rivanah took two minutes to fill her in.

'Hmm. Everything is so twisted. Do give me your kundali after this.'

'Huh?'

'I want to know what kind of planetary position a girl needs to first have a hot guy like Danny and now a sex god.'

Rivanah smirked and with a tinge of sarcasm in her voice said, 'Oh, I too want to know that because every one of them slips out of my grasp.'

The girls came out of the washroom. They ordered their coffee after which Rivanah put it straight to Ishita, 'Just tell us what happened after we returned from Hiya's house last time.'

'Okay.' Ishita took a deep breath as if she was recollecting all of it correctly in her mind and then said, 'Your mother called a few times after which you said you had to accompany your parents to meet one of your father's colleagues. We guessed they wanted you and this colleague's son to get hitched. Then I guess you went there. I went with my colleagues for an outing where there was no phone network. I came back two days later, and when I called you back seeing your missed call alert and inquired if you had unearthed something about Hiya, you surprised the shit out of me by asking who Hiya was.'

Nivan glanced at Rivanah once and then looking at Ishita said, 'That's weird. How can Rivanah forget someone just like that?'

'This isn't the only weird thing that happened. I was pretty sure I had accompanied my parents to Mr Dutta's house.'

'Obviously, the two are connected. But how?' A couple of seconds later, Nivan asked, 'Who exactly is this Mr Dutta?'

'Manick Dutta is Baba's colleague.'

'Have you met him before?' Ishita asked.

'No.'

'And what exactly happened at his place? Do you remember?' Nivan asked.

'I went there, talked to him, all the while feeling sleepy. Then he suggested I take a nap. I was reluctant but my mother insisted as well. So I went to his bedroom only to doze off. And when I woke up, I was in my bedroom. Later, when I asked Baba, he said we were supposed to go to Mr Dutta's place but it was cancelled at the last moment.'

'You are scaring me,' Ishita said. They became quiet. Ishita's phone broke the silence. She took the call and, a few seconds later, told Rivanah, 'I'm sorry, but I have to go to office now. I'll call the moment I'm free today. Take care.' Ishita stood up.

'It was nice meeting you, Nivan,' she added, before hurrying out.

'We can trust Ishita, right?' Nivan asked.

'Oh yes. She knows everything.'

'Hmm. We have to pursue this mysterious Mr Dutta you mentioned.'

'I had messaged him on my father's behalf. And he asked if I was all right.'

'All right? You ask that if someone has had an accident or . . . if they are suffering from something.'

Rivanah had no clue what to say.

'Tell me something,' Nivan said, 'Is there anyone who might know everything about you for, let's say, a week, before and after Hiya's death? Not your parents. Like someone who was always there with you in college as well.'

Rivanah didn't have to think hard for this one. The name was clear in front of her: Ekansh Tripathi. How many times would she promise herself not to go to Ekansh and how many times would she have to break it?

# 27

The next morning, Rivanah considered several times before calling up Ekansh. She had blocked him, deleted his number and yet he kept reappearing in her life like an unwanted necessity. It showed her just how much their past was intertwined. And there was no way she could undo it. *The best way*, Rivanah decided, *was to pretend there was no past.* Holding on to this thought, she typed Ekansh's number on her dialler and called him. She would finish it over phone and be done with it.

*The number you have called has been temporarily suspended,* an automated voice said in Marathi.

*What the fuck,* Rivanah lamented. She typed a message, both on WhatsApp and SMS, and sent them to his number, hoping he read it. Morning turned to afternoon with no response from Ekansh. In the evening, Nivan called her.

Rivanah told him about Ekansh Tripathi, and Nivan enquired if he was the same person who had stayed in his flat before her. When she replied in the affirmative, it piqued Nivan's interest immediately. And he was sure

Ekansh would prove to be an asset in their quest though Rivanah tried to convince him he was nothing but an ass.

'Did you get through to him?'

'Not yet. His phone is temporarily suspended.'

'And there's no other way of getting in touch with him?'

'There is . . .' Rivanah knew she could call Ekansh's parents and get in touch with him. *But . . .*

'Did you try the alternative way?'

Rivanah wanted to say she wasn't interested, but Nivan didn't know of her past with Ekansh except for the fact he had been a good friend in college. And there was no reason why he should know anything else now.

'Give me two minutes. I'll call you back,' Rivanah said and cut the line. She remembered Ekansh's landline number as well. She cursed herself for remembering every inconsequential thing about him. *Perhaps girls are like that*, she concluded, *they remember the so-called unimportant details of a relationship much more than guys do*. She called on the landline which was answered on the fourth ring.

'Hello aunty, this is Rivanah here.'

The response came after a long pause, 'Hello, Rivanah.'

'I wasn't able to get through to Ekansh. Do you have any number where I can reach him? It's important.'

Rivanah heard Ekansh's mother move away from the receiver and call out to Ekansh.

'Hello?'

'Ekansh?'

'Rivanah?'

'What the hell are you doing in Kolkata?' she asked, and knew how weird it sounded. *He could be in Timbuktu, for God's sake. How does it matter?*

'I left my job.'

'Oh!'

'Where are you? How come you are calling me on my landline?'

'I'm in Kolkata. I called you on your Mumbai number but—'

'Yeah, I cancelled that number. Do you want to meet up?'

*No, I want to finish it on phone*, she thought but said, 'Okay, we'll keep it short.'

'If you want it short, it will be short.'

*Why is he suddenly so friendly? Especially after the frivolous treatment she had been giving him?*

'Coffee house?' he asked.

'Okay. In an hour.'

'Done.'

Rivanah cut the line and messaged Nivan saying she was meeting Ekansh shortly and would call Nivan once done.

Rivanah reached the Coffee House on time; Ekansh was already there. Was it a coincidence that he had chosen the same corner where they sat whenever they bunked college? She gave him a tight smile before sitting down opposite him.

'How is everything between Danny and you?' Ekansh asked.

Rivanah looked around and said, 'All's fine.' She wasn't going to give him a reason to feel he had a space in her life.

'Good,' he said.

She could sense sadness in his voice.

'I left my job and Mumbai too. I'll be at home for some time, figure out what I really want to do in life and then perhaps . . .'

'Hmm. That's nice.'

'I miss Tista.'

Rivanah had decided she wouldn't let him use his guilt as bait to fish her guilt out. She intentionally pretended his last sentence didn't mean much to her.

'I want you to tell me something, Ekansh. And tell me honestly.'

'Is that why we are meeting now?'

'Yes.'

'Okay, tell me, what is it?'

'You remember Hiya Chowdhury?'

He thought for a second and said, 'Yes, I do. You have asked me about her earlier too.'

'I know. She hanged herself a day before Tech Sky came to recruit on campus.'

'I remember that too.'

'I want you to tell me if you noticed anything odd about me from that day onwards.'

'Odd?' Ekansh seemed lost in thoughts. He spoke after some time, 'I think all was normal. You had gone on a vacation with your family for a month or so.'

'A month? Where?'

'What do you mean where? It was Leh and Ladakh, don't you remember?'

*Leh and Ladakh.* Rivanah had never seen any photographs of that vacation nor had any memory of it. Assuming she had made it to the vacation in the first place.

'Did I ever show you any pictures?'

Ekansh frowned and said, 'Why are you talking like you are an amnesia patient?'

Rivanah didn't react.

'I asked you for pictures, but you never showed me any,' Ekansh said.

'So, I was away for a month and then I was back and everything was normal?'

'You only went with your family for a vacation. It is normal anyway.'

Rivanah was thoughtful.

'Were we in touch when I was in Leh and Ladakh?'

'There was no network in your phone.'

'Which means we were out of touch.'

'Totally.'

Neither spoke for some time. Rivanah tried to fit in the information Ekansh had given her with whatever she knew of Hiya, but it didn't make sense: Hiya's death and her vacation—two seemingly unrelated incidents. *So*

217

*many students must have gone on vacations at that time. So what?* But what kept her suspicions alive was the fact she didn't remember the vacation.

Ekansh snapped a finger to break Rivanah's trance. 'I think you are hiding something.'

Rivanah gave him a sharp glance and said, 'It's nothing. Thanks, Ekansh, for meeting up. I'll have to leave now.' She stood up. Ekansh grasped her hand rather impulsively. They looked into each other's eyes. Hers seemed to ask why and his why not. He let go of the grasp and asked, 'How long are you here in Kolkata?'

'I'm flying to Mumbai later tonight,' she lied and added genuinely, 'Stay well and take care. I miss Tista too.' Rivanah put her bag over her shoulder and walked off.

Nivan had been putting up in room no. 510 at the ITC Sonar Bangla. And though he had asked her if she wanted to meet outside, it was Rivanah who told him she wanted to be away from the noise and people for some time. She needed a quiet place to analyse the dots now that Ekansh had given her a new one—her supposed Leh and Ladakh family vacation.

'You want a tablet?' Nivan asked, noticing Rivanah rubbing her forehead as she settled on the couch in his suite.

'Perhaps some water,' she said.

Nivan brought her a bottle of water from the mini fridge.

'Thanks,' she said, taking a sip.

'What did Ekansh tell you?'

Rivanah took a minute to recount everything.

'So according to him, you tagged along with your parents to Leh and Ladakh, but you say you have no memory of it nor photographs to support it.'

'That's correct. Nor have I heard my parents ever mention it.'

'And you are confident Ekansh won't lie to you?'

Rivanah looked at Nivan. 'Why would he?'

'Okay. So after Ekansh, the two parties whom we should approach are Mr Dutta and—'

'And?'

'Hiya's parents. I remember, Ishita mentioned you two had gone to her place after the convocation.'

The mention of Hiya's parents brought back memories of the crazy-looking woman she had seen at her place and Hiya's worried-looking father. And yet she had forgotten only about Hiya and not her parents. *What. The. Fuck.*

'By comparing what Ekansh, Mr Dutta and Hiya's parents tell us, we can hope to get a solid lead.'

'Right.' Rivanah understood Nivan had a point. Nivan's phone, kept at the centre of the glass table, rang and vibrated at the same time. The vibration swirled the phone towards her. Before Nivan could pick it up,

Rivanah saw the name—Advika. Nivan excused himself and went to the other end of the room where the window was. As he stood there talking over the phone, Rivanah already had her questions ready for him. Nivan came back a couple of minutes later.

'Who is Advika?' she asked.

Nivan paused before settling on the couch again.

'I'm sorry if I'm being too personal,' she said.

'Advika is my girlfriend.'

'That's nice to know,' Rivanah said, knowing well Nivan must have guessed from her tone that she meant the opposite.

'What happened to her?' She had to ask something before the air turned too awkward between them.

Nivan reclined on the couch and set his gaze on the ceiling.

'Remember you asked me if I had a secret?'

*Which you didn't tell me*, Rivanah remembered clearly. 'Yes,' she said.

'Advika and I dated for five years and have been living together for seven.' Nivan was still staring at the ceiling. 'We met for the first time at a friend's birthday party after my higher-secondary exams. She had just passed her high school then. I remember she simply stood in one corner with a smile, not knowing I had my eyes on her all the time. I found her quietness amidst the party cacophony so very attractive. I can never forget that face . . . that moment. That evening, something unprecedented happened: I fell for a girl for the first time in my life. And it led me to do something I had never done before. I proposed to her by the time the party ended. She was so scandalized that she simple scampered away without saying anything. I became the butt of my friends' jokes. Then two days later, Advika got my number from a common friend and said yes to me on the phone. I never asked her why she took two days' time. All she told me was that, for her, I was the first. And I hope she knows that, for me, she is the last.' Nivan had a nostalgic smile on his face.

'Advika was always a non-confronting kind of girl, never found faults in others. It always surprised me. Actually, she'd always lived a protected life, never facing the harsh world ever, which ensured she had a pure heart. But it was not a practical one. During her college days, I used to pick her up from her house every day. The way she held on to me tightly every time I raced my bike amused me. And I did it on purpose most of the times.' The nostalgic smile on his face stretched at this point. He stood up and went to pick up his wallet from the table beside the television. He flipped it open, and staring at something inside said, 'Every touch of yours is a memory, each memory is an orgasm, each orgasm hides a realization and the realizations leads me to self-discovery.' He closed the wallet and came back to where he was sitting.

'It was something she had written for me after our first year together. I have kept it with me ever since. You know what, if I have to tell you about Advika in one line, she is a girl who never lost her innocence.'

Rivanah felt like she was hearing an excerpt from a romance novel. It sounded incredible and yet it urged Rivanah to believe it with her heart. The depth of a man's love, she realized while listening to Nivan, was evident in the way he reminisces about his girl.

'Advika was afraid of speed. She would never sit on a roller coaster. She always took her own sweet time to cross a busy road. Every time we took a flight, she would clasp my hand hard before take-off and while landing. That was also why she never learnt driving. I used to tease her about it, because speed was something that gave me a kick. Though I used to push her to learn driving, which she eventually did, Advika never really drove.' There was a pause akin to the one which usually preceded a storm.

'It was the fourteenth of April four years back, when we had planned to go for a movie at night. I was at work, and I had not brought my car that day. So, for a change, I wanted her to come over to the office and pick me up. She kept telling me we could take a cab, but I was adamant. After all, if one doesn't drive then how does one overcome this fear? I simply wanted her to confront her fear.' Nivan was suddenly quiet.

'And?'

Nivan's eyes fell upon Rivanah but he looked away quickly.

'She gave in to my stubbornness, drove but, before she could reach my office, met with an accident. A drunkard had hit her car. She injured her spine. The result of it,' his voice turned heavy as he completed, 'is for you to see.'

Rivanah was at a loss for words. There was a prolonged silence.

'I'm not going to marry her,' Nivan said, sounding choked.

Rivanah frowned.

'If I marry her,' he continued, 'People will make me believe that I'm with Advika because she is my responsibility. It would be my duty as a husband to be by her side. But, to be honest, Advika is neither my responsibility nor my duty. Advika is my choice. And when you choose someone, you are by default embracing all the consequences the choice may bring along.'

Rivanah tried to understand what Nivan was telling her, putting her life in context. Here was a man whose conviction in his love was so strong that it eclipsed the impossibility of it going the distance. Of course, Advika was an invalid now in every sense of the word, and yet this man sitting in front of Rivanah was confident of spending a lifetime with her. As if the tryst of destiny couldn't touch his love. As if fate was irrelevant. The realization of the existence of such a powerful love story made her feel empty. It made her feel jealous of Advika. And it made her feel insignificant too. She always wanted to be one such *choice* of one such *man*—neither responsibility nor duty, as Nivan had put it. She was happy to know such men existed, but they were the rarest of rare. And the one sitting in front of her was already taken.

'Life's unpredictable,' Nivan said, 'but if you don't stand by your choice, it will become incorrigible too. That's what the Stranger told me once.' He looked at Rivanah who was blank.

'What happened?'

Rivanah shook her head and said, 'I think I'll go home. Let's catch up tomorrow. I shall ask Ishita to join us.'

'All right.' Nivan looked thoughtful.

Rivanah took a cab. She was feeling dazed. Never before had she coveted someone's life like she now coveted Advika's. She felt an unprecedented urge to snatch Nivan away from her, to cast an evil spell so Nivan would get lured to her, would make her his choice, and make her feel everything that he made Advika feel.

With that one confession, Nivan had raised her expectations of men. When Danny broke up with her, he had given her reasons to abhor men and think of them as beings who would never understand the complexity of a woman. But Nivan pushed those reasons into insignificance and convinced her in no time to still be hopeful in a hopeless way. And it was the worst space to be in—to see someone like a horizon, visible but not attainable. What is it which decides who deserves whom? On the verge of having an emotional breakdown, Rivanah messaged the Stranger:

*I seriously need to talk. Please tell me you are there.*

A few seconds later the Stranger replied:

*At your house, Mini?*

Rivanah made a mad dash for her house.

## 28

Rivanah called up her parents on the way, fearing their life may be in danger. But they both were in New Market, shopping. They told her they would be back by evening, and asked her to take the spare key from their neighbour. Rivanah didn't let them get a whiff of her anxiety. The cab dropped her right in front of her house, and she went to the neighbour to collect the spare key. The neighbour wanted to chat, but Rivanah cut her short and walked up to the main door of her house and, looking around, slowly unlocked it. She peeped in first and then stepped in. She could smell It's Different by Hugo Boss in the air.

'You there?' The drawing room was filled with darkness since all the curtains, she noticed, were drawn. She had never been so scared to enter her own house before.

'Close the door, Mini,' a voice commanded.

Rivanah shut the door behind her trying to identify where the voice had come from.

'Take a seat.'

Now she knew where the voice was coming from. Behind the refrigerator, she could see the silhouette of the upper half of someone's head as the head rested on folded hands atop the refrigerator. The Stranger's figure was hidden by the refrigerator. Rivanah didn't move for some time, while calculating what her next move should be.

'Take a seat, Mini,' the Stranger repeated. She went to the sofa and saw a blindfold and a handcuff on it. She knew what was expected of her, but was it necessary? She was about to object when she heard him speak again.

'You move, I move out. You shout or run, you lose me. You don't listen to me, this meeting is over.'

*Damn you*, she thought and put on the blindfold first and then locked her hands with the handcuff.

'Happy?' she said.

'More than ever, Mini. Tell me, what do you want to talk about?'

'I'll be honest. Nivan told me how you were after him like the way you have been after me.'

'I guessed that.'

'Nivan also confessed to me about Advika.'

'So?'

'It made me realize that deep down I have always desired a man like Nivan. He is the personification of my idea of *the* man. Also, until today, I always thought I deserved a man like this. But do I really deserve someone like Nivan? If not, then why not? I want to know my flaw

227

and rectify it because I'm sick and tired of the hypocrite men I have had in my life. One more and I'll kill him.' Her angst mixed with envy made the Stranger smile.

'Do we deserve someone or not is a question that can't be answered. It's essentially a rhetorical question. But what can be answered is why you had the ones you had.'

'Why did I have Ekansh? Why did I fall for Danny?'

'Just like you were meant to love them genuinely, Ekansh and Danny were not meant to understand that genuineness of yours. Have you ever thought of looking at it this way: both Ekansh and Danny probably weren't meant to be in a committed relationship with you? Maybe it was your misinterpretation of it. Whoever comes in and walks out of our life always has a role to perform. We simply don't see it that way. Ekansh's and Danny's roles were to make you realize that people may claim they love you, but at certain moments of truth, it is proved that their love is superficial. Nivan's role is to make you not give up on love in the first place.'

'Will I be a bad girl if I tell you I want Nivan, knowing well he is committed for life? I know it started with him being a silly crush of mine, but today he has shaken my core. I feel like I have wasted my life seeking the kind of love Nivan has for Advika in Ekansh and Danny.'

The Stranger was quiet as Rivanah tried wiping the tears from under the blindfold with her handcuffed hands.

'Why are you sad, Mini?'

'I'm sad because after all this time that you have been asking me to know my worth—and I have probably known my worth to some extent—it still doesn't make me eligible enough to deserve Nivan.'

'You know, Mini, the toughest kind of acceptance is when we have to accept that there are certain things in life which can't be ours—no matter how hard we try. It's called growing up, Mini. It's difficult—very, very difficult, but inevitable nevertheless. Worse, growing up doesn't only happen as we turn eighteen. Growing up happens as our soul keeps swallowing these depressing acceptances little by little, one at a time. For no acceptance can happen overnight. It's a bit-by-bit process. The way a patient is given saline. If you try to accept the fact that Nivan can't be yours right at this moment, you will destroy yourself further.'

Neither spoke for a long time. Rivanah took her time to get a grip on her emotional self.

She felt a hand cupping her face. She sensed the Stranger was standing right beside her.

'The surgery will soon be over. And any surgery without anaesthesia will cause pain. Just hold on for some more time, Mini. It'll all be worth it. Trust me.' His words made no sense to Rivanah.

'What do you mean?' Rivanah said, looking up. She felt something being thrust in her hand. It was the key to the handcuff. She immediately unlocked herself, removed the blindfold to see an empty drawing room. The curtains had been drawn open and there was light pouring in.

The doorbell rang. Her parents had come back. She quickly stood up and shoved the blindfold and the handcuff into an empty drawer nearby. Her parents had purchased some clothes for her from New Market, but she wasn't interested in trying them out. Making an excuse of missing old times, Rivanah opened all the family photo albums, but found no pictures from her Leh—Ladakh trip. She couldn't ask her parents about it, now that she was slowly beginning to understand there was indeed something they were hiding from her. In the evening, she called Ishita and told her to keep herself free the next day. They would have to visit Hiya's place again.

The next day Rivanah accompanied Ishita and Nivan to Hiya's place in Agarpara. Nivan insisted only Ishita accompany him. Since they didn't know yet how Rivanah and Hiya were connected, it was better—or so Nivan thought—to keep Rivanah away from Hiya's parents.

As the two went inside, Rivanah went to a tea stall nearby and waited for them there. They came out after an hour. Rivanah strode across the road to them the moment they came out of Hiya's house.

'What happened?'

'Hiya Chowdhury had a little brother as well,' Ishita said, gloomily.

'How is he related to me?' Rivanah asked, looking at Ishita and then at Nivan.

'Let's talk in the car,' he said.

Ishita sat quietly sitting with Rivanah in the back seat of the car they had come in, while Nivan sat beside the driver. They all were silent until Rivanah chose to speak.

'What happened? What about the little brother?'

'Hiya's little brother had some kidney problem for which he needed dialysis. Her father had exhausted every bit of his savings on it, and Hiya's getting into Tech Sky was their only hope of continuing with the dialysis,' Nivan said.

'So that's why she hanged herself?' Rivanah asked.

'We don't know that yet. Mr Chowdhury showed us the pieces of white cloth Hiya had received, which means the Stranger was behind her as well. Whether he pushed her to hang herself or she did it on her own discretion is hard to say.'

Rivanah knew that any conclusion about the Stranger would be useless. His last words though—*the surgery is about to get over soon*—sounded dangerously loaded.

'Now only the third link is left—Mr Dutta,' Nivan said.

'Do we approach him today?' Ishita asked.

'Today itself,' Nivan said, and turned to look at Rivanah, 'Did you do it?'

Before going to bed the previous night, Nivan had asked Rivanah to message Mr Dutta from her father's phone and fix an appointment somewhere outside, as if it was her father who wanted to meet him. Rivanah did what was asked of her.

'Mr Dutta will meet my father at 3 p.m. at Mio Amore in Russel Street.'

'Your father?' Ishita was surprised.

'For Mr Dutta, it is my father meeting him,' Rivanah said. Ishita understood.

They reached Mio Amore before time. Nivan and Ishita took a table, and Rivanah sat at another, with her back to the entrance. Her presence would be announced only when the time was right.

Mr Dutta reached the place shortly after three. He took a table and told the waiter that he was waiting for a friend and would place his order once the friend arrived. Nivan, who kept an eye on every single man entering the place, worked on his instinct as he stood up and went to Mr Dutta.

'Mr Dutta, isn't it?'

'Yes?' Mr Dutta looked up at Nivan.

'Hi, I am Nivan.' He shook hands with him. This was a cue for Ishita to join them.

'What is this about?' Mr Dutta asked, feeling slightly uncomfortable.

'This is about a friend of ours,' Nivan said, taking a seat and helping Ishita to settle down beside him.

'Which friend?'

'Rivanah Bannerjee.'

For a moment, Mr Dutta seemed slightly taken aback but he quickly regained composure.

'I still don't understand this.'

'I'm sure you remember me, uncle?' It was Rivanah who stood up from the table nearby and joined the lot.

'We don't mean any harm,' Nivan clarified. 'We just want to know what happened the day Rivanah visited you with her parents.'

'But I'm not supposed to divulge information related to my patients to anyone,' Mr Dutta said, and immediately knew he had given a hint already.

'Patients?' Rivanah frowned.

'Mr Dutta, if Rivanah is your patient, then you don't have the right to hide anything from her, at least. Am I right?' Nivan said.

Mr Dutta understood they wouldn't take anything short of the truth. He drank some water from the glass in front of him, and said, 'Okay, I'll tell you everything. I knew it had to come out one day. But will you be able to handle it?' He was looking at Rivanah.

# 29

'I don't have a choice any more, uncle. Nobody can escape their own story, can they?' Rivanah appeared calm.

Mr Dutta seemed to understand what she meant. All three were waiting for him to speak.

'Rivanah was brought to me by her parents almost a year and a half ago,' Mr Dutta said, 'I could see it in her eyes then that she needed medical treatment. But her parents said they were done with medicine and doctors. Her mother especially was hysterical about losing her daughter. She had heard about me from a distant relative, I think. I calmed her down before focussing on Rivanah. She was acutely restless and seemed like she hadn't slept in a long time. The kind of profession I'm in, I get all kinds of patients, but looking at Rivanah I realized she was more a victim of acute remorse, more than anything else. At first I had to calm her down to know exactly what the problem was. All she kept repeating was "I killed someone".'

Rivanah swallowed. She knew Ishita had glanced at her but she was too shocked to return the glance. Nivan was calmly looking at Mr Dutta as the latter continued.

'I asked her whom have you killed and she took a name—Hiya Chowdhury. Her parents clarified that nothing of that sort had happened. Confused, I took her to my room, my work station, where I induced her into deep sleep through hypnosis.' Mr Dutta looked at Rivanah and said, 'I'm a professional hypnotist.'

There was a silence gravid with inquisitiveness.

'I understand your doubts. Hypnosis may not be talked about much socially, but a lot of people use it in their everyday life. A lot of my patients have used it to forgo labour pain during childbirth. Especially the ones who are adamant to go without a caesarean. Lot of patients also use hypnosis to counter guilt. Though I would agree that there are very few genuine hypnotists left.'

'What happened next, Mr Dutta?' Nivan asked.

'After the induction of deep sleep, Rivanah started talking to me, giving away whatever she had been hiding in her conscious and her subconscious self. I learned that Rivanah and Hiya were fierce competitors in college. In fact, Rivanah told me she'd never accepted it openly, but was actually jealous of Hiya for scoring higher than her in every semester examination. I remember I'd asked you to name one thing which irked you the most about Hiya. And you'd said it was her laughter. You thought it had a mocking tinge to it.'

Rivanah remembered how the Stranger had set Hiya's laughter as the doorbell sound.

'Over time, the jealousy turned into a grudge as if Hiya had deliberately scored higher to put Rivanah down—or so Rivanah came to believe. Belief isn't as simple a thing as we think it is. It can eclipse a lot of things from your sight. Anyway, the year in concern was different, since there were job cuts and economic slowdown all over, and only one IT MNC was scheduled to visit Rivanah's college campus—Tech Sky. The company was supposed to recruit ten students but not from one college. They were supposed to visit ten colleges and pick one student from each. There were protests against the recruitment manager but all of it came to nothing. Rivanah knew that if they could only select one candidate, it would be Hiya since she was the brightest in her batch. And she had to beat her once and for all to show who the best was.

'Two nights before, Rivanah bought some over-the-counter sleeping pills, searched on Google for the amount needed to make someone sleep for long but not kill, and experimented on herself. She had the pills at 8.30 p.m. and then woke up around 1 p.m. the next day, having slept like a log throughout. Her plan was convincing and would not raise any doubt. Do we blame someone if we oversleep suddenly one day? It was too casual a thing to seem suspicious—or so she thought. The night before Tech Sky was supposed to visit the college for recruitment, Rivanah was ready to implement her experiment for real.' Mr Dutta glanced at Rivanah. A teardrop rolled down her cheek. He averted his eyes to Nivan; he knew he wouldn't be able to continue otherwise.

'Rivanah called for a group study session to exchange notes at one of their batchmate's room in the college girl's hostel. There were four girls in total who met that night in the hostel room: Rivanah, Meera, Hiya and Pooja. The last one was Rivanah's best friend in college, or so I was told by her parents later. The four girls discussed possible questions for the impending interview until very late in the night, and next morning went to the college for the exam and interview. Except one—Hiya. She didn't wake up on time and was left behind in the hostel room. And by the time she woke up, Tech Sky had already selected their quota of one candidate from the college: Rivanah Bannerjee.'

Nobody spoke for a minute. Rivanah had her face half covered with a hand as if she might die if she saw anyone looking at her.

'What happened to Hiya?' Ishita asked.

'Hiya had overslept. Unknown to her, Rivanah had mixed sleeping pills in her coffee the night before; the same number of pills—not enough to kill her but make her sleep longer than desired. Rivanah's parents told me later that Hiya hanged herself to death. This was the trigger to Rivanah's emotional breakdown.'

'And what did you do to Rivanah? How come she never remembered all this?' Ishita asked.

'Something which I do only in rare and extreme cases. With deep hypnosis, one can push one's memories from the conscious to the deep subconscious. Some people call it erasing memory as well, but technically it's never totally erased. It is there in the subconscious and can manifest itself in the form of dreams.'

*And nightmares* . . . Rivanah thought but didn't say anything aloud.

'Because it's a part of you. Or sometimes it can also manifest itself in creative endeavours like writing or,' Mr Dutta glanced at Rivanah and continued, 'sketching.'

'You mean the sketches you drew were of . . .' Ishita said and saw Rivanah nodding gently.

'This was why your parents brought you to me the last time. They were petrified when they discovered you had sketched Hiya Chowdhury's face. They feared you would know the truth again and probably go berserk the way you had done for that one month. It was an emotionally taxing time not only for you, but your parents too.'

*One month . . . when she was supposed to be on vacation to Leh and Ladakh with her parents . . .* Rivanah was joining the dots in her mind.

'I had to push whatever you came to know about Hiya into your deep subconscious once again. That's why you forgot everything related to her quite abruptly,' Mr Dutta said. A waiter came and asked if they wanted to order anything. Mr Dutta shook his head and said to

Rivanah, 'But I have a question which I had asked your father too, but he had no answer. How come you knew about Hiya Chowdhury once again? I understand about the sketching, but what propelled you to realize there's a Hiya in the first place? I mean you are my only patient who has backtracked like this on my hypnosis. And, trust me, I have treated a lot of patients in the thirty years of my career.'

Rivanah glanced at Nivan to know if she should tell him about the Stranger.

'It was from a sketch which one of her friends identified as Hiya. It made her curious, one thing led to another and here we are.' Nivan quickly came to the rescue.

'Hmm. That's it?'

'That's it,' Nivan said conclusively.

Mr Dutta had nothing more to say. He took his leave, wishing Rivanah the best and offered his help if she needed it. Rivanah was as if in a trance, but did have a request for Mr Dutta.

'Please don't tell any of this to my parents,' she said.

'I won't, if you promise me you won't let whatever I told you break you.'

Rivanah nodded. How much further could she break? She went out with Nivan and Ishita to where the car was waiting for them.

'I'll have to leave you guys here since my boss needs me in office,' said Ishita

'We can drop you,' Nivan said.

'I think Rivanah needs to be home now,' Ishita said. Nivan agreed. Ishita hugged Rivanah but the latter didn't feel the hug.

'Be strong. What has happened has happened. We all commit mistakes. I'll be in touch.' Ishita went away towards an auto. Both Nivan and Rivanah climbed into their cab. The driver was asked to take them to Rivanah's place.

'No. The hotel,' she said. Nivan gave her a short glance and then nodded at the driver.

It was a quiet drive. Rivanah took Nivan's hand in hers, surprising him. While looking out of the window, away from Nivan, she started sobbing profusely. Nivan immediately asked the driver to park the car in a lonely lane. The driver was asked to wait outside the car. The moment the driver locked the door, Rivanah turned to look at Nivan.

'How can I be such a bitch?' she said. 'Just to show I was the best, I ended up taking someone's life?'

'You didn't intend to take her life. You wanted to secure a job for yourself.' A pause later he added, 'Just like I wanted Advika to conquer her fear and pick me up that night.' Nivan sighed and said, 'I too didn't intend her to become an invalid for the rest of her life.'

With teary eyes she looked up at Nivan and said, 'Even if I hadn't planned to kill Hiya, I had spiked her coffee in a cold-blooded manner. I was the trigger.'

'It's unbelievable how a seemingly small decision of ours can proliferate into our worst nightmare.'

'Did she really kill herself because she couldn't get the job?'

'I've a feeling this is only half the story.'

'Who would tell us the other half?' Rivanah shot an inquiring look at him.

'The one who pushed you to this half,' Nivan said. And she knew whom Nivan was hinting at.

# 30

It was a quiet drive to the hotel. The revelations had left Rivanah speechless. How do you accept such an acidic self of yours that you didn't even know existed so far? There was a cold-blooded killer buried inside her. With this realization she had lost the right to question anyone on anything. Ekansh had only ditched her, Danny had only misunderstood her, but she had pushed someone to commit suicide, however unintentional it may be.

As she walked inside the room with Nivan, he received a phone call. Rivanah heard him talk to Advika and learnt he was flying to Mumbai later that night. Once the call ended Nivan came to Rivanah who had quietly settled on the couch seemingly withdrawn.

'I'll have to fly back in some hours. Advika needs me.'

*Rivanah needs me . . . will someone ever say that?* Rivanah wondered. And answered her own question: why would someone? Now she knew why she could never deserve a man like Nivan. She deserved whatever had happened to her so far and she had no right to find solace in cribbing.

'Rivanah? You all right?' Nivan asked.

'Yeah.' Both she and Nivan knew she was anything but all right.

'If you need more leaves from office, let me know. I'll talk to the management.'

'I think I will be coming to Mumbai shortly as well.'

'To be honest, I think that would help you to move on as quickly as possible.'

*Move on from what? The ugly person that I am? Won't I forever carry the person within me?* She asked, 'What did you do when you learnt Advika paid the price of your stubbornness?'

'Though whatever happened to Advika was unintended, I still believe it happened because of my stubbornness. Advika may have become invalid, but Arun died.'

'Arun?' Somewhere the name rang a bell for Rivanah.

'Arun Rawat. He was the one who crashed his car into Advika's.'

Rivanah now knew where she had heard the name. Arun was the son of Dilip Rawat, the one for whom the Stranger had made her sign the cheque from the last bit of her savings once. *Was everything always connected?*

'I knew it would be difficult not to break bit by bit everyday seeing Advika in her present condition, but I was made to realize that if I broke down completely, so would Advika and whatever was left of us. And "us" was everything I ever had. "Us" was something I could compromise my life for.'

'You were made to realize?'

'By the Stranger. He helped me realize a bad stubborn choice may define us momentarily. Unfortunately, most of us have this bad habit of wasting the whole because of the momentary.'

'But the momentary choice ended up taking a life.'

'In my case too it ended up taking two lives. Arun was dead.'

'And the second life?'

'The life Advika and I would have lived had I not pushed her to drive that night.'

*In that case, I've taken two lives as well, Hiya, and the life she would have lived if I hadn't mixed the pills in the coffee,* Rivanah thought.

Nivan called the reception. He told them he would check out in some time and asked the receptionist to be ready with the necessary bills. Then he called someone and asked them to book a business class ticket for the next flight to Mumbai. As he finished the call, Nivan said, 'We are still assuming Hiya killed herself because of you. Maybe there's something that we don't know yet. I still feel it's half the story. And half stories often lead us to wrong inference.'

'Maybe,' she said.

There was silence. Rivanah knew she had to leave, so Nivan could pack up. But she felt too heavy to move. How could she face her parents now that she knew what they were hiding from her?

There was a momentary eye lock between Nivan and Rivanah. The moment it happened, she didn't know why she blurted out, 'May I please hug you once?'

Nivan looked at her and came forward. She stood up and hugged him with such tightness that it took Nivan by surprise, though he didn't say anything. Rivanah knew it wasn't a friendly hug—it was more, it had passion in it and a claim but she couldn't help it. The hug didn't seem like a first. Rivanah wanted Nivan to understand her unsaid claim, the way an author wants his readers to understand the unwritten. She would have prolonged the hug had Nivan's phone not rung.

'Excuse me,' he said and broke the hug. Before he took the call, she said, 'I'll see you in Mumbai. Thanks for all the support.' She left the hotel room.

Once home, Rivanah tried to be normal the way her parents did even after knowing they had made her forget that one fact which could have altered her life. She would do the same. Not let them realize she knew what they were hiding. Rivanah surprised herself with how normally she was behaving, even though she wasn't looking straight at either of them. With a blank mind, she kept watching television, talked to Ishita for some time keeping her responses simple. Ishita understood she needed some alone time on this. Rivanah booked her ticket to Mumbai and then had her dinner with her parents, pretending all was fine. The pretence scared her and also relaxed her at the same time.

245

Lying on her bed at night, she messaged the Stranger: *You there?*

For a change the Stranger didn't respond immediately.

A message from a new number popped up: *Can we meet for coffee once more?*

She checked the display picture and noticed Tista and Ekansh together.

*I told you I'm in Mumbai*, Rivanah replied.

*I too am in Mumbai. Serving notice period for two months.*

*I'll let you know.*

She saw Ekansh typing but she received no message. She didn't probe either. Waiting for the Stranger's reply, she scrolled down to Nivan's name on her WhatsApp contact list. She tapped on his display picture and kept staring at it for some time, after which she messaged him: *Reached?*

She received a reply soon enough: *Yes, I did. How are you now?*

*I'm okay. I've booked a flight to Mumbai tomorrow.*

*Good. Any intimation from the Stranger yet?*

*Not yet. I messaged but no reply yet.*

*Okay. Keep me updated. See you soon.*

*Sure, see you.*

After thinking for few seconds she typed: *May I tell you something?*

*Sure.* Nivan messaged back.

Rivanah typed: *I love you, Nivan. Not like the way one usually desires someone. My love won't limit you to choose between Advika or me. I'll only be limiting myself to you with my love. It won't attempt to own you either but only request you to make me a part, or perhaps an extension, of whatever you share with Advika. I'll be more than happy to hide myself within the shadow of your and Advika's relationship. I know it's weird but to be loved the way Advika is loved by you is perhaps my only redemption. It may sound selfish but—*

Rivanah paused for a moment and then deleted the entire message. She rewrote instead:

*Nothing important really. Goodnight, Nivan.*

247

# 31

Heading for the airport the next morning, Mrs Bannerjee was narrating to Rivanah what happened between her and Rivanah's maternal aunt.

'She was as usual being poky. All through the phone call, she was hinting that we have decided to make you sit at home all your life. She has shifted to the US but her mentality will never shift.'

Rivanah was facing the other way, not really paying attention to what her mother was telling her.

'I also told her my daughter is the best.'

Rivanah suddenly gave her a sharp look as she heard her mother say, 'And for the best, we have selected the best.' She looked at Rivanah and continued, 'I didn't take Nivan's name, but your father and I have decided that we will talk to him once you go to Mumbai. He is the best match for you.'

The last statement broke all her defences, and Rivanah started sobbing uncontrollably, holding her mother tight. Her father, who was driving the car, kept looking at his wife via the rear-view mirror, confused.

'What happened, Mini? Tell me.' Her worried mother egged her on, but Rivanah wasn't ready to speak. Her embrace only tightened. *I'm a bitch, Mumma. And I only deserve shit.* It was only when her father said if she didn't talk, he would drive her back to their house and cancel her Mumbai flight, that Rivanah said aloud, 'Nivan is committed.' It wasn't why she was crying, but then she wasn't sure why exactly she was crying. Mrs Bannerjee too had tears in her eyes as she glanced at her husband, understanding that their daughter perhaps had feelings for Nivan.

'It's okay, Mini. I'm sure there are other guys like Nivan.'

*No, Baba. There is nobody like him. Nivan is rare. And to get to him, one had to be rarer. Like Advika. Not like me.*

'I think you shouldn't go to Mumbai today,' Mr Bannerjee said.

'No, Baba. I'll have to. I don't have any more leaves. I want to work to take my mind off other things.'

Mr Bannerjee agreed that work would be the right anodyne for his daughter and didn't speak any further.

Ishita was waiting for her at the departure gate as the Bannerjee family climbed down from the car. She came and hugged her friend tight.

'Everything will be all right,' Ishita whispered in her ears.

'Yeah.' Rivanah spoke softly.

'Go for Nivan. He is a good guy. I'm sure he will keep you happy,' Ishita whispered next. Though Rivanah had said nothing about her feelings for Nivan to her, Ishita had

Novoneel Chakraborty

still understood it. Was Rivanah so obvious? Had Nivan too understood it as clearly and as correctly like Ishita did?

'He is committed,' she told Ishita. The latter broke the hug and looked deep into Rivanah's eyes. The kind of pain Ishita saw in them churned her guts. She hadn't seen it even when Ekansh had ditched her or when she had told her that Danny and she had broken up. It was the kind of pain which comes when someone's innocence is lost once and for all.

'You will be late, Mini,' Mr Bannerjee said.

'Be in touch,' Ishita said. Rivanah proceeded to the gate. She knew her parents were waiting for her to turn around and wave at them, but she didn't. She just couldn't.

The flight landed on time. She reached the Residency Enclave soon after. She glanced once at Nivan's door, as she was about to unlock her flat. But her door opened suddenly, and Rivanah saw Nivan's servant and Advika on her wheelchair inside her flat. Advika was smiling at her.

'Nivan told me you were coming, so we thought of dusting the flat a bit,' Advika said, her speech slurry.

*How can she be so damn good to others?* Rivanah thought, and said, 'That's really kind of you Advika.'

'You must be tired. I'll leave you now. We can catch up later.'

'Sure.'

'Is Nivan back?' Advika asked the servant. She nodded.

'Where is he?' Rivanah asked.

'He must be downstairs taking his karate class,' Advika said and took her leave. Rivanah watched them step out of her flat and then get into the adjacent flat, closing the door behind them. Rivanah immediately locked her flat and went downstairs. She didn't have to look for long before she found Nivan with a group of young girls in white martial-arts attire in a circle on the society ground. They were watching something. As Rivanah approached Nivan, he looked up and asked her to be quiet, gesturing her to look ahead. She did. A girl seemingly of her age was fighting a strong-looking guy. He was about to punch her but the girl flipped in a flash and kicked him on the face. The man lost his footing and fell down. Everyone clapped and cheered. Nivan had a smile on his face.

'What's this?' Rivanah asked.

'I'm a black belt in karate,' Nivan said. 'And I teach these girls the art of self-defence. He called it "share your good luck".'

The words took Rivanah back to her past when she taught ten slum kids—Mini's Magic 10.

'Hey Rivanah!' It was Smita from work.

'What are you doing here?' Rivanah asked.

'Joined here a few weeks ago.'

Rivanah remembered a pamphlet on her desk regarding some karate class. She did think about giving it a shot, but never knew it was managed by Nivan.

'All good at home?' Smita asked.

Rivanah nodded, shooting a furtive glance at Nivan.

'Great. See you in office,' Smita said and left.

'Can I be a part of it as well?' Rivanah asked.

'Sure. You don't even have to ask. From tomorrow morning?'

'From tomorrow morning,' she confirmed.

Together they went back into the building. At work, the first thing she did was to approach Argho.

'I wanted to apologize for whatever happened to you that day in the police station,' she said. Argho wasn't expecting her to apologize once again.

'It's okay. You'd already apologized the other day.'

'I know,' she said. *I wish I could tell you this apology is actually for something else. I can't face Hiya's parents, and you are her next family link I know of.*

'Did you find out who was playing games with you?'

'Not yet.'

'Let me know if you do.'

'Sure.'

The moment she was in her cubicle, she messaged the Stranger: *I need to talk. Where are you???*

The Stranger was yet to respond to her last message. She tried calling the numbers she had with her. All the ten numbers that she had of the Stranger produced the same result: *The number you are trying to reach has been withdrawn.*

Clouded by suspicion, Rivanah rushed to Nivan's cabin. Looking at her, he knew it was something urgent.

'What happened?'

'I think the Stranger won't contact me again. And I can't let that happen. I can't afford to lose him. Not now. Not ever.'

'How do you know he won't contact you?'

'None of his numbers are active any more. And he hasn't responded to my message in over twenty-four hours. This has never happened before.'

Reclining on his seat, Nivan looked thoughtful.

'You must have the Stranger's number?' Rivanah asked.

'I do. First come in and close the door,' he said.

Rivanah did as asked and said, 'Could you please dial him?'

Nivan picked up his phone from the table and opened Contacts. He scrolled down and reached the name which read Stranger. Placing his phone on the table again, he dialled the number. The screen flashed 'Calling Stranger'. He tapped on the speaker mode. Both Nivan and Rivanah could hear the rings. On the fifth ring, the phone was picked up.

'Hello,' the person at the other end of the line said.

*It can't be*, Rivanah thought. The voice belonged to someone dear to her once, someone acutely close to her, someone she loved, someone who had left her broken recently. Someone who also went by the name Danny.

## 32

Nivan tapped the mute button and asked, 'What happened?' He felt Rivanah had perhaps identified the voice. She didn't react though.

'Do you know the person?' he egged on.

Rivanah nodded. She was too shocked to talk. *Is Danny the Stranger? Both Nivan's and mine?*

'Hello?'

Danny was still on line. Nivan, who was still looking at Rivanah, tapped on the red button and the call ended.

'Is this the same voice who talks to you?' Nivan asked.

'No. But then it never was one voice throughout.'

'Same here. Sometimes it's a woman, sometimes an old man and sometimes a teenager. This time it's a man.'

*A man who feigned Danny's voice? Or was it Danny himself?* Rivanah said, 'Precisely. I'll wait till the Stranger contacts me.' She didn't feel comfortable mentioning Danny to Nivan—especially their shared past. The moment she left Nivan's cabin, she once again dialled all the numbers belonging to the Stranger. They were still not available. Frustrated, she checked her Contacts and realized she'd deleted Danny's number long back. She checked her Truecaller history and finally got Danny's number. She saved it under his name. On a hunch, she went back to Nivan's cabin.

'Could I please get the number you called for the Stranger? Just in case . . .'

'Sure.' Nivan called out the number. As she punched it in her dial pad, she thanked Nivan and stepped out to dial the number. Her phone's screen soon flashed 'Calling Danny'. The number which Nivan stored as 'Stranger' in his phone was in fact Danny's number. Going by the record, it could be a duplicate sim and a mimicked voice, but Rivanah knew she wouldn't be able to focus on anything till she was sure. The phone kept ringing and was finally picked up. *Is it because he still has my number and is in two minds seeing my name?* Rivanah wondered, and heard him say, 'Hi.'

'Hi ba—' Rivanah was about to say 'baby' but paused at the right moment. It was funny how relationships programmed a mind.

'What happened suddenly?' Danny said.

*I'll have to meet him*, she thought, but said, 'Congrats on the film thing.' She was already framing her next sentence in her mind as she heard him say, 'Thank you. I thought you would never call.'

'I thought you wouldn't pick up.'

'I thought you wouldn't think about me.'

'I thought you wouldn't talk to me.'

255

There was silence. Did Danny react the way he did because he wanted to leave her alone, because he indeed was the Stranger? Was his entire plan of coming into her life as a sexy neighbour an attempt to be close to her to know her every move? Why would he do that? And why would he behave the same with Nivan? *Things might clear up*, she thought, *if we met once.* Rivanah was praying Danny himself would mention the meeting part, as it was becoming tougher for her to say it aloud. Deep down, she knew even this time she didn't want to meet him because she was missing him, but she wanted to know if his phone really had received a call from Nivan.

'Listen, I'm shooting for a magazine. I'll have to go.'

'Can we meet for some time today?' Rivanah finally blurted out.

'Okay. I'll be with a friend in Boveda later in the evening.'

It was clear he didn't want to rekindle anything between them, or else he wouldn't be rude enough to meet her while he was meeting a friend.

'Sure.' Rivanah thought she too would make it clear she wasn't looking to go back into the past.

'Around eight,' Danny said.

Rivanah was late by half an hour due to heavy traffic. Before she could guide the cab driver to the place, she received an unexpected call.

'Is that Rivanah Bannerjee?'

'Speaking, who is it?'

'This is Inspector Kamble.'

It took few seconds for Rivanah to recollect who Inspector Kamble was.

'How are you, sir?'

'I'm good. How are you doing? Glad you remember.'

'I'm good too.'

'Listen, would it possible for you to come down to the Goregaon police station anytime soon.'

'Now?'

'Not now. But maybe tomorrow.'

'Sure, I will. But what happened?'

'There's something I want to talk to you about. Will tell you when we meet.'

'All right, sir.'

Rivanah remembered how worried Inspector Kamble used to be for his daughter, though the last time she met him, he had told her she had got a job in Mumbai itself. Rivanah guided the cab driver and reached Boveda soon. She entered to realize a karaoke night was in full swing. A guy and a girl were singing an Enrique song. It wasn't long before Rivanah's eyes located Danny. He was looking happier than ever before, talking to a girl. Danny's eyes spotted Rivanah as he stood up. She understood he didn't want her to come up to him. The girl with whom Danny was sitting had her back to Rivanah. She turned to flash a smile at her. It was Nitya. The sight of her was like a bullet through her heart. Did Danny intentionally call her there because he was meeting Nitya? Or did he meet Nitya because Rivanah wanted to meet him? Were Danny and Nitya in a relationship?

'Let's go outside. I need to smoke,' Danny said as he walked past Rivanah. He didn't even appreciate the fact that they were meeting after a long time. She was ready for a hug even if it was going to be awkward. She turned to follow Danny outside. He lit a cigarette.

'When did this happen?' Rivanah said. Seeing her glance at Nitya, Danny knew what she was talking about.

'Never you mind,' he said, looking around constantly, as if he thought someone was filming him.

For Rivanah, those three words were loaded enough to answer her query regarding Nitya's presence. They were seeing each other. A casual glance at Nitya told her she was smirking at her. I-finally-won-bitch kind of smirk. A slight anger nudged her, but Rivanah knew she didn't have the right to express it.

'What's up?' Danny said.

*If he wants to keep it to the point, I shall keep it to the point*, Rivanah decided and said, 'I want to see your phone's call list once.'

'What?'

'You heard me.'

'What for? And what makes you think you still have the right to check my phone?'

'I know I don't. That's why I am asking you. It's related to the Stranger,' she said and noticed Danny pause in between a puff, and then release the smoke at one go.

'I'm sorry, but I don't want to show you my phone.'

'Why not?'

Danny's hesitation persuaded Rivanah to believe her suspicions: Danny perhaps was the Stranger.

'A phone is a personal belonging.'

'I am not interested in your chats or pictures. All I want you to do is open your call history and show it to me. You don't have to give the phone to me.'

'Call history?'

'What's happening, baby?' It was Nitya.

'Nothing. She wants to see my call history.'

'You sure you haven't lost it, Rivanah?' Nitya said. It was quite insulting, but Rivanah didn't react.

'One glimpse, Danny, and I shall be forever gone.'

Danny and Nitya exchanged a glance. Nitya took Danny's phone and unlocked it. The fact that Rivanah never knew Danny's password made her feel inferior. But it was momentary. Nitya held the phone flashing the call history in front of Rivanah. The latter read on quickly. Nitya, Nitya, Nitya . . . some other names . . . couple of random numbers . . . not Nivan's.

'How much longer?' Nitya asked.

'Did you delete any number, Danny?' Rivanah asked.

'I really think you should visit a shrink, girl,' Nitya said.

'Excuse me, but I'm not talking to you,' Rivanah said, looking from Nitya to Danny.

'I too think you need to visit a shrink,' Danny said. Nitya almost pulled him inside. Did he delete the number or did he really not have any idea why she wanted to check his phone? A frustrated Rivanah left Boveda.

Half an hour later, she was in her flat in the Residency Enclave. Sitting on her bed, she had no clue what she should do next. Was it really supposed to end this way? The Stranger withdrawing without any notice after revealing what a bitch she had been to Hiya? The Stranger was still in touch with Nivan, then why not her? Why did the Stranger choose to talk in Danny's voice? Was Danny even speaking the truth? If he had deleted the number, she would never know. And she couldn't approach him again. Especially after the way both he and Nitya had treated her some time back. Rivanah lifted her head up and her eyes fell on the sketch stand. Hiya's face was half covered with something. She frowned. It was an A4 sheet. In fact, there were two sheets stapled together and taped to one edge of the sketch. Rivanah took it out. It read like a chat transcript between two people: the Stranger and Hiya. Before she could begin reading, something occurred to her and she rushed to the main gate. In two minutes, she reached the security guard's room. She checked the visitors' book but there was no entry mentioning a visitor to her flat. She asked the guard to show her the CCTV footage of her floor. Every corner of the Residency Enclave was under CCTV surveillance 24/7. As the guard played the footage for the day, Rivanah sat still beside him, staring unblinkingly at the screen. She could see the newspaper man, the sweepers and some residents coming into view and moving out. She saw Nivan leaving for work. She saw herself as well. She slowly started forwarding the footage until she stopped at a particular segment. Time 14.06. Someone had entered her flat through the front door and a minute later had stepped out. The person was wearing a cap, shades, jeans and a tight-fitting tee. Rivanah had made love to this man several times. How could she mistake him for anyone else? She paused the frame just before the person was about to enter the elevator.

'Do you know the person, madam?' the security guard asked, as Rivanah stared at the frozen image of Danny speechlessly.

## 33

I t was late. Rivanah walked to Nivan's door but wasn't sure if she should ring the doorbell this late in the night. She decided against it and settled on her couch, clutching the chat transcript in her hand. Finally, she knew who the Stranger was. She read through the transcript in her hand.

*Hiya: I know you did something so I couldn't go to the college on time. Tell me, what did you do?*

*Stranger: I didn't do anything.*

*Hiya: Wrong. You did. I don't know why you are after my life.*

*Stranger: I only want you to know your worth, Hiya.*

*Hiya: Cut the bullshit. You want to kill me. You knew how badly I wanted this job. My family is looking up to me to secure the job and then sponsor my little brother's dialysis. You knew it, damn it, and still you didn't let me have it.*

*Stranger: As I said, I wasn't the one who stalled you from going to college today.*

*Hiya: What's the use of lying to me now? Whoever you are, just know that you've left me with no option other than the one I'm opting for now.*

*Stranger: Hold on, Hiya. Don't be presumptuous.*

*Hiya: I did whatever you asked me to. I thought you were a friend.*

*Stranger: Hiya, you won't do anything which upsets me.*

*Hiya: Go to hell.*

*Stranger: Let me come to you.*

*Hiya: I don't care any more.*

*Stranger: Hiya.*

*Stranger: Hiya?*

Rivanah knew why Hiya didn't respond—the date and time of the message was printed in a corner. It was the same night that Hiya was found hanging in her room. Hiya died without knowing it was Rivanah who had mixed the sleeping pills in her coffee which made her wake up late. *Too late. Why does the Stranger—or Danny— want me to read this?* Rivanah tried to guess the answer. Was it because he didn't want her to feel guilty about the fact that she thought she led Hiya to kill herself? Had Hiya known it was Rivanah who mixed those sleeping pills, she would have been upset but probably not killed herself? She probably wrongly assumed the Stranger would lead her to her doom, and thus, burdened with the brother's medical condition, hanged herself? It could be true as much as it could be false. Whatever she guessed would only be an inference of the truth but not the truth itself. And the one who could tell her the truth was the Stranger—Danny—whom she couldn't contact. He had—cleverly—made sure of that by bringing Nitya into the picture earlier in the evening. But she could make sure he came to her. If he was the Stranger then Danny would definitely come to her. She eyed the last words of the Stranger to Hiya in the transcript: *Let me come to you.* And that sort of desperation happened because the Stranger was convinced Hiya would kill herself. Rivanah knew what she had to do to summon Danny to her on his own will. She had tried to do it once before too. But that was pretence. This time it won't be pretence.

The next day Rivanah was quiet in the office. Nivan asked her if she managed to get through to the Stranger, but she was cold about it. She did dial the stored phone numbers again but they were still suspended. After lunch, she got a phone call from Kamble saying he was busy that day and asked if she could meet up the next day. Rivanah confirmed she would.

In the evening, while going back to her flat, time and again she kept stretching her hand out of the cab and clicking random photographs of the traffic behind her using her phone—a total of five clicks. And as she kept checking the photographs, she broke into a smile. One biker was common in all the photographs. She was right. She was still being followed. It wasn't over yet. Rivanah intentionally got down in front of the Residency Enclave and walked inside. She sipped her tea by the huge French windows in the drawing room overlooking the sea in the distance. Then she asked one of the security guards to come up with the terrace keys. The moment the guard came, she told him she had to check her dish antenna and so wanted the door to the terrace to be unlocked. The guard unlocked the terrace for her and waited. She asked him to leave and said that she would call him when she is done. The Stranger wouldn't appear if the guard was there with her. As the guard left reluctantly, Rivanah went to the edge of the terrace. A fierce sea breeze hit her hard. She felt at peace. She was almost lost at the sight of the sea ahead when she heard the sound of the elevator coming from the main control room atop the terrace. Her hunch told her the elevator would stop at the sixteenth floor—it did. The same hunch told her the one inside would take the steps to the terrace and would stop by the main door. Rivanah didn't turn around but could feel a presence. Something hit her. She bent down and picked it up. There was a pebble in the piece of paper crumpled into a ball. She dropped the pebble and read the words on the paper:

*You don't have to do it, Mini.*

Finally, for once, she was ahead of the Stranger. Of Danny. She turned around but saw only darkness by the terrace door.

'Why don't you show yourself, Danny? I know it's you,' she said aloud.

Seconds later, another paper ball with a pebble in it reached her.

*Everything has consequences, Mini. Revealing who I am will have its own share of consequences.*

265

'Why are you still so cryptic? I thank you for making me realize what my blunder was. How I lead Hiya to kill herself, but I also want to thank you for helping me learn to live with my blunders.'

*Hiya didn't get the job because of you. But she died because of me.*

Rivanah had understood it while reading the chat transcript.

'But what is it all about? Who are you really? What did you gain by being Hiya's Stranger, then mine and Nivan's too? Why did you keep reminding Hiya and me to know our worth?'

*Can't we end this without questions?*

'No, we can't. This isn't the time to play games, Danny. I know you still love me. Whatever you did in the ATM at Kalyan or at Boveda was all an act. Wasn't it?'

A paper ball reached her after a while.

*Yes, I love you, Mini.*

Rivanah could have cried reading it. Finally, there was some hope in her life. The line reminded her of what Nivan had told her once about standing by your choices. Another paper ball hit her.

*I shall ask you one more time. Think and answer, because this choice of yours and mine will affect lives. It will be a lot of responsibility for you if I show myself. Are you sure you can handle it?*

'I'm dead sure I can handle whatever it is. Especially after whatever you have been helping me learn.'

*I'm happy, Mini, that it was all worth it.*

'I want to hug you, Danny. Right now.'

*Not now. We are being watched. We meet tomorrow, 8 a.m. sharp, at the edge of Nariman Point.*

Rivanah heard the terrace door close. Danny was gone. What made him say they were being watched? Why was he so secretive even when she knew his identity? Most importantly, why did Danny have to play the role of Stranger in her life?

One more night—she checked the time on her phone—ten hours to be precise. And things shall become clear once and for all. Sleep was a distant cry for her. She was awake till six in the morning. Then she took a bath, got ready and took a cab to Nariman Point—the tip of Marine Drive in South Mumbai. She reached at the spot ten minutes before time. There were a few people sitting at some distance on the cemented barricade of Marine Drive and some others walking and jogging on the sidetrack. She was the only one standing at the edge. The morning breeze strengthened the hope she felt when she had read that Danny still loved her. Rivanah felt a tap on her shoulder. She turned around in a flash.

'Hello, Mini, I'm your Stranger.'

# 34

Rivanah's jaw slowly fell open.

'What the—' she just began but was stopped by a finger on her lips.

'You don't get to talk today. Only I do,' the person said. Rivanah kept staring at him as if she was looking at him for the first time.

'This is more complex, sinister and pertinent than you can even imagine, Mini. And it has rules. None of this is random. None of this can be proved.'

The Stranger was finally right in front of her—in flesh and blood. It was a face all too familiar for her. But how could it be . . .

'Firstly, I would like to apologize to you for those life-threatening attacks. My intention was never to kill you but I had to push you towards finding your link to Hiya because time was running out.'

'Time was running out? What do you mean?' Rivanah asked.

'We are a highly classified network of emotional-surgeons spread across the nation, working underground for a social revolution. Nobody knows how big or small the group is or who all are part of it. Believe me, even if your closest friend or family member has a Stranger in his or her life, he or she won't ever share it with you. We manipulate people in such a way that nobody has the option to talk about us. Like you too couldn't talk about me to many. Even if you did, there was no substantial evidence. We are the best-kept secret for the public at large. Our own statistic is that every seven-hundredth youngster in India has a Stranger in his or her life, as we speak. We are committed to raising the number.'

'What do you mean by "emotional-surgeon"?' Rivanah mumbled. She was still trying to absorb it all. He looked at the sea in front and said, 'One of the weakest things about humans is we can be easily influenced. We are inherently gullible though we are one of the most intelligent creatures. This weakness is our group's strength. We initiate a change in people by influencing them. We don't perform physical surgeries on our targets but we work on their emotions. We push them to the edge. And we work within a time frame. We famish them emotionally as much as we nourish them. We alter their way of thinking, of perceiving things, their beliefs, their conclusions—in short, we alter them as an individual. You know, Mini, our everyday fight is between what we are holding on to and what we are letting go of. What we let go of changes us, what we hold on to alters us. Changes are irreversible. Alternations aren't.'

*Like you initiated an alteration in me the first time I landed in Mumbai*, Rivanah thought.

'Our social revolution is all about crushing that individual self in us, which is a product of a myopic and materialistic society, and knowing our real worth. If one observes people, one will know that people can be categorized, because there's a pattern—nobody is exclusive. Why do you think these social-networking platforms are a hit? Because deep down, we all are lonely, bitter and depressed. The extent varies, the extent of acceptance varies but we are these things. We all feel an urgent need to connect, to communicate without filters all the time, and yet we tell ourselves it isn't possible. That's where we emotional-surgeons come in. We pick our targets, we clean their bitterness by making them accept their deep-rooted mistakes, blunders which otherwise they would never embrace and always try to run away from. We sweep away their loneliness by explaining to them why one must love one's own self in the garb of the "share your good luck" endeavour.'

*Like you made me learn to cook when I was depressed, you made me teach those slum kids and find happiness in simple things, you made me offer money to Mr Rawat, which told me I wasn't a bad person, after all.*

'Everything needs time. Even sunlight needs time to explain to the seed why it is falling on it. The kind of social design we have knitted over years trains us subliminally

to see things not as they are, but as we are told they are—
no questions, no objectivity. We emotional-surgeons
push people to question, to doubt their subjectivity,
because otherwise, it makes our emotional selves blind
with time. I too was made a part of it after being pursued
by a year and a half by a Stranger who wanted me to know
my worth. Not everyone we pursue is made a part of
our group. But the ones who are—like I was—are given
a target. Hiya Chowdhury was my first target. I had to
perform an emotional surgery on her so that she could
take on life better and realize her potential to the fullest.
Our meticulous and collective planning is our strength.
And my surgery on Hiya would have been successful
had you not interfered, Mini. You drugged Hiya and
she thought it was my doing. Before I could reach her,
she had hanged herself assuming that I was some lunatic
stalker harassing her.'

Nivan had both his hands in his trousers' pockets as
he talked.

'But what about Danny's number in your phone
labelled as Stranger?'

'He wasn't my Stranger. I was his. I'd recently started
pursuing him, after the way he behaved with you inside
the ATM in Kalyan. How do you think he cracked a film
deal this quickly?'

'We all have secrets to hide, Mini, truths to confess.
Danny coming to drop the chat transcript at your place
yesterday was my manipulation, just the way I made you

271

resign from your job, compelled you to go to Prateek's place and the like.'

*Everything added up now. Danny looked anxious when he came out to smoke with me in Boveda, looking around all the time,* Rivanah thought and asked, 'But why didn't you come clean in front of Hiya like you are coming clean right now? Or did you come out clean in front of every target of yours?'

He gave her a tight smile and said, 'No, we don't come out clean in front of anybody.' A few silent seconds later, he added, 'Remember, how I had made you breathless on your terrace in Kolkata?'

*The holding of hands . . . the pressing of the mouth . . . the clipping of the nose . . .* Rivanah nodded.

'That's what you made me feel as well. Acutely desperate. Love's power of influencing us is always more than our scope of understanding it. In the quest to alter you, I fell for you, Mini, though I always believed I would never fall for anyone except Advika.'

Rivanah's lips parted but no words came out.

'Initially, I was angry with you for snatching an opportunity from me to influence Hiya. That's why I had attacked you in your flat too, but I let you go . . .'

Rivanah remembered the night clearly when she was alone in her flat, waiting for Danny, but she was attacked instead, stripped to the bare minimum.

'Why did you let me go that night, Nivan?' she asked.

'Not every pain you want to let go of, Mini. Some you want to keep by your side and watch it grow, because you know you too shall grow with the pain. You are one such pain for me, Mini,' Nivan said.

Rivanah didn't how to react. The initial shock of seeing Nivan as the Stranger had somewhat died down, but she wasn't ready for the fact that Nivan could actually love her. It was always supposed to be a fantasy. Or was this a fantasy?

'I could have told you on the first day itself that you were made to forget about Hiya through hypnosis, but I had to make sure that first you had the necessary strength to take such a thing. One can take as much shit as possible, but when it comes to one's own shit, the mind works in a different way, activating the weirdest of defence mechanisms.'

There was silence.

'Will you . . .' Rivanah stopped, feeling choked, and started again, 'Will you believe it if I say I love you, Nivan?'

'I know it, Mini.'

'What about Advika?' she asked.

The way Nivan looked at her first and then away, she knew their dilemma was the same.

'What happens next?' she asked.

'Next is this.' Nivan took out a piece of paper from his trousers' pocket and gave it to Rivanah. She was about to open its fold when Nivan stopped her.

'Not now. Before you read it, you have to listen to me carefully. I have played a big gamble on you. Don't you dare disappoint me on this, Mini.'

'What is it, Nivan?' she asked. She had a bad feeling about it.

'I told you there are rules in the world I'm a part of and one has to stick to those rules, come what may. And the foremost rule is a Stranger can't appear in front of his or her target. Come. What. May. I have already broken that rule for you, Mini. Thus there will be a price for me to pay.'

'What's the price?' The bad feeling in her guts became worse.

'It's in the note,' Nivan said, and in a flash took the note from her hand. He held it against the wind. He took out a lighter and set aflame one of the corners of the note as Rivanah watched in shock.

'Finish reading it before it all turns into ash. Don't follow me. Or call out to me. Whatever happens in the next minute happens because of me and not because of you. Remember that always and never be guilty about it. It was important for me to come clean in front of you,' Nivan said and planted a kiss on her lips, taking her by surprise. He turned and walked off. With a frown, Rivanah started reading the note which was slowly turning into ash. It read:

*By the time you read the last word of this note, you'll know what I meant when I said last night that our meeting will have consequences. Ours is a doomed love story, Mini. And the doom is planned. I know of it. So does Advika. But she won't be able to deal with it alone. So she will be your responsibility from now on.*

*The rules of our underground group of Strangers are simple: if you know who we are, then you are one amongst us. Once you are in, you can't get out. If you don't comply, you are dead. You breach, you are dead. And our biggest strength is our secrecy because of which we convince people we don't exist. Like this paper shall turn to ash, swallowing all the words in it.*

*Don't let what you see when you are done reading this note break you in any way. In fact, don't react since we both are being watched right now. Any unfavourable reaction from your end, and they won't think twice before eliminating you. Someone will contact you in the next five days to tell you what's next for you. Accept it. Take care, Mini. Goodbye. We shall be together in some other life, maybe. This one was too complicated.*

Rivanah let go of the paper as the fire licked the last bit up. As some of the ash slipped out of her hand, Rivanah heard a commotion at a distance. A car had run over someone. People had gathered. Rivanah wanted to throw up. She knelt by the edge of Nariman Point, trying to shut the noise around her. She could hear people screaming for someone to call the police. Her phone rang next. It was Inspector Kamble. She didn't take the call. He called again. She picked up.

'Rivanah, are you coming to meet me today?'

'I'm sorry, sir.' She was finding it difficult to talk. 'I'm out of the city right now.'

'Oh, not a problem. Let me get this done on the phone itself. I wanted to tell you there's one more person who lodged an FIR a few days back, claiming someone was stalking him. A little investigation told me that this guy too received messages on white cloth like you once did. Are you still getting them?'

'No, sir. They stopped coming long back.'

'Hmm. Okay, that's all. Thanks. You carry on.'

Glancing at the last piece of ash of Nivan's note being swept off into the sea by the wind, his words came back to her: *Advika is your responsibility from now.* The dreadful feeling was actually an intuition. If she knew this was going to be the end, then she wouldn't have ever asked the Stranger to reveal himself. Rivanah wanted to see Nivan for one last time, but she knew she couldn't. *We are being watched,* he had written. She stood up, hailed a cab and headed to the Residency Enclave, breaking down inside the car.

It took an hour and a half for her to reach her destination. She took the elevator and reached the sixteenth floor in no time. Standing in front of 1603, she was trying hard to not think of how she would react or in what state she would find Advika in. The servant opened the door and gestured towards the bedroom immediately. Xeno was sitting in a corner.

Rivanah went towards the bedroom. As she stood by the door, she could see Advika sitting by her window, looking out at the sea. Rivanah approached her with heavy steps. Once there, she placed a trembling hand on Advika's shoulder. The latter turned. Her eyes were swollen. Rivanah understood that Nivan must have told her about it beforehand. Advika threw a hand around Rivanah's waist and hugged her tightly. As she felt her body shudder against hers, Rivanah put her arms around Advika holding back her own tears. From someone who was always in need of a shoulder to cry on, the Stranger had turned Rivanah into someone who could lend a shoulder to someone in need. And for that, she would be forever indebted to Nivan . . . to her Stranger, whom she would never forget.

# Epilogue

## 11 MONTHS LATER

*Indigo flight 6E-332, Mumbai to Kolkata, 12.30 a.m.*

Manish Agarwal switched on his mobile phone even before the flight had landed. He knew it was against the rules, but he didn't care. One after another, messages started pouring in on different social platforms. One of his close friends had sent him a dirty MMS on WhatsApp. It was of a girl giving a guy a blowjob. The next message read: *Rohit: 13. Manish: 11*, followed by a devil's emoticon.

*Pretty soon, I'll up my score, asshole!* Manish replied.

He looked up to see the air hostess he had been fantasizing about all through the flight. Her name tag read: Anita. Manish gave her a big toothy grin. She smiled back at him awkwardly.

After the exit doors opened, passengers started moving out of the aircraft with their luggage. As Manish reached the exit, he looked at the same air hostess who was now standing beside the door.

'Have a pleasant night, sir,' Anita said in the typical I-am-programmed-to-say-this manner.

Manish stopped and looking at her said, 'What are you doing later tonight?'

'Excuse me, sir?' Anita wasn't expecting it.

'Okay, let me be straight. Are you free to hook up tonight?'

'What do you think of yourself?' Her raised voice made others shoot a suspicious glance at Manish. It made him uncomfortable and also pinched his ego.

'I'll have to file a complaint against you if you repeat it,' Anita shot back.

Manish gave her an angry look and stepped out of the airplane. He was walking furiously on the aerobridge as he called his father.

'Manu beta, has your flight landed? I have already sent the new Jaguar to fetch you,' Mr Agarwal said. He was the largest sponsor for the ruling party in the state.

'I need to get an air hostess fired. Right. Now.' Manish was fuming.

'Oh. What happened?'

'I will tell you later. She needs to be fired first.'

'I'll see to it. You come home first.'

Manish cut the call and promised himself he would make Anita his bitch in no time.

After collecting his luggage, he pushed the trolley to the men's washroom to take a dump. Stepping in, he tried to locate the light buttons since the toilet was concealed in utter darkness. Before he could find it, someone held him by his collar and pulled him right inside one of the toilets. The door was pushed closed while his hand was held behind and twisted hard. Manish opened his mouth to scream but a sock was stuffed inside his mouth. There was a strong smell of some deodorant. Manish didn't know it was It's Different, Hugo Boss. Manish tried hard, but couldn't free himself from the tight grasp. It all happened in a way he had only seen in Bruce Lee films. It was evident that the attacker, whoever it was, knew martial arts. He felt something on his groin.

'That's a nutcracker right between your legs,' a girl spoke in his ears. 'Tell me, are you going to listen carefully to what I'm going to say or . . .' Manish nodded out of fear.

'Good. You will take the next flight back to Mumbai right now. The ticket is inside a packet by the washbasin outside. And when the flight takes off, you will hold your ears and do ten squats before Anita, the air hostess, and apologize to her.'

Manish started fidgeting only to feel his arm being twisted even more. He stopped for his own good. He heard the girl's voice again.

'Or else, I will crush your nuts first and then every bone of your body.'

The sound of it made Manish freak out. He shrank like a timid dog.

'Did you get what I just said?'

Manish nodded.

'Will you be a good boy, Manu?'

Manish nodded again, sweating profusely by now.

She removed the sock from his mouth.

'Who the fuck are you?' he said, gasping for breath.

'Anonymity is power, Manu.'

'Huh? What do you mean?'

'You can call me . . . Stranger,' said Rivanah.

# Acknowledgements

I have always dreaded the moment when, after working on the Stranger trilogy for three years, the time would come for me to move on to a different story. The Stranger trilogy has been an educational journey for me. It was a deeply emotional experience as well. And as is true for every journey, there are always souls to thank when it comes to an end.

First and foremost comes my publisher, Milee Ashwarya; my editor, Gurveen Chadha; Shruti Katoch from Marketing; Rahul Dixit from Sales; and to each and every one in Penguin Random House who has shown faith in my work and supported me in presenting the trilogy to my readers. Heartfelt thanks, a loud cheer to you all!

Authors are mostly selfish about their work. And to balance it out, one needs a selfless family. My sincere respects and gratitude to my family for being there whenever I need them.

Since I'm a borderline social recluse, I would also like to thank the few friends I have, for being there, for inspiring me, for teaching me, rectifying me in innumerable ways, and supporting me too. Arindam, Rahul, Rachit, Arpit and Reetika: double thumbs-up!

# Acknowledgements

Then there are people with whom you can't define your relationship, because it is a lot of everything and a little of nothing. Yet, you learn so much. Ranisa, Pauli, Anuradha, Siddhi, Pallavi, Trisha, Titiksha and Rashi: you guys may not realize it, but I've learnt a lot from you people, especially over the last one year. Thank you!

Pallavi Jha: as the trilogy draws to a conclusion, I thank you once again for planting the seed of the concept (though unknowingly!) in my head during one of our innumerable phone calls. I hope you continue to be happy and blessed. Here's to many more phone calls, cheers!

R, for ... guess I should rest my words for once and let the dots take over ... for it's in the dots that we define ourselves the best, isn't it?

# About the Author

Novoneel Chakraborty is the bestselling author of six romance thrillers. *Forget Me Not, Stranger* is his seventh novel and the third in the immensely popular Stranger trilogy. He works in the Indian films and television industry, penning popular television shows like *Million Dollar Girl*, *Twist Wala Love*, and *Secret Diaries* for Channel V. He lives in Mumbai.

You can reach him at:

Email: novosphere@gmail.com
Facebook: officialnbc
Twitter: @novoxeno
Instagram: @novoneelchakraborty

He runs a blog—*NovoSphere*—on life and its lessons at: www.nbconline.blogspot.com

# ALL
# YOURS,
## STRANGER

## By the same author

*A Thing beyond Forever*
*That Kiss in the Rain*
*How About a Sin Tonight?*
*Ex*

## Stranger Trilogy
*Marry Me, Stranger*
*Forget Me Not, Stranger*

# NOVONEEL CHAKRABORTY

# ALL YOURS, STRANGER

RANDOM HOUSE INDIA

Published by Random House India in 2015
Fifth impression in 2016

Copyright © Novoneel Chakraborty 2015

Random House Publishers India Pvt. Ltd
7th Floor, Infinity Tower C, DLF Cyber City
Gurgaon – 122002
Haryana

Random House Group Limited
20 Vauxhall Bridge Road
London SW1V 2SA
United Kingdom

978 81 8400 685 8

Typeset in Requiem Text by Manipal Digital Systems, Manipal

Printed at Thomson Press India Ltd, New Delhi

A PENGUIN RANDOM HOUSE COMPANY

*For my father . . .*

*Thanks for that Howard Roark gene. I shall be forever indebted to you for this and a lot more.*

# Prologue

The photograph of love is sometimes so big that you can't fit it into the frame of your relationship. If you force it, you are sure to lose some of it. Maybe most of it.

Sitting at the bar, Rivanah watched as her boyfriend Danny danced with the 'other' girl in a close embrace. Rivanah had promised herself she wouldn't drink since the next day was Monday and Monday-morning hangovers made her feel the world was conspiring to bring her down. Minutes back the three of them had been sitting on a couch. It was when Rivanah had stood up to get her Virgin Mojito refilled that the 'other' girl Nitya had asked, 'May I ask your boyfriend for a dance?' Rivanah had given her a tight smile of acknowledgement.

Nitya was one of those people you could never be 'friends' with and there was no reason why. But Rivanah couldn't afford to be indifferent to her because Nitya was her boyfriend's best friend. On other days, Rivanah neither liked nor disliked Nitya but she hated her whenever she started a statement with 'May I ask your boyfriend for . . . ?' Why this seeking of permission? To Rivanah, it always sounded as if the statement was gravid with a hidden taunt for her to decipher. As if Nitya would have left Danny alone had Rivanah said no. As if Danny too would have said no to Nitya if Rivanah had said no. Rivanah would have skipped accompanying them to the nightclub but today was Nitya's birthday and Danny had requested Rivanah to join them. As usual she couldn't say no to Danny and now she was sitting at the bar, like a loser, watching her boyfriend and his best friend groove to the latest chartbuster.

'Absolut,' Rivanah said to the bartender instead of asking for a refill of her Virgin Mojito. The bartender was quick to serve her and she was quicker to gulp it. She noticed Danny flash a smile at her (did he?) and then his face was turned the other way by his best friend. *Have they slept behind her back?* Rivanah was ashamed of asking herself this question but it was not the first time she was doing so. There were questions she could never answer. Questions about loyalty, trust and infidelity in a relationship. If love was really no contract then how does cheating come into being? Or was love an unsaid emotional contract after all? She gulped three more shots of Absolut and ordered the fourth, turning her face spitefully away from the 'best friends'.

'You remind me of someone.'

Rivanah turned her head to see an insanely handsome man standing behind her. *No such man should happen to a girl when she is emotionally vulnerable,* she thought. The handsome guy was leaning sideways on the bar, looking obliquely at her: dark complexion, clean-shaven, clear jawline, sharp nose, thin lips and deep eyes. Rivanah flashed an abrupt smile which she knew was timed all wrong. A smiling girl emboldens a guy like nothing else. She should have given him a you-talking-to-me glance instead, or better still, no reaction at all.

'Your smile confirms that you indeed are that girl,' the guy said.

'Now you'll say my voice seals it.' The vodka was clearly getting to her head.

'Not if you let me buy you the next drink.' The way his smile redesigned his face took his desirability quotient to temptation level.

'I've already had enough,' she said.

'For tonight, let's presume enough isn't enough.' In the next breath, he called for another drink for her.

In a kinky way, pushy men turned Rivanah on, especially when she was a few vodka shots down. This was one major difference between her former boyfriend Ekansh and Danny: Ekansh would decide for her while the latter would always let her have her way without batting an eyelid. Even now if she stood and flirted with Mr Handsome, she was sure Danny would only smile at her. If it were Ekansh . . . well, she wouldn't have been in the nightclub in the first place.

'Do you always think and speak?' the guy asked.

'Huh?' Before she came across as a dumb person, Rivanah blurted out, 'One more shot and then we hit the floor.'

'Sounds like a plan.'

A minute later the two were grooving to the same number which, minutes back, had irked Rivanah because Nitya and Danny had been dancing to it. She did glance towards them but, as expected, her boyfriend's thumbs-up gesture told her he was happy she too had got someone to dance with. One shouldn't be *this* open-minded, Rivanah told herself, feeling the handsome guy's hands tightening around her waist. With Danny only a few feet away, Rivanah felt uncomfortable with the man's proximity to her, but the disgust triggered in her by Danny's desire to be with Nitya instead of her didn't let the feeling of discomfort last for long. To distract her mind from Danny, she focused on the handsome guy who, she now knew, was looking at her the way a predator looks at a prey. It aroused her.

The handsome guy came close to her and spoke softly into her ears, 'How about we take a stroll outside?' His breath tickled her ears. Rivanah looked at him and nodded. She could do with some fresh air. She didn't care to glance at Danny before stepping out.

The cacophony of the nightclub suddenly vanished the moment they stepped out.

'Do you believe in magic?' the guy asked.

Rivanah thought he was trying to be funny and that she was supposed to laugh. Then she found herself nodding.

'Want to see some now?'

Rivanah nodded again. He smiled at her mischievously and stood facing her. Then slowly he started retreating, one step at a time.

'What are you doing?' she gasped, not knowing what to expect next.

'Wait. And watch.'

Like a teenager, Rivanah waited for some magic trick to unfold itself while watching the handsome guy disappear into the darkness. Then she realized she didn't even know his name. She called out to him only to feel a tap on her back. Rivanah turned in a flash to see the handsome guy standing right behind her, still smiling mischievously.

'What the fuck!' She turned to look at the other end where he had disappeared seconds back and then again at him standing in front of her. She had no clue how he had come behind her so quickly.

'How did you manage to do that?'

'Magic!' the handsome guy said, raising both his hands animatedly in the air.

'Want to see me do it again?'

Rivanah nodded, this time confident she would catch him in the act. The guy yet again started walking backwards from where he stood. Rivanah took a few steps forward, curious to know if there was a shortcut or something but once he disappeared at a distance she knew there was no way he could come up behind her— not this quick. Rivanah kept looking either way eagerly. Half a minute later the handsome guy appeared neither from behind her nor from front, but—to her shock— from inside the nightclub.

'Holy shit!' Rivanah exclaimed.

The guy came up to her and said in a naughty tone, 'I know far more pleasurable magic tricks. Want to give them a try?'

Rivanah knew what he was hinting at: a one-night stand. Something she had never done earlier while involved with Ekansh or Danny. An Audi appeared from nowhere and stopped right in front of her. The front window slowly rolled down. Rivanah bent down to look inside. The same handsome guy who was standing beside her was behind the steering wheel and was also sitting in one of the back seats. *How is that possible?* Before she could decipher if she was hallucinating, Rivanah felt a pair of hands grabbing her from behind. In no time she was bundled into the car by the guy standing beside her. Rivanah found herself sandwiched between the two similar-looking guys while the third drove the Audi.

They were fucking triplets! That seemed like the only plausible explanation.

She tried shouting only to have a hand press her mouth with force. The car was speeding away on the lonely road as she heard the guys tell each other to get her under control. The one who was driving had already switched on some music at top volume to mute her cries. Rivanah was throwing her legs and hands at them in desperation. One of the guys held her hands, while the other held her legs. She tried to move but couldn't. She shouted but it didn't matter. She could now see the two guys looking at her with a sadistic smile. As if her struggle was giving them a kick. Would she able to break free before it was too late? Or was this a nightmare like the ones she had had before? The lusty stares the guys gave her told her otherwise. She felt the will to fight slowly slip away from the grasp of her conscious.

And then the car suddenly came to a halt, throwing everyone in the back seat off balance. The guys beside Rivanah took their hands off her and sat still. Everyone in the car looked out ahead through the windshield. The triplets' faces paled one by one while a bright smile appeared on Rivanah's face. Someone was waiting right in front. Rivanah knew well who this someone could be. He hasn't forgotten me after all, Rivanah thought, feeling relieved. Only *she* knew how much she had missed him all these days . . .

# 1

Rivanah's parents were pleasantly surprised when she told them she was flying down to Kolkata a fortnight after her call to her mother inquiring about Hiya Chowdhury. This was the first time she was visiting without any apparent reason since she had moved to Mumbai. Rivanah wanted to come down immediately after she spoke to her mother on the phone about Hiya, but she couldn't manage a leave because the client for her project in office was in India. And the first thing she did after her client left was book a flight to Kolkata.

Rivanah hadn't slept properly for over fourteen days. Her mind kept drifting to one single name: *Hiya Chowdhury*. All Rivanah remembered was that Hiya was her batchmate when she was studying engineering. Strangely enough, she remembered the name and even her laughter, but couldn't recall her face. Yet, she was there in her scrapbook. Why was her laughter made to substitute for the normal doorbell in the flat where the stranger supposedly put up? Why were Hiya's interests similar to what the stranger wanted her to do? It was obvious there was a link but what was the link—that was something that stole Rivanah's peace of mind. To add to it, Inspector Kamble, along with the crime branch officer, hadn't been able to trace the stranger after Abhiraj was wrongly nabbed at Starbucks. Most importantly, even the stranger hadn't contacted her in the last fourteen days.

Rivanah's mother was waiting for her on the veranda but, the moment she stepped out of her cab, Rivanah rushed to her room. She didn't even stop to greet her mother.

'*Ki hoyeche ki?*' Before her mother's words could reach her, Rivanah was already in her room upstairs. The first thing she did was go to her study table, kneeling down while pulling the last drawer. What her mother had told her over the phone about Hiya Chowdhury, she had to read for herself. What if her mother had missed something in the scrapbook which was essential in order to track the stranger down or at least activate the link that connected her to Hiya? As Rivanah pulled out almost the entire drawer, a few notebooks fell out of it. She looked thoroughly but there was no scrapbook. She opened the other two drawers above the last but didn't find it there either. She looked on top of her table.

Nothing. She called out to her mother, only to realize she was standing by the door, looking slightly taken aback.

'What are you up to, Mini?' her mother asked.

'Mumma, where's my scrapbook?'

'What book?'

'The one you read to me from, couple of weeks back on the phone? Remember?'

'Oh!' Her mother came inside the room. 'I kept it where it was. Inside the last drawer.'

'But it's not there now!'

Her mother looked as confused as she was.

'But I had kept it here only.'

Rivanah let out a helpless sigh and watched her mother search her table like she had done only seconds back. The result was the same: the scrapbook was not there.

'But why do you need the scrapbook all of a sudden?'

'Nothing.' Rivanah was resigned to her fate. 'Please let me know when you find it,' she said, throwing herself on the bed.

'How long are you staying, Mini?' her mother asked.

'Only this weekend,' Rivanah said, staring at the ceiling. Her mind was elsewhere. It couldn't have been a coincidence that the stranger had saved Hiya's laughter as the doorbell sound in the Mumbai flat. *But why?* Is the stranger related to Hiya? Or is she . . . ? But she only knew

3

Hiya from college. That's all . . . like she knew so many other students. If she had been close to her she would have at least remembered her face. Perhaps her other friends would have some more information.

'Did you get it, Mumma?' she said, sitting up.

'I'm looking for it.'

For the first time she had had one single lead to who the stranger could be and the scrapbook had gone missing! 'Misplaced', if her mother was to be believed. In the evening, an irritated Rivanah went to the house of her best friend from college, Pooja, in Kalighat. Pooja's marriage was scheduled for the next month but she had come home early to take care of her trousseau and to enjoy her pre-marriage time to the fullest with her parents and siblings. She was delighted to see Rivanah after more than a year.

'You look different, Rivanah!' Pooja exclaimed.

'Really? Like how?'

'I don't know but you do. Come in now.'

The two friends had a lot to catch up on. Pooja had so much to share and so did Rivanah. But all through the conversation, Rivanah kept getting the feeling that she somehow withheld much more than she shared with Pooja. That way she had indeed changed. Over the past year, Rivanah had understood that sharing your emotional woes didn't lead to anything.

'Won't you be working after marriage?' Rivanah asked after she learnt that Pooja had actually resigned from her job.

'I haven't thought about it yet. Right now all I want to do is enjoy this attention that I'm getting from everyone. It is my marriage, after all!'

Rivanah only smiled at her as a reaction.

'Honestly, sometimes I wonder if I even deserve so much happiness. I mean, Rishi and I have been in a relationship from some time now. From the time we first talked to actually marrying him . . . I can't describe it to you, Rivanah. I only want to live this moment as much as I can.'

'It's so important to marry the person you love, isn't it?' Rivanah said.

'Or love the person you marry. I mean, love has to be there.'

'The second option isn't for me and the first I don't know will happen or not,' Rivanah said with a hint of dismay.

'Did you talk to Kaku–Kakima about Danny?'

'I did but talking won't help much I'm afraid. They have a perception and I don't think I'll be able to break it.'

'Think positive,' Pooja said, clasping her friend's hand.

5

'Remember how Ekansh and I were labelled the fairy-tale couple in college? Everyone thought we were sure to get married. Even we thought so.' A pause later Rivanah added, 'At least *I* thought so.' She broke the clasp and drew her hand back, saying, 'I don't think I'll cry a lot this time. I mean I'll feel bad, maybe I'll be irreversibly damaged too, but still I don't think I will cry if Danny and I don't make the distance, if you know what I mean.'

'No, I don't. What are you saying? Is there any problem between you and . . .'

'Danny is alright. It's just that I haven't been able to move on from Ekansh yet. It's like every day I lie to myself that I have moved on, that I don't love him any more, that it's good that he walked out of our relationship, but whenever I go to bed at night my own lies catch up with me. And mock me in the most painful of ways.'

'Do you really still love Ekansh?' There was a hint of surprise in Pooja's voice which hit Rivanah hard. As if her friend was subtly accusing her: how could you be in love with two people at the same time?

'I have asked myself that question several times but not once have I dared to answer it.'

There was an awkward silence.

'Anyway,' Rivanah said, 'tell me, what do you know about Hiya Chowdhury?'

'Hiya who?'

For a moment Rivanah thought Pooja was kidding. When she had called her right after calling her mother two weeks back, it didn't take her one second to identify Hiya as the girl who had hanged herself.

'Now don't tell me you don't know who Hiya Chowdhury is!'

'Oh, Hiya, yes . . . What about her?' Pooja seemed to remember her, much to Rivanah's relief.

'You tell me anything that I should know about her. I don't remember much really.'

'Anything? What's up with you snooping about Hiya?'

'Why did she die, Pooja?'

The response came a tad later than Rivanah expected.

'How would I know? One day I heard she is no more.'

'She hanged herself from a ceiling fan,' Rivanah said.

'Oh, did she? Poor thing.'

'What poor thing? *You* told me this.'

'I did? Why would I say such a thing when I didn't know it myself?'

'What are you saying?'

Before Pooja could reply, her phone started to ring.

'Rishi is calling. Excuse me, please.'

Pooja went out in the balcony with her phone, leaving Rivanah alone in the room. For the next one hour she didn't come in. Rivanah didn't understand whether she wanted to avoid her or she was actually glued to Rishi's phone call. Rivanah went to the balcony after her patience ran out. Pooja excused herself from Rishi over phone and said, 'I'm so sorry. There's some problem and . . .'

'It's fine. I understand. Let's meet when you are free. I'll be going home now.'

'Okay. Do come for the marriage next month.'

Rivanah nodded and waved her friend goodbye. Seeing Rivanah leave Pooja breathed a sigh of relief. Lying never came naturally to her.

Rivanah went home from Pooja's place and took a nap. At dinner her father surprised her by asking, 'How is Danny?'

Rivanah didn't know if she should be hopeful since her father sounded grumpy rather than concerned.

'He is good, Baba. He was asking about you too.'

'Hmm. Did he bag any film roles?'

'He signed a regional film. Shooting will begin soon.'

'Hmm. And why exactly is Shantu not talking to me?'

This one took Rivanah by surprise. There was a momentary eye-lock with her father and she realized that he knew that Abhiraj was taken into custody.

'Abhiraj was stalking me.'

'You could have told us. Why did you have to go to the police yourself?' Her father's voice rose.

8

Rivanah was quiet. She knew she couldn't tell him why exactly she had asked the police to butt in.

'Mumma, did you get the scrapbook?' she asked, changing the topic.

'What scrapbook?' Her father was still not done with her.

'I need to know about a friend of mine.'

'Which friend?' her father asked with a frown.

'Hiya Chowdhury.'

Her father's frown went away as he quickly looked away from Rivanah.

'Give me some more rice,' he told his wife and continued, 'You know what happened in office today?'.

9

# 2

The next day Rivanah called Pooja inquiring about Hiya's address. Pooja had no idea where Hiya lived or who her close friends were in their batch. Or so she said. Instead of hounding Pooja, Rivanah chose to update her Facebook status: *Guys, remember Hiya Chowdhury? Anyone knows where she lives in Kolkata?*

Three hours later the status had received zero likes, zero comments. Frustrated, Rivanah called up her college. Though it was a Sunday, she knew the college office remained open seven days a week.

'Hello, Techno College? I'm Rivanah Bannerjee; I graduated last year. I'm arranging an alumni meet, so I would like to have the postal addresses of my batchmates to send them invites.'

'That's a lot of names. I can't tell you over the phone. You can come here and collect them for yourself. And please bring your college ID along. Any misuse and you will be responsible.'

'Okay.'

Rivanah reached college within the hour. Though she came with something else in mind, the sight of the college reignited her love story with Ekansh that she had been trying to extinguish for a while now. The good thing was that the emotional embers associated with the memory didn't have any flame, but the bad thing was those embers still had heat left in them. Before those embers could do any further emotional damage, she reached the office. Rivanah was made to wait while her ID was checked. Soon she was given a long printout which had the names and corresponding address of all of her forty-three batchmates. It took little time for her to spot Hiya Chowdhury's name and address. Her house was in Bangur Park in south Kolkata.

Rivanah took a cab from her college in Salt Lake to Bangur Park. She had to ask around a bit to eventually get to Hiya Chowdhury's house. As the cab driver drove away Rivanah turned around to look at the house. She pushed the small iron gate open but couldn't spot anyone or hear any sound coming from inside the house. It was difficult to say if the house was still inhabited. She noticed a white cat atop the terrace looking straight at her and casually moving away as if to inform the owner that someone was here. Rivanah

11

walked to the main door and found that the main door was not locked. She pressed the doorbell. It wasn't the normal ding-dong but had a weird buzz to it. A moment later, the window adjacent to the main door opened.

'Who is it?' asked an elderly man.

'Hello, I'm Rivanah Bannerjee, Hiya's friend.'

'Hiya who?'

'Hiya Chowdhury?'

'You know any Hiya Chowdhury?' The man turned his face away from Rivanah and asked someone inside the house. Rivanah tried to look but couldn't see who it was that the man was talking to.

'Chowdhury? She could be Hiren Chowdhury's daughter,' said a woman who sounded as elderly as the man behind the window.

'They don't live here any more,' the elderly man said, turning towards Rivanah.

'Do you know where—?'

'They were our tenants. These days one doesn't know where one's own children live; how can I tell you about our former tenant's whereabouts?' the elderly man said curtly and shut the window. A moment later she saw the curtains being drawn as well.

*So, Hiya Chowdhury and her family lived as tenants here.* And if not here then there was no way she could hunt Hiya's family down . . . except if the stranger helped her. It was a dead end as far as Rivanah was concerned. With a heavy heart and a confused mind, she caught a cab once again and went home with two questions clouding her mind. If Hiya was dead and her family was untraceable, why did the stranger lead her to Hiya? And was the scrapbook misplaced by her mother or was it stolen?

Rivanah took a flight back to Mumbai the next morning. While pushing her luggage trolley out of the airport arrival gate, Rivanah's eyes were looking for Danny. He would spring a surprise for her by suddenly appearing with a bunch of roses in his hand and that killer smile of his, she thought, looking around outside the exit gate. There was no sign of Danny.

'*Madam, wahan jakar wait kijiye please,*' said one of the security personnel by the exit gate, gesturing towards the opposite side. Rivanah didn't even care to look at him as she pushed her trolley. She checked her WhatsApp on the way. She did tell Danny about her flight timings. He should have been there. She called him but there was no answer. The second and third times too the calls were not picked up, though Rivanah held on for the entire ring. With a clogged mind she took a cab straight to Danny's friend's flat in Andheri, Lokhandwala, where she had been living with Danny for about two weeks now. Her parents didn't have a clue about it. Staying all by herself in Mumbai for a little more than a year, Rivanah had learnt that not everyone had to know about everything that happened in one's life. The more you shared your things with people, the more you invite opinion about yourself. She was in love with Danny and was comfortable living with him; that was all that mattered. You are married if you feel you are married. And if you are not, then no ritual can ever make you feel so. Rivanah never tried to explain this to her parents; else they would have taken her to some tantric, accusing her of mental imbalance.

As her cab crossed one traffic signal after another, Rivanah wondered how she had, of late, stopped weighing her relationship with Danny on the weighing scale of marriage. Being with him was more important than any other social licence. The only thing that worried her was that sooner or later her parents would ask her that dreaded question: 'So, what have you decided about marriage?' By then would she be able to muster enough courage to be honest with her parents and tell them that she didn't give a damn about anything except for the fact that she wanted to be with Danny? And he with her.

Once she reached the apartment, she called Danny's phone once again but he still didn't pick up. Going up to the seventh floor in the elevator she checked his last

WhatsApp to her: *Have a safe flight back baby. Love you.* His Last Seen on WhatsApp was when she had boarded the flight.

Rivanah came out of the elevator and dragged her luggage to the main door. In no time she unlocked it with the spare keys. The single lock told her Danny must be at home because he always double-locked the door if outside.

'Hey baby! I'm home,' she yelled.

The response came seconds later. In the voice of a girl.

'Danny is in the shower.'

Rivanah turned around to notice the girl had wet hair, as if she too had been inside the bathroom with . . .

# 3

'Nitya!' Rivanah said, not sure if she had disguised the fact that she neither expected her in the flat nor did she like it.

'Hi, Rivanah. I'm sorry if I surprised you.'

'I just didn't expect you here,' Rivanah said, putting her luggage down on the floor.

'I know. I also don't want to be here, especially with you and Danny living-in, but you know how Danny is when he gets stubborn. He didn't give me any option,' Nitya said and sat on the plush couch, switching on the television. The indifference with which she sat didn't go well with Rivanah. She knew from before how stubborn Danny could be and it always turned her on emotionally but now she learnt the stubbornness wasn't something exclusive for her. Somewhere within her the realization formed a knot.

'I hope Danny has told you what happened,' Nitya said, her eyes fixed on the television. Rivanah's eyes were fixed on Nitya. What was Danny supposed to tell her about Nitya? Rivanah guessed the worst: Nitya and Danny were a couple now, and she—Rivanah—had been conveniently ousted just as she had been by Ekansh a year back. There was no response for some time. By then Rivanah could feel her guts churning. Danny came out of the bathroom and straight to the drawing room in a vest and knickers, drying his hair with a towel.

'Hey baby! So nice to see you,' said Danny, hugging her and dropped the towel on a beanbag beside her. There's no awkwardness in the hug, Rivanah pondered, something that happens naturally when one emotionally distances oneself from the other. She broke the embrace to look Danny in the eye.

'Were you going to tell me something about Nitya and you?'

Danny shot an incredulous glance at Nitya first and then looking back at Rivanah, said, 'Let's go to the other room.' Danny pulled a bemused Rivanah into the bedroom.

'What is it, Danny? You are scaring me now.'

'Relax. It is not about Nitya and me. It is about Nitya and Nitya only.'

Rivanah gave him a bored look that said 'tell me something new'.

'Nitya had a bad, bad break-up with her boyfriend the day you left for Kolkata. She tried to kill herself. I took her to the hospital and then brought her here. The doctor said she shouldn't be alone right now because she is suicidal.'

Rivanah sighed, trying to ward off all the obnoxious thoughts in her mind and let the fact register in her.

'So, will Nitya stay here with us?' she asked.

Danny nodded.

'For how long?'

'Till she recovers a bit. The doctor said she shouldn't be allowed to stay alone for some time. She is emotionally fragile.'

There was an awkward silence between them. Rivanah didn't want Nitya to stay with them. But she knew if she was honest to Danny it would make her sound rude and he wouldn't appreciate it either. Before she could tell him her decision, Nitya was in the room.

'I'm sorry if I'm disturbing you; if Rivanah has a problem with me staying here, I'm ready to leave. It's really not an issue.'

Danny and Rivanah exchanged a blank look.

'The doctor is mad. I can take care of myself.'

Rivanah went to Nitya and said, 'Why would we have a problem, dear? Please feel free to stay here.'

'Cool,' she said, shooting a look at Rivanah and Danny alternately, and then went away.

'Thank you,' Danny said, wrapping his arms around Rivanah. Only she knew how much pain it caused her to say 'yes' to Nitya. From the day she had first met her a year back, Rivanah never got a vibe from her that said, 'yeah, we can be friends too'.

Hunger pushed Rivanah to quickly change and freshen up. Though she had eaten breakfast on the flight itself, she was famished now since it was past noon by the time she entered her flat. She had already told Danny about how she longed to have a pizza when she reached Mumbai. She joined Danny and Nitya in the drawing room after freshening up and asked which pizza she should order.

'Pizza? But I've already prepared lunch for us,' Nitya exclaimed.

'We can eat that at night,' Rivanah said.

'I was in the kitchen the whole morning preparing salad for us,' Nitya said, which made it seem like she wasn't complaining and yet she was.

'You have the salad, Nitya. Danny and I will surely have it at night.'

'But . . .' Nitya's voice changed gear.

'Can't we have pizza at night?' Danny asked Rivanah. Her jaw would have dropped had she not controlled herself in time.

'Yeah, sure we can,' she said after a moment.

'I'm sure you will like the salad,' Nitya said with a smile and went to the kitchen to fetch it. Rivanah could see a sense of victory in that smile which made her feel uncomfortable. Though Rivanah knew Danny was looking at her, pleading for peace, she chose to look at her phone instead.

For dinner it was pizza indeed but when Rivanah said she wanted to have a Cheese Burst pizza, Nitya said extra cheese gave her a headache. Danny ordered both Cheese Burst as well as a regular one but he ate more from the latter. Rivanah didn't say anything but could feel frustration brewing in her. She ate only one of the six slices and threw the rest in the garbage and she did so exactly when Danny was looking. He didn't probe; she didn't clarify.

Rivanah went to her room, switched off the lights, plugged her ears and listened to a Lana Del Ray song. A few minutes later she felt her earphones being taken off. She didn't have to turn around. She knew it was Danny as his hand rested on her tummy.

'Angry?' he whispered in her ears.

'No,' she said in a stern voice.

'I'm sorry.'

'You don't have to be.'

'Can we go clubbing?'

'Depends on who "we" are.'

'"We" can only mean you and me.'

Rivanah turned to look at him and said, 'Are you sure?'

'Absolutely.'

'Okay.'

'I know you are uncomfortable in Nitya's presence,' Danny said once they were in the car. Somebody had to talk about it. Rivanah was glad it was him.

'I'm not uncomfortable, Danny,' Rivanah said. 'It's just that Nitya and I are two different personalities with different tastes. And you know that. Personally I don't have a problem with Nitya but . . .'

'But . . . ?'

*But . . . your closeness to her burns me.* Rivanah wondered how she could dress this naked truth in a way that it didn't make her sound insecure.

Danny shrugged at her, still seeking closure.

'But . . . nothing,' Rivanah said.

'It's just a matter of a few days.'

'Hmm.' Rivanah turned the stereo on and rolled down the window to get some fresh air. Danny switched off the AC and asked, 'Anything about Hiya Chowdhury?'

Rivanah gave him a sharp glance and then, leaning back on the seat while looking outside, said, 'Nothing. I tracked down where she used to live but nobody from her family lives there any more. It was a rented place. The owners too don't know where the Chowdhury family has moved to after Hiya's death.'

'And did she really die just the way you envisioned in your nightmares?'

'Yes. Pooja said Hiya died after hanging herself from the ceiling fan.' *But Pooja also acted funny, saying she didn't remember saying so.* Rivanah didn't share this with Danny.

Danny put his hand on hers. He tightened his grasp as she gave him a relaxed smile. It was a cool night with low traffic. She leaned sideways and kissed him on his cheeks and then licked her way to his ears. The car wobbled on the road.

'Control, baby,' Danny said. Both had a naughty smile on their faces. Before they could take things one step further, his phone rang. Since the phone was lying on the deck, Rivanah could easily read the name of the caller: Nitya. She pushed the phone towards Danny and rested on her seat again. Danny slowed down as he took the call. The next second he took a U-turn.

'What happened?' Rivanah asked.

'Nitya has high fever. We have to go back.'

The concern in his voice saddened her. She knew as a friend he ought to be concerned but what was she to feel, as a girlfriend, about this? No, as an *insecure* girlfriend. Danny didn't say a single word as he drove fast to their apartment. Once there Rivanah stayed back in the car as he rushed to the flat. Sitting in the car she wanted to tell someone her point of view. That she wasn't a bitch who didn't care if a person had high fever but ... she unlocked her phone, tapped on Contacts and went to a name that read Stranger.

She typed a message: *Please tell me you are there*. She sent it but she didn't get a delivery report. She chose to wait.

# 4

Rivanah woke up to the sound of the doorbell. She looked around and found herself in her room. At first, all she remembered was sitting inside the car. Then she remembered how even after half an hour the message to the stranger had not been delivered. She had come back to the flat last night to see Danny checking the thermometer while Nitya lay on the couch. Rivanah hadn't bothered to ask anything.

Rivanah got up, tied her hair into a loose bun and went to open the door. There were two pouches of milk on the ground. She picked it up and locked the main door. It was then that her eyes fell on Danny who was asleep on the couch while Nitya's head rested on his lap; she too was asleep. There was nothing objectionable in it and yet there was something deeply disturbing. She wanted to wake them up immediately but, she wondered, why did Danny have to make Nitya sleep on his lap? Rivanah understood she was his best friend but she wasn't his girlfriend. There's a difference. *Is there?* Rivanah thought and stopped herself from waking them up. *Can a guy's girl best friend and girlfriend live together with him?* With this question probing her calmness, Rivanah went to take a shower instead of sleeping for a few minutes more.

When she stepped out of the shower, she noticed Nitya was preparing tea for herself in the kitchen while Danny was on the phone. When the call ended, he joined her in the bedroom.

'I have an important audition today for a movie,' he said, putting his arms around her from behind, trying to be cosy with her. She could still feel the coldness with which he had left her in the car last night. From that coldness to this cosiness—how was she supposed to adjust so quickly and that too with no explanation or even a whisper of an apology?

'I thought you would come to the room after Nitya slept,' she said, shrugging her shoulders a bit as if she didn't appreciate his arms around her at the moment.

Danny looked as if he was expecting something else from Rivanah.

'I dozed off. Why do you ask?'

Was she wrong in expecting an apology from him because he didn't come to his girlfriend's room at night?

'Nothing,' Rivanah said. 'When is your audition?'

'They wanted me to be there in the morning itself but I have rescheduled it for the evening.'

'Why? You have another one in morning?'

'No. I need to take Nitya to the doctor. She still has fever.'

Rivanah gave him a momentary glance and, turning her back to him said, 'I'll take her to the doctor. You go to the audition.'

Danny wrapped his arms around her once again from behind, this time tighter, and said, 'I love you.'

'Me too,' she said, removing his arms immediately. Only she knew that she had proposed to take Nitya to the doctor out of her own sense of insecurity. Pistanthrophobia was the word—the fear of trusting someone because of a previous bad experience. Thanks to Ekansh, Rivanah could think of nothing else but the fact that every girl in her man's life was a potential threat to her relationship. The closer the girl to your partner, the more active the threat was. Whether Danny was lured by Nitya or he fell for her, the result would be same: Rivanah would be single. She had suffered such a thing before. And somewhat recovered, if not fully. But if it happened again—just one more time—then nothing in this world would be able to cure her. People don't understand but heartbreak, with time, becomes a disease, a well-kept secret disease whose symptom is a deep mistrust, and that is incurable. She promised herself that she would do her part at least so that what happened between Ekansh and her didn't happen again. And thus she decided to take Nitya to the doctor.

Danny dropped both Rivanah and Nitya at the doctor's and drove off to his audition. It took close to an hour before they were done with the check-up. As they came out Rivanah called for a Tab cab. When it arrived, Nitya persuaded Rivanah to head to her office while she went home alone.

Once in office Rivanah's team lead, Sridhar, told her something which instantly filled her with excitement.

'There's an on-site opportunity coming up for two of our team members and I will be forwarding your name.'

'You mean I will go to London?'

'Yes, if selected, you'll have to work from there for two years.'

'Wow! Thank you so much.' Rivanah was genuinely thrilled. She had worked hard on the project and finally it was time for her reward. She immediately called Danny but he didn't pick up. Then she called her mother who was equally jubilant hearing this. Rivanah knew her mother would inform every close and distant relative of theirs about this in no time. After all Rivanah would be the first woman in her family to work abroad. The rest had only tagged along with their husbands on a dependant visa.

A few minutes after her mother had put the phone down, Rivanah got a call from Danny.

'Sorry, baby. I was driving.'

'It's okay. I guessed so.' Rivanah was about to share the good news when she heard Danny say, 'I'm back home.'

'Huh? Why?' The smile disappeared from Rivanah's face. A frown appeared instead.

'Some crisis came up at the production office. The audition will possibly happen tomorrow.'

'So?'

'So, I'll be at home only.'

'Oh. Okay.' Rivanah was lost. *He was at home. So was Nitya.*

'You called me, right?' Danny said.

'Yeah. Just like that.'

'Okay. Let's talk later then. I need to give Nitya some medicine.'

'Yeah, sure. Bye,' Rivanah said and cut the call. She had a constant frown from then on. Physically she was in the office with her team but mentally she was at her flat wondering what Danny and Nitya were up to. She called Danny half an hour later.

'Hey, what's up?' he said.

'Nothing. Was missing you. What are you doing?'

'I was shaving.'

'And Nitya?'

'She is sleeping. It's the side effect of the medicines.'

'Okay.'

*Was Nitya really sleeping?* Rivanah cut the call, feeling ashamed for doubting Danny's words. She went back to work but still couldn't focus. A restlessness caught up with her; she drank water from time to time, took deep breaths and tried to distract herself, but failed miserably. She called Danny again after twenty minutes. And again. And again.

'What's up with you today? Don't you have any work in the office?' Danny said when he picked up her call for the fifth time in an hour and a half.

'Why, aren't you happy I'm calling you?'

'I'm not.'

'Huh?'

'I would rather have you home if you are out of work,' Danny giggled.

'What's Nitya doing?'

'She is taking a shower.'

'Okay.'

'Listen, thanks,' Danny said.

'For?'

'For being so concerned about Nitya. I know I didn't discuss it with you before I brought her here

29

but I'm so happy with the way you embraced the whole situation.'

Rivanah could have choked to death hearing this. She only swallowed a lump, sitting on her chair in her cubicle, trying hard to pretend she didn't hear what Danny said.

'There?' Danny said.

'Yes. Let me call you later. Team lead's calling. Bye.' Rivanah cut the phone and kept it in her bag, promising herself she wouldn't call Danny again that day.

Just before she was about to leave for the day, Sridhar told her to keep her passport ready.

'Sure. I'll let you know when done.'

She couldn't wait to share the news with Danny. And when she did tell him after she reached home, Danny was equally excited.

'I'm really happy for you. But I'll miss you as well,' Danny said, hugging her tight. It was then that Rivanah realized what she had forgotten the whole time. It made her jittery. And somewhat neurotic too. What if Danny and Nitya continued to live together after she shifted to London?

'You'll come with me,' she said and immediately knew it was stupid of her to say that. Danny half broke the embrace to look at her and said, 'How I wish!'

Rivanah managed a tight smile.

'May I say something?' Nitya barged in. Danny and Rivanah together turned around to see Nitya leaning by the room's door. They awkwardly broke their embrace completely. Nitya looked at Rivanah and said, 'Don't worry. In your absence, I shall take proper care of him.' She gave Rivanah a warm smile. It hit her like a poisoned arrow.

Rivanah couldn't sleep that night even though, unlike the previous night, Danny was right next to her, sound asleep. The same relationship, Rivanah pondered, which had made her sniff freedom months back was pushing her to limit her career choice. With her in London and Nitya taking care of Danny, she wouldn't be surprised if their relationship ballooned into love. And if that balloon started flying high she would never be able to catch it and burst it. Who would she blame then: Danny or herself? Rivanah longed to talk to someone about this. She checked the messages on her phone once. Her message to the stranger still hadn't been delivered. Was he gone forever? Why did he come in the first place? Why was Hiya Chowdhury's laughter so important that he used it as a doorbell sound? Would she never know about it at all? Thoughts about Danny and Nitya, the stranger and Hiya started intermingling in her mind, creating a jumble. Out of sheer frustration she sent the same message she did a day back to all the numbers she had saved of the stranger, and closed her eyes to think: she had never been a career-oriented girl. All she needed was someone who loved her truly. And now when she had one, was it worth risking it all to go to London to work?

At four in the morning she sat up on her bed, took her phone and typed a message for her team lead: *Hi Sridhar, sorry to message you this late. I had a talk with my parents. I won't be able to get my passport in the next three months. I think I'll let this opportunity go by. Sorry.*

After sending it she checked her messages to the stranger once again. None were delivered. She called those numbers. None of them were switched on . . . yet.

# 5

Returning from her office, Rivanah got down from the autorickshaw at the start of the lane which led to her building. As she walked down the lane she realized it was unusually quiet. The adjoining shops were shut; some of the street lights were also not working while the street dogs which usually hovered around were missing. She checked her watch: 7.30 p.m. She wondered what was wrong and walked on. The moment she reached the end of the lane, she realized what was wrong. She had reached the same spot she had got out at. *How is it possible?* She turned with a fear slowly rising in her, which made her run towards the other end. She reached the spot only to realize it was the same place where she started from. She kept running from one end of the lane to the other in a loop, unable to find her building. Rivanah was sweating by now, perplexed at what was happening. She screamed for help but there was nobody around. As she for the umpteenth time tried to run to the other end, hoping to find her building this time, she noticed one of the street lights was on. Its light fell directly on a grilled manhole. And from inside it a hand came up. Accompanying the hand was a voice.

'Help me, Rivanah. Help me. I'm trapped.'

She didn't recognize the voice. With unsteady steps Rivanah reached the manhole. And through the grill saw her own self trapped inside. But as her own self saw her peeping, her visage changed into a demonic one that cried out, 'I'll get you, Rivanah. Soon, I'll get you.'

Rivanah's eyes snapped open. After a long time the nightmare had returned. Sleep had been a far cry for Rivanah ever since coming back to Mumbai the previous weekend; she didn't know when she had dozed off that night. She quickly gulped some water from the bottle by her side and, lowering the AC temperature by three degrees with the remote, she tried to close her eyes and relax. She found her mind working even more maliciously, all the while knitting imaginary tales involving Danny and Nitya. As if her mind had nothing else to think about. When did she become so insecure? She knew that the chances of Danny leaving her for Nitya were negligible but the thought still bothered her a great deal.

Rivanah sat up. Danny was sound asleep beside her. She caressed his hair. He didn't budge. Their love story wasn't a smooth one. She knew she had to still convince her parents about him but she was ready to fight it out. But this new problem, the root of which lay deep within her—she didn't know how to uproot it. Rivanah felt choked looking at the calm edpression on Danny's face. She would have burst into tears if she had not withdrawn herself away from him right at that moment.

She went and drew the curtain of the window to inhale the fresh morning air. Dawn had just broken. She looked down and noticed a jogger on the footpath. On an impulse she put on her tracksuit, got into her Converse shoes, tied her hair in a bun and looked at herself in the mirror. It was the same tracksuit she had worn to the gym when she was trying to woo Danny last year. A tiny smile touched her face. Things had moved so fast. Her thoughts shifted to how Ishita and she had tried to woo Danny together and how miserably the former had failed. Ishita was the only one whom she could call a friend in Mumbai other than Danny, but she had shifted to Gurgaon following a new job. And all that remained of that friendship was a Like and a Comment on each other's Facebook update.

Rivanah felt the morning air work as an elixir as she started jogging on the lonely road right in front of her apartment. At least the motion of jogging took her mind off the garbage she had been pondering over almost all day and night. Rivanah slowed down on seeing a young girl running towards her. She wasn't wearing a tracksuit and the way she was running told Rivanah she was in some kind of trouble. She waited for the girl to come close to her. The girl stopped right beside Rivanah.

'Didi, please help me!' the girl said, gasping for air.

'Relax! What happened?'

'I have a job interview and I live far from this place. Hence I left home early. But these two boys have been following me and . . .' The girl looked towards the end of the street where Rivanah, following her eyes, realized two guys in a bike had taken a turn. Rivanah looked around. She spotted an autorickshaw approaching.

'Quick!' Rivanah pulled the girl by her arm and in a flash stopped the autorickshaw and climbed in. The driver looked at her expectantly.

'Police station!' she said. The autowallah took a U-turn and accelerated. Rivanah peeped out and realized the guys would catch up with them before they reach the police station.

'What do you have in that bag?' Rivanah asked the girl who immediately opened the bag and showed it to her. There was a tiffin box, a file, a deodorant, a few cosmetics, a hairbrush and an umbrella. Rivanah took out the umbrella and pulled its stem out without opening it. This time she didn't have to peep out. The guys on the bike had closed in on the autorickshaw. The autowallah asked them to behave only to be rebuked in the dirtiest of cuss words. The guy riding pillion shouted to the one driving the bike that now they had two girls—one for his friend and one for him. They laughed in a lurid manner. The autowallah drove away from the bike but Rivanah asked the driver to take the auto close to the bike once more. Once that was done, she smiled at the guys, taking them by surprise, and then shoved the umbrella between the spikes of the bike's back wheel. The umbrella immediately broke but by then the bike and the guys on it were all over the road. They hurled abuses at Rivanah as the autowallah sped past them.

'Thank you so much. I hope you are not hurt,' the girl said, sounding extremely relieved.

Rivanah had felt a strong jerk in her hand but it was nothing serious.

'Fear is the most prized illusion we create for ourselves, dear. Never be afraid of such louts. They feed on our fear,' Rivanah said. A smile of realization touched her face. These were the same words the stranger had once written on one of the embroidered white cloths he had sent her.

'I'll always remember that,' the girl said. Rivanah got off the auto at the closest traffic signal, asked the driver to drop the girl at her destination, and jogged back to her apartment. She did notice a few men trying to get the two bikers to hospital but she didn't care to stop. *Next time they would remember not to harass a girl on the road,* she thought, and jogged on. While moving into her apartment building she realized that if this incident had happened two years back she would have never been able to help the girl the way she did this morning. The guts, the attitude, the confidence to tackle the situation had developed in her since the last year . . . since the stranger had come into her life. In a way, the stranger had become a part of her system. She might fear him but she wouldn't be able to sever herself from him. He was the one who had unlocked a secret Rivanah hidden within herself: a Rivanah who knew how to stand up and pack a punch.

She went to her flat, showered and was ready for office. By then even Danny and Nitya were ready. The latter had of late started working as an assistant to a famous stylist who had ample links in the film industry. There was a rehearsal for a show which was supposed to be attended by a top-notch film director and thus Danny had the right reason to tag along with Nitya. The fact that Nitya worked at a place where Danny could seek his professional break made Rivanah feel like an outcast. She was in IT and there was no reason why

Danny would ever tag along with her to her office. She didn't say much and stepped out before they did, wishing Danny luck.

In the office Rivanah didn't call Danny even once. Nor did a call or message come from him. Though it was usual for Danny to not call her when he was out for work, it made Rivanah feel uneasy. Five times that day she picked up her phone, almost tapping the Call button against his name, but she somehow didn't. She could feel a restlessness building up inside her but it couldn't locate a vent in the form of a person. In the evening she called her mother.

'Hello, Mumma.'

'Mini? What happened? Why are you calling at this time? Everything's fine?'

'Why, can't I call you just like that?'

'Of course you can. But you generally call around eight in the evening.'

Rivanah talked with her mother for the next fifteen minutes. Many a time she thought of sharing her fear about Danny with her mother, but realized there came a time when you couldn't share everything with your mother, no matter how close she was to you. *Being a grown up, you have to drink your poison yourself,* she thought. Was it time for her to accept the fact that, at twenty-three, she was a lonely soul? Something she had never thought was possible in her wildest dreams. In the evening Rivanah went to a lonely flat, had a lonely supper because Danny was still out and she didn't care where Nitya was. At around eleven at night she got a call from Danny asking her to come to Hype, a nightclub in Bandra. Just when she thought she would have to resign to her inner loneliness, there was a spark of hope. Rivanah dressed up quickly and took a cab to Hype. And there she saw Danny and Nitya waiting for her.

'Tomorrow is Nitya's birthday. So I thought we'll celebrate it here itself,' Danny said and realized the surprise wasn't well received by Rivanah. Nitya excused herself to go to the washroom and he tried to explain, 'Baby, I know I didn't tell you about this before. And trust me, if Nitya wasn't single and hadn't done the shit she tried to do, I wouldn't have done this . . .' Rivanah didn't bother to hear the rest.

'It's okay, Danny,' she said.

They cut the cake at midnight. Rivanah not only had to force herself to smile constantly but also had to click a lot of pictures of Danny and Nitya where both were either hugging or the latter kissing the former's cheek or, worse, had to pose between Danny and Nitya with the latter clicking their selfies. Once they were done with the photos, Nitya asked her, 'May I ask your boyfriend for a dance?'

Rivanah was pissed off but nodded with a tight smile. As they danced, she went to the bar with a mild headache. She ordered her drink and considered going back home when she heard a man's voice.

'You remind me of someone.'

She was emotionally vulnerable and his timing was right. To add to it he was drop-dead handsome. She couldn't resist the urge to accompany him on the dance floor. She hoped Danny would leave Nitya and come to her, at least out of jealousy. He didn't. In fact he flashed a smile at her which infuriated her and made her desperate to get out of the place.

'Do you mind taking a stroll with me outside?' the handsome guy spoke in her ears. It was like he read her mind. Rivanah instantly agreed.

Outside, she felt better till the handsome guy showed her a magic trick she wasn't prepared for. Excusing himself, he went away and then appeared right behind her. Then he went backwards, disappearing at the bend of the road and reappearing in front of her. Rivanah stood awed at what was happening. Next a car came and stopped right in front of her. The handsome guy was beside her, inside the car by the steering and sitting in the back seat as well—all at the same time. By the time she understood they were triplets she was pushed into the car. The loud music from the car's stereo muted her cries. She fought hard but before her fear paralysed her to surrender herself to the look-alike beasts, the car came to a screeching halt. The three looked in front of the car. The triplets' faces paled one by one while a bright smile appeared on Rivanah's face. There was a jeep in front of them. A siren was flashing above it. Two policemen were standing by the jeep. One of the triplets started backing their car but was soon sandwiched by a police vehicle from behind. Four policemen—two from each vehicle—came towards the car and knocked on the darkened windshield. By then the two guys had let go of Rivanah inside the car. She unlocked the door and got out, almost kicking out one of the guys who looked as if he had peed in his pants. The policemen took the three guys inside one of their jeeps. Rivanah meanwhile kept looking all around as if she knew *he* had to be around.

'Are you all right, madam?' asked one of the policemen.

'Yes. Who informed you?' Rivanah asked, still looking around.

'Someone named Hiya Chowdhury,' said the policeman.

42

# 6

*Fate is a smell, Mini. Follow it hard and you shall reach me.*

Rivanah had kept all the white cloths she had received embroidered with the messages from the stranger in her cupboard, with the last one on top. The message . . . Hiya's laughter on the doorbell . . . her nightmares . . . these were the dots which she had not been able to connect at all. And before she could ask the stranger about it he had vanished from her life.

Last night when the policeman had mentioned the name Hiya Chowdhury, her jaw had dropped. But the answer to her next question revealed the reality.

'Did she say anything else?'

'She? It was a man.'

And Rivanah realized who it could be.

'What did he look like?' she asked.

'We only received a call at our control room. The details say it was Hiya Chowdhury, a fifty-year-old man living in Byculla. The address is . . .'

Rivanah didn't bother to listen. It had to be a wrong address. But the phone call also meant the stranger had been keeping an eye on her like always, though without making his presence felt. On the one hand she didn't know why he had become so dormant suddenly—was it due to the police threat?—while on the other hand she was happy too, because she suddenly knew she wasn't as lonely as she thought. The stranger was around . . . somewhere near her. Rivanah didn't tell Danny about the incident right then. One of the police jeeps had dropped her back at the nightclub. It was the next night, when Danny and she retired to bed, that she said, 'What will make you jealous, Danny?'

'What do you mean?' Danny was lying sideways, looking at her, resting his head on his hand.

'How did you feel when you saw me dancing with a guy the other night?' Rivanah was lying on her back, looking at nothing specific on the ceiling.

'How am I supposed to feel when you were having a good time?'

'But I wasn't having that good time with you.'

'But you were having a good time, right?'

The fact that Danny still didn't get what she was trying to imply irked her. *Don't you get it, Danny?! I was jealous seeing Nitya and you dance,* Rivanah framed in her mind how she would say it, *and I don't want to see the two of you together again, no matter how much of an emotional catastrophe she is in.*

'Yes, I was having a good time,' Rivanah said aloud. She didn't know why she suddenly couldn't be honest about her feelings with him. Was it because, if she said it, there was a possibility that Danny would judge her? Or was it because she judged her own self?

'What happened? You sound disconnected.' Danny placed his hand across her bosom.

'How long will Nitya stay here?'

Danny understood the subtext of the query. He came closer and said, 'A few more days. Once her medication is over and the doctor tells me it is okay for her to stay alone, everything will be the way it was before.'

'Promise?'

Danny planted a soft kiss on her forehead and said, 'Promise. But I'm sure you will agree she isn't much of a trouble.'

Rivanah took her time before she said, 'Yeah.' She turned towards him and both of them closed their eyes together. After some time Rivanah opened hers and kept staring at Danny as if she was trying to understand herself by looking at him. She had no idea when she fell asleep.

The next day Nitya had to shop for some outfits for the stylist she was working for. She was heading from her stylist's office in Andheri to Phoenix Mall in Lower Parel. She called Danny to ask if he could drop her. He agreed to. Just prior to that Rivanah had called him for lunch at Indigo Deli in Andheri. Danny called her and asked if she could come down to Phoenix instead.

'Phoenix? That's so far from my office. Indigo is fine, Danny.'

'Actually Nitya needs to buy some stuff and she doesn't know the place well and I'm free so . . .'

Rivanah suddenly found she had no option. She could have asked Danny to skip meeting Nitya and meet her in Indigo instead, but she knew there would be numerous calls from Nitya which would make Danny rush through the lunch and leave even before she was halfway through hers.

'Let's meet at Phoenix,' Rivanah said resignedly. She immediately excused herself from her team leader saying she wasn't feeling well and had to go to a doctor. Sridhar let her leave for the day. Of late, he had found her focus at work wavering. He wanted to tell her that he found her sudden unwillingness to go on-site rather weird, and would have actually tried to convince her against her decision, if he didn't have other equally qualified contenders ready to pounce on the opportunity.

Rivanah joined Danny in Andheri after which they picked up Nitya from her office. Then together they headed towards Phoenix Mall. Though Rivanah tried to help Nitya choose the dresses she needed, Nitya's queries were all directed towards Danny. Soon she got tired of butting in with her opinion. The way Danny's suggestions were appreciated by Nitya hurt Rivanah even though she knew it was possible they weren't intended to hurt her. It was the language of insecurity that made her read their behaviour in one particular dimension only. While Danny was involved in suggesting something to Nitya, Rivanah took a couple of steps back. She saw that Danny didn't even notice it; he was so engaged with Nitya. Then Rivanah went outside the store and looked at them through the glass from a distance. The indifference in Danny triggered a sudden and strong urge in her to get his attention. As if that was the only relief she knew of to the itch that her insecurity had become. She looked around casually trying to think of a plan of action to make Danny run to her. Soon she knew what exactly she had to do.

Rivanah headed towards the lingerie section in an adjacent multipurpose store and picked up three bras and three matching G-strings. She went into one of the trial rooms and quickly stripped off her kurti and leggings and her bra. She put on the purple-coloured bra which she had brought with her and clicked a selfie with a pout. She WhatsApped the picture to Danny immediately and waited desperately for him to come online on the app. Half a minute later, he was online. He messaged back: *Where are you?* Rivanah had a mischievous smile on her face. Next she sent a picture of herself in the purple G-string. Danny immediately called up on seeing the picture. She cut the line without answering, smiling all the while. She then sent him yet another picture wearing another set of lingerie. This time when he called her, she picked up and in one breath said, 'The adjacent store, first trial room. I'm waiting.' Within seconds she could hear footsteps coming towards her. Then she looked down. From below the door she could see a shadow moving close to the trial room. On an impulse she unlocked the trial room's door and pulled Danny in by his tee. Before he could speak her lips were on his. His hands were on her butt over her G-string while hers were cupping his face. She smooched him with a deep passion that emboldened Danny to get into the act as well.

'I didn't tell Nitya that—' Danny tried to break off from the smooch for a moment to speak but Rivanah kissed him again. As their tongues slurped each other's his squeeze on her buttocks tightened. In a flash her hand was at his groin and he felt her hand massaging his semi-erect penis over his jeans. Danny had never seen such aggressive sexual behaviour in Rivanah before. On the one hand it aroused him and on the other he was worried about Nitya since he had rushed off without telling her. Danny wanted to break free but he heard Rivanah say, 'Suck me, baby.' And all he could do was rip off her bra and take her right breast in his mouth, sucking hard at the light-brown areola. Rivanah's eyes were shut tight. It had been some time since they had made love. The urgency of it only excited the sexual flame within. Their kiss broke for a moment and there was a sudden eye-lock.

'Fuck me, Danny,' Rivanah rasped.

Danny quickly unzipped, took out his fully erect penis and pulled the string of her G-string. It dropped to the ground. He turned her. Rivanah could now see both of them in the mirror in front. Her own self never aroused her more than it did at that moment. Danny slowly inserted his penis in her wet vagina. A moan escaped her. He was about to start his thrusts when they heard something: Nitya was calling out to Danny in a helpless, forlorn tone.

'Damn! I knew it,' Danny mumbled under his breath, sounding worried and crossed. He pulled out of her instantly.

'Danny! Finish what you started,' Rivanah said. But he paid no attention. In no time Danny was outside the trial room. A highly frustrated Rivanah didn't move for some time. She looked at herself in the mirror. A loser was staring back at her. She took a deep breath and then put on her dress. She went out only to see Nitya crying profusely, holding on to Danny in a tight embrace, resting her head on his chest and telling him that she thought he too had left her like her boyfriend. Rivanah didn't know what to make of it. The salesgirl who had taken Rivanah to the trial room came to her with an annoyed expression. Rivanah gave her a hundred-rupee note for allowing Danny inside the trial room. The moment she did so Rivanah heard Danny shout out Nitya's name. The latter had fainted.

In the hours that followed, Danny rushed Nitya to the doctor with Rivanah quietly accompanying him. She had never seen Danny as worried and tense as he was in those few hours. It scared her because she wasn't the subject of his worry. Rivanah knew she was being acutely selfish but she didn't know what to do if not be herself. The doctor found that Nitya's blood pressure had fallen. She was admitted to a nursing home for some time. By evening she seemed fine. It was the same doctor who had treated Nitya after her failed suicide attempt. He was angry with Danny for being negligent and strictly asked him to keep her out of any kind of emotional turmoil. While taking Nitya back home, Rivanah asked Danny if they should inform Nitya's parents about her condition. Danny gave her a stern look. It was only when they reached home and Nitya was asleep that Danny spoke to Rivanah.

'Nitya doesn't have a father. And she isn't in touch with her mother because her mother married her husband's business partner, which Nitya didn't like. So all she has right now is me.'

They were in the drawing room while Nitya had been put to bed in their room.

'Oh! I never knew that.'

'But you knew that she is emotionally unstable right now, didn't you?' he said, glaring at her.

Rivanah was taken aback by his accusatory tone.

'I did. So?'

'So what was the need for that stupidity?'

'What stupidity?' Only her mouth was moving. The rest of Rivanah was pretty tense.

'Calling me into the trial room?'

'When did I call you?'

'Yeah? Why else did you send me your hot pics?'

'I just wanted to share them with you, Danny. Am I not allowed to do that?'

'Of course you are allowed to. But why did you have to do it when I was with Nitya? You didn't even tell me before you went to the other store.'

'Since when do I have to take your permission before doing something?'

'It's not that. All I mean is just don't make it tough for me.'

'Tough for *you*? Do you know how tough it has been for me since I came back from Kolkata and saw Nitya putting up here?'

'Why would it be tough for you?'

'If my best friend was a guy and I brought him here to stay with us for whatever reason, then wouldn't it be tough for you?' Rivanah felt she could cry any moment. Their spat was fast taking a dangerous turn.

'Nitya isn't here for whatever reason. I think I told you already but it seems you didn't listen properly or try to understand. But now I'm saying it again. Nitya tried to kill herself!' Danny raised his pitch to an extent that jolted her. He had never spoken to her in such a high-pitched tone before. It reminded Rivanah of her cousin Meghna and Aadil. That, she knew, was bad news.

'Why are you shouting at me, Danny?'

'Because I have tried to be gentle and you still haven't got the point.'

'What's the point?'

'The point is Nitya is not well and we shouldn't be selfish.'

'Even if it eats into our relationship?'

Danny gave her a searching look and said, 'Till now it hasn't. But only till now. If you continue to behave like an imbecile then it very well may,' Danny said and walked out of the flat, leaving Rivanah in tears. She felt weak from within, just like she did when she had seen Ekansh with another girl a year back. Only this time she feared this weakness could be irreversible. She somehow managed to stumble towards the couch and collapsed on it, sobbing hard. This dreaded moment where she was made to feel like a loser wasn't alien to her. With Ekansh she didn't see it coming while with Danny she tried her best to prevent it, and yet here she was in the middle of it, all alone. Why was she alone? Wasn't there anyone who could understand why she did what she did? Someone who would say she did the right thing and that Danny was the one being insensitive? Someone who would not judge her but appreciate the fact that anyone in her place would have done and felt the same and whatever she was going through was absolutely normal? Absolutely human? She knew who that someone was . . .

But the question was, where was that someone?

## 7

Danny came back around two at night. He had his own set of keys so Rivanah didn't have to open the door. With Nitya sleeping in their room, Rivanah was lying down on the sofa-cum-bed. The moment she heard the door unlock, she turned around and feigned sleep. She had left ample amount of space for Danny to sleep beside her but he chose to sit on the beanbag instead. She didn't sleep a wink the entire night. By morning she had had enough. Rivanah called all the phone numbers she had stored of the stranger but found all of them still out of service. Earlier maybe it was a luxury for her to connect to the stranger but overnight it had become a need. And a burning need at that.

That day Rivanah went to office with an idea of how to connect with the stranger. Perhaps the only one she knew with whom she could talk, exposing her naked emotional self. She designed a fake document about some fictitious astrological guru with some fake numbers, took a printout and then made exactly fifty-four photocopies of it. There were fifty-five flats in Krishna Towers where she lived in Lokhandwala. When she returned from office in the evening she went to each and every flat with the photocopied pamphlet to hand it over to the residents herself. The real intention was to know if there was any flat which was locked for the world outside but inhabited secretly, just like it was when she lived in Sai Dham Apartments in Goregaon East. To her dismay there was not a single flat that was locked up. Every flat either had families or couples living in it. The probability of the stranger living with a family seemed farfetched to Rivanah. She confidently concluded that the stranger wasn't living in Krishna Towers. And yet the nightclub incident with the triplets was proof enough that he was keeping an eye on her. What was stopping him from contacting her? Could it be . . . ? She finally thought she had got the answer.

Rivanah went to the Goregaon police station. Inspector Kamble who had been helping her with the case seemed more than happy to see her.

'Miss Bannerjee. How are you?'

She found it sweet that he still remembered her.

'I'm fine, sir. How are you?'

'I'm good too. My daughter finally got a placement here in Mumbai. Such a relief it is.'

'That's wonderful!' Rivanah was genuinely happy for him.

'What brings you here? Though I'm sorry nothing has come up about that person who was stalking you.'

'It's okay. I want to take back my complaint.'

'As in, you want me to close the case?' Kamble was taken aback.

'Yes.'

'Why?'

'I don't think the person will disturb me again,' Rivanah said. Her main purpose was something else. And she hoped Kamble wouldn't outsmart her by deciphering it.

'Hmm. As you say. But do let me know if anything comes up.'

'I surely will, sir. Thank you so much.'

Rivanah was made to sign a couple of documents after which she was getting up to leave when Kamble spoke up, 'I want you to suggest something to me on a personal level.'

'Sure.'

Kamble too stood up and said, 'Come.' He led her outside the police station where he stood with her and said, 'Suppose you have chosen someone as your life partner and your parents aren't sure about it, then what should your parents do so you don't get angry with them?'

For a moment Rivanah thought Kamble was asking about her own self.

'I'm asking this because my daughter has a boyfriend whom I don't like, but she says she wants to marry him. I thought, since you are of her age, perhaps you could help me understand how youngsters think.'

'I think you should accept her choice. After all, your daughter has to live with her choice, you don't. So let her have her way. Good or bad, she will have to live with her decision,' Rivanah said, wishing someone would suggest the same thing to her father as well.

'Hmm. Thank you.'

Rivanah exited the police station and looked around for an autorickshaw. She was sure the stranger was watching her. If he could know so much about her then he would also know she had taken her case back. If the police was the reason he was hiding, he better show up now. She climbed into an autorickshaw, burning with curiosity.

Her cold war with Danny continued. She was yet to forgive him for leaving her sexually frustrated the other day. Though she didn't bring it up with him, she hadn't forgotten it. Rivanah didn't say anything when she saw him leave with Nitya. Instead of going to work in the morning, Rivanah went to Dahisar where she used to teach the ten kids: *Mini's Magic 10*. She did visit the place a day after Abhiraj was wrongly caught as the stranger. But she didn't find any kids there then. She asked around but she couldn't get a lead. Her only consolation was that she had done her part by then. She had shared her good luck . . . the kids had learnt to write basic English. Standing near the space where her classes used to take place, she couldn't locate any of the kids. In its place stood a tiny grocery store now. Perhaps the stranger had put those ten kids in some school somewhere as he had once told her he would. Rivanah stayed there for some time, keeping an eye out for any kid entering the place. A few did turn up but none were from the ten she had taught. Though she was crestfallen, standing under the sun and looking around, she somehow felt the stranger might be watching her. Or was it all in her head? Rivanah finally took an autorickshaw to her office.

All along she kept an eye around her. Whenever the autorickshaw stopped at any traffic signal she stepped out of the vehicle and looked sharply at other cars, bikes and autorickshaws till at the third traffic signal the auto driver said, '*Madam, aap utarta kaiko rehta hai? Main barabar leke jayega na aapko office.*'

Embarrassed, Rivanah quickly climbed back into the auto. She was convinced the stranger was behind her. But why was he still not making his presence felt? Especially when she needed him the most.

She got off the auto a little before her office. As she walked on the footpath she kept turning back. She thought one particular man was following her. She stopped and let the man pass by. He did. And he didn't care to look at her even once. Any other girl would have been happy to know the man wasn't interested in her. But Rivanah was frustrated. She would have been happy if the man had turned out to be the stranger. She entered her office premises, conscious that her failure to find the stranger was slowly starting to unnerve her. Why was the stranger not approaching her when it was clear that he was still interested in her? Why else would he send the police to save her? And how else would she know how the hell Hiya Chowdhury was linked to her?

Once in her cubicle Rivanah was informed by one of her teammates that their company had invited a psychiatrist for a one-hour pep talk with all its employees on how to bust everyday-life stress and improve productivity at the workplace. Rivanah deliberately skipped the pep talk but went up to the psychiatrist during the lunch break.

'I didn't attend your session,' Rivanah said, apologizing to the psychiatrist. Dr Bineet Ghoshal looked at her and said with a smile, 'It wasn't mandatory. Maybe you already know how to beat stress.'

*I wish!* Rivanah thought and said, 'I have a problem which I don't think will be solved with pep talks.'

'I'm glad you have at least identified and accepted your problem. We can meet in my clinic if you—'

'I don't want to go there.'

The psychiatrist put his plate down on the table, wiped his mouth with a napkin and said, 'Should we take a walk?' Her vulnerable appearance told him she could be an interesting case study.

Soon Rivanah found herself walking with Dr Ghoshal in the smoking zone of her office which was free from the normal office hustle of the lunch hour.

'Tell me,' Dr Ghoshal said.

'I had this person in my life last year.'

'Your boyfriend?'

'No, not boyfriend. You can say a friend. Special friend.' Rivanah chose her words carefully, knowing full well she didn't know the right word to describe her relationship with the stranger.

'He helped me a lot,' she said. 'Like, from pulling me out from a major emotional crisis to help me grow as a person.'

Dr Ghoshal listened intently.

'And now he has disappeared.' Rivanah didn't think the stranger's ways of helping her were any of the doctor's business.

Dr Ghoshal was staring at the floor, listening attentively as he paced up and down slowly with Rivanah by his side. His deep frown told her he was thinking hard. He suddenly stopped. She stopped too.

'And these days whenever you are stressed you miss this person?'

'Exactly.' Rivanah was happy the doctor knew what she was trying to say, without her having to tell him the entire story.

'You miss him because you want him to guide you or de-stress you by giving you solutions to your problems.'

Rivanah thought for a moment and said, 'Maybe.' A pause later she said, 'Not maybe. That is it. I want support and solutions from him.'

'Cinderella complex,' Dr Ghoshal said.

'Huh?'

'You said he rescued you from an emotional crisis, helped you grow as a person, etc., which means in a way he made you depend on him. And now you have developed a complex.'

'Did you say Cinderella complex?'

'Yes. The name is taken from the famous fairy-tale character where the girl needs some external support to stabilize herself. Here too you need him to stabilize your problems. But don't worry . . .'

Dr Ghoshal walked ahead while Rivanah remained where she was, too stunned to move.

Rivanah started to feel disgusted thinking about the stranger. Very cleverly and manipulatively he had pushed her to rely on him and now when she was an emotional loner yearning for him, he wasn't ready to reveal himself but was still keeping an eye like a true sadist.

After Rivanah went back home in the evening, she started searching the whole flat for possible bugs. She even squashed a couple of cockroaches but they were real ones, unlike the ones she had found in her Sai Dham Apartment. Frustrated and emotionally exhausted she cried out aloud, 'What do you want from me, stranger?' There was no answer. 'I want to share things with you. And I also want to know how I'm linked to Hiya. Or was that a sadistic joke of yours?' She hoped the stranger had heard her, somehow. Rivanah waited for a possible response, looking at her phone. There was none. She slowly collapsed on the floor, drew her legs to her chest and started sobbing.

'I loved Ekansh.' She was talking to herself. 'He dumped me. I loved Danny. He isn't bothered about

63

me the way I want him to be. I can't share everything with my parents. I don't have any friends in Mumbai any more. The ones outside are busy with their life. I thought I would have you at least.' She rubbed her eyes, took her phone and once again sent messages to all the numbers she had saved as 'stranger'.

*Please come back into my life. I really miss you. I need to talk to you. For God's sake . . .*

She kept staring at the messages waiting for them to be delivered. One minute . . . two minutes . . . three minutes . . . she sobbed uncontrollably. A few minutes later she lifted her head and unlocked her phone once. It opened directly to the message screen. There was a small tick against one of the messages. Rivanah immediately called that number. Someone answered after the second ring.

'Hello?' Rivanah said, holding her breath.

Nobody spoke.

'I know you are there so why don't you bloody speak up?'

Still no sound.

'I know I went to the police against you but you didn't leave me with any other option. Hello?'

Some breathing was audible now. Rivanah too paused for some time.

'So you won't talk, huh? You think only you can play games with me? I know I'm still important to you; otherwise you wouldn't have called the police the other night to save me. So here's the deal: I'll wait for an hour. Only one more hour. If you don't call me back I'm going to kill myself. And I'm serious about this,' Rivanah said in one breath and cut the line. Her heart was racing fast as she waited for her phone to ring. He couldn't *not* call.

*He will call . . . he will call . . . he will call*, Rivanah kept repeating under her breath. One minute became twenty with no call flashing on her phone. And with each passing minute fear ate away at her. What if the stranger didn't call? When the fifty-ninth minute came she found herself perspiring with every second. And then the doorbell rang thrice in a row, just the way Danny rang it. She was slightly taken aback. Rivanah stood up, realizing Danny and Nitya had been out since morning. Somehow she didn't desire any company right now. She wanted to be alone. Rivanah reluctantly went to open the door. As she was unlocking it she turned back when the lights of her flat suddenly went off. She turned back to the front door to see who was there but by then the corridor's light had gone off too. In the pitch-darkness a strong fragrance of Just Different, from Hugo Boss, filled her nostrils. Rivanah knew who it was but before she could call out to him she passed out.

# 8

Rivanah shifted a bit, trying to open her sleep-laden eyes. She felt something soft touch her skin, a white satin bedsheet, and realized she was lying on her stomach. In a flash she turned and sat up. Her clothes were the same as the ones she was wearing the previous night. She looked around and didn't know where exactly she was. It was a tidy room with everything in its place, the interiors were posh and the ambience was cosy. But there was a haunting silence in the room which scared Rivanah. Looking around she knew she was alone and yet she had a feeling she was not. She turned right to see a small bedside table atop which there was a lamp, a menu and a telephone. The menu card had the name 'The Taj' written on it in bold. Below it was the reception's number. She drew herself closer to the table and picked up the phone. She dialled the reception.

'Good morning. The Taj, reception. How may I help you?' said the light voice of a man.

'Hi, I'm Rivanah Bannerjee. I am speaking from your hotel . . . I guess.'

'Yes, ma'am. You checked in last night. Any problem?'

'Who brought me here?'

'One second, ma'am.' Rivanah waited with bated breath.

'Hello, ma'am.' The receptionist was back on line. 'You were brought in here last night by Mr A.K. Bannerjee.'

For a moment Rivanah thought she was hearing the name for the first time and then realized it was her father's.

'What?'

'Mr A.K. Bannerjee,' the receptionist repeated.

'But he is my father,' she blurted.

'Oh, okay.' The receptionist didn't know what else to say. It didn't matter to him who this guy was. The fact that he had already paid for her room's expenses as well as the breakfast was all that mattered to him.

'Ma'am, we have been instructed to serve you breakfast. Please let me know whenever you are ready. I'd be happy to inform room service on your behalf.'

'How did my father look?'

'Sorry?' The receptionist did have an inkling when she was brought in an unconscious state the previous night that something was wrong. Now he was sure: this girl was mad. Why else would anyone ask what his or her father looked like?

'I mean, what did the person who brought me here look like?' Rivanah rephrased the question. It sounded the same to the receptionist.

'He was tall, with a wheatish complexion, long curly hair and . . .'

'And . . .?'

'I'm sorry but that's all I remember, ma'am.'

'Hmm.' *So it wasn't Baba,* Rivanah thought.

'Should I send the breakfast now?'

'In some time,' Rivanah said and put the phone's receiver down. The last thing she remembered was opening the flat's door. She had threatened the stranger before that. And now she was here. A slight smile appeared on Rivanah's face. *The threat worked!* The stranger didn't want her to kill herself. It only meant he was still interested. And he was interested because she was important. But why here in this hotel room? Another thought dawned on her. Neither her parents nor Danny knew where she was. She looked for her mobile phone but it wasn't there. She picked up the hotel landline once again and dialled the reception.

'Good morning, The Taj reception.'

'I've lost my phone and I urgently need to make a call.'

'Please press zero first followed by the number you want to call,' the receptionist said.

'Thanks.' Rivanah put the receiver down and then picked it up again to dial Danny.

'Hello.' He picked it up pretty late.

'It's me.' She wanted to sound normal but she couldn't.

'Hi.' Danny was cold too. 'How is the seminar going?' he added.

'Seminar?'

'You messaged me last night saying you were going to Pune for a seminar?'

Rivanah couldn't believe it. And yet she believed it. This was nothing compared to what the stranger had done before to her, for her.

'Yes. The seminar is indeed going well.'

There was an awkward silence.

'When will you be back?' Danny asked.

'Soon.'

Both wanted to say 'love you' but neither said it and the call ended with a dry 'see you' instead.

She called her parents next. God knows what the stranger had told them, she thought.

'Mumma!'

'Mini, thank God that you messaged; your baba and I were really worried.'

'Messaged what?'

69

'That there's some network issue in Mumbai. And you aren't able to call. We tried to call but your phone was unreachable. Is the network all right now?'

'Yes, Mumma, how else do you think I'm calling now?' In a way Rivanah was thankful to the stranger that he did inform her parents else they would have been in Mumbai this morning. She was talking to her mother when the room's bell rang. She said bye quickly and went to open the door. It was room service.

'French breakfast for you, ma'am,' the man in the hotel uniform said, holding a tray. Rivanah moved aside as he entered the room. He went in and put the tray on the centre table. The man went to one side and pressed a button on a wall. The curtains in the room slowly began to draw themselves to a side. And the view that came up left Rivanah spellbound. She could see the Gateway of India at some distance and the bustling crowd around it. She had never seen Mumbai from this point of view.

'Enjoy your breakfast, ma'am.'

Rivanah turned to see the man leave and locked the room's door behind him. She came forward and inspected the tray. It had some fresh fruits in a bowl, a couple of crepes, a croissant and jam and cafe latte in a long glass. The timing of the breakfast couldn't have been better. Rivanah applied some jam on the croissant and took a bite—it was delicious. She was full after

70

having half of it, gazing out the giant window. Picking up the cafe latte, her eyes fell on a tiny pen drive lying below it. She kept her coffee aside and picked it up. On it was written: Mini. She frowned. Did the hotel boy know about it? Or had it been placed here without anyone's knowledge? She looked towards the big LED television in the room. She went and plugged the pen drive in, and in no time she was checking its content using the remote. There was a video there. She played it.

'Oh my God!' she gasped as she watched the video. It showed the badly bruised faces of the triplets. All three looked dazed. And all of them were muttering the same thing: *I'm sorry, Mini*. Rivanah didn't know what to do with it. Precisely then she heard a sound. She listened hard. Somewhere something was . . . ringing. Rivanah paused the video and followed the sound to a corner of the room which had a dressing table and a closet. She opened the closet which was empty except for a small old Nokia phone placed on one of its shelves. She picked it up. A private number was flashing on it. She answered the call.

'Hello,' Rivanah said anxiously.

'Hello, Mini.'

It was the stranger! The voice was deep, solid and piercing.

'Are you the . . .?'

'I'm the one you were seeking so desperately.' This time the voice changed to that of a kid. Rivanah frowned but realized instantly that the person must be using a voice morphing software and was probably calling from a computer.

'This isn't your real voice?'

'Is this your real self?' He sounded like an old man this time. The question made her recollect something: *When was the last time you made a terrible, terrible mistake?* The stranger had asked her this many times.

'What's up with this video?'

'The triplets who tried to take advantage of you the other night. They went scot-free after bribing the police. And the next weekend it was some other girl they tried to hunt. So I hunted them down and did a few things so that they never hunt again.'

A smile shone on Rivanah's face.

'Thanks for helping me the other night'.

'You are welcome, Mini.'

There was silence. Rivanah was happy to connect to the stranger. Perhaps the psychiatrist was right. She indeed was suffering from the Cinderella complex. She took her time to frame her next question and kept it simple.

'Who is Hiya Chowdhury?' she asked.

'If I had to tell you I would have done so by now.'

'So, you want me to know but you don't want to tell me?'

'You are becoming smarter, Mini. I like it.'

A tiny smile appeared on Rivanah's face. After a long time she was feeling calm talking to someone. Only she knew how much she had waited for this.

'So, you are not going to tell me anything about Hiya, right?'

'No.'

'And you won't let me rest too if I don't seek the answer myself?'

'You are not only smarter now but you are getting to know me too.'

The tiny smile stretched into a big one. She would find out how exactly Hiya was linked to her but before that she had other things on her mind.

'I have things to tell you,' she said.

The silence that followed told her that the stranger was listening. She continued, 'I presume you know what's happening between Danny and me. Nitya has come to live with us and—'

'I know.' The stranger cut her short.

'Well, I feel my relationship with Danny is slipping out of our grasp . . . maybe *my* grasp. It makes me feel miserable. I'm losing myself too in the process.'

73

'You can't hold on to something by questioning it all the time.' The stranger was back to the deep, piercing male voice.

'How can I not question it? From the time Nitya has come into our life, our house, I have almost been compelled to see what I kept myself away from earlier—Danny and Nitya together. Yes, I'm jealous. Maybe I won't admit this in front of Danny or Nitya, but I won't hide it from you. I'm jealous of the closeness they share. Somewhere it makes me feel my connection with Danny is inferior. The exclusivity I thought I enjoyed, I see Danny giving it to Nitya. And I don't like it one bit.'

'We presume that with love comes exclusivity. Since we presume it, we believe it even more strongly. With love comes only one thing: honesty. And honesty is different from loyalty. Most of us never get this difference. Most of us never remain happy in a relationship either.'

'But I'm both loyal and honest.'

'Choose your gods wisely, Mini, for they'll decide how well you fight your demons."

'Meaning?'

'If you were honest then you wouldn't have suffered so much within you. You would have expressed it all to Danny.'

'But if I do that then he would think I'm an insensitive, jealous bitch.'

'What do you have a problem with, Mini? Whether you are an insensitive, jealous bitch or Danny knowing that you are one?'

This time Rivanah was left with no words.

'Am I one?'

The stranger's response was a prolonged silence.

'What should I do?' Rivanah said, concerned. 'I don't want to lose Danny.'

'Go away for a while. Sometimes physical distance throws light on what emotional closeness conveniently eclipses. Whatever he isn't able to see right now perhaps will be clear to him once there's some distance.'

'You mean I should stop living with him?'

'Precisely.'

Rivanah thought hard and said, 'You told me about Ekansh's affair once. So . . . what I mean is . . . could you help me find out if Danny and Nitya are having an affair behind my back? Look, I just want to be sure. It will help me—'

'I can do that for you.'

A wave of relief encompassed her as she said, 'I can't thank you enough.'

'You can thank me by resigning from your job,' the stranger said.

It took a few seconds for Rivanah to understand what she had heard. She said, 'Resign from my job? Are you out of your mind?'

'This isn't your job, Mini.' For the first time he sounded threatening during the call.

'I secured this job during the campus recruitment in my college with my hard work. Whose job is it then, if not mine?'

'Do I need to name her? I thought you were becoming smarter, Mini.'

Rivanah's lips slowly parted with astonishment.

'Who the hell is Hiya Chowdhury? I don't even remember her face,' she said.

'She is the bridge.'

'Why the hell can't you meet me and clarify everything once and for all?'

'If I clarify everything, then the purpose will fail.'

'What's the purpose?'

A few silent seconds later the stranger said, 'Know your worth, Mini.'

# 9

Rivanah came back to her flat an hour after her talk with the stranger ended. Nitya opened the door, showing no pleasure or displeasure in seeing her. It was only a plain 'Hi' that Rivanah blurted which was reciprocated with equal plainness from Nitya's side. Danny came to the drawing room all dressed up.

'Hi, dear. I have to leave now. See you in the evening.' He kissed her cheek and went out. Nitya had disappeared into the kitchen by then. Rivanah went to the adjacent window and looked down to see Danny drive away from the parking spot below the apartment. He didn't even ask if she had had her breakfast, if she would rest or go to office . . . nothing! Most importantly he didn't even care to know if the seminar had actually happened or not. Had he really started taking her for granted? She could have had an affair and Danny wouldn't know. Worse, he wouldn't inquire. Had things come to such a rotten state or was she thinking too much? Or was it Nitya who was slowly blurring her presence for him? Rivanah felt a thud in her heart. Was the stranger right? Should she distance herself a bit to make herself and the problem of their relationship more visible to Danny? Considering there indeed was a problem and she wasn't exaggerating.

That day, Rivanah searched for her appointment letter in her mail's inbox. She clicked it open and read the contents carefully. It was *her* appointment letter. Tech Sky had come to her college. She had cleared the prelims first and then the HR round. She remembered it clearly, so how could it be Hiya's job? She searched with 'Hiya Chowdhury' in her mail. No mails came up. Clueless, she carried on with her office work. The pressure at office made her forget about the issue for the time being.

When she came back in the evening to her flat she found Nitya alone. She joined her for a cup of ginger tea in the drawing room after freshening up.

'The ginger tea is amazing,' Rivanah said, sipping the tea.

'Thanks.'

'No work today?' Rivanah was being kind to her and trying to strike up a conversation only to unknot whatever she had against Nitya within her. Maybe there was indeed nothing between Danny and Nitya, she thought, and tried hard to believe it.

'There was but I did it over the phone,' Nitya said with eyes fixed on the television.

'How are you feeling now?' Rivanah said, looking at the television where a boring soap was going on.

'You want me to leave the flat soon, don't you?' Nitya said, still not looking at Rivanah. The latter looked at Nitya with a taken-aback expression. She wasn't expecting her to interpret what she said this way. It disturbed her.

'Why would you say such a thing?' Rivanah said, not caring to hide her irritation.

'Because you are jealous of Danny and me, isn't it?' This time Nitya turned to look straight at Rivanah.

'Jealous? Why would I be jealous?' She was, she knew. But she didn't owe a confession to Nitya.

'I would have been. Namrata was.'

'Namrata?'

'Danny's ex-girlfriend.'

Danny did tell her about Namrata but it was in passing and Rivanah didn't remember much.

'Well, I'm not Namrata,' she said. And then added spitefully, 'And yes, I would like to know by when you can leave, if not soon.' She knew she shouldn't have been so rude but Nitya asked for it, she told herself.

'Maybe tomorrow. Or maybe never. Maybe this time you will have to leave,' Nitya said in a casual tone.

But in that casual tone Rivanah could feel a pulsating threat.

'What do you mean?' She put the cup of ginger tea away.

'I don't know whether you have understood till now or not that Danny is not the marrying type. It's not that he won't marry *you*. The fact is he won't marry anyone no matter how close he is to that person. And that way we both are similar. Even I'm not the marrying type.'

'But I'm sure Danny will change for me even if for a second I presume what you said about Danny is right, doesn't matter how much I doubt it otherwise.'

'I have known Danny for the last nine years.'

*I knew Ekansh for six years and still I didn't know shit about him.* 'I'm sorry, but you still don't know him yet. Moreover, you know him as a best friend and I know him as a boyfriend. There's a difference.' The last part was meant to injure her. The last part was deliberate.

'Why don't we test it?'

'What for?'

'Just to find out who knows Danny better?'

'Is it some kind of competition?'

'Are you getting scared, dear?'

Rivanah and Nitya's eyes remain locked for a few seconds after which the former said, 'Okay, how do we test it?'

'Ask him about marriage. If he agrees to it then great and if not . . .'

'If not?'

'Then you will know you are wasting your time . . . just like Namrata was.'

One thing Rivanah was sure of now: she wasn't wrong about Nitya's vibes. They wouldn't have had this discussion otherwise. She indeed coveted Danny secretly. It was possible she envied the closeness that Danny and Rivanah's relationship had in comparison to hers with her ex. Rivanah went to her room without stretching the talk.

Danny came home late at night. He was hungry. Rivanah had thrown whatever Nitya had cooked for him in the trash can and cooked for him herself. With a fake smile plastered on her face, she listened to Danny rave about how successful his audition was and how much the producer had liked him. There was no interruption from Nitya. In her mind Rivanah was preparing herself. Once Danny switched off the lights in their bedroom, she first closed the door and then came close to sit beside him on the bed.

'You want to say something?' Danny said, looking at her in the dark. She was glad the lights were off. She didn't want to see his reaction but only hear it.

'Let's get married, Danny.' She put it to him simple and straight.

There was a momentary silence. Her mind said it was hesitation, while her heart said otherwise. Somewhere in between she died.

'Sure, baby,' Danny mumbled.

For a moment Rivanah wanted to jump up with happiness and then realized Danny could be joking.

'I'm serious,' she said. Danny sat up.

'You can't be.'

'I am.'

'What about your parents?'

'So, are you waiting for them to give a nod to our relationship?'

'Obviously!'

'What "obviously", Danny? You know they won't ever agree to this.'

'Then why are you suddenly so gung-ho about it?'

'You and I love each other. Isn't that a good reason to be gung-ho about it?'

'It is, but why now? Why can't it wait till I get something concrete?'

'So, we will get married right after you secure a movie deal?'

'Of course we will. Why, don't you want to marry me?'

She heaved a sigh of relief. It was only now that Rivanah wanted to see his expression.

'Statue!' she exclaimed. After a long time their love story was experiencing a sunrise. She slowly kissed him all over his face while Danny tried to keep still with a funny expression on his face. She looked at him once, smiled naughtily and then kissed him again; this time harder, biting his nose. She lifted his hands and took his tee off. Lying on his back Danny tried to move but she glared at him.

'No movement, Mr Statue,' she said and pulled the elastic of his knickers, tugging down his briefs. She was excited to see his penis was already hard. She gave him an amused smile as she started blowing him slowly. Suddenly everything seemed back to normal. It wasn't the sex alone but the sense of acute belonging that it brewed in her that excited her the most. As Danny locked his jaws with pleasure, Rivanah tugged her shorts and panties down and rode him. She herself placed his hands on her butt and put hers on his chest. As she started riding him she wondered how Nitya would react if she saw them now. It aroused her even more and she increased her speed. She intentionally moaned with a higher pitch than usual so that Nitya heard them. She collapsed on Danny's chest as both climaxed together.

'Can't you statue me every night?' Danny whispered in her ears. She looked up at him and laughed. As her laughter faded they looked into the other's eyes. They spoke a truth: he was hers. She was his. So what was the problem? She gently placed her head on his chest as he wrapped his arms around her. They went to sleep like that.

Rivanah woke up after some time, took out a post-it slip from the bedside table's drawer and wrote on it: *Surprise, surprise! Danny and I are getting married. You are invited!*

She took the post-it and went to the drawing room. Nitya was sleeping there. She noticed her phone by her side. Rivanah stuck the slip behind Nitya's phone so that she would wake up to it first thing in the morning. And with a victor's smile she went back to her bedroom. Danny was asleep but she wasn't sleepy.

She opened her laptop and logged on to Facebook. She updated: *After a really long time—feeling blessed.* While checking out her friends' updates, an idea struck Rivanah. She checked for Hiya Chowdhury's profile on Facebook. To her surprise she found one. The profile picture was a girl's photo taken from a side angle. Someone she didn't remember. She and Hiya had three mutual friends. All of them were her college batchmates: Sumit, Sonakshi and Ritam. Could they know something about Hiya that she didn't? The rest of the pictures and information was locked. There was no cover photo either. On an impulse she clicked on the Add Friend button before she remembered Hiya was no more. Who would add her? There was no way she could see Hiya's other photographs. Rivanah scrolled down and saw the last timeline post by someone named Argho Chowdhury. The post said: *RIP Hiya di*. She clicked on Argho's profile, which had a close-up of him wearing sunglasses. As Rivanah scrolled down his profile, a particular piece of information caught her eye: Argho's current location. It said Mumbai. And he had updated it exactly the day Rivanah had come to Mumbai a year back. *A coincidence?* Rivanah was wondering when she received a notification which made her break into a cold sweat: *Hiya Chowdhury has accepted your friend request*.

# 10

Rivanah swallowed the lump in her throat before clicking on the latest notification on her Facebook profile. The next instant she was on Hiya Chowdhury's profile once again. Only this time nothing was locked any more since her friend request had been accepted. Rivanah clicked on the photo section. Except for the profile picture, there was no other photo. It was difficult to make out Hiya's face in the profile picture. She checked that it had been uploaded some time last year. The date didn't have any apparent significance. She checked her friends list. There were a total of fifty friends. Apart from the college batchmates Rivanah knew none. Of course there was Argho Chowdhury as well. She quickly checked her timeline. No posts except for one. And that one made her heart stop for a second. It read: *I'm super excited. Tomorrow my dream company is coming to my college for recruitment. Please pray for me.*

The message had been posted two days before Tech Sky came to their college. And they had recruited only one student from their batch: *Rivanah Banerjee*. She immediately messaged her on Facebook: *Who is this?*

The next minute a 'Seen' appeared beside her message along with the time. *Who could be operating the account? The stranger himself? Then why would he not respond?* Rivanah wondered and waited for a reply. None came. An hour later her eyes started to ache. She pushed her chair back and went to her bed with a clogged mind. She had to think about what was happening but she didn't know where to start. Bouncing off her thoughts from nothing to everything to anything, she finally surrendered to sleep.

Next morning the first thing she did was check for a reply from Hiya Chowdhury's account on Facebook. There was still none. While leaving for her office, she noticed Nitya looking at her. Her face told her that she had read the Post-it. It was Rivanah's way of telling Nitya that not only was she wrong, but she better keep her unwanted and untrue opinion to herself in the future. She closed the door behind her and walked off, feeling happy after a long time.

Once in office Rivanah logged on to her Facebook account from her desktop computer. She went directly to Messages. There was still no reply from Hiya

Chowdhury's account. She clicked on her name and realized it wasn't hyperlinked. It meant either the user had blocked her or had deactivated the account. She quickly copied the URL from her browser, created another Facebook account and pasted the URL on the browser. The profile didn't open. Hiya Chowdhury's profile had been deactivated. *Shit!* Rivanah muttered under her breath. Her gut feeling told her this account would never be activated again. But then why was it active for this long anyway? *Only for me to stumble upon it?* She answered her own query. *That's odd*, she thought. But everything about this whole Hiya Chowdhury mystery was, in one word, odd.

Rivanah kept thinking about it. During lunch the fact struck her that only Argho's comment was visible on Hiya's timeline apart from her status update about the company's arrival in college, which told her it could be a possible clue to something. Or . . . a dreadful thought occurred to her at that moment. Was Argho . . . the stranger himself? *To reach me you have to reach yourself . . . Hiya is a bridge.* Rivanah was astounded at this link. Could it be that she had finally spotted the stranger? She would know only if she met up with Argho Chowdhury.

From the canteen Rivanah went back to her desktop and opened Argho's profile. She was close to clicking on the Add Friend button but stopped. *What if this profile too gets deactivated like Hiya Chowdhury's?* Rivanah instead clicked on the About Me section of Argho's profile. It opened to tell her that he worked as an HR person in a start-up IT firm called Neptune Solutions Technology Pvt. Ltd. Rivanah googled the IT firm's name and went to its official page. She further explored its Contact Us section and came to know the office was in the Mindspace area in Malad West. There were a couple of landline numbers too. She called up and told the lady who answered, 'Hello, I would like to talk to Argho Chowdhury.'

'Certainly, ma'am,' the lady said, but before she could connect to Argho, Rivanah cut the line. She only wanted to know if there was an Argho working there or not.

In the next two minutes she made a decision. The decision gave way to a plan. Rivanah would zero down on Argho and follow him first to see what he was up to, and only if need be, she would introduce herself. The plan was put to execution. She complained to her team lead that she had indigestion and had thrown up three times. The team lead gave her a half-day. She immediately left her office and took an autorickshaw to Malad West. She located the IT firm quite easily. She didn't go inside. If Argho was indeed the stranger then he would know her. In that case, if he saw her, he would either approach her or avoid her. Moreover, how do you

89

enter a company office when you have no appointment or interview? Either way, she didn't want him to notice her just yet. Rivanah once again called the front office landline number of the firm. When the phone was picked up she directly asked if Argho Chowdhury was available.

'Yes, please hold on,' the lady on the other side said.

'Excuse me, but what are the working hours?'

'9 a.m. to 6.30 p.m. Please wait while I get Argho sir on the line.'

Rivanah immediately hung up. Her job was done. Argho was inside at the moment. She looked around and noticed a cafe across the street. She went inside and took a seat from where she could keep an eye on who was going in and coming out. She was sure to identify Argho because she had perused every unlocked picture of his.

At around 6.30 p.m., people started moving out of the building. By then Rivanah had had three cups of coffee. She stood up with her eyes fixed on the exit. She prayed hard that she wouldn't miss Argho because the chances of her missing him were more than those of spotting him in the surge of people. A few more minutes of waiting and then she saw Argho coming out, talking on the phone. He walked to the bus stop and stood there, smoking a cigarette while continuing to talk on the phone. Rivanah prayed he didn't have a bike or any vehicle; otherwise following him would be tough. Soon, he dropped the cigarette, stamped it out and climbed into an auto which had slowed down by the stop. Rivanah quickly took an autorickshaw herself and asked the driver to follow Argho's auto. The driver did exactly as he was asked to. It was only when the auto reached Andheri West station that she saw Argho getting down. She too got down, paid the auto driver and started following him on foot.

As Argho took the West–East bridge, she too did the same. There was a good hundred metres between them. All she wanted to know was where he lived. Once she knew that she could find out a lot more and most importantly if he indeed was the stranger.

Suddenly Argho kneeled down. Rivanah turned around and in a flash had her phone against her ear as if she was talking to someone. Her heart was in her mouth. She could feel her body was trembling slightly with tension. From the corner of her eyes she noticed Argho was only tying his shoelace. She relaxed. And started following him once he started walking again. He crossed the bridge and finally took the direction for the metro. For Rivanah it was the first time at the Mumbai Metro. Looking around cluelessly, she tried to do whatever Argho was doing. She took the escalator to move up like he did, went a floor above the ground level, walked straight, took a turn and saw Argho in the ticket queue. She tried but couldn't hear which station he was heading to. She took another queue and as she reached the ticket window, she turned to see him pass through the security check.

'Which is the last stop?' she asked the girl behind the ticket counter.

'Versova at one end and Ghatkopar on the other,' the girl said indifferently.

Rivanah knew Versova was towards Andheri West where he could have taken the auto itself which meant he was definitely going somewhere towards . . .

'Ghatkopar,' she said. She got the ticket and without caring to take her change rushed towards the security check, after which she proceeded to the automated gate where she touched her ticket on the top of the machine for the gate to open. She passed through it looking ahead. Argho was climbing the stairs for the Ghatkopar-bound train. Rivanah almost scampered towards it, waited by the stairs for a moment and then climbed up. She was gasping for air when she reached the platform. A casual glance to her left told her he was standing amidst other men at a distance. The metro arrived in the next minute.

Men were blocking the door through which Argho had entered. Rivanah entered two compartments ahead but walked through the vestibule and reached the same compartment as Argho's. She hid herself behind a tall man in a way so that she could keep an eye on Argho without him noticing her. One after another, stations went by and Argho finally moved out at Saki Naka station. So did she. Following him, she reached the exit. He was waiting for the elevator with a few others. Rivanah waited at a distance, knowing she couldn't risk going close to him just yet. As he entered the elevator with the others and the door closed, she hurried towards the escalator. But to her frustration she realized the escalator was going up. The only way she could go down was by the elevator. She waited with some others hoping Argho didn't go out of sight. She rushed into the elevator the moment it arrived again. In a few seconds it took her to the street below. As she came out on the street outside another set of people rushed into the elevator. She looked around. There was no sign of Argho.

*Damn!*

'Madam, is it yours?' said someone who was about to enter the elevator.

It was a white piece of cloth with something embroidered in black. It was not hers. But she knew it was definitely meant for her. She stretched her hand and took it from the person. The elevator door closed. She read the message on it:

*I'll be glad if you get to me. But once you do, you shall destroy yourself forever, Mini. The choice is yours.*

For a moment she couldn't breathe. The passive-aggressive threat that the message communicated hit Rivanah hard. She could feel a certain fear escalate right from within her guts. She took out a bottle of water from her bag and drank from it. There were two things hovering on her mind right then: one, she had finally zeroed in on the stranger; two, the cloth message also told her that Argho knew she would come after him. Once again she looked around but knew she had lost him for the time being. Or maybe he was looking at her from somewhere. She checked her phone for some message, perhaps from an unknown number. There was nothing. Disappointed, she took the escalator up and went back to Andheri first and then home.

She opened the flat with her spare keys. The silence told her there was nobody inside. She switched on the lights and was about to take off her sandals when her phone buzzed with five messages. For a second she thought it could be the stranger—Argho—messaging her. She checked the messages. A couple of audio messages from Nitya. She played the last one. Nitya's voice said, *Congrats indeed, Rivanah*. She played the second-last audio message and heard Danny's voice. What he said stole the air out of her lungs.

## 11

Rivanah was sitting on one of the two La-Z Boy chairs in the drawing room, trying hard not to think about the messages Nitya had sent, and yet she could still hear Danny's voice from the audio. Her body temperature had risen a bit and she could feel anger gushing within her like a fierce wind. And with the anger there was a certain instability that she could feel that wasn't letting her think straight. The doorbell rang after a good one and a half hour. Nitya's laughter was audible and so was Danny's. Rivanah got up and opened the door. The way she stalked back to the chair without even caring to look at them piqued both Danny and Nitya. Danny immediately sensed something was wrong.

'What happened?' he asked.

Rivanah, with a straight face, glanced at Nitya once. There was a slight hint of amusement on Nitya's face which told Rivanah she knew exactly what had happened. Rivanah gave the phone to Danny. He took it and played the audio file. He knew exactly when this had been recorded. In the morning after Rivanah had left for her office, when Danny was having his green tea with Nitya sitting on the couch in the room he was in right now.

'*I don't know what to do really!*' Danny's voice from the audio reverberated in the quietness of the room.

'*Why, what happened?*' It was Nitya's voice.

'*Whenever Rivanah talks to me about marriage it just gets to me. I want to be with her, but I don't know why she keeps harping about marriage all the time. As if we are in a relationship only to get married. Why does she do it?*'

'*Did you tell her that?*'

'*You think she'll understand? I always have to lie to her face that we'll get married, but the whole idea of marriage screws my mind up. I love Rivanah. But this one thing about her just irritates me.*'

'*So you don't want to marry Rivanah?*'

'*No, I don't want to. I mean I don't understand the need for marriage.*'

The audio was over. Danny didn't know where to look. He had said whatever he felt in the audio and that made him feel all the more guilty. He couldn't look at Rivanah. He turned to Nitya instead.

'What's this?' he asked.

'Rivanah said you would marry her. I said you won't. A little game between us which she thought she won last night.' She glanced at Rivanah and said, 'You now know who won, don't you?'

Rivanah didn't look at Nitya. Looking straight at Danny, she said, 'Why couldn't you tell me this?'

'I wanted to, but I was scared that you wouldn't understand me.'

For a moment everything about Danny seemed like Ekansh to her.

'What else didn't you tell me, Danny, safely presuming that I wouldn't understand it?'

'Trust me; I haven't hidden anything from you.'

'*Trust?* If you don't already realized it by now, then let me tell you: this "trust" becomes a funny thing once you realize the person can lie to you.'

'I didn't lie to you, Rivanah. I just—'

'Yes, you lied. And don't you try to tell yourself or me otherwise. When I asked you last night you said you were more than okay with marrying me. Why can't you men just be straight about a few things?' Rivanah turned and was about to dash towards the front door when Danny grabbed her hand.

'Let go of me, Danny.' She was fuming.

'I'm sorry, Rivanah. It's not what you think. I can explain. I love you,' Danny pleaded.

Rivanah shot a glance at him. *I can explain . . .* the same words Ekansh had once used. When you are a tourist every place is exciting but as a native every place is the same, monotonous. The first day she had seen Danny in a towel she had been a tourist. Now she was a native. She knew him better. A bud of an ironic smile stretched her lips but before it could flower further, Rivanah checked it.

'I understand, Danny, and that's why you don't have to explain anything.' She shook his hand off and added, 'Just message me when you won't be home; I will come and clear out my stuff.'

'What? Where will you stay?'

'Never mind.' Rivanah spoke softly this time. She stepped out and shut the door behind her. For some time Danny stood still, looking tense and anxious. Then he looked at Nitya who was now sitting in the La-Z Boy where Rivanah had been a moment back.

'It wasn't just a game, was it, Nitya? You wanted her place, right?' Danny said.

'No, Danny. What are you saying?' She stood up and came to him and, putting her hands around his neck, said, 'I wanted *my* place, not hers. Don't you get it? You and I were always supposed to be together. It was foolish of me to get into another relationship, but, after the break-up, I realized if there is someone who will always understand me, that's you, Danny. That's you!'

'Before recording that message, didn't you think that I actually loved Rivanah?' he said, removing her hands from around his neck and moving away.

'I did, but then Rivanah and you don't have a future. You said so yourself in the audio. You both want different things from the relationship. But you and I want the same thing. I will never ask you to marry me. *Never ever.*' She tried to come close again but Danny stopped her.

'I want you to go back to your flat, Nitya.'

'Danny . . . listen . . . you are not able to—'

'Right now, Nitya, before I forget you were my best friend once.'

Nitya staggered. Danny went into the bedroom and locked himself in.

From her flat in Andheri Rivanah took an autorickshaw straight to Meghna's place in Goregaon East. She had called her to check if she was at home. She was. Rivanah kept rubbing her tears off but they didn't seem to stop. She knew there were things that even she had never told Danny about, and she was blaming him for the same emotional crime that she too had committed. And yet she couldn't bring herself to forgive him. She wouldn't be able to go back to the flat. That was final. Would she go back to Danny? She wasn't ready to answer this because she didn't yet know if it was even a question.

Meghna opened the door for Rivanah. She was meeting her after nine or ten months. After she had left her place Rivanah had gone to live on her own for the first time. So much had happened since then, she thought, and hugged Meghna.

'You remember your Meghna di only when you need something, no? Where were you all these months?'

'I'm so sorry, Di. I always wanted to call up and meet but—'

'But time flies, I keep busy and all that. It is okay; even I give the same excuse to everyone.'

They laughed as Meghna welcomed Rivanah into the drawing room. Meghna excused herself to finish some office work on the laptop while Rivanah relaxed on the sofa-cum-bed in the drawing room. The same one on which she had had the most amazing phone sex of her life with Ekansh. Where did that time go? What happened to that Rivanah who was so happy with life? *Life kills you more acutely than death*, she thought and tried to close her eyes to sleep when the doorbell rang.

'Mini, will you please see who it is?' Meghna shouted from the bedroom.

'Sure, Di.' Rivanah stood up and went to open the door. It was a young guy with spiked hair, red tee, royal-blue denims and Converse shoes. His ears were plugged with white earphones. He took out the earplug on seeing Rivanah.

'Yes?' she said.

'Umm . . . This is where Meghna lives, right?'

His accent told her he was from the North-east. 'Yes,' Rivanah said without registering why such a young guy would refer to Meghna by name.

'Then who are you?' he asked.

'I'm Rivanah, her cousin. But who are you?'

'I stay here.'

'Excuse me?'

'I live with Meghna.'

Before Rivanah knew it, her jaw had already dropped. Meghna was standing behind her by then.

'Come in, Riju,' Meghna said. Rivanah slowly moved out of the way as Riju came in.

'Freshen up. I will make tea for you,' Meghna said. Riju nodded and disappeared inside. Meghna closed the door and said, 'Aadil and I are divorced now. Nobody at home knows. And I hope you will keep it to yourself,' and went to stand by the window in the drawing room. She knew Rivanah would come up to her.

'Aadil da and you are divorced?!'

'We tried our best but it didn't work out.' There was silence, after which Meghna continued, 'Or maybe we didn't really try our best because we knew that if we did we would have saved our relationship but neither of us wanted that. A saved relationship is no relationship, after all.'

'I don't understand it, Meghna di. Why would you not want the relationship for which you guys fought your families?'

'I don't want to go into it again, Mini. I only know that, with Riju, I'm trying to make a start. A fresh start at life.'

'But he looks like a—'

'He is a second-year college student. Thirteen years younger.'

'And you are okay with it?'

Meghna looked at Rivanah and said, 'Aadil was someone I fell in love with. Wasn't I okay with him? I have stopped bracketing relationships with good, bad, right, wrong, okay, not okay.'

The breeze coming in through the window ruffled Rivanah's hair. She brushed a few strands of hair away from her face, still unable to process what she had heard.

'I will prepare tea for all of us,' Meghna said and went to the kitchen.

Rivanah had nothing against Riju but she couldn't bring herself to talk to him properly for the rest of the night. When they sat together for dinner she could see Meghna was happy with Riju: the way they talked, touching each other at the slightest of excuses, holding hands while eating, and the way Meghna took care of him was proof of their love. And yet all of it disturbed Rivanah. She knew whatever Meghna was doing was because of lack of an option. Age wasn't the factor but the way Meghna was trying to fit into the relationship that she said she shared with Riju didn't seem organic to Rivanah. Would she too end up like this? She wanted to call Danny and tell him that she forgave him and that marriage wasn't necessary and that they should start afresh. But then she realized she was a human being after all. And with human beings everything has a ramification. Her coming to this flat would have a ramification as much as her going back to Danny now would. What if he started taking for her granted all the more?

Rivanah went to the washbasin and splashed some water on her face. Her mind was akin to a traffic signal where no thought vehicle was following any rule. And they caused one messy traffic jam. As she rested on the sofa-cum-bed and tried to sleep, she thought about what would have happened had Ekansh not cheated on her. By now she would have been living with him, making more and more memories with him. He must have applied for an MBA but before that she would have made sure they were engaged. Two more years and they would have gotten married, moved abroad to some beautiful place and spent their life happily together. But it didn't happen. What happened was that Ekansh turned out to be a dog. It taught her a simple truth: even if you love someone truly, things could still turn out badly. She turned on the sofa-cum-bed trying to force herself to sleep when she heard the doorbell. She checked her mobile phone lying beside her. It was 11.30 p.m. She remained still, hoping Meghna or Riju would come out and open the door. Then she recollected the two had gone out for a late-night movie after dinner. They had asked her but she had cited a false headache. The doorbell rang again. Rivanah got up and went to the door. She looked through the peephole. And she had her heart in her mouth.

'Hiya!' she mumbled to herself with fear churning her guts.

# 12

Rivanah pulled herself back from the door, her heart racing and hands trembling. Her knees felt weak. This couldn't be possible. Hiya Chowdhury was *dead*. People whom she trusted had confirmed this for her. The doorbell rang again. *This is not even a dream*, Rivanah thought, and once again looked through the peephole. Hiya Chowdhury was still standing there wearing a salwar suit.

'Who is this?' Rivanah asked aloud. Her voice had a scared trill to it.

'Didi, it is me . . . Swati.'

A slight frown appeared on Rivanah's forehead and she immediately opened the door.

'Swati?' she said, looking at the girl whose picture she had seen as Hiya Chowdhury's profile picture. Though the picture on Facebook was not very clear, she could tell it was her picture. A closer look and she knew who this Swati was. The last time she had seen her, Swati had been in a dishevelled and bruised state in a municipal hospital in Borivali. Swati had been gang-raped near Aarey Colony. And Rivanah was instrumental in putting those gang rapists behind bars.

'What are you doing here?' Rivanah asked. This was the first time she was actually talking to her.

'My mother asked me to thank you for what you did and give you a hug,' Swati spoke in Hindi but with a heavy Marathi accent.

'You came to thank me at this hour? And how did you know I live here?' Rivanah couldn't hide her surprise.

'I know it is odd, but my mother said a lady told her that this is when you need a hug the most. She gave her your address too. You have done so much for me. A hug at this hour is the least I could do.'

A *lady* . . . Rivanah didn't waste a second trying to figure out who this lady could be. Someone the stranger must have tipped to approach Swati's mother. By now she knew it was useless to go to her and inquire about the stranger.

'Whatever it is that is bothering you, Didi, will be over soon,' Swati said and hugged her.

At least there was someone in this whole world who knew when she craved a shoulder to cry, a hug to dissolve herself in, Rivanah thought, and hugged Swati back tightly. In no time her eyes were wet. She felt like she was emptying herself. As if those tears were words which she was sharing with Swati but in reality were intended for Danny. She could feel Swati's hand caressing her back as if to tell her: cry, if that's what you think will help, then do cry. After some time Rivanah let go of Swati.

'I shall forever be indebted to you,' Swati said before taking her leave. Rivanah was about to close the door when Swati turned back.

'I forgot. Aayi asked me to give you this. The lady gave this to her.' Swati took out a piece of white cloth from her shabby sling bag and gave it to Rivanah. She took it in her hand. By then she knew what it could be. She read the message embroidered in black: *There's a belief according to which the world of the dead and the world of sleep are connected.*

Rivanah swallowed a lump reading it. *World of the dead . . . Hiya . . . world of sleep . . . the nightmare?*

'And this too,' Swati said, giving her another piece of white cloth.

*Resign from your job ASAP.*

Rivanah was momentarily lost in thoughts when she heard Swati say, 'If you could help me fight such a terrible crisis, I am sure you shall fight yours too. All will be well. Bye for now, Didi.' Rivanah smiled at her before closing the door and wondered what Swati's picture was doing in Hiya's profile. Moreover, Hiya was her batchmate in college. Then why the hell couldn't she remember her face though she remembered her laughter? Till she saw her profile picture on Facebook she thought she had a vague image of her in her mind. The kind which clears up the moment the person or her photograph comes in front of you. But the truth was she didn't remember Hiya Chowdhury at all. And the stranger was taking advantage of it. But why would Argho comment on a fake Hiya's profile? The clouds of confusion hovered in the sky of her mind. There were too many questions and none with any lead to a solid answer. Well, there was one lead. The stranger . . .

The doorbell rang again. It was Meghna and Riju. He had his arm around her shoulder while she had hers around his waist. Something about it made Rivanah abhor them. Why was she being so judgemental about them? Was it because Meghna had found happiness with a guy much younger than her or was it because she hadn't been able to find that happiness with Danny?

'Hey, Rivanah, what's up?' Riju said.

'Still awake?' Meghna said.

'I was about to sleep,' Rivanah said and went to the sofa-cum-bed. Riju and Meghna locked the door and went to the bedroom.

Lying alone on the bed, Rivanah could see the moon outside. She wondered why the stranger wasn't telling her who Hiya Chowdhury was. Why was he playing this game with her? Then she realized the stranger was all about games to begin with. She couldn't resign from her job just like that. It was her identity, the only alternative where she could afford to immerse herself and forget other troubles. Every time she ran from something, it was work that came to her rescue. How could she simply resign? How would she sustain herself? What if she didn't get another job immediately? And then Rivanah suddenly sat up. Something struck her. The stranger had asked her one thing repeatedly: *What is the most important thing in your life?* And she had time and again told him it was Danny. But only now she knew the answer. It was her job that was most important.

She immediately wrote a message for the stranger on her phone and sent it to all the phone numbers she had saved with her.

*I need to talk.*

A minute later only one of them showed a delivery tick. And right after that her phone rang, flashing a private number.

'Hello, Mini.' It was a man's voice.

'I finally have an answer to your question.'

'I'm listening.'

'You asked me what the most important thing in my life was, right? It is my job. I can't leave it. I can't resign else my life shall collapse.'

'I know.'

'You do? If you know then why are you asking me to resign?'

'So that your life collapses.'

'I want to be really clear with you. I have nothing—absolutely nothing—to do with Hiya Chowdhury. In fact I'm sure you are the one who put Swati's picture on Hiya's profile. This proves I don't even remember her. Then how can you expect me to do away with the most important thing of my life for her?'

'It's not for her. It is for you. You have to resign for your own sake.'

'You know what that would mean? What if I don't get another job?'

'We presume a lot by merely looking at a road. But presumptions limit us, limit our life. You have to walk the road to really know what it has to offer.'

'What if the thing this road has to offer is a big nothing?'

'If you walk a road well, then it will at least offer one basic thing.'

'What's that?'

'You will know your worth a little more, Mini. Every road is an opportunity to know yourself . . . bit by bit. Tougher the road, bigger the bit.'

Rivanah took her time to frame her next question. Should she ask the stranger if it was Argho Chowdhury on the other side? He must know by now that she had been following him, so what was the harm? But what if he didn't know she was following him? Just what if . . . ?

'I need time to think,' she said.

'Think. And think fast. Maybe this road has to offer you something which you are eager to reach.'

'And that is?'

'Me.' And the line went dead.

*Dammit!* Rivanah thought. She was sure she wouldn't resign but this last bit from the stranger was just the teaser she could have done without. *Oh no, I can't resign just like that.* Her mind was quite numb. She wanted to know how Hiya Chowdhury was linked to her but she couldn't find a way to do so. She wanted to know who the stranger was and now it seemed she had a chance. But it wasn't a mere chance. Resigning from her job sounded more like a price. The stranger had told her before that the job wasn't hers. That was absurd. In fact everything about the stranger was absurd. With sleep being a far cry, she turned over when she heard a moan. Suddenly it went up several decibels. Meghna was moaning out Riju's name. Rivanah shut her ears with both her hands and then after a moment she released her hands only to hear Riju's groan this time. The moans and groans reminded her of too many things and too abruptly: of Ekansh and her, of Danny and her, of Nitya and Danny, of Aadil and Meghna, of everything she didn't want to be reminded of. She rushed for her earphones, put them on and played a random song on her phone. She finally relaxed. Earlier it was Meghna–Aadil's fights which drove her out of the flat and now it was even more irksome. She knew she would have to look for a flat for herself. She checked her phone. There were no messages from Danny. Not a single one. She hadn't messaged him either. So, going back to his flat was not even an option right now. The song she was listening to paused as her phone's screen flashed a private number. She took the call.

'What is it, Mini: yes or no?'

'I'm sorry; I can't resign. And you don't have to tell me anything about Danny and Nitya either,' she said. 'It is—'

'Yes or no?'

'No!'

There was a momentary silence.

'Just to remind you, Mini, every yes or no has . . . consequences.' The stranger cut the line.

# 13

When the stranger said 'consequences', Rivanah knew it wasn't a joke. It scared her but you don't resign from your job because you are scared of someone whom you have no idea about. More than the stranger this time, she was afraid of the one word the stranger had used: *consequences*. She had had enough of 'consequences' in her life. And she was tired of them. Falling in love with Ekansh had consequences, splitting up with him had consequences, choosing Danny, now staying away from him . . . staying with parents made her meek; living alone made her aware. Life is all about consequences and how you deal with them because Rivanah by now had understood nobody could run away from them. She would have thought more about this if her phone hadn't buzzed with a WhatsApp message just then:

*How are you?*

It was Danny. He had finally found time to message her.

*Good*, she wrote back.

The ticks turned blue telling her Danny had read the message. But no reply came. She typed: *And you?* She sent it.

*Good.* The reply was instant this time.

*Hmm.*

*Hmm.*

It was their first official cold war where ego was the deciding factor. With this particular set of messages, she knew, their relationship had entered a new phase; whether it was backward or forward she had no clue. She stared at the WhatsApp message for some time. Danny was online and so was she. But neither communicated. On an impulse she tapped on the phone and it went back to the home screen. Suddenly furious, she switched off her data network and shut her eyes.

The next morning Rivanah left for work before Meghna and Riju had opened their bedroom door. The first thing she did was log on to Facebook to search for flats. Unlike a year ago, now she knew exactly how to talk and negotiate with dealers. She was happy with one particular flat in Goregaon East itself. The dealer had told her the place would be shared by only one more girl. It was a 2 BHK where they would have a room each for themselves as well as a drawing room. Her share was to be twenty-five thousand rupees a month but she managed to bring it down to twenty-two a month. She told the dealer she would be there in the evening after office to check out the place and finalize it if she liked it.

'Hey, Rivanah, did you see this?' It was her team lead Sridhar. Before she could turn and look at him, Sridhar leaned to show her something on her desktop. Though Sridhar had this indecent habit of gaping at her breasts while talking, never before had he come this close to her. His face was too close for Rivanah to be comfortable. She tried to push her chair back but found Sridhar's leg blocking it. He was showing her some Facebook video he could have easily asked her to see from his seat. Why this sudden inclination to come close? 'I'll just be back from the washroom,' Rivanah lied, excusing herself before he could come any closer. Sridhar moved his leg from behind her chair and she pushed it to stand up.

She turned to look at Sridhar who was gaping at her. Till then a mere eye-lock always made him look somewhere else but this time it was Rivanah who looked away.

Right through the day Rivanah caught Sridhar looking at her in a manner she couldn't decipher. It was as if he wanted her to say something. She kept wondering what it was the whole day in the office. After work, Rivanah went to see the apartment in Goregaon. It was on the twelfth floor. The view of the distant hills from the bedroom window made her waste no more time. She told the dealer she would complete all formalities the next day and move in the day after.

'That will be great, madam.' The dealer was happy to have sealed the deal in a day.

'But do you have any idea who will stay with me in the flat?' she asked.

'Not yet.'

'I don't want any weird girl as my roomie,' Rivanah said, remembering Asha from her previous flat. And at the same moment she missed Ishita too. It had been some time since they had had a talk. She made a mental note to contact her soon as she heard the dealer say, 'The other room is still not occupied. And don't worry. You can ask anyone. My record is clean as far as tenants are concerned. No weird people ever.'

Rivanah flashed a plastic smile and said, 'See you tomorrow morning at the registrar's office.'

That night when Rivanah told Meghna about the shift she said, 'Let me know if you need my help.'

'Sure, Di,' Rivanah said, hoping she wouldn't need any such help. Meghna had started to remind Rivanah of what she could pretty well become in the near future. And she didn't like it one bit. Severing herself from Meghna was her priority.

The next morning Rivanah took her luggage to the registrar's office where an eleven-month contract was drawn between the landlord and her, after which she gave the landlord eleven post-dated cheques, went straight to the furnished flat with the keys, put her luggage there, and immediately left for office.

In the office Sridhar yet again kept looking at her expectantly. And during lunch he WhatsApped her: *I'm okay with it.* What was he okay with? Rivanah had no clue. She was about to ask him when someone cleared his throat and asked, 'Are you Rivanah Bannerjee from Sridhar's team?'

She looked up to see a middle-aged man with a slight paunch and a receding hairline looking down at her. His ID was hanging from his neck. She read his name in a flash: Bitan Dey.

'Yes, that's me.'

'Hi, I'm sure you don't know me. I just wanted to tell you that it's okay with me. We can meet after office if you are free. See you.' And he walked off.

*It's okay with me*—the phrase struck Rivanah hard. Something was wrong. She immediately WhatsApped Sridhar back: *What are you okay with?*

*Whatever you wrote in the email*, Sridhar replied.

*Which email?* Rivanah's heart was already racing. She was expecting a WhatsApp reply but Sridhar called her instead.

'The email you sent me a couple of nights ago.'

'But I didn't send any email to you.'

'Come on, Rivanah. It was from your office ID. You don't have to feel shy. It's okay with me.'

Knowing fully well who had sent that mail, Rivanah was disgusted.

'I want to read the email. I'm coming to your desk,' she told Sridhar and cut the line. Before she went to Sridhar, she quickly went to her desktop and checked her Sent Items folder in her office mail account. There was no email from her side to Sridhar or Bitan—by now she had guessed why he had approached her. She dashed to Sridhar's cubicle. The latter was waiting for her with his email open on his desktop.

'Now don't tell me it's not you. See, it has come from your official email ID. Dated day before yesterday; the time was 7.30 p.m.'

Feeling a knot in her stomach she went close to the desktop computer and read the email that she had supposedly sent Sridhar:

*Hi Sri,*

*I have a confession to make. I've started having this thing for you, like a wild animal has for a forest. Will you let me explore the forest?*

*XOXO*

*Rivanah*

The first thing she did was delete the mail.

'What are you doing?' Sridhar said, trying to push her away but by then she had deleted it from the Recycle Bin as well.

'Why did you do that?' Sridhar looked at her, clueless.

'My office mail was hacked. I never sent this email,' Rivanah said.

Sridhar looked at her for some time and knew she was telling the truth. The email was too good to be true.

'Hmm. You did the right thing by deleting it. But we must catch whoever executed this vulgar joke. I'll register a complaint with the HR.'

'I know who did it,' Rivanah said in one breath.

'You do? Who is it?' Sridhar sounded amazed.

'I don't know the person yet.'

Sridhar frowned and said, 'You know who did it but you don't know the person yet?'

'Never mind. You can complain if you want to, but I don't think it is going to help.' Rivanah turned and slowly walked back to her cubicle, leaving a confused Sridhar behind.

*Every yes or no has consequences*, the stranger had told her.

In the evening, when Rivanah opened the door to her new flat and stepped in, a whiff of something familiar stopped her dead in her tracks. It was the smell of Just Different from Hugo Boss. The next instant she groped frantically for the switchboard, realizing the obvious: the stranger was in the room; but none of the switches were working. Her first instinct was to run but the stranger's voice stopped her.

'Chill, Mini. I won't harm you,' the stranger said. It was a male voice not matching with any of the ones she had heard till now. Though the voice was slightly mechanical, she could sense he was in the room, only a few feet away from her perhaps.

'Just close the door.'

Rivanah took her time but eventually closed the door to let the darkness engulf the room and her totally.

'You hacked into my office email,' she said, knowing that was obvious. And also knowing how much her voice trembled with fear. Add to it her temporary blindness.

'I could have done worse. You know that.'

'Can you, for God's sake, tell me whether you are a friend or a foe?' Rivanah slowly pushed herself against one of the walls in the room, feeling slightly claustrophobic in the darkness.

'If I was a friend then I wouldn't have hacked your email.'

'Exactly!'

'But if I was a foe I would have sent Sridhar the video I have of you. You know which video I'm talking about, right, Mini?'

Rivanah knew it was the same video that he had made when he attacked her in the flat, tearing her clothes off and tying her up.

'Then what are you?' she gasped.

'I'm neither a friend nor a foe. I'm what you want me to be.'

There was silence. Rivanah could feel her throat drying up as she said, 'What if I still don't resign?'

'People in your office will get more emails. Maybe this time with a video attachment.'

Exactly what she had feared a moment back, Rivanah thought as she swallowed a lump.

'This is blackmail,' she mumbled.

'This is me for you.'

A moment later Rivanah said meekly, 'Will you actually send that video out?'

'Don't you try me on this, Mini.'

Rivanah knew the stranger had made her helpless once again. She would have to resign. She would have to let go of the most important thing in her life. Her job. Her identity. A symbol of her independence. And who knows when she would get another job? What if she did and had to return to Kolkata? No, she couldn't just resign. The dormant rebel in her suddenly woke up. The stranger was only few feet away. If she rushed at him while screaming, he could probably be caught.

Yes, he could be caught! And in all probability, it was Argho Chowdhury standing somewhere in the darkness around. On an impulse Rivanah sprang forward without really knowing where the stranger was in the room. She hit a centre table and fell to the floor shrieking out in pain. The lights came on. She turned to look all around the room and at a corner by the window she saw a mobile phone and a tiny speaker attached to it. Her leg throbbing, she almost crawled to the phone. She picked it up only to notice the call was still on.

'Exactly by noon tomorrow you should resign.'

# 14

Rivanah went to office an hour later than usual. From early in the morning she kept looking at her watch every minute. And with every second she only had one question in her mind: would she actually resign?

The protocol for resignation at her company was simple: anyone wishing to resign had to log on to their internal company portal, log in with one's unique credentials and then click on the Resign button. The employee could revoke it only within twenty-four hours after he or she clicked on the Resign button. She kept staring at the button but couldn't summon enough courage to click on it. Yet. At 11.30 a.m., she messaged all the numbers she had of the stranger.

*Can we please do without my resignation?*

The next second came a reply from one of the numbers: *Sure, we can.*

For a moment Rivanah couldn't believe her eyes. She relaxed, gulping down some water from the bottle on her desk. She finally started her work for the day. Sometime later she got a message from another number which too she had saved in the stranger's name.

*But whatever we do . . . has consequences, Mini.*

Rivanah glanced at the watch. It was 12.01 p.m. *Past noon!* She looked around to see if she could spot something amiss. *The stranger won't circulate the video. He may say whatever he wants to but he isn't her foe*, she thought. It was precisely then she saw Sridhar walking towards her. Had the stranger forwarded him the video? *Damn,* she muttered under her breath, feeling her throat go dry.

'What's up, Rivanah?' Sridhar inquired.

Rivanah stood up from her chair.

'Why did you resign?' he said.

'What?!'

Rivanah turned in a flash and logged on to the company portal as quickly as she could. As the page loaded, her phone flashed a private number. The page loaded and she noticed her Resign button actually read Revoke which meant someone had already clicked on the Resign button. She immediately was in two minds whether to pick the call up or not. Slowly she answered her phone while taking the mouse to the Revoke button.

*'You click the Revoke button; I'll click the Send button on the email with the video attachment.'*

The line was cut.

'Now don't tell me someone hacked the system and resigned on your behalf,' Sridhar said, expecting Rivanah to come up with a valid explanation.

A few seconds later, Rivanah removed the cursor from the Revoke button and looked at Sridhar guiltily. The latter shrugged.

'No, it wasn't hacked. I've actually resigned.'

'What? Why?'

'I don't know. I'm sorry. Please excuse me.' Rivanah stumbled to the washroom like a ghost and, locking herself in one of the toilets, cried her heart out. Her notice period would begin soon: a total of thirty days. After which she would have to stop coming to office. What would she do after that period?

When she went back to her cubicle, two of her teammates told her the same thing: *This is your worst decision, Rivanah.* Sometime later, another teammate came to her and said, 'I know you must be joining another company, otherwise who resigns just like that? Could you please forward my CV there too? I won't tell anyone here.'

'I'm not joining anywhere else.'

The teammate stared at her and then went away, probably sensing something was wrong with her, and acting as if that something could well be infectious.

Rivanah knew she would soon have to find another job for herself or else it would be difficult for her to survive in Mumbai. And this thought gave way to another thought which felt like a stab: did the stranger want her to leave Mumbai? She sent a message—*I want to talk*—to all the numbers she had of the stranger. But didn't care to check if the message was delivered or not. Her mind was trying to crack the reason behind why the stranger would want to push her out of Mumbai. And where to? Kolkata? Or . . . wherever Hiya Chowdhury's family was?

She got a call from a private number. She took the phone and moved out into the smoking zone where there were only a few people. Once there she answered the call.

'Hello, Mini.'

'Why do you keep giving me such pain?' she asked.

'Let me tell you an amazing thing about pain.' The stranger spoke in a woman's voice this time. 'You give it; you'll get it.'

'How have I given pain to anyone?'

There was silence.

'Okay, now that you have made me resign I want that video of mine. I can't allow this blackmail to continue. Or else I'll be forced to involve Inspector Kamble once again.'

'It was you who said you will kill yourself if I don't come back. It's not good to complain about the chicken you hatched yourself.'

'Every time I start to believe you are a dream, you push me to believe that you are a nightmare. Why?'

'I'm neither your dream nor your nightmare, Mini. I'm what you want me to be.' With this the line went dead.

Rivanah realized it was useless, simply useless, to talk with the stranger about what his intention was. The sooner she reached the truth behind Hiya Chowdhury, the quicker she would be able to decipher what the stranger was all about. But how could she know the truth about a person she remembered nothing about? Not even how she looked. And Hiya Chowdhury was supposed to be her batchmate in college. Or so she had been told.

# 15

Rivanah came straight to her flat after office. Without caring to switch on the lights, she slumped down on the bed in her room. On her way she called Danny once but there was no answer. But a minute later came a WhatsApp message saying he was in a shoot and would call her at night. Reading the message she did feel bad that she hadn't responded positively when he had messaged her a few days back when she was in Meghna's flat. She didn't even know if Nitya was still living with Danny or not. It was not that if she wasn't, Rivanah would go back to live with him again. Somehow, living in the flat alone now, she was having contradictory feelings. A major part of her was happy to get a private space for herself where Danny and Nitya were no longer in her sight. That somehow plugged her insecurities to some extent. It made her happy. But she was also scared because she didn't know whether she should be really happy about it.

She yearned for Danny's lap, but she didn't want to call him. She wanted him to realize it and come to her. And the last few messages between them told her it wasn't going to happen anytime soon.

'They say my tea has magic in it.'

Rivanah was startled by the sweet voice she heard. She immediately sat up on the bed. By then the tube light had stopped flickering and was on. She saw a young girl standing by her bedroom door with a smile which was even sweeter than her voice. She was slightly frail but had a radiant face and looked like she was twenty or twenty-one years old.

'Who are you?' Rivanah asked.

'Tista Mitra. I shifted here this afternoon.'

'Oh, hi. I'm Rivanah Bannerjee.'

Tista came forward and shook Rivanah's hand.

'Nice to meet you, Rivanah di. I'm lucky to get a Bong roomie. Should I prepare my magic tea? I think you need it.'

There was a pleasant aura about Tista which Rivanah found herself envying instantly. An aura which existed only in those people who were yet to lose their innocence, who had not seen the ugly face of life like she had a year and half back.

'It's okay. I don't—' Rivanah started but was cut short.

'I will make it for myself anyway.'

'Okay.' Rivanah found herself smiling at someone after a long time.

Tista disappeared into the kitchen. Rivanah washed her face and went to the drawing room to find Tista sitting on the couch, stirring one of the two cups of tea with a spoon.

'Here,' she said, holding a cup up for Rivanah. The latter took it and sat down beside her. She was about to sip the tea when Tista stopped her, saying, 'The first sip should always be with eyes closed. Your system should feel that something amazing is going to invade it.' Tista herself took a sip closing her eyes. Rivanah did the same. The tea definitely had something different in it. It made her feel refreshed with the first sip itself.

'Isn't it good?'

Rivanah nodded with a smile.

'It is wonderful!' She was happy to have someone who made her smile for a change.

'Are you from Kolkata, Rivanah di?'

'Yes. And you?'

'Same. But originally I'm from Tezpur, Assam.'

'Working or studying? You look very young.'

'Thank you. I just turned twenty-two. I'm working in Stan Chart. What about you?'

'I'm in IT.'

The more Rivanah started knowing Tista, the more strongly she realized that Tista was what Rivanah had been a year back: naive, simple and ignorant. And because she was all those things she seemed happy all the time. Had she not come across someone like her, Rivanah would have concluded happy people didn't exist.

Tista worked as a relationship manager and had fixed working hours. She was there in the flat when Rivanah left and she was there before Rivanah came back. Though Rivanah hadn't opened up much to her, with each passing day, Tista did so without much fuss.

Neither of the girls entered the other's bedroom without knocking. This was something Tista did to begin with, which Rivanah followed because she liked it. No matter how close one gets to someone, they should always respect the other's privacy. One night, however, was an exception. Rivanah had left a particular book on the dining table but couldn't find it.

'Tista, did you see the book I put on the dining table?' Rivanah said, pushing the door of Tista's room open to see her lying on the bed in front of her laptop. Tista looked at Rivanah once and then at her laptop screen to say, 'My roommate is here. Give me a minute.' Tista climbed down the bed and came to Rivanah.

'I have the book with me.' She picked it up from the table beside her bed and gave it to Rivanah who took it without much curiosity about who she was speaking with. Half an hour later, when Rivanah was reading the book in her room, she heard a knock.

'Yes, Tista.'

Tista came in and sat beside her roomie on the bed.

'It was my boyfriend.'

'Huh?' Rivanah didn't know what she was talking about.

'When you came to my room I was Skyping with my boyfriend.'

*Skype . . . boyfriend . . .* it wasn't an unknown territory for Rivanah but it was definitely one she did not want to think about.

'It's okay,' she said, hoping Tista wouldn't prattle further on the topic.

'I love him a lot.'

'That's good,' Rivanah said and wondered why Tista wasn't shutting up. She was in no mood to discuss boyfriends.

'But I find him very cold towards me,' Tista said. A silence fell which told Tista that Rivanah was trying to understand what she had told her.

'Doesn't he love you?' Rivanah found herself asking.

'He does. I'm sure he does, but there's something that stops him from surrendering to me completely.'

'Where did you guys meet?' It was for the first time since they met that Rivanah had asked her new roomie a personal question.

'Actually, we are engaged. He is my fiancé. It was an arranged thing which our parents decided.'

'Nice.'

*Some people go the simple way by letting the parents choose their life partner*, Rivanah thought. And probably that's better than trying to go after the illusion of getting Mr Right and ending up in a shit pool like she was in.

'Can you please guide me, Rivanah di?' Tista said, breaking Rivanah's trance.

'Guide you?'

'This is my first relationship. And I really don't know what guys want or like when they are in a relationship.'

Tista's innocence made her wonder: how nice it would be if Rivanah too could marry the one with whom she was in a relationship for the first time! Suddenly that fairy tale called first love seemed so painfully desirable.

'Why don't you talk it out with him?'

'I tried to, but he says all's good and that he loves me a lot.'

'Hmm. Are you sure there's no other girl involved?' This came out straight from her experience. A year back she wouldn't have asked Tista such a question.

'I trust him.'

Rivanah looked at her for a moment. That was when she fully realized the difference between Tista and her: Rivanah could no longer say that for anyone even if she wanted to. A momentary sadness clouded her but she was careful not to let it show.

'How long have you guys been in a relationship?'

'It has been three months since our engagement.'

'When is the marriage?'

'Early next year.'

Rivanah thought for a while and said, 'I think you guys should know each other more. Maybe he is the kind who takes time to open up.'

'You know, I also thought of this. Thanks for confirming my idea. I am ready to give him all the time he needs,' Tista said with a smile. 'You read now; I'll leave.' She was about to move out when Rivanah stopped her, saying, 'You are a very good girl, Tista. I am sure the guy is lucky to have you in his life.'

'I hope he knows it too,' Tista said.

*That's the problem with guys: they rarely realize how lucky they are when they get the girl who is perfect for them,* Rivanah thought and smiled back.

With Tista gone, Rivanah put the book aside. The thought that her notice period had begun in office was a torment. And worse she had nobody to share her stress with. She picked up her phone and messaged Danny. He was supposed to call her but he hadn't.

*Do we need to take appointments now to talk to each other?* she messaged.

What she actually wanted to say was: *Asshole, call me. I want to talk.*

Danny's response came in the next instant: *Sorry, was busy the whole day.*

Rivanah's next message read: *What did you have for dinner?*

What she actually wanted to say was: *Is Nitya still there with you?*

Danny responded: *Ordered from Faaso's.*

Rivanah replied: *Hmm.*

What she wanted to say was *Why can't you just tell me if Nitya has left or not?*

Danny messaged: *What else?*

Rivanah's replied: *I shifted to a new place.*

What she actually wanted to say was: *Look, I don't need you all the time for everything.*

Danny's response read: *Good.*

Rivanah thought: *You won't even ask me where I'm staying? Great!*

But she messaged back: *What else?*

Danny's reply came in a second: *Nothing.*

What Rivanah thought while reading it: *Why can't you simply ask me to meet up? I will come, but just ask me first.*

Rivanah messaged: *Okay.*

So the cold war continues, Rivanah thought and stretched herself on the bed.

'Yippee!' Suddenly Tista barged into her room.

'Shit, Tista, you scared me!' Rivanah said, sitting up once again with her heart suddenly beating fast.

'I'm so sorry. Actually my fiancé is coming here tomorrow. He stays in Navi Mumbai. I'm so excited.'

'All right. That's nice. Now may I please sleep? I have office tomorrow.' Rivanah knew her rudeness was an outcome of the frustration that her current equation with Danny was brewing in her. Though Tista didn't show any sign of hurt, Rivanah herself felt bad. The next instant she went and apologized to Tista in her room. And asked what the plan was for tomorrow.

'I don't know. We don't like to go out much. Probably we will be in the flat itself. Let's see,' Tista said.

The next day Rivanah went to office and applied for some job openings on various job portals. Her notice period was on and she desperately hoped she could secure another job before it was over. In the evening she returned to her flat and saw that Tista wasn't there. On other days, she was the one who reached first and kept her magic tea ready for both of them. Rivanah didn't care to prepare any tea for herself and changed to lie down on her bed. She received a call from Tista.

'Look at my luck. My fiancé is coming today and of all days I am loaded with work today.'

'When will you be free?'

'Around nine. I think I will be at the flat by ten. My fiancé will be there in half an hour or so. Hope it is not a problem.'

'It is perfectly fine. I have reached the flat so he won't have to wait outside. Don't worry.'

Rivanah cut the line and checked the time on her phone itself. It was 7 p.m. She decided to cook for herself. Around 7.35 p.m. the doorbell rang. Rivanah went to open the door. Her blood froze when she saw the visitor. She realized he too had a similar expression on his face. He was talking on the phone.

'Yeah, I have reached. Yes, okay.' He handed the phone to Rivanah and mumbled, 'Tista wants to talk.'

She took her time to take the phone with her heavy hands and spoke into the phone, 'Hello.'

'Rivanah di, that's Ekansh, my fiancé. I shall be home soon. See you both.'

# 16

The moment Tista ended the call Rivanah dashed to the kitchen without saying a word, leaving the main door open. Standing in the middle of the kitchen doing nothing, she heard the main door lock. They were alone in the flat now. The last time they were alone in a flat she had lost her virginity to him. The scene flashed in front of her in disturbing detail. The last time she saw him was in Oberoi Mall where she had lost a life to him. And of all people Ekansh had to be Tista's fiancé? How can a cheat like him marry a naive soul like Tista? Trying not to think, she moved towards the oven.

'I'm sorry,' she heard Ekansh say. *Why was he even talking to her? Couldn't he just pretend they were strangers until Tista comes?*

She could sense he was standing by the kitchen door. His sorry still sounded the same. Fake. Why did she expect anything about him to have changed by now? With her back to him she didn't know if he was looking at her or not. For a moment she did try and look from the corner of her eyes. He was looking at her. Then she sensed he was moving towards her. Out of sheer nervousness, she tried to light the gas burner. She wanted to scream out to him to stop and not come close, but she didn't. She couldn't. She saw a reflection on the tiles in front of her. Ekansh was right behind her. The next moment she felt his breath on the back of her neck. All her muscles stiffened. She couldn't even press the lighter's button.

'I'm sorry,' he said almost into her ears. With all her energy she pressed the lighter button again and the burner lit up this time. She felt a hand on her waist. Rivanah immediately turned around to stop whatever she sensed could begin.

'Ekansh, we shouldn't . . .' She wanted to say more but he stopped her with a kiss. Right, wrong, should, shouldn't—the lines between them were blurring. She started to live in the moment and thus welcomed Ekansh's initiation by putting her arms around his neck. She wasn't waiting to kiss him all this while and yet she smooched him hard as if she was hungry for it. As if she was claiming him back in her life with it. As if through the hard smooch she was asking him: how dare you left me? As if she was trying to spin the wheel of time back and by the time the smooch would end they would realize they were still a couple, faithful to each other. She felt his hand on her butt as he lifted her up. She reciprocated by wrapping her legs around his waist. He carried her to her bedroom. It was dark and hence they could be what they were not in the light of the kitchen. In no time their skin was exposed to the other. Rivanah was surprised how deep the echo of the friction of their skin still reached her. And this surprise was the best aphrodisiac she had ever encountered. There was a hunger in Ekansh that matched hers in intensity. She would have stopped everything if she knew there was life waiting after this, but their mutual affinity convinced her otherwise. And sometime in the darkness when Ekansh was inside her she did hear him gasp, 'I love you.' The worst part was she was moaning out the same words. And with each thrust all the good times they shared in the past flashed in front of her. Every time she felt his mouth sucking her breasts Ekansh's face from college came to her. Every time his mouth caressed her lips she was convinced their break-up was only a bad dream.

It was almost an hour later that they moved away from each other, still lying in bed half naked.

In the silence of the room Rivanah could only hear their breathing. And the sound stifled her.

'Please leave the room,' she said, not sure whether she was angry with him or herself or with life or love. Ekansh

141

stood up after some time, pulled on his underwear, got into his jeans and, adjusting his tee, was about to move out when the doorbell rang. Both Rivanah and Ekansh knew who it was.

Ekansh went to the drawing room and opened the front door. It was Tista who had excitement written all over her face.

'I'm so sorry to be late,' she said, spreading her arms and preparing herself for a hug.

'It's totally all right,' said Ekansh, hugging her and speaking into her ear.

She stepped into the flat holding his hand and closed the door behind.

'Your bus reached earlier than I thought it would.'

Ekansh gave her a tight smile and said, 'Yes.'

'What happened? You seem a little . . . off.' She looked into his eyes. He averted his eyes.

'Nothing. It is really nice to see you.'

'Same here. Did you have tea?'

'Not yet.'

'Wait, I'll make some.'

'You must be tired. Freshen up first.'

'It's okay,' Tista said with a smile that said she was already refreshed seeing him. She went to the kitchen and came out immediately.

'Where's Rivanah di?'

'Hmm?' For a moment Ekansh thought Tista had said, 'Why Rivanah?'

'My roomie. Didn't you meet her?'

Tista went to the kitchen. Ekansh was about to say something when Rivanah came out of her room in a different dress. She joined Tista in the kitchen.

'Hi.'

'Did you leave the burner on?'

'Oh shit! I went inside to change and forgot about it.'

'It is okay. I'm preparing my magic tea for us.'

'I'll make it.' Rivanah took over from Tista.

'Thanks,' Tista said and, turning towards Ekansh who had joined them, said. 'Even you haven't changed. I thought you reached here a while ago.'

'I was waiting for you to come back.' His voice betrayed guilt.

Rivanah called Tista to the kitchen when the tea was ready.

'We don't have a problem if you join us,' Tista said.

'Another time.' Rivanah made it sound as warm as possible. Tista was about to go into the drawing room with the two cups of tea when Rivanah asked her, 'By the way, how did you know about this flat?'

'As in?'

'I mean, who gave you a lead to this rented flat?'

'An agent called me saying someone told him I was looking for a flat.'

With bated breath Rivanah asked, 'Who was that someone?'

'I don't know. I didn't ask.' Tista shrugged and said, 'Why are you asking suddenly?'

Rivanah nodded, saying, 'Just like that.'

Once in her room Rivanah pushed the teacup aside. By then she had guessed it couldn't be a coincidence that Ekansh was Tista's fiancé. In fact nothing that had happened to her in the past year or so had been a coincidence. Tista was sent as a roomie to Rivanah so that she could meet Ekansh again. So that she slipped. She picked up her phone and messaged the stranger: *Why did you do this to me? WHY? Wasn't it enough that I resigned from my job? Ekansh and I fucked each other as if there was no before or beyond.*

She sent it to all the saved numbers in her phone but a response came from only one of them: *I only guided Tista to your place. The rest you did to yourself.*

*Don't pretend you didn't know Ekansh wasn't her fiancé,* an angry Rivanah was typing on her smartphone with hot tears in her eyes.

*I told you to choose your god wisely, Mini. I only knew you were confident about your god. And I wanted to test your confidence.*

Which god you are talking about?

*Our god is what we think we are, and our demon is what we actually are. We are often blind to the difference till a situation brings it up. And I told you earlier, Mini, to choose your gods wisely. You chose loyalty as your god. Somewhere you thought you were loyal. Now it is time to face your demon. What you actually are.*

*I didn't want to do it. Trust me, I really didn't want to. I love Danny very much.*

*Now you are choosing convenience as your god, Mini.*

*How will I face Danny? How will I look at Tista? What will Ekansh think of me? And how the fuck will I look at myself in the mirror?* Though the questions were for her, she typed them and sent them to the stranger as if it was her deep-seated conscience she was talking to.

*Don't you think it is time to accept the obvious? You genuinely love Ekansh. You always did, you always will. Love is about attachment, Mini. You understand attachment? It is that chain which even if you break free from, or think you can, you will never be able to do anything about the marks the chain leaves on you. Those marks you take to your grave.*

The message made Rivanah sob profusely. She didn't know what was more disturbing: that she still loved Ekansh, or that she would always love him, no matter what. What was more disgusting: that Danny may or may not have cheated on her, or the fact that she had already cheated on him? Which was filthier: the presumption on which she had initiated a cold war with Danny, or the lie she had used to convince herself that Ekansh was no longer important?

There was a knock on the door.

'Rivanah di, what should we prepare for dinner?' It was Tista.

Rivanah didn't move for a moment. Tista knocked on the door again. Rivanah rubbed her eyes and abruptly stood up. She took a few steps to open the door. And immediately hugged Tista tight. The latter didn't know why Rivanah did that. She still hugged her back as a reflex.

'I'm sorry, Tista. I'm very, very sorry.'

'Why are you crying, Rivanah di?'

'I'm a bad girl, that's why.'

Tista broke the hug and looked into her roomie's eyes which spoke of only thing: contrition.

# 17

'Any problem?' Ekansh came into the small passage between the drawing room and bedroom with a concerned face. He paused, seeing Tista and Rivanah in an embrace. Tista turned to look at Ekansh and said, 'Rivanah di is crying.' There was a momentary locking of gaze between Rivanah and Ekansh. Her eyes had a story. His had the moral of that story.

'I left the burner on,' Rivanah muttered. Tista looked at her in disbelief.

'Oh God!' Tista said with one hand on her forehead. 'You have been crying for that? Come on, Rivanah di.'

'There could have been an accident,' Rivanah said.

'Accidents are not in anyone's hand,' Ekansh replied, looking at Rivanah cautiously.

'But one should be alert especially if there already has been an accident in the past,' Rivanah said.

Tista glanced once at Ekansh and then at Rivanah, with no clue what they were talking about.

'I think I have a solution to this. How about I prepare a lovely dinner for us all?' Tista said, displaying her cute smile to the full.

'No, I will,' Rivanah said.

'You cook?' Ekansh blurted.

'Why do you sound surprised?' Tista asked. 'Rivanah di cooks better than I do.'

Rivanah didn't wait to listen to her praise. She simply walked towards the kitchen, saying, 'You two carry on. I'll tell you when dinner is ready.'

'Let me change and freshen up quickly. Then Ekansh too can change,' Tista said.

Rivanah went into the kitchen. Ekansh stood still for some time till Tista locked herself in the bathroom. Then he ambled to the kitchen.

'It is so nice to know that you can cook now,' Ekansh said.

Rivanah pretended she didn't hear him. Pretence was the only jacket she had to save herself from the winter of guilt. Ekansh stood there for some time and then said, 'Won't you even talk to me?'

'There's nothing to talk about, Ekansh. Not now. Not any more,' Rivanah said without looking at him. She was chopping an onion.

'I'm in need of someone who is ready to listen,' Ekansh said softly.

Rivanah gave him a sharp glance and said, 'Why? Are you now done with Tista because we just met and fucked and you enjoyed it so much that now you think you are in love with me again?'

The spite with which she spoke was enough to silence Ekansh. He turned and went back to the drawing room. Rivanah ate her meal separately even though Tista pestered her several times to join them.

Next day in office she received a call from Danny. She wanted to pick up but an ineffable fear stopped her from answering. She was wondering if she should call back when he called again. This time she took the call, pressing the phone against her right ear.

'I want to meet you,' Danny said. They were talking on the phone after quite some time. And with those words Rivanah understood the worst had already happened. The stranger must have told Danny about what exactly had happened between Ekansh and her in the flat. She shouldn't have blurted that out in a fit of emotion to the stranger. Screwing her up emotionally was the stranger's favourite pastime. This she was sure of by now.

'Are you listening?' Danny said.

'Yes. I have some work . . .' Rivanah's attempt to postpone the meeting sounded pretty unconvincing.

'It's important.'

Rivanah couldn't remember the last time Danny sounded so grim over the phone.

'Where?' she asked.

'Candies, Bandra. Around seven in the evening.'

'Okay.'

'All right, see you.'

He cut the line. What do I tell him? That whatever the stranger had told him was rubbish? There couldn't possibly be any proof of it unless there were hidden cams in the flat. *Were there?* Rivanah held her head which had started to throb slightly. One of her colleagues came and asked her if she had got through any company. She shook her head. And followed up with all the job portals and consultants through phone and mail but there wasn't any opening that suited her profile. Frustrated, she continued working with no interest in work whatsoever.

In the evening Rivanah reached Candies on time and found Danny already waiting for her. They were seeing each other for the first time after Rivanah had walked out of the flat. He looked preoccupied. She didn't know if he had already noticed that she wasn't looking directly at him.

'How are you?' she said, sitting down opposite him.

Danny only took out a large envelope and put it on the table without saying a word. Rivanah frowned. Were there photographs inside? The damned stranger had actually sent Danny photographs of Ekansh and her together? With trembling hands she took the envelope, opened it and took out its contents. There were papers. Legal papers, she noticed. In fact, stamp papers on which was an agreement between a production house and Danny. She looked directly at Danny for the first time in the evening. He was already beaming.

'I have got a movie deal finally!'

'Oh wow!' Rivanah couldn't control her instinctive reaction and she half rose from her seat to hug Danny and congratulate him.

'Though it is not the lead, the production house is good and I'm sure the role will lead to better deals.'

'I'm sure too. I'm so happy,' Rivanah exclaimed. For a moment she actually thought all her problems were solved and that life was smiling at her. Then Danny grasped her hand tightly and said, 'I'm sorry for the last few weeks.'

She swallowed a lump.

'I know I ignored you,' Danny said and continued, 'but I wanted to surprise you with this. The production house got in touch with me a day after you left. I was waiting for the contract to happen. They gave it to me last night.'

Rivanah managed a tight smile. She wanted to know if Nitya was still there with him but somewhere her guilt told her she had lost the right to ask Danny about Nitya.

'Nitya has left too,' Danny said, as if reading Rivanah's mind. 'In fact, I asked her to. I know you were never comfortable with her around. But I hope you understand, being her best friend, I too was duty-bound.'

'I understand,' Rivanah said, her throat feeling bone dry. She turned around and asked a waiter to bring some water for her.

'So, when are you coming back?' Danny asked with that typical charming smile of his which time and again made her feel funny between her legs.

'I have just paid all eleven months' rent. I don't think the landlord will refund it,' Rivanah said and noticed disappointment eclipse Danny's face. He slowly pulled out his hand from hers. Did she say so because she actually wanted to stay away from Danny or did she say it because now she knew she could be close to Ekansh? It was one of those grey questions which one never asks oneself, and if one does, then one evades the answer at any cost.

'Or else I would have,' she said but this was more of an attempt to convince herself that she wasn't choosing Ekansh over Danny. Had she not given the rent she would have definitely shifted, she thought once again.

'Okay. You can always come over, right?'

That I'll anyway have to whenever Ekansh comes to meet Tista, Rivanah thought, and said, 'Yes.'

'Or maybe I could come over,' Danny said with an amused face. She knew what he was hinting at.

'I have a roomie at my place. So, it'll be better if I come over,' she said and shuddered at the thought of what would happen to her if and when Ekansh and Danny were in her sight together.

'That's cool with me as long as you are near me,' he said and leaned forward to whisper, 'I love you, Rivanah.'

Rivanah kept looking at him.

'Why are you crying?' Danny asked. She didn't know when her eyes had flooded.

'Any problem?'

Rivanah nodded and carefully pressed a paper napkin against her eyes so that her eye make-up didn't smudge.

'Did that bugger disturb you again?'

Rivanah paused and looked at him inquiringly.

'The stalker,' Danny clarified.

Should she tell him the stranger had compelled her to resign from the job, had manipulated the situation in a way that she ended up fucking Ekansh?

Rivanah nodded. The stranger may have made her resign but the latter happened because of her own indiscretion. It had to happen, it didn't matter that she had met Ekansh a day before or was meeting him in the future.

'Let's go.'

'But we didn't order anything,' Rivanah said.

'Doesn't matter. I have tickets for the night show of the new Hobbit sequel. Let's get going.'

As Rivanah stood up, Danny held her hand. That one gesture made her feel relieved as well as protected. As if her demons wouldn't be able to get to her in Danny's presence. Danny was almost pulling her along when she called out to him. He turned.

'I love you, too,' she said. Danny came close and, in full view of everyone, caught her lower lip between his lips and sucked it for a few seconds. He looked at her. Rivanah wondered if he had tasted her or tasted Ekansh through her. He smiled and the question lost its relevance in Rivanah's mind for the time being.

They reached the multiplex in the nick of time. In the dark theatre Rivanah kept glancing at Danny time and again. She was happy the cold war between them was over. She was saddened by its timing. If Danny had met her a day or two earlier, she wouldn't have done what she did with Ekansh. It was irreversible. But so was her love for Danny. The stranger had told her she genuinely loved Ekansh and hence she couldn't get over him. Did that mean she had never loved Danny truly? That was absurd because she was ready to marry him, to fight with her family to be his. Would anyone do that if he or she wasn't truly in love?

'I need to go to the washroom,' Danny said and went outside. Rivanah toyed with her phone and then, unable to resist her urge, messaged the stranger. After all she was the one supposedly suffering from the Cinderella complex. And the stranger was one helluva mystery prince.

*What exactly is cheating in a relationship?* Rivanah messaged.

The response came a little earlier than she anticipated:

*Your answer is waiting in the third toilet inside the men's washroom beside the multiplex entrance.*

It could only mean the stranger was in the washroom right at that moment. There was no way he could guess her question. He must be writing the answer there right now for her to find later. Rivanah sprang to her feet and scampered out of the theatre. She walked briskly to the first washroom by the entrance. The door had a man's silhouette pinned on it. All shows were on and nobody was either going in or coming out. She held the doorknob, looked around, took a deep breath and pushed the door open. There was nobody in sight. She entered the washroom. And then she saw someone peeing with his back to her. The guy turned and shrieked.

'What the fuck are you doing here?' Danny said.

*Shit!* Rivanah thought. In the utter excitement of getting to the stranger she forgot Danny had excused himself to the washroom. She had to tell him something, anything but the truth.

'What are you doing here?' she said, feigning surprise.

'It's the men's washroom.' Danny, done answering nature's call, turned to her.

'Oh! I thought this is for girls,' Rivanah said. She was about to turn around when the door to the third toilet opened. Rivanah paused, holding her breath. Danny followed her eyes and looked at the door too. And then at the guy who came out of the door. He didn't know him. Rivanah did. It was Ekansh. She instantly turned around. Her heart was racing like never before and she could feel her body shudder.

'I'll see you outside, Danny.' She rushed out of the men's washroom. She hoped Ekansh had not seen her. But what was he doing there? Or was it another of the stranger's sadistic manipulations?

Rivanah came out of the men's washroom and went straight to the girls' washroom. It was empty except for her. She wasn't able to think properly. The fact that Danny and Ekansh were right there in front of her together had made her go blank. She heard the washroom door being pushed open. It was a female cleaner. She came right up to her and handed her something, saying, *'Kya yeh aapka hai? Darwaze ke pass pada tha.'*

Rivanah looked at the white piece of cloth which the female cleaner was holding. She took it from her and opened it out to read the only word written on it in black thread: *LOL*.

## 18

The first thing Rivanah did after coming back to the theatre with Danny by her side was message Tista to ascertain if she was with Ekansh or not. She was. The film was ruined for Rivanah. She knew Ekansh was there with Tista in another hall watching another film. It stressed her out to think: what if Danny and Ekansh came face-to-face once again while exiting?

'Did you see anyone else when you went inside the washroom?' Rivanah asked Danny in a whisper. He gave her a curious look and said, 'Anyone else?'

'With long hair?'

Rivanah had Argho Chowdhury in mind. Danny frowned for a moment and said, 'Nope. I only saw the guy who came out of the toilet when you were there.'

Rivanah immediately averted her eyes from Danny, knowing he was talking about Ekansh.

'Why do you ask?'

'Just like that. A friend messaged me saying he was here with his girlfriend.'

'Oh, okay.' Danny said and went back to watching the movie. Rivanah didn't like the fact that she had to lie to him. But she knew this was probably the beginning of a series of lies. Why couldn't she simply turn and tell Danny she had cheated on him but it wasn't planned, it wasn't something she thought she would do? It simply happened. He loved her, she loved him. He would understand her. The momentary slip on her part wouldn't affect their relationship. In fact the confession would only cement the break in the relationship which at present only she could see.

'Danny . . .' she blurted, turning towards him.

'Hmm?' He turned towards her. Eye to eye. And the guilt pulled her will to tell the truth somewhere deep within her.

'I'll be back,' she said instead.

'Don't get into the men's washroom again,' Danny said with an amused face. Rivanah gave him a tight smile and stood up. Soon she was out of the theatre. She felt weak within. She sat down on one of the stairs outside, burying her face in her lap. Her phone vibrated with a message. She lifted her face and read it.

*People think cheating is an action like sleeping with someone, kissing someone or whatever. Wrong. Very wrong. Cheating is when you feel the pressure of being faithful to someone because of someone else. When you suddenly realize there's an option. That realization is cheating.*

A couple of teardrops fell on her mobile screen. Another message popped up. It read:

*You are a cheat, Mini.*

Rivanah buried her face in her lap again and sobbed. A couple of passers-by did notice her but nobody approached her. Her phone beeped with a WhatsApp message.

*Where are you?*

It was Danny. She replied: *Coming.* Rivanah wiped her tears, regained her composure and went back inside the theatre.

From the time Danny dropped her at her place that night she wanted to leave Tista and shift to another flat where there was no Ekansh and no Danny. But she had already paid her eleven months' rent which also put pressure on her savings. While signing those cheques Rivanah had had a job. Now she had resigned; she was yet to appear in any interview; and she had only three weeks before she was totally jobless. She felt like a fort that was being attacked from all sides and, though it was standing its ground, Rivanah knew it would be taken over soon. And she had no idea what she would do then. She made it a point to tell Tista to inform her in advance whenever Ekansh was coming over so that she could give them the privacy every couple needed. She now knew from Tista that Ekansh had shifted from Bangalore to Pune and now to Navi Mumbai. He generally came over on weekends. But he didn't stay over. Was it because he too was as sorry as her for whatever happened? Did he tell Tista about it? On the one hand she was avoiding Ekansh because he knew too much about her, while on the other she started ignoring Danny because he knew too less. Though Danny too didn't have time owing to the new film he had signed, she started saying no to him whenever he asked to meet up. Holed up inside her flat alone, Rivanah first tried listening to music at full volume and cooking. It didn't help. She needed something more visually engaging. She watched all the latest American sitcoms till the wee hours of the morning every day, plugging her ears and fixing her eyes on the laptop screen. The content seldom registered with her, but she still used to follow the serials because it somehow kept her mind distracted from the emotional hurricane that ravaged her heart. In office, she lost her interest in work. Every time she sat down to work she knew time was running out. Soon she would have no office to work in. She kept applying to other places but in vain. The only time she forced herself to smile was during the two-minute phone calls to her mother after reaching office, after lunch and post dinner. She developed dark circles in no time and also lost five kilos in twelve days. Her appetite for life was waning. One evening she ended up writing a suicide letter as well, but she tore it up knowing she wouldn't be able to do it. She sat down to watch yet another television series when she realized it could no longer keep her hooked. Time and again her thoughts went back to the fact that she was a cheat. That something which she hated in people had become her definition now. It disgusted her. Tista only acted as a reminder whenever she came to her and tried to talk about what Ekansh and she did. Rivanah tried her best not to sound rude and pretended to listen to whatever she said, but in reality she began to shut herself out. One night while she was idling in her room, Tista came in and said, 'I need to talk to you, Rivanah di.'

There was a grimness in her voice which Rivanah rarely associated with Tista. She only gave her a silent glance. That was enough for Tista to come and sit on the bed.

'Ekansh is still in love with his ex.'

Rivanah could almost feel her heartbeats stop suddenly. Then she relaxed. She was *one* of his exes.

'How do you know?' she asked.

'I don't know. I feel it at times. Like last weekend he and I were in Marine Drive, and we were getting into the mood but suddenly he went off. I asked him but he said the place reminded him of someone else.'

Chances were it was Rivanah he was missing, she thought.

'Who is it? Did you ask him? Did he mention any name?' Rivanah asked.

'No. I thought he may get upset. His past isn't something I should be concerned about, I think. I'm sure if I had a past, I too would have reacted in the same manner.' Tista thought for a moment and then said, 'Can I ask you something, Rivanah di?'

'Hmm.'

'If you had a past would you share it with your boyfriend or keep it within you?'

Each word of that question injured her. She was too stifled to even frame her thoughts.

'Oh wow!' Tista, said catching hold of the electricity bill behind which Rivanah had been sketching.

'I never knew you could sketch too.' Rivanah didn't even realize when she had grabbed a pen and had started to sketch on the bill.

'I didn't know either,' Rivanah said and looked at the sketch. It was a pair of eyes. *Not bad for a first-time sketcher*, she thought. The good thing was that the sketch took

Tista's mind completely away from the question Rivanah dreaded not only to answer but even to consider.

That night, instead of watching yet another TV series, Rivanah sat down to sketch. She used to sketch as a teenager too but she didn't know when she grew out of it. And now sketching a pair of feet, with focus, she felt energized after a long time. Revelling in the rediscovery of her lost hobby she forgot that the day after was going to be her last day in the office. She was reminded of it when she was given a farewell lunch by her teammates the next day. When she came back to her apartment, the security guard handed her an envelope. By the time she reached the elevator she had already taken out its contents: a cheque for fifty thousand and one hundred rupees. The exact amount she was left with in her savings bank account. There was no signature in the cheque nor was there any name written on it.

'Hello, Mini.' Someone spoke the moment she stepped inside the elevator and closed its doors. She turned around in a flash. She looked at the floor of the elevator where there was a mobile phone on speaker mode. She picked it up and said, 'What is it now?'

'You sound as if you are angry with me.' The voice didn't sound like it had the last time.

'You haven't given me any reason to be happy with you,' Rivanah said as the elevator stopped on her floor.

She stepped out.

'The choices were yours, Mini.'

'Yeah, sure. And you had nothing to do with my choices. Anyway, just tell me, what is it?' Rivanah said, pacing up and down her corridor. She knew something was up. The cheque and its amount couldn't be a coincidence.

'I want you to sign the cheque.'

It was then Rivanah realized the cheque was from her own chequebook. Her account number was printed on the left side.

'How did you get my chequebook?'

'I have my ways, Mini. Just sign on it.'

'Who is it for? And why would I sign it? It is my money. The last of my savings.'

'You will sign it because I want you to.'

'You want me to go back to Kolkata, don't you? Why don't you say it?'

'Write on the name section: Mr Dilip Rawat.'

'Who is—?' she was about to ask when the line was cut. A baffled Rivanah kept staring at the cheque.

# 19

After entering her flat, Rivanah was about to chuck the envelope with the cheque in it when she found a SIM card inside. She immediately put it in the phone she got in the elevator. The SIM memory contained a few messages which she read one by one. The first message had an address of a certain Dilip Rawat. It was an apartment in Borivali West. *But why the cheque?* Rivanah wondered, slumping into the sofa. If the stranger wanted money from her then why would he wait till now? Was this Dilip Rawat a way to divert the money to Argho? If the stranger was Argho then he obviously wouldn't give his true name to her. If this was true then whoever this Dilip Rawat was, he was linked to the stranger or Argho as well. And if it was all because of squeezing money then the stranger could have threatened to share the video he had made long back; there was no reason for him to wait this long when he knew she had given more than half of her savings in rent. Rivanah held her head, trying to think as she scrolled down to another message stored in the SIM. It had Tuesday written on it and a specific time. So, Rivanah thought, the stranger wanted her to deliver the cheque to the address on Tuesday—which was the next day—at I p.m. Did she have the option to say no to the stranger? Not as long as he had her video, she told herself. After the attack on her by the stranger in her flat and the subsequent filming of it, Rivanah wasn't confident about going to the address alone but she was curious. She called Danny immediately and asked if he was free in the afternoon.

'So Ms Busy Bee finally found time to meet me,' Danny said. His sarcasm didn't hurt Rivanah for it was justified. It had been more than a fortnight since they met, when they had watched the movie together. She always gave him some excuse or the other and postponed their meeting. Danny's presence brought her guilt to prominence as much his absence blurred it.

'I'm sorry, Danny. Been a little hectic, that's all.'

'When did I complain? I'm free tomorrow afternoon. Where should we meet?'

'Pick me up from my place around twelve. We need to go somewhere.'

'Where?'

'To a friend's place,' Rivanah said cautiously.

Next day afternoon they headed to IC Colony in Borivali West. Danny parked the car inside the complex. It was the second building from the main gate they had to go to. Rivanah and Danny together climbed up the stairs.

'So you won't tell me why we are here?'

'Told you. I have to give this to a friend,' Rivanah said, flashing an envelope she took out from her bag.

'All right.'

They were on the second floor. The second flat from the stairs. Rivanah looked around for the doorbell. Danny spotted it first and pressed it. They heard the bell ring distinctly. Half a minute later the door was opened by an elderly gentleman. He looked at Danny and Rivanah in a way as if he was sure they had lost their way.

'What is it?' He said. His voice quavered.

'I was asked to deliver a cheque to Mr Dilip—'

'Oh! Please come in. I'm so sorry to have kept you waiting.'

Danny and Rivanah shared a glance and stepped inside the flat.

'Give me a moment, please,' the man said, closing the front door and then he disappeared inside.

Everything in the flat seemed old and untouched. There were lots of photographs on the wall. A particular one caught Rivanah's eye. It was a picture of a boy along with a lady and the man who opened the door for them. Danny was by then ensconced on the sofa. He pulled her by the hand and made her sit too. The next second the man who opened the door came out with an elderly lady who smiled at them. The two sitting on the sofa smiled back. Rivanah guessed she was the lady in the photograph. The elderly lady came and sat by the sofa in front of Rivanah.

'How is my son?' she asked, still smiling, looking at Rivanah and Danny alternately.

*Which son?* Rivanah for a moment was clueless. She noticed the elderly lady was still looking at her expectantly. She looked at the man. He looked a little tense.

'I don't know . . .' Danny started but was cut short by Rivanah.

'I'm your son's friend. He is doing fine,' she said and saw how the man too smiled now.

'I told you he is fine. Just that these days work is so much that he doesn't get time to come and meet us. But he will be here soon,' the man told the lady.

'Only I know how difficult it is for a mother to keep waiting for her child.' The woman sighed, looking at the floor. 'Anyway,' she continued, 'at least this time Arun sent his friends, otherwise it is always some errand boy delivering the cheques.'

'Did you say Arun?' Rivanah asked.

'Yes. Didn't Arun send you?' the woman asked.

'He did. But we call him by his nickname so I got confused.' Rivanah gave an unsure smile and thought hard. No, she didn't know any Arun. Something about the elderly woman told her it would hurt her if Rivanah was honest with her about having no clue about her son.

'I had given the nickname. Though he doesn't like it much.' The woman had a nostalgic smile on her face. Then she looked at Rivanah and said, 'What will you have? Tea or—?'

'Nothing, Aunty. We are—'

'They will have tea.' This time the man spoke a little assertively. The woman looked at him and said aloud, 'Let me prepare it.' She got up and went to the kitchen.

The man came and sat down adjacent to Rivanah. He looked at her and said, 'Thanks.'

'What happened?' she asked.

'I don't know whom to thank. I was a junior-level government employee. Now all I have is a meagre pension, no medical cover and literally no savings. Whatever I had invested in my son's education, thinking . . .' He was too choked to speak. 'Every three–four months someone or the other keeps coming with the cheque. And thus my wife and I continue to survive.'

'Are you . . .?'

'I'm Dilip Rawat. And I know you aren't my son's friend nor has he asked you to bring in this cheque.'

Rivanah's lips slowly parted. *Does he know the stranger then?*

'But Aunty said it is Arun who sends the cheques.'

The man looked at the floor for a moment and said, 'My son Arun died few years back.' He kept staring at the floor as if he had just got the news.

Rivanah and Danny shared an awkward glance.

'We are sorry to know that,' Danny said and made a mental note to ask Rivanah about the matter. *If Arun was dead then why did she not know about it, since she said it was a friend's place they were visiting?*

The man suddenly looked up at them with a smile and said, 'It is okay.' The smile curtained a pain. 'The problem is, my wife doesn't know about it,' he said.

'She doesn't know her son Arun is no more?'

'She once did. But the shock was too much and she developed Alzheimer's in no time.'

'The disease where you lose your memory?'

The man nodded.

'I have packed roti and aloo-matar for your tiffin,' the woman cried out from the kitchen. 'Take a bath now. I'll look after the kids.'

The man looked at Rivanah and said, 'She doesn't even remember I have retired from work.'

171

'Why don't you tell her?' She asked.

'I need to go after lunch today,' the man said aloud to his wife who was still in the kitchen. Rivanah got her answer.

'Where do you go if not office?' Danny asked.

'I travel from here to Churchgate on the local train and then roam about here and there. And then come back home on time in the evening.'

'But how long do you think this will go on?' Danny asked.

'I don't know. I'm okay even if I can keep her away from reality for one more day. You see I told her something years back. I'll do my best to live up to it.'

'What did you tell her?' Rivanah said curiously.

'That I love her.' The man sounded slightly choked again but he controlled himself well. The reason the stranger sent Rivanah here slowly dawned on her.

'Don't you wonder, Uncle, who these people are who bring you the cheques?'

'I only know that there are still good people in this world.'

Rivanah understood that the stranger asked people to visit with the cheques, pretending to be Arun's friends. Just like he had sent her.

Mrs Rawat came out with tea and some snacks on a tray. Rivanah and Danny had it with Mrs Rawat talking for most of the time. Before Rivanah left she gave the cheque to the man, Dilip Rawat. She had only one thing on her mind: with the delivery of the cheque she had officially become broke. What was she going to do?

Danny asked her if he should drop her to the office. In order to not arouse his suspicious she agreed.

'So, who is this friend of yours whom you don't know and yet you went to give money to?' Danny asked while driving her to her office.

She knew this question would come. She was ready with an answer that wouldn't raise further questions.

'Arun's friend is a friend. I thought it was his place.'

'And the money?'

'The friend will return it.'

'Okay.'

This was one thing Rivanah always liked about Danny. No complicated questions. He was always satisfied with what she told him. Would he be all right if she told him the guy in the multiplex toilet the other day was Ekansh, her ex? That he was now her new roomie's boyfriend? And that he fucked her the day they met in the flat with her giving in to him so easily, something she would have never thought possible?

Danny dropped her right in front of the office building and went off to his film's acting workshop. She was wondering if she should go back to her flat when she got a call from a private number. She picked it up on the fourth ring.

'Let's have coffee together, Mini,' the stranger said.

For a moment Rivanah didn't know what to say. Then she said, 'Yeah, right.'

'I'm serious. Krishna Towers terrace in half an hour?'

*Was the stranger seriously going to have coffee with her in Krishna Towers? Did he live there?* Rivanah thought as she felt excitement run through her veins. She found herself saying, 'Yeah, okay.'

Rivanah took an autorickshaw and rushed to Krishna Towers. Fortunately for her there wasn't much traffic and she reached her destination a few minutes before time. She knew the terrace keys were kept with the security guard. She asked for it, citing the excuse that she needed to check her dish antenna.

'The terrace is open, madam. A few minutes ago a television mechanic took the keys to check the dish antenna.'

Was it really a mechanic or . . . the stranger? Before the guard could say anything more Rivanah dashed inside the apartment building, took the elevator to the fifteenth floor—the topmost floor—after which she climbed a set of stairs to come face-to-face with the terrace door. It was indeed open. She checked her watch. One minute left for it to be half an hour since the stranger had cut the phone call. She took a deep breath. One more step and she would be able to see the stranger. Rivanah exhaled and crossed the terrace door to step onto the terrace. She looked around. There was nobody. She heard a phone ring. She followed the sound and reached a corner away from the door where a mobile phone was lying on a table. A private number was flashing on it. Rivanah picked it up.

'Hello, Mini.'

'Where are you?'

'Look to your right.'

Rivanah obliged but still couldn't see anybody. The stranger asked her to look again at the table on which the phone had been left. Rivanah noticed there was a pair of binoculars on the table. She picked them up and, as directed by the stranger on the phone, looked to her right again. This time she could see a figure on the terrace of one of the high-rises adjacent to Krishna Towers. Rivanah adjusted the zoom to the max but realized it still gave her only a vague outline of the person. She couldn't be sure if it was a man or a woman. If she ran out, she wondered, and got to the opposite terrace, by then the stranger would be gone. She could make out the person was waving at her. *Very smart!* she told herself as a smile touched her lips.

'There's more,' said the stranger. Rivanah found there was a cup of coffee right under the table, covered, so that it didn't lose its steam. She picked it up, all the while pressing the binoculars to her eyes. The person lifted one of his hands. She did the same, lifting the coffee cup up.

'So won't you meet me ever?' Rivanah said on phone.

'Only when the time is right.'

'And when shall that be?'

'You'll know.'

'Hmm. Thank you, by the way. Thanks for leading me to this amazing couple. Though I felt sad for them, I felt good about myself after a long time.'

'I had to do it.'

'Why "had to"?'

'How else would you have known that nobody is always good or always bad? For example, the girl who cheated on Danny is also the girl who is now the reason why the elderly couple shall survive for the next two– three months.'

A sadness eclipsed Rivanah's excited self. She removed the binoculars from her eyes, lost in thought.

'Have your coffee, Mini,' the stranger said.

Rivanah took a sip and said, 'Why did I slip in that moment in the kitchen with Ekansh? I was so sure I loved Danny till that slip.'

'We all have this special talent for hiding a truth by adding layers of lies on to it.'

'What's the truth?'

'That you genuinely love Ekansh. You can't escape it.'

There was a silence which Rivanah broke by saying, 'Does that mean the lie is I don't love Danny?'

'The lie is: you love Danny . . . only.'

Rivanah sat down on the table, holding her head. She wasn't able to think clearly.

'What should I do now?' she said in a choked voice.

'Ekansh already knows the truth. That you love him. It is time for Danny to know that as well. That you love him too.'

'But Danny knows I love him.'

'You have to tell Danny that you still love Ekansh, even if it means that you want to live with Danny.'

'That's absurd! I will never say that. Danny will leave me for sure. I don't know if you know this or not, but I'm not in touch with Ekansh after the kitchen incident.'

'When we hide something from our partner a part of us is never with them. And in your case a very important part won't be with Danny. Understand this, Mini: when

177

you are attached to one and attracted to another, then one's truth becomes the other's lie as long as you keep the truth away from each other.'

'What if Danny leaves me? I simply can't take a break-up now. I'll die.' Rivanah's eyes had tears in them.

'From when did love start to concern itself with who is leaving whom? Love is whether someone truly belongs to someone or not, be it for a moment or for a lifetime.'

There was a prolonged silence. In that silence Rivanah understood she was staring at an abyss which was her life. Everything she thought was dear to her was finally gone. The last bit left was Danny.

'I will not only tell Danny the truth but also go back to Kolkata. I am anyway jobless and after Danny hears what I did I am pretty sure he will leave me. Mumbai won't have anything for me. Nor will my life.' She was sobbing by the end.

'Before you start to pack your bag, do check your email, Mini.'

The stranger cut the line. Rivanah immediately checked her email on the phone. What she read made her smile through her tears. She would have given the stranger a tight hug if he was near her.

# 20

The email was from the HR team of Zeus Technology Pvt. Ltd, asking if she would be available for an interview the next day. Reading the email Rivanah couldn't decide whether it was real or just one of stranger's jokes. She looked through the binoculars and was about to say something on the phone but the line was dead by then. There was nobody on the distant tower as well. To be sure Rivanah immediately called the HR's number that was provided in the email itself. They confirmed a time for an interview the next afternoon.

Rivanah thought of sharing the news first with her parents but stopped herself. It was only an interview. She must get an offer letter first, otherwise there would be a barrage of questions from her parents, the most important of which would be: first of all, why did you leave your job, Mini? She didn't want to share the news with Danny either till she had an offer letter with her.

Instead Rivanah shared the news with Tista on the phone right away. She had to tell someone about the interview in order to calm her thrilled self. She knew it was stupid because an interview did not necessarily mean a new job, but for her even this was welcome news.

'That's wonderful, Rivanah di! All the best,' Tista said, equally excited. Rivanah adored how genuine Tista always was. Whatever she said or did was straight from the heart; no filters, no pretension. Like she had once been. It also made her sad because the kitchen incident wasn't only about cheating on Danny. It was also about cheating on Tista and the bond they had formed as roomies. What would happen if she ever came to know about it? *She too will have filters from then on*, Rivanah answered herself in her mind.

'Thanks,' Rivanah said.

'But I will need a treat.'

'It is only an interview. I haven't got the job yet.'

'You will. I'm sure,' Tista said. Rivanah only hoped she was right.

The next day Rivanah reached Zeus Technology's office on time. Zeus was in Mindspace, Malad West, and it was not as big as her previous office. She remembered the place well since she had been here following Argho once. Would she stumble upon him again? This was the first time she was going inside the building. She found out that Neptune Solutions was two floors below Zeus. Once on the desired floor Rivanah was asked to wait for fifteen minutes after which a junior HR came, the one whom she had already spoken to, and set her up with a technical person who interviewed her for close to an hour. Once it was done, the same HR junior told her that she would be interviewed by a senior at 2.30 p.m. Though Rivanah wasn't hungry, she couldn't resist the idlis a vendor was selling just outside the building. She ordered a plate and was promptly served steaming idlis with a dash of coconut chutney. She finished her food and was wiping her hands using a tissue paper, when her phone rang. It was Danny.

'Hi, I have something to tell you,' he said.

'What happened?'

'I will tell you when we meet. Let's have dinner tonight.'

He had sounded the same when he had surprised her with the film contract. Was it a surprise again or . . . ?

'Okay,' she said.

'I will message the place. Be free around eight.'

'Sure.'

Danny didn't ask her more. *I have something to tell you . . .* Rivanah feared the worst. It could either be about Nitya or maybe the stranger had told Danny the truth before she could. Her phone rang again but this time with a landline number. It was from Zeus. Her interview was about to start in a few minutes. Rivanah rushed inside.

She was asked to wait in one of the glass-walled cabins where she would be interviewed. She looked around. Everyone seemed to know exactly what they were supposed to do without a hint of bother on their faces. Rivanah prayed she would get through the interview. Suddenly she sniffed something. Just Different, Hugo Boss. Her heart started racing and precisely then she heard someone say, 'Hi.'

Rivanah turned her head to see a clean-shaven man with long hair which was tied in a pony, sporting carbon-framed glasses. Before she could notice any other feature her jaw had already dropped. It was . . .

'I'm Argho Chowdhury. Senior HR at Zeus.' He extended his hand.

*What the hell is he doing here? Isn't he with Neptune Solutions?* Rivanah thought without knowing she was looking stupid. Argho shrugged, waiting for her to stretch her hand and shake his hand. Rivanah slowly lifted her hand. They shook hands. He sat down on a chair right beside her.

Argho took a moment to check all her certificates, payslips and other documents to see if everything was in place. While he was doing so Rivanah kept wondering if the man sitting only inches from her could be the stranger.

But why was he acting like he had never seen her before? Was it because he didn't know she had tracked him to Neptune Solutions before and followed him some time back? Or was he actually a damn good actor?

'Weren't you in Neptune Solutions before?' Rivanah blurted out. Argho stopped leafing through her documents and looked at her. It was obvious what he was thinking: *how do you know?*

'I'm sorry. What I meant was I gave an interview for Neptune Solutions too and someone there resembled you,' Rivanah quickly improvised. It wasn't convincing enough.

'I'm sure I'm meeting you for the first time though I did work for Neptune Solutions till a month back,' Argho said and went back to her documents.

'I'm sure you are,' Rivanah quipped, thinking how well he was faking it. And it would be better if she played along too just to be absolutely sure whether Argho was the stranger or not. She was itching to ask him about Hiya as she clearly remembered he had written 'RIP Hiya di' on her profile. But she knew this wasn't the time. One little slip and she could very well spoil her chance of solving the mystery behind Hiya Chowdhury for ever. Perhaps, she wondered, Argho was her only chance.

Argho Chowdhury asked her a few basic HR questions at the end of which he offered her the position of senior programming analyst with a salary hike of 45 per cent over her previous job. He said she would get an email with the offer letter the same evening and she would have to revert by the next evening. The rest of the formalities would follow once she accepted the offer.

'Have a good day, Ms Bannerjee. Hope to see you here,' he said and turned his chair around to face the table. Rivanah took her documents and left. Before she left the HR space she turned back to look at Argho. She quickly averted her eyes because he too was looking at her.

*Finally, relief!* She wouldn't have to go back to Kolkata just yet. There were two other things she had on her mind. Argho came to this company a month back. And now she would too join. Was it a ploy by the stranger? Or should she say *Argho*?

Once outside Zeus, she entered the elevator with two men and a lady. The men stepped out on the floor below while the woman stepped out a few floors before ground level. Rivanah was now alone inside the elevator. She was trying to check her email when the 3G connection failed. Then the network too was wiped out. She waited for the elevator to reach its destination. It didn't. It suddenly stopped and the lights went out simultaneously. Rivanah immediately remembered how the stranger had done the same thing in her Goregaon apartment once. She started banging the closed elevator door with force while crying out for help. She could hear people outside as well. Someone asked her to back off if she was near the door since they were opening it from outside. Rivanah shouted back to them that she was away from the door. The elevator door was manually opened. What she saw was a tall guy in a blue formal shirt neatly tucked into his black trousers. He had a strong jawline, and a sharp nose and chin. His hair was thick. His eyes were a bit greenish. The man was looking at her expectantly. It was then she realized the elevator had stopped at quite some height from the floor. She would have to jump down.

'You can jump. It's safe,' the man said. He had sexy voice. And an infectious confidence. Even if she knew she would be hurt, she would have still jumped because of this man's confidence. Rivanah bent down slightly, hurled herself into air and landed right into the man's arms. The way his hands squeezed her muscles while holding her evoked a feeling of desire. The man quickly placed her on the floor.

'Thank you,' Rivanah said.

'You are welcome,' the man said and walked off briskly. Rivanah couldn't help staring after him in a schoolgirlish way. Once he was gone she took the stairs this time.

Later in the evening Rivanah reached Hawaiian Shack at Bandra. Danny had told her he would join her there. She didn't know what it was he wanted to talk about, but her mind was busy with what the stranger had told her: *When we hide something from our partner a part of us is never with them.* And, to be honest, Rivanah wanted every part of hers to be Danny's. She felt an arm around her. Before she could turn, Danny planted a kiss on her cheek and took the seat in front of her.

'Here,' Danny said and put an envelope on the table. It was way smaller than the one which had the movie contract.

'What's this?' Rivanah said, a little wary of opening the envelope.

'See for yourself.' He was still not giving her any clue.

Rivanah slowly drew the envelope towards her and opened it, still looking at Danny sceptically. She looked down and broke into a huge smile. It was a cheque. Danny had officially secured his first film. Rivanah leaped up and hugged Danny tight.

'Congrats, baby.' She kissed his cheek.

'Thank you so much. I was so waiting to see this reaction of yours,' Danny said, kissing her on her lips.

They settled down in the chairs after a prolonged hug.

'I am feeling so alive right now,' Rivanah said.

'So am I.'

Rivanah picked up the seven-lakh cheque in her hand and looked at it closely.

'Let's celebrate by being together. It's been a long time!' Rivanah said.

'I have something on my mind.'

'Like what?'

'You'll see. Get a leave tomorrow. The acting workshop is closed tomorrow but day after I will be busy with it again. So let's make use of tomorrow.'

As Danny talked on about leave Rivanah quickly checked her email on her phone. There was a mail from Argho Chowdhury: the offer letter. Before reading it herself, she showed the attachment to Danny.

'New job?'

'A 45 per cent hike! Do I need to give any other reason?'

'Double whammy!'

'I was so waiting for this offer to happen.'

'Now we better celebrate tomorrow our way.'

'Sure,' she said and sent a confirmation email immediately. She looked up at Danny and saw he was going through the menu. Should she tell him the truth? Rivanah wondered. They were so happy right now; what if the truth disturbed this state? No, this was not the time to spill out the truth. They drank, had dinner and danced a bit too, all the while Rivanah convincing herself that the time for not right for the truth. When they came out of Hawaiian Shack, they walked for a few seconds to reach a little lane where Danny had parked the car. They got in.

'Where's my phone?' Danny said. Rivanah had no idea.

'Shit! I guess I left it inside. Give me a second.' Danny went to get his phone. Sitting alone in the car in the quiet street Rivanah called her mother and told her that she had finally hopped to a better job with a higher pay package. She also told her about Danny's success at securing a film. Her father wasn't in; her mother said she would convey it to him first thing when he came home. As she was talking she heard someone bang the back of the car.

'Mumma, I'll call you later.' Rivanah cut the line and turned. There was nobody. It was the first time she realized how quiet the lane was. She leaned out of the window to get a better view. At that instant someone banged the front windshield of the car. Rivanah turned in a flash. Her heartbeat suddenly quickened. There was a vehicle in front whose headlights were switched on and the light fell right on her and thus she could only see a silhouette in front of the car. Was it Argho? She swallowed a lump, shielding her eyes from the headlight. Was the stranger going to tell Danny the truth? She felt fear tightening up her muscles. And what followed made her go numb. The figure broke Danny's car's windshield with one single blow. With squinted eyes she tried to see who it was, pieces of glasses all around her. She shut her eyes again. She knew how to unbuckle the seat belt but she wasn't able to move. The other car's headlights went off. There was no figure visible now as Rivanah opened her eyes completely. Rivanah was about to open her seat belt when she noticed a white cloth on her lap.

*Certain lanes are so attractively safe that we don't realize when it leads us to a busy highway. And it is only then that we have to decide whether to cross the highway or not. It is a decision that is seemingly momentary but is actually life-altering. When will you cross the highway, Mini? When will you tell Danny the truth? I won't repeat my question.*

'What the fuck happened?' It was Danny. Before saying anything Rivanah grabbed the white cloth with the message, hiding it from him.

## 21

Rivanah lied to Danny that it was an urchin who had hurled a brick at the car probably assuming there was nobody inside the car. When she screamed the urchin had run away. Though Danny didn't quite get why someone would do such a thing, he didn't probe any further. He drove immediately to a service station where they asked him to leave the car overnight so that the windshield could be fixed.

'Are you sure we shouldn't report it to the police?'

Rivanah gave Danny a sharp glance, trying to understand if he had unmasked the fact that she had lied to him about the urchin. But she wasn't sure. Perhaps the fact that she had not let go of Danny's arm from the time he came back to the car after fetching his phone told him that she was indeed scared.

'That won't be necessary.'

'Hmm, okay. Can't you stay at my place tonight? We are leaving for Khandala first thing in the morning anyway. We are going to a resort.'

This made sense to her. Staying with Danny would be the perfect cushion for her fear. The aggressive move from the stranger had seriously rattled Rivanah. Was it necessary? She would have anyway told Danny the truth. Would she have?

'That sounds good to me. Though we will have to go to my place in the morning to collect my clothes,' Rivanah said.

'That's fine,' Danny said and called out to a cab. Rivanah called Tista but she didn't pick up. She left her a message that she would come to the flat in the morning.

An hour later she stepped into the same flat from which she had moved out many days ago. It brought back memories for Rivanah. Nitya wasn't there any more. As she looked around she heard Danny say, 'Nitya is in Paris with her designer boss.'

She liked the fact that Danny had clarified the matter without her asking the question.

'Hmm,' Rivanah said, moving into the bedroom.

'Can't we pretend the Nitya episode never really happened?' Danny said, coming into the bedroom after her.

*Can't I pretend Ekansh didn't happen to me?* Rivanah wondered and said aloud, 'I have something to tell you Danny.' She was facing him. He came a tad closer and said, 'What is it?'

*Should she say it now?* Rivanah kept looking at Danny hoping that he would simply read her mind and understand her heart without her having to use words to express it aloud. Danny shrugged.

'I love you' was all she could come up with.

'I love you too,' Danny said and hugged her tight. And in the embrace Rivanah understood that a simple truth carries the potential of destroying a relationship in a far more irreversible way than a complex lie. Sleep was a far cry for Rivanah and she spent the whole night staring at Danny who slept soundly.

In the wee hours of the morning Danny and Rivanah went to her flat. She didn't see Tista there, which seemed odd to her. She wasn't the kind of girl who would not come home at night. Maybe she had gone to Ekansh's place. At least she should have intimated her about it, Rivanah thought, and called her once again while packing her stuff. The call went unanswered while she realized she was yet to get a response to her last night's message to Tista. Rivanah messaged her again, asking her to call or message back as soon as she read her messages. Done with packing Rivanah left with Danny for the service centre from where they got their repaired car and then drove to Khandala. On the way she kept wondering that on the one hand she loved Danny—she knew it—and on the other she was questioning the authenticity of that love by not sharing an important happening of her life with him. Her only excuse for it: how will he react? What if the truth triggers an emotional landslide? The fear of consequences—is it too part of loving someone with all one's heart? Or is love about being fearless even it means choosing your own doom? They reached the resort close to afternoon. They freshened up, had a sumptuous brunch and then they were back in the room.

'I have something to tell you.' Rivanah summoned all her energy.

'What is it, honey?' Danny said and came to rest his head on her lap, looking at her directly. All of Rivanah's resolve went away.

'I love you,' she said, disappointing herself.

'I love you too,' Danny said and kissed the tip of her nose, raising his head a bit and closing his eyes. As Rivanah caressed his hair he said, 'Life seems so peaceful right now.'

*Should she tell him the truth and rob him of the peace?* Rivanah wondered and looked down to realize Danny was asleep. She rested her head back while continuing to run her fingers through his hair. Rivanah slept like a log. When she woke up she found herself lying on the bed alone. She sat up. The sound of water was audible to her. She looked around but Danny was not in the room. The digital clock in the room displayed the time—11.15 p.m. *Shit! I slept for ten hours.* Rivanah got down from the bed and, putting on her slippers, went towards the balcony from where the sound of water was coming.

Rivanah stepped outside the room. It was relatively quiet. The distant view was of covered mountains and a silence which had a sheath of moonlight over it. There was nobody in sight except for Danny taking a bath under the open sky shower at the edge of the balcony. A naughty smile escaped Rivanah as she saw the water from the shower cascade down Danny's naked back. The next moment Danny turned around.

'I knew you would come,' Danny said with a tempting smile that Rivanah read as an invitation to join in. The sight of Danny showering alone stark naked aroused her after a long time. She moved towards the shower and stopped. Their eyes remain locked while their faces had a tinge of naughty amusement. The steam around the shower area told her the water was warm. The way it was trickling down Danny's naked body made her already slightly wet between her legs. A small light was on right above the shower which covered that particular area with a bluish light. Rivanah could see the details of Danny's nudity. It had been some months since she had seen him this naked. With eyes fixed on Danny, Rivanah first stepped out of her slippers. The ground below was cold. It added to the sensual feeling which from a brisk wind had turned into a storm now. She raised her arms next and took off the black top she was wearing, to expose her black bra to Danny. The top was dropped on the ground. She tilted her head, unbuttoned her white capris and pulled them down seductively. She stood there, looking teasingly at Danny. With a sexy pout Rivanah took her hands to her back and unhooked her bra. Before she could drop the bra on the floor Danny came out of the shower. He came to her, smooched her hard and then, kneeling down, tore her panty off. Then he rose and picked her up. He took her under the shower. Rivanah by then had surrendered totally to him.

The extreme passion with which Danny made love to her under the shower was something she had never experienced before. It was as if he was sucking the soul out of her and making it a part of his. Since it was an open shower, there was no wall for support on either side. They were each other's support and it made the sexual act all the more intimate. With Danny's hands supporting her butt she wrapped her legs around his waist and her arms around his neck. As he finally penetrated her, she reached the zenith of pleasure. In the distance she could see the mountains, moon, some clouds, trees . . .

darkness beyond them. And each of them seemed to be talking to her.

*You love Danny . . . you should tell him the truth . . . you love Danny . . . you shouldn't tell him the truth . . . tell him the truth . . . shouldn't tell him the truth . . . the truth . . . truth . . .*

'Will you marry me, Rivanah?' Danny said, pushing himself deep in her and digging his teeth into her shoulder. It was the most intense marriage proposal she knew of. She yelled out in pleasure and pain and said, 'Yes, Danny . . . I will, Danny. I will.'

A prolonged moan and a grunt escaped both Rivanah and Danny respectively as they climaxed together. By then she had scratched his back to her heart's content. He had even bitten her lips, sucking the blood from it. Finally, as he came inside her, he let her feet down on the floor. They stood in a quiet embrace with the warm water gushing over their intertwined bodies. Sometime later Danny broke the embrace, saying, 'I'll wait for you inside.' And he ambled away to the room. Rivanah switched off the light, shivering a bit in the coldness of the night. She was about to move out when a light fell on her. For a moment she thought the shower light had been switched on but in a flash she realized it was not the case. The light that was on her came from a distance beyond the fence of the resort where there were some dense bushes. Rivanah was quick to cover her privates with her hands.

'Is that you?' Rivanah blurted, knowing well who it could be. Had he been watching her copulate with Danny all this while?

The flashlight went off for a second and was on again. *So he is talking in binary. Off means a yes, on means a no*, Rivanah thought. Would the stranger come out in the open now? It wasn't the first time the stranger was seeing her naked. She couldn't see much in the light. Or in its absence, when it was abruptly switched off. *Was it really Argho standing a few metres from her?* This was her best chance to unmask the stranger. And the only way to do so was . . . seduction. The fact that she was naked was also her power. She stood her ground firmly with no more communication from the stranger except for the flashlight which was on at that point of time. Rivanah closed her eyes and with a shiver slowly raised her hands, exposing her privates and saying aloud, 'I'm . . . all yours, stranger. Come, take me.'

Rivanah was sure the seduction would work. She waited with bated breath. *Was Argho approaching her?* She couldn't tell. Her eyes were closed, senses alert and muscles tense. She was praying for the stranger to come to her. She was craving to open her eyes and see the stranger's face and confirm her suspicion that it was Argho. Seconds became a minute but nobody approached her. The flashlight was still on. Driven by impatience

Rivanah opened her eyes and was dumbfounded with horror. A noose was hanging from the shower right in front of her. The stranger had tiptoed right up to her and she hadn't even realized it. The flashlight went off. In the darkness Rivanah's voice returned to her and she yelled out to Danny. He rushed out of the room.

'What happened?'

Rivanah swallowed a lump. By then she had pulled down the noose and thrown it away into the bushes in the dark.

'Bring me a towel please.' She knew she was unconvincing but it was still better than telling him what had just happened. It wouldn't help her cause if Danny knew the stranger was still stalking her.

They drove back to Mumbai the next day. When Danny dropped her by her apartment building he asked, 'Can't you shift back?'

Rivanah only wished she could say yes, but the distance that the stranger had talked about, she didn't want to kill it just as yet. That distance was giving her the space to place her guilt. Staying together would only nurture it.

'Give me some time,' she said. Danny nodded, saying, 'I'll wait.' He drove away.

Rivanah unlocked the door and stepped inside the flat, only to hear someone weeping inside Tista's bedroom. It sounded odd. More so because it wasn't Tista but a man.

'Who is it?' she said, not closing the front door. The next moment Ekansh came out to the drawing room, rubbing his eyes. This was the first time she had seen him crying this way.

# 22

'What happened? Where is Tista?' Rivanah said, trying to look beyond him and hoping Tista was there as well. She didn't want to be alone in the flat with Ekansh. The latter simply sat down on the couch, hiding his face with his hands, and said, 'She is not here.'

'Why are you crying? What's wrong?' Rivanah was herself surprised with the genuine concern she showed for him. Some people will burn your world into ashes and yet the smoke from the singe would still be in love with them, Rivanah thought.

Ekansh sat still for some time and then said, 'I can't live without her.'

Rivanah sensed the obvious. Tista must have left him just like he had left her a year and a half ago. A sense of satisfaction invaded her. Tista didn't look the type who would ditch a guy, but if she really had ditched Ekansh, it must be his fault and not hers.

'She is your fiancée. Who is asking you to live without her?' The last part was deliberate. If Tista had left him then it would hurt him. Rivanah wanted that. At that moment she only wanted to hurt Ekansh. She closed the front door, feeling confident of the fact that there wouldn't be any more slips on her part. Ekansh's weakness was her source of confidence.

'She is not well,' Ekansh said, still not looking at her.

'As in? What happened?' Rivanah preferred to stand against the wall facing Ekansh.

'She has acute pancreatitis and some problem in her small intestine as well.'

'What are you saying? She never told me.' Rivanah took her phone and immediately called Tista. A phone lying beside Ekansh began to ring.

'What the . . .'

'She left her phone with me.'

'What? Why would she do that?'

Ekansh looked up at her and said, 'She used to save voice notes on her phone.'

'What voice notes?'

'About her thoughts on us.'

'Us? She knew about you and me?' Rivanah's heart was in her mouth.

'Us as in Tista and me.'

'Oh, okay.'

There was silence. *Did you ever cry for us, Ekansh, like this after we broke up?* Rivanah wanted to ask. *I did*, she wanted to confess. Instead she spoke aloud, 'Has she gone for a check-up? When is she returning?'

'She is in Kolkata. She may not return even if she becomes all right. I came here to give the remaining rent cheques from her side and the flat keys. Here . . .'

He gave the cheques and the keys to Rivanah. She took them quietly. She didn't know how to react. She was feeling bad for Tista, but for Ekansh . . .?

'You know,' Ekansh said, 'before you came here I was on the phone with her. She asked me what I would do if she died.'

'But why would she die?'

'She may have to undergo a surgery soon and the doctor said there's a 70 per cent chance she may not . . .' Ekansh didn't say the rest.

'I want to talk to her now.'

'She is sleeping. I will arrange for you to talk to her when she wakes up,' Ekansh said and hid his face with his hands yet again. Rivanah was about to ask Ekansh if he needed some water when he spoke up, 'Life has been tough since the time I wronged you.'

Rivanah shot him a sharp glance. For the first time she heard him clearly accepting that it was he who had ditched her. No excuses, no reasons. A simple confession.

Till then all Rivanah had wanted to do was laugh at his situation. But the moment he confessed she felt like forgiving him. Not for what he did to her but for what he did to himself, perhaps, after what he did to her.

'I realized I made a mistake when Vishakha left me for someone else like I left you for her.' Ekansh was talking with his face in his hands while Rivanah was listening with her eyes closed and resting her head on the wall.

'I still don't know why I chose her over you. I was so happy with you. Maybe I was happy with you but I wasn't happy with *us*. Those are two different things. People jump into a relationship when they experience the former.'

Rivanah was itching to ask if he really thought they had jumped into a relationship and maintained it for over four years without it being genuine. But she kept those words to herself as she heard him say, 'After Vishakha left me I was pretty sure I would never fall in love again, for I understood that, if I could never appreciate the kind of love you had for me, I probably didn't deserve to be in love.'

Rivanah could feel tears oozing out from her eyes but she knew it was futile to wipe them away. Even if she wiped those tears out she could never suppress the feeling which was triggering them.

'Then Tista happened to me. She was the younger sister of one of my colleagues. I went to his place in Kolkata last Durga Puja. We met there. Since our parents knew each other, the proposal came from her parents and my parents accepted. I honestly didn't care any more whom I got married to. We were soon engaged. I discovered the best part about Tista was that she never demanded anything. She loved me. That's all. I wish I could love her or anybody else like that. So absolutely.'

*I too loved you absolutely, Ekansh. And you are the reason why I won't ever be able to love someone else absolutely*, Rivanah thought.

Ekansh stood up and said, 'I'll ask Tista to call you from her father's phone when I talk to her next. I'm taking her things with me.'

'Won't she come back?' Rivanah asked.

'I hope she does. But she would need rest so I asked her to resign for the time being.'

Ekansh went to Tista's room once again and reappeared with a suitcase.

'Thanks for listening,' he said and left.

Rivanah sat still, fervently wishing that Tista came out of the surgery alive and healthy. For the first time after her break-up with Ekansh she prayed for him too. Sometime later she freshened up and left for her new office.

In the office she had to meet the junior HR to talk about her leaves and submit hardcopies of some documents. The truth was Rivanah actually wanted to see Argho. Her plan was simple. She wouldn't let him know she suspected him. The irony was she had to meet him as a stranger to know if he was the real stranger or not. She asked the junior about Argho.

'You can tell me whatever it is. He hasn't come to office yet,' the junior said.

'It is okay. I will wait for him.'

'He isn't well. He was absent yesterday too.'

Rivanah's jaws dropped. He was absent. Did he follow her to Khandala?

'In case he comes in I'll tell him,' the junior said.

'No, no, it's all right. Don't tell him anything,' Rivanah immediately blurted. The junior gave her an as-you-wish shrug.

It was during her post-lunch casual walk around the office building, while talking on the phone with Danny, that Rivanah noticed Argho entering the office premises.

'I will call you in a bit, Danny,' she said and cut the line. Rivanah rushed inside the building and saw Argho taking the stairs. *Is he going to climb the eleven floors?* She reluctantly took the stairs as well.

As she reached the first floor she saw Argho move out of an exit door. She reached the door before it closed and found herself staring at a corridor which led to the emergency backstairs. *Should she or shouldn't she?* Rivanah decided in a flash and took the emergency backstairs like Argho who by now had already climbed a floor. Since these were the backstairs there wasn't anybody there. She could hear Argho's footsteps climbing up. She took care he didn't get an idea someone was following him. On the fifth floor Rivanah slowed down, typed a 'Hi' on the message section of her phone and sent it to all the numbers she had of the stranger. She raced up and could see Argho standing on the seventh floor checking his phone. She checked her phone. One of the numbers had a delivered tick next to it. *Damn!* She sighed. How she wished she could call the number. It would have been all clear if he was the stranger or not then and there.

Rivanah soon felt the fatigue and thus was taking her time to climb up. Finally she reached the office floor. She saw Argho had entered the door from where a corridor would lead them to the front stairs. Rivanah was exhausted. She took a deep breath and, summoning all her residual energy, climbed the last set of stairs to reach the door. She turned the doorknob but it didn't open. She turned it a few times and then her eyes fell on the red indicator on the right which would turn green only when a magnetic ID was tapped on it. And Rivanah didn't yet have her ID. Her breath was getting back to normal as she stood there thinking what to do. She turned back and got the scare of her life. A man was standing right behind her. Perhaps a finger away. As she pressed herself against the door, she realized it was the same man who had rescued her from the stuck elevator a few days back.

'I hope I didn't give you a fright,' the man said. There was an air of decency about him. And it was irresistible. He was tall, wheatish-complexioned and handsome, but Rivanah wouldn't have described him with these words to anyone. If she had to describe him it would be simpler than that. She would use the word 'sexy'. Period.

'I don't have the—' she started but the man took out his card and tapped it on the red light. It turned green. He pushed open the door.

'Thanks,' Rivanah said and thought: she had met this man twice now. And both times he had rescued her. *Who the fuck is he?*

'I'm Rivanah Bannerjee, Zeus Tech. I'm new here so I don't have a card yet,' she said, hoping he would introduce himself as well.

'Nice to meet you, Rivanah Bannerjee,' he said and walked away, pushing the door further. His secretiveness made it even more tempting to pursue him. She ran after him, took the corridor and reached the front stairs. He was nowhere. Rivanah went inside her office wondering why he hadn't introduced himself when something struck her. She had told the man she was new here. It reminded her of the offer letter. She opened her Gmail on her phone, opened her offer letter. It was from Argho Chowdhury. She scrolled down to the bottom of the email and checked Argho's signature. It had his name, his designation and . . . his phone number. She copied it, saved it on her phone and dialled. Her screen flashed the name Stranger 10. It was the tenth number she had saved of the stranger. Rivanah cut the line, feeling a chill down her spine. She was finally sure Argho was the stranger.

# 23

Rivanah didn't get a chance to get back to Argho throughout the day. She wanted to follow him in the evening as well to know where he lived. She wanted to know everything about the stranger as he did about her, before she revealed to him that she now knew who he was.

At seven in the evening she went towards the HR cubicles and noticed Argho was wrapping up for the day. She went out and waited by the elevator so that she didn't arouse suspicion. Even if he took the stairs, she would take the elevator and wait for him outside the office premises. This time Argho took the elevator. She stood right behind him. The scent of Just Different, Hugo Boss, coming from him and the thrill of knowing the stranger made her smile to herself. Ground floor. Argho stepped out. So did Rivanah.

She would have followed him and crossed the road, just like he did, had Ekansh, who was standing by a bike by the office building, not called out to her.

'Ekansh? What are you doing here? How did you know I work here?'

'Chuck that. I need to talk.'

Rivanah's focus was still on Argho, who had by then taken an AC bus and was out of sight. She averted her eyes to Ekansh.

'Talk about what? How is Tista?'

'Can we please sit somewhere?'

Rivanah looked at his troubled face. *I will never be able to say no to his face*, she thought, *all because, once upon a time, I loved this guy with all my heart*.

'Okay.'

Half an hour later, Rivanah found herself sitting with Ekansh inside a CCD close to her place.

'Tista didn't call me. I was waiting,' she said.

'Wait,' Ekansh said and dialled a number. They exchanged a look as the phone kept ringing.

'Hello, Aunty. Is Tista awake?' Ekansh waited and then said on the phone, 'Hi, all good? I'm good. Okay, talk to Rivanah.'

'Hi, Tista,' Rivanah said, taking the phone from Ekansh.

'Hi, Rivanah di.' Tista sounded pretty weak.

'You never told me!' Rivanah said.

'I'm sorry, Rivanah di. It all happened so fast.'

'It's okay. You just take care. We'll meet soon.'

'Will we?' There was a deep doubt in her voice.

'Shut up. We certainly will.'

'I hope so too. Can you go a little away from Ekansh?'

'Yeah, sure. Excuse me,' Rivanah said to Ekansh and went towards the washroom.

'Tell me, what is it?'

'How is Ekansh handling it? Like, he doesn't tell me anything and tries to make me laugh all the time but I know he is deeply affected.'

Rivanah took a moment to respond.

'He indeed is,' she said, feeling uncomfortable saying it. She didn't know the exact reason for it even though she knew what she told Tista was true. Ekansh clearly was affected.

'I knew it,' Tista said and added, 'Can you just tell him I love him more than anything else in the world? I won't be able to say it because, if I do, I shall break down on the phone and I really don't want to do that.'

For a second Rivanah felt choked. She looked at herself in the washroom mirror and realized her eyes were swimming with hot tears.

'Rivanah di?'

'Yes, yes, I will certainly tell him that. And don't you worry. No true love ever goes unfulfilled,' Rivanah said, fighting hard to believe it herself.

Rivanah came out of the washroom and gave Ekansh the phone.

'What happened? Why did you have to go to the washroom with the phone?'

'She loves you, Ekansh. She said she loves you more than anything else in the world,' Rivanah said. There was silence. Rivanah didn't look at Ekansh. How time changes the dynamics of a relationship, Rivanah thought. A year and a half back she was with Ekansh in Marine Drive and they were telling each other how much they loved the other. Now she was sitting right opposite him and informing him how much another girl loved him. And in between she supposedly went through the I-hate-you phase as well. A break-up doesn't necessarily end the love two people have for each other. In fact some love stories never end. They only end something within the people involved. Rivanah knew she was still in love with Ekansh and it didn't matter how much she denied it, because otherwise she wouldn't be sitting with him in the cafe. She looked up and saw Ekansh was looking out of the glass door with tears rolling down his cheeks. *Had he ever cried for her after their break-up?* she thought again and was about to pass on a tissue paper to him when she stopped mid-air. Something was written on the tissue. She read it: *Truth?*

Rivanah instantly turned to look around. Argho had not taken the AC bus. He must have followed her here.

'Did you see a guy with long hair in the cafe?'

'Huh?' Ekansh turned to look at her. He had no clue what she was talking about. 'No.'

'Did you leave the table at all?'

'I went to smoke outside when you were in the washroom.'

'You smoke now?'

Ekansh nodded. 'But what happened?'

Rivanah shook her head keeping the tissue with her while giving another one to Ekansh. He wiped his tears off and said, 'I know why I'm going through all this.'

'Why?'

'People who ditch true love once don't deserve to get true love again.'

Rivanah could sense a confession in Ekansh's words but didn't know what to say. The confession gave her as much pleasure as it pulled her emotionally towards Ekansh.

'I need you, Rivanah,' Ekansh said out loud. She wasn't ready for this. Even though she had suspected he may say it, she hadn't expected him to do so right then. What did he mean anyway by 'I need you'?

'Don't worry; I won't force this friendship on you. It will only happen if you want it too. None of my friends know about Tista's condition except you. I don't feel like sharing it with them. I am too tired to unwrap myself in front of them. With you it is easier, you know me well already. I want you as my friend, Rivanah. Someone on whose shoulder I can cry. Someone with whom I can share my wounds. Someone with whom I can be emotionally naked.'

*And what if our emotionally naked selves ask us questions we can't handle? The kind of questions which slowly deconstruct us and in the quest of finding answers to them we get constructed into someone we never thought we could be.* The only question, at that instant, however, was this: was she ready for such a deconstruction?

Rivanah let go of a deep breath. She was about to speak up when she felt someone's presence by their table.

'Hey!'

Both Rivanah and Ekansh looked up. It was Danny. Rivanah's throat instantly went bone dry. *Had Argho told Danny the truth?*

## 24

'Danny?' Rivanah exclaimed and immediately knew she shouldn't have made her surprise so overt.

'As if you didn't know I was coming here. *You* texted me!' he said. He side-hugged her, planted a kiss on her forehead and sat down between her and Ekansh.

*You texted me* . . . Rivanah knew who this 'you' was. Argho was back to his sadistic best.

The next moment was the most awkward of Rivanah's life. She had her ex and her present boyfriend staring at each other for possible introductions.

'Danny, this is Ekansh. Ekansh, this is Danny,' she said. The men shook hands wishing the introduction was longer than that for them to know who exactly they were.

'Wait a minute,' Danny said and seemed thoughtful. 'Aren't you the guy from the washroom?'

'Which washroom?' Rivanah quipped.

'The multiplex washroom.' This time it was Ekansh.

'Yes!' Danny was happy that he was right.

'Ekansh is a good friend from college,' Rivanah told Danny and to Ekansh she finally turned and said, 'Danny is my boyfriend.' From the corner of her eye Rivanah saw Ekansh withdraw into himself on his seat. She had told him she was single. The silence that followed had a probing energy to it which made Rivanah uneasy like never before.

'So, why did you want to meet so urgently?' Danny asked Rivanah.

'Though of watching a movie,' Rivanah blurted.

'Christ! I thought it was something more serious. Anyway, am free. So we can go.'

'Yeah. Let's go,' Rivanah said and stood up.

'It was nice meeting you, Ekansh.' Danny said and, putting his arm around Rivanah's waist, was ready to leave.

'See you,' she told Ekansh. He only nodded with a tight smile. And watched her walk away with Danny.

In the next minute Rivanah was in the car with Danny. He was driving towards the nearest multiplex.

'Tell me something,' Danny said. 'Wasn't your ex's name Ekansh too?'

'Yes,' Rivanah said and hoped he would ask all the important questions she was running away from and all she would have to do was say 'yes' or 'no' and that would be the end of the story.

'Is this the same Ekansh?'

'Yes.'

'Were you looking for him in the gents' washroom that day?'

'No!' She glanced at him once.

'And today too you met him coincidentally?'

Rivanah didn't like his interrogating tone but she couldn't do much realizing that, somewhere, she deserved that tone.

'Pretty much,' she said. Danny didn't ask anything further. Rivanah zoned out during the whole movie, conscious at times of Danny laughing out. She did text Argho on all his numbers saying that she wanted to talk. She didn't care if it was Argho or not. She wanted a sounding board. But there was no response. After the movie Danny dropped her at her flat.

She skipped dinner and was busy sketching when she got a call from a private number. She put on her earphones and took the call.

'Hi.'

'Hello, Mini.'

For once she was tempted to say, 'Argho, please cut the crap and tell me it's you, because I now know it is you.' But she didn't say anything lest it disturbed her connection with him which, at that point of time, she was more in need of.

217

'I know you want me to tell Danny the truth and even I want to. But before I do that, I have a question for you.' Rivanah was furiously sketching as she talked over the phone.

'What's the question?'

'Why can't I love both of them?'

'You can but you will have to live with one of them,' promptly came the response.

'Who made that diktat?'

'People who tried to do what you now desire and failed miserably.'

'Is revelling in the attention you get from more than one person a sin? When Ekansh and Danny both had their eyes on me I felt powerful in a way I have never felt before.'

'Attention is an aphrodisiac, Mini. The more you get it, the more important you'll feel. The more important you'll feel, the less you'll know yourself.'

'But will I be very wrong if I claim such attention from both?'

'All of us define right and wrong in relation to the other. If this is right then that is wrong. That way nothing is wrong, nothing is right.'

'Then why do you want me to tell Danny the truth if nothing is wrong or right?'

'Some people can only be your horizon, Mini. You may crave them, you may burn, you may die but you will never get to them. But also understand this: when someone is your ever-eluding horizon, the sun of your emotions shall always rise and set in their lap. If that can't give you peace, nothing in love will.' The stranger spoke slowly, giving Rivanah the time for the words to register along with its subtext.

'You mean Ekansh is my horizon?'

'I mean either Ekansh or Danny will eventually be your horizon. You'll have to learn to live with it.'

'But before I know who that horizon is, why can't I have the attention of both guys? How do I know Danny has told me everything?'

Rivanah by then had finished sketching. It was a pair of eyes that she had sketched. She went towards the open window in the room and inhaled some fresh air. The phone call was still on.

'You can either give yourself excuses, Mini, or you can tell the truth,' the stranger said.

'I don't want to tell Danny the truth. Not right now.'

'Your yes or no will have consequences, Mini.'

'Why do I have to listen to you all the time? I have asked you a million times who Hiya Chowdhury is but you never tell me. I told you to meet me but you won't. But I have to do whatever you want me to. Sorry, but that's not possible,' Rivanah blurted impulsively. Why couldn't the stranger tell her that what she had in mind

219

was perfectly all right? She heard the line go dead. For once she didn't care if the stranger was angry. She, after all, had the right to live her life the way she wanted. The rest of the night she continued to sketch without feeling sleepy.

Next day in office she kept wondering what was wrong in revelling in the attention she got from two people. It wasn't that she was interested in Ekansh sexually. The kitchen incident was a slip. Period. It wouldn't happen again, Rivanah told herself with confidence. Ekansh needed her as a friend. Danny needed her as a girlfriend. Why couldn't she fulfil both the roles without merging them? And then it struck her: Danny was perhaps doing exactly the same with Nitya when she had come to stay at their place. It had made Rivanah leave the flat. There was a greater truth that she had to accept before she told Danny about the little truth that happened in the kitchen with Ekansh. The greater truth was: she needed both the men in her life. Roles didn't matter, their presence did.

In the evening she received an email on her personal account. It was an invite for the convocation cum alumni meet of her college that was supposed to happen the following weekend. *Could it be another of the stranger's games?* She called Ekansh.

'Hey, did you get an invite for the convocation and alumni meet from our college?' she asked.

'Yes, I did. Few weeks back. It is next week.'

Rivanah was relieved to know it was a genuine invite.

'Oh, I got it today only. Are you going?'

'I'd anyway have to. I had applied for leave before. Tista is getting operated the next day.'

'Oh.' Rivanah took a moment to think and then said, 'When is your ticket? And which flight?'

'It is on the Friday night. Indigo flight.'

'Message me the details. I shall book tickets on the same flight if available.'

'Give me a moment.' Ekansh said. As Rivanah waited she thought her motivation to go to Kolkata wasn't the convocation or the alumni meet. She wanted to meet Tista once for sure before the operation but she also wanted to see if someone from Hiya's home was present at the convocation or not.

Danny dropped Rivanah at the airport the following Friday evening. He didn't ask if Ekansh was also attending the convocation; she didn't tell him either. She kissed Danny goodbye and entered the airport. She met Ekansh at the gate. Soon they collected their boarding passes, passed the security and boarded the flight.

'I want to thank you, Rivanah, for being there,' Ekansh said once they had taken their seats. He tried to grasp her hand. But she was alert. Anything that could lead to a probable slip turned her off. She withdrew her hand and said, 'I think we are meant to be in each other's lives always. If not as lovers, then at least as friends.'

The last part was deliberate. She wanted to underline the fact for Ekansh.

'Let's not go to the convocation together,' Rivanah said, looking out of the window.

'As in?'

'As in,' she looked at him, 'let's not enter together. Let's not behave like friends in front of everyone.'

Ekansh thought for a moment and then nodded, saying, 'All right.' He understood it would call for unnecessary questions that even he didn't want to answer.

Once in Kolkata they took separate cabs for their respective homes. She called her mother and told her she would be at home in some time. While she was talking she had received a message on phone. She read it after she was done talking to her mother.

*Time's up, Mini. Now be ready.*

Her throat dried completely as she read this. The last time the stranger had messaged 'Time's up', he had exposed Ekansh's infidelity. What now? Did she piss him off a little too much by not obliging him earlier? Was the stranger going to finally going to unveil Hiya's link with her?

It was a new number from which the message had been sent. She checked the number on the Truecaller app but it didn't show any record except that it was a Kolkata number. She had called it five times by the time she reached home but no luck. She didn't have much option but to wait and watch.

Rivanah was relieved to be home at last and have mom-made food. Mumbai for her was a battlefield where there was no time to rest, to be oneself and, most important, to live life the way one wanted to. Her father impressed her by gifting her a sketch stand. She had only mentioned in passing that she had started to sketch again.

'I haven't given you anything from a long time,' her father said. She hugged him, realizing how much she missed being pampered by her parents. It all seemed like a fairy tale now.

After the best dinner she had eaten in a long time, her mother joined her in her bedroom while she was sketching.

'I told your father that Danny has been signed for a film. He seemed to welcome the idea.'

'That's good, Mumma, but I'm in no mood to get married now.'

'Don't tell me you and Danny have broken up!' Her mother sounded scandalized.

Rivanah stopped sketching and looked at her lovingly. 'No, Mumma. Nothing like that. We both are still getting to know each other.'

'I think I will never understand this getting-to-know-each-other thing that you keep talking about. What is there to know so much?'

'You won't get it, Mumma.'

'Yes, I won't and I don't want to. Thank God I am not your age now. So confusing you youngsters are. Now sleep early. Don't stress yourself,' her mother said and left her alone. Her phone beeped with a message. It was Ekansh.

*I'm going to meet Tista tomorrow in the hospital. Would you like to join me?*

*Of course*, she replied.

Next day Ekansh met her below the Ultadanga footbridge and together they drove to the hospital on EM Bypass. The visiting hours had just started when they reached. They arrived at Tista's cabin only to find her family present there. On the bed was Tista, looking pale and weak. She tried to smile but it was clear she was very unwell. Ekansh greeted everyone and went to stand beside Tista. Rivanah introduced herself to Tista's family and stood by her bed on the other side. Tista raised her hand on seeing Rivanah who grasped it warmly.

'I can't live alone in that Mumbai flat. I want you back soon,' Rivanah said, trying to boost her morale.

'I . . . too . . . want . . . that,' Tista stuttered. Rivanah smiled at her, caressing her forehead, as Tista's father asked her not to talk much.

'You get well soon first, then we'll talk as much as we want to over a cup of your magic tea.' Rivanah said. Her phone beeped with a message. Rivanah excused herself as Ekansh started talking with Tista's parents.

Rivanah read the message. It was from the same unknown number that she had received the message a day ago.

*Food court, City Centre 2. In 30 minutes. Your only chance to know who I am.*

A chill ran through Rivanah's spine. *Will Argho actually reveal his identity?*

Rivanah spoke up, saying that she needed to go home because of some emergency. Ekansh glanced at her but she averted her eyes quickly and took her leave. Coming out of the hospital she took a cab to City Centre 2. She reached a few minutes late. She looked around trying to spot Argho when she got a message from the same number:

*You are late, Mini. I don't like that. I will see you in Mani Square now. Food court. In exactly 40 mins.*

Rivanah was enraged reading this. She replied to the message: *This better not be a game.*

And rushed out. She took a cab and clocked herself this time. She reached Mani Square mall's food court exactly ten minutes before time. She took a seat and waited for Argho to show up. She messaged on the number that she was there. The response which popped up infuriated Rivanah further:

*You are early, Mini. I don't like this. Meet me in South City, food court, in an hour.*

*If Argho doesn't show up in South City mall this time, I will never ever talk to the stranger again,* Rivanah promised herself and hailed a cab.

Ekansh called her in between, but she was too distracted to talk to him properly. She reached South City mall before time again but went inside only two minutes before the fixed time. This time she stepped on to the food court exactly on time. Few seconds later she got a message: *Look to your left.*

Rivanah did but couldn't spot Argho. Someone tapped on her shoulder from behind. Rivanah turned in a flash. *It can't be . . .* she thought and said, 'What the fuck are you doing here . . . Ishita?' Rivanah's eyes widened seeing her old roomie after ages now.

'I'm sorry, Rivanah. I never told you this.'

'Told me what?' Rivanah thought she was almost losing her voice.

'That I had a crush on you, Mini.'

All of the mall's cacophony around Rivanah turned into pin-drop silence.

# 26

'Please tell me this isn't true,' Rivanah said in a resigned manner. She had never seen Ishita look so serious before.

'But it is true, Mini. I love you,' Ishita said with no change in her expression.

Rivanah pulled up a chair and sat down on it with a thud. She hid her face with her hands. Nothing was making sense to her. She looked up and said, 'What's with Hiya . . .?' And noticed Ishita had an amused face.

'What?' Rivanah shrugged.

Ishita burst out laughing. For a moment Rivanah was clueless and then she got it. Her ex-roomie was kidding. *She was fucking kidding.*

'I will kill you, Ishita. I sure will,' Rivanah said, watching Ishita who was in splits by now. 'This isn't funny, Ishita.'

Realizing Rivanah was actually cross and extremely serious, Ishita stopped laughing.

'I am so sorry, babes. I thought I would surprise you.'

'But this is not the way.'

'Okay, I am sorry, yaar. What's the big deal? Don't tell me the stranger is still behind you,' Ishita said, and, looking at Rivanah, her jaw fell.

'Are you serious?'

Rivanah nodded.

'Then I'm seriously sorry.'

Rivanah took a few minutes to relay to Ishita what all had happened since she left for Gurgaon.

'So the stranger is still there somewhere? Unbelievable! What does he want?'

'I have no idea!'

'And that Hiya Chowdhury thing you told me about is fucking scary, dude!'

'Tell me about it.'

'What is the police saying?'

'I revoked my complaints.'

'Why?'

'Cinderella complex,' Rivanah lamented.

'What the fuck is that?'

'A psychiatrist told me that I constantly need a saviour in my life or else I'll go mad.'

'Holy mother of God! What have you landed yourself in?'

'And that is not all.'

229

Rivanah told her about Ekansh and the kitchen incident.

'Fuckin' shit! When I met you for the first time you were a girl who used to take permission from her boyfriend to go out and enjoy herself, and now, in a span of a year or so, you are telling me that girl has fucked her ex while he was in a relationship with someone else? I can't believe it.'

'Frankly, I wouldn't believe it either. Anyway, enough about me. What's up with you? How come you are in Kolkata?'

'Been here for a month. I changed jobs. Gurgaon is history now. I so wanted to contact you before but time just kept flying and here we are now.'

'I know. Even I wanted to buzz you but it just didn't happen.'

'I saw your Kolkata update on Facebook and thought of playing this prank. I had your number but I was sure you didn't have my new Kolkata number.'

'Wait. Let's go to my place. We can catch up there,' Rivanah said.

'Sounds great.'

The two girls took a cab and went straight to Rivanah's place where they caught up with their past, lessons and life.

'You know, men just don't excite me now. I mean, I am straight,' Ishita said, 'but the idea of being with a man is something I have grown out of. All are the same, they all stink. Mom and Dad want me to get married within the next year. It is only to avoid them that I came to Kolkata. I have relatives in Delhi but none in this part of the country.'

'Marriage is something I am confused about as well,' Rivanah said.

'Okay, Danny or Ekansh?' Ishita said. 'Just one name.'

'Danny.'

'Did you pick Danny because Ekansh anyway will be a part of you, but if you go with Ekansh you may end up forgetting Danny?'

Rivanah was amazed at how well Ishita knew her.

'Yes. But I don't think I will forget Danny.'

'You may get used to his absence.'

'Perhaps.'

'At least you have someone to live with,' Ishita said and sighed. The girls sat in silence till Rivanah's mother called out to them for lunch.

Post lunch, Rivanah had to go for the convocation ceremony. She dressed up and asked Ishita to join her.

'Are outsiders allowed?'

'Family is allowed. I will tell them you are my cousin.'

'Great. By the way, Ekansh will be there too?

'Yes, why?'

'Last time I had a talk with him, it wasn't really nice.' Ishita remembered how she had abused and pushed him in the mall after Rivanah had slapped him and left.

'Don't worry,' Rivanah said with a smile.

Rivanah's parents too accompanied her to the convocation ceremony. Ekansh was there but alone. They maintained a distance from each other, fearing someone would suspect the truth. The ceremony went on smoothly. The dean and a few other senior members of the college were dressed in black cloaks. And so were the students. One by one their names were called out and the dean gave them their degree, posed for an official college picture, after which the next name was called.

Rivanah was waiting impatiently for her turn. They were all standing in a line with a staff member coordinating their on-stage entry and exit. She looked at her parents once. The pride on their faces made everything worthwhile. She smiled at her mother who was beaming at her. She nudged her husband and together they signalled a thumbs-up sign to their daughter. Ishita, sitting beside her parents, too looked happy for her. Rivanah turned to look back. Ekansh was standing in the queue after some students. He was busy talking to another boy. She was happy she was done with I-hate-Ekansh phase and it wasn't exactly substituted by I-love-Ekansh. Which phase was it?

She couldn't define it. And she was happy that she couldn't. A definition brought with it its own set of problems. The next announcement made Rivanah turn to look at the announcer. He repeated the name: Hiya Chowdhury.

For some time nobody turned up. Rivanah glanced at Ishita who was already looking at her.

'Anyone from Hiya's family here?' the announcer asked. Someone in the crowd raised a hand. Rivanah leaned a bit to see Argho Chowdhury stand up.

'Please come here and receive the degree,' the announcer said. Dressed in casuals Argho came up to the stage, passed Rivanah, but he didn't seem to see her, or so she thought. He went, collected the degree from the dean and immediately walked out. She wanted to keep track of Argho. It could lead her to Hiya's family. Rivanah WhatsApped Ishita asking her to keep an eye on the guy who had just collected the degree on behalf of Hiya—Argho. Reading it, Ishita immediately stood up and went backstage, where Argho was.

After a couple more students, Rivanah's name was announced. She went and accepted the degree from the dean. Her father clicked a picture. She smiled, wondering if Ishita had Argho in sight or not. The moment her turn was over she rushed backstage. Neither Ishita nor Argho was there. She called the former.

233

'He is moving out. I'm outside your college gate.'

'Wait, I'm coming. Just keep an eye on him. It could be my only chance of finding out about Hiya.'

As Rivanah walked out, she told her parents on the phone that she would join them at home and that she was going out to celebrate with Ishita. Before they could ask where exactly they were going, Rivanah cut the line.

She joined Ishita outside the college and found her in a cab.

'Hurry up! He took a cab seconds ago.'

Rivanah climbed inside the cab and asked the driver to follow the white 'no refusal' cab ahead of it.

'How is Argho linked to Hiya?' Ishita asked. During the cab ride, Rivanah told her how she stumbled upon Argho on Facebook first, followed him and now she was working with him in the same office, which, by no stretch of imagination, could be a coincidence.

Argho's cab stopped at the Bidhan Nagar railway station. They bought tickets and followed him into a local train towards Barrackpore. They were one compartment away. And each time the train stopped, they got down and then climbed up again to make sure Argho didn't get down. Finally they saw him get down at Agarpara. He took the bridge which was rather empty for this time of the day. Once over it he took a cycle-rickshaw. They quickly got into another rickshaw with strict instructions to follow his. It took close to twenty minutes through quiet lanes before they stopped one house away from the house in front of which Argho stopped.

'Now what?' Ishita asked.

'We can't go inside now,' Rivanah said.

'But we don't even know if it is Argho's house or Hiya's!'

'Or, if Argho's and Hiya's family live together. He had written "di" on her Facebook timeline, so chances are they are siblings.'

'Hmm.'

'I will have to come here tomorrow to check,' Rivanah said conclusively.

'We!' Ishita said firmly.

Next day both the girls were back in the afternoon at the same place. They had planned a lot—how they should introduce themselves to whoever opened the door even if it was Argho. But in the end they thought it would be best to tell a partial truth. Rivanah was Hiya's batchmate and she got to know about her death during the convocation. And hence decided to visit her home.

Ishita was the one who pressed the doorbell. They exchanged nervous glances as the door was opened by a girl.

'Is this Hiya's house?' Rivanah asked.

*'Mashima! Didi ke chaiche.'* The girl was the housemaid, Rivanah understood. She asked the two girls to come in. A woman came out. Her hair was dishevelled, her sari had been draped around haphazardly, and she had a weird twinkle in her eyes as if she was looking for someone. Ishita and Rivanah stood close to each other. The woman scared them. A man came out quickly after her and asked the maid in a strict voice to take the woman inside. The maid used some force but eventually was able to take the woman inside.

'I'm sorry for my wife's behaviour. Who are you?' the man asked. He was wearing a simple half-sleeved shirt and trousers.

'Uncle,' Rivanah said, 'we are Hiya's friends.'

'Okay. I'm her father. But how did you find us here?'

'A friend told us,' Rivanah said. 'We didn't know she died because we were not in college at that time. Yesterday we had our convocation and got to know there about Hiya's death.'

'What happened to her, Uncle?' Ishita asked. This dialogue was part of their last night's plan to get to the real news.

The man paused before he said, 'She hanged herself.'

'We are sorry,' Rivanah said.

'But why did she hang herself?' Ishita asked.

'I don't know,' Hiya's father said and then added, 'I only know that someone was following her for some time.'

Rivanah and Ishita looked at each other with horror.

'Who?' Rivanah managed to ask.

'I don't know,' Hiya's father said and then added, 'One minute.' He went inside.

'I don't get it,' Ishita said. 'Was this the same stranger who was following Hiya? And if Argho is the stranger then was he following his own sister? Wait a second; we aren't sure they are siblings, right?'

'Right,' Rivanah said, trying to think clearly but failing miserably. Hiya's father came out and said, 'I found these in her room where she hanged herself.'

What Hiya's father held in his hand were white paper chits which had messages on them. As Ishita read those messages aloud one after the other, Rivanah hoped it was a dream, or else she wouldn't be able to take it. They were exactly the same messages the stranger had given her from the moment she climbed into the Meru cab on her first day in Mumbai.

'But weren't these sent to . . .' Ishita said and stopped. Rivanah had already realized the obvious. Hiya was stalked by the stranger, and she too had received the same messages. And then she hanged herself. Where was this stranger leading her? Was Hiya's death even a suicide or did he kill her?

'What happened?' Hiya's father asked. Neither was able to respond. Rivanah's phone buzzed with a message. It read: *I'll soon free you, Mini.*

# 27

Rivanah and Ishita took leave from Hiya's house. They were supposed to go back to Rivanah's house, but Rivanah's head started reeling, and she collapsed on the road, muttering, 'The stranger will kill me too.' Ishita took her to her PG lest Rivanah's parents become worried and ask all sorts of questions. After resting in Ishita's PG for a while, Rivanah finally felt somewhat normal.

'This is far more serious and sinister than we ever thought, Rivanah,' Ishita said. The two were alone in the PG at the time.

"I'm sure the stranger killed Hiya and made it look like a suicide. And perhaps he wants me to take the blame for it; otherwise he would have killed me too.'

'But why you? If it was only about taking blame then it could have been anybody,' Ishita argued. 'Try to connect to him and ask him for a talk,' she suggested. Rivanah sent a message to the numbers she had of the stranger. None of the messages were delivered.

'Damn, we forgot to even ask if Argho was Hiya's brother,' Ishita said.

'How does it matter now? I'm in the line of fire. I will soon be dead like Hiya.'

'Shut up, Rivanah. You have to be strong. If the stranger gets even a hint of your weakness he will not spare you.'

'He won't spare me anyway.'

'The only way ahead is cracking this whole puzzle,' Ishita said and heard Rivanah's phone ringing. It was her mother.

'Pick up the call and don't sound grim,' Ishita said, giving the phone to Rivanah. She took it after a moment's hesitation.

'Hello, Mumma.'

'Mini, when are you two coming home? Should I prepare lunch or you both are eating out?' her mother asked.

'Mumma, we will eat out and also I will come home tomorrow as I am at Ishita's place.'

'In Kolkata itself, right?'

'Yes, in Kolkata itself. You don't worry. Let Baba know. I shall be home tomorrow morning.'

'Okay Mini, take care. I will call at night.' Her mother put the phone down and continued to clean her daughter's room. She arranged the bed, the bookshelf and finally moved the sketch board to a corner in order to make space in the room. As Mrs Bannerjee held the sketch board her eyes fell on the last sketch. Her lips slowly parted in disbelief as she gaped at the sketch. She immediately called up her husband.

'Hello, what is it?' Mr Bannerjee asked.

I . . . I saw something.' Mrs Bannerjee sounded as if she had seen a ghost.

'What is it? Tell me quickly. I'm in a meeting.'

'Mini has sketched . . .'

'So?'

'Mini has sketched Hiya Chowdhury's face.'

There was a pause.

'I'm coming home now,' Mr Bannerjee said and added, 'Just keep it away from Mini.' The line went dead. Mrs Bannerjee's hands were still trembling but she somehow managed to get the paper off the sketch board.

At Ishita's PG, they were still discussing Hiya.

'And you know the worst part?' Rivanah said. 'I don't even remember Hiya. Like, I don't know how she looks.'

'What are you saying?'

'That's true.'

Rivanah's phone buzzed with a message. It was from one of the stranger's numbers. It read: *Know Your Worth, Mini. For all your answers lie within you.*

*To be continued . . .*

# Acknowledgements

A huge thank you to Gurveen, Shruti and each and every one at Penguin Random House for bringing out this book and my previous ones just the way they should be.

When you have very few close friends you don't really have to name them: they know it without being mentioned. Thank you for being there. Sometimes that's all that matters.

Thanks to each one of my readers who has overwhelmed me with appreciation mails and messages for Book One of the Stranger trilogy and has kept me on my toes to make sure Book Two is equally good. I hope you love it as much as you loved Book One.

Special thanks to all those 'strangers' I come across every day on the road—at traffic signals, in trains, flights and where-not—whose names I don't know, and yet they help me knit stories.

Last but not the least, love and gratitude for my family for standing by me and my decisions.

# About the Author

Novoneel Chakraborty is the bestselling author of seven romance thrillers. *All Yours, Stranger* is the second in the immensely popular Stranger trilogy. He works in the Indian films and television industry, penning popular television shows like *Million Dollar Girl*, *Twist Wala Love*, and *Secret Diaries* for Channel V. He lives in Mumbai.

You can reach him at:

Email: novosphere@gmail.com
Facebook: officialnbc
Twitter: @novoxeno
Instagram: @novoneelchakraborty

He runs a blog—*NovoSphere*—on life and its lessons at: www.nbconline.blogspot.com

# Book Three in the Stranger Trilogy . . .

When Rivanah finds out that Hiya too had received the same messages she did, she freaks out. More so because Hiya was found hanging in her room, and Rivanah has good reason to believe it wasn't a suicide after all. Maybe Hiya was murdered in cold blood . . . and maybe she is the stranger's next victim.

But why would the stranger intend to kill Rivanah? Is Argho the stranger? Will Rivanah be able to find her link to Hiya, whose face she says she doesn't remember but is able to sketch? And if this was not enough of a mess already, Rivanah will have to choose between her first love, Ekansh, and true love, Danny, as well. Whom will she choose?

As the stranger closes in on Rivanah, leaving her with no options but to piece this elaborate puzzle together, the series finale races towards a heartbreaking finish . . .

# MARRY
# ME,
## STRANGER

# By the same author

*A Thing beyond Forever*
*That Kiss in the Rain*
*How About a Sin Tonight?*
*Ex*


Stranger Trilogy
*All Yours, Stranger*
*Forget Me Not, Stranger*

# NOVONEEL CHAKRABORTY

# MARRY ME, STRANGER

RANDOM HOUSE INDIA

Published by Random House India in 2014
Fifth impression in 2016

Copyright © Novoneel Chakraborty 2014

Random House Publishers India Pvt. Ltd
7th Floor, Infinity Tower C, DLF Cyber City
Gurgaon – 122002
Haryana

Random House Group Limited
20 Vauxhall Bridge Road
London SW1V 2SA
United Kingdom

978 81 8400 596 7

Typeset in Requiem Text by Saanvi Graphics, Noida

Printed at Thomson Press India Ltd, New Delhi

A PENGUIN RANDOM HOUSE COMPANY

To you...

...the girl living alone in a big city full of strangers.

# Prologue

## FEBRUARY, 2014

She shut the elevator gate behind her and took a couple of steps to stand in front of her boyfriend's flat. She took out the duplicate key from her bag and put it inside the keyhole rather swiftly. With two full rotations, the door unlocked.

She was supposed to come two days later but the situation in Kolkata was such that she had to cut her trip short. She would have gone straight to her flat but she didn't want to miss an opportunity to surprise her boyfriend the way he would all the time. In fact, there were times when she would wonder if she deserved the kind of maniacal care her boyfriend showered on her. The extent he went to bring a smile on her face scared her because she knew she was getting used to his attention. She knew well-enough that this getting-used-to is to a relationship what pollution is to air—nothing happens immediately, but when you inhale the polluted air for long, you make yourself vulnerable to sickness. But she also thanked her stars that he happened to her right when she was on the verge of doubting the authenticity of love as a concept and kill something valuable within her forever.

Once inside the flat, she found herself standing in a pool of mess. *Typical him!* she thought and panned her sight around the room: the ceiling fan was switched on, the windows were open, the old pedestal fan had an underwear on top of it, a chips and biscuit packet was carelessly lying on the mattress, a pair of jeans had been thrown on the television stand while the doors of the almirah were wide open. From somewhere inside the flat the sound of running water was distinctly audible. One by one she sorted the mess. After cleaning up the room, she called him to check his whereabouts.

'Hi baby, I've reached my place,' she lied.

'Great! I'll come there directly,' he said. There was a hunger in his voice that turned her on. As if he would eat her up the moment they met. Not that she would complain.

'No sweetheart. I have some work in office. You go to your place. I'll come there.'

'Aye aye, princess. But don't be late.'

'I won't.'

Ending the phone call, she closed her eyes and let out a sigh. She then envisioned herself cooking Chinese for him, then dining with him in the soft candlelight that she had brought with herself from Kolkata after which they would...

She opened her eyes and blushed reminiscing about her first orgasm he had introduced her to on her birthday a month ago. She never thought her body was capable of giving her such ridiculously intense pleasures. Until that night, she had never felt so weak and strong at the same time. She smiled to herself imagining his athletic physique—strong broad shoulders, a pronounced worked-out chest, and a narrow waist. He was much taller and broader than her and she always felt safe in his arms. There was a magnetic manliness about him, a smell of sex that he carried which made her seek out lust in the love she had for him. She could respond to her lust with to-the-point-answers whereas love always asked her questions for which there was no specific answer. It was easier to generalize lust than love.

The possibility of a carnal encounter that night made her opt for a Brazilian wax the day before. Her roommate had once told her it would increase her pleasure during foreplay.

She took a shower in his bathroom; it was not the first time she had done so. Applying his used soap made her feel more connected to him. She was in the middle of her shower when she heard her phone ring. She stepped out of the shower and grabbed the phone kept on the cemented pedestal by the bathroom window. It was him. She swiped her thumb on the screen and pressed the speaker button.

'Hey, where are you?' he asked.

'I'm going to office. And you?'

'I'm in the middle of something. I'll reach home late. Just wanted to check on you. See you soon sweetheart. Bye.'

She ended the call and stepped back into the shower after placing the phone on the pedestal. As the water drops cascaded down her body, washing away the white froth of the soap, she wondered if her boyfriend was trying to outsmart her. *Was he going to come home early?*

After a prolonged shower, she rummaged through the clothes in her bag and pulled out a yellow tank top and a pair of denim shorts. She prepared some coffee for herself and, relaxing on the bean bag by the window, took leisurely sips while surfing her Facebook newsfeed on her mobile phone. There were a few 'comments' from her friends who wrote saying they loved her new profile picture. She thanked them and logged out. In no time, sleep snatched her from reality.

She woke up late and wasted no time in preparing her boyfriend's favourite cuisine—Chinese. Once the smell started teasing her olfactory senses, she thought of checking on him. The moment she picked up her phone, there was a power cut. *That's strange*, she thought. It was the first power cut she had encountered in the area. She unlocked her phone quickly and checked the time: 9:05 pm. She was contemplating whether to call her boyfriend or not when she heard the main door unlock.

*I was right! He is being smart.* She switched the light of her phone off with an amused face. With cat-like alertness, she trotted toward the drawing room. As she stood by the entrance, waiting to pounce on her boyfriend and take him by surprise, she sniffed a certain masculine fragrance approaching her. It came from a cologne— 'Just Different' by Hugo Boss—which her boyfriend always used in abundance. She could smell him close now. She knew if she stretched her hand, she would feel him. And she did exactly that.

'Caught you!' she said and before she knew it, she was blindfolded with a ribbon. She immediately recollected sharing a similar fantasy with her boyfriend once: making love blindfolded. *Was it going to be fulfilled tonight?* she wondered and suddenly started craving for a quick communion. She lifted both her hands to feel him but they were grabbed with an empowering strength and handcuffed.

'What's this?' she said with mixed emotions. In a flash she was lifted up by a strong pair of arms, flipped, and literally thrown on the mattress in the drawing room.

'You are really in the mood tonight, aren't you, hon?' she said and lifted her leg up, not allowing him to come on top of her immediately. Her feet touched his clean shaven face. He was sweating. She liked it. Slowly she took her feet down to his bare chest. She liked the fact that he was already out of his tee. She hadn't witnessed such aggressive behaviour from him before. He was always powerful but soft with his lovemaking. And the fact that he wasn't talking was making it all the more intense.

A hand grabbed her right leg and moved it away from his chest. Then she felt something like a rope being tied around her calf. It was only when she felt another rope being tied on her left calf that she felt something was wrong. *Very wrong.* With one strong pull, her legs were parted. She called out her boyfriend's name but there was no response. If he wanted to be rough, he could have told her. She needed it as much as he did. But now he was scaring her more than pleasuring her.

'Talk to me dammit!' she said, exasperated, only to feel a piece of cloth being stuffed into her mouth. She used all her energy to revolt, to free herself, to plead. In the dark quietude she heard her phone ring. She went numb when she heard the ringtone. It was the customized ringtone she had set only for her boyfriend. He was calling her. Was her boyfriend playing a game with her by calling her from within the room? Or, could it mean the person she was with was not her boyfriend? She felt like her guts were falling out. The phone ring stopped. The nerves on her neck became tense as she started screaming her lungs out but no cry escaped her mouth. She tried to sit up but was again pinned down on the mattress with one push. She felt a cold metal touch her outer thighs. She realized her shorts were being cut into half, probably, by a pair of scissors. She wanted to move her legs but knew she would only injure herself in the process. She remained still, holding her breath, as the scissors slowly cut her tank top open. The next moment her breasts juggled out as her top and bra was taken off with one single pull. Embarrassment clouded her mind. Before she could fidget, she felt the last bit of clothing—her panty—being torn apart. For sometime nothing happened. She prayed hard in her mind it was a nightmare. Why would anyone do this to her? It couldn't be her boyfriend. Or could it still be him? Except for her stark nudity, she was sure of nothing. It was only when her breathing turned back to normal that she felt someone sniffing her face. She could feel his breath—it smelt of mint—but she couldn't do much. The sniffing tickled her and made the hair on her nape stand right up. Then he rubbed the nose on her throat, her nipples, dipped the tip of his nose on her belly button, once, and lastly blew out a gentle breath on her waxed vagina. She knew she was wet and it added to the concoction of arousal, fear, and embarrassment that she found herself in. She felt the palm of his hand cover her vagina. It made her feel warm and acutely aroused. She wanted to draw her legs as a reflex but couldn't. Again, nothing happened for some time after which she felt the tip of his tongue circle her inner thighs, her navel, her nipples, and her arm. A sensual tickle made her body wriggle. The tickle also made her listen to certain music within her whose notes were grossly sexual in nature. And these notes had distracted her enough to stop fighting back.

'Ummm...mmmm...mmm...' she exclaimed in a muffled voice, at the zenith of her arousal. Something told her she would be penetrated any moment. The wait made her crave for it even more. But the moment never came. Next she felt her face being dabbed by something soft, as if the person was taking off the light make-up that she had donned for her boyfriend. It postponed the obvious and added to her sexual ache all the more. *Cotton?* she wondered. After the make-up had been rubbed off, she felt a cloth being pressed on her nose. Within seconds, her consciousness deserted her slowly. *This isn't my boyfriend...this can't be my boyfriend...this has to be...*

# 1

Rivanah opened her sleep heavy eyes with a yawn, the saliva rolling down her mouth. Just before she could get out of her bed, her heart almost stopped seeing her own body hanging from the ceiling fan in her room. The hanging figure was wearing the same nightdress as her, looking dead straight at her with a lurid vengeance. As their eyes met, the hanging figure started chuckling. Rivanah wanted to get up and run out of the room but felt herself glued to the bed. Soon the ominous chuckle got so loud she thought she would go deaf. She woke up for real just before the dream could get any worse.

It was the month of May and Kolkata was both hot and humid. Irrespective of the weather, Rivanah had a habit of keeping the air conditioner on at the lowest temperature it could be set to, using a blanket to cover herself up with. She let go of a heavy breath as if she was letting go of the dreaded feel that the nightmare had built inside her. She had seen the same dream one more time before. It had made her break into a cold sweat then. She stretched her hand and picked up her Samsung S3 phone from beside her pillow. It was 4:44 am. She knew the alarm would go off in a minute and it would be time for her new life: *Rivanah Bannerjee, Programmer Analyst, Tech Sky Technologies.*

Four months back, Rivanah had successfully cracked the campus interview for two IT companies during her penultimate semester of B. Tech at Techno Asia College of Engineering in Salt Lake, Kolkata. One company had placed her in Bengaluru while the other in Mumbai with almost the same salary. When the company based in Bengaluru delayed its offer letter after she graduated as a computer engineer, Rivanah decided to join the one in Mumbai. Initially, her parents were apprehensive about her living away since she was their only child and had never stayed away from them before. Eventually they coaxed themselves because that was the demand of present times.

The alarm screeched for a microsecond before Rivanah silenced it. She tried to forget the bad dream by saying a short prayer, asking God's blessings for her new beginning. She climbed down from the bed and went out of her room, into the corridor that took one to the floor below. She leaned down from the staircase and noticed that the tubelight of the kitchen was on. Her mother, as usual, was up before her.

'Mumma, keep my clothes on the bed,' she ordered with the air of a princess and went to the attached bathroom in her room. She quickly took a shower and came out of the bathroom to notice there was indeed a kurti and a pair of leggings on the bed, as demanded by her, but the outfit wasn't the one she had picked out in front of her mother the night before. What irritated her more was that the kurti wasn't from BIBA, her favourite kurti brand. It was one of those low priced kurtis her mother had purchased from a cheap store in Hathibagan.

'Mumma!' she screamed.

'What happened Mini?' her mother asked. She could tell her mother was climbing up the stairs.

'Where's the blue kurti, mumma? I told you I'll wear that today,' Rivanah asked making a face as her mother walked into the room.

'I had given the blue kurti to Bishnu yesterday to get it ironed,' her mother said with guilt, 'but he didn't return it last night. You'll look good in this maroon one too.'

'It's not that, mumma. You know how particular I am about brands. If you would have told me the blue one was not available, I'd have chosen something else. Baba has already packed all my clothes.' She sounded rude. Even Rivanah knew it. She saw her mother leave the room quietly. She immediately followed her downstairs to the kitchen to find her in tears.

'I'm sure,' her mother said wiping her tears with the loose end of her sari, 'when you'll stay alone in Mumbai you will be able to wear whatever you want to.' Rivanah held her by the shoulders and turned to face her, saying, 'I'm sorry mumma. You don't know how much I'll miss you and baba.' She then kissed her mother's cheeks and gave her a tight hug. Her father appeared by the kitchen door, yawning.

'Did you miss your flight, Mini?' he said wiping the sleep off his eyes.

'No baba. But I will if I don't hurry up now. And please take out the new off-white kurti from my bag.' she said and went to her room.

It took her another twenty minutes to get ready. She joined her mother on the breakfast table where a steaming boiled potato meshed in rice and butter along with an omelette was waiting for her in a dish. She wanted to complain because rice and butter would add some extra kilos to her already voluptuous frame but she made a happy face instead and ate it. God knew when she would be back from Mumbai to have her mumma-made-food.

'What should I tell Shantu Mukherjee?' her father asked standing by her chair and gulping his normal quota of lukewarm water with a squeeze of lime in it.

'You tell Shantu Mukherjee what you told Mrs Ganguly and everyone else who comes asking for my hand in marriage. I have a boyfriend, and even if I didn't have one, I won't ever marry a stranger,' Rivanah shot back shoving a spoonful of the rice in her mouth.

Both her mother and father stared at her.

'What?' she shrugged. 'Why are you looking at me like that? You have already met Ekansh.'

'We have and neither your mother nor I have objected knowing well he is not a Brahmin like us,' Mr Bannerjee said.

Rivanah couldn't believe her father had brought up such a trivial and dated matter. 'How does it matter if Ekansh is a Brahmin or not? He doesn't intend to earn his livelihood doing Durga, Saraswati, or Kali Pujo anyway.'

'It matters to me,' he said putting the empty glass down with a thud. 'You don't even let me talk to his parents.'

'Baba, times have changed. I love Ekansh and he loves me too, but we haven't discussed marriage yet.'

'Not yet? Then what do you guys talk so much about?' her mother chipped in.

'About everything but marriage,' Rivanah said finishing the rice and saw her mother shoot a furtive glance at her father.

'I'll tell you both when we are ready. Till then, no more marriage talk or proposals please.'

'Abhiraj is an IIM pass out and...'

'Who is Abhiraj?' Rivanah stood up.

'Shantu Mukherjee's son.'

'Baba, please!'

The parents sighed watching their daughter saunter to the washbasin.

'Good that at least you went from Mrs Ganguly's school teacher son to an IIM pass out. God, who marries a primary school teacher!' she said rinsing her mouth with water.

'Okay!' she said and raised her hands in the air animatedly. 'I will talk to Ekansh about marriage but don't give me that look now.'

Her parents heaved a sigh of relief.

Mr Bannerjee drove her to the sprawling new Netaji Subhash Airport in their Alto. The moment he halted the car near one of the departure gates, he turned to Rivanah and said, 'Mini, I called your Meghna di last night. She won't be able to...'

'...come to the airport because she has office so I'll have to take a Meru Cab from the airport itself and go to her place, take the keys from the security guard, and get in. This is the fourth time you've told me this baba.'

She climbed out of the car along with her parents.

Her mother shot a sly smile at her husband and murmured, '*Meye boro hoye geche, bujecho?*'

Mr Bannerjee nodded in agreement. Their daughter had indeed grown up.

He tried to hide his anxiety and said, 'Take out your PAN card and the print out of the ticket. You will need to show it at the entrance gate.

Rivanah flashed both the ticket and the PAN card at him with a smile. They walked her till the entry point after which she touched their feet and kissed them goodbye. She had not thought this moment would feel so heavy before but now, looking at her parents waving at her with sad faces, she thought it would have been better had she been placed in Kolkata itself.

Rivanah slept through most of the smooth 2 hour, 40 minutes flight to Mumbai. She woke up when the sun's rays kissed her face through the aeroplane's window. The view outside made her stealthily click a couple of pictures from her phone which was on airplane-mode. *I will send them to Ekansh once my flight lands,* she thought. It had been two months since they had last met each other. She checked out pictures of them together on her phone. One album contained pictures they had clicked the night before he flew to Bengaluru to join a software company. As she tapped on the pictures, every moment seemed to come alive as a memory. They had had dinner in Peter Cat restaurant in Park Street that night. He was looking dapper in a black round-neck tee and jeans while she was in an Anarkali salwar-suit. Post dinner, they had silently walked hand-in-hand giving each other furtive romantic glances without really talking. Finally, they had kissed standing behind a fused street lamp near her place.

'A kiss means a part of me will forever trust you. A kiss means a part of you will forever reside in me. A kiss means a part of us will forever forgive each other,' Ekansh had said looking deep into her eyes right after their short kiss. Then they had smooched while her eyes cried warm tears. The flight attendant tapped on her shoulder lightly to take her order for the in-flight meal. Rivanah, realizing her eyes were moist, quickly took out her shades and covered her eyes. How much fun would it have been if she was employed in Bengaluru too? She was ready to wait for the Bengaluru-based company's offer letter and let the Mumbai one pass but Ekansh told her about an impending recession and asked her to join the company she had got an offer from. Then later, she could perhaps move to a different company in Bengaluru. It made sense then but sitting in the flight all she wished was if she could spend all her life in his arms; no work, no reality, nothing to disturb them.

Her mother called the minute the flight landed. Rivanah kept assuring her the journey was fine and that she was alright.

'Now keep the phone down, mumma. My phone's on roaming. I'll call when I reach Meghna di's place.' She disconnected the phone and asked around for where the pick-up point for Meru cab was. She found her pre-booked Meru cab waiting to take her to her destination. The driver helped her keep the luggage in the trunk and soon drove her out of the airport.

'*Goregaon east mein kahan, madam?*' the driver asked.

'Vishnu Dham,' she said and quickly updated her Facebook status: *Travelled alone for the first time. Mumbai feels awesome!*

Next she called Ekansh from her phone.

'Hey babu, I'm in *aamchi* Mumbai!'

8

'How does it feel?' he asked.

'It's...it's...' She was about to respond when her eyes fell on something beside her on the cab's seat. It may have been there when she got in, but she didn't notice it before.

'One second,' she told Ekansh and took her time to grab the neatly ironed blue kurti. It seemed like an exact replica of the one that she wanted to wear in the morning. *Or was it the same one?* She was intrigued.

'I'm calling you back,' she said and cut the call. Rivanah checked the kurti's brand: BIBA. Size M. Her brand, her size.

'Yeh kiska hai?' she asked the driver. He quickly flipped his head for once but seemed clueless about it.

'Mereko nahi pata madam.'

*Maybe it's another passenger's,* Rivanah guessed though doubting her own thought. She was about to keep the kurti back where it was kept when the driver responded that she was his first passenger for the day. With a frown she averted her eyes back to the blue kurti and unfolded it this time to examine it properly. Something fell off from its fold. It was a piece of white cloth with something embroidered in black in the middle. She picked it up and saw it was a message:

*Be ready Mini.*

Her throat went dry. Only her parents called her by that name.

# 2

The first thing Rivanah did after stepping inside Meghna's one bedroom-hall-kitchen flat, taking the keys from the security guard, was call her mother up.

'Did you send the blue kurti, mumma?' She had brought the kurti with her and was looking at it sitting by the couch with one ear pressed to the phone.

'Blue kurti? Which blue kurti?' Her mother sounded clueless.

'The one I wanted to wear this morning but you said Bishnu hadn't returned it.'

'Oh, don't ask about that. I went to Bishnu after you left but he said he had lost it.'

Rivanah felt a lump in her throat. How, or more importantly, *why* was the kurti in the cab with her name stitched on that white cloth? A blue kurti from Biba could have been a coincidence but a blue kurti with a cloth having a message for someone by the name of 'Mini' couldn't be just a coincidence.

'But why are you asking this?' her mother asked.

'Just like that,' Rivanah blurted. She knew if she told her mother about the sudden appearance of the kurti, it would only worry her and she would ask a series of questions after that. It was only a kurti and a message—nothing more. *Does the incident deserve my attention? Does it even matter?* Rivanah thought and heard her mother say, 'How is Meghna?'

'I have just come, mumma. Meghna di is in office.'

Meghna was Rivanah's paternal uncle's daughter. She worked as a senior copy editor with an advertising agency and had married a Muslim colleague of hers. The marriage was considered blasphemy in her family and most of the Bannerjee family had boycotted her except for Rivanah's parents. Though they didn't support her decision, they did stay in touch with her for their own daughter's sake. They knew one day Rivanah would get a job and if she had to travel to Mumbai, then Meghna could be of help.

It was late evening when Meghna returned home from office. Rivanah was never close to her cousin but she secretly admired her for the stance she took—especially the way she stood up to her parents for her love. It wasn't easy to do so. Meghna inspired her to listen to her heart, so if anyone stood against her and Ekansh's love, she too would follow in her footsteps.

'So nice to see you di! After...' 'Three years,' Meghna said. 'We haven't met since I got married.' There was

11

an awkward silence which Rivanah eventually broke by saying, 'When will jiju be home?'

'He will be late.' Rivanah strongly felt the sense of indifference in her voice but she didn't probe.

After dinner, Rivanah pulled out the sofa, turning it into a bed. Aadil, Meghna's husband, was still not home.

'Won't you wait for jiju?' she asked Meghna when she saw her getting ready for bed.

'What's there to wait? He'll come when he has to. You sleep tight darling,' Meghna said and went to the bedroom.

Rivanah's mother had categorically asked her not to tell Meghna anything about Ekansh. Though she wasn't in touch with the Bannerjee family, her mother didn't want to give any relative a chance to talk ill about her daughter, especially when she knew Ekansh wasn't from their community. Rivanah had agreed. It was only when she heard Meghna's soft snores, standing stealthily by the bedroom door, that she dialled Ekansh's number from the drawing room. The moment he picked up the phone, he showered non-stop kisses, amusing her in the process. He sounded like an adorable puppy who had been missing its master for long. She was happy to be in love with a boy who was so crazy about her.

'Statue!' she said and Ekansh went quiet. Rivanah took over from him and continued with the non-stop 'muah-shower'. He should also know the girl he wooed in college was as crazy as him.

They had studied in the same college but had met each other for the first time during a hunger strike in their college ground against a professor's heinous beating of a student. Ekansh Tripathi was from the Mechanical branch and she was from Computer Science. It was while screaming her lungs out during the protest with a large group of students who had assembled in the ground that she noticed Ekansh, sitting diagonally from her, put his hand inside a sling bag and then swiftly transfer something into his mouth. He was putting up a pretence of shouting the slogan when he was actually eating something! Rivanah slowly moved toward him and said, 'Shame on you!'

Ekansh turned sideways and gave her a guilty look.

'Finish it fast.' Ekansh quickly swallowed the rest of it and then quipped, 'I'm sorry.' He had to shout into her ear to mitigate the shouts of the other students.

'Don't you know we are on a hunger strike? What were you eating?' Rivanah said with a suspicious face. Ekansh put his hand back in his sling bag and drew out a closed fist. Rivanah knew it had something. He forwarded his hand as she opened her palm. It was a dry laddu.

'Mom gave it to me this morning,' Ekansh's smile had two shades to it—stupidity and nervousness.

'Such a mumma's boy you are,' she said with sarcasm and gobbled the full laddu like Ekansh did a moment back.

13

'Please don't tell anyone,' Ekansh pleaded.

'Only if you give me one more laddu.'

He quickly took out another one and gave it to her.

'God, I don't know when this stupid strike will get over. I'm so damn hungry,' she said to herself and gobbled the second laddu as well. With a mouthful of laddu, Ekansh felt like she was the cutest girl he had ever seen in his life.

'Want to have more?' he asked. She nodded. He quickly gave her another and said, 'I'm Ekansh Tripathi. First year, Mech. And you?'

Every laddu was followed with a question from him and an answer from her. Before they knew it, the noise around stopped being a distraction and they hit it off like a house on fire. Everything in him seemed to be complimenting everything in her. Once done with the laddus, they added each other on Facebook from their phones and by the time the students dispersed from the ground, they had fed each other's numbers in their phone book as well. For the next three years in college, both became a source of hope for other couples. People broke-up, ditched, deceived, toyed right, left, and centre but their bond only grew stronger. They were tagged as FTC by their batch mates. FTC meant a Fairy Tale Couple. There were students who, looking at them, longed to be in love and there were students with multiple heartbreaks who were envious of them. Students in their respective batches were confident

14

that if ever their story would be written, it'd turn into a runaway bestseller. True love, they often told their batch mates, was like stardom; anyone can get it but not everyone.

Ekansh was the most balanced boy Rivanah knew existed. He never shouted at her, never abused her, never even touched her the wrong way. There were times when she would go hyper about a matter but he would help her calm down, making her understand how unnecessary it was. Ekansh not only loved her, he inspired her, encouraged her, and in a way spoilt her emotionally as well by making her believe that there was someone for her to fall back on.

During their fourth year in college, they introduced each other to their parents as each other's best friends. They were young and both agreed on the fact that it would be better if they let their parents know about the seriousness of their relationship only after they were financially independent. One incident Rivanah would never forget was the day she met with an accident on her way to college. A bus had hit her while she was standing with her back to the road. She was immediately rushed to the nearest hospital. It was one of her exam days. When one of her friends messaged Ekansh about it, he left his exam midway and rushed to the hospital. He got a 'back' on that paper, which he could have topped otherwise, but he never complained to her about it. His selflessness made her love him even more.

The first major twist in their story came when he got a job in Bengaluru after college and had to stay away from her; the first time in four years. They were momentarily happy when Rivanah too cracked a company which would have placed her in Bengaluru but with the sudden turn of events, she was now in Mumbai while he was still in Bengaluru.

'I can always come down to Mumbai. It's not that far,' he said to Rivanah on the phone as she ensconced on the sofa-cum-bed.

'And what exactly will we do here, Mr boyfriend?' Rivanah had a naughty tinge to her voice.

'I have a friend who lives alone in Mumbai. He has office on Saturdays,' Ekansh giggled on the phone.

'My naughty baby. It's been so long. When will we get to stay together?'

'Why? What can we do staying together that we can't now?'

'Oh no, we aren't going that way tonight. Di is here.'

For the next half an hour, had the most amazing phone sex. With her eyes on the small passage leading to the bedroom, hoping Meghna doesn't appear there all of a sudden, and her mind fuelled by Ekansh's dirty words, she kept touching herself till a gigantic pleasure wave swept her off her conscious self. She didn't know when she fell asleep. She woke up with a start after hearing someone screaming. It was only then that she realized there were not one but two people in the room. One was her sister and the other was her jiju. She could hear Aadil hurling abuses at Meghna and she reciprocating equally. She wanted to go inside the bedroom and see what the matter was, but their pitch scared her and she remained put. She picked up her phone to check if Ekansh was awake. It was 4:15 am. She was about to call Ekansh when she noticed a message on her phone from an unknown number. She opened it. It read: *Beware of the darkness that engulfs you in the form of light.*

Rivanah frowned and typed a reply: *Who is this?*

After sending the message, she checked the phone number. As she read the digits one by one, she could feel her heart beat ascend. It was the same as her phone number! She immediately called back at the number. The voice at the other end said exactly what she was expecting: 'The number you are trying to reach is busy. Please try after sometime.'

Just then, another message popped up. *Don't waste your time, Mini. Know your worth.*

# 3

'Can two people have the same phone number?'

It was the next morning and Rivanah was in an autorickshaw on her way to office. She had called Ekansh in the autorickshaw itself.

'Two people with the same phone number? Maybe if the SIM card is duplicated, but I'm not sure if it can be done. Why are you asking?'

For a moment, Rivanah was lost in her thoughts. Why would someone duplicate her SIM? Even if someone did, the question was how? She had changed five mobile phones from the time she bought her first, but the SIM card was the same since her first phone in standard eleven. She used to keep her phone with her twenty-four-seven. Only thrice had her phone been away from her for a considerable amount of time. One was when she had forgotten it in a cab but later found it thanks to the honest driver. The second time was when she had misplaced it somewhere in college. She had to buy a new phone after that but was able to reactivate the same phone number for herself. And third was when her purse was robbed in a local train while she was travelling to a friend's house to Khorda from Bidhan Nagar station a few days after her graduation. But she only thought it was stolen. She had found the bag in the train's compartment itself while getting down.

'Hello? You there?' Ekansh asked.

'Yeah, sorry.' Rivanah's trance broke. She tried to get all this out of her mind and focus on her new life ahead. It was her first day as a working professional.

'Why are you asking about the same phone number?' Ekansh said.

'A friend asked,' she lied so he wouldn't prod further and said, 'Anyway, I'm on my way to office. It's my first day. Wish me luck babu.'

'My best wishes are always with you. Have a great day ahead. And be confident.'

'Thanks!'

'Call me whenever you are free.'

'Sure.'

◆

Tech Sky Technologies had three branches in Mumbai but luckily for Rivanah, she had to join the Goregaon east branch which was two kilometres from her sister's place. She climbed out of the auto and paid the driver. She then came and stood right in front of the humungous building, clicked a quick selfie, and Whatsapped the image to Ekansh with three kiss smileys. Five kisses came in as a response. She smiled and took a deep breath looking high up at the Tech Sky building. She had been waiting for this moment since a long time and it was finally here. For an outsider it was just a building where people came and worked, but for her it would give her an identity that she had studied hard to attain. It was also a symbol for her impending financial freedom.

'Rivanah Bannerjee, you are a corporate girl now,' she said to herself as she entered the premise feeling jubilant.

The first day was more about submission of documents and certificates, meeting some of the other freshers, and undergoing an orientation programme where an HR personnel from the company briefed the newcomers about Tech Sky's corporate goals, ambition, and what the company stood for. The appraisal process for the employees and other benefits and rights were discussed too. Coincidentally, the HR person who presented the company profile to the freshers was Prateek Basotia—Rivanah's senior from school.

'I thought I knew this face when you came in but then I wasn't sure if it was really you,' she said once Prateek came over to her with a guess-who smile after the presentation.

'But I was looking forward to meet you today,' Prateek said.

'Huh?'

'I have been following you on Facebook since a year now. I read your post about Tech Sky's recruitment.'

'Oh, then why didn't you message me?'

'I wanted to but I thought maybe you won't recognize me.'

'Come on!' Rivanah exclaimed and recollected her last meeting with Prateek. She was in the tenth standard while he was in the twelfth. He had proposed to her a day before Valentine's Day that year, but his geeky image in school and caution from friends that he was a weirdo pushed her to publically turn his proposal down. She had not seen or heard from him since. And even now he seemed as unsure in front of her as he did in school. He rarely looked straight at her while talking. As if he was running the danger of getting slapped by her anytime.

'I was there with you on the flight to Mumbai a day before. Your seat number was 17 A while mine was 19 D,' he said in a matter-of-fact manner.

'What? Why didn't you approach me?'

'It would have spoiled today's surprise,' he smiled. 'I was in Kolkata on a holiday. Anyway, where are you putting up here?'

'At my cousin's place in Goregaon east itself. Do you stay here with your family?'

'No. Mom and dad are in Kolkata. I stay in Andheri west. I've been working for Tech Sky for over a year now.'

21

An awkward silence followed whereby neither knew what else to talk about.

'This is wonderful,' Prateek said with a sudden animated gesture, 'Never knew fate would let us meet again.'

Rivanah found the last statement bordering on it's-my-chance-to-impress-you-again.

Prateek received a message on his phone and excused himself while Rivanah went back to her desk. She stumbled upon him later in the evening inside the office elevator when she was about to leave office for the day. He requested for her phone number.

'This sounds like a Kolkata Vodafone number,' he said saving the number on his phone.

'I didn't get time to switch to a local number yet.'

'I would suggest you go for a corporate post-paid connection, otherwise it may take time.'

'Okay.'

'Don't worry, I'll help you out with it.'

*He still loves me*, Rivanah concluded, feeling good about herself.

'Should I drop you home? I have a bike,' Prateek asked with childlike enthusiasm once they stepped out of the elevator.

'Thanks but I'll walk.'

She could sense the disappointment in him.

'Okay. See you.'

He was about to leave when Rivanah stopped him on a hunch.

'Is there any opening in Tech Sky for someone with a three months' experience?'

Prateek thought for a moment and said, 'Not right now.'

'Okay. If I forward you a CV, could you please let me know whenever there's an opening?'

'Sure. Mail me. My id is prateek.b@techsky.com'

Rivanah typed some gibberish on her phone to show she was indeed jotting down the id and said, 'I will ask my boyfriend to mail you directly.'

Prateek's response came a little late.

'Great! Take care.'

Rivanah knew Ekansh would never mail him his CV nor would she ask him to but it was her way of telling Prateek that she was in a committed relationship in case he still harboured any thoughts of proposing to her again. School was still manageable but working in the same office, she didn't want to end up in an awkward situation.

She came out of the office premises and was looking for an autorickshaw when Prateek slowed down his bike in front of her.

'Say hi to Ekansh,' he said.

For an instant she was flummoxed. 'How do you know his name?' Rivanah couldn't help but exhibit her surprise a little too overtly.

'I told you, I've been following you on Facebook since a year.' He drove off before she could see his expression.

*He already knew she was committed and yet...*

23

# 4

Rivanah was supposed to 'officially' join Tech Sky Technologies on the Monday of the following week, giving her a lot of free time to kill before that. All that time made her realize she had no friends in Mumbai. There were some people from her college and a few from her batch working in the city, but they weren't really 'friends' with whom she could hang out. And Ekansh had categorically told her before she left Kolkata that once she was on her own in Mumbai, she shouldn't trust anybody.

'When you move out of your home everyone connects to you with an agenda. At times the agenda is clear from the beginning and at times it is clear only when the person has fulfilled it through you. But by then it's often too late for damage control,' he had said.

Though Rivanah was 22-years-old, she still didn't have a natural instinct of judging the real face of a person. Ekansh was her only help. This was yet another thing she loved about him. He was what she was not. As a couple, it's the one thing that becomes important once you go out in the real world. Two blind people can never cross the highway of reality together. She was the one who did things on an impulse and then thought what went wrong whereas Ekansh was the cautious one who weighed the pros and cons before going ahead with anything. His maturity was uncommon for boys of his age and she adored that about him. One thing he always told her was to be extra alert of guys who always took the first initiative to talk to her.

'Then what should I do? Should I take the initiative instead?' she said.

'No stupid! What I mean is if you find a guy trying to talk to you all the time, even when he knows you aren't interested, stay cautious.'

'Hmm. Do you do that too? Talk to a girl even when she isn't interested?' she teased him.

'Only when she is as hot as you,' he giggled back.

'I'll kill you,' She shot back.

Two days before her official joining, Prateek Whatsapped her in the morning and asked if she was free in the evening for coffee. She was a little apprehensive in the beginning and didn't know what to say. The last time she didn't comply when he wanted to drop her home. Now this. Rivanah didn't want to come across as a snobbish bitch. School days were fine but now they were in the same office and more importantly, he was in the HR department. Rubbing someone the wrong way even before she joined office was something she couldn't afford at this point. She thought of asking Ekansh once. She even typed a message but deleted it on second thoughts. She knew he would never say yes to her going out for coffee with any other guy. But why was she being so uptight about it? It was only coffee! Being in a relationship with Ekansh had dissected her from within into two Rivanahs: the impulsive Rivanah and the trying-to-be-mature-like-Ekansh Rivanah. While the two were duelling it out, Prateek messaged again saying they would be in Goregaon itself (in Oberoi mall to be specific). The impulsive Rivanah won.

*Great! I will pick you up by 6. Okay?* Prateek messaged immediately after she said yes.

The trying-to-be-mature-like-Ekansh Rivanah thought for some time and messaged: *I'll come there on my own.*

She reached Oberoi mall on time. They went to Moshe's and took a table for two.

'This colour doesn't suit you,' Prateek said pouring two sugar sachets onto his coffee.

For a moment Rivanah didn't know what he was talking about. Then she noticed him looking at her top. 'But I love blue,' she said.

'But I think you will look good in black.'

'I don't like black,' Rivanah shot back. She loved black as well but she said otherwise as a reflex action. She didn't like Prateek's patronizing tone. And it was right then that the trying-to-be-mature-like-Ekansh

Rivanah taunted the impulsive Rivanah: *I told you it will be a mistake meeting Prateek for coffee. Who knows he may still be harbouring feelings for you. Don't you know people always remain vulnerable toward their first love and interpret any unintended action as a positive signal to proceed?*

'Don't mind but I feel Indian attire suits you more than western. I loved the way you looked in office on the first day. The kurti fit you just perfectly.'

*Mr School-lover trying to play Mr Husband, huh?*

'Is that an S3? You could have bought an iPhone instead. It's better,' he said and forwarded his iPhone to her.

She excused herself to go to the washroom where the impulsive Rivanah convinced her to leave as soon as possible lest she said anything unpleasant. She came back and told Prateek that her sister had called and that she needed to accompany her to the vegetable market because she was all alone.

'Please don't mind,' she said picking up her Vera Moda bag.

'But your coffee?'

'Di is waiting. I'm so sorry.'

Before Prateek could say anything more, she was gone. On her way down the escalator she promised herself: *No more coffee with Prateek. Phew!*

By the time Rivanah reached her sister's place, the cook was done preparing dinner: chapattis which were as thin as papad, a dry bhindi ki sabzi, and a bland dal. It was the same thing Rivanah had been having since the past five days. She didn't know why her cousin never complained. How can someone eat the same dull food every day? She decided she wouldn't eat that night. But soon the tumultuous hunger in her took precedence and she ate the food silently. Seconds later, she spat out the bolus in the dustbin and proceeded to prepare Maggi noodles, burnt the pan where she was boiling water, hid it in the sink amongst other utensils in utter frustration and called her mother.

'The cook here is such an idiot mumma,' she said.

'At your age I used to cook for my entire joint family, Mini. I used to tell you so many times to learn to cook basic food so you could at least sustain yourself in situations like these but...'

'Mumma, I'm a programmer analyst not some home-maker.'

'Youngsters like you only think of careers all the time. Now boil your career for two minutes and have it for dinner.,'

'Oh mumma, I'm hungry and you are lecturing me instead of providing me with a solution.' There was a beep on the phone. Ekansh's call was on waiting.

'Maybe I'll order something. Call you later.'

'But what will you order?' Before Mrs Bannerjee could get a response, she switched the call.

'Hey babu, why are you calling so early tonight? What

happened?' she said. Usually Ekansh called her after eleven at night.

'I...I...' Ekansh drawled as if he was choking on something. Rivanah had a bad feeling about this.

'Ekansh?' Her heart missed a beat. 'Are you crying?'

'Just...look outside,' he said.

Rivanah rushed to the window in the room with her heart in her mouth. Ekansh was standing on the footpath across the building, waving at her excitedly with a huge grin on his face.

'Come down. Quick!' he said and cut the line.

Rivanah changed from her shorts and tank top to jeans and a tee and rushed down the building.

'Ekansh!' She was exhilarated to see him. She crossed the small lane to reach him and hugged him tight for a minute before she heard him speak.

'People are watching,' he said softly into her ears.

'I don't care.' She broke the hug and looked deep in his eyes.

'I missed you.'

'Tell me about it. But how come you are here?' Rivanah was yet to believe she wasn't imagining Ekansh's Mumbai visit.

'Because my life is here,' he said with a smile which made her all the more excited.

She immediately kissed him on his cheeks and said, 'Idiot, you could have told me. I would have come to receive you at the airport. I'm totally free till Monday, remember?'

'I wanted to surprise you, but why the hell are you crying, stupid?' Ekansh said rubbing her eyes. Rivanah was a tad conscious. 'Thanks for coming,' she blurted, adding, 'I'm hungry. Let's have dinner.'

'I can eat a horse myself,' he said.

They laughed and took an autorickshaw to Goregaon railway station and then took the local train. Before getting down at Churchgate, Rivanah called her sister and told her that she was with friends and would be late. Meghna didn't care much.

Ekansh took Rivanah to the famous roadside eatery Bade Miyan in Colaba where they ordered Badi roti and mutton rolls.

'The food is awesome. How do you know about this place?' she said finishing the hot roll in no time and burning her tongue slightly in the process.

'One of my colleagues is from Mumbai. I flew down with him this evening. He told me.'

'And when are you leaving?'

'Early morning tomorrow. I have office. I'll go to the airport directly after dropping you home tonight. I was just dying to meet you.'

'Awww. Me too,' she said giving him a soft hug.

After a sumptuous dinner at Bade Miyan, they walked till Marine Drive and sat there by the cemented barricade looking at the distant city line and feeling the cool breeze orchestrate an urge for companionship within them.

'I'm sorry,' she said.

Ekansh frowned and turned at her. 'For what?' He budged as she moved her head from his shoulder and matched her sight with his.

'I didn't tell you but I met a guy this evening.'

'What do you mean?'

'He is just this school friend I met in office.'

'Office?'

'Prateek. He is in HR. He means no harm. I was feeling guilty that I didn't tell you about it, that's all.'

Ekansh looked at her for a moment and then leaned forward to kiss her forehead.

'Honesty is the essence of every successful relation-ship.'

'I know. And I won't ever hide anything. I promise,' she said and quickly touched her lips to his, once, and then quickly looked around to see if anyone had seen her. By the time she looked back at Ekansh, she felt her lips being sucked by him. She reciprocated for a few seconds and then pushed him back.

'When will we be in the same city?' she said.

'Just complete six months here. I'll then forward your CV to a few contacts I have made in office. Then we both shall be in Bangalore.'

'Same place?' she said.

31

'Same place!' he responded looking at her with an amused face.

'Same room?'

'Same room!'

'Same bed?'

'Same bed!'

Rivanah clasped his hand warmly and with a puppy face said, 'Let's get married.'

Ekansh looked at her as if she had just confessed she was an undercover agent.

'What? Why do you look surprised?' she quipped unable to interpret his looks.

'You know my plans. I want to complete two years in this company first and then pursue MBA. That's two more years and then we'll happily get married.'

'I know. I said it just like that. We are anyway too young to get married,' she said resting her hand around his waist and head on his shoulder again.

'Exactly. And what's there in a marriage? As long as we are together, that's all that counts.'

'Right. There's nothing more genuine and worthwhile than true companionship. But who will explain this to our parents?'

'Seriously! A few days back my mom said they wanted to talk to your parents.'

Rivanah burst out laughing. Ekansh looked curious.

'My parents always do that. Good God! I think we are the first couple caught up in a situation where our parents want to talk and get us married, but we are not letting them.'

They laughed in unison. It gave way to silence.

'Ekansh, do you think love can die?' Rivanah said with a tone which was a little serious for the occasion. Ekansh took sometime before replying.

'If love is based on priorities and conditions, it can certainly die because priorities and conditions keep changing in life all the time.'

'What is our love based on then?' she said tilting her head up and looking at him directly.

'Our love isn't anything specific. I think when love is something specific, there's a chance of losing it.'

'What do you mean?'

'I mean, if life is night, then our love is light bulbs. If life's a power cut, then our love will be a candle. If life's a traffic jam, then our love will be patience. It's nothing specific and yet it's something without which we won't ever be comfortable. Our love is a solution.'

'Wow!' she exclaimed and kissed his cheeks.

They sat there clicking selfies together; sometimes talking, sometimes silent. When Meghna called her around 11:30 pm asking about her whereabouts, she realized she had to get back home before her parents found out who she was with. They had asked her to be at home by 9 pm sharp, no matter what. A couple of hours back she had called her mother and told her that she had eaten dinner and was preparing to go to sleep.

They walked till the Baskin and Robbins outlet near Marine Drive, bought her favourite ice cream, and ambled till the Churchgate railway station. They took a Borivali bound slow local train whose compartment was mostly empty. They took a corner window seat away from the few other passengers.

'Can I tell you something?' Ekansh said.

'What?'

He took her hand and put it on his groin. Rivanah immediately pulled her hand away nervously feeling his hard-on.

'What are you doing?' she whispered.

'Remember what you did in the bus on our trip to Mondarmoni from college?'

Rivanah clearly knew what he was talking about.

'I can't do it now.'

She was blushing. She looked away from him and out of the window with a sly smile.

Ekansh brought his sling bag and kept it over his lap so that it would cover her hand when it slid inside his pant. Rivanah turned to look at the bag once and then at him. The next instant, she slowly slid her right hand under the bag, unzipped his jeans, and grabbed his hard penis. She had felt it after months. Slowly she started jerking it looking around with an amused expression. Nobody had a clue what was going on. Ekansh laid his head back in bliss. Then she pinched the top and he shrieked out. The few passengers at the other end of the compartment gave them a nonchalant look. Rivanah already had a naughty smile on her face as she jerked it with more force. Ekansh came within two minutes.

'Give me something to clean up,' she whispered. Ekansh gave her his handkerchief. She cleaned up with a face that was ready to burst out into laughter.

Someone on the opposite side of the train's compartment smiled looking at them. Neither Rivanah nor Ekansh knew that the person had ordered the same food which they did in Bade Miyan, had sat on the same cemented barricade of Marine Drive some distance away from them, and had bought the same flavoured ice cream which they did from Baskin and Robbins.

When Rivanah moved inside her sister's flat using the spare key she had given her on the first day itself, she received a message on her phone from her own number like she had a few nights ago.

*You have a month's time to learn to cook Spanish Omelette, Kadhai Paneer, and Butter Chicken for yourself.*

It wasn't funny anymore. She messaged back:

*What? Who are you?*

The reply came instantly:

*Else I'll make you cry.*

A deep frown appeared on Rivanah's face. She re-read the first message. All the three mentioned dishes were her favourite. On a hunch, she messaged back:

*Is that you Prateek?*

The reply came after a good one minute.

*LOL.*

35

# 5

Rivanah's team in office consisted of three men and herself. Her team lead was Sridhar Ram who was the most amicable man she had ever met. In the morning, he would tell all his team members what his expectations were of them and added that his only concern was if they did their work well. If they were able to do so before office time, they were free to use the residual time to their liking and he would save their asses in case senior management probed about it. Making time flexible for an employee, Sridhar believed, increased the overall productivity. But every person has a flaw and Rivanah soon realized Sridhar's flaw was he would never look her in the eyes while talking to her. It was always her breasts as if they had a mouth of their own. It made her feel uncomfortable and irritated, and she wanted to complain to her teammates but couldn't since they themselves were a weird bunch. Bijoy was a porn addict who would watch dirty videos on the office computer and forget to minimize the window whenever

Rivanah approached him. Somehow he scared her and she maintained a safe distance from him. Shantanu was someone who would give her furtive glances all the time but rarely spoke to her directly. And Rohit always stared at her in a way that made her feel naked, even if she was covered from top to bottom.

The office canteen didn't have quality food, and Rivanah knew she would have to get food from home. But she was done with the maid's dull stuff that her sister and her husband had developed a taste for. And cooking didn't interest her, or so she thought, so it was out of question. While munching the somewhat stale burger in the canteen, she wondered about the message she had received asking her to learn to cook else the person would make her cry. *How audacious! Cook, my foot!* Out of sheer angst, she had deleted the message immediately after reading.

She knew that if the situation peaked to another level other than the messages, she would have to involve Ekansh and do something about it.

After she came to her desk post lunch, she found some fresh red roses waiting for her. She counted them: twelve. It was her birth date. She immediately called Ekansh.

'Thank you mister. You really caught me unprepared.'

'What are you saying?'

'The twelve roses.'

'Which roses?'

Rivanah was quiet for a moment. She looked at the roses and then heard him say, 'What are you talking about?' Ekansh genuinely sounded like he knew nothing about it.

'Oh, nothing. I was kidding,' she said feeling an irk brewing in her. She talked to him causally for another minute and then ended the call. Before she could hide the roses inside her desk drawer, her team lead, Sridhar, immediately asked, 'Hey, is it your birthday?' He was looking at her breasts.

'No,' she said picking up the roses without caring to look at him.

'Then? Boyfriend?'

Rivanah nodded with an uninterested smile and brought the roses close to her to inspect them. The fragrance was strong. She kept the entire bunch inside one of the drawers and resumed working. An hour later, Prateek pinged her on the office messenger:

*Hi! You there?*

At first Rivanah thought she would not reply. She was committed and there was no point giving air to the friendship that Prateek was covertly seeking since she was confident he would interpret her friendliness for love. Then another message popped up from him and she had to reply. If she didn't, she knew this passive wooing would continue.

*Did you like the roses?*

He knew she had a boyfriend so what was he doing sending her red roses? Did he believe she could still be lured? A sudden rage filled within her. She could have punched Prateek in the face if he was there in front of her. She took a deep breath, relaxed herself, and then typed on the messenger chat window:

*Please meet me at the smoking zone NOW.*

'I'll be back in a minute,' she told Sridhar and moved out of her cubicle.

The smoking zone was not an official smoking zone but an open extension to the office space where people would smoke and indulge in casual and sometimes—as the office lingo went—*tharki* talk. Prateek joined her after two minutes.

'I don't want to be rude Prateek, but you are not going to send me any more roses, okay?'

'Why? What happened? You don't like roses?' Prateek looked around nervously for once. There weren't many people around.

'I like a lot of things, but that doesn't mean you will gift the mall to me.'

'What's wrong with gifts?'

'Wrong? There's nothing right in it,' Rivanah said helplessly. 'I told you I have a boyfriend.'

'So? Just because you have a boyfriend doesn't mean I can't gift you something? I'm not asking you to leave him. I only sent you simple, harmless, and fresh smelling roses.'

39

'I don't appreciate all this,' Rivanah said and dashed back to her place.

In the evening Prateek pinged her on the office messenger again.

*I'm sorry, Rivanah. Don't be angry with me.*

Rivanah was talking to Ekansh on the phone when she saw the message. Once her phone call ended, she read the message again. She knew she couldn't be too rude with him.

*I'm not angry with you. And it's okay. I'm happy you understood what I meant.*

*You are happy, I'm happy. So, coffee after office?*

An irritated Rivanah logged out of the office messenger. While moving out of the office in the evening, she stopped by the office's main gate. Prateek was standing there with two paper glasses of coffee.

'What's this, Prateek?'

'Coffee. I asked you on the messenger and you...'

'I logged out.'

'Yes. So I thought you are okay with coffee. We can sit and have it in the office premises itself if you have a problem going out with me.'

The guy was slowly getting on her nerves now. She was all too glad she had rejected his proposal in school or else by now she would have either killed him or admitted herself to a mental asylum.

'Okay, let's have coffee.' She wanted to be done with it. 'But Prateek, you have to promise me something.'

'Anything!'

'You won't do something for me unless I request you to do so.'

He gave her a long stare.

'Say something,' she urged.

'I was waiting for you to request me to talk.'

'Very funny! Come now.' They stood at a corner inside the office premises with Prateek who kept talking endlessly while Rivanah did her best to sip off the hot coffee as quickly as she could. Finally, she took an autorickshaw and went home. On her way back, she tried calling Ekansh up but his line would always be busy. So she called one of her close friends from college, Pooja Haldar, who had been placed in a software MNC in Hyderabad. Pooja was the gossip queen of their batch and talking to her was always fun.

The autorickshaw dropped Rivanah right in front of Vishnu Dham. She walked in and took the elevator, still chirping on phone with Pooja. Once the elevator ascended, the call disconnected abruptly because there was no network reception. Rivanah was about to unplug her phone's ear piece when the elevator suddenly stopped a little above the second floor. There was darkness inside the elevator. Rivanah tried but could see nothing through the elevator gate either. She understood it had to be a power cut.

'Hello, anyone there? Hello?' Rivanah said raising her voice. Her eyes were slowly getting used to the dark but she could still see nothing except for the elevator switch-board. Suddenly she heard footsteps coming toward her. *The security guard?* she thought and said, 'Excuse me, I'm stuck here. Could you please get someone to turn on the generator?'

The footsteps stopped as a response. She thought the person might have gone looking for where the generator was. She waited impatiently, wiping the sweat drops off her forehead with her handkerchief. With every passing second she felt the elevator doors were closing in on her in the dark. Then there was a loud noise, as someone kicked the elevator gate hard. Rivanah shrieked out in fear.

'Who is this?' she said in a fragile tone. Nothing happened. Her short, jittery breath could now inhale a certain fragrance. She could tell it was a deodorant but didn't know which one. She hastily tried switching on the flashlight of her phone. The moment she held it in front of the collapsible gate of the elevator, there was another kick on it. This one was stronger than the earlier one. A nervous Rivanah lost her grip on her phone and it fell.

'Please don't do this,' she pleaded trying to bend down to retrieve her phone. Someone now held the elevator gate and shook it hard. Rivanah started shaking in fear and sweating profusely.

'Please!' she somehow muttered.

Silence. The power came on and the elevator started

moving up again. Rivanah felt her muscles relaxing slowly. She tried to look through the gate but there was nobody. Instead, she noticed a white piece of cloth lying on the elevator floor. She picked it up. It was similar to the cloth she had found in the cab on her first day in Mumbai. She flipped the cloth and found something stitched on it in black thread:

*28 more days: learn to cook or learn to cry.*

'What the fuck is this?' As the elevator stopped on her floor, she quickly opened the gates. She climbed down the stairs as fast as she could and went rushing to the security guard who was smoking by the building entrance.

'Bhaiya, did you see anyone enter or leave the building right now?'

'No. Why?'

'Were you here all the time?'

'I only went to switch on the generator madam. But the power is back now.'

'Why did you leave the gate?' she said rather annoyingly.

The security guard gave her an incredulous look and said, 'Who would switch on the generator then?'

Rivanah trotted back into the building, holding onto the piece of white cloth. This time she took the stairs to reach Meghna's third floor flat. When she reached, she saw that taped on the door was another piece of white cloth with words stitched in black:

*Know your worth Mini.*

43

## 6

'I received a message from a phone number identical to mine when I came to Mumbai.'

Rivanah was on Skype chat with Ekansh. Meghna and Aadil, for the first time since her arrival, had gone out together to one of Meghna's friend's wedding in Thane. And it was the right time for Rivanah to catch up with her boyfriend.

'What do you mean? Who is it?' Ekansh said, concerned, and thought for a moment before adding, 'Is this why you asked me about the duplicate SIM?'

'Uh-huh,' Rivanah nodded.

'What did the message say?'

Rivanah thought for a moment and said, 'I don't know.'

'You don't know?'

'It said something like get ready.' She wanted to tell him about the elevator incident too but she could see how worried he already looked. She didn't want him to skip office and fly down once again to Mumbai for something even she wasn't sure about.

'What? That's absurd. Listen, why aren't you getting a new local number?'

'I have applied for a corporate connection. I'll get it in a day or two. I will stop using the Kolkata number then.'

'Just break that SIM card, okay?'

'Okay.'

The call got disconnected, so Ekansh called her again.

'Babu, will you like it if I cook for you?' she said projecting a puppy-faced expression.

Ekansh came close to the cam and said, 'Can you pinch yourself?' He knew what a disaster she was in the kitchen and also how much she hated to cook. All her life she had only prepared a boiled egg. Once.

'Dhat! Tell me honestly. Will you like it if I cook for you the next time we are together?'

'Which guy won't like it if his girl cooks for him? It's a major turn-on for any average Indian guy.'

'Is it? Why didn't you tell me this before?'

'I knew how much you hated cooking. But there's no need to cook.'

'Why?'

'When we'll be together, I don't want you to waste time in the kitchen. I would rather want you to do something useful with me in the bedroom.'

'You are incorrigible!' she said and blushed.

'Please don't blush like that. I can't afford a hard-on when I'm alone.'

'Shut up!' she said turning a darker shade of red. 'I love you.'

At the back of her mind, the elevator incident had shaken her up a bit. She wanted to take the message seriously. But now, with Ekansh telling her it wasn't important for him if she knew how to cook, the message and the sender stopped mattering. But she also promised herself that one more threatening incident and she would tell Ekansh everything honestly.

'Hello!' Ekansh said waving his hand and trying to break her trance. Rivanah was about to speak up when the doorbell rang. She immediately cut the Skype call, shut her laptop screen, and went to open the door. It was Meghna and Aadil. The latter was drunk and both were shouting at the top of their voices.

'So what if I shook hands with him? I'm not sleeping with him like you do with your colleagues. Do you think I don't know about it?' Meghna said with a pitch that Rivanah was now somewhat used to.

'What happened di?' she asked with a dry throat. She had heard them fighting a couple of times more but this was the first time she had said something.

'Stay out of it, Mini,' Meghna roared and walked inside the bedroom. Aadil followed her. Rivanah shut the door quickly. Inside the bedroom, a two-hour long blame game began, with abuses galore. Rivanah thought there would begin a fist fight any moment but thankfully nothing of that sort happened. She couldn't sleep that night and kept exchanging messages with Ekansh over the phone. *It was one thing when an arranged marriage went wrong but when a love marriage goes flat like Meghna's and Aadil's,* Rivanah thought, *it makes the entire institution of marriage sound scary and loathsome.*

*We will never fight, okay?* she messaged Ekansh once the fight in the bedroom subsided.

*Of course we won't. Fights happen when there's misunderstandings or if one takes the other for granted. We won't do either of the two,* Ekansh responded.

*I have seen Meghna di and Aadil da go against the entire family for their love and now they are fighting with each other all the time. Where's that love that made them leave their family?*

*Relationships do change with time dear,* Ekansh messaged back.

*I know and that's why I'm scared. Please don't ever change, Ekansh. I won't be able to take it. I love you too much.*

*I love you too much as well.*

Unfortunately, it wasn't the only night that Meghna and Aadil fought. Almost every alternate day they would end up fighting over trivial issues but the accusations were serious and most of the time forthright cheap. Soon Rivanah concluded that perhaps both Meghna and Aadil knew the relationship was over but were too afraid to acknowledge it because they were each other's choice to begin with. Rivanah shared her conclusion with Ekansh one night after installing Whatsapp on her new local phone number.

*I agree,* replied Ekansh.

*Maybe neither wants to take the blame for the break up since they both are to be blamed for the relationship anyway.*

*Jesus. What happened to you? You suddenly sound so mature!*

Rivanah sent him an angel's emoticon.

*On a serious note Ekansh, their fights are simply getting on my nerves now.*

It wasn't only her cousin and her husband who were getting to her. The office had seemed exciting at first, but within a fortnight, the thought of going to office and working in the cubicle where she had to grind herself all day made her cringe. At night she came home feeling weak and exhausted. The food cooked by the maid was so repulsive that many a times she skipped dinner or simply drank a glass of milk and slept. Weekends were worse. Ekansh was in Bengaluru while she had no friends to hang out with in Mumbai. Prateek was there but she kept avoiding him, citing one excuse or the other. If she stayed back at home, there was her sister and brother-in-law to make life miserable for her. She preferred to sleep than join them for a movie or dinner outside because she knew peace would eventually be a far cry with them around. Once, during a dinner at a restaurant, Aadil ended up fighting with the waiter only because his idea of a Peking Soup was different from what the restaurant served him. When Meghna tried to calm him down, the fight steered direction ruining the evening all together.

On the second last Saturday of the month, Rivanah woke up late in the evening with hunger cramming her stomach. She opened the refrigerator but there was nothing to eat. She called Meghna who told her she was in a movie theatre with a friend and would be late. She also informed her that the cook had taken a day off. The late relaying of information angered Rivanah but she didn't say much. She called the Borivali Biryani Centre and ordered a Chicken Tikka Biryani for herself. It was only after she had ordered the biryani that she realized she had run out of cash. She changed quickly and went out to the ATM across Vishnu Dham. She took out the cash, tore the receipt slip, threw it in the dustbin, and turned to go back to the flat when she noticed a piece of white cloth taped on the glass of the ATM's door from outside. It wasn't there when she entered.

'Dammit!' she muttered removing the tape on the cloth.

*7 days more.* It was stitched on it with black thread.

Rivanah looked around crushing the cloth in her grasp and exclaimed loudly, 'Fuck you!'

Few passers-by gave her a what's-wrong-with-you glance and then forgot about it.

Rivanah was sitting alone in the office cafeteria, during one of her monotonous days, tossing the fruits in her bowl when Prateek approached her.

'May I please join you?' He said it with such politeness that Rivanah couldn't say no. All these days Prateek had maintained a distance even though she knew he was keeping an eye on her.

Prateek thanked her and sat opposite her with his plate of masala idli and a paper-glass of filter coffee.

'Please don't scold me, but these past few days I have been noticing you looking pensive and disturbed about something. Is everything all right?'

*So he was noticing me, after all!* Rivanah thought and looked at him. If both of them didn't have a history in school and he was a tad less psychotic like he was in that moment, she would have found him cute.

'Anything troubling you?' he asked with genuine concern.

She wasn't sure if she could trust him with any personal information.

'You can tell me,' he said grasping her hand. The psycho Prateek was back. Rivanah instantly pulled her hand back and said, 'It's just that I'm finding it difficult to live with my cousin and her husband.'

'Why, what happened? Aren't they good people?'

'They are but I think they need space and more privacy which they don't get with me around.' Rivanah lied on purpose.

'Hmm.' He cut a piece of the Idli, dipped it in sambar, and put it in his mouth.

'Why don't you shift home?' he suggested.

It did occur to her to shift to some PG but when she told her parents about it, they vehemently opposed it saying staying alone with unknown people wasn't safe. Though Rivanah wasn't convinced, she agreed only since she didn't want the trouble that comes with shifting houses.

'It's too much of trouble,' she lamented to Prateek.

'I agree, but when you have a true friend, you don't have to worry about it.' It was the mild Prateek again.

Rivanah had to take a decision within seconds; yes or no. If she said yes, Prateek would invariably tell her he would take care of her shift and if she said no, then she would have to go back home—day after day—and try to adjust with her volatile cousin and her maniacal husband which she knew had tested her patience to the hilt already.

'Can you really help me?'

'Of course! All you need to do is check the availability of flats on sulekha.com or magicbricks.com. You can also check certain Facebook pages for availability.'

It sounded easy. It also meant she wouldn't have to work as hard as she thought earlier.

Once home, she called Ekansh and discussed her plans of moving out with him.

'Wow! The next time I'm there, we shall stay all alone.'

'I'll have roommates hon.'

'We shall lock them out.'

After the nod from Ekansh, she logged into the websites Prateek had told her about, posted her requirement on one of the 'Flat for rent in Mumbai' Facebook pages and shortlisted five places in Goregaon and Malad that were reasonably close to her office and within her budget. She called on the phone numbers listed in the advertisement on the websites and got a favourable reply from some, deciding to check out the places for herself the coming weekend. The next day when Prateek asked her if she had zeroed in on any place, she said, 'Few of them. I'm thinking of checking them out this weekend.'

'Wonderful. I'll be there with you. You shouldn't go around alone.'

Rivanah didn't say no because she indeed was sceptical of visiting the places alone and had hoped that

Prateek would come forward to help her on his own. She responded with a smile of acknowledgement. By Sunday evening, Rivanah was sure where she was going to shift: Sai Baba Apartment in Malad west. The agent informed her that she would share the fully furnished flat with two other girls. When she told Meghna about her shift, Meghna didn't ask her the reason for leaving and instead apologized to her.

'Please don't apologize Meghna di. You let me stay here for so long. I should thank you actually.'

Meghna smiled at her, the first time she had done so since Rivanah moved in. They were boiling milk in the kitchen to prepare some coffee for themselves.

'But you have to do me one last favour, Meghna di,' Rivanah said.

'Tell me.'

'Please talk to mumma and baba. They'll never support my shifting,' Rivanah pleaded.

'Don't worry. I'll talk to them,' Meghna said caressing her cheeks. Rivanah hugged her tight.

'Can I ask you something di?' she said breaking the hug.

'Sure.'

'Were you sure you loved Aadil da when you married him?'

Looking into her eyes, Meghna tried to decipher the reason for the query. 'Completely,' she said after an instant.

'And what do you think now?'

'I think love is complicated. It doesn't let you leave your partner alone when you actually should and it makes you own him when you really should not.'

'Does marriage change a relationship, di?'

'It's not about marriage. It's about time. Dating and all is fine, but when you start living with someone twenty-four-seven it sure does test one's true feelings for the other. Also, how you handle monotony in a relationship says a lot about how you basically feel for the other person. Not every couple fights like we do. Moreover, Aadil and I were too young when we married, so all of it seemed like a magic carpet back then but now we know our relationship is nothing but a dirty doormat.'

Rivanah sensed remorse in the last sentence.

'I love someone di. He works in Bangalore. We are college friends.'

'I know.'

Rivanah's facial muscles tightened hoping she didn't hear the phone sex sessions she had with Ekansh.

'Don't worry, nobody will know,' Meghna assured her. Rivanah gave her a tight, awkward smile.

'Do you guys want to get married?' Meghna poured the boiled milk in the two cups containing coffee powder.

'We do. Not immediately but we definitely want to get married. But I'm always scared what if something bad happens and I can't marry him? It's not good to be so emotionally dependent on someone, is it di?'

'Why not, especially if both of your eally love each other?' Meghna said stirring the cups with a spoon.

'Hmm.'

◆

The following Saturday, Rivanah shifted to the furnished two bedroom flat in Malad west. Though Prateek offered his help, she turned him down politely because she didn't have much luggage. It was Aadil who drove her to the flat. This was the only time she was alone with him. During her time in Vishnu Dham, she had always spoken to Aadil in Meghna's presence. He seemed to be a person who took his own sweet time to open up. So far she had not understood what he was really like.

The elevator was undergoing maintenance when she arrived with her luggage at Sai Baba Apartments. The flat was on the second floor so she didn't have much trouble climbing up. Rivanah pressed the doorbell of her new flat and waited. Someone opened the door for her and said with a straight face, 'Welcome Mini.'

Rivanah wasn't prepared for this.

## 8

By Mumbai's standard it was a rather spacious flat. While Rivanah got the drawing room, the other two girls—Ishita Rana and Asha Pradhan—took a room each. Both girls seemed to belong to different planets. Rivanah instantly took a liking to Ishita even though she did not have a lot in common with her. Ishita was fiercely independent and audaciously modern. She consumed an average of a box of cigarettes a day and all her water bottles contained 80 percent Vodka and 20 percent Sprite. Ishita worked in a travel company and would turn up in her office half-drunk saying she couldn't focus unless she tasted Vodka. Though she hailed from a small place—Pathankot—she could give any big city girl a run for their money. She was debonair, sharp, and a fashion freak. She had six tattoos and two piercings on her body. There were people who merely exist and then there were people who lived, Rivanah observed, but Ishita seemed to fly through her life with no attachment, no care, and absolutely no plan.

'People judge the unknown with their knowledge of the known. I take up the unknown head-on because the known is so damn boring,' Ishita told her ten minutes after their first meet. Rivanah didn't exactly know what she meant but understood probably it only meant she loved to live without any rules of the society.

Asha Pradhan, on the other hand, was someone who was acutely secretive. She cooked her own food even though Ishita and Rivanah had opted for a cook. Neither knew where she actually worked or hailed from. She was out before the two woke up in the morning and when she returned in the evening, she kept herself locked up in her room. When Rivanah came to the flat for the first time and Asha referred to her as 'Mini', Rivanah had asked her how she knew her nickname.

'I looked at your profile on Facebook. A comment on one of your cover pictures had that name. I always have to know everything about my flatmate.'

*But you share nothing about yourself*, Rivanah thought. She wouldn't have been surprised if one day someone told her that Asha was part of some occult group who were perhaps conspiring to bring the devil into the world.

In fact, one night, when Rivanah found the door to Asha's room slightly ajar, she peeped in to take a look out of curiosity. She saw her surrounded by candles sitting in a vajrasana pose in the centre of her room with a towel wrapped around her bosom and her dishevelled hair covering her face. She maintained a distance from her since then.

While Rivanah secretly admired the free bird that Ishita was, the latter became protective of her because she knew Rivanah hadn't seen life as one should in order to stop taking it seriously. Rivanah had got a non-judgemental friend in the form of Ishita while the latter had got a soul-sister in the former. Within a few weeks, the girls bonded deeply.

One Friday, after Rivanah was done with her dinner, she saw Ishita dressed up like a sexy doll in a short yellow dress and matching stilettos.

'Where are you going?' Rivanah asked.

'Hype, Bandra,' Ishita quipped clicking a selfie with a pout standing in front of the wardrobe mirror in Rivanah's room.

'Shopping?'

'Bleh!' she said. 'It's a nightclub, yaar. And listen, I may not come back tonight so don't panic. Sleep in my room and keep the door locked. I don't trust this Asha, okay? For all you know, she may be a despo lesbo!'

'Alright, but where will you be for the whole night?'

'Wherever my boyfriend takes me.'

'I never knew you had one.' Rivanah's surprise was genuine.

'One? Excuse me, I have two healthy ones,' Ishita said adjusting her breasts with her eyes fixed on the mirror.

'I meant boyfriend!'

'Lol. I know. But then I myself didn't know I had one till a night before. Connected with him on Facebook.'

'And you love him?'

'Love?' She turned around to look at Rivanah as if she said something blasphemous. 'Who said anything about love?'

'Do you mean you are going to have a one-night stand?' Rivanah said in shock. Ishita laughed out.

'God! You sound so terrorized! Yes, I do mean exactly that; a one-fucking-night-stand.'

'It's not worth it.' Rivanah couldn't believe how quickly she had turned judgemental of her roomie.

'Oh-ho, someone's experienced, huh!' Ishita teased her.

'Shut up! I have a boyfriend. And I'm loyal to him. I hate one-night stands anyway.'

'You hate something you haven't even tried yet. That's why I say society is such a bitch. It prepares us to have an opinion about something we have no clue about.'

'I hate it and that's why I never had it.'

'Well, to each his own. Can I borrow your perfume darling?' Ishita asked after she was done honing herself in the mirror.

'Yeah, okay.' Rivanah opened the wardrobe and gave her the perfume. Ishita applied it quickly and left.

Ekansh had a night shift that night, hence he wasn't available on phone. Asha didn't turn up that night either, so Rivanah slept in the drawing room with the lights on. In the morning, she woke up with a strong urge to pee. Still sleepy-eyed, she went to the bathroom to relieve herself. She opened the door of the bathroom and saw a butt-naked guy standing with his back to her and peeing. She let out a loud scream and scampered to Ishita's room.

'Ishu wake up! There's a naked man in our flat.'

Ishita didn't budge a bit.

'Ishu!' She shook her hard.

Ishita turned to look at her drowsily. 'He didn't have a place to go to. I brought him here,' said Ishita casually and flipped the other way.

'Is he retarded? Doesn't he know how to shut a door and pee?' The sight had truly robbed Rivanah off her sleep.

'Ask him,' Ishita said and closed her eyes. The guy peeped inside the room. Rivanah shut her eyes tight.

'Sorry. My underwear is lying beside you. Could you please...' he said.

Rivanah opened one of her eyes, picked up the underwear in disgust with the tip of her fingers, and threw it at him. When the underwear clad guy came into the room, Rivanah stood up, turned around, and with her back to the guy slowly moved outside. It was for the first time she had seen a stark naked guy that close. The image stayed with her. Later in the morning she shared the incident with Ekansh.

'Ishita brought home a guy last night,' she told him over phone.

'Is she mad or what? Doesn't she know there are two more girls living with her?'

'It's okay. The guy had nowhere to go so...'

'It's not okay. Ask your roomie not to repeat it again or else you would complain to the landlord. Alright?'

Rivanah was quiet. She thought she would tell Ekansh how funny it was to see a butt-naked guy but she decided to omit it lest he ended up asking her to shift some place else immediately.

'Alright?' Ekansh repeated.

'Alright.'

Rivanah agreed with Ekansh but she couldn't confront Ishita about it. Somewhere deep within her, Rivanah felt Ishita did what she herself wished to do but couldn't: going to nightclubs, dating guys on a hunch without emotional attachment, living a carefree life with nobody to question. She remembered how at the end of every term-exam in school students were provided with report cards. As an adult too she carried a report card for every action of hers. If she went to a nightclub, she knew, her parents and Ekansh would fail her. Of course she could have gone without telling anybody but that was something she wasn't prepared to do. Or trained to do. Even if it was talking to a boy during her teenage years, her parents had to know who exactly the boy was and what his parents did and where they lived. Coming from that kind of a life and now looking at Ishita, she only could adore her. Rivanah knew she would never be able to approach the edge on which Ishita lived her life. It wasn't that she wanted to make that edge her life but she did miss the kind of freedom which allowed one to do as his or her heart said. Maybe if she was given the freedom, she wouldn't have gone to pick up guys at random but that freedom, that right to live the way she wanted was what she coveted. More so after knowing Ishita.

Rivanah did try once to talk about it with Ekansh telling him that she too wanted to go to a nightclub, but he came down on her in a way she didn't expect him to.

'Promise me you aren't going to a nightclub. I'll take you when I'm in Mumbai or when you come to Bangalore.'

'Will it make you insecure if I go there alone or with friends?'

'Shut up, it's not about me. It's not safe to go there alone.'

'I won't go alone. And not everyone who goes to a nightclub gets brutalized. Even you go but I didn't say anything ever.'

'I'm a guy. Do you have any idea what you are saying?'

That was the end of the discussion. She didn't like the chauvinist streak in Ekansh. It was something which was there in her father too. Whenever she wore a dress which was slightly bold, her father made sure to complain about the younger generation's dressing sense. It disgusted her but in the end she consoled herself saying perhaps her father and Ekansh were right—that it wasn't a safe place for girls. But she also knew the fuzz that made life all the more attractive was beyond that line of safety. Every time Ishita showed her the selfies she clicked at pubs and nightclubs, Rivanah would get upset. Soon an opportunity arrived when Ishita came home with two passes to a show one Saturday night.

'Darling, I have passes for DJ Notti tonight. Get dressed up doll, together we shall fall!' Ishita said in a rapper's tone.

'Sorry, I can't,' a gloomy Rivanah said.

'Can't? Why?' Ishita couldn't believe someone was saying no to her favourite DJ.

'If my parents or my boyfriend found out about it, I'd be screwed!'

Ishita ogled at her for some time and then said, 'Are you someone's pet?'

'It's not about being a pet. I love them and I'm only respecting their wishes.'

Ishita didn't argue any further since she felt it was pointless doing so. Later that night she Whatsapped Rivanah a snap of hers snuggling up with DJ Notti. She was about to delete the snap when she heard a sudden noise. It was too near to have happened outside her flat. She sat up on her bed trying to listen hard. A few seconds later, she heard it again. It sounded like a moan. Rivanah moistened her dry lips feeling a tiny bubble of fear form in her gut. She had fallen asleep in Ishita's room for a change after talking to Ekansh on the phone. The door of the room was open. And worse was she had watched a horror film with Ishita the night before. All her mind could conjure was a headless figure scampering up to her with a dagger. Her heartbeats gained speed in no time. She didn't know why but she was anticipating a sound in the stillness of the night. Something fell somewhere in the flat. *Had someone broken in?* She could feel small beads of perspiration started forming on her forehead and her throat started going dry. She called out, 'Asha!'

Rivanah wasn't even sure if Asha had come home or not. There was no response. She stood up and sneaked toward the switchboard.

'Shit!' she said pressing the switch. There was a power cut. Or...had someone cut the power off? She swore she would never watch horror films again. She took her phone and dialled Ishita's number. Nobody picked up. She dialled Ekansh. It was switched off. She wanted to call her parents but didn't want to disturb them at that hour. She checked her mobile phone's clock: 2:15 am. Even if her parents' phone gets a missed call from her at this time, they would go paranoid. She dialled Pooja's number. Call waiting. What else was she expecting for someone who had made a new boyfriend? Another noise tore apart the dreadful silence. This time she was sure it came from the toilet. The mug must have toppled...but why? She inched toward the window and stood still, prepared to scream her lungs out if she saw something...anything. An hour went by—neither anyone appeared nor any sound came. The strength in her legs were wearing out. It was a Saturday—the only day in the whole week where she could afford to sleep till late in the morning—but for this stupid sound she couldn't go to her bed either. She was about to sit down on the floor when she heard a meow. She shone her phone's flashlight toward the door. Another meow. Rivanah feared all kinds of pets; especially cats. If it was really a cat that had come in—from God knows where—then it would not go away easily. She peeped outside the window and saw lights in the nearby apartments. *The power is probably back* she thought. It gave her an impetus to stand up and amble toward the room's switchboard. She pressed the switch and the tube light was on within few seconds. She stepped outside the room swallowing a lump and peeked inside the adjacent toilet. Rivanah noticed the small bucket was on the floor along with the jet spray. Also, on top of the flush tank sat a pitch black cat. The way it looked at her made her swallow multiple lumps together. The toilet window was open. *It has to be Asha,* she wondered, *who always leaves it open.* Rivanah noticed that around the cat's neck was a red ribbon which had a white piece of cloth at its centre. The kind she had been receiving for some time now. Rivanah guessed the obvious. She was too scared to go near the cat so she took couple of steps and switched on the toilet's light. She strained her eyes to read:

*Fear is the most prized illusion that we create for ourselves.*

The cat suddenly flipped and jumped out of the toilet window. Rivanah stepped back with her heart in her mouth. As she relaxed, she found a rage gripping her. She dashed to the toilet window and screamed, 'You don't scare me. You can't scare me, alright!' Except for a few stray dogs that started to bark, there was nobody else. She calmed down and went to her room where her phone buzzed with a message:

*Time's up, Mini. Be ready to cry.*

The message this time came from an unknown phone number. She called back but it was switched off.

'Even I want to see how you are going to make me cry,' she told her stubborn self and then saved the unknown number by the name of 'Stranger'.

## 9

Rivanah unlocked her flat's door and came in. Instantly a rotten smell hit her. She pinched her nose but could see nothing because it was all dark. She kept the main door open to allow some light from the passage into the room as she went toward the switchboard. Before Rivanah could reach it, the door shut with a loud bang. She turned in a flash and felt trapped in the darkness. She took a few steps to reach the switchboard but felt something around her neck. She touched it with her hands and realized to her shock that it was someone's feet. She wanted to scream but found she had lost her voice. She ran to the main door but couldn't open it. There was a chuckle in the air and she saw herself hanging by the drawing room's ceiling fan. The eyes seemed demonic while the chuckle was vibrating in her eardrums. As she started losing her sense, she heard a rather familiar sound. It was a Skype video call waiting to be answered. Rivanah opened her eyes wide with a jerk on her bed and took some time to understand what was happening. *Yet again the same dream*, she thought, and hastily took the Skype call on the laptop kept beside her.

'What happened? You look messy,' Ekansh said appearing on her laptop screen.

'Nothing. I just dozed off waiting for your call,' she said tying her hair in a bun and regaining her balance.

'I really miss you a lot, Ekansh, especially when Ishita tells me about her escapades,' Rivanah said. 'We have to be in the same city soon otherwise I'll go mad.'

'Why don't you tell me straightaway that you want to make love to me?' He was trying to cheer her up.

'Shut up. I only want to be with you.'

'Really?' Ekansh said with amusement.

'Yes, really. Long distance is a killer.' She sounded acutely emotional. Ekansh turned serious too and said, 'Bring your forehead close to the cam.'

She did and he planted a kiss on his cam.

'I know long distance is a bit trying, but if we can pass this, it will be so good for our relationship,' he said.

'Hmm. I was wondering that my shift to Bangalore is a far fetched thing as of now. Why don't you shift to Mumbai instead?'

'Do you think I'm not trying? But the platform I work in isn't there in the Mumbai office of ours. But still I'm on the lookout. I would grab a change of location on the first opportunity. You wouldn't have to tell me.'

'I know I don't have to. But...you know you shouldn't have come here last time.'

'Why do you say that?'

'I have started to miss you all the more now. I had accepted our long distance relationship when I was at home but ever since you came to Mumbai, a weird kind of restlessness has invaded me. Also, this stupid loneliness is making me crazy.'

'Why, where are your roomies?'

'Ishita has gone to her hometown to attend a cousin's wedding.'

'And the other one?'

'I have no clue about Asha. All I know is she hasn't come home on weekends since the last two weeks.'

'Is she a ghost?'

'Don't scare me, Ekansh. I stay alone here. Moreover, I have been having this recurrent dream which is really scary.'

'What dream?'

'That I'm hanging from a ceiling fan. I have seen it like four-five times now in the last few months. Only the location changes but rest of it is all same.'

'I'm sorry.' He blew a flying-kiss to her via the laptop screen. She kissed him back.

'Even I'm lonely here,' he said dejectedly. 'I mean I have friends here but you know what I mean.'

'I do. How I wish you were here with me right now.'

'What if I fly down to Mumbai?' Ekansh said in a tone which meant business.

'When? Tell me before hand so that I can take an off from office.'

'Now dumbo! What if I come down tonight?'

'OMG! Really Ekansh?'

'Wait and watch.'

The Skype call was abruptly disconnected. It was 8:15 pm. At exactly 3:20 am Ekansh pressed the doorbell of Rivanah's flat in Malad.

'I don't believe this!' she said opening the door. Ekansh came in and kicked the door with his heel. Then he cupped Rivanah's face and smooched her deeply. She could feel his hunger in the ferocious way his tongue explored her mouth.

'I don't want you to stop us tonight,' he said in a whisper breaking the smooch as he took off her top. The urgency in his voice and his demeanour was supremely sexy. They had always discussed it amongst themselves; no penetrative sex before marriage. But that was when they hadn't stayed away from the other for this long. They hadn't realized the urge for an emotional union through a physical communion could be this necessary.

'I won't Ekansh. I won't stop you,' she responded with another whisper as she got rid of his shirt. She had seen him topless but he had never seen her in a bra. He groped her breasts over her bra and squeezed them hard. Then his hands went behind and unhooked the bra.

'How do you open this stupid strap?' he gasped. Rivanah managed a short giggle and unhooked the bra looking naughtily at him. Once the bra came off, her instinct was to cover her breasts with her hand while Ekansh pushed her against a wall and pinned both her hands apart on the wall. Her firm succulent breasts were right in front of him in all its nudity.

'Ekansh, leave me,' she said out of shyness closing her eyes.

'I will but first look at me.'

Helpless, Rivanah opened her eyes only to find him staring at her. Looking directly at her, Ekansh dived down a bit and took her left nipple in his mouth, sucking it gently at first and then hard to the extent that Rivanah cried out in pleasure.

'You are so loud,' he said leaving her left nipple and shifting focus to the right one.

'Shut me up then.' The way she said it compelled Ekansh to smooch her once again, this time mauling her breasts with his grasp. She unbuckled his belt and unzipped the jeans he was wearing. Her hands slipped inside his underwear and grabbed his penis.

Ekansh broke the smooch and looked deep into her eyes.

'It is so hard.' She seemed bewildered.

'Now you know what you do to me when I miss you.'

His hands untied her pyjama and tugged them down till her knees along with her panty. She hurriedly stepped out of both. He put his hands on her vagina, with the tip of his middle finger just about entering it. A moan escaped her as she grabbed his hand.

'You are so wet,' he exclaimed.

'Now you know what you do to me when I miss you,' she said jerking her head a bit to let her hair fall sideways to her face.

'Rivanah Bannerjee, I want to make love to you. Right now,' he said coming out of his shoes and socks. His eyes were set ablaze with a lusty fire whose flame was love.

'Stop talking, start doing me,' she gasped.

Ekansh picked her up in his lap and took her to Ishita's room, where he threw her on the bed and got on top of her. They kissed while he tried to insert his penis inside her vagina with one hand.

'Slowly Ekansh. It is hurting me,' she said spreading her legs as wide as she could while holding onto him tight.

And before she knew it, her virginity was gone. The love of her life became one with her. She could have cried at that moment as she felt Ekansh's penis slowly make its way inside the tight and juicy walls of her vagina and then thrusting his pelvis against hers. Rivanah closed in her legs around his hips, rubbing his butt cheeks with her heel and clawing his back with her nails while kissing him each time the thrusts brought him close to her face.

Since adolescence, Rivanah had fancied about the moment she would become someone's the way it has been designed by the cosmos. She only prayed that whenever it happened, the body in the whole process would be a means for her to surrender her heart and soul to that someone. Making love to Ekansh was an oblation from her side to the holy idol that they had both created and named 'love'. He soon took her legs over his shoulder, bending her a bit and penetrating even deeper. His thrusts turned harder and faster now. She held his arm and dug her nails into the flesh of his arm. In the heart of this pain, there was a pleasure which each thrust was connecting her to. Each time his penis rubbed her vaginal walls, it felt like some forbidden waves were eating away the shores of morality; bit by bit. Soon his body went stiff. He gave three full and deep thrusts, one after the other, and then remained rock still. A prolonged groan escaped Ekansh's lips as she felt a warm discharge flood her vagina. He collapsed beside her. She could feel an ache in her hip bones as she brought her legs together. They lay still for some time. Next, she slowly cuddled into his arms.

'It was awesome,' he said.

'Sshhh.' She put a finger on his lips and said, 'Just feel it.'

He kissed her finger and they lay awake naked in the quietude of the dissolving night.

It was one in the afternoon when Rivanah woke up the next day. She felt sticky in the warm morning sun rays that were falling on her. They had forgotten to switch on the fan last night. Ekansh was still asleep. She sat up arranging her hair in a bun. She climbed down the bed, naked, and went to her room where she checked out this new non-virgin self in the full-length wardrobe mirror. There weren't any external changes except for a few bite marks around her breasts but she knew she had taken a leap last night. She had never been so happy in her life and so sure of her commitment before.

Ekansh stayed over the whole of Sunday as well since none of the flatmates returned. They made love again in the evening but it was less intense and more sensual.

'Last night was a dream,' she said sipping a hot cup of coffee with Ekansh sitting in front of the French window of her flat wrapped in a bed sheet wearing only their inners. They had only one coffee cup from which they were alternating their sips.

'I swear it was,' Ekansh said.

'What if I get pregnant now?' Rivanah said looking up at him.

'Huh?'

'I'm in my unsafe time of the month. It's quite possible.'

Ekansh caressed her forehead and said with a warm smile, 'Then I would marry you this very moment.'

She kissed his chin feeling emotional. They continued to sit in silence. She wanted to tell him about the messages she had been receiving since her arrival in Mumbai but she felt the time they spent was too beautiful to even bring up a morbid subject like that.

The next hour Ekansh left for Bengaluru. Rivanah was passing time by surfing her Facebook profile on her laptop when her phone buzzed with a message.

*Coming Saturday, Cafe Basílico, Bandra. 8:30 pm. Meet me.*

Though it was from another unknown phone number, Rivanah knew only one person could have sent it. The Stranger.

## 10

'Come on!' said Bijoy. He was one of Rivanah's teammates in office.

'Where to?' Rivanah asked.

'It's your boyfriend's cake cutting time,' said Shantanu. The two guys giggled among themselves and went ahead. A confused Rivanah put her desk computer on sleep mode and followed them wondering what they were talking about.

They went to the HR department's room where there was already a large assemblage of people. As Rivanah entered, everyone looked at her as if she was star of the occasion and they were waiting for her arrival. She had no clue what was going on. There was concealed laughter and a few nudges.

'Let her come in the front,' one of the HR personnel said from amidst the crowd. Everyone made space for her to come to the front. Rivanah ambled to the centre of the whole hoopla and saw Prateek wearing a designer birthday paper cap, holding a plastic knife, and standing behind a desk with a chocolate cake on top of it.

'I was waiting for you,' Prateek said with a grin.

Rivanah felt like a fool. Everyone started clapping and singing the birthday song as Prateek sliced out a piece of the cake and offered it to Rivanah. With everyone around staring at them, she couldn't refuse and reluctantly allowed Prateek to stuff the piece of cake in her mouth. Someone captured the moment on his camera phone. As the two moved aside, everyone else jumped on the cake. Some ate it while others smeared the cream on Prateek's face. Rivanah slowly severed herself from the crowd and stood at a corner in the room waiting for Prateek to be free. So this is what Prateek had been up to all along! Labelling her as his girlfriend to all his colleagues.

A few minutes later, when Prateek went toward the washroom to clean his cake smeared face, Rivanah caught hold of him.

'Did you tell people you are my boyfriend?' She sounded livid.

'No! Why would I?' Prateek feigned innocence.

'Then why would my teammates tag you as my boyfriend?'

A moment later Prateek slowly hanged his head down in guilt.

'Why would you do such a stupid thing Prateek?'

'I love you Rivanah.'

*There!* He knew next to nothing about her but he loved her. *When will men stop interpreting attraction as love,* she thought and said, 'Does that mean you will go around telling people we are a couple? Did I ever tell you that I love you too?'

'I didn't know it will reach your ears.' He was still staring at the floor.

Rivanah's jaws dropped. She understood she was talking to a crazy person with whom one couldn't talk sense. Did he really think the rumour won't reach her and if it did, would compel her to make him her boyfriend? And all this after knowing well enough that she was committed. Zero tolerance was the only way of keeping this lunatic off her, she decided.

'I want you to go and announce it in front of all your colleagues that you are not my boyfriend.'

'Please Rivanah.' Prateek looked up at her pleadingly. 'They will make fun of me.'

'I don't care! And you deserve it if they do so.'

'I'm sorry Rivanah.' Prateek collapsed on her feet. 'Please forgive me.'

It made her feel awkward: an HR person from her office pleading to her by touching her feet. It can't get more absurd than that. This guy *was* a psycho. Period.

'Get up Prateek. What nonsense is this? Don't make a scene now.' She tried walking away but Prateek refused to leave her. Another employee came in and stopped when he saw his HR on his knees in front of a junior.

'Forgive me please,' Prateek pleaded.

'Yes, okay,' Rivanah somehow managed to say and sauntered away uncomfortably.

Prateek stood up and smiled at the employee who was looking at him aghast.

'One has to plead mercy when your girlfriend is angry,' Prateek said with a smile. The employee shot him an acknowledging smile before entering the washroom.

Later that evening, Rivanah shared the incident with Ekansh on the phone.

'I just don't get it. I have told him clearly that I'm committed and yet he keeps pursuing me.'

'Then all you need to do is lodge a complaint with the authorities. This is a kind of passive harassment,' Ekansh remarked.

'Hmm. I will if he repeats it again.'

From the next day onward, thankfully, she saw Prateek maintaining a distance as he had been doing before. She was relieved. But it only lasted till the Friday evening of that week.

'I know I did a bad thing. May I make it up to you with a nice dinner tomorrow? It's Saturday after all,' he asked. They were alone in the office elevator.

'It's okay Prateek. As long as you don't repeat what you did, it is okay. And sorry, I can't come. I'm busy tomorrow.'

'Boyfriend?' he asked.

*None of your business*, she wanted to tell him.

'Yes.'

She saw his face go pale.

'Is he coming to Mumbai?'

*God, his questions never end!* 'Yes,' replied.

'Great. How is he coming—train or flight? Let's go and fetch him together?'

*Why can't I kill this person? RIGHT NOW.* Rivanah feigned a fake call and excused herself.

It wasn't her boyfriend she was supposed to meet on Saturday. She had planned to meet the stranger— someone she knew nothing about. But somehow she kept getting the feeling that the stranger knew a lot about her. Who was this person? Someone she knew? She was itching to share this with Ekansh but she knew he wouldn't take it well and would refrain her from meeting the person. She promised herself she would tell him everything once she met the stranger.

On Saturday morning, Rivanah was reading the newspaper when she came across a report about a young techie's brutal murder in Bhandup by an unidentified person. *What if this stranger is a serial killer?* she thought and freaked. As Ishita walked into the room with her cup of green tea, Rivanah finally decided to share the whole story with her. Ishita listened to her patiently and said, 'So, this person wants to meet you because you didn't cook the three dishes he asked you to, even after he gave you a month's time?'

'It's not that simple. I told you one of the messages said I would be crying soon.'

'Confusing indeed but intriguing nevertheless.' A naughty smile appeared on Ishita's face. 'I so love mystery men. What if he looks like Ian Somerhalder?'

'Ishu Please! I'm not in the mood for this.'

Ishita seemed pensive for some time and then jumped up, clapping her hands in excitement.

'Wow, you have a secret admirer daring! You know secret admirers are awesome in bed because day and night they only think about fucking you and when they finally get hold of you, they don't let you go. Don't you remember SRK from the movie *Darr*? That K...K...K... Kiran thing was so damn sexy!'

'Come on, I'm not going to fuck him. I only want to know who the hell this person is and why he is leaving messages for me. And I'm not sure if he is an admirer or not.'

'Trust me he is one. This crying business is all a farce. He said so to gain your attention. Now that he has your attention, he wants to meet up. And I'm so damn sure he'll be hot looking.'

'How are you so sure?'

'Gut instinct. Tell Ekansh he has some competition now.'

'Shut up! If I tell him about this person, he will ask me not to meet him.'

'Oh yes. And once he tells you something, you will have to obey it, right my Bhartiya nari?'

'Whatever! But I'm a little scared too. What if he is some creep or a killer or something?'

'But it isn't a secluded house or a garage that he has asked you to meet him at. It's very much a public place. So don't worry. I have been to Cafe Basilico before so I'll go with you,' Ishita said.

'Thanks sis,' Rivanah said giving her a relived smile.

'But if he turns out to be someone really hot, he is mine then, okay? You can have him only when I'm done. Deal?'

'Oh please! You can keep him for all I care. But what if he doesn't meet me if he sees you with me?'

'He won't know we are together,' Ishita winked at her.

Rivanah reached Cafe Basilico in Bandra on time. She had stepped down at the Bandra station along with Ishita but they took two separate autorickshaws to reach the restaurant. The guard outside asked her name and immediately took Rivanah to a table reserved for her. The cafe had both an outside seating arrangement as well as an air-conditioned area inside. The waiter took Rivanah to a table which was in the open. She made herself comfortable, looking around to see if she knew anyone there. Ishita came in minutes later and sat by a table opposite her. Minutes passed but nobody approached her. The stranger had asked her to meet at 8:30 and it was already 8:50 now.

*What should we do?* Rivanah Whatsapped Ishita.

*Wait. And don't look tensed.*

Rivanah looked around smiling.

*Don't smile like a fool too,* Ishita Whatsapped.

Rivanah giggled and sent her a smiley emoticon.

At 9 pm sharp, a message popped up in Rivanah's phone from an unknown number.

*Call Ekansh.*

Rivanah frowned reading the stranger's message. She had a bad feeling about this. Was Ekansh alright? She looked at Ishita once. She hurriedly called Ekansh. He picked it up on the third ring.

'Hey babu!' He sounded busy.

'Hi, are you alright?' She couldn't hide the tension in her voice.

'No!'

Rivanah immediately missed a heartbeat.

'I'm fucking my life sitting in front of a computer in my office,' he said.

'Oh okay.' She relaxed a bit.

'But what happened?' he said.

'Nothing, just wanted to hear your voice,' she said quickly conjuring an excuse. 'I'm with Ishita. I'll call you later.' She cut the line and noticed another message had popped in by then from the same unknown number before.

*I'm waiting inside.*

Ishita's eyes followed Rivanah as the latter stood up taking a deep breath. There was momentary eye contact between the two girls. Ishita understood she had received some communication from the stranger. She kept her eyes fixed on Rivanah who ambled inside the air conditioned sitting area. Standing by the entrance, what she saw almost made her hurl. Ekansh sitting with a girl, their hands clasped on the table as they sipped on a single blue coloured mocktail together. There was a certain spark in their togetherness which made Rivanah feel they were long time lovers. She collapsed on the ground before Ishita could reach her.

## 11

*The love that seems true isn't always true love.*

The stranger had sent Rivanah this message sometime after Ishita, with the help of the restaurant staff, put her into an autorickshaw and took her back to their flat. Ishita had identified Ekansh from the pics Rivanah had shown her. Before the staff reached them, she glanced pleadingly at him a few times but Ekansh, for reasons best known to him, didn't leave his seat or the girl he was with. His face said he wanted to help but his action conveyed his reluctance. Ishita understood that perhaps he had kept the girl he was with in the dark about his relationship status as well and approaching Rivanah would call for a lot of explanation.

Rivanah was semi-conscious in the autorickshaw and Ishita was trying her best to keep her awake.

'Should we go to a hospital?' Ishita asked slapping her cheeks softly.

'Home. Take me home,' Rivanah mumbled.

Her mother called. She knew she had to take the call. Summoning every ounce of energy left in her, she took the call.

'Hello mumma.'

'You don't sound good Mini.'

'Nothing mumma.'

'Is everything okay?'

She would have almost cried out when she stopped herself, 'Yes. Everything is okay. I have an exam tomorrow at office so I'm studying. I'll call you later.'

'But tomorrow is Sunday.'

'I have an exam,' she repeated and asked Ishita to switch off her mobile phone. After reaching their apartment, Ishita helped Rivanah to the bed where she slept for an hour and then, in her sleep, started crying. A disturbed Ishita woke her up only to find her cries transform into howls. Ishita tried her best to console her half-heartedly knowing well nothing could mend a broken heart except, maybe, time. Sometime later, when Rivanah had still not stopped sobbing, Ishita mixed a few sleeping pills that she often took with milk and coaxed Rivanah to have it. In no time, she was sound asleep.

A little after midnight, the doorbell rang. Ishita opened the door to find Ekansh.

'What is it?' she asked in disdain.

'I want to talk to Rivanah.'

'She is dead. How do you care?'

'You don't know anything about us, so don't judge me.'

Ishita looked intently at Ekansh and said, 'You work in Mumbai itself and not Bangalore, right?'

Ekansh was quiet.

'And you would have never told the girls about each other till you were done with one of them, isn't it?'

'Look I wanted to...'

'You, or for that matter every other douchebag like you, are still alive because it is illegal to kill else I would have castrated you in the restaurant itself. Do you have any idea how much Rivanah loves you? If I see you around this place again, I'll call the police. Get lost,' screamed Ishita and closed the door on his face with a thud. She looked through the peephole only to see him wait for a minute and then leave.

Ishita went inside to check on Rivanah and heard her blabbering in her sleep: *I love you Ekansh. Don't leave me. Don't walk away. I won't do anything wrong. I have listened to you and I always will. I'm yours forever. Be mine always.* The verbal ramblings continued all through the night. At times when she was quiet, Rivanah's body suddenly shuddered while her eyes oozed out tears. Ishita sat beside her all night, caressing her forehead whenever Rivanah spoke or cried. There was a moment when Ishita too broke down looking at her roomie pleading for love in her sleep. When she couldn't take it anymore, Ishita finished every drop of Vodka she had with her and slept.

Rivanah woke up in the morning feeling unpleasant about herself and about life in general. She heard Ishita talking to someone over phone in the other room. It was her mother.

'Why is Mini's phone switched off? Is she alright?' a worried Mrs Bannerjee asked on the phone. She and her husband had finally allowed Rivanah to stay in a PG only when Meghna explained how common a thing it was for young girls.

'She has a little fever, aunty.'

'Fever? She said she had an exam today.'

'Wait, I'll give the phone to Rivanah.' Ishita pressed the mute button on her phone, went to Rivanah's room, and saw she was lying on her bed staring at the sunny day outside through the window with swollen eyes and messed-up hair.

'It's your mother,' Ishita said. 'Talk to her.' She passed on her phone to Rivanah.

'I told her you have fever,' Ishita whispered and sat beside her grasping her hand with assurance.

Rivanah sat up, cleared her throat, and said feebly, 'Hello Mumma.'

She was having problem suppressing her pain.

'What happened, Mini?'

Those were the words her mother said to her as a child whenever she went to her with a complaint. These words would make Rivanah howl till her mother hugged her tight and convinced her everything would be alright.

And everything indeed would become alright. But now she was a grown up. She couldn't go to her mother for every little problem no matter how much she wanted to. She simply couldn't tell her mother that Ekansh had turned out to be the asshole that she thought he could never be. That their fairy-tale romance had come to a brutal end. That true love indeed was like stardom and it didn't happen to everyone. Just that until yesterday she thought Ekansh and she didn't belong to that 'everyone' category. The sight of him clasping hands with the other girl flashed in front of her eyes, and she felt like her head would explode.

'Mini?'

Rivanah locked her jaws, took a deep breath, and said, 'Nothing mumma. Just a little fever.' She glanced at Ishita once.

'What about the exam?'

'It has been cancelled. My battery was exhausted so the phone got switched off automatically. I'll charge it and switch it on in a minute,' she said and talked as normally as she could for the next two minutes before cutting the line. She gave the phone back to Ishita, released her hand from her grasp, drew her legs close to her chest, and sat looking out of the window. Ishita took her roomie's phone from beside her and switched it on.

'Get up!' Ishita said. 'Take a shower. Shit happens. Flush it before your emotional room starts to stink.'

'You don't get it, Ishu,' Rivanah said without looking at her. 'I loved Ekansh from all my heart and soul, and whatever there is that constitutes the core of me. He was my world, my everyfuckingthing. There was nothing beyond or before him.' Tears announced their presence in her eyes again.

Ishita scuffed and said, 'I won't understand?' She let go off a heavy breath. 'Some years ago,' she began, 'there was a prince charming who came into my life. I was nineteen then and he was thirty two. He was a smooth talker who pampered me silly. He made me feel like a princess who was born for good things. I was simply clean bowled by him and he knew it. Everything was so perfect. And all of it happened so fast that I felt I was living a dream. I even lost my virginity to him and after my graduation, I told my parents about him who took an instant liking to him. He was even ready to get married to me. Invitation cards of our engagement were printed and were about to be distributed when he vanished all of a sudden.'

'Vanished?' Rivanah now turned to look at her roomie.

'Three months later, my father located him with the help of the police. He was living in Jalandhar with his wife and a kid. Basically, he began the affair with me when his wife was pregnant. But when he was confronted about it, he insulted my dad and called me a whore. And his wife supported him on this. Can you beat that? All these prince charming types that we read about in books are actually prince chutiyas in real life. I cried, I sulked, I was depressed, I was angry, and then I accepted a simple fact: what shopping is for girls, sex is for guys. It's too basic an itch to be controlled with the dog-collar of loyalty.'

There was silence after which Ishita continued, 'Do you think it is possible for me to fall in love after this? The kind of love where you prefer to remain blindfolded because you trust your heart too much? Do you think it is possible to even live after knowing you won't ever be in love again because you will never ever trust anyone? Every time I think of him, I hate myself. I feel wasted.'

Rivanah stretched her legs, leaned forward to reach Ishita, and hugged her tight. The emotional storm brewing in Ishita calmed down.

'Ekansh was here last night,' Ishita said. Rivanah broke the hug and looked at her, 'What did he say?'

'He works in Mumbai.'

And she thought he was flying for her from Bengaluru.

'I don't believe this.' Rivanah's jaws dropped.

'You know I did slap my prince *chutiya* in front of his wife. That was my only comeuppance. You have to get yours otherwise you will keep crying forever.'

'Hmm,' Rivanah said. As her phone turned on, it started buzzing with continuous messages. There were fifty Whatsapp messages from Ekansh. Each of them said he was sorry and that he could explain himself.

Rivanah immediately blocked him. She tapped on her Facebook app, next, and blocked him from her friend list as well and threw away the phone on the bed in disgust.

'At least you guys weren't physical. I can't tell you how good I felt when that bastard made love to me for the first time. And now I feel like a fool thinking about it.' Ishita observed how Rivanah hid her face with her hands.

'Oh dear, when did that happen?' The last time Ishita inquired, Rivanah was still a virgin.

'He was here last weekend. We did it then,' she said crying profusely.

'Bloody mother-fucking faggot.' Ishita said and consoled Rivanah caressing her back. 'It's okay. It's not a big deal. At least your feelings for him were genuine.'

A few seconds later Ishita added, 'By the way, you should be grateful to the stranger who disclosed this truth to you.'

Rivanah picked up her phone again and showed Ishita the stranger's message: *The love that seems true isn't always true love.*

'It's so correct,' Ishita said, 'We all are in love with the fictitious version of a real person; our self-made illusion. We commit ourselves to what's going on and not to what really is. But...' Ishita paused and then said, 'Who is this stranger? And why doesn't he help me out the way he helps you?' Rivanah tried to smile looking at her roomie's mischievous face.

'I think you should at least thank him,' Ishita said.

Rivanah was about to type a 'thank you' on her phone when Ekansh's call came.

'It's Ekansh,' Rivanah said.

'It's asshole; that's his real name from now,' Ishita said. 'Take the call and ask him to meet you today at the Oberoi mall.'

The call turned to a missed call. Rivanah relaxed and said, 'If he calls again...'

Before she could complete, Ekansh called again.

'Pick up the call, girl,' Ishita urged.

Rivanah picked up the call and said nothing.

'I want to meet you and explain...' Ekansh said but was cut short.

'Today at Oberoi mall around two,' Rivanah said in one breath and ended the call.

'Better!' Ishita quipped.

'Are you sure I should meet him? I don't want to.'

'You don't have to after this. And trust me, just give it back to him. You owe this much to yourself.'

Rivanah understood. Next she typed a 'thank you' and sent it to the last unknown number the stranger had sent her a message from. She waited but got no response.

Ishita had asked her to reach the mall an hour late than the fixed time. Rivanah did exactly that. Ekansh was a bit worked up when she reached the food court of the mall around three. Ishita too was with her.

'You are late,' Ekansh said.

'You are an asshole,' Rivanah retorted. 'You have been in Mumbai all this time and I thought you flew from Bangalore for me. Only for me! What a fool you have made out of me Ekansh. Congrats!'

'I swear I was going to tell you everything but...'

'But your love for me stopped you, isn't it? And exactly when were you going to tell me? When my dad had printed our marriage cards?' She raised her voice to a level which he had not heard from her before.

'Please, let's talk like adults.' He sounded defensive.

'Stop patronizing me. And answer me, when were you going to tell me?'

'Can I talk to you alone?' He glanced at Ishita.

'She stays with me.'

'Okay, look I know I didn't tell you that I was in Mumbai but that was because I didn't want to upset you since you were about to join your new office. So I was waiting for the right time.'

'Does it mean you never went to Bangalore?'

'Of course I did. And that's where I met Vishakha. I don't know why or when I fell in love with her. I couldn't believe it myself when it happened. Her company gave her a Mumbai location. I couldn't stop myself and followed her here. But that doesn't mean I can afford to lose you. Please try and understand.'

'You were with me for four years Ekansh, and Vishakha's been with you only for four months. You chose *her* and still you want *me* to understand?' Rivanah said, appalled. Did he think she would hug him and say she still loved him because he cared so much about her happiness that he didn't tell her he was cheating on her? Who was this person that she had been in love with? He suddenly seemed like someone whom she didn't know one bit.

'I came to your flat with the intention of telling you last week but you wanted to make love and I thought of not disappointing you since you had been waiting for it from a long time,' Ekansh said.

Rivanah noticed how 'we wanted to make love' had comfortably become 'you wanted to make love'. She also noticed the way he was passively tagging himself as a poor guy who had made love to her only out of sympathy for her. If he was seriously the same person she was thinking of getting married to at some point in life, then there was something wrong with her.

'Look, I think we can handle this without a break up,' he said.

'Does Vishakha know about us?'

'She doesn't know. But her knowing won't change anything, will it? What's going on between us is none of her business anyway,' Ekansh said avoiding eye contact. 'I love you and...'

Rivanah slapped him hard right across his face to shut him up. His jaws dropped. A few people in the food court stopped short in their tracks. Ishita's face glistened with a smile.

'You have no idea what it is to be in love, Ekansh. My parents were ready to accept you as their son-in-law. What will I tell them? I thought you were mine. Only mine. What shall I tell *myself*? That I'm an idiot who doesn't even know how to choose someone good for herself?' Rivanah was choking.

Ekansh's phone rang. Before he could hide it, she noticed the caller's name was Vishakha.

'Yes, I'm coming,' he said and cut the line.

'Someone's waiting for you Ekansh and that's not me. Goodbye and have a happy life with your girl,' said Rivanah and walked away. As Ekansh gaped at her walking away from him, Ishita pushed him by his chest and said, 'She doesn't know how to abuse so I say this on her behalf; you are a mother-fucking-monkey, a cunt with an STD, and an impotent bastard.' Saying this, she dashed off.

Rivanah knew forgetting someone was easier said than done. Emotional investments are subject to life risks. But it was something she thought she wouldn't have to care about, after all Ekansh and she were the hyped FTC—the Fairy Tale Couple. Once inside her flat, she opened her wardrobe and one by one threw out all the gifts that Ekansh had given her into the dustbin and burnt the love letters he used to write for her in college. When she thought she had destroyed everything that reminded her of Ekansh she sat down in silence. In no time their memories started haunting her. And she knew this was something she would never be able to burn, delete, or throw away. The time they spent together, did it mean nothing to him? He said he didn't know how he fell in love with Vishakha. Did he ever think about her when he was with her? Was she so much better than her that he forgot about her totally or did he purposefully subject her to this kind of insult by being in a relationship with another girl? And why did he make love to her when he wasn't interested in her? It was like he had brought her to the room of love by promising her a beautiful future after which he locked the room and threw the keys away. And now she had nowhere to go. Ishita was right: what shopping is for girls, sex is for guys. Ekansh must have made the other girl feel beautiful as well by fucking her.

With Ishita gone for a rave party, Rivanah felt all the more lonely. She logged on to her Facebook account to distract herself, but all she saw was her friends posting happy pictures with their loved ones. She hated them all and she hated herself more for hating them. She impulsively deactivated her account. She was tossing and turning on bed, telling herself repeatedly it was not the end of the world and the next moment doubting it herself when her phone buzzed with a message:

*Welcome.*

It was the stranger's response to her 'thank you' in the morning from a new phone number.

Rivanah immediately messaged him back:

*Why didn't you tell me this before?*

Prompt came a reply: *You can simply talk. I can hear you. I'll reply by message.*

Rivanah sat up on her bed the moment she read the message; startled. For the next one hour she left no corner of the flat unturned—under the bed, the kitchen, the television stand, the balcony, the wardrobe, and where not. Finally, she moved the wardrobe to see if there was anything behind it but shrieked seeing several cockroaches. She put the wardrobe back in place. Sweaty and tired, Rivanah's mind was still trying to guess how someone could hear her without being in the flat? She heard her phone buzz with a message:

*If you are done searching, you can talk.*

With a chill in her spine she spoke aloud looking nowhere in particular, 'Since how long have you known about Ekansh and that girl?' It was weird talking to someone she couldn't see. Seconds later, the stranger's message came:

*Since the time he came to Mumbai following her.*

'And why didn't you tell me this before?'

*I wanted to hurt you real bad.*

'What? Why? What have I done to you?' she said aloud.

*You didn't learn to cook.*

'What nonsense!'

*If you are not badly hurt, you don't learn. If you don't learn, you don't grow. If you don't grow, you don't live. If you don't live, you don't know your worth. If you don't know your worth, then what's the point?*

'You would have shared this even if I had learnt to cook, isn't it?'

*Maybe.*

'But my love for Ekansh was true. You know what the worst thing is? Not that I have to live with the fact that Ekansh cheated on me but the fact that I won't ever be able to love anyone with the kind of blindness, innocence, and selflessness that I loved him. How do I come to terms with that?' She didn't know why she was saying all these things to a stranger but she wanted to talk, she wanted a vent and some sort of answers.

*How: that's your business. I'll tell you why: heartbreaks are like those pestering advertisements that make you believe a particular product is important for you. They create a false space in you and convince you that it's your need. Ekansh isn't important. You are. There's more to you as a person and in your life than cribbing for a guy who can only limit you from reaching your real worth.*

'What is my real worth? I'm a simple girl who only wanted to work till she got married to the guy of her dreams and then raise a family with him, grow old with him, and probably die in his arms. I know it sounds like a story from *Mills & Boons* but that's me.'

*That's NOT you. You shall soon know who you really are.*

'Huh? But who are you? Why are you helping me?' Rivanah said and after a hiatus added, 'I want to meet you.'

*Anonymity is power, Mini,* the stranger replied.

# 12

The sudden break-up led to a certain organic change in Rivanah. She abhorred spending time alone, knowing well her 'me-time' would invariably be accompanied by the memories of Ekansh. And it always put her in the middle of a dichotomy: to cry or not to cry.

Both Ishita and Pooja asked her to move on but nobody told her how. Human beings are designed in a way that they always live with one half of their self in the past and the other half in the present. For Rivanah, the problem was that the past was about Ekansh's presence and her present was about his absence. She couldn't forget her past and she couldn't accept her present. Though Rivanah had blocked Ekansh on Facebook, time and again she would first activate her profile, unblock him, check his latest profile and cover pictures and whatever that she could see without being in his friend list, and block him again conveniently. It only meant he still mattered to her. It made her hate herself even more. She knew he ditched her and still he mattered to her. What depressed her the most was the fact that Ekansh never understood that in love one's own choice affects the other the most. With one single choice of his, he had turned her life upside down. Whenever the thought of Ekansh and Vishakha invaded her, she used to put heavy make-up on and click selfies only to post them on Facebook in order to garner more and more likes. The likes and comments made her feel important. It was her way of defending her own pride which had been punctured.

In office, Rivanah started working even harder. She robbed her own free space and time for herself. She had secretly bought the same sleeping pills which Ishita used to take once in a while. Almost every night after dinner, Rivanah would pop one before crashing on the bed. The pills gave her a sound sleep even though she knew it would harm her in the long run. *But then, who gives a damn about the long run,* she thought, *when living one single day without feeling miserable about myself is becoming an achievement?* The truth was the roots of her commitment to Ekansh had entered so deep within her that pulling them out wasn't possible without developing cracks within her own self. And she knew well those cracks won't let any other root to develop,no matter how much time went by.

As days changed to weeks, Rivanah discovered certain behavioural changes in her as well. Earlier, if any guy would glance at her fishing for her attention, she would pretend the guy didn't exist. Now she would glance back as if she was hooked to him and wouldn't mind if he came and talked to her. She would reciprocate politely but later would take pleasure in avoiding the guy as if nothing ever happened. Ekansh's action had taught her how unimportant she was to him and the one thing she would never let any guy do to her again was make her feel that way, she promised herself.

As a mark of gratitude to the stranger one day, Rivanah decided to cook something simple. She made dal, rice, and aloo-matar. It was below satisfactory but tasting her own preparation made her happy and worthwhile. Her mother couldn't believe when she told her about it.

'Did Ekansh ask you to cook?' Mrs Bannerjee said.

'Why does Ekansh have to tell me everything? I did it myself,' Rivanah said in irritation.

'Don't get angry Mini. Your baba will be so happy to know that you have started taking interest in cooking.'

'It tastes nothing great but by the time I visit Kolkata next, I shall surely improve.'

And improve she did. Listening to songs and preparing a new dish in her free time worked as a therapy for her agitated soul. In a span of a month and a half, she became an expert at preparing mouth-watering butter chicken. Ishita was floored when she tasted it for the first time.

'I would have married you right now if I was a man,' she said.

Rivanah laughed out and messaged the stranger that she now knew how to prepare the dishes he had asked her to. But there was no response.

On weekends, following the break up, Ishita made sure Rivanah accompanied her to the nightclubs.

'At least have fun before your parents get a husband for you.'

The edge that Ishita balanced her life on was a temptation to begin with for Rivanah and now she had the perfect motivation to go ahead and anchor her life beside that edge.

While Ishita danced and openly hit on men in nightclubs and pubs, Rivanah preferred drinking alone sitting by a corner and return to her flat totally sloshed, cursing Ekansh with newer and unapologetically vulgar slangs every time. Once she had written the name 'Ekansh' on her pillow with her lipstick after coming back zoned-out by Tequila and then had spent an hour cutting the pillow into innumerable pieces wailing to herself.

The noise at the disc, the disconnection that booze brought her, and the freedom that she chose for herself opened a new world for her, both outside and within. Lying to her parents on the phone became a habit. It was like a rebirth for her. The earlier Rivanah was someone who used to live by rules. The new Rivanah lived by fucking those rules. She soon developed severe mood swings because of which she sometimes skipped her meals for days and at times ate like there was no tomorrow. She didn't look sick but she didn't look normal either. She laughed her heart out at trivial matters, embarrassing everyone around, while remained neutral on actual jokes. One day Prateek spotted her in the office canteen sitting alone by a table and with a huge pile up of food that aroused his suspicion.

'Hey, is there anyone else with you?' he asked, not sure whether to sit down or not.

'No. Why?' She was talking to him after a long time. They did greet each other once or twice during their casual encounters in office, but that was about it.

'Nothing,' he said deciding not to probe her about the extra food. 'May I?' He placed a hand on the chair opposite her.

'Sure.' Rivanah didn't look at him. Prateek took his seat beside her.

'Anything the matter? You look...different,' he said.

'Where have you been all these days, Prateek? I didn't see you much in office,' she said this time linking her eyes to his.

'Thanks for asking.' A halo of happiness appeared around him. 'I went home for a cousin's marriage,' he said, 'But what's up with you really?'

'Nothing, why?'

'I can see something is wrong.'

Really? Can he really feel my pain? Is he that special? Rivanah thought and quietly continued with her heavy lunch.

'Ekansh has broken-up with you, isn't it? I don't see him in your friend list anymore. In fact you too are sometimes there and sometimes not on Facebook,' he added without knowing how she would react to his covert stalking.

*He hasn't stopped snooping around,* Rivanah thought and then spat out the bolus on her plate. She gulped a mouthful of Coke, rinsing her mouth once.

'Ekansh didn't break up. I broke up. He cheated,' she said with a straight face.

'Wow, sounds like one of those campus novels written by college goers these days; *I Broke Up, He Cheated*' Prateek said beaming to himself.

'Would you have cheated on me Prateek if you were my boyfriend?' She didn't know why she asked him that.

For a moment Prateek thought he didn't hear her correctly. His stare urged her to repeat it.

'Forget it,' she said. 'Now I know how you must have felt when I rejected you in school.'

'It's okay Rivanah. Even if you don't love me, I'll always love you.'

With that one statement, Prateek changed the way Rivanah looked at him since her joining Tech Sky Technologies. Here was a guy who loved her even when he knew she probably would never be his. And there was a guy who knew she was his and yet...she smiled at the irony of it.

'What are you doing this evening? Want to catch the latest superhero film? Heard its better than its first part,' he asked with the same excitement that he always exhibited in front of her, the excitement she earlier interpreted as dangerous but which was now turning infectious.

'Let's go,' she said.

◆

After that evening, going out with Prateek became a habit. It introduced her to yet another side of her own self: Rivanah realized that with Prateek she could choose when to be good and when to play a bitch. Such a choice wasn't there with Ekansh because she loved him. She was with Prateek only because she wanted to prove to her own self that she wasn't as undesirable as Ekansh made her feel. That she too was capable of having a pet who could do whatever she wished him to only to gain a little attention from her. She knew it was mean of her to be doing something like this, but the forbidden pleasure of doing it overcame the morals associated with it.

They went out only when she wanted to, but when Prateek would request for some coffee-time together, she had her excuses ready. When she Whatsapped him that she was feeling like having an ice cream at midnight, Prateek would ride his bike to her apartment carrying two cones. But when he'd ask her to dine together, she'd have a sudden headache. There were times of self-introspection too when she asked herself if what she was doing was at all justified. After which the sight of Ekansh clasping the girl's hand in Cafe Basilico would flash in her mind and she would convince herself if what Ekansh did to her was justified, then this too was more than justified.

One day while sitting in the Barista cafe at Band Stand, Prateek asked her, 'Have you forgotten Ekansh totally?'

'Yes,' Rivanah replied promptly lest her lie be caught.

'Then is there any place for me now?'

This was the propose moment which she knew could happen anytime and thus she had her answer ready.

'We should take it slowly, Prateek. I just had a break up. I don't want you to be my rebound.'

Prateek sat gloomily for some time and then said, 'I think you are right, but I'm scared too.'

'Scared of what?'

'What if someone else takes the place before I do? I lost my chance once in school. I don't want to lose you again.'

Rivanah sat in silence sipping her coffee and looking at the horizon far across the Bandstand on whose lap the sun was setting. She would have to convince Prateek to give it some more time without being obvious that she didn't really love him.

'Do you believe in destiny Prateek?' she asked.

'I do.'

'So do I. And if we are destined to be together, then we will. Let's not kill our friendship trying to force things upon it.' She tried to sound as mild as possible. Come what may, she didn't want to disturb what she had formed with him over the course of a few weeks; a relationship with no stakes from her side.

'Alright,' Prateek said. 'By the way, can we please have dinner together? Last week you had a headache so we couldn't go.'

'Oh dear. I would have love to, but I'm menstruating, and my stomach hurts real bad on the second day. In fact, my abdomen is already aching a bit.'

'Can I do something to ease the pain?'

'No, thanks. Not tonight. Let's have dinner some other time. Okay?'

Rivanah had had her periods two weeks ago. The real reason why she avoided going out with Prateek was that she had to accompany Ishita to a private party at one of her friend's place.

'But what will I do there!' she had complained to Ishita a few hours ago.

'You will get free ka daaru. Do you need any other reason?' Ishita had argued. A happy Rivanah gladly nodded.

The party was in a luxurious flat at a posh apartment in Aarey Milk Colony in Goregaon east. The two stayed there till 2:30 in the morning. Ishita was wrong. The alcohol was actually beer, which was no alcohol for someone who had developed a fetish for whiskey in the weekends. Rivanah was cross with Ishita when they finally left the party.

They were walking alone, abusing each other on a lonely road looking for an autorickshaw but there was not a single one in sight. They walked ahead a little further till the main road. Ishita felt a strong urge to pee.

'What else will you do if you drink five mugs of beer!' Rivanah exclaimed. Ishita excused herself and went toward the bushes on the left side of the road. With Ishita gone, the scary silence around suddenly made its presence felt to Rivanah.

'Don't go far,' she said. Ishita didn't reply.

Rivanah stood alone checking her Whatsapp friend list on her phone. Some muffled noise called for her attention from beyond the dense bushes on the right. With an ominous curiosity that fear sometimes brings forth, she took a few steps toward the bushes. Little away beyond a tiny bush she could now see a guy kneeling down trying to force his mouth on...Rivanah tilted her head a bit and saw a young girl. She was trying to set herself free from the clutches of the boy. Her mouth was tied so all that came out were helpless muffled nothings. There was another guy too, naked from waist down, trying to force himself on the girl. For a moment Rivanah couldn't move, think, breathe. The power with which they held the girl was frightening.

'Hello?'

She heard Ishita's voice. Before it could reach the guys' ears, Rivanah ran out into the road, took Ishita by her hand, and simply started running toward the main road.

'What's up girl?' Ishita said, feeling her friend's tight grip on her arm.

'Be quiet and keep running,' was all Rivanah could whisper. Ishita didn't know why she was looking back from time to time.

They finally got an autorickshaw. Once the vehicle was at a safe distance, Rivanah heaved a sigh of relief. Ishita looked at her inquiringly but Rivanah didn't share what she had witnessed a minute back. Reaching home, sheupdated her status on Facebook: *Every rapist's balls should be chopped off!*

Plugging her ears with her headphones and playing a Taylor Swift number, she forgot about the matter in no time.

# 13

Every day after getting up in the morning, Rivanah would first check her Facebook profile from her phone. The morning after she posted her opinion on rapists on Facebook, Rivanah saw the post had received over one hundred likes and several comments echoing her sentiments. She felt happy to have updated her status, for the first time, with a cocky message.

Rivanah was reminded of the dastardly incident when her mother mentioned it to her on the phone after she reached office. She was surprised the incident had been reported in a national newspaper. Rivanah took a copy of the newspaper from one of her colleagues and found the article on the second page.

## TEENAGER GANGRAPED

*Mumbai: A 15-year-old girl was gangraped last night in the Aarey Milk Colony area in Goregaon east. She was found by a sweeper in the morning who informed the authorities. The girl was admitted to a municipal hospital in Borivali in a comatose state.*

*The hunt for the rapists is on. Police is waiting for the girl to regain her senses.*

*The girl's mother works as a maid in one of the nearby residential colonies.*

Rivanah had a sinking feeling as she finished reading the article. She had witnessed the beastility. She didn't remember their faces clearly, but she was confident of identifying them if someone brought them in front of her; both the rapists as well as the girl.

The memory of the incident didn't let her focus on her work. At lunch, Prateek came to her looking rather excited.

'Joyita and Dilip are getting married.'

Joyita was from the HR department whereas Dilip was from one of the software developing teams. Rivanah didn't know Joyita, but she had met Dilip a couple of times.

'That's great!' she said.

'What is even greater is that they are throwing a pre-wedding party for all of us tonight.'

'Us? They don't even know me that well.'

'Joyita knows me and I know you. I told her you'll join me.'

Rivanah's instinct didn't want her to go.

'Where is the party?' she asked.

'Trilogy, Juhu.'

Trilogy was one of her favourite places.

'Okay,' she said. Prateek could have jumped with joy.

'I'll pick you up around nine from your place,' he said and left.

◆

Prateek arrived a little after nine and waited on his bike outside Rivanah's building. When she came out, he almost fainted. She looked ravishing.

'At least shut your mouth, for God's sake!' Rivanah said and climbed on his pillion.

'Why do I have to drive the bike? Why can't I just admire you?'

'Ho gaya? Now please drive.' It was one of the few times Rivanah would allow Prateek to flirt with her mildly when she was in a good mood.

There were a total of ten people from the office at Trilogy. Rivanah knew none of them personally, except for Prateek. A cake was brought out for Joyita and Dilip and after the cake cutting session, Rivanah, along with some others, ordered their favourite poison. She gulped hers in one go. Then she ordered another. And another. Totally inebriated, she hit the dance floor grabbing Prateek by the hand. Dancing beside her, Prateek sensed alcohol was slowly taking control of her. She smiled at him, then casually put her hands around his neck, and turned to gyrate her hips against his groin. It aroused him. As she turned once again to face him, he gave her a sly smile, placed his hands around her waist, and brought her close to him. Looking into his eyes, Rivanah suddenly felt the DJ had lowered the volume even though she could see everyone dancing around her. With every second, she seemed to be getting closer to Prateek. Or was it he who was getting close to her? Prateek tilted his face and leaned forward. She knew what was going to happen but the alcohol's spell was so strong that it didn't let her pull away. Prateek's lips soon pursed hers and for the next two minutes, they smooched each other hungrily. When the music stopped, Rivanah pushed Prateek away and went towards one of the couches. The music changed as Prateek followed her out.

'Drop me home, Prateek.' Rivanah suddenly sounded rude. She knew something wrong had happened, but her mind was too numb to know what.

'Let's stay for sometime more,' Prateek pleaded.

'No!' she said trying to stabilize herself.

Joyita came to Prateek and said, 'I think you should take her home. She seems wasted.'

'I have a bike. And she does look sloshed. Won't it be risky?' Prateek argued.

Dilip joined them and suggested Joyita and he would drop her in his car on their way back.

The next day, Rivanah came late to office. She had a vague remembrance of what had happened between Prateek and her in Trilogy. She found a few men looking at her in an amused manner during lunch hour, laughing in hushed tones. When Prateek didn't join her for lunch, she called him to ask him to join her. By the time he reached, her lunch was over.

'What happened?' he said without caring to sit down. She could sense a change in his overall demeanour.

'Is anything wrong?' she asked.

Prateek kept a straight face for some time and then broke into a chuckle.

'What is it Prateek?' Rivanah asked in a stern voice.

'Say, "What is it Prateek, sir".'

'Are you out of your mind?'

Prateek handed her his phone. She took it and pressed on the play button of the video on the screen. She stopped it mid-way even before she could see the details of her smooch with him. Whoever had recorded it had used the zoom-in and out option to a vulgar perfection.

'I waited for this moment for a long time,' Prateek said. 'Remember how you made a mockery of me when I proposed to you in school? "Rejected piece"—that was my nickname for the rest of my school life. If you wanted to, you could have said no in a sober way but you didn't. You had to make a scene out of it. Now the same Rivanah Bannerjee who turned me into a rejected piece in school will be my bitch.' He scoffed in a way that scared Rivanah.

'I have already apologized for that Prateek. I...'

115

'Are you going to fall on my feet now, Rivanah?' Prateek's voice had a loathsome condescension.

'I'll complain about it to the higher authority. You can't record me without my permission.'

'Sure, do complain. The clip doesn't show me raping you. And my colleagues have seen you getting close to me. So yes, go ahead complain and meanwhile I shall waste no time in circulating this clip on the internet and telling people how much you wanted to record our private moment. And you know what happens when this kind of thing hits the virtual world? The girl's real world gets fucked.' He chuckled and left whistling a raunchy Bollywood item number.

Rivanah sat down on the chair with a thud, holding her head which was reeling. How could she have not seen it coming? How could she trust Prateek so much? How could she be such a fool?

At night, a sobbing Rivanah shared the incident with Ishita.

'If it was not for the clip, I would have squashed his balls tonight itself,' Ishita said clenching her jaws.

'I think I should go back home.' Rivanah said wondering how she had cried more than smiled in the last two-three months.

'Stop talking like a retard! I'm sure there's some way out. Nobody can blackmail a girl like that.' Ishita was pacing up and down the room.

'Why don't you ask the stranger to help you?' It was

Asha who surprised both Ishita and Rivanah with her appearance.

A glimmer of hope shone on Ishita's face. 'That's a good idea!' she chirped. 'But how do you know about him?'

'I know about my roomies more than they know about me,'Asha said and went inside the washroom. Ishita and Rivanah exchanged a blank look.

'She must have overheard us discussing the stranger,' Ishita said.

'Should I?' Rivanah asked a pause later.

'Well, we don't have much option. We can go to the police and I'm sure they will burst Prateek's ass but what if he circulates the MMS before that...'

Before Ishita could finish, Rivanah sent a message to the stranger.

*Hi! Are you there?* Rivanah could have spoken it aloud, but she did not want to disclose every little thing to Ishita. It was something between the stranger and her. *The stranger and her*, that sounded so much like a relationship with no name. A minute later a reply came:

*Always.*

*I need some help,* Rivanah messaged back.

*I can get you the clip,* the stranger replied. Rivanah read the message aloud.

'So he already knows about it,' Ishita said in wonder.

*By when can you get it for me?* Rivanah asked.

*For now you do yourself a little favour. What favour?* she asked.

The stranger's reply turned Rivanah's face pale.

# 14

Rivanah sat at her office desk the following morning, staring miserably at her computer screen. Her colleagues were discussing something with the team lead but she wasn't interested. She felt devoid of any motivation to work but she had to. For a 22-year-old like her, working away from home in a big city, life behaved like a spoilt brat. In the few months that she had been in Mumbai, she understood that nothing came for free.

Rivanah had not shared with Ishita what favour the stranger had asked of her.

'He didn't respond,' she told her. But a message in fact did come and in the message, the stranger had asked her to do an impossible task. A message popped on her office messenger from Prateek interrupting her thoughts.

'I want to see you in the no-smoking zone in a minute.'

The message turned her livid enough to want to smash Prateek's skull into pieces. But all she did was take a deep breath and diffuse the anger within her. She was a fool for having trusted him. Ishita had told her once: people judge the unknown from the known. Rivanah was fooled by Prateek because he looked like a *lalloo* and she believed he was one. The same mistake that she committed with Ekansh; she thought because Ekansh loved her, he would be loyal to her. When she couldn't catch him even after knowing him so well, how could she have known Prateek's intention? Ekansh and now Prateek had taught her well that the known and the unknown are two different things. Rivanah didn't know whether to feel miserable, laugh, or cry because of the mess she had got herself in.

*Waiting.*

Prateek whatsapped her this time. Rivanah stood up, turned the desk computer on sleep mode, and went out into the no-smoking zone.

Rivanah could see Prateek standing alone, smoking a cigarette. This was the first time she was seeing him smoke, but she didn't care to inquire about it. Prateek flashed his Samsung tablet when she approached him.

'Red or black?' he said.

Rivanah couldn't believe her eyes. On the tablet's screen was a page from a popular online lingerie store website displaying a particular brain both red and black colour.

'I'm buying this for you,' Prateek said pointing to the red bra. He looked pleased to see Rivanah's bewildered face. 'I want you to wear it this weekend when you come to my place.'

*Should I admire his audacity or slap the indecency out of his system?* she wondered but she was too shell-shocked to do either. A moment later, she found her voice.

'I told you Prateek, I'm sorry for rejecting your proposal in school, then why...'

'Red or black?' He meant business.

'Prateek, please don't do this to me. I'm your friend now and...'

'Red. OR. Black?'

Rivanah went quiet.

'Prateek!' one of Prateek's colleagues called out to him.

'Okay. I'll order both,' he said. 'We will have lots of time for you to wear both as well as not wear any,' he said winking at Rivanah.

'And by the way just in case you are still considering your option of complaining about me then let me tell you that I have located all your cousins on Facebook. I don't think they will like it seeing you smooch in a video, will they?'

Rivanah swallowed a lump. Prateek turned and went away.

Rivanah went back to her desk feeling disoriented. Reaching her desk, she unlocked her phone and opened the message inbox. The stranger's message was still in her phone. What he was asking her to do was impossible! She checked his message again:

*Be the eyewitness in the gangrape case.*

He had asked a simple favour of her in return for the clip that had stolen her sleep. She read the message for the umpteenth time. A night before, she considered telling her father everything by sending him a message because she knew she would never be able to confess it verbally: 'Baba, I was drunk when I became intimate with Prateek in the disc but I didn't know that he would record it. I don't know what to do now. Please help me.' Reading the message, she thought of the number of questions that would be hurled at her by her father:

'What were you doing in a disc Mini?'

'Haven't we asked you to get back home every day by nine at night?'

'Did you say you were drunk? Since when have you started consuming alcohol? Even I haven't done that in my whole life.'

'Who is Prateek? Does Ekansh know about him? How can you be so mean to him?'

'Why is Prateek blackmailing you?'

The queries would give way to her father's eventual decision: Pack your bags and come here. No need to work anymore. We'll get you married off soon.

Rivanah, in the end, had decided to keep it all to herself. But little did she know Prateek would actually

121

stoop so low as to blackmail her into being his sexual slave for the weekend. She left her cubicle and rushed to the washroom. By the time she glanced at herself in the mirror, the kohl in her eyes had already been smudged by her tears. She splashed some water on her face. Why couldn't the stranger arrange for the clip without her being the witness in the gangrape case? What was his stake in it? She immediately messaged him:

*Why does it matter to you if I become the witness in the case? Is the girl related to you?*

She waited for a few minutes but got no reply. Rivanah was about to move out when her phone buzzed with a message .

*She isn't related to me. But by that logic I shouldn't help you out with the clip either because you too are not related to me.*

Rivanah typed a reply and sent it back hurriedly.

*Do you even know how much of a hassle it is? It involves the law. My parents as well as the media will know and what if I get threatened by the men who raped the girl? Just so you know, I did make people aware of it by posting how I felt on my Facebook profile. I did my part.*

The stranger replied:

*Your part? What you did on Facebook is called bullshitting. Social networking sites are nothing but virtual commodes for people to shit their opinion on and then conveniently presume their job's done. Their only agenda is to feel good about themselves by convincing themselves that ejecting thoughts is as responsible an act as producing an action. How many of them really go out of their way in the real world and do something about a matter? Did anyone who liked your post buy the girl medicines? Did anyone come forward to sponsor her hospital bill? Did you?*

*How do you know I was a witness? Were you there too? If yes then why don't you become the witness as well?* Rivanah typed back.

*I didn't see the faces of the rapists.*

*May I know what your stake is if I become the eyewitness in the case?*

*You are my stake.*

*Why me?*

*Why not you?* he shot back.

*Okay, if I become the witness, what's the guarantee you will give me the clip? Why don't you give me the clip first and then I'll see what I can do?*

*What's the guarantee that I won't take the clip from Prateek and circulate it on the internet myself? The world doesn't run on guarantees, Mini. It runs on faith.*

*I don't have faith on men anymore.*

*LOL. How are you so sure I'm a man?*

Rivanah swallowed a lump. She had yet again repeated her mistake of judging the stranger too soon based on someone else's judgement. Ishita only guessed the person was a secret admirer. And was there a diktat every secret admirer of hers had to be a man? God, she didn't even know if he admired her or was it something else! Another message.

*Be Prateek's weekend bitch or stand up for the girl: take your call, Mini.*

Rivanah took a moment to think: the police was not an option lest Prateek circulated the clip, her parents were not an option lest they asked her to come back home, and being a weekend bitch to Prateek was definitely not an option either. Her hands shook subtly as she typed her final decision to the stranger.

*Okay. I shall be the eyewitness but promise me you will get me the clip before this weekend. Otherwise, I won't fullfil my side of the bargain.*

*Have faith*, replied the stranger.

Rivanah picked up a local English tabloid during lunchtime. In a couple of days' time, the news of the gangrape had travelled from the front to the fifth page. The tiny article said the girl was still admitted at the municipal hospital in Borivali where she was initially taken and the police were yet to identify the rapists because the girl was unable to give them any leads.

Rivanah called Ishita asking if she could join her without telling her the reason or the destination. Ishita said she had a night shift in office and would be free only the next morning. It was Thursday and Rivanah didn't want to waste a single day now that she knew what Prateek had in mind for the weekend.

She left her office an hour early to avoid the office crowd. She took an autorickshaw from Goregaon east and went directly to the municipal hospital in Borivali.

The scene in the hospital was abysmal. The place was dirty, with a pungent smell of medicines lurking in the air. There were people who were either howling or running around or sitting helplessly, waiting for their turn for check-up to come. Rivanah tried to locate the reception amid the crowd, but to no success. She soon located a police constable chatting with a middle-aged man who was carrying a camera around his neck, with a glass of tea in his hand. She went to them.

'Excuse me,' she said. Both the constable and the man with the camera looked at her with an expression that said they didn't expect her to be there.

'*Kaye paije?*' the constable asked in Marathi.

'What do you want?' the man with the camera translated. He seemed educated as well as less terrifying than the pot-bellied constable.

'I have come to see the gangrape victim. Do you know which room she is in?'

The constable and the man exchanged a surprised look.

'Are you a relative?' the man asked.

'No. I'm an eyewitness in the case.'

Both the men suddenly turned alarmed.

The constable asked her to follow him. Rivanah and the man with camera followed him closely behind.

It was not a private room as Rivanah had thought it would be. It was the general ward housing people suffering from all kinds of problems—fractures, bullet wounds, animal attack, and burns. In the middle of all this was a young girl who lay in the silence of her sleep. There was a middle-aged lady sitting beside her on the dirty bed itself. Rivanah guessed she would be her mother.

'She wakes up, screams, and then the nurse has to make her sleep,' the constable said. 'Did you really see the guys who did this to her?'

Rivanah couldn't speak or move. She had a strong urge to throw up. The newspaper said the girl was fifteen but she looked much younger. She wondered if the girl would ever be able to come to terms with the wounds that had been inflicted on her soul without any fault of hers. The hair on her nape stood up thinking what would have happened if she was in her place. The girl suddenly woke up as her body started shuddering vehemently. Though her eyes were shut, she was screaming her lungs out as if the devil had possessed her. The constable yelled something in Marathi. A nurse came running towards them, blabbering something in Marathi as well, and quickly gave her an injection. The girl gradually went quiet once again. By then, Rivanah had tasted bile.

The constable took her to the Goregaon police station with him and documented her statement. The man with the camera, who Rivanah later learnt was a small-time journalist with a Marathi newspaper wanted to click a picture of her but decided not to on her request.

Soon police inspector Mohan Kamble joined them and inquired about what Rivanah had witnessed. She hadn't sipped any alcohol the night of the incident unlike Ishita and that made her claim all the more strong.

'Sir,' Rivanah said glancing first at the journalist and then at Kamble, 'I don't want to be named or exposed in the media or in front of the rapists. Is that possible?'

'Don't worry madam. I'll take care of that,' Kamble assured her. 'Your gesture is really commendable, otherwise who cares these days?'

She felt like a slap of shame hit her. She knew well that the real intention behind her appearance at the police station was selfish, but a small part of her also understood what the stranger had meant when he asked her to know her worth. Though there was a dichotomy in her situation, the fact nevertheless was she did give her statement as an eyewitness. She *did* decide to help the girl.

'Do your parents know you go to late night parties?' Kamble asked.

'No,' Rivanah replied meekly.

'That's what worries parents these days. It doesn't matter how close you are to your children, they will never be completely honest with you,' Kamble said. 'I actually have a daughter your age.' The fatherly warmth in Kamble's demeanour was evident. 'Her name is Smita. She works in a software company in Bangalore. It's tough to live in a big city all alone, isn't it?'

*With a stranger trailing me, a colleague trying to blackmail me, and me presenting myself as an eyewitness in a rape case, tell me about how tough it is living in a big city,* Rivanah thought to herself and said with tight smile, 'It indeed is. But one can't really help it.'

'I remain tensed about Smita all the time. These days, anything can happen,' Kamble said in a worried tone. 'Please do let me know if you ever have any opening in your company. I want her to work in Mumbai itself.'

*Parents will be parents.* 'Sure,' Rivanah said and a moment later added, 'How long do I have to stay here?'

'Some time more. All you have to do is identify the two men from a group of people we have rounded up from the area. They'll be here shortly. You can hide your face while doing it,' Kamble said and gestured to the female constable who escorted her to an adjacent room. She waited there for some time. In-between her mother called.

'Did you reach home Mini?' she asked.

'I'm on my way mumma,' Rivanah lied. 'Tell me something mumma, would you like the rapists to be caught and punished?'

'Which rapists? What are you saying?' Her mother sounded tensed.

'The ones who raped the teenager in Mumbai a few days back. Remember you told me about it on phone?'

'Oh yes! I definitely want them to be caught and punished. They spoilt the life of an innocent girl.'

'Hmm.' Rivanah took a long breath. 'I will call you mumma when I reach home,' she said and cut the line.

When the rounded-up men arrived in a police van, she was made to wrap a cloth around her face. One by one, two constables brought in the men. It wasn't difficult for her to identify the two rapists amongst the fifteen men. She later learnt from Kamble that they worked as labourers in the nearby construction site and weren't from Maharashtra.

Kamble gave her his contact number and also took her office number as well as home contact information and asked her not to leave the city without informing him. Kamble had started seeing his daughter in her and wanted to safeguard her from danger. She was told that she would have to appear in the court and testify against the men once the charge sheet was submitted.

'Will it take time?' she asked.

'I hope not.'

Rivanah soon left. Kamble arranged for a police jeep to drop her home.

At night when she messaged the stranger saying she had become the official eyewitness in the gangrape case, the stranger replied with an address in Andheri west and asked her to be there on Saturday night at nine sharp.

'Why?' a worried Rivanah asked. She was again talking aloud sitting in her flat alone when the stranger messaged her on the phone.

*Prateek lives there.*

'What? That's what he wanted anyway; for me to visit his place this Saturday night. Please tell me you are kidding,' she said sounding nervous.

*Do you trust me?* the stranger asked in the next message .

*Trust a stranger?* She had trusted both Ekansh and Prateek before when she thought she knew them well. Should she trust someone she knew nothing about? Rivanah took her time before she said aloud, 'Yes.' She hoped and prayed nothing would go wrong this time.

# 15

There was still one more day to go before Saturday night arrived. Rivanah kept leading Prateek on. She gave him forced smiles whenever he was around and accompanied him to the canteen or the no-smoking zone whenever he asked her to for some fake love talk. He asked her to come to his place on Friday night itself, but she lied to him saying she was having muscle spasms owing to an early period and would visit him on Saturday night for sure. Prateek took the bait and agreed to wait for one day more.

Saturday arrived. Rivanah was feeling apprehensive. She had a bad feeling about what she was going to do. She wanted to share it with Ishita but didn't because one thing she had learnt in the last few months was not to trust anybody beyond a certain limit. You never know when that person will go against you. And a friend who knows your secret can be far worse than an enemy. She had also decided this was the last time she would listen to the stranger too. She didn't know why the stranger was so hell-bent on helping her. There had to be an agenda. But at that moment, she only cared about the clip and nothing else.

Sipping the evening tea while standing by her room's window, she wondered if the stranger would really help her with the clip or not. What if the stranger was Prateek? Would it be safe to go to his address at night? The world runs on faith, the stranger had said and it was faith that, owing to her experience in the past months, had depleted from her core. Well, almost.

Rivanah finished her tea in a rush and waited for the clock to strike eight. Once it was time, she dressed herself in a jeans and t-shirt, took a knife from her kitchen and kept it in her bag as a safety precaution, and put inspector Kamble's phone number on speed dial number one. It took her thirty minutes in an autorickshaw to reach the Andheri west address. It seemed like a posh colony from outside. The stranger had said nine so she waited at a corner outside the colony till 8:55 and then went in. The security guard asked her to write her name in the visitor's register. She wrote a false name, a fake phone number, and a fake address after which she went inside the building looking for the flat the stranger had messaged her about.

Once she climbed up the stairs to reach the first floor of B-wing, she came and stood in front of flat 103, the flat where Prateek lived. Rivanah prayed hard in her mind that the stranger lived up to his promise. She stood nervously by the door contemplating whether to press the doorbell or not. Her phone pinged with a message from an unknown number.

*The key is inside the dustbin.*

Rivanah looked down and saw a small dustbin by the flat's main door. Making a face she bent down and picked up the key from the almost empty dustbin. With fear forming lumps in her throat, she gently inserted the key into the keyhole. There was a slight noise as the door unlocked. She pushed the door open with the tip of her finger. It was dark inside. She took an unsure step forward and then immediately pulled out. Should she enter? She closed her eyes for once, took God's name and after a moment of resting her pacing heartbeats, advanced inside.

*To the left is the switch board*, the stranger messaged. Her own phone's beep scared her. Rivanah turned around to see if there was anyone behind her, watching her. There was nobody. Extending her arm to the left, she found the switch board. She pressed all the buttons at once. The next instant, three lights in the room came on along with two ceiling fans. She saw Prateek lying on the floor in an unconscious state. He was stark naked except for a bra around his chest. Rivanah didn't know what to do. She went close to him to check if he was dead or alive. She noticed something was written on his stomach: *world's tiniest wonder*. An arrow was marked below which aimed toward his flaccid penis. Rivanah's first instinct was to laugh, acknowledging the stranger's sense of humour. But she controlled herself. She now understood why the stranger had asked her to be there. She took out her phone and made a three-minute long video of Prateek. His phone was lying beside him. Once done, she quickly kept her own phone in her bag while taking out the memory card and SIM from Prateek's phone stamped the phone out of shape. Even if he had transferred the clip somewhere else, she now had stuff to barter and shut him up permanently. Rivanah was about to get up to leave when the lights went off. She could smell the same masculine deodorant which she once did in the elevator before. She turned around but before she could see anything, Rivanah felt someone press a cloth to her mouth from behind and within seconds she was unconscious.

Rivanah woke up when a middle-aged woman slapped her cheeks gently.

'Hello! Wake up. Can you hear me?'

She sat up and looked around to realize she was inside her apartment's elevator with no memory of how she came there. The woman who helped her lived in the same floor as her.

'Are you okay?' the woman asked.

'Yes,' Rivanah said holding her head which was mildly aching. She stumbled out of the elevator and went to her flat with the thought: did the stranger leave me in the elevator?

Ishita had gone to Matheran with a guy from her office while Asha was not there in the flat. Rivanah was dying to share the entire incident with someone, but since there was nobody at home, she kept watching the video on repeat until her stomach started cramping with all the laughing. She wanted to watch Prateek's reaction when she would show him the video in office. She was so happy that she decided to cook a new dish. Then she called her mother with whom she talked for a good one hour, the first time she had talked to her mother for so long since Ekansh left her. Her mother was immensely happy to hear her daughter speak like her old self after a long time even though she didn't know what was really happening in her life.

'Is Ekansh coming to Mumbai?' her mother asked trying to guess the reason for her sudden enthusiasm. Rivanah had never told her of his earlier visits.

'No mumma.'

'Then what has happened? Are you getting a promotion?' she egged on.

'No mumma! It's nothing. I'm just happy.'

After the phone call with her mother ended, she spoke aloud finally. 'Thank you stranger!' As an impulse, she immediately stared at her phone for a response. It came soon enough.

*You're welcome.*

'I think I'll soon fall in love with you,' she said and giggled to herself. She knew she wasn't making any sense but she didn't care.

*You don't know me. You can only fall in love with the illusion of me. And illusions are fragile. Illusions are breakable. Illusions are dangerous.*

'Hmm, that's true. But really, I can't thank you enough for this one. I want to meet you one day. Possible?'

*Very much.*

'Thanks. By the way, why did you knock me out?'

*Nothing is for free.*

'Meaning?' An MMS came in from an unknown number. She downloaded it and played the video. It showed her capturing Prateek in the compromising position earlier in the evening. Soon her happiness turned into anger. Did the stranger record her so that she didn't backtrack on the gangrape case? Or was he planning to enslave her just like Prateek?

'You could have given me the clip or recorded Prateek yourself, but you wanted me to record him so that you could record me?' Her voice choked as she added, 'I thought you were a friend but you are no different from Prateek. In fact, you're probably worse because I don't remember doing you any wrong to deserve this.' Rivanah cursed herself to have trusted the stranger.

*I never said I'm your friend.*

## 16

The MMS showing her recording Prateek in a compromising position did mar her happiness but when Monday arrived, it brought with it a sense of excitement. Rivanah was looking forward to Prateek's reaction when she would show him the recording. She went to office early and impatiently waited for him.

When Prateek turned up, Rivanah went up to him and said, 'What happened? You didn't call me on Saturday? Not on Sunday either. I was waiting for your call.'

Her extra eager demeanour took him by surprise.

'I...I wasn't well actually,' he said. 'This coming weekend you will come to my place, okay?'

Rivanah stretched her hand and gave her phone to him.

'What's this?'

'Something I recorded for you.'

Prateek thought she was going to show him something sexy. With blood rushing to his penis, he pressed the play button. For the next two minutes, he stood in a frozen position.

'You bitch. It was you who...how did you...?'

'You and your indecent games are over Prateek.'

She snatched the phone from him and added, 'In case you want to play the game of online video circulation now, count me in on it too.'

Prateek wanted to say a lot more but all he managed to blabber was, 'You...you can't...but how...shit...'

'I told you I was sorry to have rejected you in school. Still you had to come out with your filth, isn't it? Now follow me like a good boy,' Rivanah said and walked away. After a few seconds he followed her to her department. His submissiveness told her their intimate clip was only on his phone and nowhere else, otherwise he wouldn't be playing meek. .

Once they reached her department, Rivanah instructed, 'Now. I want you to scream and say you are sorry.'

Prateek made a pleading face. Rivanah stood rock steady, ignoring him.

'I don't have all day,' she said.

'I'm sorry,' he said softly.

'Louder.'

'I'm sorry.'

A few colleagues turned to look at them.

'Louder,' Rivanah egged on.

'I'm sorry.'

Now almost everyone present in the room was staring at them.

'Get lost now,' Rivanah said. 'If you come near me again, I shall register a case of sexual harassment against you with the higher authorities here. I should have done that on day one anyway.'

◆

It was in the evening when Rivanah went back to her flat that she decided to share the entire smooch incident and the subsequent blackmail exchange with Ishita.

'Did you kick his balls?' Ishita asked. She was busy drying her nail polish, while Rivanah was choosing which nail colour to apply from her vanity box.

'No.'

'You should have.'

'It's okay. My job is done. I'm not interested in anything more.'

'But seriously, did the stranger help you get the clip?'

'Yes.'

'He is such a hero.'

Rivanah thought about the MMS he had sent her and said, 'I don't know what he really is. I mean I don't even know if he is even a man, if you know what I mean.'

'Huh? What do you mean?' Ishita looked at Rivanah for a moment and then started fanning her feet with her hand saying, 'Of course he is a man. Don't spoil my fantasies now. And he is a hero. He helped you out of a situation that could have fucked your life, yaar. What else do you want?'

Rivanah was tempted to think on the same lines as Ishita but after he had sent her the MMS, she was more confused than ever.

'I don't know. Do you know what he made me do for helping me with the clip thing?' she said picking out a nail paint of her liking.

'What?' Ishita looked at her again.

'Promise me you won't speak about it to anyone, come what may!' The secret was killing her and she had to share it with someone.

'Just tell me, what is it? You are scaring me now.'

'I'm the witness of the gangrape case that happened in Goregaon few weeks back.'

Ishita couldn't believe her ears. 'What the fuck! Seriously?'

Rivanah nodded saying, 'I did witness it.'

'You did? When?'

Rivanah took a few minutes to relay exactly what had happened when Ishita had gone to pee that night after the boring beer party leaving Rivanah alone on the street. She also apologized for not telling her about the matter before.

'God! And now you are an eyewitness?'

'Yes. The inspector told me I'll have to make myself available whenever the police or the court summons me. The police have promised that my identity won't be disclosed in front of the media or the rapists or anybody else.'

'That's such a brave thing you did, darling. I mean don't mind but I always thought you were a fattu kind of a girl but this is superwoman stuff, yaar.'

'I didn't do it of my own accord. The stranger made me do it,' Rivanah said continuing to apply the nail paint.

'That's even more interesting. He could have asked you to sleep with him like perverts do, right?'

'That's why I said I don't know who he is. He had his chance and still...' Rivanah was about to tell her roomie about the MMS when the doorbell rang.

'I'll answer it,' Ishita said and went to open the door. Rivanah waited for her to come back. When she didn't come back for almost five minutes, Rivanah called out loud, 'Ishu, who is it?'

There was no response. A few seconds later she heard the main door lock. Ishita walked into her room like a zombie.

'What happened?' Rivanah urged her.

Ishita looked at her as if all the air from her lungs had been sucked out.

'What is it Ishu? Don't scare me.'

'We have a new neighbour,' Ishita said with a straight face.

'So?'

141

'He came to check if we had eggs since there were none in the shops nearby.'

'So?'

'I gave him all the eggs we had.'

'What? Are you mad?'

'I wasn't. But now I'm. He was wearing a pair of black knickers and a red-black gym vest,' Ishita said lost in her thoughts.

'So what's the point?' Rivanah was piqued.

'He is the sexiest, hottest, and the most handsome male specimen I have ever seen in my entire life. What a height, what looks, and what a presence. One look at him and I turned into a 16-year-old in an instant. I was checking him out shamelessly and I don't care if he noticed. He looked soooo edible,' she drooled.

'And he is mine, okay?' Ishita said coming out of her trance.

'You can have him.' Rivanah stood up and out of plain curiosity said, 'I also want to see this hot male specimen.'

'How?' Ishita said and followed her.

'Wait here,' Rivanah said. She checked herself in the wardrobe mirror once. She was looking more than presentable in a pair of denim hot-pants and a green spaghetti top over which she had donned a black shrug.

'He is in the exact opposite flat,' Ishita said.

Rivanah cleared her throat before unlocking the main door and then proceeding toward the concerned flat.

While she pressed the doorbell, Ishita closed their flat's main door. As seconds ticked by, Rivanah could feel the embers of curiosity form a smoke of desire in her. She pressed the doorbell again while turning to look toward her flat. The door was closed but she was sure Ishita was behind the peephole watching everything. Rivanah was about to press the doorbell for the third time when a guy pulled it open. It looked like he had just stepped out of a shower because his body was completely wet and he was naked except for a towel wrapped around his waist.

'Yes?' His voice was deep.

Rivanah swallowed a lump noticing his four-pack abs. She hadn't seen such a perfect male physique, that too in the same building as hers. He understood she was uncomfortable so he tried to make things easy for her.

'I'm sorry I'm taking a shower right now,' he said in a polite manner.

*Gosh, Ishita was right. He is hot*, Rivanah thought. *Such a hot guy shouldn't take a shower alone.* Quickly thinking of an excuse, she said, 'I want your eggs.'

'Excuse me!' Rivanah couldn't believe she had jumbled up her words so bad.

'Actually,' she said, 'My roomie gave you all the eggs we had. But we would need two of them if you don't mind.'

'Oh, it is perfectly fine. I told her I would only need three.'

143

*I don't blame her*, Rivanah thought, and stood there with a stupid smile on her face.

'One minute,' he said and disappeared inside. Rivanah quickly turned to give Ishita a thumbs-up sign.

'Here,' he said handing two eggs to her.

'Thanks. By the way I'm Rivanah,' she said stretching her arm.

'I'm Danny.'

*Danny what? Full name please. I need to Facebook you*, Rivanah thought but couldn't say it aloud lest she was labelled a despo. Never before had she been so eager to know more about a guy. Not even Ekansh did this to her on their first meeting.

'See you,' was all she said.

'Sure. Bye.' Danny closed the door behind her. Even before she could knock, Ishita opened the door. Rivanah came in and locked it.

'Okay, it's not alright. I think he can't be yours just like that,' Rivanah declared.

'Bitch, I knew it!' Ishita hissed.

'Chances anyway are that he already has a girlfriend,' Rivanah guessed.

'Whatever, I'm open to competition,' Ishita declared.

Rivanah hadn't done such a thing before; woo a guy. With Ekansh it was love and not a going-weak-in-the-knee kind of attraction like Danny made her feel almost instantly. She had had many crushes, but most of them were celebrity crushes and there was nothing she could do about it except acting like a crazy fangirl. Danny's wet abs, his smile, the eyes—everything flashed in front of her.

Ishita snapped her fingers in front of her face and said, 'Are you on for competition?'

'Like hell I'm.' They shared a high-five and distributed the days in the week between them so that both get to woo Danny separately. Monday-Wednesday-Friday went to Ishita while Tuesday-Thursday-Saturday went to Rivanah. Sunday was common. The coming day was Wednesday.

The two met the following evening in the flat after they were back from office.

'Any luck?' Rivanah queried.

'I got my information.'

'Like what?'

'The guy is a model, a struggling actor, and a gym freak. Goes to Full On Fitness, the one in Malad. By the way his name is Danny Abraham.'

As Ishita went in to change, Rivanah located Danny on Facebook after creating a fake profile for herself. She liked almost all his pictures, which were open to all, after having a close look at them. There was something magnetic about him. Especially the eyes; they seem to fish for her soul directly. After she logged out of Facebook, Rivanah called Full On Fitness gym and enrolled herself, ensuring that she starts working out the next day onward.

Full On Fitness was a unisex gym. She would go there right after her office. On the first day, Rivanah was taught a few stretching exercises by her trainer and then asked to hit the treadmill. It was while running on the treadmill for ten minutes that she noticed Danny come in. Their eyes met for once and a faint smile was exchanged, but she soon understood it meant nothing. She saw him come out of the men's changing room in a pair of blue denim knickers and a black gym-vest. His body looked unbelievably chiselled with no ounce of fat anywhere. Unlike the last time she saw him in his flat when he was completely clean-shaven, his face now had a stubble which added a certain wildness to his otherwise pleasant personality.

Danny started running on another treadmill opposite to her. The two set of treadmills for men and women were kept on two opposite sides of the room facing huge mirrors against the respective walls. Rivanah could see his back in the mirror in front of her. And soon, she noticed, he was sweating. He removed his vest in no time. As sweat drops trickled from his scruff to his broad shoulders to his narrow waist, so did Rivanah's sight. For the next half an hour, she tried to exercise but in vain since all her focus was on him.

Done with her cardio, she was waiting for her trainer to help her with the crunches but he was nowhere in sight. She didn't complain for she had a delightful distraction. Danny was pumping both his biceps with a barbell and all Rivanah could do was drool looking at the way his muscles flexed as he pulled the barbell up to his neck. *Bless the maker of this wondrous creation,* she thought. Danny kept the barbell down and was about to pick up a set of dumbbells when he noticed her standing by the treadmill doing nothing.

'Any problem?' he asked.

*Lots!* she thought and said, 'I need to do my sit-ups but I don't know where my trainer has gone.'

'I can help if it's okay with you.'

'Umm, sure,' she said.

She took out a floor mat from a nearby shelf and sat on it with folded legs. Danny came and pressed his palm on her shoes to give her enough pressure so that she could sit up easily without lifting her feet. And every time she sat up, as Danny kept a count, she could smell his musky body odour, revelling in it as she lay back. She would have loved to continue but after fifteen sit-ups she could no longer lift herself up.

'First day?' Danny said.

'Yeah.'

'One more set?'

'Yeah, okay.' She would have given up had it not been for the endearing twinkle in his eyes when he asked her for another set. This time Rivanah dared to go beyond revelling in his odour. She started breathing heavy and each time their faces came close, she deliberately blew her breath on his face. Not for a single time did Danny move his face though.

After few more exercises, it was time for Rivanah to leave the gym for the day. She knew the next day was Ishita's. She was contemplating how she should approach him when Danny came up to her.

'Hey, leaving?'

'Yeah,' she said nervously.

'Are you working somewhere?'

'Yes. In Goregaon.'

'Saw you last morning leave the building in haste,' he said with a sharp smile. She felt like a butterfly of desire was hovering in her tummy. What was this spell that imprisoned her in such an embarrassing and yet arousing manner? Rivanah wondered and said, 'What about you?'

'Don't you think this is the wrong place to answer such questions? I mean how about coffee on Saturday?'

And she knew Ishita was out of the game. 'Why not? Saturdays are my off anyway,' she said with a renewed confidence.

'Great!'

'How do we connect?' She hinted at him to give her his phone number. He took the hint well. Rivanah was imagining Ishita's face when she would show Danny's number in her phone contact list. For the first time after her break up with Ekansh, the prospect of a date excited Rivanah.

She reached her flat and was impatiently waiting for Ishita to come home from office when she received a message from the stranger.

*Be free on Saturday.*

*Why, are you meeting me?* She preferred to message back than talk aloud.

*Your good luck is needed,* the stranger messaged.

*Good luck? What do you mean?* The stranger's words never stopped to baffle her.

*I call it the 'share your good luck' endeavour. It was your good luck that you were born to parents who could sponsor your education. Now, it's your turn to share the result of that good luck with children who don't have it.*

Rivanah read the message a couple of times and understood the social implication of it but still missed the point.

'So?' she spoke aloud.

*So, you need to go to Dahisar east on Saturday. There's a small slum there. There will be ten kids waiting for you. You'll teach them every Saturday till they learn how to write their names in English.*

*Good joke! I seriously don't have time. Moreover, I have other things to do than teach slum kids,* Rivanah message again.

*Other things like dating Danny?*

'None of your business,' Rivanah cried out sounding crossed. Did this person have nothing else to do except for following her around? *Be free Mini.*

'Why don't you get it? I have a life of my own!' Frustration was evident in her voice.

149

*Why don't YOU get it? I have a clip of yours that can be transferred to Prateek's mobile any moment with a press of a tiny button.*

Rivanah's face contorted with disgust followed by helplessness.

# 17

'I'm sure you resorted to black magic? Asha helped you in this, didn't she?' said Ishita when she learnt Danny himself had asked Rivanah out.

'Look I'm sorry,' Rivanah said, 'If you like him...'

'It's okay, yaar. I was not going to marry him anyway. He is only a guy. Two soul-sisters can't get mad with each other because of a guy,' she winked at Rivanah and continued, 'But tell me something seriously: do you like him? I mean like really "like" him? You know what I mean.'

'I think I do. For the first time after my break-up, I feel like giving it a try. But I'm scared too. Like should I really give it a try? What if we too break-up later?'

'First, stop thinking about the future all the time. That's one thing we girls do wrong. The moment we come across a desirable guy, we start knitting the possibility of a future with him. For us, it's always the destination in a relationship. But thinking about the future with someone only begets false expectations. And you know what harm expectations can do. Supposing you didn't expect Ekansh to be loyal to you, it wouldn't have hurt you as much as it did otherwise. Obviously you would have left him then too, but I guess you got my point.'

Rivanah nodded as Ishita said, 'So, don't think, don't expect and see where it goes. I guess you'll know it yourself when the time is right to think about the future.'

'Hmm, I guess you are right. I'm just twenty-two. Why should the future bother me so much? Thanks darling.'

The girls hugged.

A day after was Saturday. By then she had forgotten what the stranger had asked her to do. Danny called her in the morning and said he was already out because of a film audition and would wait for her in the food court of Infinity Mall in Andheri, west, around 12:30 in the afternoon for he had another audition in the evening. Rivanah promised him she would be on time but the Mumbai traffic made sure she was half an hour late.

'I'm so sorry,' she said the moment she walked up to him in the food court of the mall. They took a seat by the Subway outlet instead of Gloria's as planned.

'Don't mind but I'm a bit hungry. Can we update the coffee thing to a quick lunch?' Danny asked.

Rivanah smiled and said, 'Please! Even I'm hungry.'

Danny went to Subway and bought two 6-inch subs.

'Here you go. Do you need anything else?' he asked.

'Nope!' she said drawing one tray toward herself.

'How long have you been in Mumbai?' he asked.

'Been around eight months. What about you?'

'Close to three years now.'

'How long have you been a model?'

Danny frowned at her. 'How do you know?' he asked.

'Err, my roomie told me,' Rivanah answered. She couldn't help but portray an amused face. His smile told her he understood.

'I've been modelling for small products and print ads in local newspapers and magazines. Nothing big.'

'And you want to be an actor too?'

'An actor is always an actor. What I aim to be is an employed actor,' he said munching the sandwich.

It started as a Q and A session, turned to a discourse mid-way and before they realized it, they were having a warm and honest heart-to-heart conversation. With every piece of information they were divulging, Rivanah found the colour of her liking toward him getting darker. Her first opinion about Danny was that he was at one level a simple, sombre, disciplined person and yet there was a sublime wildness about him which could lure any girl to the cave of sin. His eyes had a sexual longing in them. Also, the way he looked at her...it was never a casual look. Once they were done with the sandwiches, Danny received a message on his phone. Rivanah watched dejection perch on his face. She wanted to inquire if the message was from his girlfriend. She wouldn't have cared for this question if it was the first time she was interested in a guy. She didn't want someone in her life anymore who would give her divided attention. And she definitely didn't want to invest emotionally in a committed guy. She wanted a person who would respect her presence in his life, who would be honest with her, who would not continue to waste her time even after being done with her. Too good to be real?

'What happened?' she asked.

'I had booked two tickets for a movie. But now she says she won't be able to come.'

If Rivanah's heart was a calm sea till then the word 'she' was thrown at her like a boulder. Was it over with Danny even before it had started?

'She as in? Your girlfriend?' Her heart was praying to hear a no.

'No. My bestie Nitya,' he said.

Rivanah heaved a sigh of relief. *A girl best friend,* Rivanah thought, *that's manageable.* She didn't want to tell him directly that she was free for the day and would love to watch the film with him.

'What are you doing after this?' he asked.

'Umm,' Rivanah feigned thinking about it and said, 'Actually...nothing much.'

'Do you mind joining me for the movie?'

Rivanah deliberately waited for a few seconds to show she was not so eager.

'Okay, yes...I think I can squeeze in time for a movie.'

Danny flashed her a warm smile. Rivanah had a good feeling about it all.

During interval, Danny went to fetch a bucket of popcorn while she went to the washroom. She came back to see Danny talking on the phone outside the theatre's entrance. He gave her the popcorn bucket and asked her to go inside, telling her he would join her soon. She complied. Rivanah went inside and made herself comfortable in her seat, dipping her hand into the bucket of popcorn. Along with a handful of popcorn came out a piece of white cloth, surprising her. She switched on her phone's flashlight and saw a message was stitched on it with black thread:

*Don't piss me off Mini.*

Rivanah immediately stood up, looking around for the stranger and then realized she didn't even know whom to look for. Danny joined her and found it weird that she was standing.

'Looking for someone?' he said taking his seat.

'Nay!' she said and immediately typed a message on her phone:

*Stop bugging me. I'm trying to enjoy myself.* Rivanah was burning with rage. As she sent the message to the last unknown number the stranger had messaged her from, she panned her sight hoping to see if anyone looked at his or her phone. The next second, she let out a sigh of despair. It was useless. She wouldn't spot the stranger like this.

'Something's wrong?' Danny asked.

'No, nothing.' She flashed him an unconvincing smile. The lights slowly went off and the movie started. Rivanah's phone vibrated with a message: *Okay, let's enjoy the movie as of now.*

*Damn! He is in this theatre,* she thought, and still she could not get to him. While moving out, Rivanah did try to register as many faces as she could but soon started forgetting the initial ones. In the end, she accepted the futility of it.

Days passed but there wasn't any more communication from the stranger. She knew what he asked of her was not a bad thing but who would take the pain of going to a slum every Saturday to teach some kids? It all sounded good on paper but the reality was that Rivanah wanted to enjoy her life too. Weekends were the only time she felt alive after the five brutal office days. And more so since the time Danny had stepped into her life.

The good thing about Danny's line of work was that he didn't have any formal office timings. Sometimes he dropped in during her lunch and many a times she waited for him in the office after work hours and left with him. On weekends they would go out for movies, clubbing, shopping etc. Since they were neighbours, there were times when she felt they were literally living-in together. Danny was a natural when it came to messing up his flat while Rivanah took it upon herself to arrange everything. They were getting emotionally close and it was happening fast. It scared her. Was it her own emotions that rebelled because she was trying to move on from Ekansh and create a space for someone else that had earlier been occupied by Ekansh? She had no answer. Worse was she couldn't ask Danny about it. When they had a discussion about the number of people they had in their respective lives, Danny was quick to respond: five, while she said it was only one, Ekansh. Rivanah couldn't understand how someone could move on so easily? Five relationships meant he must have had to move on five times and here she was finding it difficult to move on from the hangover of one single relationship. Was it that he never loved any of the five girls truly or was it that she loved Ekansh a little too much than necessary?

Soon Rivanah started getting insecure and more possessive about Danny than was necessary. She made sure whenever Danny didn't look, she checked his mobile phone for suspicious messages, checked his pockets, and even sniffed his clothes for any foreign fragrance. She had never done all these things with Ekansh. Probably that's why she never saw it coming when he cheated on her. Even when she saw Danny's pictures with his best friend Nitya, it made her uncomfortable, but she never took it up with Danny. Even if she had to draw a comparison, she knew well Danny was a better human being than Ekansh. Danny, for one, had no strict emotional uniform for her like they do in most relationships. I-want-you-to-be-like-this; that's the phantasmal emotional uniform people make their partner wear—directly or indirectly. Unlike Ekansh, Danny never asked her to show him her phone or pester her about her Facebook password or inquire about unnecessary details if she attended an event with her male colleagues. He never asked her to change her dressing style if she wore a dress that was revealing or asked a single question if she went to a nightclub with Ishita. In the end she concluded Danny wasn't insecure about her. It was enough for him that Rivanah was there for him, beside him. Nothing more worried him. He took her along to his shoots whenever she was free where she could sense he repelled temptation in the form of gorgeous girls he shot with. And yet, in a tiny corner of her heart she still fanned a possibility where Danny could cheat on her. And the culprit of such a compulsive nesting of this cheap possibility was not her but what she shared with Ekansh and how it was broken. The biggest damage that Ekansh did with that one choice of his was snatch away the innocence out of her system; once and for all. Though she did seek that innocence in whatever Danny and she shared, Rivanah knew she would never get it. Not even a hint of it. Some things are irreversible in life. It was sad but it was the truth.

One night Rivanah was all alone in her flat, experiencing a bout of depression, when she suddenly spoke up loudly, 'Are you there?'

A blank message popped up on her mobile screen from an unknown number. She understood it was an indication of the stranger's willingness to listen.

'Thanks,' she said and continued, 'You know how Ekansh and I ended. Do you think whatever we shared until then was not love at all?'

*Love doesn't always happen to strengthen our beliefs. Sometimes it happens to destroy all our previous beliefs and faith and gives us a chance to re-look at our own conclusions.*

'I can't tell you how much I burn every time I'm told by myself that Ekansh and I couldn't make it.'

*Some relationships don't have roots but you still expect them to blossom into fruits and flowers. Why?*

'I think you are right. But can you please tell me why I can't love Danny the way I loved Ekansh? I want to but there's this emotional vertigo that scares me all the time which wasn't there with Ekansh.' She kept staring at her phone. A reply came after a minute.

*Can apple and orange taste the same?*

'I know they can't but I'm still not able to come to terms with the fact that Ekansh still resides in my heart while I'm pursuing a relationship with Danny. We haven't proposed to each other but I have special feelings for him and I know he harbours the same feelings for me. But Ekansh is still alive within me.'

The reply from the stranger was an address. The message ended with: (*do visit alone if you want to find an answer*).

The address was very close to where she lived. Out of plain curiosity and in search for her answer, as the stranger had said, Rivanah strolled to the address during daytime the next day, a Sunday. It was a slightly dilapidated apartment. According to the address given to her, she was supposed to visit the third floor to flat numbered 302. Once there Rivanah pressed the doorbell. A middle-aged lady soon opened the door.

'You must be Rivanah Bannerjee?' she said with a strong Bengali accent. The fact that the lady was expecting her surprised Rivanah. Then a thought struck her: is this where the stranger lives?

'Yes,' Rivanah said to the lady.

'Please come in,' the lady said and opened the iron-gate ahead of the wooden door. Rivanah entered the flat. The sight of the lady had washed away all the apprehensions in her mind. It was a small flat and its contents told her it belonged to someone from a middle class background.

'Please sit,' the lady said. 'Oh, by the way I'm Malati Raha.'

'Nice to meet you ma'am,' Rivanah said and sat down on an old looking couch whose cover was torn at places.

'I was told that you would be coming.'

'Who told you?'

'It's weird but we don't know the person who changed our life by name or face. Ratna calls him captain miracle.'

'Captain Miracle?' Rivanah repeated.

'He connects with Ratna through emails.'

Rivanah was sure it had to be the stranger.

'Come let me take you to Ratna. I was asked to introduce you to her,' Malati said and went inside. Rivanah stood up with an air of uncertainty and followed her in. The bedroom was smaller than the drawing room and seemed stuffy. By the window sat a young girl who had a smile on her face that spoke of strength and honesty. Rivanah guessed she should be at most fifteen-sixteen.

'This is my daughter Ratna. My only child,' Malati said.

Rivanah smiled at her and forwarded her hand and said, 'Hi Ratna. I'm Rivanah.'

When her hand met hers, Rivanah understood it was an artificial hand. A quick glance and she noticed the other hand too was artificial. Rivanah felt a knot in her stomach. She had never seen an artificial hand so closely before. 'She and her father were coming to Mumbai from Kolkata on May 28, 2010 in Jnaneswari Express when the train derailed. Ratna's father died while her hands had to be amputated in order to pull her out of the debris.'

For a moment, Rivanah felt a lump in her throat. When she spoke she said, 'How...how old is she now?'

'I'm eighteen,' Ratna said. Her voice was sweet and without any sorrow.

'Thanks to her captain miracle we could afford these artificial limbs,' Malati said.

'Is the person a male?' Rivanah queried.

Ratna and Malati exchanged a blank look.

'Male. I have had a voice call with him over the internet once but we haven't seen him as yet,' Ratna said.

'But then, we don't see God as well,' Malati added caressing her daughter's forehead.

Rivanah managed a smile. Ratna told her about her dream to be an IAS officer. She showed her the sketches she had made before losing her arms. As she spoke, Rivanah could sense how faithful Ratna still was toward life. The accident had changed her life but couldn't touch her spirit. She wanted to hug her tight once but didn't. Sympathizing with such a strong soul would be insulting her.

Malati went into the kitchen to prepare some tea for her but Rivanah requested her not to, excused herself, and left. She could sense something was building up inside her. On her way back, she climbed the lonely skywalk, sat down on an empty seat, and started sobbing. She knew the reason but was too ashamed to admit it to herself. Meeting with Ratna had made her feel insignificant and her problems as unimportant. Her phone buzzed with a message from an unknown number. Wiping her tears away, Rivanah read the message:

*Do you think Ratna can ever forget what happened to her for no fault of hers? Understand this Mini: we all are designed to remember things. So, if you try to forget, you will suffer. Accept and you shall shine like never before. The greatest lesson love can give you is how to live a complete life by accepting its incomplete ways. If you can't hope in love, you can't live.*

*Thanks*, she replied back.

*Accidents happen Mini but that doesn't mean you stop travelling,* the stranger messaged again.

She stared at the message and sometime later left the spot with a new sense of determination.

The incident almost gave a new lease of life to her feelings for Danny. Those bestselling concepts that she had read in romance novels during her teens about love happening only once slowly faded away from prominence. There was more to life and real love than those bestselling gibberish. She understood as human beings we love to read about and accept those things as real which made us feel good about ourselves even if it is far from the truth. And when that far-from-truth meets the real truth in the real world we suffer realizing the huge gap between the two. Ekansh is Ekansh. Danny is Danny. Ekansh was past. Danny is present. And why would her love for them feel the same? Why would she seek night in day and day in night and not live the day and night as they individually are? Her feelings for Danny grew stronger once he proposed to her on phone. He was out for a photo shoot and she was at home that Friday night when he called her unexpectedly.

'Hey, what happened? No shoot?' she asked.

'The photographer has some work. And I'm starving,' Danny said.

'Then why don't you take a break and eat something?' Rivanah suggested.

'How do I? My food is not here?'

'What do you mean?'

'I mean I'm starving of you, Rivanah. I'm missing you like hell.' There was a genuine restlessness in his voice that hit her emotionally. It was for the first time that Danny was being so direct about his feelings with her and she didn't know how to exactly react.

'Say something!' he insisted.

'Like what?'

'Like...I love you?'

'I love you,' she blurted on an impulse and realized they were officially in a relationship.

'I love you too Rivanah. I was so waiting to tell you this since the time I first saw you!'

'With that towel around your waist? Liar!'

'I swear.'

'Then why did you choose to say this over phone?'

'We have been so close friends from some time now and I wasn't sure how you would react. So...'

'Really? Then come home tomorrow after your shoot and I'll show you my reaction.'

'I'm sorry if...' Danny turned serious but his words were cut short by her.

'We talk next when you come home tomorrow.' And the line was cut with a giggle that soon turned in to a blush as she looked at herself in the wardrobe mirror right ahead of her. She could sense rain-laden clouds hovering above the sky of her heart. Will it rain true love finally?

The next day was a Saturday and Rivanah promised herself that she would make it the best Saturday for the two of them. The first thing she did that morning was go to the parlour. Then she bought herself a new outfit from Zara after which she bought some vegetables, some chicken, and a few candles from Hyper City. Before she started cooking in the evening, she took out a condom from Ishita's wardrobe and put it in her bag. Though her roommates would be home at night, Danny and she would use his place. While taking out the condom she noticed a strip of I-pills as well. She cut out one tablet and kept it with herself just in case. Once the cooking was done, she dolled herself up for Danny. She kept messaging him every hour to know his location but didn't take his call to increase the sexual itch in him which was creating an ache in her privates as well. At around ten, the doorbell rang. Danny! Rivanah sprinted to the door with a naughty smile. When she opened the door, every ounce of naughtiness vanished from her face.

'Mumma?'

# 18

'What are you doing here?' Rivanah said rubbing her eyes hoping that she was dreaming. She was not.

'Are you going to let us get in or not?' Mrs Bannerjee said. A quick glance over her shoulder and Rivanah saw her father come out of the elevator with two heavy bags.

'Sorry mumma,' she said and gave her mother a hug. Then she moved aside to let her mother in the flat. As her father came to the door, she hugged him praying hard Danny didn't turn up now. She quickly closed the door once her father stepped inside.

'How is your health Mini?' Mrs Bannerjee asked.

'My health?' Rivanah was confused.

'Why else do you think we came here?' Mr Bannerjee said keeping the bags on the floor.

'One of your friends called us and said you were terribly sick and couldn't even take our calls. Your baba took an urgent leave to come here.'

'Why didn't you guys call me?'

'We were told you are too serious to take our calls. But you seem alright.' Mr Bannerjee touched her forehead with his palm to check for fever. Then he noticed her dress and make-up and added, 'In fact more than alright.'

'One second,' she said and rushed to grab her phone. She wanted to inform Danny not to come to her flat. But before she could call him, she noticed a message from an unknown number was waiting for her:

*Messing your life is easy.*

Rivanah immediately understood who this 'friend' of hers was and why exactly her parents had been summoned: to complicate the situation.

'Which friend of mine called up?' she asked.

'Your roommate Ishita,' Mr Bannerjee said.

Rivanah didn't dig further. She was sure it wasn't Ishita. Must be some random girl the stranger had employed to call her parents up, she thought.

'Anyway, what happened to you Mini? You know all along the flight I was praying to Baba Loknath. I was so tensed,' said Mrs Bannerjee coming to her.

'Food poisoning,' Rivanah lied and added, 'But now I'm perfectly fine.'

'Thanks to Baba Loknath,' her mother said and touched Rivanah's forehead with her palm. 'Joy Baba Loknath,' she mumbled to herself.

'When are you leaving?' Rivanah asked. The longer they would stay, the more uncomfortable things would get.

Both her parents gaped at her.

'We are seeing you after so many months, Mini. You should ask us how the journey was, if we want to drink water or not, and here you are asking our return date instead? I don't know what's up with your generation. No sense of attachment at all,' her mother complained and went to sit on the bed in the drawing room.

'No mumma, it's not that!' Rivanah went to her, kissed her on the cheeks, and hugged her tight saying, 'I was asking so that I could apply for leave. Actually an important project is going on in office so I need to inform them at the earliest to get a leave.'

'Don't tell your mother about office leaves. She won't get it,' her father added sitting down clumsily on one of the beanbags. 'By the way why are you so dressed up?'

'I was out with friends. Just came back.'

'You are looking pretty but I think you have lost weight,' said her mother kissing her on her cheeks.

'Oh mumma, I told you I have joined the gym.'

Her mother caressed her daughter's forehead lovingly.

'Don't you have proper chairs, Mini? This is so...' Mr Bannerjee was finding it difficult to sit on the beanbag.

'I'll get some water for you,' Rivanah said and went to the kitchen. The doorbell rang. And she face palmed. Informing Danny escaped her because of the stranger's message. Before she could move out, her father had opened the door. Rivanah stood frozen by the kitchen door hoping it wasn't Danny.

'Yes?' Mr Bannerjee said looking at Danny.

'Is Rivanah here?'

'Who are you?' Mr Bannerjee asked as if he was the investigative officer of an important case.

'I'm her boyfriend,' Danny said.

Rivanah could have collapsed in the kitchen itself. *It's a dream, it's a dream. Please someone wake me up,* she told herself. She heard her father call her name out. She went outside and smiled uncertainly at her father first and then at Danny.

'Hi Danny! Meet my parents,' she said.

'Danny?' Her father looked at his daughter once and then at the guy. He was still the investigative officer.

'Hello uncle. Hello aunty.'

Mr Bannerjee only nodded his head acknowledging the greeting while Mrs Bannerjee gave him a warm smile.

'One second,' Rivanah said and went to her wardrobe in the drawing room itself.

'What do you do Danny?' Mr Bannerjee asked.

'I'm a model and an actor, uncle.'

'Model and an actor?' Mr Bannerjee frowned as if Danny had said he was an alien.

Rivanah came back quickly with a key and gave it to Danny.

'Here, we'll talk later,' she said. Danny took the keys and left. Rivanah closed the door behind.

'He lives here?' her father asked.

'Let me bring your water baba,' she said.

'Answer me first Mini.'

'Yes.'

'What's his full name?'

'Danny Abraham.'

Her parents exchanged a worrisome look as if they had just discovered their daughter had been infected with a deadly virus.

'Where is Ekansh?' her mother asked. 'He was such a good guy. Though Danny looks better than him.'

'One minute,' her father cut short her mother. 'Is it true that he is your boyfriend?'

Rivanah was quiet.

'Answer me young lady—where is Ekansh?' Her father's voice was strict.

It took Rivanah a few minutes to tell them under what circumstances Ekansh and she had broken up. She went and embraced her mother who had tears in her eyes.

'I don't know why bad things happen to my daughter,' she said and kept crying.

'It's okay mumma. Things like these happen. They are beyond our control. Plus it's not like Ekansh and I were married,' she said. Her mother caressed her daughter's face.

'But why Danny?' her father interrupted.

'Why not baba?'

'Firstly he is not from our religion and secondly he is a model and an actor.'

'So? Like I'm a software engineer, he is an actor.'

'You can't trust actors Mini.' Mr Bannerjee took his seat on the beanbag again and said, 'Even his arms are waxed. It looks so strange. Also, I remember a guy like him had destroyed a girl's life once.'

'Which guy? Which girl?' Rivanah was confused.

'I saw it in *Crime Patrol*.'

'Baba, please! Danny is a good boy. We love each other.'

'Where's your room? I need to take rest,' her father said sulking further.

Rivanah looked at her mother who gave her an assuring look. Her parents stayed on for two more days. On one of the days, Rivanah managed to take them out for Mumbai darshan and on the second day the mother and daughter went out for shopping in Colaba causeway. Mr Bannerjee stayed back in her flat snooping around her daughter's wardrobe. The kind of dresses and accessories he saw told him that it was time to accept that times have changed, that a daughter no longer needed a different protocol to live her life than a son. He was surprised to see a bottle of Black Dog in her wardrobe. He took it up with her when she came back with her mother in the evening.

'Have you started drinking Mini?' he said displaying the bottle of Black Dog in his hand as if it was a prized discovery of his.

'This is Ishita's. The girl who called you up, remember?'

'Where is she?' he asked.

They did meet Asha a day before but Ishita had not turned up for three days straight. She had told her before that she was going to Goa with a couple of guys.

'She has gone home. Actually she had bought it for her father but forgot to take it with her,' Rivanah lied with an expertise that impressed her own self.

'But why your wardrobe?'

'There's no my or her wardrobe baba. We share things. She isn't just a roommate now but a friend too.'

'Hmm.' Mr Bannerjee wasn't convinced.

That night her mother insisted she invite Danny over for dinner.

'If they talk more, your baba will get to know him better and things will ease out. I like Danny. He looks so much like Uttam Kumar,' her mother said with a grin.

'Every good looking guy looks like Uttam Kumar to you. Uttam Kumar never had muscles mumma. Say Salman Khan,' Rivanah pointed out.

'*Oyi holo!*'

Rivanah kissed her mother hard on the cheeks and Whatsapped Danny to come over for dinner.

He pressed the doorbell right on time. The dinner lasted for a good twenty minutes and every minute of it was a disaster as far as bonding between Danny and Mr

173

Bannerjee went. For every question that Mr Bannerjee threw at Danny, he gave her an honest answer. That only made the matter worse.

'What do your parents do?' Mr Bannerjee asked.

'My father is a chef in Hong Kong. And my mother is an investment banker in New York.'

'That's nice. But how do they manage with such a long distance between them? It must be difficult.'

'Not really. They live with their respective partners,' Danny quipped. Mr Bannerjee choked on his food. Rivanah gave him a glass of water that he drank in one go.

'Are you the only child?'

'No. We are five brothers. The eldest one is absconding and I really don't know why. I haven't seen him since a decade now. The second one is at a rehab centre in the US for drug abuse. The third works in a hotel in Dubai while the fourth has become a lama and stays in Tibet. I'm the youngest,' he said.

That was the last time Mr Bannerjee spoke to Danny. Mrs Bannerjee on the other hand asked him about all her favourite film stars and whether he had been to Dilip Kumar's or Amitabh Bachchan's or her all time crush Dharmendra's bungalows.

'Mumma,' Rivanah said, 'Danny is still struggling to get a break. How can he go to the bungalows of these legends just like that?'

'But I have seen Emraan Hashmi up close, aunty,' Danny added with pride.

'Who?' Mrs Bannerjee looked for help at Rivanah.

'Serial kisser,' Mr Bannerjee replied and excused himself. He was done with the dinner. He didn't talk much with his daughter after Danny left.

The next day Rivanah dropped them off at the airport.

'Whatever you do, think about the repercussions. Marriage is a serious thing.' It was all her father told her. She gave him a warm hug and said, 'Don't worry baba. I won't do anything that will put you to shame. And Danny and I haven't discussed marriage yet.'

'Just like Ekansh and you had not discussed it either,' her father said. He glanced at her mother and added, 'That's why our generation was better. We married and discussed other possibilities. And today youngsters live all the other possibilities and break-up even before discussing marriage.'

Rivanah shot her mother a helpless look.

'If only Danny was Danny Ganguly or Danny Mukherjee or...' mother lamented. When her parents went inside the airport, Rivanah relaxed for the first time in three days. The first thing she did was text the stranger.

*What do you want from me?* She was pissed off at him for having called her parents to her place and putting her relationship with Danny under constraint.

*Be free next Saturday. The kids are waiting,* the stranger replied.

175

*For how long do I need to do that before you delete that clip of mine?* she asked.

*You will continue with it till the time it doesn't become your habit. And don't worry about the clip. If you lend me your ears, I shall lend you peace,* the stranger responded.

## 19

The following Saturday Rivanah went to the slum pocket in Dahisar east along with Danny. He didn't understand why exactly she was doing what she was doing.

'It is part of an office project of mine,' Rivanah said. She knew if she told Danny about the circumstances that pushed her to visit the place, she would have to tell him about the stranger. If she told him about the stranger, she would have to tell him about the clip. With the clip Prateek would come into the context. If Prateek came in, so would Ekansh because it was after the break-up that she started going out with Prateek. She would have to do a lot of explaining which she wasn't ready to do. After Ekansh she didn't feel it was right to be an open book in front of one's partner. A personal space was always necessary, it didn't matter how much you love someone. Moreover Rivanah and Danny were only in the February of their relationship.

'What is the project called?' Danny asked.

'It's called share-your-good-luck. Since I was born to well off parents who could sponsor my education, now I need to impart that good luck to ten kids and help them learn to write their names in English.'

Danny looked at her admiringly and said, 'Wow! You don't stop to impress me girl.'

Rivanah gave him a hug. They soon reached the place and the first thing they noticed was that it wasn't exactly a proper slum but a single line of twelve-thirteen shanties. As she stood clueless about her next action, a kid came running up to her and said in Hindi with a heavy Marathi accent, 'Are you Rivanah tai?' He was wearing a fresh white shirt and a pair of blue half-pants.

Rivanah exchanged a furtive glance with Danny and said, 'Yes.'

'Please come with me,' The kid said and turned to walk on.

'The kids know about you?' Danny said perplexed.

'So it seems,' Rivanah said and followed the kid to a nearby place—a square piece of sheltered space that looked like a godown. On one side a heap of watermelons were kept while on the other side, a few kids were sitting with folded legs; six girls and four boys wearing the same outfit as the kid who brought them there. A smile appeared on their faces seeing Rivanah. The boy who brought her went ahead and sat down beside the other kids. A moment later, Danny too went and sat behind the kids folding his legs just like them.

There was a hush-hush laughter. For Rivanah, it was the first time that she was going to teach. All her life she had been taught things. Being on the other side of the line, she felt different in an intriguing and powerful way. As she went and stood in front of the students, she noticed there was a blackboard beside her. All eyes were on her. All the kids seemed to come from below poverty line. The only thing that stood out in their appearance was their brand new uniform. It was while looking at the dress of one of the students that she noticed the emblem for the first time. She gestured that particular kid to come up to her. The girl stood up and went to Rivanah. On her shirt's pocket, she could see a smiley was stitched in a way as if it was an emblem. At the centre of it was stitched: *Mini's Magic 10*. A faint smile touched her face reading it.

'What's your name?' She asked the kid.

'Divya,' The girl said.

'How old are you?'

Divya started counting on her fingers and then said 'Nine' in Hindi. Rivanah tapped her cheek lovingly and asked her to go and sit.

It was the first day so Rivanah hadn't come prepared with anything. She asked the kids their names and asked them a few general questions to test their IQ. They were sharp kids; she concluded. That's when she felt nice to be a part of the stranger's 'share your good luck' endeavour. A little time on her part wouldn't really take much from her life but it would, she now knew, give a lot to the kids in the long run. It was one of those rare moments where she felt she was doing something worthwhile. She arranged for the kids to have chocolates from a nearby shop and told them that from next Saturday she would start teaching them properly. Their smile told her that they liked her.

'I didn't know you were so good with kids,' Danny said while returning to their place.

'Even I didn't know myself,' she said.

'Sitting in the class,' Danny said, 'I had a feeling that if we all are committed to small things like this, only then can a big and positive change happen.'

Rivanah couldn't agree more.

'What after these kids learn to write their names?' Danny asked.

Rivanah looked at him but realized she had no answer. *The stranger must have a plan after that,* she thought, and sent him a message right then.

*What after the kids learn to write their names?*

It was when Danny was paying the autorickshaw fare that the reply came:

*They will start going to a government school. That's my way of sharing the good luck I was born with.*

'What are you smiling at?' Danny asked as the auto left.

'Nothing,' she said reading the message aloud and went inside the building with him.

'Danny, do you think we all are striving in lives in our own little ways to derive more than what we need to live a decent life? Maybe 99 percent of the time, we don't need something and are still ready to die to procure it in order to either stand out from the others or stand in with them?' she said when they were in the elevator.

'Why do you ask??' he said.

She immediately knew she shouldn't have asked him this.

'Nothing. Just leave it?'

'I think,' he said, 'It's an individual who decides how much he needs. This thing called need is subjective, right? Sometimes we confuse need and necessity, I guess.'

'Necessity is common to all but need is person-specific. Like a simple kurti would pacify my necessity of covering up but a kurti from BIBA would satisfy my need for affluent brands, of looking high-maintenance. The latter is an innate need for city-bred girls like me who grow amid a bombardment of advertisements, fashion, and materialism.' A pause later she added, 'Though for some, necessity and need is one and the same thing and that's when we lose our depth I guess.'

'We lose our worth,' Danny corrected her. The word 'worth' reminded her of one of stranger's early messages: *Know your worth Mini.*

If Rivanah was honest with herself, then the untouched and pure faces of the kids that day actually

181

made her realize maybe she did take a little more than what she needed to live in peace. And to top it, she also took her need to be a necessity.

'It's the same in show-business,' Danny said.

'I think every business is show-business today, if you know what I mean. We are taught Moral Science lessons in junior school but it is Market Science that we need to handle all our life as a grown up.'

'Actually!' Danny agreed.

The next Saturday Danny had a shoot for a print advertisement and so he couldn't accompany her. This time Rivanah went with ten fresh alphabet books and distributed them among the kids along with basic stationery like pencils, erasers, and pencil-cutters. Teaching those kids connected her to an unprecedented freedom in her which allowed her to forget herself, her irks, and her own complaints from life. She felt like floating when she was with *Mini's Magic 10* whereas otherwise she fought hard to swim in the sea of life.

Rivanah also made sure she interacted with the kids beyond her academic involvement. She asked those kids about their background, where they came from and also listened to their innocent dreams. One kid had an alcoholic good-for-nothing father and a mother who worked hard cleaning people's houses and all he dreamt of was to see his mother spend twenty-four hours with him. A girl had both her parents working hard as daytime labourers at a construction site and she believed they were actually building a palace for her because she was their princess. Their aspirations, their zeal, and their will to smile amidst their grave reality taught Rivanah more than she taught them. She could forget neither the kids nor their stories. Over weeks, they became a part of her.

'I wish I could make you meet my kids?' she told her mother one night over phone.

'Your kids?' Her mother sounded scandalized.

'The ones I teach mumma.'

'You gave me a heart attack. First you changed from Ekansh to Danny and now suddenly these kids.' Her mother tried to calm herself down.

'I didn't change Ekansh. It didn't work out. Anyway.'

'I'm happy you are teaching poor kids. Last week your pishi and pisha had come with Mou and Bunty. I told them that you do a lot of things in Mumbai like working in an American-based company and teach poor kids as well.'

'Why do you have to advertise what I do to everyone?' Rivanah sounded crossed.

'What's the harm? People should know about it.'

Rivanah knew that the real reason behind such advertisement was to project her as someone better than her cousins.

'Do you know why they were here?' Mrs Bannerjee asked sounding mischievous.

'Who? Pishi and Pisha? Why?'

'Yes, yes. They were here to invite us for Mou's wedding.'

'Mou's wedding? What are you saying? She is only...'

'Twenty!' her mother said completing her sentence. 'But they said they got a bright boy who is working in Singapore and is from a good family so they couldn't say no. In fact your pishi was taunting that Mou is getting married before you.'

'I don't care how much she taunts me but I'm not getting married so don't ask me about it either.'

'Alright I won't. Do what you feel like but come down for Mou's marriage in February, okay?'

'Yeah, okay.'

'By the way who gave you the idea of teaching the kids Mini?' her mother asked. It was then she realized she hadn't talked to the stranger for some weeks now.

'A friend,' she said and quickly added, 'I'll call you later mumma.' She cut the line and typed on her phone: *Thanks.* She sent it to the stranger's last unknown number.

*What for?* prompt came the reply.

By now Rivanah had stopped being baffled at the prompt responses.

*For letting me teach the kids. It's one of the best things that has happened to me,* she messaged back.

*I told you before. I'm not important, you are.*

*Why do you say that? Why am I so important to you?*

*Not to me. You are important to yourself.*

*Everyone is important to his or her own self.*

*But not everyone knows it. All our life we destroy and waste ourselves the most.*

*Why don't you show yourself? I would really appreciate it if you meet me once. Like seriously.*

No reply came for two hours. Then five minutes before midnight, her phone beeped with a message from an unknown number:

*Meet me tomorrow at Tiger Point in Lonavla. 8 pm sharp.*

*Tomorrow is my birthday!* she messaged back immediately.

No more reply came.

*Answer me.*

Still no reply. Rivanah wondered if the stranger really meant what he said. Was he actually going to meet her?

At 12 am sharp, Danny called her.

'Happy birthday babe.'

'Thanks baby.'

'Sorry, I couldn't be with you right now but let's plan something for tomorrow.'

If the stranger really was going to meet her this time, she wouldn't let the opportunity go for anybody.

'Umm, baby actually I need to go for an office meet to Pune tomorrow. Can we please meet the day after? I know it's my birthday but this office thing...' Rivanah was upset about lying to Danny but she thought she would tell him everything once she met the stranger. An instinct told her if she took Danny with her, the stranger may not reveal himself.

'Oh! But I thought we would have fun and...'

'We definitely would baby. Don't be sad. It's just a matter of one day. Even I'll miss you.' Rivanah consoled Danny and convinced him they would party whole night once she was back. He agreed. She had to end the call sooner than she would have liked because her parents' call was on waiting. She took their call and birthday wishes. On a whim she checked her message, whatsapp, Facebook, and email. Last year Ekansh had flooded her Facebook inbox, Whatsapp, and email with all sorts of birthday messages, e-cards but this year there was nothing. Suddenly she realized Ekansh wasn't there in her life anymore. She was finding it difficult to accept the fact that from now onward he won't ever wish her on her birthday. For reasons unknown to her, she logged on to her Facebook account from her laptop and unblocked Ekansh after a long time. She wanted to give him a chance to get to her if he wished to on this day. Rivanah checked his profile picture on Facebook once and immediately logged out.

Rivanah was thankful that her roommates where not there to wish her. It was her first birthday where she just wanted to be by herself. Since the break-up Ekansh, more than just being a past, had become an experience for her. And when someone becomes an experience, it becomes difficult to severe oneself from it.

The next day, after Rivanah learnt that Danny would be at his flat in the afternoon, she moved out early lest he saw her at her flat instead of the false office meeting she told him about. She hired a cab early in the evening which drove her to Tiger Point. Just to be safe, she had messaged Ishita before leaving.

*I'm going to Tiger Point in Lonavla to meet the stranger. Don't tell anybody.*

*OMG! Best of luck girl. Be safe,* Ishita replied.

When Rivanah stepped out of the cab, she could still see tourists loitering around the point clicking pictures and having fun among themselves. As per the deal, the cab was supposed to wait till ten after which it would take her back to Mumbai. The driver moved out while she went to sit on a plastic stool by a small shop selling corn. She passed her time by receiving calls wishing her birthday from distant friends and relatives and then answering messages on Facebook. She kept refreshing her Facebook inbox, but no message came from Ekansh. Feeling stupid to have unblocked him, she blocked him again. With time, the other tourists went away and the corn stall too shut down. By seven in the evening, there were only the cab driver and Rivanah in sight around Tiger Point.

It was around 8:30 pm but there was still no sign of the stranger. The silence and emptiness of the place made her heart race. Though Rivanah had dared to come far from the city, standing alone at a distance from Tiger Point she realized perhaps she shouldn't have.

She wanted to call Danny but messaged the stranger instead.

*Are you coming? I'm already here.*

There was no reply. Fifteen minutes later, she noticed a Xylo take a turn and approach her. Rivanah swallowed a lump as the headlights fell on her eyes, blinding her. She blocked her eyes with her hands. The next instant, the lights went off. She strained her eyes to see who it was but it was pitch black. Slowly, she saw a man walking towards her with a bouquet in his hands and a smile on his face. As he reached closer, she could tell it was a smell she had inhaled before.

'Happy birthday baby,' the man wished.

As his face became clear, an astonished Rivanah blurted 'Danny?'

# 20

'What?' Danny said. 'Don't tell me you came here without knowing it was me. I wanted to surprise you, but I knew you had understood my prank.'

No, she didn't know it was him. The message had come from an unknown number like always and there was no way she could guess it was a prank.

'Now will you take these?' Danny urged forwarding the bouquet to her. She took it with an expression unlike the one Danny was expecting.

'What's wrong?' he asked. Rivanah realized she would have to think of an excuse fast. She immediately hugged him tightly and whispered in his ear, 'I was feeling scared.'

Danny hugged her back and said, 'I was watching you all along, so there was nothing to worry about.'

'Did you follow me here?'

Danny broke the embrace and gave her a you-caught-me smile. 'How did you guess it was me who messaged you from an unknown number?' he asked.

'Who else could it be?' she quipped and gave him a forced smile.

'Yeah! It was actually Nitya's number. When you lied to me on the phone that you were going to Pune, I knew you were playing smart.' She smelled his deodorant again.

'New deodorant?'

'Yes. "Just Different," by Hugo Boss,' he said. 'How is it?'

'I like it.' The same deodorant was of course a coincidence, she told herself and said aloud, 'By the way whose car is that?' she said eyeing the Xylo.

'A friend's.'

'One second,' Rivanah went to the cab driver and asked him to leave after paying his dues. She came back to Danny and said, 'Why Tiger Point?' Switching on the car's headlights they leaned on the front of the car, looking at each other.

'I wanted to be away from everything today except you. I was here a month back for a short film and that's when I had decided we would celebrate your birthday here in the serenity and silence of the night.'

'Celebrate?'

Danny gave her an amused smile, went back to open the car's door, and brought out a cake, two glasses and a bottle of champagne. He placed them on the car's bonnet. She glanced at the cake, the champagne, and then at Danny. Why did she subject herself to momentary depression when she had such a caring boyfriend? She could have cried seeing Danny fixing two small candles making up the number 16 on the cake and then light them with a lighter.

'Blow them,' he said.

'Why sixteen?'

'My love for you shall be forever young, that's why.'

Wearing a white round-neck tee and jeans Danny looked his most handsome self in the aura of the candle light. Rivanah came forward, blew the candle, and cut a piece with the plastic knife. She picked up the piece and brought it close to Danny's mouth. He took the piece from her hand and pushed it back in her mouth instead, taking a bite from the other end and licking every bit of it from around her mouth just like she did from around his.

Then they poured some champagne in the glasses and sipped on it sitting in front of the car by the edge of Tiger Point as Danny briefed her about his meeting with a film producer who was willing to give him a chance in a regional film. Rivanah was more relieved than happy to hear it. She had decided that once Danny had signed a film, she would discuss marriage plans with him before telling her parents about it. Her mother did have a point when she said that sometimes one should know the current status of a relationship and the direction towards which it is headed.

'I have had many girlfriends in the past, but they meant nothing to me. You are slowly becoming my everything, Rivanah,' he said after a prolonged silence. They had switched off the car's headlights. Under the soft romantic moonlight, he resembled the Prince she had dreamt about as a kid and believed some day would come and sweep her off her feet. Did she deserve such goodness? The break up with Ekansh had somehow convinced her nothing good would ever happen to her. Though Danny's presence proved otherwise, she wasn't sure. When you have seen dry days for too long it becomes difficult to believe that rain is awaiting you. And even if you see a rain-laden cloud all you tell yourself is perhaps it is an illusion.

To blur the line between illusion and reality, Rivanah leaned towards him and locked her lips with his. Danny responded by sucking her lips hard. She soon felt his big hands on her breasts over her white shirt. His demeanour told her he wanted control and she willingly gave him that. With his tongue licking the cavity of her mouth and her hands around his neck, Danny picked her up in a flash. The power with which he did so acted as an aphrodisiac for Rivanah.

Once the smooch broke, Danny placed her on the roof of the Xylo and looked arrow straight at her as he doffed his tee, shoes, jeans, and socks. This was the first time she was seeing him in his briefs. She missed a heartbeat as he climbed up to the car's roof to join her.

The trees and the other surrounding flora started to dance to a mild breeze. Rivanah's mind went numb as he stripped her off her shirt, trousers, undergarments; one at a time. Every touch of his was also stripping the clothes of hurt from her soul. Soon she felt his bare skin rubbing her bare body. As they smooched again her heart gave her a hint in the form of two tear drops that she was finally happy after a long time.

For a moment Danny stopped and glanced at her inquiringly. She nodded bringing herself even closer to him and continuing to kiss him all over his face. In no time, her hand went down and grabbed his hard penis along with his taut balls while he cupped her breasts and caressed her erect nipples with his thumb. The cold car's roof and the warm grab of his hands took her sexual itch to a certain level which turned her into an immoral beast. Rivanah pushed Danny and made him lie down flat on the car's roof. She carefully put his hands above his head.

'Don't move,' she said and started kissing her way down. Her hair glided over his skin as she moved down, pushing his erection to the maximum. She tugged down his underwear and sucked him for long after which she rode him with her legs on either side of his waist, guiding his hard penis inside her puffy and wet vagina with ease.

Rivanah moaned out as the thick penis entered her tight vaginal walls. As she started subtly bouncing on it, the car made a funny creaking noise feeling their movement. They exchanged a smile as Danny, still inside her, flipped Rivanah to come on top of her.

She felt like she was flying as he looked straight into her eyes while she held on to him tight. Though she was enjoying herself, soon the car's surface started to hurt her back. Danny understood her dilemma and, once again, changed position. Placing his hand on her butt, he sat up stretching his legs. They both were now sitting up with Rivanah on his lap with her inner thighs wrapping his waist. As she started to ride him, she put her hands around his neck. The position made him hit spots inside her which had never been probed before. And it released unprecedented pleasure. Her breasts rubbed his face every time she went up and down. Danny's above average strength that lasted for more than an hour gave her the first real orgasm of her life. Rivanah moaned out loud in ecstasy, feeling all her muscles curl-in together. During the orgasm, she felt her soul leaving her, traversing the entire cosmos, and then return to her, gravid with everything she ever desired. Danny held her butt and stood up on the car's roof along with her. He then allowed her to keep her feet down and then flipped her without warning. He placed his hands on her breasts and took her from behind. She actually felt she would die of pleasure and knew well that this pleasure death would be her real birth.

Danny came thrice that night, while Rivanah

orgasmed twice. She couldn't believe how exhausted she was once they were eventually done. Lying naked on the car's roof in Danny's strong arms and staring at the star studded night sky, she couldn't believe what had just happened.

'I didn't tell you this but I dreamt of making love to you like this.'

'When did that happen?' Rivanah sounded surprised.

'Obviously I don't remember the exact date, but I guess it was a couple of weeks back. And I thought whenever we'll do it for the first time, we would do it on top of a car,' Danny said.

'On top of a car?' Rivanah giggled.

'It was a fantasy of mine. Why, don't you have one?'

'Umm,' Rivanah thought and said, 'Maybe making love blindfolded.'

'Ahan, we shall do that soon.' Danny stole a kiss from her forehead.

There was silence. And in that silence their own selves told them a lot about the other.

'I love you Danny,' she whispered.

'I love you too,' he gasped kissing her cheeks.

'I never knew I would say these words to someone else as well.'

Danny gave her an inquiring look.

'I told you about Ekansh. ButI never told you I loved him with all my heart. I never thought I would be in love again.'

There was silence.

'Do you want to ask me anything?' she asked.

'Do you love me Rivanah?' Danny said turning and taking her face in his hand as if she was an infant.

'A lot and that's why I'm scared of things going wrong.'

'God forbid if something does go wrong, will you regret this night we had?'

'Never.'

'Nor will I and so we have nothing to be scared of. I know it's difficult to predict the future but what I can promise is I will leave no stone unturned to be by your side.'

'I want to believe you Danny. I really do, but when you lose a person whom you once loved with all your heart and soul to something as cheap as adultery, then an important part of you simply stops believing in love. Everything that comes after heartbreak doesn't seem worth it anymore.' A pause later, she asked looking into his eyes, 'Do you think I'm the most beautiful person you have ever met?'

'I think you are the only one who makes me believe that everything is beautiful.'

She smiled, proud of her choice this time.

'What will you say,' Danny brought his face so close to hers that his lips brushed hers as he talked, 'If I tell you that no temptation can ever snatch you from me?'

Rivanah touched his face with her fingers and said softly, 'I'll believe you but there are so many things we have to fight.'

'Life itself is a fight. But the point is: are you willing to take it on for us?'

Rivanah nodded and said, 'I'm willing to otherwise I wouldn't have been lying here naked in your arms.'

Sleeping in his fragrance she discovered a new hope.

Late into the night, they woke up with a start as they heard their car honking loudly. Danny jumped down naked and found a chewing gum pasted on the horn. As Rivanah joined him covering her privates with her hands, they took a round of the car to see if everything was okay. She noticed all their clothes had been arranged neatly on the bonnet of the car to form a smiley.

'Must be some jerk,' Danny said.

'Must be.' Rivanah looked around trying to spot the obvious someone who could have followed her to Tiger Point. Danny quickly wore his jeans and was about to go ahead to look when Rivanah stopped him saying, 'Forget it.'

## 21

'I won't be able to come next Saturday so it'll be a holiday for you all,' Rivanah told the kids in Hindi. 'But when I'm back, I'll take a test. I want you all to write A to Z without looking at the books so prepare well. There will be a special treat in store for those who complete the test successfully. Understood?' There was collective yes from the ten beaming kids.

Rivanah was scheduled to fly to Kolkata the following Friday. On Wednesday morning, she received a phone call from inspector Kamble who told her that she would have to appear in court to identify the two rapists in front of the judge. She felt relieved to know that her face would be hidden from the rapists and the media as per her request. The next day she did what was asked of her. Since it wasn't a high profile case, there was not much media present anyway. The court was nothing like what she saw in films. Things went smoother and quicker than her expectation. The judge announced the date on which it would relay the final verdict. The date was a month and half away. While returning back to her office in an autorickshaw she realized that the meter in the autorickshaw seemed tampered with. According to the new meter rates of autorickshaws in Mumbai, for every one kilometre 11.33 rupees would be charged after the initial one and a half kilometres for 17 rupees. This had happened many a times before but she had given the extra fare without any qualm. But that day when she was about to get down from the autorickshaw, she noticed the meter showed three rupees extra. Rivanah immediately barked out at the auto driver. More than the driver, she surprised herself. As her voice ascended, a traffic policeman joined them and asked her to pay three rupees less. Walking into her office, she understood it wasn't about those three rupees but about taking a stand on a matter. Sitting in her cubicle, she drank some water wondering if it was only because of the stranger that she got to know a side of her which was alien to her before. For someone who would pay extra money to avoid any kind of a tussle, she fought for a mere three rupees? For someone whose social conscience was restricted to a Facebook post, she actually stood up so that a girl could get justice? Rivanah was sure even her parents who knew her so well would not believe it. Just like teaching the poor kids made her more compassionate, this minor incident with the auto driver made her realize there's more substance in her than she initially thought.

She typed a message for the stranger:

*It's been long. I think we should meet now.*

*Come back from Kolkata and we'll meet,* the stranger replied.

Was there anything in her life the stranger wasn't aware of? The stranger did seem a little scary at times but till now he had been harmless. Maybe because till now she had listened to whatever she was asked to do. This relationship—or whatever it was that she shared with this unknown person—had its own troughs and crests but if someone asked her now, Rivanah would say she was happy the person was there for her. He knew all her weaknesses but like a true friend kept it a secret. At least till now.

The next morning Danny dropped her off at the airport. They hugged for a good two minutes before they waved each other goodbye. It was a matter of one week. She would have cried if it was her first relationship but by now she had prepared herself for separation. It was important because that was the only immunity she could have for herself against any possible heartache. Attraction depletes itself with indulgence contrary to attachment. What started as an intense physical attraction in the case of Danny had, over time, transformed into an attachment. Danny Abraham was not only her love interest anymore but an emotional cover against the disaster named Ekansh Tripathi that happened to her once upon a time. For the world she had forgotten Ekansh long back, but for her she would always remember him. The good thing was that she was at least out of the denial phase or she thought.

Once in Kolkata, she saw that the arrangement for Mou's marriage, Rivanah's cousin, was going on with aplomb. All the relatives were stationed at her Pishi's place in Behala. There was a tent that had been put up at the terrace where the entire family's breakfast, lunch, and dinner was being prepared for the past two days before the marriage. Rivanah was happy to meet most of her cousins but talking to them, she realized she couldn't connect to them anymore. They were what she was before she went to Mumbai to work. They had only seen the world that was provided to them by their affluent parents and not the world that was for real. Hence their biased and myopic conclusions about everything under the sun which they were always ready to throw at everyone as the truth irked Rivanah all the more. She somehow tried to mix in and wished time passed soon so that she could go back to Mumbai to work, to teach the kids, to be with Danny, and most importantly to be herself.

One by one, the rituals were conducted—from 'ayiburow bhaat' to 'gaye holud' till the evening arrived when the marriage was supposed to take place. Rivanah had a spat with her mother who wanted her to wear a heavy Banarasi saree and put on proper make-up.

'I'm not the bride mumma. I don't need to look good,' she said.

'I don't know what has gone into you ever since you started working. Earlier you used to pester me for all this.'

'People grow up mumma. We think these superficial things make us happy when in fact they don't.'

The duel went on for half an hour after which Rivanah was emotionally blackmailed to wear not only the Banarasi saree but also heavy jewellery and make-up. Her mother seemed overjoyed when her father said she was looking even better than her mother in her hay days.

The borjatri came with the groom and were welcomed wholeheartedly by the girl's side. Rivanah kept her distance from her cousins who were making up silly plans of embarrassing the young men accompanying the groom simply because she found the whole exercise disgustingly silly. In no time she was feeling completely out of place. It was while sipping Pepsi standing alone by a pillar in the corner that she noticed a particular guy aiming his mobile phone at her. The moment their eyes met, he moved the phone away. She understood he was clicking her or maybe videotaping her without her permission. She didn't know the guy which only meant he had to be from the groom's side. She avoided him and went to be by Mou's side. The same guy was there too aiming his phone at her. She excused herself from Mou and went straight towards the guy.

'Any problem?' she asked.

'That doesn't sound like a Bengali name to me,' the guy said. Rivanah honestly didn't anticipate such a smooth response from a guy who looked studious in a boring way from a distance. Standing a couple of inches taller than her, Rivanah observed, the guy was clean shaved except for a tiny dot of hair under his lower lip. He was wearing a suit and had very short but spiked hair. He adjusted his rimless specs as he talked and spoke with a slight American accent too. Overall, he looked suave and very corporate.

'Is that how you show your admiration for a girl? Using your phone's camera?' There was a hint of flirtatiousness in her voice that could have aroused any guy instantly.

'The phone is going to be with me all night, not you. So I thought...'

Rivanah blushed slightly at the comment and said, 'But it is indecent to click a girl without her permission.'

The guy took a few seconds, came closer and showing her his phone, deleted the five pictures he had clicked of hers. Rivanah was impressed.

'I'm sorry,' he said with a smile.

'It's okay,' Rivanah said without making anything obvious.

'Thank you. This guilty guy would appreciate it if the gorgeous girl let's him know of a proper way of admiring her?'

'Why is it so necessary to do that?' she teased maintaining a straight face.

'The necessity is a guy thing,' he said maintaining the naughtiness.

'Does the admirer have a name?' she asked.

'Abhiraj Mukherjee,' he said bringing forward his hand.

'Rivanah Bannerjee,' she said shaking his hand.

'Oh no!' he quipped looking at his hand; astonished. Rivanah shrugged at him inquiringly.

'I may melt anytime now,' he clarified.

'What?'

'You are so hot!'

'Shut up!'

She blushed, he giggled. They walked up to the dining place where a large buffet had been arranged. She took a plate and a spoon for herself. He was close behind as he noticed her put some salad on her plate.

'Are you single?' he said picking the same salad as her.

'How does it matter?' She turned back for a trice and proceeded to take a scoop of mixed vegetables on her plate.

'It's not that I'm afraid of competition but it will help me to know if I need to prepare for one or not.' He put a little amount of the mixed vegetables on his plate too.

'Your questions are always direct but your answers are always twisted,' she said and skipped the Shahi Paneer, taking the Malai Kofta instead.

'Glad to know you've been noticing me as well,' he said skipping the paneer and choosing the Kofta as well.

Once they were done filling their plates, he repeated himself, 'Are you single?'

'Maybe,' she said with such a teasing smile that Abhiraj could feel a tickle in his loins.

Rivanah enjoyed the rest of the marriage ceremony with Abhiraj by her side. He didn't waste a single moment to blatantly put forward a cheesy line appreciating her beauty. She asked him to stop every time he did so but somewhere inside she was enjoying the appreciation too. Ekansh used to do that in the beginning but with Danny she missed it. The latter was the quiet, caring lover to whom flattery didn't come naturally. By the end of the night, Abhiraj asked her for her phone number but Rivanah didn't show any interest in sharing it.

The reception was scheduled two days later in north Kolkata where the groom's family was based. Right after the 'phera jatra' where the bride was officially taken away by the groom to his place, everyone started dispersing from Mou's place. Once home, Rivanah finally felt relieved. But it didn't last long since in the evening her mother asked her to dress up once again.

'What for mumma?' She sounded irked.

'Some guests are coming for dinner. I don't want you to look like a depression patient.'

She had to doll up once again against her wishes. Her parents were happy when they noticed her helping her mother prepare dinner. It was her father who opened the door when the guests arrived. They were made comfortable on the couch while Mr Bannerjee called out to his wife and daughter.

'They have come,' he said.

Mrs Bannerjee welcomed them with folded hands and a warm smile.

She was followed by Rivanah who put up a pretence. Her fake smile suddenly vanished when she saw Abhiraj sitting on the couch with a sly smile.

'This is Mr and Mrs Mukherjee,' she heard her father say. 'And this is Abhiraj; their only child. He worked with Microsoft for three years in the US and has now come back to India. He is a topper from NIT, Ranchi.'

She already knew all this about him since their banter at the marriage hall a night before. But the way her father took pride in relaying someone else's son's resume told Rivanah the obvious—Abhiraj was his probable son-in-law.

'Remember I told you about Shantu uncle?' Mr Bannerjee asked Rivanah. 'This is him. It was such a pleasant coincidence to meet his family at Mou's marriage.'

Now it was all clear: Shantu Mukherjee and her father had studied together in college. A month after her graduation, he had asked for Rivanah's hand for his son. She had not met them then. And now meeting them at Mou's marriage, Shantu uncle must have pushed the marriage proposal again. Or was it her father this time? Rivanah greeted Mr and Mrs Mukherjee and said a soft 'Hi' to Abhiraj. Within minutes her mother started telling everyone how her daughter was doing a great social service back in Mumbai by teaching poor kids along with her job at an MNC.

'Our daughter believes that working in an MNC is not everything. Sometimes one needs to live for others too. She has been a compassionate soul right from the time she was a kid,' her mother said smiling at everyone present there one by one.

'Commendable!' Abhiraj's father said.

'Do you want to study further or...' Abhiraj's mother asked.

'She'll do a BMA,' her mother shot back.

'BMA?' Abhiraj's father frowned.

'She means MBA,' Rivanah said. 'I may pursue an MBA but haven't decided yet.'

To mitigate the awkwardness Rivanah excused herself to the kitchen and brought water for the guests.

'Come let me show you around our house,' her father said to the guests. The elders stood up and followed him. *It was the grand old Indian plan of leaving the boy and the girl alone to talk,* Rivanah thought with locked jaws. The more she said she wouldn't marry, the more they didn't let go of any opportunity to get her married. She saw

Abhiraj beaming from ear to ear as if he had just been declared the winner of *Kaun Banega Crorepati* without going through any questions.

'I can't get married to you,' she said.

'Ouch! Why?'

'I love someone else.'

'But you were single till last night.'

'I said maybe.'

'Maybe means you are single.'

'Maybe means I could be single or committed as well.'

Abhiraj was silent for some time. He looked genuinely hurt. Then suddenly he turned cheerful.

'It doesn't matter really. Even I have a girlfriend.'

'You do?' Rivanah hoped she didn't sound too surprised.

'Yeah, back in the US. We are only sexually compatible but not emotionally.'

'What does that mean?'

'It means she likes me in bed but otherwise she thinks I'm a loser and I think she is a bitch.'

Rivanah made an offensive face and said, 'Anyway, the point is we can't get married. So please tell your parents that. I'll tell mine.'

'Hmm. By the way what's his name?' he said.

'Did I ask your girlfriend's name?'

'Sulagna Mitra.'

Rivanah looked at him intently for a moment and said, 'Danny Abraham.'

Abhiraj broke into a smile.

'What?' she said.

'I'm sure your parents won't allow it.'

'Allow what?'

'For you to become Mrs Abraham. Come on, I know Bong parents. When it comes to emotional blackmail, nobody can beat them. So this Danny Abraham won't be yours.'

'You have some audacity.' Rivanah sounded stern.

'To state a fact I only need a mouth and not any audacity. That's the truth and I'm sure you know it.'

Rivanah knew her parents would never allow her to marry Danny. The fact that they had arranged the Mukherjee's visit was a signal enough what they thought of Danny and her after their Mumbai visit.

'I'll make it work,' she said in an unconvincing manner. Before Abhiraj could respond, their parents joined them laughing aloud on some archaic joke.

The dinner went well with the parents discussing IPL, politics, and the new Rajarhat housing projects. While walking them up to the gate after dinner, Abhiraj asked, 'May I now have your phone number please?'

Rivanah had already denied him that luxury.

'I think I...'

'Don't worry. I'll tell my parents to look for someone else but can we be friends at least?'

Abhiraj seemed to mean what he said. She exchanged phone numbers with him before the Mukherjee family left.

At night, she talked with Danny for a long time since her arrival in Kolkata. She wanted to distract herself from Abhiraj's words: *Danny won't be yours.* It injured her. She sounded happy to Danny on the phone but inside her there was a storm raging. It didn't stop even after talking to Danny. Soon she found herself typing a message to the stranger:

*What to do when you are in love with the journey but at the same time scared of the undesirable destination which you know is going to arrive sooner or later?*

A response came after half an hour:

*If you are really in love, then no destination should scare you.*

Rivanah read the line over and over again. Each time, it renewed her confidence in her relationship with Danny. She was happy to have asked for the stranger's advice.

*Have you ever been in love?* she messaged.

*It's impossible to go through life without being in love,* the stranger messaged back.

*What is love for you?* she asked.

*Love is when someone else protects you from your own self.*

Rivanah couldn't understand what the message exactly meant.

*What do you mean?*

*Each one of us is our own worst enemy. Every moment we harm ourselves; sometimes through the choices we make and at times with the ones we don't. It's a continuous process of emotional and spiritual corruption. And love is when the God in someone heals us from the hurt that the devil in us caused.*

The profundity of the statement was now clear to Rivanah. She was lost in thoughts when her phone beeped again.

*I too have a question for you: when was the last time you made a mistake, Mini? A terrible, terrible mistake.*

Rivanah thought hard for some time and typed:

*Trusting Ekansh was a mistake.*

A minute later, the reply came:

*LOL.*

# 22

The next day Rivanah went to City Centre Mall with her mother who made her buy an expensive lehenga-choli for Mou's reception because Abhiraj's other relatives would be present there.

After the Mukherjee family left the other night, Rivanah decided not to talk to her parents about the matter. Nothing was said to her directly so why should she confront them about it either? If Abhiraj was to be believed, then he would anyway tell his parents that he won't marry her and if he doesn't, then she would talk to her parents about it.

'Didn't you talk to baba about Danny?' she asked her mother while having ice cream by the Gelato counter.

'I did,' her mother said sounding a little grim.

'What did he say?' Rivanah knew what her father's response would have been but still she was keeping her hopes up.

'It's impossible.'

'Why mumma? Just because he is not a Hindu? Just because he is a struggling actor?'

'This "just because" is not as insignificant a thing as you are making it out to be. Nobody from our family would support you or us. Don't you know what happened with your Meghna di? Her parents still haven't recovered from it. Your pishi didn't even invite them for Mou's wedding.'

The mention of Meghna brought back the images of her verbal spats with Aadil. Rivanah immediately convinced herself even if Danny and she got married, they would never tire of love. And then her innermost insecurity told her: you thought the same about Ekansh too, remember?

'I would suggest you forget Danny,' Mrs Bannerjee said wiping off the ice cream from the sides of her mouth with a napkin.

'Tell me mumma, what's the most important thing in a marriage now that you have been married to baba for close to twenty seven years? Isn't it love?'

Her mother seemed lost in her thoughts for some time before she said, 'Not love. I would say ignorance. A successful marriage depends on ignorance.'

Rivanah shot her an incredulous look.

'If it was love, your baba would have respected my decision of being a working woman. I chose to ignore my own desires otherwise it would have been difficult to stay with him and raise you. And I'm sure he must have also ignored a lot of my things.'

'I disagree with you mumma. You two couldn't have possibly been in love because you married a total stranger. I love Danny because I have been with him for some months now and will be till we get married.'

'You were with Ekansh too. Did you know him well? Mini, you have to understand this dear that we can only know a person from what he is and not from what he can be. He can be a lot many things besides the thing that we see, the thing that we are in love with.'

Rivanah knew it was futile explaining anything to her parents because they would never understand where she was coming from. They were from a different generation. They grew up in a different world and thus had a different perspective toward life. The best would be to fly off to Mumbai right after the reception. As they say out of sight, out of mind.

The next evening, the entire Bannerjee family went to Mou's reception. The way her parents introduced her to every member of Abhiraj's family made her feel embarrassingly conscious all through the evening. It was as if a pair of eyes was always on her, ready to judge every move of hers.

'Did you tell your parents that you are not interested in the marriage?' Rivanah asked Abhiraj when she met him alone by the Fuchka stall.

'I haven't yet,' he told her.

'You know...' she started only to be cut short by him.

'I really want to marry you Rivanah and I can't lie to my parents about it,' he said in one breath.

'Do you want to marry someone who loves another guy?'

'Give me a chance,' he said with pride.

'What makes you think you deserve one?'

'I love you, that's why.'

'You love me? Because we talked for some time last evening and an evening prior to that? I thought you were smarter than that.'

Abhiraj was quiet.

'You don't have to lie to your parents. I'll do the needful.'

Rivanah was done with her Fuchka. She simply walked to her mother and complained that her head was aching and that she wanted to go home and rest. She took the car's keys from her father, asked him to take a cab while returning, and drove herself home.

The first thing she did was prepone her previous flight ticket to Mumbai for the next morning. When her parents came back home later that night, she told them that her team lead had called and asked her to report to office the next day because an important client was visiting them. Though her parents understood their daughter was miffed with them, they couldn't talk about it because she too didn't bring up the subject. Rivanah was tired of explaining the same thing to them over and over again. She loved Danny; her parents had to accept it. There was no other option she was giving them. Whether they wanted to do so wholeheartedly or not was their call.

The next day she decided to go straight to Danny's flat first from the airport. When he called up, she lied to him saying she was still in Kolkata. She wanted to give him a sexy surprise. Danny was supposed to come to his flat in the evening. She cleaned his flat, cooked for him, and was waiting with bated breath for the love of her life to return. It was while waiting for him that there was a sudden power cut. She was about to call him back when she heard someone unlock the door. Rivanah presumed it was Danny and stealthily walked to the drawing room. Holding her breath, she was waiting to jump on him when someone put a ribbon around her eyes and blindfolded her. She could smell the deodorant that Danny wore all the time: 'Just Different' by Hugo Boss. Before she could talk, her hands were handcuffed as well.

# 23

Danny kept calling Rivanah's phone for an hour but nobody answered. Arriving at their apartment, he found her flat was locked. A nervous Danny eventually relaxed when he saw her in the drawing room of his flat lying on the mattress with a blindfold. Though her pose was a casual one, the fact that she wasn't responding to him told him something otherwise. He removed the blindfold, shook her up, and sprinkled some water on her eyes after which Rivanah started moving her limbs slightly. She looked at Danny in an unfamiliar way. Seconds later, she hugged him tight.

'What happened? Don't tell me you were asleep?' Danny held her in his strong arms, stroking her hair.

'I don't know,' she said. What she meant was she didn't know what happened after someone made her sniff something on a piece of cloth after which she was tied and stripped naked. She quickly checked the clothes she was wearing: it was a white tank top with black pyjamas, not the clothes she had been wearing before she lost her senses. And she could feel fresh inners too. Rivanah clearly remembered the one she was wearing before had been cut by...it had to be the stranger. Did he fuck her as well?

'What do you mean you don't know? What happened here? Why were you wearing a blindfold and sleeping?' Danny questioned, holding her strongly by her shoulders.

'I was attacked,' she blurted out holding the blindfold without wishing to share the incident with Danny.

'Just calm down and tell me what really happened?'

'Please give me some water.' Danny left her and sprang toward the kitchen. Should she tell him about the stranger? What happened a few hours back in the darkness of the power cut was not something that a well-wisher would do to you.

'Here,' Danny said extending the glass of water towards her. She gulped half the water in the glass at one go and said, 'There was a power cut. I heard the door unlock and when I came to this room I was blindfolded and attacked.'

Danny looked around.

'But everything looks in place. Why would someone attack you and then leave without touching anything. In fact, even you don't look hurt. Are you?'

Rivanah nodded quietly. She was still not willing to tell Danny what really happened.

They had a silent dinner after which they slept

together. Though Danny had to meet Nitya in the morning, Rivanah didn't let him go till she was ready for office herself. She would have messaged the stranger about the incident but couldn't because neither Danny nor she could sleep all night.

Once in office, she sat down by the cubicle and had just opened her phone's inbox to type a message when a security guard came to her.

'You have a parcel,' he said and kept a big brown envelope on her table along with a box covered in brown paper. He gave her a piece of paper where she signed next to her name. The guard went away. She kept her phone on the desk and took the envelope in her hand. She tried to feel it. Something soft; she thought. There was no return address written on it. A curious Rivanah cut open the parcel.

*I'm sorry*, the paper note said.

Inside the box was a lavender coloured lace negligee. Rivanah frowned. Is it from the stranger? For the first time he had given her a gift. She wasn't surprised he knew her favourite colour. Rivanah kept the negligee inside lest someone saw it and picked up her phone to type a message to the stranger:

*Why did you do what you did last night? Is that all that you wanted: to tie and fuck me?*

It was during her lunch that the stranger replied:

*I told you we shall meet once you are back from Kolkata. BTW, I didn't fuck you.*

219

*Then why did you blindfold me, tie me up, strip me naked, and rub my make up off?*

*I wanted to see how you really look like without any kind of a mask.*

*Mask? What are you talking about?*

*When was the last time you made a mistake Mini? A terrible, terrible mistake?*

*I have answered that already. Ekansh was a mistake.*

*Think hard and be honest.*

*I'm being honest.*

*Sometimes we lie not to cover the truth but to cover that side of us which the truth may strip to bareness.*

*I don't understand.*

*You better do else I'll have to make you understand.*

*Why is he suddenly sounding threatening?* Rivanah thought. *What does he want from me? Why is he asking the same question again and again when I have answered him honestly?* Rivanah didn't message back nor did she receive any message till evening when she was buying milk from a shop right opposite to her place.

*I hope you liked the dress.*

*That's my favourite colour,* she responded.

*I'm sure when you will wear it, you shall be my favourite.*

A smile touched her face as she took the milk pouches and crossed the lane to reach her building. The stranger sure knew how to flatter and impress a girl after being rude to her. Or was it some sort of a mind-game he was playing with her?

Rivanah showed the negligee to Ishita that night.

'Wow! So the stranger is finally starting to dote on you, huh?'

'Well, I don't know,' Rivanah said. She thought Ishita wouldn't have said all this had she known how threatening the stranger sounded during the day. Was he a schizophrenic?

'What if he proposes to you next? Whom will you choose—Danny or the stranger?'

'Come on, I love Danny!'

Ishita gave her a mean look and said, 'That's the problem with you moralistic girls. You don't know how to enjoy.'

'What would you have chosen?'

'Me?' Ishita said with pride, 'I would have dated the stranger.'

'And Danny.'

'Please don't mind girl, but I don't think Danny is the marrying kinds yet.'

Rivanah knew Ishita was being honest at the cost of sounding rude. Danny was still a struggling actor and model. But would she date the stranger in spite of being in love with Danny? Then a thought occurred to her: Why the hell was she even considering it when she knew well the stranger never did what she expected of him?

## 24

Rivanah didn't know who she was more proud of—herself or the kids when all ten of them passed their test of writing the alphabets from A to Z without looking at their textbooks. A couple of them even wrote basic but correct sentences with the simple English words given to them. She clicked pictures of all their papers with her phone and sent them to Danny. She also uploaded a few on Facebook with a status update: *Happiness is when your students score full and you score high.*

As a treat she arranged for the ten kids to have a sumptuous dinner at KFC in Infinity Mall in Malad west. While she was wiping her fingers with the napkin one of the kids asked, 'Tai, when is our next test?'

Everyone laughed out aloud. Rivanah knew how much this one dinner meant to them. The bill of that one meal amounted to eleven hundred and fifty rupees: an amount with which she would have purchased a single dress before. The irony of it weighed on her. She smiled at the kid who had by now pushed the burger down his throat.

'Very soon. Now nobody leaves the table till I'm back, alright?' Rivanah said and went to the washroom. She came back to notice the kids were crowding around something kept at the centre of the table. She soon noticed there was a small box inside from which shone two diamond studs. Rivanah was more than surprised.

'Who kept these here?' she asked the kids staring at the diamond studs.

One of the kids looked around and gestured at a woman. Her uniform told her she was one of the cleaning ladies. Rivanah picked up the box and scampered to the cleaning staff.

'Did you keep this on that table?' Rivanah asked holding the stud box.

The woman nodded.

'Who gave you this?' Rivanah said.

The cleaning lady looked around for a moment and pointed toward a middle-aged man who was busy buying Dosa from a South Indian eatery. She went to him.

'Excuse me, did you give this box to that woman there?'

The middle-aged man checked out Rivanah once in an annoying manner and nodded.

'Why did you give it to her?'

'I was asked to pass it on, so I simply did.'

'Who asked you to pass it on?'

The man pointed out toward a teenager who was busy having ice cream with another girl in the food court. Rivanah rushed to the boy and asked him the same question: who gave you the box? The boy looked around like the others and aimed at a woman who was sitting with her kid at another corner. Rivanah rushed to the woman. When she inquired about the box, the woman told her an old woman had given it to her and asked her to pass it to the young boy. Rivanah looked around but there wasn't any old woman in sight anymore. The ten kids had joined her by then.

'What happened tai?' asked one of them.

Rivanah said, 'Nothing'. She understood it was useless to spot the stranger. He had used a chain of people to reach her. And some of them must have left the food court by then. As her breath came back to normal, she looked at the studs. They were gorgeous. Was Ishita right about the stranger developing a soft corner for her?

'What's that tai?' a girl in the group asked her pointing toward the roller coaster on which people were screaming their lungs out.

'Do you guys want to check it out?' she asked the group lovingly.

There was a collective nod. Rivanah arranged for the kids to experience the roller coaster ride while she stood near its gate waving happily at them and making a video recording of it. She stopped in-between when she received a message from an unknown number.

*Hope you liked the studs.*

*Why are you doing this?*

*What do you think?*

*Answer me straight.*

*When does a guy gift a girl a pair of studs?*

*You know that I'm committed, right?* she messaged.

*That makes you all the more tempting.*

Rivanah couldn't help but smile at the message. It momentarily made her feel good about her otherwise confused self. It wasn't that the stranger wanted to have a physical relationship with her. That she was confident about, otherwise he would not have spared her the night he tied and stripped her. Does it mean that he intends to be more serious with her? And in the past whenever he was helpful to her, was it because he wanted to make her feel emotionally accountable towards him? Was this all his grand plan to make her fall for him? Rivanah's thoughts were interrupted when she heard the kids scream out with joy as the roller coaster turned upside down. She forced a smile and thought she would tell him straightaway she wasn't in any mood to cheat on Danny. She was about to type a message when another came in:

*Forget Danny.*

Rivanah didn't like the tone of the message. She didn't reply but once she came home after dropping the kids at their place, she showed the message to Ishita. The latter gave her phone back after reading the message and turned quiet. Rivanah had intentionally brought her up to their building's terrace lest the stranger heard them talking. It was humid outside and from time to time, she could see Ishita wiping the sweat off her forehead while Rivanah allowed her perspiration to soak her.

'Are you going to say something or not?' Rivanah said feeling impatient.

'I think you ought to stop it,' Ishita finally said.

'Stop what? I never started anything,' Rivanah argued.

'Why did you have to respond to the stranger in the first place?'

'I thought he was harmless. And he proved to be harmless and quite helpful. You know that! In fact he did some beautiful things to me which I wouldn't have done myself and which I shall never forget,' Rivanah said. There was no denying the fact that there had been a remarkable change in her since the time she first came to Mumbai and the reason for that difference was the stranger.

Ishita knew about the kids Rivanah used to teach every Saturday. Rivanah also told her about Ratna and how it made her believe that the stranger was a good human being.

'Tell me, what happens if you don't respond to him from now on? Can he harm you in any way?' Ishita asked.

Rivanah thought about her clip that showed her recording Prateek in a compromising position. Ishita read her mind.

'The clip right? Even if we suppose he hasn't deleted it, how does it matter? You are not naked in it. If it comes out, you can always say Prateek was blackmailing you. And where is Prateek anyway?'

'He left the company a few months back.'

'So? That's even better,' Ishita wiped her sweat again and said, 'For God's sake we could have had this conversation in our air conditioned room as well. Asha is also not there.'

Rivanah swallowed a lump.

'The stranger can hear us talking.'

Ishita was quiet for a moment trying to understand what Rivanah meant and then she dashed out of the terrace. Rivanah joined her soon as they took the stairs to reach their flat. Ishita started searching for possible mikes in the flat while Rivanah closed the main door and stood beside it watching her roomie go berserk. Ishita was doing what she had done the first time she learnt the stranger could hear her. But all in vain. Twenty minutes later, Ishita had still not found anything that looked minutely suspicious.

'How can he hear you?' Ishita said exasperated.

Rivanah immediately put a finger on her lips urging her to be quiet. Ishita realized her mistake. She typed in her phone and showed it to Rivanah: *How?* Rivanah whispered in her ears, 'No idea.'

Ishita whispered back, 'This guy is dangerous.'

The doorbell rang. The two girls exchanged a nervous glance. Ishita quickly went to her room and returned with a bottle of pepper spray

'Open the door,' she said mentally preparing herself for a surprise attack if need be. Rivanah unlocked the door and peeped to see who it was. Ishita's grip on the pepper spray tightened. When the door full opened, both girls relaxed. It was Asha.

'Close the door,' Ishita said. Rivanah complied. Asha gave both the girls a skeptic look.

'Our flat is bugged,' Ishita gasped.

'How do you know?' Asha asked looking at both of them with a confused expression on her face.

'We just know,' Ishita said.

'Did you guys check?'

'We did but found nothing,' Rivanah said. This was the maximum Asha had talked to them in the last ten months.

'Where all have you not looked?' Asha asked in a whisper.

Ishita looked at Rivanah and after a thoughtful pause said softly, 'I didn't check the bathroom, the toilet, the attic above, and behind that wardrobe. There are a lot of cobwebs and cockroaches behind it.'

Asha started with the toilet then the bathroom. She brought a stool and stood on it to have a look at the attic above the bathroom. It was dark and covered with dust, dirt, and cobwebs.

'Give me a torch,' she said. Rivanah switched on the flashlight in her phone and handed it over to her. Asha flashed the light into the attic but could see nothing suspicious. She stepped down and went to the kitchen. The same result. The last place that remained was the tiny space behind the wardrobe. With the help of the others, Asha was able to move the heavy teakwood wardrobe. They could see a thick layer of dust on the base of the floor, clearly telling them that the wardrobe had not been shifted since a long time. Asha peeped back and saw a network of cobwebs. Give me a duster. Ishita soon handed over a piece of cloth that they used to dust the flat with. Once Asha dusted off some of the cobwebs, she saw a cockroach. Behind the cockroach were a couple more like him.

'Be careful,' Ishita remarked.

Asha tried to scare off the cockroaches but none of them moved. They were deadstill in fact. She found the whole thing weird. She stretched her hand and reached for one of the cockroaches. There was still no movement. The next instant she held it by its antenna and brought it out. Both Ishita and Rivanah shrieked out.

'What are you doing?' Ishita cried out looking at Asha who was dangling the cockroach in her hand.

229

Then suddenly she threw one of them at the girls. Both scampered inside the other room screaming. The next minute they peeped out and saw Asha had a whole lot of cockroaches by her feet. She squashed one of them. The girls couldn't believe their eyes. As they came forward nervously, they saw there were other squashed ones too and each of the cockroaches, which were clearly made of plastic, had a tiny mike hidden in its belly.

## 25

Danny had ordered pizza for the girls on his way to their flat. By the time the delivery came, he too had arrived and had gone to his flat to freshen up.

Once the girls smashed all the plastic cockroaches and ripped out the mikes from them, Rivanah made them promise they would keep the discovery to themselves.

'But why?' Ishita was confused. Someone tried to compromise her private space and yet Rivanah was not ready to do anything about it. By then Asha had retired to her room.

'I agree he shouldn't have bugged our flat but he hasn't harmed me yet. Have you forgotten how he helped me get the clip from Prateek?'

'I remember all of it but...'

'Then I think we should give him one chance,' Rivanah pleaded.

'Are you sure you aren't suffering from some kind of Stockholm syndrome?' Ishita asked. Rivanah gave her a clueless look.

'It's a syndrome where the victim falls in love with her captor,' Ishita clarified.

Rivanah remained quiet. Ishita was about to say more when the doorbell rang. It was the pizza delivery boy. And behind him stood Danny.

'Girls, it's a pizza treat from my side. I'll join you in two minutes,' he said exhibiting his typical charming smile. Ishita took the pizza while Rivanah closed the door and said, 'Ishu, please try to understand.'

'It's okay. I won't tell Danny anything about it unless you want me to.'

'Thank you.'

'But between the two of us; if you don't do anything soon, you will be in a situation which you will be unable to handle. If you know what I mean,' said Ishita and kept the pizza on a table.

'I do. And don't worry, nobody can take me away from Danny. I love him.'

'I hope that's enough.'

'It is.'

The pizza dinner went well. The girls gave no hint to Danny about the discovery. Once done, Danny went to his flat while the girls took to their respective beds.

Rivanah didn't know what time it was when she woke up hearing the doorbell ringing continuously. She called out to Ishita and Asha but neither came out from their room. She soon realized the peculiar thing about the doorbell. It was gaining decibel each time it rang. How could that be possible? Rivanah climbed out of her bed and went to open the main door. She was dumbfounded. It was her own self by the door who was pressing the doorbell with a noose around her neck. As the two Rivanah's eyes met, the one with the noose gave the other a diabolical smile. Rivanah opened her eyes wide, feeling herself soaking wet with perspiration. It had been some time since she had last seen the nightmare. But this time she felt the chill of it the most. Before her mind could calm her down, her phone's alarm started ringing. *But why at midnight?* she wondered and checked her phone. The alarm screen showed her the note she had once put but forgotten to delete it.

*My shona's birthday,* the alarm note said.

It was Ekansh's birthday. She wouldn't have remembered it had the alarm not buzzed. But the alarm did what she had once wanted it to. She held her head down knowing well that now the memories of last year would stalk her, torture her, bleed her, and won't leave till they had emotionally raped her. She tried sleeping but couldn't. Ekansh's smiling face was in front of her. In the end, she thought of giving in to her urge of checking out Ekansh's profile on Facebook. That was her only link to him. She logged in to her Facebook profile, unblocked Ekansh, and went to his profile. The last time he had a photograph of him with a girl as his profile picture. It was the same girl Rivanah had caught him with. This time he had a single picture.

She clicked on it but it didn't open. She clicked on the message option and as it opened she could well see her last message to him which was thirteen months back. It read: *Not able to call you. Missing you. Call me back asap.* He had indeed called her within minutes of that message. Her fingers, quite involuntarily, started scrolling down the inbox and she spent the next two hours reading all the twelve thousand, seven hundred, and eighty eight messages they had exchanged in the last four years of their relationship. Her fingers didn't come off the laptop's mouse scroller till she reached the first message which was from Ekansh: *Thanks for accepting my friend request. How are you?*

Those all-day-long messaging, late night phone calls, bunking classes to meet up, going for secret dates, the naughty acts in movie theatres, convincing the parents about fake college trips and what not. They meant nothing now. In one of the messages she had written: *I won't ever be able to live without you.* And he had responded with: *Me too.* Rivanah laughed out amidst tears in her eyes. The break-up had happened and she was indeed living. And so was he. On an impulse she wrote: 'Happy Birthday asshole. You are such a pain in the ass.' Immediately after sending it to Ekansh, she realized she shouldn't have done it. It would only tell him that he still mattered to her. She was about to close her Facebook message inbox when her eyes noticed the 'other' section where sixty five unread messages were present. She clicked open the section and went through some of them which were from boys who wanted to be her friend on Facebook. The messages were written in terrible English and projected equally funny thoughts. Some of them had even attached their Kundali for marriage while some had written poems in praise of her photoshopped profile and cover pictures. Rivanah had a constant smile as she read the messages one by one. The smile totally dried up when she reached the forty seventh message. It read:

*Hi Rivanah, I made this new id of mine because you have blocked my other id. Happy birthday. I hope you are doing fine. Take Care. Ekansh.*

He did remember her birthday earlier in the year. Did it mean he missed her too? Did his message mean she still mattered to him? Did it mean he was willing to stage a comeback given a chance? Or did it mean he only wanted to make her life miserable by sticking on to her like a predator? Rivanah cursed herself for having opened the other section. The message doesn't mean anything just like she didn't mean anything to him, she told herself. The past can be a part of us but not the whole of us, she reminded herself. After refreshing the page, she noticed that he had changed his profile picture a minute back. It meant he was online at the same time as her. She could connect to him with one click of her mouse but she held back. Rivanah didn't know if he had seen her message or not but she did look at the new profile picture of his: a selfie with a girl she didn't know. They were beaming. She realized the picture was not locked and thus she quickly dragged-dropped it on her desktop, opened the paintbrush application and blackened all their teeth. She blocked Ekansh next, logged out of Facebook, and messaged Danny on Whatsapp. There wasn't any reply. She checked the time: 2:30 am.

Rivanah stood up, took out Danny's duplicate keys from her bag in the wardrobe, and went to his flat. In the darkness, she could see Danny lying on the mattress in the room on his back wearing only a pair of Jockey knickers. She went to him and gently lay down on his back holding him tightly. The touch of his skin relaxed her. Danny woke up but didn't budge.

'Is it a dream or a reality?' he asked with a sleep-heavy voice.

Rivanah kissed his ears softly.

'A dream,' he quipped.

She bit his ears.

'Reality!' he shrieked out.

Still lying on his back she said, 'Do you miss your ex Danny?'

'Which one?'

She bit his shoulder.

'Ouch. Okay, I don't.'

'Why? Have you forgotten them?'

'Can anyone forget a person with whom you once had a serious relationship?' he said opening his eyes and looking at nothing in particular.

'Then?'

'Then what?'

'Then how come you don't miss them?'

'Maybe because I'm at peace with whatever happened between my exes and me. Maybe because I know for a fact that nothing else could have happened.'

'Hmm.'

*Perhaps he was right,* Rivanah thought. She was yet to be at peace with what Ekansh had done with her. But the question was: will she ever be at peace with it?

Danny's phone vibrated.

'Who is messaging you so late?' Rivanah said and picked up his phone.

'1218,' he said aloud the password. It was his and her birth dates together. With a smile, she unlocked the phone. There was an MMS link. She downloaded it. Her blood froze the moment it started playing. It was from the night when she was attacked by the stranger. It showed her all tied up, stark naked, with a piece of cloth in her mouth.

'Who is it?' Danny said groggily.

Rivanah couldn't speak. The message was clear. If the clip can go to Danny's phone, then it can go to anybody's phone.

'Danny...' she said. The fragility in her voice made him sit up.

'I need to tell you something.'

This time it was her phone that beeped with a message from an unknown number.

*Forget Danny. I love you more.*

# 26

Neither Danny nor Rivanah slept that night. After she told him everything that had been happening with her since her shift to Mumbai, Danny couldn't help but rebuke her for the first time since their relationship.

'What were you waiting for?' Danny said after giving her a patient hearing.

'Does it also mean that you went to Tiger Point on your birthday not because you guessed it was me but because you thought this psycho called you there? You went just like that? Or did you guys have a real date and I spoilt it for you?'

'It's nothing like that Danny. You know I love you and won't do anything to compromise it. I haven't met him. I don't even know what he looks like.'

'And still you hid him from me Rivanah. And all I know is this isn't how a healthy relationship progresses. How could you not tell me? This guy attacked you inside my flat and you still did not tell me about it? Don't you trust me or what?'

*I did not want to disturb the equilibrium I have developed with the stranger*, Rivanah thought, but didn't say so lest Danny concluded she was mad.

'I fought for you with my parents,' she said instead. 'So please don't say I don't trust you. I know I shouldn't have hidden it from you and I'm sorry about it. Now can you please tell me what I should do?'

They both waited quietly for the morning to arrive. And by then they had decided: they would go to the police.

Rivanah called inspector Mohan Kamble around nine in the morning.

'Yes Miss Bannerjee, what can I do for you?'

'I need to meet you, sir.'

'Regarding?'

Rivanah glanced at Danny once and then spoke on the phone again, 'There's someone who is harassing me.'

'Come to the police station anytime. I will...'

'Can we please meet elsewhere, Kamble sir? The person I'm talking about follows my every move.'

'You mean a stalker?'

'Yes, you can say so. I don't want to give him an inkling that I'm going to the police.'

'Hmm,' Kamble seemed to think for some time and then said, 'Let's meet at your office then. I'll come in plain clothes. Fine?'

'That will be great sir. At what time?'

Kamble met Rivanah at the smoking zone of her

office around one in the afternoon the same day. She couldn't show him the video that was sent to Danny's phone, not only because of the obvious reason, but also because she had deleted the video immediately on a whim. She didn't even remember the phone number through which it was sent. After she briefed Kamble about what the stranger had been doing, she showed him the messages she had saved on the phone and also gave him all the unknown numbers that she had received messages from in the last eleven months or so. Kamble tried calling on a few of the phone numbers but each one of them was switched off.

'Look, Miss Bannerjee, it's quite clear from the messages that he is in love with you. In fact, he himself has confirmed it in one of the last messages he sent.'

'I know.'

'In these cases it isn't that difficult to trap the stalker. All you need to do is smooth talk him into revealing himself to you and that's when we nab him.' Kamble sounded quite confident.

'I have asked him to meet me several times but he doesn't.'

'Hmm. The only thing that is confusing me is that if he only wanted to be in a relationship with you, why would he make you teach the kids or encourage you to be the witness in the gangrape case? These aren't things for which we can charge him but still...'

'Maybe he is a psycho?' Rivanah suggested.

'Even psychos have a pattern. If he loved you, he would have at least kissed you once the night he attacked you.'

'Maybe he did.'

'But not when you were conscious.'

'No.'

'Hmm,' Kamble scratched his chin thinking hard. 'Guess he will answer all our questions only when we nab him,' she said.

Another silent pause followed.

'Should I text him now and ask him to meet up?'

'Do it,' Kamble said instantly.

Rivanah immediately typed a message: *I want to meet you.* She sent it to the number from which the last message had come. There was an awkward silence as the two waited for a reply. In between Kamble excused himself to answer some calls on his phone. When Kamble was advancing back toward her, Rivanah's phone buzzed with a message.

*What's the hurry?*

She showed the message to him. He frowned reading the message and then said, 'You keep trying to get him to meet you while I try and get the location details of these phone numbers. Let me know without delay if he agrees to meet you.'

'Okay.'

'I will send couple of plain clothes constables at the place you are staying to get information about the residents there. You told me about the mike inside the cockroaches. Chances are he is living somewhere close by. Maybe in the same building.'

'What?' Rivanah swallowed a lump.

'I said maybe. I will be going now but don't be afraid. He won't harm you. I'll also need all the white pieces of cloth with the messages on them that you have been getting. Keep them ready with you. Remember this: if he contacts you, just involve him in some talk and don't enrage him. And most importantly, call me,' Kamble said.

'Yes, sure sir.'

Kamble took a start but suddenly stopped and turned to her.

'By the way, is there any opening in this company?'

For a moment, Rivanah thought Kamble wanted to work in Tech Sky Technologies. Then the obvious occurred to her.

'Please ask your daughter to mail me her resume. I'll pass it on to my HR team for sure.'

'Thanks,' Kamble was gone after noting her email id.

◆

In the evening Rivanah received a message from Danny forsaking if she was free to come to the McDonald's outlet near the Kora Kendra bus stop in Borivali after his audition around nine where he would be waiting. They would have dinner there and then go home

243

together. Rivanah messaged back in the affirmative. She came to her flat, freshened up, and then went out in. On her way out, she did notice two men talking to the guard of her building. Were they the constables? *Could be*, she thought and took an autorickshaw to reach the Kora Kendra McDonald's.

Rivanah reached before time and bought a Coke and some French Fries for herself to kill time. She opened her Whatsapp chat window. Pooja had surprised her by sending her a picture of her wedding card in the morning. Rivanah checked the card again and sighed. Some people had all the luck. Everything in their life happened at the right time and for the right reason. Rivanah was happy that Pooja was settling down with a guy she had been dating since college. Such life wasn't for her because the universe had reserved all the life's lessons exclusively for her. Pooja's marriage was scheduled for the next month in Kolkata. Though she had promised her she would be there without fail, Rivanah had already decided she wouldn't be going. In fact she would stay away from home till her parents accepted her relationship with Danny.

Rivanah put her hand in the paper box and realized the French fries were finished. She tried to sip the coke but nothing came up the straw. She checked the phone clock: 9:15. There was no sign of Danny. She went to the last dial section of her phone and tapped on the dial button. The next moment she took out her ear piece with a frown. She could hear Danny's phone's ringtone from somewhere behind her. She turned in a flash but couldn't see anything. And precisely then there was a power failure. Rivanah immediately heard one of the McDonald's staff shout out to people to remain where they were and that the power would be back shortly. But Rivanah had a feeling this was no coincidence.

As Danny's phone stopped ringing, she could smell the 'Just Different' deodorant close to her. Every muscle in her body stiffened. The outside chaos suddenly muted and all she could hear was her own breathing and heartbeat. Soon the fragrance kept getting further away from her. Rivanah slowly relaxed as the power came on. She turned back and found Danny's mobile phone on the empty table. She looked around. Nobody seemed interested in her. Was Danny playing a prank on her? Suddenly her own phone rang. An unknown number flashed on the screen. Was the stranger calling her finally? As she moved her hand to answer the call, she felt the presence of something. Rivanah shrieked and stood up simultaneously, pushing her chair back. There was silence in McDonald's. Everyone was looking at her. Around Rivanah's forearm there was a rope smeared with something red. And the rope was in the form of a noose. The kind she had been having bad dreams about where she saw herself hanging. The buzz returned as one of the staff attended her.

'Any problem madam?'

'No,' she said and noticed her phone was again ringing with the unknown number. She picked it up.

'Hello,' she said.

'Hey baby,' Danny said. 'I somehow lost my phone this evening. And...'

'I have your phone,' Rivanah cut him short.

'What?' Danny was stunned.

'Come down to McDonald's, Kora Kendra. I'm waiting,' She said.

Danny reached a little after ten. The staff there had tried to calm Rivanah down, offering her some water. They wanted to throw the noose away but she didn't let them. It was a tangible proof. She kept it at a distance from her and kept staring at it, wondering what could be its implication.

In Danny's presence Rivanah called Kamble. This time he arrived at McDonald's in a uniform with couple of constables who confiscated the noose.

'Most of the phone numbers that were used to message you don't exist anymore and hence it will take more time to spot the last tower they picked for use,' Kamble said after Rivanah told him what had happened in the last one hour. 'Except for the last two or three numbers. The SIM was last used from Andheri west area.'

'Andheri west?' Rivanah mumbled under her breath.

'Do you know anybody living there?' Kamble asked.

Rivanah nodded. Prateek used to live there. But how

could he be the stranger? He wouldn't let her record his own compromised self like that. Or would he to shift her suspicion from him? Another person who went to that area often was Danny. Was that a coincidence as well just like the deodorant Danny and the stranger wore was the same? Rivanah was perplexed.

'This is going a bit too far sir,' Danny said. 'I hope you catch this guy soon.'

Rivanah looked at him. He looked genuinely concerned.

'Did he message you or tried to get in touch in any way after I left from your office?' Kamble said.

'No. Except the one I got from Danny's number.'

'Hmm. Anything you can make out of the noose?'

'Nothing.' Rivanah kept her dream a secret.

Kamble scratched his chin for some time.

'Tomorrow is Sunday,' he said looking at Rivanah. 'Update your Facebook status saying you will be in Infinity Mall, Andheri with your boyfriend. Make it public.'

'What for?' Danny said.

'If this guy is a genuine stalker, he would be present there for sure.'

'But we don't know who he is,' Rivanah chipped in.

'We will. But before you reach the mall tomorrow, Danny needs to be present there with another girl. Ask one of your friends. You go there Rivanah and catch Danny with a girl. An ugly verbal fight ensues, at the end of which you break up with him. Make sure it all seems real. I'm hoping it will be the stalker's bait for making himself visible.'

Rivanah understood Kamble's point. She was anyway experienced about catching a guy with a girl.

'And then?' Danny said.

'I'll tell you that later, but first enact this scene properly. My constables will be present in the mall in plain clothes but they will intervene only if need be.'

'I'll ask Nitya,' Danny said. Rivanah nodded.

'Now you come with me Danny,' Kamble said. 'You will have to file a report with us against the stalker. My constables will drop Rivanah home.'

'May I bring my roomie with me tomorrow?' Rivanah asked.

'If it helps you in any way,' Kamble said.

'Thank you so much sir.'

◆

The moment she reached home Rivanah did two things: One, she relayed everything to Ishita and two, she updated her Facebook status.

*Yippe! Can't wait to watch the first show of my favourite actor's movie tomorrow @ Infinity, Andheri!*

She checked her Facebook friend list once. There was no suspicious looking profile. Then she checked her followers—a total of 88—out of which she knew nobody.

The next day, as per Kamble's plan, Rivanah went to Infinity Mall along with Ishita. She spotted Danny with Nitya in the food court and made a hue and cry over it. She surprised herself with her acting skills. She left the spot making sure everyone present in the food court remembered her well.

Once home, she was confused about what would happen next. She called Kamble once who asked her to relax and wait for the stalker's message. His confidence surprised Rivanah. Kamble wasn't wrong because a message did come late in the evening from the same unknown number that had asked her to forget Danny.

*So, Danny is history.*

Rivanah immediately called Kamble who told her over phone what exactly her reply to the stalker should read like.

*I didn't know Danny would turn out to be such a dog. Why are men like that?* she messaged back.

*Not every man is a dog.* The response came. Rivanah shared it with Kamble who again framed her response for her.

*The ones in my life were. And I have lost hope now.* She messaged.

*You deserve someone who can give you lifelong loyalty.*

*Do loyal men exist in real? If yes then will I get that lucky?*

*Of course. A girl like you deserves all the luck.*

*Really? Where will I get such a man?*

*Right here.*

*OMG. I don't believe this.*

*And I promise I won't leave you mid-way.*

She called Kamble again, asking him what her next response should be. Briefed by Kamble Rivanah messaged:

*Are you saying you will marry me, stranger?*

A smiley came in as a reply. When she told Kamble about it, he assured her the stranger was on the verge of being caught.

The next message from the unknown number read: *how about meeting up tomorrow?*

# 27

At around 3 pm the next day, Rivanah was on her way to Infinity Mall in Malad west, the place where the stranger said he would meet her.

*I will be waiting for you inside Starbucks. I will order my coffee in your name,* said the last message for the night read.

Finally, the time had come to meet the stranger and to know why exactly he was so interested in her. Was he someone she knew from before? Or was he really a stranger? Sitting in the autorickshaw all by herself, Rivanah was nervous. It would have helped if Danny had accompanied her, but Kamble had strictly asked him not to.

'This guy now knows that you have broken up with Danny. I don't want to take a chance. What if he follows you to the mall?' Kamble had said. He had a point. In fact, this time he didn't allow Ishita to accompany her as well.

As the autorickshaw halted itself at a traffic signal, Rivanah peeped out and looked around. There were no familiar faces. Her phone rang. It was Danny. She picked it up immediately.

'Thank you for calling. I'm petrified,' Rivanah said.

'Just chill sweetheart. I know it is tough for you but it's a matter of only some more time now. After this, that bugger won't disturb you ever again,' Danny said.

'I know. I just hope it all goes off smoothly.'

'It will. I had a talk with Kamble a few minutes back. They are already there in Starbucks in plain clothes. I too shall be there.'

'Oh! Did Kamble ask you to?'

'No but I want to smash the rascal's face when he approaches you. Don't worry I shall be incognito.'

'Take care baby. I don't want you to get hurt.'

'And I don't want any scoundrel to hurt you.'

'I love you Danny.'

'Love you too Rivanah.'

The phone call ended.

'Idhar roku?' The autorickshaw driver asked her looking at her in the rear-view mirror.

'Peeche wale gate par,' she instructed. He stopped the auto at the mall's back gate. Rivanah wished the ride had not come to an end. She paid the driver and walked inside the mall.

Once the security let her pass through, she literally stared at every male that her eyes could spot. She took the escalator to the left of the entrance. Nobody in particular seemed to be looking at her. The guys who were indeed looking at her were actually checking her out; she knew that look well. Soon she reached Starbucks. She took a deep breath and went inside.

The order and payment counter was inside, so she slowly ambled towards it. She wanted to look around but her neck felt stiff. She removed her shades once reaching the order counter.

'Good evening ma'am,' the boy at the counter said.

'Hi,' she replied back.

'What would you like to order today? Anything hot or cold?'

For a moment she felt tongue-tied.

'Ma'am?'

'A simple cappuccino.'

'Certainly ma'am.' As the boy busied himself punching the amount on his machine, Rivanah turned her head. She spotted Kamble and immediately turned her face away. A sweat drop trickled down her scruff. When the boy handed her the bill, she took out her wallet from her purse and handed him the amount. As she kept the change back in her wallet, she noticed the boy write 'Rivanah 2' on a plastic glass.

'I ordered only one coffee,' she said.

'I know ma'am but coincidentally someone else also has ordered with the same name.'

It meant the stranger was already in Starbucks. She felt the stiffness in the neck now travel to her back. Somehow she managed a stupid smile at the boy behind the counter. She went ahead and took a seat by a table for two from where she could see Kamble from the corner of her eyes. She put on her shades to look around without being watched. She nervously started toying with her phone. Seconds turned into minutes. Then someone shouted, 'Rivanah 1'. She wanted to turn and see who approached the counter but was too nervous and shaky to do so. She dropped her phone on the table as her hands began to tremble. *By now the coffee must have been taken,* she thought, because there wasn't a second announcement. Slowly she turned her head toward the counter and her jaws dropped immediately.

By the payment counter, Kamble and his men had pinned a guy by his collar. The guy was trying hard to free himself but in vain. Rivanah focussed on the guy's face and identified him soon enough.

*What the fuck is Abhiraj doing here?* was her first thought. Her muscles instantly relaxed. She suddenly felt energetic. Rivanah stood up and went to him.

'Abhiraj? Don't tell me you are the one who...'

'Rivanah, please I can explain. Please ask these men to leave me,' Abhiraj was fidgeting helplessly.

'Let's take this mister-secret-lover to the real love den.' said Kamble to his men. They almost dragged Abhiraj out. Rivanah too followed but slowed down when she met Danny by the entrance.

'Do you know him?' Danny asked.

'Yes,' she said and briefed him about Abhiraj as they followed the police team out.

◆

Abhiraj was taken straight to the police station.

'You will be charged with section 354, d, for stalking, section 354 for assaulting a woman with intent to outrage her modesty, 506 for making an indecent video of hers, and also 509 for having gestured intending to outrage the modesty of a woman,' Kamble said thrashing him hard.

Abhiraj was given a chance to clarify only when Rivanah told Kamble that she knew him and his family well. By then his nose was bleeding, his lips were bruised, his face had a red texture from thrashing, and his left eye was somewhat swollen.

'I give you five minutes to clarify whatever you have to say and then willingly accept whatever you have done. After which I want the clip you recorded of Rivanah,' Kamble said in a threatening voice.

'Clip?' Abhiraj looked at everyone present there one by one with an expression as if someone had told him that he didn't have a dick.

'Abhiraj, why are you making things difficult for you? Just tell me why were you after me since I came to Mumbai? I promise I won't let them punish you severely,' Rivanah said politely.

'I don't know what you are talking about Rivanah. I didn't follow you.' Abhiraj was weeping like a kid. 'When we met in February I didn't tell you that the new company I joined had its headquarters in Mumbai. So I had to come here anyway. I had your phone number and honestly after I met you at the marriage I couldn't forget you. I wanted to pursue you since I knew your marriage with Danny had a big "if" in it.'

Rivanah and Danny exchanged a stern look and together looked at Abhiraj again who continued saying, 'I thought of seducing you away from Danny. So I gifted you the studs and the negligee. When you seemed to respond to the messages I sent you from the unknown number, I was convinced that you didn't love Danny as much and that if I pushed you a bit, you may actually be mine. I was happy when you two broke-up in the mall. I thought after Danny, you would give me a chance. And I swear I don't have any clip of yours.'

Does it mean it was a coincidence that the real stranger and Abhiraj's message came in one after the other? And did she link it all like a fool because both came from unkown numbers? Rivanah wondered.

'What's the password?' Kamble said taking Abhiraj's mobile phone from the constable who had confiscated it from Starbucks. Abhiraj told him the correct password. Kamble searched his phone but didn't find any clip. He kept it with himself to be checked by an expert team.

'Do you believe this guy?' Kamble asked Rivanah.

Abhiraj looked pleadingly at her.

'I don't know,' she said.

'Please Rivanah. My career will be over. I did what I did only to woo you. Nothing else. I never in my wildest dreams thought it will all come down to this,' Abhiraj said.

Kamble gestured to the constable who held Abhiraj by his arms to take him away to the lock up when Rivanah stopped them. She went close to Abhiraj and sniffed him. It was not the deodorant that she was expecting.

'Answer me honestly Abhiraj. Do you use "Just Different"?'

'What's that?'

Rivanah looked at Kamble and said, 'I don't think he is the man.'

'Why?' Kamble said.

'If he never used "Just Different" deodorant then he isn't the stranger.'

'How are you so sure?'

'I have smelled him closely thrice. In McDonald's as well as the night I was attacked and also once when he approached me in the elevator of my building. He uses the "Just Different" deodorant from Hugo Boss.'

'Who approached you?' Abhiraj asked.

'A stranger.'

'Hmm,' Kamble looked at the floor once with one hand on his hips and the other scratching his chin and then told the constable in Marathi to go and search

Abhiraj's place for the deodorant.

'Can I call my father?' Abhiraj pleaded. Kamble took his father's phone number and called him himself. Mr Mukherjee promised him that he would take the next flight to Mumbai.

'I think you should inform your parents too,' Kamble told Rivanah.

She looked at Danny for help.

'Excuse us please,' Danny told Kamble and pulled Rivanah to a corner.

'What is it?' he asked.

'I don't want to tell my parents about this.'

'But Abhiraj's parents may tell them about it.'

'I don't think being arrested for stalking a girl is something his father will tell my parents. But if I tell my parents about all this, I'm sure they will emotionally blackmail me to resign from work and get back to Kolkata. I just know it. And then...'

'What are you more scared of really?'

'I don't want to lose touch with you. I know you won't be able to shift to Kolkata even if I do.'

'Hmm. Can't you just request Abhiraj's father not to tell anything to your parents?'

'That's the only way out, it seems.'

'And what is it about the "Just Different" deodorant. You never told me about it before? Even I use it.'

'You don't have to tell this to the police,' Rivanah cautioned him.

'Come,' Danny said and together joined Kamble again.

'Sir, I think we will not divulge the matter to her parents as of now.'

Kamble first looked at Danny and then at Rivanah. Studying their faces he said, 'As you wish.'

'It means the stranger is still out there watching me,' Rivanah said.

'Relax. Let's first confirm if what Abhiraj is saying is even true. Then we will think about what to do next,' Kamble said.

Rivanah knew Abhiraj was correct. He couldn't have followed her since the past eleven months. It was only a matter of wrong timing that his messages were construed as being the stranger's. Perhaps, knowing this, the stranger had intentionally kept a distance from her all these days. He had been watching this comedy of errors silently, she thought, feeling her dry throat.

'May I have some water?' she asked.

'Sure,' Kamble said and asked a constable to get her a glass of water. As she finished drinking the water, she kept the glass on the table. Danny was at a corner answering an important phone call. They were asked to wait till the constables brought Abhiraj back. Kamble went to check on another thief who had been brought in. Meanwhile Rivanah checked her phone. There was a message and a few Whatsapp messages. She viewed the message first:

*Inky pinky ponky,*
*Mini had a donkey.*
*Donkey caught, Mini smiled a lot,*
*Inky pinky ponky.*

'Kamble sir,' Rivanah stood up holding her phone. Kamble as well as Danny rushed to her.

'What happened?' Kamble said.

She handed him her phone. Kamble read the message and said aloud, 'Mother fucker!'

'What happened?' Danny said.

'This is my wife's phone number. She told me she had lost it yesterday.' Kamble sat down on his chair feeling angry and frustrated.

# 28

*When was the last time you made a mistake Mini? A terrible, terrible mistake?*

Rivanah read the message again for the umpteenth time that morning. She had answered it for the stranger but he didn't seem to accept it. Could this have the clue to the puzzle that this stranger was?

Five days had gone by since Abhiraj's arrest in Starbucks. Ishita was in her office while Asha had gone to her hometown. Rivanah had her bags packed since morning. It was time to shift someplace else. Danny had a friend who was shifting to the UK for six months and was more than willing to rent out his friends the two-bedroom flat that his father owned in Lokhandwala.

The constables didn't get the concerned deodorant at Abhiraj's place. When the analysis of the messages sent to Rivanah from different phone numbers came in, it was clear that the clip was sent from a different location that was closer to Rivanah's place while the message that Abhiraj sent was from Andheri west. The last message that was sent from Kamble's wife's phone number confirmed that Abhiraj was not the stranger. It was indeed a coincidence that Abhiraj started luring Rivanah using unknown numbers and she misunderstood him to be the stranger.

On Abhiraj's request, and with slight help from Rivanah, the police agreed not to tell his father on what ground was he brought into custody. He was allowed to leave when Rivanah withdrew her complaint. Kamble promised her that he would not rest till the stranger was caught even though they had no leads as such. Kamble did question the slum kids but again reached a dead end. Rivanah could have told Kamble about Malati and Ratna but didn't. The police would harass them and it was something she didn't want them to go through, knowing well the innocent mother-daughter duo had nothing to do with all this.

The stranger had not messaged or tried to contact her since Abhiraj was caught. That was five days before. She hoped it was finally over because now the stranger knew the police was involved. Pursuing her in spite of it would be a risky affair.

The doorbell rang. Rivanah sprang up on her feet and picked her bag up. She was ready to leave with Danny to the new flat.

She opened the door to see Kamble beaming.

'Congratulations,' he said.

For a moment Rivanah thought the stranger had been caught.

'Where is he?' she asked.

'Oh no. We haven't been able to catch him yet. I'm congratulating you because the honourable court gave its verdict today regarding the gangrape victim; life imprisonment for both the men. You will read about it in newspapers tomorrow.'

Kamble had told her earlier in the week about the verdict date but she had forgotten about it completely since the incident at Starbucks.

'That's great,' she said.

'By the way, meet inspector Suresh Patil of crime branch,' Kamble said.

It was then she noticed the man standing beside Kamble. Patil shook Rivanah's hand .

'Did you get any promising leads?' she said looking at Kamble.

'The stranger lived on the flat above yours.'

'What? How do you know?'

'We located every owner of the flat in this building.' Patil preferred to answer. 'Some live here and some have put up their flats on rent like the one you stay in. Only the owner of the particular flat above yours lives in Australia. When my team contacted him, he clearly said he had not given it up on rent whereas the guard told me he had seen the flat unlocked many a times and yet he didn't exactly know who lived there.'

'Shit! Is the flat open now?'

'Yes. Come with me. I need to show you something.'

Kamble said. Rivanah was about to lock the door to her flat when Patil stopped her. He said he'll take a look around while she followed Kamble upstairs.

Rivanah noticed the flat above hers was completely empty. Kamble called a constable who came to him with a plastic packet inside which she could see few pieces of cloth as Kamble dangled the packet in front of her. She didn't take time to realize it was a set of undergarments; a bra and a panty cut into pieces.

'Do you...'

'They are mine,' said an embarrassed Rivanah. She was wearing the pair on the night the stranger attacked her.

'Hmm, I guessed so.' Kamble gave the packet to the constable. He got a call on his phone. He went outside to talk. Rivanah went to the window in the drawing room and looking down at her flat below wondered: whenever she was there talking, he was here listening. But he never made himself visible. Anonymity is power, he had once told her. What did he want with such power? She was lost in thoughts for some time. A girl's laughter echoed in the empty flat taking her by surprise. There was nobody. She was about to turn toward the window when she again heard the laughter. She rushed to the bedroom but found nobody. Then she went to the toilet, the bathroom, the kitchen; there was nobody anywhere. She ran to the main door calling out to Kamble. He was checking the doorbell along with a man who was unscrewing the doorbell's socket on the wall beside the main door.

'What happened?' he said looking at a worried Rivanah.

'That girl's laughter...' she said.

'It's the doorbell,' Kamble said and pressed the doorbell again. The girl's laughter echoed in the empty flat. The laughter reminded her of something. Rivanah had heard it somewhere before or so she thought.

'We are wondering if it has anything to do with the stranger,' she heard Kamble say. 'Do you know this laughter by any chance?' he asked.

Rivanah thought hard. And then a name occurred to her. How could she forget it? The person used to be a good friend of hers in her engineering college.

'I knew there would be something.' Kamble exclaimed. He took out a small roll from inside the doorbell socket which unfolded to a small piece of white cloth similar to the ones, which he too knew, Rivanah had been receiving from the stranger. Kamble read what was stitched in it in black thread before handing it over to Rivanah.

*Fate is a smell Mini. Follow it hard without struggle and you shall reach me.*

'Never before in my service have I seen someone communicating with the means of embroidery,' Kamble remarked.

Holding the cloth in her hand, Rivanah quietly recollected every major thing that had happened to her since she came to Mumbai for the first time. Certain dots formed in her mind and to join them she called her mother purely on an instinct.

'Hello mumma, are you at home?'

'Yes, why?' Mrs Bannerjee was taken aback by the urgency in her daughter's voice.

'Please go to my room.'

'What happened?'

'Please don't waste time mumma. It's important. I need you to find something for me.'

Her mother did as asked. Half a minute later she said, 'I am in your room.'

'Go to my study table and pull out the last drawer.'

'Now in the end you will see a slam-book. Can you see it?'

Her mother moved some of the college text books to get to the slam book.

'Yes. It's in my hands now.'

'Open it and look for a girl named Hiya.'

'Hiya?'

'Hiya Chowdhury.'

There was silence.

'Mumma?'

'I forgot my specs downstairs.'

'Oh mumma, be quick.' The impatience was killing Rivanah.

Another minute went by before she heard her mother say, 'I have found Hiya Chowdhury on your slam book. Now?'

'Now read whatever is written on it.'

'Name: Hiya Chowdhry. Friends call me...' And her mother went on till she reached a particular section.

'Favourite dish: Spanish omelette, Kadhai paneer, and Butter chicken.

Hobby: embroidery.

Ambition: To work in an NGO for rape and domestic violence victims.

Favourite pass time: To teach kids.'

Mrs Bannerjee finished reading Hiya Chowdhury's profile in the slam book. The uncanny resemblance of the incidents that had happened since she was in Mumbai with the information in the slam book had turned Rivanah cold.

'Anything more?' Rivanah's throat had gone bone dry.

'There's a note for you where she signed her name. Should I read that too?' her mother asked.

'Yes.'

'Know your worth,' her mother said.

Rivanah swallowed a big stifling lump. She cut the line immediately and called her friend Pooja in Hyderabad. The latter picked up the call on the fourth ring.

'Hey, what's up?' she said.

'What do you know about Hiya Chowdhury?' Rivanah asked.

'Who? The girl who hanged herself to death from a ceiling fan last year?'

*Death...hanging from a ceiling fan...* As the nightmare that has been haunting her from sometime now flashed in front of her, Rivanah struggled to find her own voice.

(To be continued...)

# Acknowledgements

Gratitude to my family for negating my weaknesses with their strength all the time.

Thanks to my friends who have been a constant source of inspiration and support.

Heartfelt thanks to my readers who, time and again, have maintained unconditional thirst for my work.

A sincere thank you to my publisher and editor for making the book look amazing.

Special thanks to Pallavi Jha and Paullomy Chowdhury for...well, let it be.

# About the Author

Novoneel Chakraborty is the bestselling author of seven romance thrillers. *Marry Me, Stranger* is the first in the immensely popular Stranger trilogy. He works in the Indian films and television industry, penning popular television shows like *Million Dollar Girl*, *Twist Wala Love*, and *Secret Diaries* for Channel V. He lives in Mumbai.

You can reach him at:

Email: novosphere@gmail.com
Facebook: officialnbc
Twitter: @novoxeno
Instagram: @novoneelchakraborty

He runs a blog—*NovoSphere*—on life and its lessons at: www.nbconline.blogspot.com

# Book Two in the Stranger Trilogy . . .

After learning about Hiya Chowdhury's scrapbook details from her mother, Rivanah is left dumbfounded. The eerie similarities between her nightmares and Hiya's death don't let her rest in peace. She immediately books her ticket to Kolkata. She'll have to go to Hiya's house to find the truth behind it all. With such a blatant reference to Hiya Chowdhury, has the stranger finally given Rivanah the lead to find him? But why would he do that? And what does he want from her?

Rivanah can't wait to get the answers, but will her search really lead her on the right path or take her further down into some sinister labyrinth designed by the stranger? Along the way, Rivanah will discover dark secrets about her own self...those that may resurrect her or destroy her forever.

All this and more in Book 2 of the Stranger trilogy...